Hello.
Thank you for taking an
interest in this early work
of mine. Please treat this
book well as it is quite rare.
If it is not to your liking,
Just pass it along. It you want
more info about my work;
Just email
Richi1052@gmail.com

TOBIAS & OSAZE
By
Riqi Roze
2014

This book is dedicated to its readers.

THE FORWARD

What do you expect right now? Rhetorical
questions? Have you heard about this book? Already I'm
asking questions? What is happening here? Read
assured for your enjoyment is secured; I try not to ask
too many rhetorical questions in narratives. Richard
Matheson loved rhetorical questions(it seems) and I was
turned off by the result. Rhetorics are an easy way to
make a point, and that's why I feel such questions tend
to weaken good writing. I was younger when I wrote this
and I didn't know better. I apparently used a lot of them
in this so even after all the editing them out, a few still
remain. One day I hope I can write a story with a
grotesque overabundance of questions and call it,
Morbidly Rhetorical(I don't hope this. It would be lame.
Rhetorical questions blow, period.). To answer my
original question for you- instead of rewriting this
introduction to the forward- I would say you are
expecting an interesting and unusual book. Indeed, I'll
say it myself, you have chosen a good one. Maybe you
heard this book is an elaborate philosophical fiction
about an apocalypse that was supposed to happen but
never did. Perhaps the apocalypse did happen and I
wasted more time than I thought possible. From where I
sit, there is no way to know. I can say that if you're
reading this then the revolution must have done alright
for itself and I got published(not necessarily related
events). By the way, there are mistakes in this book.
Please don't get on my case about it. Books with no
mistakes have like six people working on them. This is
all your's truly right here. Props to all my cover artists.

Future people can't imagine how the people in my
world are trapped under the weight of themselves. They
don't care whether you never live. It's too much work for
them to change the world and they all have a moral
belief that tells them to do nothing. But do not fear. The

people are docile, but not inherently evil. They have been made evil but by the same degree I hope we can make them good. But these crises are for me. You live in a beautiful world I hope. I hope you live in a world that has recovered from this time and learned to love. You can't imagine how badly I want that for you. It keeps me awake at night. I will do everything I can to give it to you. I can swear that much.

My book mainly exists to give you a surreal experience of the very real fear we all felt, and of the doom most people accepted as an inevitability. I want to show you the way people felt as they all attempted- or accomplished- suicide together.

I saw the end times coming when I was young- we all saw them coming- and I started writing this book. I was 21 I believe when I began this project. I am 24 now and writing the Forward having just written the Afterward to the second book. This first book was also meant to describe my journey from literary apprenticeship to journeyman. I am not yet a professional writer basically only because there is no industry for what I do. It ain't there. I can write a book, but this is where it ends, with me; exactly where it began. When the internet came along my specific niche was basically consumed by every other form of entertainment. Even the appeal of poetry beat out my brand of fiction in the competition for the limited resources available to writers. Also, I try to be humble and avoid self promoting and my methods are not exactly a recipe for 'success.' So I apologize for not doing better. Luckily, I needed no industry to create the book, only to distribute it. If you're reading this now I must have improvised in a beneficial way to get this out there. Otherwise you're reading a stack of papers I probably handed you myself.

This book began as a project trying to document the horror of prime-time news stories. Our media, the givers of information, insist on only showing the worst, twisted, most dismal, unfortunate, horror stories they can find. Our world is fucked up in the head. It's a bad place getting worse fast, for real. See history for more on that. As I was collecting these news stories I also was learning more about how to write good books. Basically this book was inspired by equal parts; write what you know, write your times, do it your way, let it tell itself, and that is all. Any similarity, real or imagined, to any persons, living or dead, is either real or imagined. I used people I knew to model the characters around.

In fact, I owe this book in its entirety to the charity of 'Gari' and 'Crystal.' If it weren't for them I'd be dead. This is a common theme in my life that involves all kinds of people, but throughout writing Tobias it was those two that helped me most. Also, the character of Olivia helped me out tons. She is always a major ally in my war against oblivion.

My mother is not in this book. Tobias' parents have nothing to do with my parents. But I can't possibly thank my mother enough. She gave me the books Tobias learns out of in this story. This first book is all based off of what I could glean from a closet full of new age metaphysical books from the 1970's. Do you still use that calender? Don't answer me. I can't hear you.

Speaking of calendars, I should mention the Mayans. It was their calendar that spawned the weird subliminal apocalyptic panic we are currently trying to separate from reality and the government is trying to exploit. Currently the Mayans actually say the new dawn is upon us and that we are entering an era of peace and love. I do hope so. Because it doesn't seem like it. Maybe it is truly darkest before the dawn. At least metaphorically.

At the time I wrote this I did not understand the Mayan calendar. I still likely don't. I've researched it thoroughly and yet somehow I suspect everything I learned was wrong. If I had waited to write this book, or updated the scene, Tobias would be more informed about what the calendar actually means. The research he does on the subject is 2008 research and not 2012 research. Just pretend he lived under a rock. He sort of did anyhow, so it works... kind of.

This book was exciting to write. I was beginning to learn about the influence an unknown talent carries over the other 'artists,' who, though basically worthless, will gain all the exposure you require to flourish properly. The talented artists are always the smallest trees in the forest. In my time this is how writing is: If you are an unknown talented artist, you are a lion. If you are a lion you exist around hyenas trying to eat you alive; bit by bit. The hyenas are the untalented unknowns. In writing I know only one other lion. Her name is A.R.Martinez and she is the only other writer writing right now that can do what I do, I promise you that. What do I do? I write well. Well enough at least. It is not how well you write that matters. What matters is who you are and what you write. Especially with poets- a writers writing is no more or less interesting than the person would be face to face; that is the measure. To say that I am interesting is understating it. Normally I would type something here then delete it in an attempt to stay humble. I'd rather just say something humble. I'd also want to not be humble but humility is the life line of humanity, so I'm trying to get over my wants and if you people are like us people you should too.

Speaking of humility, let's discuss the beginning of this book. It might aggravate you. I don't know. It aggravates me. It may have needed more pizazz. You'll want me to get to the good stuff, but trust me when I say that Tobias wrote itself from front to back. The entire book was a learning experience for me. I had written a novels worth of stories, but I had never written a novel. You'll find two short stories toward the beginning; one about a rampage murder spree, and the other is about autism. I left those in there for a specific reason. My original intention was to acclimate the reader to how intense my writing is, but in the end I realized these stories, like every chapter, were part of the real story being told. Like every fictional book the real story is, on some level, the story of me, the writer.

The story of the rampaging killer represents my frustration and the stifling inexperience I was combating at the time. I wrote it because I had always wanted to write it. To feel it as well as I could without doing it. The story is sick and twisted because I needed to know how disturbed and wrong I could possibly make a story. The phone call he makes to his girlfriend is an homage to an actual similar killing spree that took place. The murders take place on Valentine's Day and I can't remember if that had something to do with the killing spree I just mentioned or with the actual St. Valentine's day massacre that occurred in Chicago. It isn't actually relevant unless you were involved in either of those incidents. Sorry to those people.

The story about autism is based on my own experiences. I mean, the environments I've worked in were practically horror stories unto themselves- not as bad as they'd been before Geraldo busted into Willowbrook and created my day job industry(people with mental, physical, and developmental disabilities used to be kept by the 1,000's in understaffed under budgeted state hospitals and I can't imagine the monstrosity of such places) but not much better either. The point is I am aware the subject is touchy; or at least it was when I wrote it. Maybe there are no autistic people in your society because when we banished capitalism some fiendish culprit went away as well. Did the Chinese ever take over the disunited status of amerika? I bet they did. I hope they did not. I was hoping the citizens of this country would inherit it.

There really isn't much we could do. Most people would rather everyone and everything die rather than change their ways. Like I said, they are only docile, dumb, and pliable- not evil (depending on your definition of evil).

Part of this book was written with the use of tarot cards to decide what happened next in the plot. I don't want to give anything away but as a hint I will tell you that it seemed like an odd place for a vulgar display of violence. Except that describes at least some point in most chapters. I should thank Eileen Connolly for teaching me the tarot. Thanks Eileen. And I should thank Parker for teaching me astrology. Thanks Parker. My computer just erased the diatribe I wrote on why I won't justify astrology when I don't have to, and I would hate to retype that considering the central thesis was a disdain for repeating myself. Astrology is wonderful and that is that.

To date tarot and astrology have never been used in literature the way I've used them, but I am sure that is changing(hyenas). As I wrote Tobias I watched the hyenas chew up astrology and do it no justice in their lazy poems and brief prose, just because they were interested. Same with tarot. They had all this knowledge left over from when they dropped acid with dinosaurs, but they weren't serious enough as writers.

As I wrote these books a renewed interest in tarot magically appeared in the territory of these profoundly flawed hyenas. I was hoping for a little Buddha space but I guess nothing is sacred. The question is; was it my right to exclusivity in using these two occult arts for literary purposes? The answer is no. But I became an astrologer as I became a writer and I became a tarot reader shortly thereafter. It made sense for me to write about this stuff because it was what I knew. They weren't popular practices when I began the books and granted, as time went on, the popularity of tarot and astrology increased, I doubt any writer will have done what I've done as well as I've done it (plus astrology always rises and falls in popularity over time. It never goes away, though). If they tried to rip me off than they've earned their misfortune. They shouldn't have tried. Either way, it is stupid I've had such a hard time publishing this considering the big deal the industry made about tarot usage in T.S.Elliot's The Wasteland. People as a whole can't really get too into tarot. The knowledge isn't exactly accessible. It is, but it is not. Tarot simply isn't easy. Astrology is fun for all levels of interest. Tarot is fun for beginners with books, then it is no fun for a really long time until you get good at it and don't need books anymore(the trick is you didn't need the books to begin with- the imagery of the Ryder Waite deck is enough to read the cards). Even then tarot still isn't fun because you've realized nobody gives a damn what you know or what you're doing. To quote Superjoint Ritual, "Everyone hates everyone." Regardless tarot is the truest wisdom available and my aim was to especially communicate that with Osaze.

Tobias has an astrological chaos that is more akin to tarot reading, and Osaze has an exacted finesse that is more akin to astrology. This is intriguing because the plot of Tobias is paced by astrology, and the plot of Osaze is paced by tarot. In retrospect I am amazed I was able to use these practices for such an obscure purpose. A word to artists; astrology. Another word to artists; tarot.

At some points in the story I use a few lines from songs that I was listening to at the time. I'd like to thank those bands here; (Hed) P.E. - I used the line, 'nothing lasts forever when you're flesh and bone,' and maybe another I've forgotten- Jah Red you and your band were a true inspiration and a major coping mechanism for me; Cake – I used the line 'It's coming down,' which I say all the time anyway, so who cares?; Dax Riggs, I may not have used any of your lines, but your philosophies defined the way I interpret and process my worst emotions, and I cannot thank you enough; Rage Against The Machine- if Dax defined me you guided me where I needed to go since I was young. I don't know whose lines I used where right now, but there is no more than four instances. If I did use a line from a song it was because I was listening to the song at that very moment, am a fan, and wanted the message to be ushered by me to the readers of the future. I also hope these musicians are still available to you for your listening pleasure, particularly Dax Riggs and his infinite projects; he is easily the most talented and probably the most under appreciated musician I've ever encountered. I also need to thank Dax for the term, 'Agents Of Oblivion;' one of his band names that I used within. And also, one of his songs turned me onto the term Endsville. I have to thank Edgar Cayce for the quote, 'We resent those we're indebted to.'

I've gone through at least 4 computers to write these two books. The one I am on now isn't very reliable, and I am sure I'll go through another one or two before I ever get published. They are always really old and under powered and cause problems. Problematic. That is a good word to describe writing. My computer just crashed, but unlike in the story, since this is only a forward, I can tell you about it. The event was lame, inconvenient, and happens way too often. That's all I have to say about that.

I really want you to like my book. That's why I wrote it, so you would like it. There is a lot to like about Tobias and if you read it, there is even more to like about the next one. Osaze is very much the second half of this. If someone picked up Osaze without first reading Tobias, they would have no idea what is going on. Birth is like that. I remember being born. Did I ever tell you that? It's true. Before birth there was this knowingness. That thing I was before conception knew everything and he placed me quite delicately into the womb. I was only in a womb for an instant, then there was a brief period of blackness, then I started having nightmares, then I was aware around age two. Is that interesting? Sort of? Yeah.

It was unfortunate when the world became a worse place than my books could anticipate. For obvious reasons, but also because all these traumatic events kept happening but it was too late to incorporate them into the story. If I had waited to write them there would be more history in the books. But, firstly, that was not an option, and secondly, maybe the fiction wanted me to work for the story, instead of just having my tragedies handed to me, like writers writing today. The ocean water is basically acid and oil now. Things are looking grim. The government might kill us all. It's bad. That's all I want to say about that. The revolution takes enough of my time as it is, and it has hardly even begun. For me the revolution begins when all my editing is done. It's the dead of winter now. In the spring I'll be going to New York City to do as much good as I can.

Almost time to begin the book. One last thing; I want you to think of me as your friend. I could use a friend like you. I lost all of mine writing these books. I want you to imagine that I am there for you alone. Indeed, I am. If you don't live in a beautiful utopian society and nothing has changed, or if you live in a bleak fascist murderous hell hole like me, just remember where to find me. You matter most to me. If you live in utopia, I am happy for you, but my writing will be severely discordant to your existence. So, if people aren't giving you the respect you deserve; if you messed up in your life and you're feeling like a reject because of an honest mistake- or even a dishonest mistake- I want you to know I am your friend no matter what and unconditionally; if you are feeling lower than you've ever felt just read my work, because I live down here. The more the merrier.

This paragraph is for people who get suicidal or might; everyone else can skip it. Listen. I know about pain. I know how it feels to come so close to death and still have people wonder why you changed. I know how it comes back again and again and each time it is worse and worse. I know how hard it is for you. So do others. I can't imagine what your pain is like. Mine was from alcohol, women, and writing. I could have been fine if it wasn't for these books. The ironic thing was these books were the only things that kept me alive. So many passages, especially in Osaze, were written during those times when all I wanted to do was bleed out. You'll see it in the writing. Some need what I can't give, and I can't really help them. If you need somebody, and you don't have someone, my books are here specifically for you, and really nobody else. Maybe the ladies, but that's my business. Remember that I love you unconditionally. No matter how bad the thematic elements of this writing make me look. That ain't me. I'm your friend the author. It's all I can be. That is unconditional love- to give all you have even when you have nothing. To give love when all you feel is hate. I don't want to lecture you, just read. It isn't even me who will become your friend, it is Tobias.

Another point: My intended audience is basically young people. I write with the sensibilities of a 15 year old boy so keep that in mind. I would like for adults to enjoy my book, but most adults have lost their sense of wonder so my writing will probably irritate that fleshy patch where it used to be.

Either way. We're here together, right? That is so awesome to me. You can't imagine the odds of this never happening. They were truly staggering to the imagination, but so is life. This is truly a dream come true. It is an honor to have you read my work- even this Forward. I seriously thought no one ever would. Don't forget that my writing gets better and better as the story goes on. I think the writing is always good, but, gauging by my experience levels, common sense dictates the beginning of Tobias just won't be as good as the end of Osaze. It's all good. And I mean that literally not figuratively. I wouldn't write if I wasn't constantly amazing myself. The passages I write in my opinion are the most beautiful ever written, except I don't expect my opinion counts toward that decision(I am a reader, too).

I know you had a lot of options in choosing a prolific author for you literary indulgence, thank you for choosing RRRoze. 'We' here at the 'me' know you'll be very pleased with your choice. This is the best work I've ever done(the second I am pretty sure is a majorly significant literary masterpiece, but time will tell). I'll be back to say goodbye Afterward. With no further ado: Welcome to Tobias & Osaze.

Love,
RRRoze

TOBIAS

Winter Of Fond Farewells

Back Story

Out the bay window he could see Federal Hill alive with window shoppers and restaurant goers wearing light jackets. In the midway courtyard flowers of pink and blue had not yet bloomed and the circular fountain had not been turned on for the first time after the winter; dormant stalks clung to the ankles of the concrete angel. A moment earlier he had finished doing two Tarot readings for a couple of ditsy college girls who had stopped in.

He stood watching the street and drinking a

cup of tea; taking it in with an uneasy stomach. Always he felt uneasy on such a nice day; turned off by the intrusions brought by daylight. He valued his privacy and the feelings of isolation afforded in the middle of the night. Desires far removed from the there and then of the situation; days like that one. Sometimes he didn't even answer the door when customers came knocking. If Olivia were home she might not answer it either. Of course she could do that. His benefactor's clientèle was such that she didn't really need the extra business. The potential clients simply left disappointed.

Tobias had sixty dollars in his pocket for half an hour's work. He put his tea down and removed his shining wooden guitar from where it hung on the wall and sat on the white microfiber sofa to play it; plucking the strings melodically, sort of upbeat, building a song in his mind. For instance; what should come next? Power chords? A certain progression? Or maybe that other one in between the two. He added more funk to offset the obscurity. And rolled around in the riff trying variations and settling back to what it had been originally. He counted with pick strokes to strike back into the chords he had been plucking. With hair hanging over his face and his eye closed Tobias struck the strings, applying pressure with his left fingers and then letting off and on and off, for some counts, then maintaining pressure, strummed less spastically and more dramatically. Over and over, changing the chords; going through motions of strum and change. Strum and change. Pick up the pace. Drop it, throw it, pick it up, pick it up, pick it up, pick it up, drop, solo.

Around and around the notes with his fingers. Looking to his hand picking up and down, and then looking back to his fingers on the neck. Making guesses as to which note would provide optimal melodic benefit, finding the right one through trial and error. Playing with it. Pulling it apart like putty and crushing it back together to return to the basic chords. A little more pronounced that time around, deeper, more personal. Harder and Faster. And harder and faster. Ring out. Back to the funky power chord riffs. Eight measures the same. And then into the original chords, with a new found tragedy for a crescendo.

Strum them away into nothing. The song was over and he picked strings at random to cleanse the instrument as if it were a deck of cards. He put the guitar back on the wall; hanging the black acoustic from its mount of molded iron and horseshoe wrapped in hemp that Olivia had made out in the garage.

His step mother's laptop was set out on the coffee table. He sat back down and opened it, finding in the list of internet favorites the 6000 year on-line ephemeris; planning to get a feel for the next couple days from the tables of logged information that serve as a map of the ever circling skies.

There were places on the web to receive this information typed and wrapped in a little package. Tobias found it better to figure the stars out for himself. Critical thinking kept him level and tuned into the world. It allowed him to know what to expect in an "unpredictable" universe. He would be in tune with the rhythms of the lives of others. For the purpose of knowing what aspects of a life, his or another's, should be pursued and at what points in time. When the energy from the skies may provide a boost in whatever endeavor is the case. Or tuned in and aware of certain unpleasant emotional realities that may present themselves. Most of all, it had taken him years to learn all the glyphs and symbols and meanings, why not use the knowledge? Let others buy what can be learned for free.

On that Friday the Moon was in Pisces, which could explain the general strangeness he had been feeling at work and throughout the day. The sun was in

Aquarius. It was not yet a new year astrologically. Not until Aries in March. He wasn't doing much by the way of taking on any new endeavors. Mercury was in Capricorn. That could explain the spike in business the past week.

Tobias considered his own sun; there was a lot of Leo in his blood. And the opposition between the two signs, any Aquarian influence and his own Leonine traits, had always been evident to him through his understanding of certain aspects of Aquarian nature that mirror aspects of his own sign as always is the way with oppositions on the wheel. He found certain Aquarian behavior to be bothersome in large quantities. While he was envious of their social openness, he wouldn't sacrifice his Leonine integrity and strength for it. For that "lost without others" need inside of the Aquarian. Not to be confused with his deceptive need to be noticed. As if he could change his astrology. As if a Tiger could change its stripes.

Olivia was out soaking up the energy of the sun. He looked over the aspects for a moment. Positive energy between the Moon and Mercury in water and earth signs. She was out on a date. Who knew who with? Some day date. In Boston maybe. Enjoying the January thaw. Doing any of her favorite trivial pursuits. She had gotten all dolled up for somebody.

Tobias had been awake and reading under a blanket on the couch when she left earlier that morning. She would come home soon though. It was sometime after two in the afternoon then. And she never stayed gone long. Her prime motivation for those dates was in her bedroom.

He stood in Olivia's bedroom doorway. Looking in for no reason other than he had been pacing around the apartment. She kept her room as clean as he kept his. Set up in the same practical design for her business affairs; bed against the wall, small round table and chairs tucked in the corner; walls lined with furniture. A crystal ball set upon her pine table. The golden brown hue of the wood color coordinated with her bed, dresser, and bookcase. White cotton strewn around; the bedspread, the curtains. The same shade carpet as in the living room, but much softer, vacuumed into rectangles and curving lines like on some data graphs. Her jewelry, silver necklaces and turquoise beads, was strewn in random places over corners. Mostly bare walls. Black framed pictures of flowers and her far away family. A hair straightener and beauty supplies were tucked away somewhere. This informed him she would be bringing a man home for sure. Those items would be splayed out otherwise.

As for him, in his own room, Tobias gathered Pluto, his black cat, into his arms from the floor and sat down on his mattress, straining the painted white metal of his 1950's nut-house twin bed frame. Cross legged with his back to the wall facing East; Tobias petted his fluffy cat, who barely seemed to notice he had been moved at all; both their eyes closed. It felt, then, to him, like a good time to meditate. Instead of the traditional posture, he held the feline in his hands; taking it along. That was of minimal significance.

Tobias oriented himself with the seven directions, East and a breath, West and a breath, South and a breath, North and a breath, Below and a breath, Above and a breath, brought it all together in his heart; centered, he went off into himself.

Pluto went limp with his head propped on Tobias's hand. Purring very shallow and subdued.

Hours passed. Tobias was doing a natal chart interpretation for a new customer. For two hundred twenty-five dollars he typed up a five to ten page report about the individual and gave an hour session the following week. The one he was working on was for a regular's daughter. Industrial techno music played on the silver living room stereo, the surround sound keeping his soul submerged in a more comfortable environment and his mind free from anxiety. He could focus better if he didn't have to hear the street. The music was not blasting. He wouldn't mind having the music louder; nobody liked to come home to blasting stereo though.

Olivia arrived right then. He looked up from the warning. Always, she let him know when she had gotten home by way of a tug in his solar plexus. A sensation that he was completely used to by that point but had amazed him earlier on in history. She walked in through the door from Atwells avenue with a navy blue day bag around her arm. She must have spent the day in Boston.

"Oh, my god Tobias you should have seen the bug that hit my windshield today," she said.

"Oh yeah?"

"Yeah it was like this." She came into the living room doorway and held her two long fingers together to make a circle representing the size of the bug. Tobias was oddly impressed by the thought of that much smashed insect.

He silently admired Olivia for a moment before even acknowledging her male friend. Her long flowing limbs. The way she moved gracefully as though projecting herself through the kitchen; putting items away or into the sink; wearing a lacy white skirt, and a hooded sweatshirt of the same color, zipped to the midsection over a tight red shirt. Her hair was done like an Egyptian; the bangs cut into a flat line over her brow and very straight pigtails hanging over either shoulder. She had a sharp face and cat like features of tan skinned. Like a runway model; there was an intoxicating feeling in looking upon her. Inebriated by her crystalline aura of pure white light; like Jesus.

Surely, this guy with her could testify to that.

Another tall guy, with a large muscular frame. Stupid inside his pretty head with the strong scruffy jaw. How many of these guys did they make?

"How's it going, man?" Tobias asked him.

"It's going good man. What about you?"

Tobias answered him, "Fine," and then looked back to the work at his computer.

Olivia was pouring herself and the man red wine in the kitchen. Tobias wouldn't see her for a couple hours. She pulled the guy into her bedroom and shut the door.

Moments later there was a knock from the street.

"Can I help you?" He opened the door to two pudgy teenage girls.

"Um. What kind of psychic are you?" said one with dark smooth rock and roll hair. They were dressed in black and bright colors.

He explained that he was not a psychic. The psychic was indisposed, he informed them. Instead he offered them tarot readings for 30 dollars apiece. Only one girl was getting it done, but the other wanted to watch.

Throughout the reading the familiar sound of Olivia's headboard slamming into the wall remained ever present. Her moans and whimpers, or the gasping of "harder, harder," as the headboard slammed louder. They all heard it clearly. Tobias ignored it and the girls looked to each other smirking, but he carried on as though it were not happening. After the reading he got paid and they left.

The charade used to bother him; how he loved his Olivia. He was not meant to be with her romantically. She told him the future on that one. He was not a large man with a scruffy prominent jaw. He was just a boy of regular size with an eye patch and a tendency to feel sad. Apparently, this did not get her juices flowing. If anything it made her heart pump peanut butter. He used to sit alone in the living room digging razors around in his flesh while she got fucked. When it was all over and the man was kicked out, she would bring Toby a bowl of chocolate fudge brownie ice cream and cuddle up close to him to ease the pain of his breaking heart.

Until the day when Tobias fell in love with a girl who loved him back. And finally he no longer felt that ache for Olivia.

In one instant, one night, coming home from spending that first full day with his love, he had been cleansed. Only with no emotion did he think about the love he used to feel for his foster mother.

That girl who had returned his love eventually broke his heart. Distance sprouted between them and grew larger. Her tolerance of his maniacal spats wore thin. She got sick of his ways and moved on, like women often do. She left him ruined; shattered by a new pain. Olivia once again held the charge of nursing him back to stability; picking up the pieces. He had since healed from that injury and moved on; had an active sex life, a rebound, and dated others as well.

As a bachelor, Tobias was somebody who accepted that part of Olivia. For he would never have a say in the matter anyhow. The ties to his former love had all but decayed with time. His feelings for Olivia settled into their rightful place; adoration. Infatuation for the sake of infatuation. No motives. He would always be more important to her than these objects she manipulated for sexual gratification. She would always be his personal lord and savior. For Olivia, Tobias would climb mountains, cross oceans, kill with his bare hands, and bend reality to travel through time and space.

Tobias paced through the apartment in a momentary lapse of preoccupation.

In the bathroom he removed the designer eye patch to clean his socket out. Unnecessary ugliness. The deformed children in elementary school had always had his sympathy. To be so different?

He pushed the black hair from his face to check for crusting, or the ooze that occasionally secreted and dried. The eyes of others would never identify with that part of him. Leaving him to identify with midgets and cripples. What unjust higher power would create such a thing as deformity? He was like those schoolmates now. In that notion he found his strength. On some level he knew losing an eye had gained him his heart of a lion.

The eyelid opened in a restricted fashion. A nerve cluster fuck. He removed the prosthetic green eye made of plastic; differently colored from his real brown eye; he wore it to feel comfortable. To not feel like he did those months in that old house. He washed the socket clean with soap and water.

His father, the demonic red neck crack fiend, out of his head on whatever, acting on an impulse that defied logic, threw Tobias's head into the rocks of the basement wall; knocking him unconscious and then the man removed his son's eye so mindlessly. The mother upstairs heard a commotion from below. The surgery had been done with a buck knife.

Tobias regained consciousness to the searing pain of the nerves severing. He could feel the dirty fingers clenching the eye, the tugging, the mutilation, and then nothing. Black again. Coming to after only a moment; gasping for air. Inside his face there was a searing flood of pain. Like boiling water pulsing through his face and skull. He staggered to the stairs, glimpsing his father rubbing the eyeball, crushed, into the packed dirt. Tobias slowly got up the stairs.

His mother, sick and dying on the couch did not move. He called the police. Distorted with pain and disorientation; that was the last time he ever saw that man. His mother stirred from her rest, struggling between rooms of the old rundown shit box, trying desperately to get her son a cloth soaked in hot water; moving in her haggard expressionless way. The father was now upstairs too, throwing himself into walls and pacing, muttering to himself, rattling the old wood of the walls; raising dust.

Tobias, newly fifteen, was sitting on his mother's couch, clutching his face and doing little to stop the blood gushing through his hand, down his wrist, and dripping over his jeans and onto the floor. His remaining eye looking frantically for any weapon to use against his father. Anything. His body reactively breathing deeply and quickly to ease the pain.

His mother came to his aide, wiping away the coagulated substance and soaking up what flowed after. She had that absent mind of her disease. Eyes into him. Thoughts removed. Warm water on the wound muffling with no effect the alarms going off in his head.

On the floor in the corner the thin tattooed man was throwing his head into a wooden beam. Smashing his head into an exposed support beam only a couple more times before going limp. Hopefully he had detached his retinas.

There was no extended family for Tobias to live with when his mother died only a night or two later. She was stage IV HIV positive. She suffered in her brain. In her eyes. Her thoughts lost in a vast vacancy. Movements; routine, minimal. A shell fulfilling past wishes: to die untreated. Into the unknown not knowing why. Or what.

Tobias lied to the authorities, he lay her down before they arrived. She passed out drunk, he told them. Then he walked the 4 miles home from the hospital, worrying that his mother had wandered away.

When he got home she hadn't moved from where he left her "napping" on the couch. She stared into the ceiling from eyes hidden behind her mummified leather skin; behind a mask of frail hair; through a thick hanging stench.

A sad and mystifying sight was her disease; lying in

bed awake or walking out into the street for no reason, tripping over nothing and looking around wild eyed to find what had pushed her, never violent, but often crying to god through tears and dry heaves. And then again moments later, horizontal on her back, the comatose eyes wide open.

Tobias did the best he could for her. There was no insurance, so there was no treatment. Cindy, of course, wished it to be that way. She had been waiting to die her whole life. Tobias nursed her in the way she had taught him when she first took ill over a year before. A solemn son doing his duty.

The parents did not work. His mom had been addicted to opiates for as long as Tobias could remember. No one was sure when she contracted AIDS except her.

Tobias would have guessed it had been a couple years prior when she stopped sharing drinks with him and began to disinfect everything she came in contact with.

The father kept money around and would send Tobias walking through town for groceries. Happiness was a dream he had had only once when he was younger.

All his life he had talked to his mom about the world he was born into. His soul was curious and she had the answers. No matter how doped up she was, she would always listen; asking the right questions and saying the right things. Losing her was a lot like losing his eye. The two incidents happened more or less simultaneously and were tied together in a serendipitous way. In dreams she would appear with an eye-patch.

Tobias arrived home to his mother's aide high on painkillers and disoriented from walking such a distance with no binocular vision. He sat with her and dragged himself to and from the sink as he kept her clean. The next evening she was dead. She crossed over silently in a deep sleep. The instant gripped him from spine to skull; her life-force moved through the room and away to somewhere beyond.

His father, Alexander Squires, had been addicted to crack cocaine and amphetamines for as long as Tobias could remember. Only truly breaking as Cindy's sickness progressed; perhaps he knew the end had arrived and his violence was his way of expressing sadness. The theory made about as much sense as anything else. His dad was a twisted individual who would routinely torture Tobias's weak mother, cutting into her with knives and burning her with lighters when she was too high, or too sick, to react. He would be perched like a wraith over her. Hurting her. Beating Tobias into submission when he tried to put a stop to it.

Life hadn't always been like that. Only after his parents had fallen too deep into their hole to climb out. Those people had always been addicts, he knew, but functioning ones. And then; they stopped functioning. She got sick, usage increased and they lost their jobs. His father would leave for days. Driving his old trucking routes to Florida and back, or to Indiana.

Tobias never had much food around to eat and was rarely sent to fetch it.

Upon his admission to the halfway home he weighed 95 pounds. Tobias told the staff he had been malnourished for longer than his memory could accurately recall. At night Tobias had been breaking into churches and stealing donations. Filling jackets with lunch meat in super markets when he could find the strength. Thinking and paying attention had become a near impossibility. Constant disorientation was the only memory of his first days at St. Mary's.

Alexander went to jail the night of the surgery. Tobias's eye was crushed on the dirty basement floor. Cindy died a day later. Tobias had her body removed and lived alone in the house for months until social services came for him. The school didn't notice.

Visitors, friends, came and went; ignored. He abandoned what friends he had. More so he abandoned the idea that there was anyone alive outside of himself. No power; no heat for the chilly fall nights. A cold and hungry darkness. When he didn't feel anything but grief, or think about anything other than his mom, or care about his crushed eyeball life; or move in the daylight, or weigh more than 100 pounds. He destroyed furniture and cabinets and anything else he could. He lay in his bed covered in every blanket; biting holes into his lip. He flooded the basement with a garden hose and took comfort in feeling the mold grow around him. He kept his mushy eye socket clean.

His mother was gone. His only true friend, the only person who mattered was gone. The voice of joy. The sweet conversational junkie who left only mold behind.

Then they came; the blue van. Social services. He went away with them willingly. His loss had been mourned appropriately, nearly killed him, and he was ready to move on.

Moving on was to be done in North Providence, at the St. Mary's Home for Children. Although his residence there was not for very long. Which may have been his own luck. But he didn't mind it there. He was happy to be fed. And happy to be warm. It felt good to be around other people. Most of the time the kids spent entire evenings in silence just enjoying the company of others, and the peace of safety.

Tobias told the nice people his fucked up story; relishing in their sympathy. To be cared about. Cared for. It was new. It felt good. It felt good to feel.

He was in a facility for damaged, or traumatized, youth. Except there was no trauma inside Tobias. The trauma was in jail. No. What Tobias felt was freedom and a certain eagerness to move forward. After a short two weeks he was released into the custody of Olivia Athens. His new foster mother.

An angel, nay a god in the flesh opened her door to him. Giving him safety. A clean bedroom and food. He was given every last thing his heart desired. Safe and warm; apart from the cold winter outside. She radiated kindness and warmth.

Olivia always knew when to give him his space or when he needed somebody to talk to. The most appropriate time to take him to Thayer St. for ice cream and the hookah bar. Always knowing.

The woman was a psychic like he had only ever imagined before. He didn't understand her, but he wanted to know everything. Eventually realizing that Olivia was stingy with the things that she knew; weary of giving information for no reason. She insisted it was better that way but never explained why. An apprehension he could not understand. Or a selfish habit that annoyed him perpetually.

Except whatever. Because this woman, the master of making everything perfect, gave Tobias the greatest gift she could. The quintessential knowledge one needed to know to understand the universe and reality. The secrets of the stars and the ability to harmonize and flow with the vibrations that control everything. She taught him underlying advantage of harnessing the psychic energy that flows along the magnetic poles and the ability to manipulate the ether.

She taught him everything an apprentice of the Occult would need to know. As well as the most appropriate metaphysics. Teaching him with tact and extraordinary skill the language of the stars and the tarot; the art of divination and prediction.

Tobias consumed the knowledge like somebody who had lost everything would. Like a soul seeking a body. Like a balloon released to the sky or a rock dropped in the sea.

For all his sacrifices, the balance was too clear to him. This life on Federal Hill and his beautiful psychic foster mother? Happiness? Joy! The reactionary opposite after all the suffering. An end to an event he had assumed would be endless. Jolted straight from hopelessness to harmony.

Foster mother was such a joke. Olivia was simply a 20 year old girl with a fake identity and the desire for a companion. Working as a counselor at the home, under the alias Sylvia Trinidad, she waited for Tobias. His face in her skull late at night. A feeling of love hovering around it. The visions preluded his arrival. His figure in the crystal ball. His arrival at St. Mary's signaling her to prepare for his adoption. Feeling his pain coming to her from Cranston she had refused to seek him out or interfere. But she contemplated it and desired to. Ultimately knowing, for his development, she must wait.

On Monday, the 10th of December 2007 Tobias was admitted into the care of St. Mary's and never during his stay did he see her face. Though she watched him with a joy that was that of an expecting mother who for years thought she could not get pregnant.

The problem for Olivia was that she was aware of her own death. What it looked like, even. She had been dreaming it since she was a little girl. And it became clearer every time. Eventually the image of the Moon tarot appeared on the wall. Now, the dream was a solid, tangible entity of the night. A visitor, like a creditor using the mail system.

She would sometimes spend hours sitting on her bed and holding her shard of broken glass. The brown neck of a broken beer bottle. She called it her "life shard."

A little girl on a beach in a beautiful country far away. At the beach house of her family. With the warm air blowing water vapor across the long shoreline. There, she first had the dream. At the time, it was more a sense of where a dream used to be; more a sense of absence; where a dream should have been but did not remain and could not be found.

Like flustered girls living on beaches often do after a bad dream, she wandered out to the sand; in her plaid pajamas and rubbing her eyes. She felt a sting in her step. When she looked to her foot a small line of blood leaked from an inch long cut. There in the sands was the glass from the dream she had just awoken from. She brought the shard inside.

Olivia knew at once that it had been her own distorted presence in that dream of the terror of an unknown encounter, not visible. And for some reason she could feel the crushing grasp of human misery whatever that could possibly be. Only seeing her adult face as her body developed closer and closer to its actual figure, clearer and clearer over time.

All she had ever wanted was a baby of her own. But she could never bring a baby into a world where she would be dying so young. There was more to life than child birth but she didn't care what it was. At least not until she was forced to confront the matter as the sand slipped through her hourglass.

So what then?

For years she did not have an answer. Until, shortly after she first heard his voice in dark places and focused on the matter; deciding ultimately what she would do.

Once she had drawn together a hypothesis; her god given powers of intuition made it clear to her. On the night he lost his eye she lay in her soft covers listening to the sounds of people moving about outside the window. Then, inside her bedroom, in the quiet, Tobias said, "Tell me about the stars."

An apprentice. An heir to her everything. An apt pupil. And in return for his service to her he would receive a new lease on life. True happiness by her side. Love, patience, and gentleness; to receive all he needs to succeed; promise of growth; the beautiful symbol of the star in tarot. Hope.

In those early days together, it was not about the stars, or cards, or love. It was about a lifetime's worth of catching up. The kindest girl being everything for a damaged boy. Togetherness, in the apartment overlooking Federal Hill. Wrapped up in a blanket, holding one another, watching movies at night and reading books in the day.

His love was there from the first day. But it had not mattered until Olivia was ready to confront the issue. She supervised and controlled the elements which she knew were necessary for Tobias to move past the natural roadblock. She knew it would be hard on him and his rejection was done with tough love. Culminating in an introduction to a cunning peach who swept his desires away from Olivia like a rogue wave.

That mind altering love of a sixteen year old. Charged with magnetism. Explosive like TNT. An all-encompassing feeling of the new. The kind of love that leaves one on cloud nine wondering what could go wrong.

That girl tore him apart.

And he recovered.

Her picture to be glimpsed less and less with time.

In the summer of that first year together Olivia began talking about astrology. Little things. Anecdotes about the moons influence on crime. Following time according to the new moons. The spring airs effect on children. He was a Leo. She was a Leo. The Lion. Fantasies and metaphors of a human pride.

Tobias began questioning the signs of others. The birthdays of those closest to him. His mother and father. His father, a Gemini. His mother, a Sagittarius. At first not fully grasping what it all meant. So, searching for answers, he started looking through Olivia's collection of unusual New Age literature that filled a bookshelf in the living room. Books. Reading about all the signs, one by one. And browsing through the pages, it dawned on him- what a complexity it truly was. For a lifetime he had considered it a meaningless section in the newspaper. A Chinese finger trap.

But then there were those charts. Circles, divided into twelve sections called houses; that represented the sky as viewed from Earth. Something called aspects too. And those seemed more involved with numbers and degrees than with words. Houses, the planets, everything meant something. Either very literal or completely under the surface. Some was common sense. There were thousands of complicated concepts he could only begin to fathom.

To Olivia's perfect delight it began to preoccupy him. More and more the questions he asked increased in frequency. Or he would spend full days reading texts in the living room.

And on his 16th birthday, August, 6th of 2008, Olivia gave Tobias his very first tarot reading. She had kept the tarot a secret from him. He had asked about it early on and she immediately dismissed the subject and redirected his focus.

Olivia had him go out to the garage, clean off the pine table, and bring it upstairs. Then she instructed him to move the glass coffee table aside, and place the pine one in the center of the living room.

She wore a beautiful sun dress of white cotton and lace. Her hair was cut short to her shoulders and done straight with volume, lifted out at the bottom. The Opal stone of her ring had a green tinge to it from the turquoise of her necklace and bracelets. He hadn't ever seen her as excited as that moment. Her smile was illuminating the room when she came to the table with those cards. In her lovely brown box. The midnight blue silk spread over the table. Tobias nervously struggled to shuffle the cards; peering down at what he was doing with his head cocked to the right.

"You have to shuffle them really well. You have to break the vibrations of the last person and rebuild them with your own," she said.

And she gave him her interpretation of the cards from the top of the deck as he had handed them to her once they were cut. A dazzling display of grace. Her voice fell quiet, void of any usual regional speech patterns; in harmony with a consciousness apart from herself and still part of herself. As if playing a guitar. She explained to him the events of his near future. He wondered- but eventually learned- what she was reading in those cards. How could something so simple bare such great meaning? As he was thinking this Olivia was explaining to him that he would be shown the answers to the questions he had by somebody very close to him. His education would be surfacing as the greatest common divisor of what was to come. She told him of a new love on the way.

He was in awe. Enraptured. She let him into the places of her mind that were normally off limits. At 6:15 the power would shut off for ten seconds. The next day, he would injure himself in a minor way. And in January he would be employed by the Dunkin Donut's center as a janitor.

The power did cut off. The next day he sprained his ankle tripping up the stairs. And in January of 2008 he responded to an ad in the newspaper for a custodial position at the coliseum down the road.

He never went back to public school. He learned from Olivia instead. On the night of his birthday in the unusually quiet East Side hookah bar she unraveled her plan for him. She would teach him astrology, the tarot, and all the other Occult ways that had been long suppressed and rejected by their culture.

In the spring she would open a business and accumulate clients. And when he was ready he would take over control of the areas he had learned. This would leave her free to strictly perform the various divinations only she could do.

That excited him. School was out. Over. To himself he vowed to never stop learning. But he did not need a school for that purpose. Nor did he need a vow. Books. Those arts. Knowledge. Skill. Ability. Legitimacy. Comfort. To live comfortably until he died. With something to offer. Functioning in society. Forgetting where he came from for his own benefit. Knowing his mother would have wanted that for him.

Olivia taught him astrology first; the natural jump off point. She had the texts for it from when she had taught herself long before when she was much younger. Astrology teaches about the self and to know the world one must first know themselves. To draw natal charts was the first thing he was taught. He already understood the glyphs from his own learning. Olivia taught him to make the effort and coordinate location of birth. Then convert local time to Greenwich Mean Time. Then sidereal time. All the information sheltered in graphs. The ephemeris of dates. It what sign and to what degree each heavenly body would loom or had loomed in the sky on any given date. Calculations and formulas to find the location of each planet in the sky from the point and time of birth.

Learning to interpret that information with ease proved to be the most difficult task at hand. There was meaning to everything; for every combination of planet, house, sign, and aspect. Then the big picture task of combining each planet's individual interpretation into one amalgamated interpretation. But Tobias managed fine.

Before he learned to progress charts by following planetary movements in lives over time, or the methodology of Synastry; comparing the charts of two people to gain insight into the positive and negatives of

a given union- or even to do day for a year future
readings; before all those things he was taught the tarot.

Again it was necessary to learn quantities of
meanings and combinations of meanings, to understand
the new language fluently. Seventy-eight cards; what
they mean alone or together while alone or together in
the reading as a whole. How the divination works. The
importance of wood and silk.

The faces of each suit. Skin tones, the meanings of
the pictures. When to, and when not to, use the major
Arcana. The royalties. Prominent meanings. Accents to
higher themes. Pip cards.

Once he learned the basics of each, Olivia gave him
little assignments. Deciding herself when his skills were
complete enough in one area to move on to the next.
Until his readings became precise, and his
interpretations accurate. Then she made him study
harder.

He loved the requirement of perfection the craft
entailed. And when the business was running and she
was seeing the clients coming in from the street, he did
not envy her. Even in his 19th year he did not feel his
skills were adequate. To him they may never have been.
But Olivia knew when he was ready. When he could
finally give a reading someone would not mind paying
thirty dollars for.

He still studied and probably always would; trying
to understand more and more; make connections
quicker and with more detail. Always training his brain
to decode the meanings quicker. To speak the language
more fluently.

At the kitchen table Tobias was drinking a cup of
tea. The darkness had fallen. And from Olivia's room
emerged the guy from earlier.

"See you later," the prominent jawed man said to
Tobias on his way out the door. Tobias didn't respond.

Moments later Olivia skipped out into the kitchen clad in purple silk pajamas.

"To the willful winds he will weep," she recited. "His hung to dry heart will hurt. Tears will try to tame the torment. And sadly another man is satisfied with a fleeting fulfillment until he finds himself worse off than he'd have been before, had he not come through my door."

"You are such a tool," Tobias said. Olivia poured herself hot water and dropped the tea bag into it, then sat across from her companion.

"You want to know something?" she asked him.

"You know it."

"Pawtucket." She said the word and looked at him, her chin resting on her arms on the table; eyes open wide.

"I hate it when you do this. Are you going to tell me?"

"No. You have to wait or you won't be surprised." How she toyed with him.

1

Simultaneously the co-anchors took their seats behind the desk. A middle aged man with big white teeth and classically handsome looks, dressed in a black suit with a gold and green diagonally striped tie. He had dark hair and fake tanned skin radiating orange in the bright studio lights.

Also dressed in a fine suit of black with red lapels exposed was a woman of roughly the same age. She had blonde hair and half hidden crow's feet. Her age was a representation of all the years she had worked for the network, in that studio reporting from that news desk or one like it.

The man was Paul Allen, senior news anchor. The woman was Danna Parker, senior news anchor.

Behind them there was a photograph of the Providence skyline as seen from WaterPlace Park during an orange dusk. The Bank of America tower stood on the right; an art deco building the locals refer to as the "Superman Building" for its comic book appearance. To the left was the Sovereign Bank tower; of international style, four flush walls and a flat top. The building's walls illuminated pink for Valentine's Day. In between the two was the post-modern style 50 Kennedy Plaza with its uppermost portion resembling two stair cases meeting at one landing.

There was commotion everywhere in the studio as the live broadcast was being prepared. Paul had positioned his microphone on his jacket.

"We're ready for air," the floor director informed the director.

"Ok people! Let's do it!" shouted the director.

Beside the camera aimed at the two anchor persons the count was given.

"Five, four, three..." And hand signals for two and one.

Paul spoke, "Hello. We go now to Crystal Gold live on the scene covering the breaking developments of a tragedy unfolding in Pawtucket. Crystal, what can you tell us?"

In Pawtucket, Crystal's cameraman gave her the go ahead. They were live and recording.

"I'm here live outside of the Apex shopping center in Pawtucket where less than an hour ago a gunman opened fire with an automatic rifle and a hand gun inside the mall as well as in several shops further off on Main Street; before finally taking his own life. It is not known who the gunman was but as you can see behind me he has set these fires in many of the places where the killings occurred earlier."

Behind Crystal there was a parking lot and a burning mall. The rain was falling hard and she reported from under an umbrella at the edge of the lot making sure to give ample space for emergency rescue vehicles. Smoke was pluming out from two different separate areas and being wisped away by the gusting wind. Ambulances gathered in swarms at either of the two prominent entrances and sirens could be heard as emergency vehicles came and went. Fire crews set up equipment and more black smoke could be seen further in the distance being released in greater amounts.

"The gunman *is* dead and including him the death toll stands at 24 right now, including four law enforcement officers, but that number is expected to rise. The amount of injured stands at fourteen; some of whom are in critical condition.

"He began his assault shortly after noon in a coffee shop on Main Street; shooting patrons and employees and allegedly lighting fire to his victims. Then he moved next door to an Allied Insurance Agency and repeated his actions of killing and burning the bodies. Several eye witnesses fled into the rain and escaped unharmed. After which he went to a small clothing boutique and shot several people in there as well, before setting the store on fire and leaving.

"At that point he got into his vehicle and drove the short distance to the mall where he entered through T.I. Bailey's department store and proceeded to open fire.

"According to an eye witness he was a caucasian male of about 5'11" height wearing all black and firing into his victims at random. The police were involved in a gun battle with the killer just before he took his own life on that very sidewalk in front of the mall.

"You can see here the ambulances are still arriving and departing; taking the injured victims to the Memorial Hospital of Rhode Island. As well there are fire crews trying to contain the flames that have broken through the roof of the shopping center.

"There has been severe fire damage done on Main Street as well, and we can only hope that nobody is harmed by those spreading fires.

"We cannot begin to imagine the full scale of this tragedy right now. You can see the crowds of witnesses still standing together; consumed in tears and drenched from the rain.

"Of course, we will keep you posted as the events unfold and become clearer but for right now, I'm Crystal Gold for NBC news, reporting a tragedy in Pawtucket."

The Shooter

My last songs. This is what it is all about for me. I chose the Union Underground and how nice that my speakers can make my ears bleed the way they do.

Shrieking guitars and those eerie lyrics. What if I was your god? Yeah. South Texas death ride. Sounds almost right. South New England death ride?

I light my cigarette as I get onto the highway from the side streets. I almost went through Providence to cruise around and to see if my AK riding shotgun would get me arrested. But it's not like that. I just want to be there. I want to take life.

And what monster am I? I will give my life to take theirs. Am I not a dishonest fiend? I would give fifty lives to take fifty, but I have only got one. And who cares about that anyway. Always so human; always bestowing upon life some value. There is no value. There never has been and there never will be. The Spanish inquisition.

Let this be what it is. Huh? I have loved in my life. I have done good- with my life. I have done bad things too. I like to think only religious freaks have not. So now what?

The hate. An epic tsunami of hate. Like the

terrorists got. But less. Obviously.

This is fucking bad. This is so bad. I am really here. Here and now. And my body is a mechanism. Deep panic breaths off of my cigarette. Ok. This is the reason I brought the whiskey under the passenger seat.

"What if I was your god?" the man in the band asks.

What if, huh? What if *I* was *your* god?

My ride to be god. My appointment with power. My first, only, and final moment of power.

Why is this my destiny? Coming up on the exit now. Oh, fuck. My cigarette's done. Light another over violent heartbeats. The shaking in my hands subsiding to nothing. Try to tune into the music. I adjust the treble and bass for any more noise. The speakers are maxed out and it doesn't matter if they explode.

"All I see... is apathy... in this world, I won't be. I will be the better man. I won't

be a bitter man," I sang along.

En route to Main St., Pawtucket. I'll park at the pawn shop. Go right and hit the bohemian coffee shop. Then the insurance agency. The clothing boutique.

"Listen while I load my gun... said to me. Something bout a chosen one is coming back. Look what you've done! Watch this while I taste the sun."

Start that song over again. Revolution Man.

"One more time and you'll be dead. At least I think that's what he said. Revolution. Revolution man. Imagine all the people."

There's not a lot of sunlight down here on Main St. The rain is falling hard. Good. Muffle screams. Your god wants me to do this.

I can see them hustling up the road; parked here on the right. With an umbrella, or an arm raising a jacket; they cover their heads. The down pour around them is blinding. They will not see my rifle sitting here. They won't see me here with their heads facing down. They will only see the whites of my eyes piercing the rain and looking out from behind my cigarette.

Maybe for just a moment they will notice my stereo. That Hispanic girl has got a pink shopping bag. The pretend fur of her jacket is keeping some rain from her face. In my mind's eye the fur is binding together like the hair on a furry wet dog.

Another shot of whiskey and one last cigarette.

"So what if I was your god? South Texas death ride."

After dialing the numbers I turn down the radio.

"Hello?"

"Baby."

"Oh, hi. What's up?

"I love you very much. You've got to go and have a happy life from now on. Alright?"

"Jeff. I don't understand."

"You have got to forget about me. I love you."

"Jeff. Wai-..."

One more shot of whiskey. I'll drink to that phone call. Turn up the stereo- turn off the phone.

"I get a kick out of this. Watch you run like a bitch. I wanna break you... I can't even fake it... I'll say it again. You're on a downward slide my friend"

That's right you Texan son of bitch. Whatever you're talking about. That's right.

Looking away from the bottle and out the window, I see two Hispanics tearing through the rain away from me. They won't be there. That drop in my stomach again. Those butterflies. The nausea. I cough and my shots chuck up all over the passenger floor.

What if I was your god?

Light another cigarette. Vomit lingers in and out of my facial cavities. I get out of my car, leaving the rifle, and stand next to it in the street. A delivery truck is coming and I make my way, slowly, to the sidewalk. Rain blows relentlessly across my face, pours down my cheeks. The gusts collide with my chest and arms.

I walk past the clothing boutique. I walk past the insurance agency and flick my cigarette onto the street.

A little weak in the knees and light in the head, I walk into the coffee shop and lock the deadbolt behind me. One Hispanic youth notices me in the dim lights and then looks away. Nobody noticed me lock the door. The kid appears to be on edge. A coffee addict? A girl, curly blonde haired young one, stares at the menu over the counter. Is the boy on edge over her? And the girl with the choppy black hair and the tattoos growing up her arms is taking the order of a frumpy man in a suit. These thoughts happen instantly.

I flip the counter over at the right and walk into the back. My hand is clutching the pistol under my unzipped coat.

"What the hell do you think you're doing?" The girl was angry. My taser is charged in my left hand and I plunge the 100,000 volts into her cheek. Her feet fly from the floor and she lands flat on her back on that counter. Clat! I put the bullet into the underside of her chin and the rear of her head explodes out over the dark tiled floor. The bullet cracks the floor on impact.

"Oh my god!" The little blonde screamed as she ran into the wall.

The Hispanic ran into a table.

"Jesus Christ!" The pudgy man dropped to the floor.

I am backed into the corner in the employee area. I shoot the Hispanic in the chest and he falls over the furniture and crashes to the floor. More screams from the girl.

Clat! I shoot her in the side of her panicked and crying head and she falls dead.

The man remains on the floor making some kind of guttural grunt to himself. I move to the back room and find a chubby girl, college aged, cowered in the corner holding a frying pan. Clat! I shot her once in the chest before rushing back out. The pudgy man is struggling with the door and he throws the lock as I put the two bullets into him. He falls out into the street. I hurry over to him and give a strong pull on his ankle and he comes back into the establishment.

I hear a scream from the street before I notice the black girl running away. Throwing myself through the door I steady the pistol and aim. The rain blowing in my face makes it difficult. I don't miss targets very often. Clat! Clat! Clat! Click. The silenced bullets betray no position; the rain trapping and stifling what noise there may have been. The second shot crossed the street and pierced the window of some other main street shop. The down from her puffy jacket hung in the air for only a second before the rain pushed it to the ground.

I reload and holster my weapon and retreat back to the coffee shop taking my kerosene in hand. The Hispanic boy is crawling to the door and gasping deeply and leaving a slug trail of blood. I reach in for my gun raising it high to clear the silencer through the holster. I shoot a bullet into his head. Clat!

Next I squeeze some kerosene onto all these victims except the girl in the back. My pistol is secured. I reach into my right front pocket for my lighter and ignite the bodies one by one. I squirt kerosene onto the wallpaper and light that.

Under the energy of the rising inferno a voice catches my ear; "Help!" the girl in the back chokes out through the blood. I leap between the flaming bodies into the back and find her coughing up dark coagulate, sitting up and spilling her tears into the portion that has accumulated in her lap, and into pools all around her. I aim one shot into her head, Clat!, and she goes silent and limp.

"What if I was your god!?" I yell at her carcass. Then with a wrench in my gut I make my way through the flames, back out into the rain and rushing wind.

Hustling; I burst through the stained wooden doors

of the insurance company while raising my pistol and I fire the first bullet into a tall man working some admissions desk. Clat! Blood covers the old stone brick wall and I make my way into a centralized area of cubicles.

I am taken aback by how many heads are in here. They are shocked to see me this surprised. I see the fear; the blood clearly emanates its own presence from my throat. I open fire into a modestly dressed woman. She falls into her cubicle wall and the screams catch my attention from all around. I am disoriented as I kill the next two. Only really firing into their blurry colorful figures. Clat! Clat! Clat!

I planted my feet and caught my bearings to look around. A younger man is cowering against a wall with tears in his eyes. The others are running out the back.

I aim for their spines. Clat! Click.

Then I look to the boy as I reload. I get his attention, "Hey! Listen while I load my gun. I hope you'll remember the chosen one." More Union Underground quotations.

The kid has not moved. Only whispering, "Don't kill me. Don't kill me," at the floor between his legs.

I put a bullet into him before I chase the others. Clat! Through twisting halls I chase their screams. A larger, whiter, more modern office and more screaming people. I should have had the AK.

"Get out! Run!"

These people had caught the hysteria easily.

I stop.

The ones I've been chasing have made it out a glass door and into the rain. But there are others here. Clat! Clat! Clat! Two down close together. Over in the corner. Clat! A child? A boy of about ten. Dead now. That was new and unexpected. I have to go. In corners and crevices they cower.

"I'll be back," I say as I walk away.

I run back through the building to that initial scene. There is an old woman leaving her desk and running for the exit. Clat! Clat! Clat! The rounds penetrate her body and she falls.

I retrieve the kerosene and squirt out some onto the bodies. Missing a couple on the far side. I light them on fire. One by one. Along with the cubicle walls. I drop the empty clip, reload, and hurry the fuck out of there.

More rain. People milling around outside the smoking coffee shop. Turning their heads to the cries from the distance coming from over the buildings. Screams completely audible.

The sheets of rain blow with me as I am walking. The wind is at my back and I climb up three little steps into the white walls and amongst the practical and stylish casual wear. There are two twenty somethings looking at the slimy blood on my face. They haven't seen the gun at my side. There is shit in the way!

"You've got to help me. Please," I said desperately. And I raised the gun and Clat!, shot one in her face. Her prettiness gone with a gory impact. The patron dropped to the floor. The girl working screamed and ran out the back. I moved around the clothes and shot the other girl on the floor twice while moving over her; Clat! Clat! Not paying much attention to the placement of the bullets. I shimmied over her.

Sirens. Close.

I stop my chase and move back into the clothing racks. I ignite kerosene on the clothes, push one rack into the curtains, and another into a wall. My heart is pounding. I ignite the two victims and rush out the door; out into the running water of the streets.

I run for my car and get in fast. The keys in the ignition, I start the thing.

The cops are coming from the way of the coffee shop. I am not going that way. I am going to the mall. Up the way and around the corner.

I put the car in drive and push the accelerator into the floor. I fly through one intersection at 60 miles an hour. I keep that speed and the road dips down a hill and I drive past a bank with huge red signs and go up another hill and through another intersection and a red light.

"What if I was your god? South Texas death ride," speakers drowning me in sound.

I approach the Apex shopping center on the right and throw my car into the 90 degree turn with a cautious flick of the foot. At the sight of the first department store entrance I see, I rip the emergency brake, twist the wheel, and lock the rear tires, spinning the car 360 plus degrees.

The cigarette burns quickly at my deep and frantic inhalations. I take the rifle strap and throw it over my shoulder, the barrel smacks the back of my head when I open the door and step out into the rain. About four shots in my pistol. One drum on the rifle, one clip on my calf. 75 on the drum. 30 in the clip. 75 for the civilians, 34 for the police. Is this the last time I'll feel the rain? No, not the last time something tells me.

The sliding glass doors oblige my entrance. I come into a far corner of the store. My mom used to take me here to get clothes. Here it is. I see all the pink everywhere immediately, right before I notice the older woman who works here occupied with a rack of soft pastel shirts.

"You!" and I point the gun in her face.

"Oh my god!" she yelps. Immediately crying.

"Go. There!" And I point with the barrel down to the entrance to the actual mall.

Another girl cowers by a wall of clothes for baby.

Turning the rifle in my hand I say, "Wait! Right here!" And I throw the butt into her nose when she turns to face me.

I approach the girl from behind. "Stand up! Go with

her." I point to the lady cowering in the main isle. This girl is tan and attractive. Early twenties. Dark hair. There's another one a stone's throw away.

She runs screaming when I catch her eyes watching me. I raise the rifle and aim at her. The rifle jerks hard in my hand and three rounds explode from the chamber. The sound is absorbed quickly by all the clothe surrounding us.

"You two!" I fire into them on the ground where they are holding one another. Five or six rounds. A head bursts across the tile and carpet. The young girl lies limp. God fucking damn it!

Screams in the distance. In the mall; rising all over. I catch the location of one That is unlucky for somebody.

I run. There is a woman cowering behind a jewelry case. I move around and fire into her. The violence of the shells piercing is insanity. It seems to punch the life out of them.

I find another woman and her daughter. Cute kid. All these people react the same.

"Don't kill us. Don't hurt my daughter."

I blow the little child's head from her jaw and shoulders. The mother screams. That's grizzly. She runs toward me and I drop to the ground aiming for her heart and fire.

Trying to get out of this store is proving difficult. I see others but I ignore them. I have got to get to a shop. In the main foyer there are still people running panicked from all the different stores. I raise the gun to my eye to aim and shoot a man. Three quick shots. Another one. A teenager in baggy clothes. The bullet pierced his throat and his eyes went wide as he spun to the ground. I move through the gun smoke. A man tries to leave a music store. He caught my eye and retreated. I chase him back inside. And he made it to the back before I shot him down.

Screams quickly silenced at the rear left. I hustle over there. Two girl employees, one chubby, one ugly, and that guy's wife, clearly, and a kid of about 13. Dorky little fucker in his glasses and dirty Lego blue sweatshirt.

"All of you stand up right now!"

They all kind of whimper out their little cries and hold tight to each other, feeling for what someone else might be doing. Prey. People acting like fish.

"Get on your fucking feet now!" I shoot a CD rack twice. The little plastic packages fly through the air.

They all stand.

"Face the fucking wall!"

They do, only a little reluctant.

I fire into the bodies. The employees necks. The second in line goes to pieces in place as the other girl falls next to her. I kill that girl the exact same way. And then place shots to the back and head of the wife who had tried to throw herself in front of the boy. I shoot the frazzled boy in the head, once, also.

Nice to have that out of the way. A weight has been lifted. My homage complete. I had wanted to do it in the department store.

I turn away from the corpses and make my way back to the main hall. It is a one story mall. They are running toward the far exit. I aim and it takes five shots to drop a twenty something guy in a pink dress shirt. Had to be a cell phone salesman. There is an exit directly to my left. No one runs for that one. Another goes screaming down the way. I aim and fire. Two shots. They ring out through the terrifying silence. Ricochets make amazing noises and drift into the top 40 hits droning from above.

Across the way is a clothing store for women I go into it and look around and don't see a soul. I fire one shot into the ceiling.

"Oh!"

Every time. Just like the movies. Do they want to

51

die? The dressing rooms. Too easy. There is a pretty little number hiding behind the desk with her hand over her mouth. She looks up at me through her beautiful teary eyes. Sorry. Not a parking ticket bitch.

"That won't work this time." I shoot her in the face from point blank range. The moist cavity sparkles. Of course.

She tries to run to the employee door at the other side of the store and I take her down with two shots then walk over to the body. She looks like a gypsy, in that delicate red phosphorous skirt, and that obscure Indian looking silk blouse. Her straight greasy hair is swimming in the gathering blood pool. She writhes on the floor. I put the gun to her ear and pull the trigger before I go and investigate the dressing rooms.

There are beige curtains and ignoring the urge to look under them for legs I tear them open one by one.

Hello. The pretty girl with freckles and braces. She'll be a knockout in a few years. Her arms wrapped around her still budding body. She only has a bra on. And jeans.

"Hold on." I tell her.

I find one other woman hiding away and shoot her twice through her arms and into the chest as she lay curled up in her fetal position. And then another into her head.

This little one has given me an impulse. Returning to her, I drive the rifle butt into her temple. When she falls to the floor I tear the bra from her back, from her uncooperative bodice, and disregard it. I retrieve the kerosene and squirt it over her perky little boobs. She writhes. I punch her in the nose; blood flows instantly. I light her breasts and stand up to watch them burn. I throw the butt into her head once again as she tries to regain consciousness. Letting the smell of burning flesh linger in the air I take aim and shoot her right through the eye. The flames lick in and out of existence and

finally expire. Leaving only greasy and cratered flesh.
The pink nipple gorgeously deformed. Moist.

I start fires on certain clothing racks that can be
shoved into the walls that look flammable. And that was
the last of my kerosene. I throw the bottle and waste
two shots shooting at it.

No more screams now. There is actually a dead
silence. How many escaped? Having a partner might
have been nice. Double the fun, I guess. There is one of
those super savings superstores at the other end. I'll be
neglecting an entire wing. But this will just have to be
accepted. Surely, I can find people hiding in there.

I make my way; firing a shot into the greeting card
store. Nothing. Look around. Dead bodies here and
there in the hall. I fire into the toy store. Nothing. I fire
into the bookstore.

"Eee!"

Yup. Hiding. I light a cigarette real quick, go in, and
look over the counter. A scrawny gay guy wearing
pastels and those black rimmed glasses that are hot on
quirky girls, but make guys look like queer book
pushers. And he's wearing pastel. I walk around to
where the counter flips over itself.

"Why did you hide here? Why didn't you run out
the back door?"

"Please don't kill me." Tears on his squished up
face. Choking his words out. Why is there no fucking
variety here?

I shoot him in his foot. "Why didn't you run?!"

He cries out, "I don't kn- It seemed safer!"

I shoot him in the shoulder, tearing him away from
the clutch of his foot; exposing his stomach.

"What, are you retarded?"

"Why are you doing this?" He cried out with spit
flowing like a faucet. I shot him in his gut. He coughed
blood and went limp as he fell back but his eyes kept
looking. Past me; at the ceiling.

Yeah. This isn't doing it for me. I threw the gun over my shoulder and went behind me to pick up hardcover books and throw them at the guy. One by one.

"Who... the fuck... reads hardcover books... anyway!" Lots of people, probably, actually. I shoot him through his heart. His eyes stopped seeing anything after that. I drag my cigarette, shoulder the gun, and leave.

To the god damn super mart bullshit. I hate these fucking places. I go over to the main entrance foyer on this end and poke my head outside the second set of doors. Cops flooding into the parking lot.

Aiming the rifle I fire shot after shot at the oncoming squad cars. Not close enough to hit a driver. But they'll feel the bullets hit the cars. The rain on my skin. On my face. One more round. Back inside to the super store.

Does Pawtucket have a swat team? How are they going to handle this?

It's bright in here. Harsh. Shit. I wish I started here and ended back in the department store. Fire. What can I burn here? Clothes. I go that way. A men's room. I enter the tile area. There are feet right there.

"Come out here. I won't hurt you. Just come out."

"No." A solemn man. Good for him. I fire into the toilet and the ceramic flies around his feet.

"Get the fuck out of there!"

He steps out timidly. Awkwardly. An old black man. Fucking Curtis Loew. I shoot him in his heart and turn away before he even falls.

"Old Curtis was a black man... with white curly hair... when he had a fifth of wine... he didn't have a care. Play me a song Curtis Loew Curtis Loew."

While setting clothing racks aflame with a can of air freshener I see a man moving cautiously out the corner of my eye. He is against a rack of candy, not chancing running, and completely exposed. Like lightening, I hoist the rifle and fire at him. A neck shot. He lays gurgling, choking, coughing, gasping, and dying.

I walk up to him. He looks like a teacher in a short sleeved dress shirt and a tie. I pull the rifle up by the barrel, grasp the butt by the trigger, and throw it down into his skull feeling the crack. Blood splashed out in all directions.

Sirens are screaming through the walls. Through the light rock hits boring me dimly from the speakers. Oh god. My fucking stomach hurts. My eyes spin in my head. Things become blurry and almost fall away. I sit down by the teacher against the candy rack. Deep deep breaths. In and out. Breathe in the bad. Breathe out the good. Light a cigarette. Breathe in the bad. Breathe out the worse.

Oh god. Is this happiness? There is no time to think about it. Is this that feeling I spent my whole life searching for? A finality. An end to that beginning I have always known. I stand up and meander away through the store.

The sheer volume of actuality involved. Perhaps I destroyed the man who would cure cancer. All these people had families. How many will cry after I am gone? How many are crying now? The tears mounting in volume. Creating a great crushing weight on the hearts of so many. A weight so heavy it can only be borne by the strength of thousands.

My attention turns to this flak jacket. Who the fuck am I kidding? Fuck this. What does it matter? I should get on with my death. Do I even really want to shoot it out with the cops? I remove my coat and abandon it. I throw away the pistol. Then drop the heavy vest to the floor and it lands with a thud. Oh, it would.

My fun is over. I don't want anything to do with this anymore. I throw the rifle over my shoulder, light another cigarette, wander into the aisle full of cleaning products, pick up two cans of disinfectant aerosol; placing one in my back pocket, holding the other, and then walk through the field of indoor pyres. I create more flames on the clothes racks. But my eye is on the exit.

It shouldn't be long. They should be heading in here by now I would think. I am only burning clothes. I haven't seen any patrons around lately. I haven't searched for someone either. The fire is really pretty. The heat is hurting my face. I am having fun spraying flames from my aerosol can.

This will be the last time I have fun. I think. Oh shit. The rain.

I throw the can over my shoulder and light a cigarette. Making my way with a purpose over to the entrance.

From beyond the row of cash registers I take a general aim out of the entrance to the mall and fire off what rounds are left in the barrel. Bursts of tile rain from walls. Windows shatter; some close, and some far off. About six windows leading to the exit. I move in a semi-circle to the left so I can hit all of them at least once; pumping my finger furiously to get the rounds out.

Click click click through the echo. Crack the release, with my fist jar the drum loose so it clangs on the floor. I put down the gun, equip my knife and flick it open. Pulling up my pant leg; the mess of masking tape and full clip bound to my calf are exposed. I cut away the tape to free the magazine and tear it off like a band aid.

With the clip loaded I drag my cigarette and hear more sirens arriving. The police already out there have turned theirs off. But the blue and red still dances on the walls of the mall entrance. Masking tape bounces in the air as I move with the gun raised to my eye to peek around the corner. Two cop cars stationed. I see one face aiming a pistol out of his cruiser window. The other cruiser is empty. The rain is clearly falling as heavy as it had been all day long.

Keeping to the floor, I move around the threshold of this super store and into the mall. My back against the wall. Just a ferret in the corner. There are two cops in the distance scanning from left to right. Looking to, and away from, my recent positions; caught up with the sight of the corpses. I can only hit one from here; there are kiosks in the way of the other. I aim real fucking good and take my shot. He falls with the burst of sound. I see the other cop dive into a store.

Standing up I run within 5 yards of the glass entryway. I take aim of the cop in his car and just before I fire the glass shatters in front of me. I pull the trigger rapidly, struggling to maintain my initial aim. I move into the automatic sensor and the door is opening as from the right an officer enters the foyer taking aim at me with a shotgun. Four shots right into him. His weapon discharges once and the glass rains down all around me.

The cop in his car hangs over the door. Clearly dead. Shots over my shoulder. I return the fire but I cannot see where it came from. Glass exploding all in front of me. The door the cop had come in by opens and I run through it.

Through the rain just running. Ambulances and cop cars; there are red and blue lights everywhere I can see. I can hear the shots. The sidewalk and brick walls are bursting in points all around. There is a good distance between me and the officers shooting at me from one and two o clock. Vehicles are gathered around my car really far away. And around the other entrance still a good distance away. The pistol strikes are not even close now. They can't hit me from where they are any more.

No one can get me now without me getting them first. So I turn and aim to the cop shooting from besides his flashing lights. I can see the flames burst from his gun. That's a target. Aim. Fire. Aim. Fire. He is still shooting at me. I can hear him missing. Aim. Fire. The brick chips over my shoulder. Aim. Fire. He fell. I seen it and turn my attention to the advancing squad cars; three of them.

I fire sparingly as they advance. It is all I can do to aim for the steering wheels. The wind and water are ripping past my face and I just pull the trigger slowly. Methodically. One car is pulling ahead of the others. He turns his sirens on and his headlights are closing in on me. For a moment I kind of stare into them. But he is going to drive into me.

I fling the rifle butt down and put the barrel to the underside of my chin and pull the trigger.

2

Tobias Squires' work shift had ended. He left through a rear maintenance door of the Dunkin Donuts Center on a side street and walked out to the area where Broadway and Atwells turn into downtown; heading away from the city to his hill. The weather was pouring rain but he didn't much mind it. Anything for an excuse to look downward and not pay attention to the world. Nonetheless his head jerked this way and that keeping his eye on traffic. He walked past the Seattle spawned coffee shop and past the Hilton Hotel; heading up to Federal Hill. His hair blew across his tilted face and hid that disfigured part of him from the world.

Walking over interstate 95 he turned his head with an over emphasis left and right; checking the traffic entering the highway before the overpass, and exiting the highway after it. Hanging from a concrete arch over Atwell's avenue was a large stone pineapple. A symbol of salutations erected by the Italian community in that old Italian neighborhood. The streets were lined with fancy restaurants and upscale clothing boutiques. The neon signs shined softly in the overcast afternoon while dully illuminating the colorful walls of the storefronts.

Tobias didn't much fit into the environment. His stiff and stained jeans were wet to the shin with street water, and his dark blue polo two sizes too big poking out from under his bundled black wool coat reflected a working man appearance seldom beheld in the area. The others on the street around there were wearing finely tailored black suits, and holding umbrellas over the heads of beautiful blonds in clothes made of expensive materials, getting into big black luxury cars or awkward SUV's.

Still, Tobias was as much a part of this neighborhood as the highest ranking Mafioso, or the playboy with the nicest Ferrari. He turned his head a full 180 degrees left right and left again to look before crossing a busy side street.

His apartment was marked with a sign chained by the ankle to a wall. It read, "Astrologer," in big red letters. With smaller print underneath, "Psychic readings, Palm Readings, Tarot, Crystal Ball, Walk Ins welcome." Who would be walking in today he wondered knowingly. Through a door in the brick he walked up the stairs into his apartment.

The place was immaculately clean. High end furniture and glass tables. Dull metal wall sculptures of stars and the moon and the sun that rattled a little when a large enough truck drove by. Tucked away at a corner was a round wooden table with no items on its surface.

From his kitchen to the right a thin all black feline with fluffy fur walked in to greet him. The cat released a prolonged and high pitched vocalization.

"Pluto! Hi kitty," said Tobias in his cat voice. Much like a voice one would use when talking to a child. Only not as obnoxious. It moved slowly toward him before crouching down and looking up at him and pouncing into the air to land in his arms. The cat started purring as he stroked it. He walked to the window holding his pet close to his face, talking to it as he looked down at the soaking wet street from the bay window in the living room. "My day sucked Pluto. But I bet yours was nice. Where's Olivia? In the garage?"

He walked to his bedroom at the back left through the kitchen and put the cat down on his black and white polka dotted comforter. From his pocket; he placed on a chest height bookshelf his keys and his wallet. From a black backpack he removed one clove cigarette, lit it, and undressed to put on jeans and a t-shirt that were not soaked and did not have toilet water in their fibers. He removed the patch he wore over his right eye and replaced it with another. That one, also black, had a white infinity symbol stitched into it.

Pluto hopped off the bed and stayed close to his ankle while Tobias walked around barefoot on the beige tiles of the kitchen. His feet collecting only a little grime on the soles.

While making rice in the microwave the digital tones of his cell phone started piercing the air and rupturing the afternoon quiet. On the ID he read a name and a number.

The call was expected. He had seen the news at work. A couple people in the break room had been gawking at a television screen when he walked in.

Any of his clients may have been affected by this in one way or another. Some people cry for the tragedy of others. And some of those are the types who look to the stars for answers or, in her case, relief.

"Hello... I know. I saw you on the TV. Come right over... Ok. Bye."

Crystal Gold had been his client since he started drawing the natal charts for Olivia. Long before he learned the tarot.

For a long time he had had clients coming to him

for answers and in that right he fancied himself a therapist. Like a shrink without the mundane, and of a higher significance. Naturally. His service was rare. Something for the privileged enlightened.

It was exceptional that the day's events happened so close by. He always thought things like those killings were reserved for those in states far away, and in areas he would never visit. The settings for single tales within his memory.

But he was not immune to the excitement building within him. There was a large death toll in Pawtucket. The part of him that was tuned into the homeostasis of humanity could feel the displacement of energy. Only after he learned of it, of course. Olivia had known about it though. In Pawtucket? She had even said something.

He looked up at the corner of the room and thought for a moment; projecting his words into the space around him. Sensing the energy spread through the quiet until he knew she would hear it. "Olivia. Come here." He didn't need to go all the way to her with the thought. For all logic and reason, she probably knew to come when he had first thought of her.

Picking up his cat, Tobias leaned against the porcelain counter and pushed the microwave open, and then closed the door so it was only cracked, he ignored the food for a minute. All was very still. The rain dribbled on the windows as night fell and the house grew darker.

From a door in the kitchen wall Olivia Athens appeared. With black grime on her exquisite face and skin, dressed down in an old gray college hoodie, unzipped over a tight pink t-shirt and jeans; her hair was only a little out of place from the face shield she had been wearing. Wiping her face with her forearm and standing attentive, she looked at him knowingly, with a hint of sorrow, and an identification with Tobias on the matter that these murders had happened as close as

Pawtucket.

"What up, homie?" she asked.

He looked at her for a moment before speaking.

"Can you guess who just called me about a reading?"

"Crystal."

"Yup."

"You excited?"

"I don't know. How much do you think she saw?"

"How upset did she sound?"

Tobias, still holding Pluto, walked past Olivia to the living room couch and sat down.

"She sounded like she had seen dead bodies earlier."

"Did you hear about the other one? Denver?"

He hadn't heard. Olivia informed him. Rhode Island was the first. She had seen it right before on the tv out in the garage where she was working; another killing very similar to that of Pawtuckets was reported on the national news. The connection hadn't yet had a chance to be broadcast locally. Crystal would need to be there for that. That meant she must have left from work only to see Tobias.

"But don't mention the coincidence to Crystal. She won't know yet and we want her to be attentive. If you tell her, she'll go running off back to work."

"Alright. Whatever," said Tobias. Thinking how remarkable it all was. Two?

"Just wait," Olivia said ominously.

Tobias was stunned silent by the certain way in which his foster mother had said that, and had meant it. He recognized the rise in intensity she was suggesting. He knew she couldn't distinguish most causes. Or wouldn't. He didn't ask. He only reflected on something unknown and heavy that was going to drop. And then the knowing that that could only be a foreboding of something much worse.

He stared to the ground and tried to think of the future. She knew. And in the empty doorway of the kitchen, Olivia smiled a little smile and laughed at him, at their little understanding of the world.

The cat jumped from his lap, went to Olivia's foot, and she picked him up and held him in her arms. Not acknowledging him further than the strokes of her hand. She just looked to her apprentice.

"What are you making?" he asked her.

"A fountain."

With spacey eyes he disregarded her reply.

"Oh. Did you know this was coming?" he asked.

"No. You know that." She was his height but, leaning against the wall her head was kind of looking down, though her eyes stayed on him.

"And you know what I mean."

"Then yes."

Getting to his feet he walked past her, touching his cat as he moved. And he removed the bowl of wild rice from the radiation machine. And with a juice box from the fridge he sat down at the kitchen table between the two bedrooms to eat.

"Come tell me about it when she leaves." She walked back out the back door to go and work with her torch in the garage downstairs.

He put another spoonful of boiled grains into his mouth and got up to turn music on in his room. He pushed power on the CD player, set CD 4 to play, and turned the volume to low; techno music, electronic sounds and beats squirming like vibrations as they rolled through the atmosphere, nothing more than an ambiance. No lyrics whatsoever. Number four that day, for its particular dark trance effect. He turned on his black lights, and then aimed a spotlight at his mini disco ball. Small statues of flying witches, and angels, and demons made by Olivia hung from his ceiling by string. Catching the light fragments. His walls were lined with

white and black posters of rock stars and Edgar Allen
Poe. Or tapestries with anti-establishment messages.
The motif was entirely particular to his tastes in an
important way. Other than the disco ball there was only
a lamp to provide natural light and it was turned off.
Strong black light bulbs were installed in the fixtures
overhead and four, four foot, ultra violet bulbs were
screwed to the walls. It was his intention that in this
space his clients knew who the mystic was.

He needed to possess the attention of all of a
client's major senses. He lit nag champa incense on his
bookcase. And in the kitchen he boiled water for
decaffeinated tea. He moved his low circular table of
ebony to the center of the room. And the two bean bag
chairs were set. That covered the five major senses. The
center of his room kept open and free of clutter for his
sessions. That room was of complete order. Anything of
importance either hidden or displayed.

In his room he had the ability to take a person away
from themselves so they could see for their own eyes the
things that he knew about them. The will he presented
provided confidence to those clients who arrived with
any skepticism. An effect not to be under-appreciated.
His intent made it easier for them to trust the tarot; a
big part of his work, and of his life too.

The bedroom was set for Crystal's arrival. He stood
in the kitchen and watched the water boil for a moment.
He watched the steam rise from the shining metal
kettle. From the cabinet he took two black mugs with
white Asian characters embedded in them. He took
down two chamomile teabags from a shelf behind a
glass door and placed them into the mugs, clicked the
heat off on the stove and poured the hot water into the
cups. He added half and half and sugar to Crystal's glass
before putting those items away. Pluto hovered about
his ankles for a moment; Tobias picked him up and
walked to stand in the kitchen doorway, staring at the

street door. The cat purring in his arms.

At the bottom of the stairs the first door opened. Her feet clunked in heels climbing the stairs and she knocked on the door twice. Quick hallow noises.

Tobias opened it and Crystal stepped into his apartment. She wore a long soft coat the color of lion fur. Her hair was wavy and resting on her shoulders, only a little blown around by the wind. Her long face was softened, stressed, and solemn with old tears. Brown eyes looked at him and through him. She handed him her umbrella and he took it; she closed the door.

"Hi," he said.

"Hey."

There was sadness about her that day. To the astrologer, that she had been affected by the events was clear. He knew enough about her that the fact was not news to him. He knew of her capacity to feel for others and of her tendency to do so. Her compassion was such that a long time ago, when he was first coming to know her through his study of her natal chart, he wondered why she would be a street reporter in the first place if she responded poorly to situations of duress. Though he knew; her Gemini moon and Venus in Cancer said it all. She was good with words and had a strong desire to share them with everybody. Her sun sign was in Leo and that placed her in front of the camera. But she cared too much; it was not the first time a story had brought her to Tobias.

If there was a murder close to her house she would see him. If there was an epidemic of some sickness and someone close to her was affected she would see him. She would see him if the mayor she had voted for was going to jail. All of those instances had occurred. Now it was the mass murder.

Tobias put Pluto on the floor and handed the tea to Crystal; they went to his bedroom and he closed the door after she and Pluto had entered.

"Toby!" she cried out, breaking into tears and looking at the floor in front of her. "The bodies were everywhere. They were bringing them out one by one. And some were still alive, and they were in shock..." she broke off; weeping into her hands.

"Crys, sit down."

She removed her jacket and obliged; cross-legged on the bean bag chair. Pluto crawled into her lap and she held him close, stroking him, still looking down. Her black turtle neck fading into the dim, her hands wrapped in a cat, her focus in a steady stare with teary significance. Hiding behind her sandy hair and dark highlights.

Tobias reached under his small bed and retrieved an ebony cigar box. Then he sat across from his client; placing the box on the floor by his side and opening it. From the box, a white silk cloth was removed and placed over the center area of the table. Four semi circles of wood remained uncovered. Stitched into the fabric was a black Lemniscates. He removed another white cloth. This one wrapped into a bundle. The flush surface of the bundle was placed on the table and he unfolded the white material corner by corner. Facing up was the fool card. The joker of the tarot. Tobias's own requisite to always be greeted by the fool. He picked up the deck and put aside the blank measure of silk. Crystal took a single sip of her tea and he was delighted by it. They were ready to begin.

From under the bed behind him, he removed a red colored pencil and a small notepad opened to a blank page. These items he handed to her.

He watched as she wrote her question. She did it blankly. Expressing the emptiness. A revulsion. As though something had been seriously misplaced within her. Pluto moved over to his side. Crystal tore the slip of paper and gave it to him. He placed her question in the left circle of the symbol for infinity.

Putting the Gothic Vampire deck in front of her he said, "Break the cards please."

"Can we use a different deck today?"

Tobias laughed to himself about that and said "Oh yeah. Sure." From under the bed he retrieved another pine box with a Ryder Waite deck in it. He placed the cards on the silk and said, "K. Break them please."

She did. Into three proportions; large, small, and medium. He took the tarot cards and shuffled them. Looking up from the cards for a moment's glimpse of Crystal; at the terror within her. This terror was what must be expelled. "Why does it have to be this way?" was written on the paper.

He thought briefly. She needed to hear her own voice of security. She needed to see what part of her was going to guide her to the future; through the jagged winds of despair. Tobias needed to know what had happened in Denver. What exactly. It was easy to worry him too. He could feel the cosmic disruptions permeating through the ether. The connection. Seeing Crystal there sent him a single message: Tobias needed to know what Olivia knew. There was a vicious coincidence that day. He could not ignore it the disruptive presence of the knowledge within him, distracting him

Tobias handed the cards to his client. "Please shuffle them and think of your question while you do."

The music rang under the surface. The electronic thuds in rapid succession, gaining speed and drawing Crystal's awareness to nowhere. She handled the cards with a sense of what she would receive from them; going through the motions to tear the terrible memories away from her conscience. She wanted to move on as quickly as possible. Her compassion was to be overcome.

"Can you cut those into three stacks please?" she did.

"And now pick them up." So she did; right to left.

"Hand them to me. Thank you."

Tobias took the cards, careful to maintain their handed position, to his solar plexus; to focus his energy on nothing other than the cards in their relation to the client. He came into the cards and the cards came into him. Now the cards were of Crystal- through Tobias- for Crystal. Tobias and his cards were almost the same.

He lay them down. The first, the second, and so on into a Celtic cross spread. To answer the question: why does it have to be like this? Seven, eight, nine, ten; the other cards were put to the side.

Crystal took another sip of tea and Tobias was given another moment to look everything over. He lifted the first card. This was what covered her. They both knew it.

"King of Wands. This is Gerri." Gerri was the man in her life. In her world; the end all be all of everything she was until the point she had met him. The position covered her.

"In this position Gerri is going to be present throughout your life permanently. No doubt. He will be there through all of anything to come. You are deeply longing for his comfort.

"The Tower. This tells me right now is only the tip of the iceburg. This tells me that you and I have not seen anything yet."

He went on to explain the next cards. The High Priestess. Handling it better than worse. The whole picture could not be seen at that moment. Something was wrong in the distance. Behind her was the two of cups. Achieving their goals was in the past now for the couple. As was the strongest period of their love. If this were a positive occurrence it would not have been in that position.

Castles in the sky. The Empress reversed. Her big thing and what was to come of it. Again, Gerri. And her being taken care of to the stretch of her desires. All of her dreams came true. She had found happiness. She had found money. And she had found the happiness that came with money. Living such a glamorous life and to bring children into that world. Crystal as a future soccer mom of only the highest standard. A Jewish lady then. Though she had been born Catholic. It had meant everything to her for a long time. The second of two fantastic achievements. She acquired her dream position of working for the news. Being out in the middle of things. All of it was in jeopardy.

Crystal would be searching for a deeper meaning more than ever before. For Tobias that was a signal flare to pay absolute attention. He would take extra interest for the sake of a business opportunity. She'd be coming back more often.

But even still she was wrapped up in material concerns that would come to the surface as her ideals were forced into an upheaval as materialism lay waste before her.

The Ten of Swords represented those surrounding her. Unhappiness and depression, and a sense of loss. Deep distress.

Queen of swords was representing her own positive feelings. He kept a certain revelation to himself. Instead he informed her that her wit would be solid and there was a desire to be helpful to a mutual party

Then came the absolute reason why it had to be that way- from all the previous angles- where she herself was actually standing; that, was the hanged man.

From his memory of texts he quoted, "Blessed with truth and has no fear; Faith holds strong when trouble's near."

"Do you get it?"

She sniffled, "Can you explain it?"

"Yeah."

"Everything I see points in the direction of more catastrophe. I see that it will be this way because there is a powerful reckoning coming toward us. And of course, your work mandates that you be there for it. The events will be extraordinary and that is your life's work. The reading I just gave you showed me how you are going to handle it. But I'm sorry I can't tell you anything positive. These show me an avalanche of terrible things. And they show me how you are going to cope too. This reading is wicked tuned in. There is something deep inside you showing me this. And I don't understand it fully. Faith holds strong when trouble's near. Blessed with truth and has no fear. You better be on your toes.

"Because basically you are in for a rude awakening. I see upheavals. There is no way for *me* to know what they will be. What I think happened is that; in your proximity to today's events, you have been exposed to the foreshadowing energies involved in certain events yet to come. These cards would support that. The hanged man took this reading pretty far away from only today.

"I am not being the harbinger of doom here. My source told me that this is only the beginning of something much greater. I think I had something to do with the merging of your feelings and thoughts with the actual fact of the matter; informing you regardless of the reading that the future will not be a gentle one."

"Can I talk to Olivia?" Crystal asked him.

"Crys." She had insulted him a little. But he understood her duress. It had been a long enough while since Crystal ever thought it necessary to seek a second opinion. It was Toby's mention of his source that even brought the idea to her attention. "Call me in one day and I can tell you. Ok?"

"Ok." The old agreement.

However, under the surface he was ignoring something. He saw himself indicated within her cards and made no mention of it. He couldn't understand it and he kept the issue to himself.

Why was he so relevant in her life and the things to come? The Hanged Man? She was the Hanged Man. Gerri was the hanged man for some reason too. He did not tell her that.

Instead he looked into her eyes and said, "It's coming down, Crystal."

Afterward they talked about the shootings. They talked about her sadness. She told him about the burned corpses and the other terrible actions of one man.

The shooter was a worker at an upscale Italian restaurant downtown. He had called his girlfriend to say goodbye before he started shooting.

Toby was amazed by what he was hearing. There in the ultra violet lights, he was picturing it all in his head. The mall where it happened. Machine guns. The offices. The fire. The rain. Wondering what his sign was. Gemini? Scorpio rising?

He waited until she finished talking and said, "I need to go on-line and see what the stars are doing."

From under his bed he pulled out his laptop computer, opened it, and set it on his lap.

"Are you going to charge me for that?" Crystal asked, smiling for the first time.

"Um, no." Tobias said. Only a little embarrassed at his past business faux pas; charging for every little thing rather than giving them as good faith. Crystal was good for him in that sense. There was a lot about the world he didn't understand, things Olivia couldn't teach him; for she was set in her own ways. Crystal told him all about the business world.

Olivia did not actually facilitate his entrance in the family business. Nor did she shun it. She simply let him come into it for himself. As he became ready the day for a year natal chart progressions she didn't feel like doing were sent his way. Her tarot customers who decided they wanted astrology work done were sent to him as well. And when he felt confident to do Tarot readings himself, Olivia gave him two of her regulars.

One was a middle aged woman who naturally stopped coming very often over time. He did not worry that she didn't enjoy his readings. In the beginning he was rough around the edges and that lady stuck it out until he got better. They had a very comfortable association. The woman was mostly happy to be getting the discount. Sometimes she would stop by out of the blue; usually around the change of the seasons. Over time those visits lessened and eventually stopped.

Also given to him as a customer was Crystal. Madame Money Pants; she was sometimes referred to as. As long as Toby had known her she had been dating a rich man. His name was Gerri Goldstein and he was the vice president of The Hexatron Company. Crystal did not actually need to work but she liked to. Her contract with the television network was almost up and she didn't even pursue a continuation.

Tobias was greatly amused by Crystal. Of his six regular customers he was closest with her. He enjoyed listening about how she threw money around like candy to a child. The extravagant vacations she was always taking. The plastic surgery. He had advised her, more or less absent mindedly, that converting to Judaism was a positive thing. She'd tell him about the conversion classes she took and he'd laugh because it all seemed so silly. To merge with a foreign system of religious beliefs for an obscure reason like money. Becoming Jewish, not for a desire to be closer to god, but for a measure of convenience in her family life. That was the way of the world. People did strange things all the time. Especially with religion concerned. The conversion to Judaism was amusing but not surprising.

"Can you get me the killer's birthday? My guess is his rising sign is Scorpio. There were negative aspects between the sun and the moon earlier. And the moon is in Scorpio today. It would make sense. Mars is in Virgo?

A Mercury conjunction with Neptune. Which means we are all doing something that is part of who we are. You're reporting something terrible. I'm working with you. That guy was killing random people. Olivia is burning metal. But never mind. I would still need a birth time."

"Are you sure? I could probably get you that too."

"No. No. Forget it. It's not important."

"Ok then. I have to go back to station Toby."

"Yeah. Ok."

Tobias recapped her reading for her. Looking it over and making a few points he had missed about some old acquaintances of hers and an unexpected trip. She was holding Pluto, and Tobias stared at the cards trying to come up with anything else to tell her. An anxiety to give her more information than he already had nagged at him. But he knew she appreciated his readings.

"Here." She handed him a fifty dollar bill. Twenty dollars more than a stranger would pay. Crystal paid well because she could. Tobias accepted the money for much the same reason.

"Ok. Um. I'll talk to Olivia and give you a call tomorrow. Do you have any questions?"

"No. I'm good. I want to try and wrap up the evening edition quick and get home. I'm going to lie down, and have some wine, watch myself at ten."

"Ok."

He stood in the kitchen as she was leaving. She had her jacket on and she picked up her umbrella and turned the doorknob...

"Crystal," he said.

She turned and looked at the astrologer. His head was cocked to right, looking at her through his hair. "Try not to think about it. Alright?"

"Ok. Bye Toby."

"Bye-bye."

Crystal opened her umbrella, walked down out

onto Atwells Avenue, and got into her expensive new Cadillac. An upgrade from the Audi she had been driving. The rain poured down and she flicked the windshield wipers. There were cars coming by. All the windows were fogged over. She couldn't see well; gaging traffic by headlight reflections on the other cars around her. Eventually she was able to pull out into traffic.

She was listening to the Beatles. Julia. "Julia... Julia... So I sing the song of love... Julia... Julia." Her station was in Cranston and she took the highway. Driving slow; not wanting to be back there. Not wanting to cover the story. She dug her fingernails into the steering wheel and gritted her teeth.

"It will only take an hour. Two hours at most. Two hours."

It took her fifteen minutes to negotiate traffic and arrive at the studio.

As Crystal parked her Cadillac; she reached into the back seat to grab her purse. And from the passenger seat she picked up her cellular phone. It had been left there while she had her reading done and it had not yet occurred to her to check it. The touch screen informed her of a missed call and a new voice mail.

*   *   *   *   *   *   *   *   *   *   *

A big screen television mounted on the wall portrayed the image larger than life in plasma. Crystal was reporting from the newsroom. Sitting amongst a lot of gray. The network logo on the wall behind her. Shades of blue were prominent. She wore a red pant suit. Her hair had been redone; beauty kept modest for respect of the sensitive subject matter. The anchors had introduced her.

"Hello. I'm Crystal Gold. Today, shortly after noon, a gunmen opened fire in Pawtucket..."

She quickly retold the events of earlier that day.

The updates. The new death toll: 35 dead, 9 wounded. The charred bodies were omitted from the report. Memorial services were announced.

"And it is with deep sadness that I report that this was not the only tragic event that occurred today. Across the world atrocities such as ours have been reported. In virtually every European nation and in South America; Brazil and Columbia. In Mexico. In South Africa. Countries through the Middle East and Asia."

There was a montage of images from all over the world playing on the screen while she spoke. Showing crime scenes in Australia and Spain, and in Japan and Croatia. Helicopter shots of parking lots filled with flashing lights.

Too many to list verbally. In the US there were more killings. In Denver and in Columbus similar shootings had occurred. In Denver 17 were dead at a shopping mall. The killer also took his own life there.

"Possibly some of the worst news of all comes from Ohio where 13 young children are dead and three adults as well. The gunman opened fire on a restaurant and children's arcade. He was eventually subdued by patrons and died later in police custody. It is uncertain how the Ohio gunman died; we will get you that information when it is made available to us.

"We do not know at this time if the killings abroad are connected in anyway as it is too early to tell. But currently the thinking is yes, they are connected. We just don't, um, know at this time."

"I am fucking scared Gerri."

"It's really scary. But there has got to be some kind of explanation for everything. The government maybe. Or an internet cult."

"An internet cult?"

"I saw it once, all these people that wanted to kill themselves going to a website and getting together to

figure out how to convince other people to commit
suicide. Something like that."

It was late; the ten o clock news was on. Crystal lay
curled into the arms of her fiancé Gerri Goldstein. Both
were adorned in white Turkish bath robes. Gerri in the
corner of a lusciously soft Italian leather sofa. She had
rushed home to him. At work she did the evening news
live, and recorded a report for the 10 o' clock show.
Against network head wishes she insisted on recording
the story early, far before it would air, and not sticking
around for developments. Blind to the significance
through a compulsive denial; there was no way she
would report on this anymore and she abandoned the
story in a spoken proclamation.

Gerri had been home waiting for her. Through the
day he had watched it unfold from his office in the
Northwest corner and 26th floor of the Hexatron World
Headquarters. He had counseled Crystal over the phone
and she talked him out of coming to visit her while she
stopped home to cry after seeing the bodies.

At Hexatron all talk was of the news and there was
a very distracted necessary productivity all throughout
the building. The employees could not stop. It was a
designated tax time and there was a lot of information
to be moved around. Gerri watched her privately from
his office; somewhat removed from others who may or
may not have been viewing. She had phoned him just
before going on the air live.

He was smoking a light cigarette and very unnerved
in the few moments after he had gotten the call. She was
so upset. And a mass murder? In Pawtucket? Why?

He sat on his desk with an arm on his knee. The
pink cuff of a well-tailored blue shirt about his wrist and
his hand took uneasy drags from his cigarette. The black
hair of his head was curling thin and sparse; bald much
of the way back. His body was more trim and slim than
it had ever been from the diet Crystal had him on.

Behind his prominent cheeks; his blue eyes were shining and staring off into the gray of the Sovereign Bank Building. No view; just a contrasted image of rain against glass and concrete. For times like this, he thought in the back of his mind.

She came on the television against his wall. He saw the hidden sadness in her face. Then he focused on the quantity of rescue vehicles; he realized where his love actually was. He didn't know what to do so he sat at his desk, put out the cigarette, and took a sip of coffee. He used a mug with a picture of the warped web cast by a spider introduced to caffeine. And he went over documents mindlessly.

There was a knock on the door and James came into his office without waiting. James was an older man and a personal mentor to Gerri.

The company belonged to James Harrington. But Gerri had been running it for the better part of 15 years. James stood tall and had the way about him people get when discussing tragedy. Quiet and frank, aware of others pain in a vicarious way. Unconsciously aware of the disruption in life's interconnectivity. He was a British gentleman and an intellectual at heart. He too wore a blue business suit and his gray hair was combed neatly with a part.

"Did you see your fiancé on the tele just now?"

"Yeah. Did you?"

"Most of it. My secretary told me about it as soon as she saw Crystal. Of all the people that work there how did Crystal end up with that story?"

"I don't know," Gerri said, "luck of the draw."

"Well it's a terrible thing that happened."

Throughout the day Gerri talked to few people about it. Only the guys working directly under him and his secretary. But he never had much to say.

Crystal and Gerri lived on a cul-de-sac named Tulip

Drive in Hope Valley, RI- 29 miles South East of
Providence. In a 3,500 square foot McMansion. A home
with a décor that represented the countless hours of
shopping Crystal had logged to furnish it. Only the
finest everything. Guest rooms furnished for children
and adult relatives. The master bedroom smelled of the
mahogany woodwork. There were high ceilings in the
living room with a piano and a sitting area of white sofas
with a unique break away design. The layout was a flow
of numerous rooms and spaces and hallways. Light
hardwood floors and beige walls.

Upstairs was a loft area where the television hung
from the wall. She was drinking her wine; Gerri was
having orange soda. They both watched the news for a
little while longer.

It had taken Gerri a few hours but he had finally
calmed Crystal down. The worldwide events had
overwhelmed her. What she had seen in the afternoon,
and then what she learned of others later on had fused
her mind pretty well. It made her unable to focus.
Worried. Tobias' words echoed silently in her mind,
"more catastrophes."

She was beside herself. A lifetime of reliability in a
world with comprehensive events. And then that. The
widespread mourning in the air. She had told the world.
Mothers had heard it from her.

He made her dinner and got her to relax. Gerri
helped her to feel like herself again.

*　　*　　*　　*　　*　　*　　*　　*　　*　　*　　*

The massacres stayed the top news story for
another three weeks. Crystal swore to never speak
another televised word about them. And she took
several days off as stories from around the globe
surfaced one after another until February 18th when the
reports trickled to a stop. With most incidents occurring

late on the 15th and early on the 16th, by Eastern Standard Time.

In the United States there were incidents in almost all the major cities. Austin, Miami, NYC, Albany, Detroit and so on. Also a few isolated instances in low-population towns in places like Kansas and Idaho.

It was no different in any other civilized area. Or rather; the killings did not occur, or were not reported, in third world and tribal nations. Around 85% of populations over 900,000 were affected by a lone killer. 95% of all cities with a population over 6,000,000 experienced two killings. Shanghai experienced four; most likely due to its population of over 20,000,000.

A worldwide death toll was rumored to be in the progress of being formulated. A task doomed to fail; proving impossible for those that tried to collect such information from so many locations. A goal was set to have the number created by the same time the next year, and a race was on after a reward was offered by multiple wealthy families of victims and the contributions of others. When they heard about the fund Gerri and Crystal donated fourteen hundred dollars themselves to the search for a number, with a high percentage of the money going to those 'left without' after the tragedy.

Medias were reporting different numbers from their various sources. Some the same as others, and others wildly different from the rest. Some said 3600 hundred dead. Others reported 90,000 and 115,000. Eventually a lip service estimate of around 5650 was temporarily agreed upon by the major news organizations of the United States.

The natural stages of grief followed on a world wide scale. International mourning unlike any seen before was done over the internet, in civic centers, and at candle light vigils in the streets which could be seen from outer space.

Once the news of continuous random mass murders had spread initially; riots were reported in many areas, taking advantage of distracted police.

In Mexico City, Mexico; Delegate Zero and the Zapatista Army of National Liberation rose up to take hostages; giving them the leverage necessary to make the changes they desired. In a week long period of direct action and forceful politics the Chiapas were returned the indigenous people of the region by the government. They had their victory. Changes were set in stone to give them the autonomy they had never actually received but had long been promised. No hostages were harmed in that event. The people of the Chiapas were finally free to govern themselves.

The correlated events went on and on. Crystal didn't know each one, but she wanted to. She felt obligated to be more informed than anyone else. But she felt ill, too. Stressed. Afraid. And deeply confused. Everything she'd ever feared had happened all in a single day practically.

The St. Valentine's massacres, as they came to be called would certainly live on in infamy. People everywhere would remember where they were when they first heard of them, and what they did for those days while the killings went on. The police would remember that strange high alert. Rescue workers would remember the bodies. And Crystal would remember them too.

3

Ahead of her the van drove dangerously fast; a hazard to the other vehicles on the road; jerking and accelerating; it's satellite dish quaking in place. Driving her black Cadillac, with its powerful motor, Crystal stayed impatiently on their tail.

Something had happened. Only two or three hours

prior, on a Monday morning. She had already heard of the bizarre repeating of individual events; involving details not clear to her at that time.

A disaster at a facility for people with autism. Manton Avenue curved through residential neighborhoods. She was anxious to get there and uncover the details of what had happened. There were multiple ambulances at the scene. The police would be there. Fire? What was the scoop?

They arrived at a long driveway on the right barricaded by the police standing guard. The van parked as close as it could; her cameramen got out and began setting up equipment. She drove past them and parked her car on the far side of the driveway mouth, grabbing her notebook and getting out of her car.

The blocked off driveway curved down a hill through leafless trees and to the institute below. The emergency rescue vehicles were down there; all three branches. Behind flashing lights was the ominous presence of the black government vehicles.

The heels of her Gucci shoes clunked on the cold street as she walked; approaching the closest officer.

"Hi. I'm with Channel 11. Can you tell me what happened here?"

The middle aged cop seemed a nice enough guy; had that blonde haired soft skinned family man persona. Immediately recognizing Crystal, he told her what he knew.

"It's like been happenin' all over the place. I guess these disabled people are freaking out everywhere. We got injured people missing noses, or dead, brains bashed in. The workers said they 'lost control of the population.' 'Overwhelmed' they said. So now, we've got a good percentage of the entire population down there in restraints. Some are isolated locked in rooms. The poor PR lady of that place hasn't regained consciousness yet. Some of the others down there are trying to figure out what's going to happen next. There's no sense in arresting these people. But we're going to have to do something with em. Gotta find out how they handled it at the other places."

"Can I go down there?"

"Oh, I don't know Crystal. I mean, maybe once the ambulances clear out of here."

"Ok. Um. Do you think you can have someone from the inside sent up to talk to the press?"

"Yeah. Yeah, sure. I can do that."

"Thank you so much."

One more look down at the scene then she walked back to the van.

The cameraman was dressed in khaki and a maroon letterman jacket. He had a dark blue cap on and a scruffy beard. He looked up as Crystal approached him.

She said nothing until she got close, "Give me the binoculars."

Addressing the young sound guy, Lenny, who came around to see what was going on, she said, "Get on the phone to the station. Tell them to get employee names off this place's website and call cell phones, call immediate family, call anybody else who might know something. The government is down there and we won't be talking to anybody here."

The cameraman handed the compact optical instrument off to her. The wind was blowing her long buttoned black jacket about her thighs. The sky was gray and her cheeks red with cold.

From the right side of the barricade she peered down at the commotion in the valley below. The building was a colossal concrete block. Five stories including the basement. Lots of windows on the higher floors. A half dozen groups of people huddled together. The paramedics rushed to and from the front doors and at the side doors as well, further away. The witnesses were wrapped in blankets sitting in the vans and being questioned by men in black trench coats. An ambulance pulled up the driveway and the police pulled the blue barriers to her left aside letting the truck through. There were two other ambulances down there as well. And paramedic SUV's.

The incident had taken place roughly an hour and a half ago. The call to the station had come from a young black man who had answered his door to a crying woman with a bone showing through her right arm. He had called the police, though they'd already been reached from inside. And the woman had told him to call the news. People needed to know, the woman said.

The decision to interrupt programming had not yet been made; an absurd judgment call. That was Crystal's concern. Her job was to relay what was happening to her bosses. The government had not yet addressed the phenomenon. But that woman's concern was for the wellbeing of anyone inhabiting space around a person with autism; concern toward the drastic nature of the event.

The connection was clear. It was exactly what happened on Valentine's Day. In some incomprehensible way. Some connection she could not fathom.

Regardless of whatever way autism was involved; it was a crisis. People had to know. She took her press badge from her pocket and walked past the police car blocking part of the entrance.

"Crystal. You can't," said the cop she had spoken with.

She kept going. Rushing down the sloping road. Trying to find somebody who might know something. And leaning against a tree was a wiry young man with very tan skin and dirty golden hair that sat short and shaggy on his head. He had a gray sweatshirt on and blood drenched khakis. He was smoking a cigarette.

"Were you inside?"

He looked at her for a second and said, "Yeah. I was in there."

"Do you work here?"

"Yeah. I work here."

"What's your name? Can you tell me what has happened?"

"Alright. Yeah. I'm Mark." He paused, "They all lost it at once. They got savage- some of them- and some of them were just scared, they got wild, like scared looking, out of control."

"Why do you think this happened? Why would they act this way? What is it about them and not regular people?"

"Well. Some of them are always like that. That's how we had the restraints hanging around. We use 'em. But this happened so suddenly all at once, almost all of them. All the middle to lower functioning ones, and that's most of them we've got here. It just happened all at once. I can't explain it. They wouldn't organize this kind of thing. It wasn't planned. They couldn't. And we were being told to watch out for it. We were having a meeting about it when it happened. Happened in Ohio and everywhere between, moving over this way they said. Which I still don't understand how that makes any sense. But we didn't realize cuz everything we heard sounded like rumors and then there it was. Watching the people I work with get laid out; bloody, broke. The residents were out of control. Attacking each other. My kid I work with threw his head into the floor and knocked himself out. And we're trying to restrain them. We eventually got drugs into some of them. But these guys are big, and strong, not usually this forceful though, but today; today they were unstoppable. It was a really scary thing that happened. We were fighting for our lives."

"And you got out alright, it seems like? Are you

hurt?"

"My leg got bit. And some of this isn't my blood. I did get out alright. But that's because I'm badass. Others weren't that lucky. When all of this blows over, we're going to go back to work and the dead people won't be there. People we all knew this morning are gone now. I mean, it was a really frightening place for a long time. Until the police showed up. Hah. There were about a half dozen people that ran upstairs that had to be talked out of there by the police. They wouldn't come down."

He paused and dragged his cigarette.

Crystal saw her opportunity and asked, "How severe is this Mark? Everyone is wondering how urgent it is that we address the public. Will this be happening more?"

He wiped away the tears that had been trying to break through his eyes. "Ha. Yeah. Tell the world. Now. Better safe than sorry. This is a serious danger to anyone with their condition and anybody else around those people. America needs padded rooms and tranquilizers on hand until somebody figures out a better solution."

"Thank you, Mark."

"Yeah. Sure. But, hey, I wasn't supposed to tell you anything."

"Ok," she said. Then she turned and walked away; back up the hill. The cop was looking at her carefully as she came up to the barricade.

"Thank you for that. You probably saved a lot of lives."

"Of course Crystal."

She walked to the van and sat in the driver's seat to make a call on her cell phone to her boss at the station. Now was the time to go live. There was a crisis and regardless of how little she understood it, she knew that the gist of this issue was an urgent matter of public health and wellbeing.

The station arranged the broadcast. Crystal was

given 10 minutes until air. Phone calls were pouring into the station from all over Rhode Island. In five minutes she would receive a call from the research team giving her the sum total of what was known to be, and regarded as, the latest information. For the time being the first task was to inform the crew. They were adjusting equipment at the back of the van.

Her cameraman was gnawing on gum in his cheek, grinding his teeth and focused on the large camera he was working on.

"What's going on?" asked her sound man.

"We're on in ten," she said.

"Oh. What'd you find out?"

Crystal told them what she had discovered; spouting the details as exactly as she could piece them together. She'd be repeating the task in nine minutes. There was an inexplicable wave of "savagery" or "violent outbursts" coming from the autistic community; apparently this was happening everywhere this side of Ohio she told them. As far as they knew it all started earlier today. No reports of locations west of Ohio. But countless reports East of Ohio.

"What is actually happening with them?"

"Something about the nature of autism, from what I can tell. These people are exploding violently. But they usually behave like this. Some of them, I guess, sometimes. Except now they are going off all at once and the staff are getting beaten to death.

"The clients affected at this facility are all in restraints, and everybody is kind of figuring out what to do with them. I'm getting a call from research in a few. David you have to call production right now. Lenny, do my microphone now in case the call cuts close."

Lenny handed the microphone to Crystal and he checked the feedback inside the van. Vehicles were coming and going. Civilians were being allowed to enter the perimeter. Minivans and sedans; families they looked like. Down below she could see the arriving people segregated and waiting for the situation to sort itself out. Some were consumed with tears. Others were talking in clusters. Men in black suits and jackets were always talking to somebody or other. She looked to Mark standing by the same tree and exhaling drags off of his endless cigarette. She noticed the body language of his posture. Like a man after a battle. Weathered, worn and hard. The sharp electronic tones permeated through the air and she answered her phone.

"Yeah."

She wrote notes on a small pad.

The call was from a familiar production assistant relaying the shorthand research. A lot of calls were originating from private residences. Phone trees within the communities worldwide were already in effect and assessing damages. Consequently it was hard to decipher what was rumor and what was not. The station advised that Crystal report only the most basic facts; though reports coming in ranged from theories of conspiracy with sound technologies to entire families dead in their homes. The point to mention was that the nature of autism is inherently volatile as well as misunderstood. As such, they did not know what was causing the crisis, but there was a very real threat to most "middle or lower functioning" individuals with autism, as well as anybody in proximity to them. Crystal was to always use people first speak. The woman with blonde hair, not the blonde haired woman. People close to someone afflicted should keep to a safe distance and develop a solid defense strategy that is beneficial to the wellbeing of both parties. Immediate examples were to keep a distance using a broom stick or a pole for protection. Or to lock the person in an isolated room or area that can be monitored, via a window or a gate, as they may become self-injurious and will need to be coerced back to stability if at all possible. Anyone involved was to exercise extreme caution. More when they had it.

"Alright. Got it. I'll call back on the flip."

Crystal went over to Lenny and pulled the cigarette from his lips and took a couple drags.

"Guys ready?"

Mark: Inside the Institute

It's 8:40. I pull into the parking lot and get out of the car with my coffee in hand. Late to work and not feeling like hearing about it. The damn drive-thru was packed and backed up. I'm not usually late like this. My boss is going to flip. As if it's a big deal to sit with my guys for a few minutes while they bounce up and down on a rubber ball until I get there.

A van pulls in front of me heading around back to drop some clients. I finish my cigarette, put it out on the bottom of my shoe, throw the butt into a bush by the door, and walk into the security foyer.

"What's up Phil?"

"Heya Mark. Running late?"

"Yeah. The drive-thru at D&D wasn't even moving."

"Ah man. I hate that shit. Have a good one."

"You too." The older black guy buzzes me in.

I walk past a couple of clients selling coffee. I can't drink the stuff they make this early on. I usually have a cup after lunch though. Their staff attendant says hello and I say hi back and keep going down a long hall with all the administrative offices, to the stairway, and down the green steps to grab my guys.

There isn't a crowd around the unloading doors today. But then again I'm late. I see Greg with my clients. He's a big guy who wears a lot of black. One of those death metal types with his hair buzzed on the sides and the rest grown into a pony tail running down to his mid back. He has four of our guys hanging around him. His two and my two.

"What's up Dexter? What's up Ryan?" I give Ryan a high five and Dexter doesn't really notice I'm there.

Ryan makes some kind of noise like he always does. It starts with a "P" sound. He is saying "pee" and signing toilet to me. He doesn't actually have to pee.

"Hold on," I tell him.

"What's up?" I asked Greg.

"Ha. That's a funny question man. You talked to anyone around here yet?"

"No. Why? What's up?"

"There's a mandatory meeting for all employees. Everyone in the building. Fourth floor too."

"What the hell for?"

"From what I've heard, there is some kind of disaster with autistic people. They're freaking out and killing people all over the place. In Ohio and Pennsylvania. Down south and everywhere between."

Holy shit. This doesn't make any sense. "Are you serious?"

"Yeah man. The meeting's at nine in theater and leisure."

"What do you mean 'killing people'?"

"That's all I know. That's all I heard."

"Shit. I'll see you later. Dexter, Ryan, let's go."

Nine's about ten minutes from now. I have to do my morning routine. Get all my papers in order at my classroom. Killing people. Places like this exist so that that kind of thing doesn't happen, let alone all over the place. I have never heard of isolated incidents like that. I mean I have heard everything else. Forks in eyes. Or whatever. People are getting messed up here all the time. Personally I've been knocked out by a bigger guy from some white trash family. We are trained; people like me are trained to subdue them; get them in restraints until they chill out.

I say hey to the other guy, Ike, sharing this room

with me. He is a big bald black guy and we never talk very much. Just kind of share the quarters. We chat a little about the meeting and what has been happening. But he is even less informed than Greg was. I told him how the attacks have happened in more than one place. He can't make anymore sense of it than I can.

Our classrooms have lots of colors and pictures everywhere. They look a lot like kindergarten classrooms. There are extra communication books of pictures lying around; little square pictures for eat, drink, toilet, etc. Circular tables and cabinets full of all the things we use to keep them occupied. Sensory toys like children's fun foam or squishy balls. All sorts of things of that nature.

Dexter is bouncing up and down on his ball. He is a pretty normal 17 year old. For being autistic that is. His parents are Jewish and he looks just like his father. As most of them do. He's got darker white skin and a high and tight hair cut; puffy cheeks and eyes set deep that always seem to be judging everything. He frickin ruminates his food all the time, and I have had a little success curbing that behavior, but he'll still do it whenever he gets the chance. He is non-verbal but he makes these bird noises. Oh oh oh's and ah ah ah's. What is really great about him is the way he mirrors my attitudes. It is really easy to get him excited. Like when we need to impress parents that visit, or the higher ups, I can always demonstrate that my clients are enjoying themselves. All I have to do is put a smile on and jump around a little bit and he'll be right there smiling and jumping with me. Or when I'm pissed off, tired or whatever; he'll sit there with his arms crossed and be grumpy with me. He isn't aggressive or dangerous so I don't have to watch him too too closely.

I used to work with the aggressive ones. That's how the directors break you in, one on one with them. In restraints, out of them. Put them in isolation with the weight blanket. Temple Grandin's theories of pressure therapy in practice. It's definitely strange at first, but you get used to it like anything else. You get used to them. I love these people. No two ways about it. I sympathize with their plight. How the gift of cognition has been stolen from them in some strange way. Replaced with an inhuman essence of awareness. Like how animals perceive the world. Thinking in pictures. Socially inept. Even the higher functioning ones.

Some; you can talk to them for hours. But they aren't always all there. They won't respond to this or that question. Or they go off on a random tangent about completely new subject matter. And then you're all bummed out because you liked the shit you had been talking about before. That's how it is with them.

My other guy, Ryan, is playing the keyboard. He's tall. Pale. Kind of looks like an emu or some kind of bird. What is cool about him was that before he came to me nobody knew he was into music. His parents had raised him so into sports, because the father was. And he took to it. Memorized all the players, all the scores of every game ever. He functions about in the middle. He can talk but not very much. You can ask him a question and he'll give you a slurred near incomprehensible response.

I would be listening to music and I saw him keeping beats with his hand. And he'd sing with little sounds that were only sort of words. I was listening to Sweet Home Alabama and he was singing the words of Pop Goes the Weasel to it. So I put him in front of a keyboard for a half hour a day and he fell in love with it. He comes up with his own rhythms and gets pissed off when it's time to move on to a different activity. Academics are the worst with him. He hates them. He throws the counting materials and rips up papers all the time.

The meeting happens in a few minutes. If everybody is going to be there that means the clients will too. It'll be stuffy in there. I've got all my papers ready for when it's over. I guess I'll go now. I'm kind of excited to hear what the higher ups know.

I tell my guys we are going and grab my clipboard and head off to the theater; also on this lower level. A few people are hanging around already but I got here early.

A power point presentation on the screen at the front of the empty room reads in big red letters "High Alert." Really?

I sit down against the wall with either of my guys on each side; Dexter on the left. They are really pliable (some of them) in their actions. Over the years they learn to obey the commands of the people working for them. And I like the symmetry that comes along with keeping myself in-between the two.

Soon everyone starts flowing in. The tough ones they keep by exits on far sides. Like usual. The room is more or less part of the main hallway; half empty space, with chairs stacked against the side wall, and its half work out space with the usual varieties of exercise equipment.

Our director, Kara, is standing by the screen. A pretty blonde woman just barely thirty. Her hair is cut short to her cheeks and she has these pouty lips that have got to taste like a cherry lollipop. She's wearing a black skirt and a maroon blouse. She spoke closely to the older large unattractive woman who handles PR I think.

And by the treadmill was a milk crate full of arm and leg restraints. There was one by the stacked steel folding chairs also. More people come in and sit together on the floor, as per our custom. Tough guys are sat in chairs because they are too volatile to sit on the carpet. The big girls and the big guys sit in chairs too.

Tina sits down next to me in the same way I am positioned; two clients are between us. Tina is the little number I associate with. We date. We don't date. We don't care and we get fucked up together a lot. She's a college girl over at URI. But she works here pretty much full time. Takes mostly night classes I think. Her dark hair is tied back in a ponytail and she's wearing denim overalls over a pretty tight, black, long sleeve shirt. Tina's got those big brown doe eyes. She's got that little kind of body you can throw around till the neighbors call the cops.

She quietly asks me, "What have you heard?"

"I heard they're killing people. All over the place."

"Me too. Anything else?"

"No. You?"

"No."

The room swells with a crowd all sitting on the floor, shoved close at the front of the room. Staff is also congregated at the back too; crowded, but not jam packed. This looks like everyone.

All these heads holding fingers over their ears resemble, well, they resemble autistic people really. But they're different. They are on edge. It's a sensory thing. They hear everything better than we do. But there is something different about them now. It is almost as if they are attentive. Which is too strange to think about. Not attentive to any one area or direction. More focused on the air in a given place; looking up and straight ahead. Dexter and Ryan too. And Tina's kids Lucy and Michelle. Cute little girls. The kind that fill you with wonder and a sense for the beauty in this world. Well. Michelle at least. Those chipmunk cheeks. But they are just staring at one spot. And it's quiet. It should not be quiet like this and it is.

I look to Tina. She is noticing the very same thing.

"Tina." I glance with my eyes to our kids. And in return she shot her eyes over the whole room to our director who had noticed of course. I am not reassured. The entire day staff is staring in awe at the room full of clients. I return my gaze to Kara at the front of the room. She lifts her eyes to mine and addresses everybody.

"Ok. Guys. Listen up!" There is no wariness in her voice. She clearly is not eliciting a reaction to what is going on. Good for her.

She continues, "If you have not heard the rumors. Let me recap what we know." The screen behind her flashes to say in big red letters "What We Know." The first bullet read. "People with autism are becoming aggressive against themselves and others at a crisis rate."

"People with Autism are becoming aggressive against themselves and others. That means exactly what it says. People are dead and people are injured," Kara said.

Another bullet, "It is happening all over the place." And another, "Only east of Ohio currently."

"I don't know why only east of Ohio. We do not know why; nobody knows why. This is uninhibited aggression, Ok? It will not be like what we deal with on a normal basis. We have been on the phone all morning trying to get information about what is going on and we have not had much luck. All we know is that people with autism everywhere are now being held in restraints and in padded rooms; tranquilized. Emergency services are tied up in all areas as a result and it is very difficult to actually speak with anybody about it. From what we know we are calling this a crisis and we expect you all to behave accordingly. They will be self-injurious as well as aggressive. You are all to take an extra set of restraints if you already have a set, and two sets if you do not. We want everyone to have two sets even if you work with only one client."

The screen behind her changed to read, "What to do now." Three bullets said, "Take restraints. Return to a quiet room- an isolation room if possible. Await instructions over the intercom."

"Having said that can we pass around the restraints?"

An older staff member, lanky white guy with long greasy gray hair, who has been here for about 15 years moves to pick up the milk crate and six different screams flood the air. Including chipmunk cheeks piercing screams. I haven't taken my eyes from the man I am watching, and from the corner of the room- oh fucking Bulldog! The huge client is on his feet and he brings the metal chair down over the old guy's head with a crushing motion. Fuck. And my hair! He is pulling my hair out of my skull. Ryan, backwards into him. What I can see is through searing eyes. Dexter throws his head into the wall. Weak walls for this reason; they crumble easily and in an instant Dexter lifts his head and brings it down with so much force into the floor and goes limp immediately.

"Fuck!"

Tina has chipmunk cheeks in a head lock and another pinned to the floor by the neck with a knee on the back.

"Mark!" she cries. I throw my arms over my head and my two fists into Ryan's ears. He lets go immediately. Rolling away from him I see the scene clearer. Everyone is wrestling with the clients. There is a panic. Staff are tripping and falling; running for their lives. Screaming. There. The crate of restraints is still there on the floor. Getting to my feet I leap at it. And somebody's back collides with me midair. But I have the crate.

"Mark." I see a hand reaching and I give him what is hopefully a full set up. Ryan is charging at me. I jump up and into him throwing him off balance and using that advantage to bring him to the ground by the crate. He is fighting against me and I am straining myself keeping him to the ground trying to get these wrapped around his wrists.

Oh god. There is blood everywhere. Coworkers and clients falling and fighting. People not moving. Got his hands. Sitting on his legs I reach to get restraints for Tina. She is looking right at me and she is clearly losing her struggle. Her client is overcoming her from underneath. I feel a sudden weight on my back and crumple to the floor on top of Ryan. I am pinned between a heavy weight and my guy.

I can see Tina is in a bad place too. Tangled up and wrestling with her girls. My free arm has restraints in it.

"Tina!" I call. "Here." And I throw the leather at her hand.

There is a crushing pressure in my shoulder. In the tendon. My neck spasms uncontrollably and with a jolt of all the strength I have I push the person biting me off and rise to my feet. Ryan tries to get up and I push him over with my foot.

I see who bit me. A harry behemoth. He's getting to his feet. I shove him over onto his side. Oh fuck. Tina is limp and gushing blood from her leg.

I throw the two girls off of her and pick her up. I have to kick a head as the person grabs my ankle. Tina is dead weight. I run out to a nearby classroom and kick a restraining mat over from the wall and lay her down; closing the door behind me.

I get back to the scene; making eye contact with Greg across the way; he is rising from placing somebody in restraints. I look around. People are wrestling on the ground. I see the shuddering wounded. The limp. The restrained and those entangled. The dead behind everything.

"Get hurt staff out!" someone shouts.

"Yeah. Good idea." And I do that. Helping a guy with a bloody face out of the room. I don't think he can see. His fucking forearm is twisted up like a noodle.

"Here man. Sit against this wall."

I turn to get back into it all. And from this point I

can see a younger one rushing at me head on. I throw myself into him, placing my shoulder at his waist and I use his momentum to throw him over me and I keep moving then pull a pair of restraints from between bodies and turn back to him. He is again charging at me. I use my leg and upper arm to stop him and bring him to the floor and kick him hard enough in the ribs to stun him. He fights against me hard as I get him tied up; kicking his legs into my back.

Moving back to the theater I am thrown down on top of an unconscious person who does not respond to the impact. My breath has been stolen. Again I jump up and the new attacker is there, he had chased after me but has fallen. I kick him in the ribs; this is fucked up. But really I don't care anymore.

I drag an older woman out of there. She is limp and my upper body is pushed to it's limits; but I get her to the other room.

Going back to hell I say nothing as I pass a big girl with blood on her face helping a limping smaller girl away.

Much of the population has been subdued. Three of my coworkers are now moving freely between the bodies. I cannot distinguish between them.

"Are we keeping the autistic ones in here? Get the hurt staff out?" I ask.

Greg said back, "Yeah. Let's do that."

There was an old woman with a battered face. The jolly old nurse sitting quietly. I lean down to help her.

From the crowd I hear, "Watch out for broken backs and necks."

My director's voice coughs out from the back, "Tranquilizers! Get tranquilizers."

That's you Mrs. Sparrow. "We have to go to your office," I say to her. I help her up. "Can you make it up the stairs?"

"Yes. Yes, I can" she said.

I walk to and up the stairs with the woman; nervous about leaving it all behind. She moves at a quick pace for an old gal. We get up to the door of the first floor and I hold it open for her behind me. Across the way in an open lobby for the offices is the twisted body of the security guard. Fuck.

"Stay against the wall. If I say run, then run. And gather everything we need that you can," I say to her.

We move cautiously toward her office at the end of the hall.

The client jumps at her from an adjacent door and mid-rush I grab him by his large shoulders and pull him away from the nurse. His momentum rammed him into the wall.

"Run!" I yell.

I jump back from him to see what he will do. Of course he gets right up and bolts after her. He is tall so I leap high wrapping my arms around his neck and pull him down onto the ground. And the nerves in my thigh erupt. Fuck. He's biting. I punch him in his ear as quick as I can, and pull my leg away in that moment. His powerful arms strain my puny grip when he simultaneously pulls his head away and throws me from him. Again he starts after the nurse; who is now in her office.

I run through the searing pain tripping me up. Oh fuck. I cannot see any kind of weapon. He is huge, old, and dirty. Leaping onto his back I wrap my fingers around his neck and clench my fists. He keeps on his feet and moving. I dig in my knee and throw the weight of my back around and this takes him down. I keep squeezing his throat and he is tossing me about like a rag; into the walls and floors. When from doors a little further off bursts a giant pear shaped girl who lumbers quickly toward the office. I drop this one's gasping body and rush after the big girl who is quickly approaching the nurse.

Taking her upper arms in my arms I pull back on her. The nurse retreats to a corner. And I pull the girl backward until her balance gives out and she falls to the floor. I open up a door to my right and as the girl stands up I push her into the isolation room, closing the door and locking her in.

"Restraints. Now," I say to the nurse.

She is behind her desk and retrieves a set from the lower right drawer and hands them off to me.

And the fat one comes through the door. I throw the leather past him, out the door, and put an uppercut into his chin; sending him right back into the hall. As he gets up I kick him over onto his stomach and jump onto his upper back landing with both my knees. This takes a lot of the fight from him and it is easy for me to get the restraints on his arms first and then, using my weight to gain control, his legs.

I look in on the isolated girl. Unconscious on the floor. Aw fuck. Ok.

There is another crate of restraints by a filing cabinet. That comes with us.

"Are you ready?" I ask her.

"Yes." She loaded a final few things into big blue cloth tote and handed me a large first aid kit. We hustle back to the stairs and down the stairs to the lower hall. Past the two girls I had seen earlier. The big girl I had orientation with has someone small pinned and under control. I hand her a set and keep going.

Weariness is rising from under the surface in the form of pain. Tina.

"That room there." I point to where Tina is. "But wait," I say, tearing off my buttoned dress shirt and I wipe what blood I can out of the nurses eyes, then turn back to the theater, shirt in hand along with the medical box and the crate of leather straps.

There are five or so people riding the backs of the clients. Some two to one. There are many restrained and seemingly more not moving but those could be staff. So I make my way over violently thrashing people quick as I can; dodging the thrusts of flailing torsos. I hand restraints to reaching hands and search for hands that cannot be moved from their position and place them as close as possible. I stop to help some tiny girl bind a large female client.

"Where are the injured Mark?" My director asked.

"Out that way. First classroom. The nurse is there. I have the first aid though."

"Leave it here and help Michelle to that room. Send the nurse back. Stay with them in there. I think we'll be Ok here."

"There are two upstairs. One is restrained and the other is unconscious in isolation at the nurse office. Could be more."

"Ok. Gregory. Go up there and bring restraints. Search the halls."

I turn away to go to the room. I heard her ask, "Has anybody called 911?"

I ask the room full of injured, "Has anyone called 911?"

Tina does not move her head but speaks up and says, "I did."

To the nurse I say, "They want you out there with the tranquilizers."

She takes the bag and rushes away. I go over to Tina and examine her body. Others are being attended to by a couple of the ladies that usually work in the office. Tina has a hole in her pants. And dark black blood is pouring from a ragged open wound on her inner right thigh. Oh no.

I take my belt off quick and wrap it around her thigh tight. I don't remember the trick to tourniquets. But treatment should be here soon. I lift her into my arms and take her out of the room, out to the hall, up the stairs and into the main hall where I see Greg.

"Did you find anyone?" I ask him.

"No. Just the two you said. I think the security guard is dead. I'm going upstairs."

I bring Tina over to the main lobby and I open the doors to the security booth with my back. Tilting her body, careful not to hurt her head. I put her down in the corner sitting up. From behind me a woman runs outside like a bat out of hell. She has a crooked injured gait.

"You'll be safe here," I tell Tina, whose face is flush and unresponsive.

I rush to the door and yell after the woman to come back but she does not respond and continues to hurry up the driveway to Manton Ave.

Going back to Tina's side I don't know what to do. There is a jacket hung over the chair which I retrieve and lay over her front; tucking it behind her back. I kiss her cheek and run back to the basement. The director is moving about through the fallen with the nurse. Someone is pulling a body by the underarms. I go back to the classroom.

I see a woman with a broken leg. The two girls from the hallway are in here now. About three women are tending to about seven damaged. A younger guy I work with is slumped in a corner with his eyes closed behind glasses and he is taking deep breaths. Hand tight around his left forearm. The blood is spilling out onto his lap.

There is gauze and creams and sprays laid out in the center of the room. I take two sterile pads, a gauze pad, and a gauze wrap.

"You have to move your hand," I tell him.

He reluctantly does and I see the area were flesh has been removed. He grits his teeth and moans as I clear the coagulated and wet blood from the wound and tear open a sterile pad which I press to the wound and wrap gauze around; using the entire roll and tying it off clumsily.

"Come on man. Let's go up stairs."

"Concussion," he whispers. And he still hasn't opened his eyes once.

Alright. He can't weigh much more than Tina. I pick him up. A heavy weight. I feel the deep pain in my thigh which draws attention to the blood staining much of my right khaki leg. I ignore it and carry him, all the same, up the stairs.

The big guy who had been trying to kill the nurse has squirmed his way into her office now. In the security room I put this little guy down next to Tina and lean his weight straight back so he won't fall.

I look at Tina. Her expression hasn't changed. But that's Ok for now because I can hear the sirens getting louder. Propping the door open with a rock I go outside to greet them and light a cigarette.

The first person to arrive is a cop. I put my hands in the air; holding my tag in one hand.

"What's happening?"

"I work here. It's really bad inside. We need ambulances! People are unconscious and bleeding. Some are dead. Everyone is in the basement. There are broken bones, and we've got about 30 people with autism; either injured, unconscious, dead, or in restraints."

He looks at me like I am lying. "I'm serious!" I said. He went back to his car. An ambulance was coming down the road. I want him to see Tina and Mark first so I ran back inside and downstairs.

I got to the theater and announced that help is here. Kara got up and ran upstairs telling another guy to help the nurse hold them down for shots. On the far side they had started laying out the ones that aren't moving. There looks to be about eight bodies laid out next to each other. At the back of the room it looks like the half dead and the unconscious. But fuck if I can tell.

My leg is tearing away at me now. I don't know

what to do. I walk into the crowd of flopping and thrashing people. I can't tell-

Dexter. Oh my god.

"Who's seen Dexter?" Where is Dexter?

"Over here."

He is where I last saw him; didn't move even a little. His body crumpled on the arms, face pressing into carpet. I lean down next to him and move the shoulder to get a look at his face. He is alive. His face retained color and I can see him taking breaths. Unconscious, but alive. I roll him over onto his back. And move to the next person at my ankles.

The nurse is working on Ryan right now. Injecting the needle into his butt.

Another client. There is a wound on his cheek; gaping but mostly coagulated. The blood leaks. He isn't moving.

Around my feet are wounded and writhing autistic people. And my co-workers. There are the dead over there. I walk to them. A desire within is telling me to do this before help arrives. What has happened here is going to be represented in the dead.

Fallen to an implacable force no one will understand. Why would this happen? They are lying on their backs. I notice their expressions first. They have all died with different thoughts and now it is frozen in their faces. What the fuck?

Kara has not come back yet. But the first couple of paramedics have got down here now. I don't know what to do with myself. There is a client thrashing around unattended to. I hurry to him and squat over his lower back. Holding his thighs down with my calves and his shoulders down with my hands. They are giving in to the drugs now. This one included. Much of the fight has left them. It is not so intense now but I can't really think straight. I am aware of all those around me. Paramedics hovering behind me. I allow my head to fall to my chest and I take a deep breath.

Leaving this client to his own sedated devices I get up and go outside. Out the basement exit to smoke a cigarette. What the fuck? Paramedics are rushing in past me. Across the way are the transport vans. I go over to them and sit down against a tire and smoke. My leg.

Getting up I pull down my pants on the right side. And I pull up my boxers to expose the wound. It isn't as bad as others I have seen but I'm going to need stitches. That can be done later. I wonder if there is any gauze left in that classroom.

*   *   *   *   *   *   *   *   *   *   *

Tobias had been reading a novel on the couch and ignoring the sounds of Olivia having sex in her room when the doorbell rang.

He hopped up to answer it and was surprised to see Crystal standing there. She hadn't even called. She always called first.

"Hey Crys," he said with inflection.

"Hi. Toby. I have to talk to Olivia about today."

Putting a finger to his lips he motioned her to be quiet and tilted his head and pointed to his ear to signal her to listen. The repetitive thump of Olivia's headboard slamming into the wall was clearly audible.

"It'll be about a half hour. Sit down and I'll make you tea."

They both walked to the kitchen, Pluto followed catlike behind them, and Crystal sat down; putting her purse on the table.

"Tell me what happened," Tobias said.

"I don't even know what happened. Well, I know. But it doesn't make any sense. It's all really twisted in a way I don't understand."

"Yeah. But what *happened* Crystal?"

"There were autistic people and they freaked out.

And they killed people, a lot of people."

"Where?"

"Right down the road on Manton. And everywhere too. First it was only east of Ohio. But now reports are coming from all over the country. From all over the world. It is just like those killings."

"What do you mean they freaked out?"

She told him everything she knew; or had learned; about their habits and why the violence itself wasn't actually that strange. Instead what was really important was the widespread and drastic nature of what was going on. How they all attacked at once was what the world at large could not comprehend.

"They were banging their heads into the walls?" Tobias interrupted her.

"Yeah," said Crystal and then continued to recount the tale.

Partially repressed images of his father broke down the doors of his thoughts and he pushed them back out; listening intently to Crystal attempting to not think about those things.

The time was around 7:30 at night and outside the sky was dark. Crystal had had a long day filming different reports at the studio. Later on the station confirmed that she was the first reporter to interrupt broadcasting to report the issue. Shortly after her live broadcast; the United States government declared a state of emergency.

FEMA, acting hastily after the Valentine's Day massacres, reacted to the situation in an effective and expansive manner. After cross referencing assessments via the internet, it was ordered for any individual experiencing symptoms of the as yet undefined illness be isolated, placed in restraints if possible, and drugged if necessary. Medical units were completely overwhelmed. The military and Red Cross had set up housing facilities in empty hospital wings and furnished gymnasiums with the appropriate equipment as well as makeshift equipment.

Tales were rampant about murder in the streets, people with autism rampaging and unstoppable having to be beaten to death. Awful tales that were all too real in company with the disaster itself. The scope was hard to imagine because autism was practically everywhere.

Temporarily the severity of the condition was being classified in five levels by FEMA. Level four being potentially fatal self-injurious behavior and five being potentially fatal aggression towards others. Rough figures extracted from various locations were averaging about 65 to 85% of individuals with autism in any form, including young people never diagnosed, falling into the level 4 and 5 classification.

Lower levels represented characteristics of shock, comas, and partial to full paralysis of their bodies. They wouldn't speak, move, eat or even relieve themselves; the individuals sat stone still.

"If this is the reckoning, I don't care. But I do not want to be in the middle of something like this again. Because I don't think the Christians are very far from the truth. All I see is a pissed off lord and savior. No one told me it was going to be like this." And with that Crystal broke down into tears. Whimpering over and over, "It wasn't supposed to go like this... Not like this."

"Crystal," said Tobias, "let me give you a tarot reading, on the house, in the living room."

"I'll do it!" Olivia yelled from inside her room. "Give me a second!"

"Here Crys. Take your tea and go have a seat on the couch."

And she did. Pluto followed her. Tobias watched her. He was lost in thought. Are these really the end times, he wondered? The apocalypse had always been something close to his heart and never far removed from his mind.

Humans had been around for thousands and thousands of years. And for the last two thousand of them; every time anything out of the ordinary occurred the Christians assumed that this was it; that it was the end of days.

But looking around, there they were. Worldwide horror stories. It had to be a plague; the terrifying notion. He wasn't sad. He wasn't happy. He'd always despised the human race. Humans; destroying forests, polluting water and air, polluting land. Always killing and never changing no matter what. Never advancing toward the light. White men especially. White greed destroying and killing and no one could love one another for very long. They were certainly far from enlightened. Truly ferocious underneath all the glorious complexity. The life they had removed, the balance they had broken, only to replace with an overpopulated race of idiots. Was there a justification there? Didn't they deserve what was happening to them? Every bad thing that ever happened in the world was the karmic reaction to some action that had upset the balance. Since when was comeuppance a bad thing? Complacency after all was guilt by default.

"Tobias. What do you think is happening?"

"What do I think is happening? You're asking me? Hah. I think. Hah. What I think, is that. I think. Hmm. I think the Christians are right. For once. No. Autism? How am I going to have any thought about that? I think it's sad and horrible. Maybe next time it will be all those NRA fucks. Somebody who deserves it. I don't know how I feel. You know what I think is happening? Whatever the cards tell *you* is happening. That's what."

With that a tall man with a strong jaw, looking like a hippie; dirty and disheveled, emerged from Olivia's room. He left with a smile as Olivia sang from behind him, "To the willful winds he will weep. His hung to dry heart will not heal. Tears will try to tame the torment.

Another man is satisfied with a fleeting fulfillment until he finds himself worse off than he'd have been before; had he not come through my door."

The man went down the stairs and Olivia, dressed in silky white pajamas, approached Crystal; who looked up at her with expecting eyes.

"Crystal baby. Tell me what's wrong." But Olivia already knew.

"Oh. Olivia. You know what I saw today. You know how I feel. I don't want to talk about it and you know that too. I only want you to tell me everything will be Ok."

"Alright." Olivia knelt down before Crystal. "Everything is going to be Ok," she said.

Crystal smiled a little and said, "Liar."

"I know," said Olivia, continuing, "We'll ask the cards, right? That's always a good idea," and she smiled.

Crystal put her head down and began to weep to herself. Tobias took this as a cue and brought the circular pine table to the center of the room and removed the cards from the shelf under the television. He set out the silk on the table, put the wooden box on the floor to the side, and gave the deck to Olivia.

Olivia put the cards down in front of Crystal who was hovering over the edge of the table.

"Ask me a question," Olivia said.

"What is happening?"

"Ok. Can you cut those, please?"

Crystal cut the deck into three different sized stacks and Olivia gathered them up before handing them back to her for her to shuffle.

Crystal shuffled the cards and handed them back to Olivia, who was still smiling as though it would rub off on Crystal, and she gave them a quick shuffle before putting them in front of Crystal and asking her to cut them once more.

She did and Olivia gathered them up into a deck

once more.

Olivia asked, "Are you ready?"

"Yes."

Tobias watched her as admirably as ever. She threw the first card down in front of Crystal, face up. Her voice adapted that tone so familiar. Soft, tuned in, and consistent. A voice that would be strange in it's fluidity only if one did not understand that when she spoke in that way she was channeling a psychic energy that existed in the air everywhere, connected to everything.

She said, "I see a growing association between your name and the important events today. It is your destiny to be there on the front lines, so to speak, of the changes taking place.

"These changes are not of a human effect on anything, no, more of an outside influence on us. But this change is happening on the level of organisms, in the basic sense of the evolution from micro-organism to homo sapiens. Or from micro-organism to fish, bird, reptile, insect, or cat. You name it."

Crystal noticed Pluto shift in her lap at the words and she felt her throat fall into her gut. The weakness that had come over her receded immediately as her attention was again drawn back to Olivia's reverberating lips.

"And the same goes for the environment; the trees, the air, and the very ether we exist in will all be effected also. That being said, this is not the last time you will be exposed to our new terror. The first time of course was the shootings in Pawtucket. But soon it will be coming from all directions." Olivia said these things as Crystal appeared to be choking on her attempt to hold back the tears and the desire to cry hysterically.

"Alternatively; you will go through a period of comfort now. But in the distance, you see, this comfort cannot last. It will only last long enough for you to become removed from the prominence of these events.

Though the whispers will be there always now. Your life with Gerri will continue and I can see you two on that island in the far away sea.

"This vacation will draw your focus from today and Valentine's Day, tomorrow, and from this reading. But shortly after your return another story of a sexual nature will bring a frightening realization."

Olivia continued to throw the cards down face up onto the silk before Crystal. Seeing into them with a skill Tobias would never possess.

"Right now there is a fetus of connection growing inside you. You can call the shootings the egg and today would be the sperm and they are both incubating in a hyper changing world. These things will become clear when more and more people begin coming to you for answers. And these people will be many. But you will take on this burden with the love of a parent for a child.

"Because of the work you do this is your new status. At that time you will come into a position even I had not expected. This will call on Gerri's efficiency in networking.

"When the people of Rhode Island try to make sense of these worldwide horrors it will be your identity placed alongside them in many a mind's eye.

"But as I have said; you will welcome this. You will find the purpose of your life in your work over the next few months.

"I see Toby here in a big way toward the suns passage through Virgo this year. There is a symbiosis between you two later on. The world will be bringing you together. Not in any sort of romantic way but by way of survival. At some point toward Virgo you will be depending on one another to survive."

She threw down more cards.

"I also see you moving Crystal. To someplace with an exquisite view. Ask Tobias about it when the sun is in Aries. I know that's soon. This move will be made in a rush and it will be made urgently but that is not to say you won't have time to prepare."

"You are going to find yourself in contact with others from the furthest points of your remembrance. Your finances will guide you through your affairs. If it were not for your immense bank account you would find yourself in a very scary place indeed.

"Now," Olivia threw down a few cards and stood to her feet. "Do not underestimate the significance of today. Rather let it guide you through your every endeavor in the coming months.

"Here we have three lions on Federal Hill. And do not discount the scorpion working late in his corner office. I trust we all know how we treat our Scorpions?"

She looked to Crystal when she said this, who understood perfectly, and then to Tobias and he nodded appreciatively of the notion.

"Good. Three lions and a scorpion. And know that here is our strength. Here is the necessity. If it were not this way, we could all succumb to this."

With sudden and short movements of her feet Olivia spun her body into slow circles. She threw down a few more cards continuing to solemnly dance to herself in place.

"On a planet that is bleeding it will be our strength that protects us. Nothing else."

Tobias felt a wrench in his heart at those words. That last part was clearly for him.

"I suppose that is what it will look like from space. I wonder if maybe the president will be up there with the aliens watching the blood flow as if through the bites of that many vampire bats.

"It will even feel like the days are getting shorter. Like time itself were running out of time. And perhaps that will be the case."

Crystal coughed out her held back sobs. She was taking deep grasping breaths with her long hair hiding her face. And Olivia ran to her side wrapping arms around her.

"There there," Olivia said; handing the deck to Tobias to lay down cards for her. He did so one at a time as he was signaled by Olivia's glancing downward eyes.

Olivia continued, "Your family will be of an incredibly high concern to you. And although they may have been somewhat distant in the past; they will now be brought to the forefront of your life.

"At work; passion will overcome your bleeding heart. You will be on a crusade my dear. And I do not advise you to seek so desperately for the answers you desire because my dear; these are not for you to know. You will do what it is that you do best, and that is showing your community the same thing that every Crystal Gold in every community will be showing; the apocalypse.

"But it is your trip to the island that will define these things in a more general way for you. You must go to the island in order to experience an important shift in your consciousness.

"I cannot tell you what is happening. For I do not know. It is too early to make any sense of these things I can see. I will tell you that some things I see are absolutely repulsive images that make me truly sad for any world where they may occur."

The tears in Tobias' eye did not go unnoticed to Olivia. And she became silent. We will have our talk later, was the message she sent to him with a look and a solemn smirk. He understood. Tobias was not about to let on that he was afraid. Not to Crystal anyway. Nor around her. But Olivia knew. Olivia had seen how this would end for herself since she was only a young girl. Tobias threw down the last card on the table. The Tower.

"This karmic force will clear away the debris caused by yesterday," Olivia said. Letting out a little laugh. And then the tears swelled in her eyes too. She crumpled into Crystal weeping.

Tobias got up from his black folding chair and moved close to the other two. He hugged both of them and rested his head on Crystal's back. He was not crying. His good eye was obscured by being shoved into Crystal's hair and he could not see. The familiar blackness welcomed his taken aback mind. His upper body cringed with Martian energy, ready to tear apart the universe for the two lionesses of his pride whom he loved so much.

4

During Crystal and Olivia's question and answer session about the reading Tobias stayed quiet. Usually he was the type who would have something to add; taking an active interest in his surroundings. Not then; not that night. Not that moment. Not about that.

With a swimming head, he only sort of noticed Crystal searching for some reassurance from Olivia, for an impression that did not exist; that everything was going to be Ok. Crystal had sat with tears in her eyes asking questions. Why? What was going to happen? Would they live through it? Only, once the reading had ended, Olivia gave no more insight.

Olivia would draw Crystal's attention back to the more important aspects of the reading. Reinforcing what had been presented; to ask Tobias for advice in April, take the vacation soon and be prepared for a turbulent homecoming; embrace her new status. Crystal was lucky and destined to escape the horror with her life.

This cheered the wealthy reporter up some, causing Olivia to use it as a platform to revive her from her distraught state of tears. Olivia told her things like; whatever happens you will get out alive; Tobias will be here to help you.

Then when Crystal asked Olivia where she herself would be Tobias noticed the subtle way in which the psychic tweaked her client's attention. Olivia mentioned Gerri. How he would be there for her always. Except the statement did not warrant the acceptance elicited by Crystal in her reaction.

Crystal should have been skeptical. Instead she accepted it blindly. Tobias noticed the familiar anomaly. One of the only ways he ever saw a glimpse into Olivia's mind was when she let something slip. He knew she was holding back. Some vision she could not share; forced to blind Crystal's eyes to some hidden truth almost discovered.

And with the same resolve Olivia raised her by the hands from the seat and whispered something into her ear. Tobias retrieved the client's coat and helped her put her arms in. The two women embraced for a moment and when Olivia opened the door leading down to Federal Hill Crystal gave Tobias a kiss on his cheek and said farewell with a wave.

Olivia closed the door and about faced; puckered her lips and squinted voluminous eyes at her apprentice.

"Let's talk about your feelings," she said.

Tobias smiled bashfully and said, "I feel thirsty for blood wine."

"Well pour me some too."

In the kitchen Tobias uncorked a half full bottle of Merlot, poured two glasses, corked the bottle, and brought both glasses back into the living room. He handed one to her and sat down on the comfy couch. He allowed himself to sink close to her in the seat.

Olivia bit, "You couldn't be happier could you?"

"It makes sense and you know it. This is finally happening. I have always wanted this. Seen the mushroom clouds in my dreams. What's gonna happen Olivia? Is the government finally killing us off? And this is their sick way of hiding it; so cutting edge."

"I really don't know. That isn't it though. I can see the essential functions of government crumbling the same as the rest of society."

"Then it's a plague. A mutated organism nobody prepared for."

"That could be it but I doubt it. I'm hoping it's aliens but I don't see them anywhere. But it's logical right? Aliens could do all kinds of weird shit that we won't know about or understand," Olivia said while sipping from her glass.

"That's sort of the plot of the Andromeda Strain. But Olive. Guess what year it is."

"Oh... 2012. I've been waiting for you to bring that up."

"It's really coming down then, huh? And ya know what? Do you realize how glad I am? I mean. As long as I am with you until the end, what do I even care? I have always wished on Armageddon. I've prayed for it. Have my wishes and prayers come true? I have to be stoked. There's going to be peace on Earth.

"But you know how sad I really am," he continued, "And I can understand why this sadness matters. And I can understand why I should be happy. I think I will be happy once I get used to it. It is going to take getting used to. I'll be singing the doom song a lot.

"What are we going to do?" he asked her.

"Well, Toby. That's a good question. I know the answer and I'm not telling you. You cannot ask me for the answer. If you know the answer it will not work and you'll be fucked, I'll be fucked, and Crystal will be fucked. Ok?"

"Yeah fine. Crystal is involved?"

"Yes."

Nothing made any sense to him. It wasn't supposed to. What would having Crystal Gold in his life really be like anyway? He didn't want to find out. He was missing something. She was holding back from him. He could see it in her subtle sneer.

"How are you going to spend your last days my darling?" she asked.

"Consulting that fucking fractal line graph I was telling you about. The charts! Oh my god. The charts. Have you looked?"

"Uh-huh."

"What do they say?"

"Figure it out for yourself. It's pretty cool though. The whole mess was all figured out through Mayan astrology. Which is wicked different but really intense. Everything still applies. I think it'll blow you away. I want you to call Crystal and tell her what you find out once you do."

"Ok. No. Wait. You wouldn't tell Crystal where you would be either."

"Go get me my life shard."

Tobias got up, heavy with despair, and removed the brown broken bottle neck from her dresser and brought it back to her.

"Thank you." She held the glass in her hands rubbing her fingers over it. "My dream, Tobias. That dream I have always been dreaming. I can see the similarity in my figure now. I know it is coming. It is all very clear."

"Olivia no!" Tobias cried in protest; putting his glass down on the silk, throwing the shard from her hands, and flinging himself upon her lap.

"Tobias. There is going to be a parade of inconvenient truths in your life. In everybody's lives. This is only the first. And you don't have to worry. I am going to take care of you. I will carry on through you and I promise you happiness. I can see it. All you must do is not interfere. You must carry on as you would otherwise.

"Which is not to say that we won't be making changes around here. Our doors are closed to all new clients. First thing tomorrow I want you to put the sign in the garage. There can't be any confusion; because the world will notice the autism tragedy. The government will play it down in the media as much as possible. All that is left is to move on as one unified and terrified world.

"You and I are watchers of the universe and what good would we be if we do not stay fluid with its desire. Our purpose would be snuffed out like the cigarette butts of our lives on the ashtray of time. Once we flowed calm and comfortable like a river through the forest of life. Now we are approaching the rocky waters of death's canyon. This spring will be the most significant of your life. Or even of history and earthbound time. There is still the time to prepare for the fall equinox and decide which seeds you want to plant to harvest.

"Your clientèle must be dissolved except for Crystal. I will be doing the same."

He rolled onto his back and looked up at her. "Then this is it," he said.

"Yes. Do you want to know what I see?"

He shook his head yes.

"I see you in love with a beautiful and virtuous Scorpio. I see a union of two wills destined to overcome all trials but one." She had adopted her tarot voice. "I see blood flowing like a fountain. I see the same death and destruction you wished for. I see a change in everything from the air to the oceans to the core of the earth to the heavens; all of it."

"How will I survive that?"

Her tone returned to normal. "That is my point dear. You are going to die. Crystal too, and me. Just like you wanted."

"I don't want that. No one wants that."

"I thought you didn't want them to suffer in Africa, right? You wanted peace in the Middle East. You wanted the murdering and marauding United States government thrown away. An end to the evil?"

"And all these things will go away?"

She brightened up. "Oh. I assure you. There will be peace on earth."

Tobias wondered why she would tell him this. It was not her way to reveal what she knew. How could that compare? Her rules must have changed.

"No one is to know these things," Olivia continued. Crystal knows because she has to know for your sake. And come to think of it, I don't want you to call her. I need to call her and tell her to keep it to herself. So easily these things leak into the universal consciousness and then you lose your head start on everybody else. It's like native gift giving; when you give a gift you give away a little piece of you and somebody can affect you with it however they'd like. If you ask for that something back then it can't be used against you after you do. And if you keep other's aware of your desires than the universe will acquiesce to those specifications. Anyway, you will not reveal these things to your clients either. Matter of fact. Have one more session with each, tarot or not, and lie through your fucking teeth. Tell them everything will be Ok. There will be a time when your knowledge will save your life but for now it is your enemy. Distance yourself from all your clients except Crystal. Ok?"

"Yeah." Tears welled in his eyes and he felt the tingle and shiver of sobbing in his cheeks. He said, "Olivia. I can't live without you. I revolve around you. I need you like the moon needs the earth."

"No Toby. It is I who am the moon. And you will have to accept that you are losing me. Remember what I said; tell no one what you know, and attach yourself to Crystal like a fucking crab on a rock. Tomorrow you and me will spend the whole day together. But I want to be alone right now. Excuse me," Olivia said. She kissed Tobias on the head and then walked away to her room; closing the door behind her.

He stared off sitting on the couch for a minute and then opened the laptop computer. Pluto crawled over him and he stroked the soft fur. Then the cat hopped down and walked to the door that lead to out back and let out a meow.

Tobias got up and went to the door and picked up his cat who meowed again as he did so. "I wish you would stay in with me tonight," he said firmly squeezing the animal. "I need you. But I understand if you want to be alone. Doling out bad luck just got a whole lot easier." He put the cat down and opened the door for it, saying, "I love you," as Pluto walked downstairs and out the open back door.

Tobias closed the door after him, stood in place for a moment, and shut his eyes. He put his forehead to the door and in his mind he visualized his adored creature walking the nearby streets of Providence. Then he imagined the most glorious and pure light coming down from heaven and surrounding the cat. The white light of protection. Or god's light, as he'd heard it called. He could feel the light, gathering loosely around the animal, with a certain knowingness. As though if he let it, the light, which was under his control, would move away from the animal like a fog in new wind. He concentrated on the image more; Pluto stalking vividly; the light undulating around him. With his presence of thought he wrapped the light around the animal rolling it into an ever firmer concentration. Until he could be certain the light was firmly secured to his pet, and only when he was convinced that no harm would penetrate this cloak of safety, he stepped away from the image. Leaving Pluto alone gently; out prowling the back streets as he actually was.

He opened his eyes and went back to the couch to surf the internet. First he researched the actual date that the Mayan calendar ended. That date was December 21st of the current year, 2012. The web pages were all adorned in ugly green and orange colors and image schemes on a speckled night sky background; he found the information he wanted. He began to read the page, which was an in depth explanation of the Mayan's logic and astrological theory.

First they referenced certain periods of time. Many Mayan terms which seemed to only throw him off rather than help him follow along. Soon he realized they were simply referencing basic astronomical terminology; the sun, the solar system and the galaxy. 5,125 years was the measure of one of the five stages of the cycle the solar system takes to travels around the Pleiadian spiral of stars. There was a star cluster of seven stars forming the Pleiadian spiral; the central star was Alcyone, in the middle there was the star Maya, and the sun as they described it, was the star that resembled a sheep that wandered away from the herd too often. But the sun is a Pleiadian star nonetheless. The page stated that it takes 25,625 years to make that journey around Alcyone. These enormous periods of time represent the overall consciousness of humans as a species in one way or another. The Mayans are the keepers of this galactic schedule and they sprinkled this knowledge all throughout their land in Central America. For the first time he was at least somewhat understanding the nature of time as relevant to the entire development and consciousness of his species and not just the advancements of technology or art between one culture and civilization and the next or something simple like that.

Also during the coming period of time, if not already, the solar system would be at the same position in its travels around the Milky Way galaxy as it had been 225 million years ago; the completion of an entire journey around the greatest circle he could imagine.

And that made sense. But he had never thought of any astrological concept beyond this solar system. All the information he was reading was completely new information.

The five cycles of the journey around the Alcyone spiral represent five periods of light similar to one of our days. Or, at least the culture had related them in this way. The closer the solar system is to the central star is considered day and the further away is night. In 3,113 B.C. the solar system entered the metaphorical night and now the coming period is the symbolic morning. As with any change of degrees in the sky, any transition, from sign to sign or winter to spring, there were inclination's of themes there. Currently they were exiting the night. A new day.

But it didn't match up. Mankind was supposed to be making decisions on an individual level. But these single decisions were to stack to a much larger change of direction in everyone. A change in the orientation of the collective consciousness and of all reality.

Apparently the solar system was entering and had been in, for some time, something called a photon band. The photon band is pure thought and light energy, it seemed, emanating throughout the galaxy in band form the black hole at the galactic center. An event that had occurred in the past and caused problems with Atlantis.

He read on. An earlier part that had referenced a twenty year cycle- one with an unfortunately accented name- began to make sense.

Because, the website warned seven years prior, if man continued on a path of hate, ego, destruction of nature, and greed, which would have happened even without the new events; they would enter the new cycle into a time of chaos and destruction which would cause them to no longer be the dominant race on Earth. Apparently that role would be played by the trees.

That seemed right to him. The government came to his mind. If those fascists weren't so caught up with taking lives and fucking with money, and they would just drop the capitalism bullshit, they could do something about the state of affairs worldwide. If they even put a little thought into it and used the resources to save the world they could set an example and others would follow. That would never happen because Tobias knew one thing about the United States government: it never changed for the better. It only went through brief periods of respite while the democrats were in power and nothing happened until the republicans came back in and fucked it up worse than the last time.

However, and this would also clearly not happen, there was the opportunity for rejuvenation. If man was to realize that they were part of one great organism, and learn to treat everyone's lives with the same respect as our own, and learn to love and harmonize; they could enter into a golden age. That was the potential of the human spirit. But humanity wasted that potential. All for the sake of social contact it seemed. Humans all needed to be around each other all the time. And the more manipulative members of the race found power in that social need. A small number of people created the first government and it's been a downhill ride since that time.

The damned government. How could he cry for this place where the only people with the power to right the wrong couldn't give a fuck less? His entire life he had watched as worldwide matters worsened and nothing changed. Everybody knew the system was warped and still nothing changed. The 44th president promised change but the system wouldn't allow anyone to change because everybody superficially or ignorantly believed in the illusion and thus could never transcend. Tobias screamed at them to systematically organize then philanthropize, but no one heard him whispering alone at the useless newspaper.

Tobias checked the ephemeris of planetary positions for that day; 12/21/2012.

The sun was leaving Sagittarius for Capricorn. The Moon was in Aries. Which seemed appropriate. A decent quantity of Martian energy. On a day like that he would suspect unexpected realities could break out easily. Mercury and Venus were both in Sagittarius; images of himself sitting by a warm bonfire under the stars discussing oblivion alone. Mars in Capricorn; trying to hold your feet on 70 degrees of mud.

A look at the aspects showed negative energy between the moon and Pluto which was just eerie. But positive energy between the moon and Mercury meant time to discuss feelings. He imagined himself at the bonfire scared and alone telling himself it would all be Ok.

Looking closely at the aspects he couldn't find any explanation for the particular significance of the day. Though he noticed the sun actually entered Capricorn on that day. Not the day after, like the other page had shown. Which page to believe he did not know. Either way, it would be the winter solstice. A winter wonderland of death.

Ignoring the outer planets for a while; he was anxious to read on about the Mayans.

The website continued to explain the significance of the Mayan Calendar. Calling it not only a system to mark the passage of time, like any calendar; more so it was prophetic in nature and could help people to understand the past and foresee the future. The Mayan calendar was an exact schedule of all things to come into and pass through existence. He noticed the title of the page: Mayan End Times. His right ear spasmed in revulsion and the motion caused the ear to become momentarily deaf, setting off a high pitched ringing in his brain in place of sound.

Oh good, he thought. They were all so fucked.

He read on about this guide to the evolution of consciousness. Like in astrology, everything was affected; science, religion, life, and everything in between. The Mayan calendar was sacred astrology and as he read on he discovered what was missing from the ephemeris. The Mayan observations were tuned into elements of the skies his astrology had never even touched on.

The same way he had never considered astrology in terms outside of the nine or ten planet solar system, he had never considered what he read next.

Concerning the ecliptic, which is the line the sun draws across the sky; it is about thirty degrees removed from the equator; to the north in that hemisphere, and to the south in the other.

Concerning the Galactic Equator, or the Milky Way as seen from Earth, and the path the solar system followed around it, he was led to imagine those two lines make an X (and they do); the sun would rise on the morning of 12/21/2012 to conjunct, or fall upon, that exact intersection.

The Sun. Tobias imagined it shining upon earth from so far away. Then he brought it to the forefront of his focus. In his mind he was staring into a sun that occupied two thirds of his vision. The sun. Undeniably the most significant figure in astrology. The giver of life.

The center of everything.

But only as far as man were concerned. If man orbits the sun and call it a god like him and the Aztecs do and did, would the Sun not call the Milky Way it's God? Are galaxies controlled by black holes, he wondered? Yes. If that was fact; the hole in the center would be god, and perhaps the dense collection of stars the galaxy is comprised of are the Sun's sibling angels. That was the Heaven that had had always been spoken of. A heaven they created for themselves. Hoping to live vicariously through their god the Sun. In all actuality there was no heaven, only cold vacuums waiting for them when they die.

However, where the planets gave no hope for meaning in death; there was an abundance of meaning that could be found in them in life. Because existence so had it that gravitational forces had developed, shaped and formed all life throughout the history of living organisms.

Creatures tuned into every reoccurring gravitational force from thousands and millions of year cycles alike. Everything reoccurs due to the nature of gravity and space. Moving in circles; the same way his life behaved in circles and history repeated itself.

What a strange enigma it all was. An organism intelligent enough to know these things and ignorant enough to discard them.

Gravitational forces of objects. Forces of aspects between fields of energy. Forces of the varying degrees of forces in a given orbit, or rotation too. The fields of a track left by an energy. Or an energy at its most concentrated potency.

The Sun, the most significant object in Astrology, would form a conjunction, the most potent aspect, with the point where two incredibly significant influences were already in a conjunction.

No wonder that the set pace of change was on such an incomprehensible scale. His astrology did not cover those time tables, or regard those influences. But no astrologer would ever deny them their true due respect.

Tobias could not begin to predict what was going to happen on that day. Did Olivia even know? Either way, any day where the sun conjuncted the intersection of the ecliptic and the Milky Way; when it did something for the first time in 26,000 years; was sure to be one magnificent cosmic event.

The cards were showing them the meanings of these things anyhow.

The manifestations of those cycles could be seen through them. They could be seen in the news. Certainly

Olivia must be watching it all through her third eye.

From behind her closed door Olivia farted loudly.

"You're fucking gross!" Tobias called out.

"Keep reading!"

But Tobias was too taken aback. He got it. He understood. All that was left was to skim the article for factoids. Weird points about a mutation of living organisms. Time appeared to be collapsing due to something about Extremely Low Frequency waves that tied into worldwide lightning strikes and probably the photon band. Effectively increasing the Earth's rate of rotation and since 1980 the hours in the day had become closer to sixteen rather than the 24 of the past. Time had been accelerating and in retrospect that made sense. Look at all that happened in recent history compared to all the nothing that happened in the distant past. It was all working toward the pin point at the bottom of a spiral. They were upon it.

Olivia walked out of her bedroom a moment later and said, "Tell me what you learned."

He recapped to her all the things he had read. Olivia was right there listening as he spoke but she had researched those things already, during the St. Valentine's massacres. She wanted to make sure that he understood them. And he did for the most part. He was tempted to ask her about the practical aspects of the ecliptic but refrained.

When he had covered most of the points he stopped midsentence.

"And any astrological event this important will sure as hell have a serious impact here on- wait- it's all astrological isn't it?"

"Isn't everything?" she asked him.

"Yeah. And humans have never experienced this shit before. And this fucking planet is too fragile to handle it. It's no wonder they call it the apocalypse. They call it the time between worlds too. So technically we are in the apocalypse now and have been since 1992. Or since harmonic convergence in 1987."

"That makes sense, doesn't it? Bill Clinton comes into office. The 'sex fiend' or whatever? Then George Bush the murderer. And now this one. The final United States president."

"Wow Olive. I can't believe it's all coming down. I mean. I can. I always knew it would happen."

She curled up close to him and put her head on his shoulder. And he laid his head on hers. She said, "I know about the sorrow you are feeling better than you do. I promise you that you will move past it. My death will be nothing more than a signal flare that will guide you to safety. I gave you all this time to get used to the idea. You might be the only person alive allowed such a luxurious loss of a loved one. I am giving this to you on a silver platter so I want you to be alright with losing me. Because it's not just about you you know. I can't go quietly into the night until I know that you are going to be Ok.

"It is the time for you to become strong Simba. Because Mufassa is falling into the thunder of hoofed feet."

He closed his eye and they sat quietly together; wrapped into one another. Inside him was the inevitable sadness she had delivered to him. What good was a why anyway, when the why was irrelevant to the awful how of this unspeakable when? Instead of dwelling on it he actively chose to focus on the amazing moment. A moment so precious and fleeting, and absolute. To have his savior so close and holding him tight until she fell away into the abyss on either side of the razor's edge path to the light at the end of the tunnel.

"Let's play with the Ouija board," he said; opening his eye.

"Ok."

Tobias went and retrieved the device from his

bedroom, turning off all the lights but only dimming the living room one. He sat next to her on the couch and put the glow in the dark board between them resting on their combined thighs.

Each of them placed two fingers on the planchette and moved the object three times in a clockwise circle and then three times in a counterclockwise circle.

"You go first," she said.

"I want to talk to god. Is god available?"

The clear plastic disk moved over to the word YES in the upper right corner. Their fingers rotating the object to keep one of the three legs from falling over the corner.

The street outside was quiet, and inside the air was humming with a human frequency of attention.

"Ok," said Tobias, "How come you won't let us live?"

The pair watched as the spyglass moved over these letters: Y-O-U- D-O-N-O-T-D-E-S-E-R-V-E-I-T."

"And who are you to decide that?" Tobias said.

I-A-M-G-O-D.

"Won't you be lonely without us?" Olivia asked.

I-T-W-I-L-L-B-E-Q-U-I-E-T

"I hate you. Do you know that?" said Tobias.

I-D-O-N-T-C-A-R-E-H-O-W-Y-O-U-F-E-E-L

Tobias noticed the small hairs of his body being drawn upward and towards Olivia. And his breath was taken deeply; his body exhausted from the lack of the energy she had drawn out of him with her focused intentions and concentrated energy as she made a mockery of the idea of the board itself. Commanding the maximum potential of the device with her will.

Olivia asked it, "What is going to become of the beauty in this world when there is no one left to enjoy it?"

I-W-I-L-L-E-N-J-O-Y-I-T-F-O-R-Y-O-U

"Are you fucking mocking us?" asked Tobias,

laughing a little.

G-O-T-O-H-E-L-L-T-O-B-Y

They kept chuckling. "Can I stab you in the face, God?" he asked.

O-N-L-Y-I-N-D-R-E-A-M-S

"God," said Olivia, "I don't mind this apocalypse. The time is right, I totally agree. But I want you to know that I never loved you. Because I always knew that you were not there. I always suspected that the closest thing to what you were supposed to be was the collective consciousness' worshiping of a ball of fire; the oneness we share with other organisms, like sunflowers for instance. Like how one of the few things every living organism has in common is the way that we all reproduce. Having said this, tell me, what are you going to do when you cease to exist? Because if we go, we are taking you with us and you know it."

The planchette moved to the bottom of the board and rolled across the words Good Bye; first to the left, then to the right before it moved no longer.

"That shut it up," said Tobias.

5

A week later and everything appeared to be back to normal; life went on in Providence. The still undefined phenomenon being referred to as OVA, or "The Outbreak of Violence in Autism," had become a non-entity. Only the aftermath remained. The condition that lasted between two and four days, depending on the individual, seemed to have subsided universally.

Autism communities around the globe had been shattered to their very core. As could be expected there was a breakdown within all parties involved. In the United States and elsewhere, many facilities for care of the afflicted had temporarily or permanently closed their doors. Mostly due to periods of mourning or short staffing. But these reasons were seemingly unimportant when one considered the sadness and disillusionment that was inherent with this outbreak.

At that point many individuals were locked in gymnasiums under the care of the government. While those who had been released had been so into the care of close family, or distant family, and in some cases volunteers who opened their doors out of sympathy to the massive worldwide troubleshooting effort. Many had become homeless.

FEMA, in a combined effort with the United Nations, had gathered a panel of experts in New York to assess the state of emergency on the planet. The effort, called SAWT, or Solving Adverse Worldwide Trends, was investigating all corners of Earth and gathering data which it would then process and attempt to discover conclusive reasons for what they had deemed Negative Worldwide Occurrences.

Once data had been gathered, the new charter said, experts would be enlisted in specialized fields to devise a plan of action to counteract that which was unknown.

An informative pamphlet was put together and distributed to any person or organization involved with anybody diagnosed with any of the Autism Spectrum Disorders and was available for viewing and mailing by request on a government created website.

Crystal Gold sat at the desk in the den of her home looking halfheartedly through the pamphlet. It included a diagram of how to bring a violent person down to the ground and how to place them in restraints. The pamphlet told where restraints could be acquired and there were two hot line numbers; one for emergencies and another providing information as to where the people with Autism were being held in all areas, and to answer any questions from the public.

She folded it up and looked at the cover page. There was a blue square that read in bold white lettering, "General Management of the Autism Crisis of 2012." And under that it said FEMA 613/ March 2012; with the FEMA seal in the bottom left hand corner.

She had been in that room doing research nearly all day long. They didn't need her at the studio and she was glad. The past week she had done four reports on the current status of the state of emergency, including an interview with Kara; the director of the institute where she'd initially reported the tragedy from. For one technically illegal report she even ventured into one Providence holding facility in a previously empty wing of the St. Paul Living Center located on Federal Hill.

At the peak of the epidemic Crystal viewed first hand row after row of tranquilized and restrained people of all ages, sizes, sex, and colors. Most lay as still as statues in their beds. Of the ones that were moving; some drooled while others looked about frantically. Certain individuals would require entire team efforts to manipulate their bodies trying to clean their spaces, and they had created makeshift upright restraints to place and hold an individual to the toilet. Other individuals were as pliable as soft clay. Hoses ran down throats of cocked back heads tied to chairs.

Over several glasses of wine she had been researching the tragedy over the internet. On the screen she clicked through the reports she had already known about of farmers in Europe who had been forced to kill a person who wandered onto their property and attacked their family. Or the facility in Japan where there were no survivors. Articles she was already familiar with but could not help but read a second or third time.

There were web pages chronicling articles by country and she skimmed them all. In more than a dozen backward countries the residents had taken to "putting the afflicted down."

In her gray walled and stainless steel trimmed office she sat sipping wine and staring into the computer screen. The nausea of the times was distorted and far more real than all the reporting she had been doing, more or less absent mindedly. The days were stewing together. The alcohol created a receptive haze of wonder to mask the nausea. Numb; she wondered about the end of days. As though man had worn out their welcome in the world. And what did they do to deserve it, the human race? Who was she to ask those questions? Year in and year out she had been blind to a world that she hardly knew existed outside of her personal materialistic concerns.

For years Tobias had told her that the cost of her lifestyle was the livelihoods of people less fortunate. She worked with them every day in the streets but in their faces all she saw was her own career. Compassion escaped her for all that time. She glared into images of bodies on the screen.

A week before she would not look at them. Upon touring the containment unit she instantly developed a stomach for it. No use looking away. Some new sense of mortality and her old morality were nagging at her. Only the wine quieted the burden. Her insides pulled outside to think of these people who only days later behave as if it never happened. Some of them even talk about it.

"Very bad thing that happened. Yeah, it's a really bad thing," one was saying.

Every day she put herself in front of that camera and told Rhode Island about the local state of affairs; that Rhode Island, while hit very hard, had managed the crisis better than a lot of other places. If only by pure luck.

Counseling the endless phone calls of frightened friends of friends. Asking if she knew anything. What did she know? Yes, she was more informed, because the government wasn't overly on her ass about what to show. A matter of a simple meeting in the lobby where they went over the guidelines they wanted her to follow for national security and slipped her an envelope with the press package inside.

She knew that what the masses were told by the 24 hour media was played down to an incomprehensible blurb of both terrible and illogically brief points. Reports designed to draw your attention to inconsequential FEMA rif raff; about solving detrimental trends and simultaneously throwing the term OVA around crudely.

Olivia's words had been rolling around Crystal's head since she heard them. The Earth bleeding. Imagining it from space. Countless bites into the flesh of the face of the earth; bleeding and clotting everywhere.

Talking with Gerri about it had proven difficult. And she understood why. Personally he was sort of removed from the issues. He donated to the causes. What else could he do? He didn't understand anything better than she did. And it was really sad because in the past Gerri always had all the right answers. That was the way his brain worked. But there were no answers. Crystal had been keeping the things Olivia told her the first night held tight like a forbidden amulet in her arms.

Gerri suspected, and it did seem reasonable, god knew it was the case, but to what degree they could not know; that the stories she reported were affecting her. She could not let him get through to her so easily any longer. He watched her stay kind of drunk all the time when she wasn't working.

Crystal. So confused about how to behave and about how she felt. She loved her Gerri. But if she could not make sense of her own self how could he ever help her? She felt so alone.

She heard the front door close and looked at the silver analog clock on the desk. It was 5:42 and Gerri had gotten home from the office. Crystal sat allowing time for him to come to her. From under the stack of newspapers she had been rifling through she produced the flight and hotel receipts she had printed out earlier.

"Babe!" he called out.

"I'm in the den," she said.

She heard his steady steps on the hardwood stairs. And still wearing his blue Armani suit jacket he came through the door, leaned in, and kissed her on her up tilted cheek.

"How you doin' sweetheart?" he asked.

"I'm fine. How was your Monday?"

"Oh you know. Eddy asked about you again. I had told him this things really getting to ya."

"What did you say?"

"I told him you're doing good, ya know, getting massages or whatever."

"Ok. Baby. This is really important to me. And to us."

She handed him the printed receipts and he looked them over before handing them back to her.

"Easter Island?" he asked.

"Yes."

"Again? Are you serious?"

"Yes."

"You have really got to stop listening to that cockamamie girl all the time. I get it that she and Tobias have been really beneficial for you over the years. But last time you went to this Island the weirdo guy you went there to see was completely incomprehensible; he was like 'a hummingbird on speed' you said. What did he even tell you? Anything?"

Crystal, a little turned away by her fiancés words, said, "Well that's not even the half of it. We are going together this time because I want you to be there to talk to him yourself. You should be happy about this because I am really scared and you should be too Gerri. Do you remember when the other time I went there was?"

"Not really. No."

"When I couldn't figure out if I was going to convert to Judaism or not. And do you know that I was leaning closer to not doing it? I wasn't going to do it, and he showed me in a bonfire what my life would be like if I didn't convert. I would have lost you.

"We both have to go Gerri. We need guidance," she said through deep sobs. "We have to go together. I'm so scared."

Gerri stood her to her feet and pulled her into his arms. Rubbing her back and saying, "We'll go, Honey. It'll be alright. You need to understand that as a race we have been through all kinds of horrible things. And every time we persevere."

"But it's not like that this time. What about the Mayan calendar?" she sobbed into the crook of his neck.

"It doesn't matter Crystal. It is not the apocalypse. It's just a marker of time. Time doesn't matter. Time is as tangible as we make it out to be."

"That's not true."

"I know that you believe these things. And I know that your cockamamie friends on Federal Hill have put all kinds of doomsday *bullshit* into your head and if it will make you feel better to go to Easter Island then of course we will go to Easter Island. Whatever you want to do babe. You know that."

"Ok." She sniffled and stood up straight. Her eye make-up running softly in place. "It's this coming Monday. Our flight leaves at 6 am. We arrive at six am the next day. I want to call my mother now."

"Alright. What do you want for dinner."

Crystal sat in the chair again and thought about it, " Sushi?"

"Really?"

"Yeah."

"Alright. I'll leave you alone. I love you Crystal."

"I love you too."

Crystal dialed her mother's number on the portable house phone, letting it ring into her ear. Eventually her parent's answering machine picked up.

She hung up the telephone and sitting back took another swallow of wine. The image on the screen caught her eye; an image of a person with autism lashing away from his handlers at a police officer. Everyone's motions were resigned to movements toward or away from the man with a reaching hand like claws and a crazed look in wild eyes.

"Oh." Escaped from her lips. And she hung her head and cried more as quietly as she could.

She thought of Forgotten Eagle out on the Pacific. Stationed dutifully on his cliff side ocean view veranda and hanging lazily in a hammock waiting for those who seek him out to arrive. Then like an explosion he would be dancing and talking her ear off.

Forgotten Eagle had greeted her with platters of exotic fruit and drink and he wined and dined her during their evening together; feeding her Polynesian meals unlike anything she had ever before tasted. And at the right moment of their single, and very expensive, night together he got her tripping on tea and showed her the vision through a fire in his yard.

The trip... she looked over the paper receipts again for a second before placing them back on the table and taking another drink.

6

With the cold weather breaking, furious March winds became nothing more than an electric chill lingering under the seemingly perpetual gray skies.

Tobias hesitantly awoke to the sound of Olivia rustling around in her room and the creaking of the back door opening and closing, over and over. It was about 10:30 am when he got out of bed, grabbed a towel, and walked in his pajama pants to the bathroom for a shower. He removed his anarchy eye patch and plastic eye, placed these items on the sink, turned on the hot water, and stood leaning against the wall with his eyelids closed; only having slept with the patch on and prosthetic in because he had been drunk when he fell asleep. He felt for the water to heat up and when the temperature was acceptable he dropped his pants and got in.

The water flowed over his head and body while he cleaned himself thoroughly with the soap and loofa. He finished up, dried off and went back to his room with the towel wrapped around his waist, turning some industrial rock music on. Tobias searched through the dresser drawers until he found a decent pair of jeans and he grabbed an old black little league t-shirt from a thrift store. No underwear.

In the kitchen there was coffee made but it was cold. He poured some into a clear mug and threw on his jacket then went out the back door with no shoes on and removed a cigarette from his inside pocket. Walking to the landing out back he lit it.

All around were the crummy houses of the back streets. The lot their appartment was built on was also used by an Italian restaurant for valet parking, but at that time of day the parking area was empty. Ally ways ran between every house and the single story buildings; the wind blew gently through the cold air. Pluto scurried up to his feet and Tobias knelt down and stroked the cat along it's arched back. And then he went into the garage.

Olivia was buried under the back of her old white Volkswagen Bug with some tools lying around her.

"What are you doing?" he asked.

But he felt stupid when he saw the jug of motor oil next to her right then.

"Changing the oil," she said.

Olivia hadn't used her car since early last summer. It ran fine, but she didn't usually drive anywhere. She always had someone else drive; or she would walk.

"Why?"

"I'm taking a road trip."

"Oh. Can I come?"

"No."

"Damn. Where are you going?"

"I can't tell you."

"Why not?"

"Take a guess Toby."

"Cuz you're a fucker."

"No. I've got shit I have to take care of."

He thought on it for a moment. If she wasn't going to tell him, she wasn't going to tell him. Pluto was chasing around what looked like nothing.

"How long are you leaving for?"

"A few days, Ok?"

"What do you mean a few days? Where in the hell could you possibly be going?"

"Toby. It doesn't matter. You'll know where I went today when the time is right."

"This is about December then, isn't it?"

"Right now December is the least of your problems. Go sit on your hands or something. I'll take care of it."

He wasn't comfortable feeling helpless. And the air was getting to him. His nausea for the times had become a constant companion. What else was new? Everything made him nauseous. From what he observed, Olivia wasn't handling it much better. Sometimes she got irritable; but Tobias noticed it happening all the time and tried to adopt a speak only when spoken to method of conflict avoidance.

She pushed the oil pan slowly out from under the car and crawled out herself; standing to her feet and stretching her back. Her gray BROWN sweatshirt and jeans had grime all over them. She undid the oil cap and placed a blue funnel inside, then carefully poured the big jug of oil in.

"What am I doing about Crystal?"

"Nothing. She's leaving on her vacation tomorrow."

He'd have the house to himself. The phone number he had gotten from a walk in client came to mind. But that didn't matter. How would he entertain the girl? What would they talk about? Did anybody even feel romantic anymore? She didn't seem like an exceptional girl. Only really attractive.

"When are you leaving?"

"Right now," she said and then removed the funnel; putting the oil cap back in place. She walked around the car and got inside. It started with a lawnmower like roar. She revved the engine a couple times and Tobias watched the small dual exhaust pipes move with the jerking of the engine; in and out in an opposite sync.

The engine turned off. He saw the suit case already packed on the back seat. She came back around. "Hold this," and they poured the old oil into the empty oil jug.

"You're not going to take a shower first?"

"Not right- 'right now.' I have to take a shower first."

"What if something happens while you're gone?"

"Nothing's going to happen. Well. Nothing too serious. Just watch the fucking news like everybody else."

Olivia finished putting all the objects away where they should be and she walked past Tobias up the stairs and into the house. He picked up his cat and followed behind her, stopping in the doorway waiting to see if she planned on saying anything. But she only walked into her room and closed the door.

There didn't seem to be any reason to be awake right then. He went over to the window and peered down at the street; only a few people bundled up in the cold. Walking with quick steps and red cheeks; small puddles were hardly there, and looking up, he could see strange clouds were gathered in bulbous wisps against a gray backdrop.

The bathroom door closed, he snapped back to reality, walked to the coffee table, and removed the leather bound Poe from underneath. After taking his shoes off by the door, he laid back the long way on the couch; skimming the table of contents in the book; Duke De l'Omelette, Morella, Lion-izing: A Tale. That seemed good. He turned to that story.

Tobias dove deep into the reading of Edgar Allen Poe- the only way he knew to read the author; with absolute concentration.

Nosology. The study of noses. A father kicks a son out of the house. Son writes pamphlet on nosology. Critics rave. The son gets in with the rich folk by selling an artist some kind of nose for a thousand pounds. But Tobias could not figure out what kind of nose was worth a thousand pounds and the story did not make it clear. The father "declares" the main character, the son, and the rich people, to be Lions and Recherché. Whatever a recherché was. A "Turk" says something about a 400 horned cow in the sky. A lot of intelligent people are saying a lot of intelligent things at this dinner.

A reference to the name Price. Who was Price? Vincent Price? He looked up the name in an on-line encyclopedia. Vincent Price was an actor. And he did bad horror movies until he did the House of Usher. That's a Poe story. What an odd synchronicity. The actor did other Poe stories as well. Pit and the Pendulum. The Raven. He also made movies of H.G. Wells' stories.

Tobias researched him further and found a link to a video of The Raven. He started to watch. Vincent Price roaming around the chamber. A window to be opened and red velvet chair to be sat on. Raven to be stared at and spoken too. This was an actor roaming around a room reciting Poe eloquently and convincingly. The story was simply a man talking to himself and to the raven; freaking out about his lost Lenore. Quite genius on both sides. A little more so on Poe's end naturally.

Olivia walked out of her bedroom showered, dressed, and ready to go. He muted the sound of the video.

"Ok. I'm leaving. Give me a hug."

Tobias put the computer down and walked over to her and they embraced.

"I'll be home Tuesday night. Call me if you need anything," she said.

"Ok," he said.

She kissed him on the cheek, knelt down to say goodbye to Pluto, and was off out the door with her purse on her arm.

He walked back to the computer and turned the sound back on. The nine minute film was coming to an end. And floors, shadows, lifted, nevermore. The character was dead.

He went back to reading Lion-izing. Grace of Bless-My- Heart visits the nosey son to deliver an invitation. Everyone was really happy about the nose guy. Celebrating him for whatever it was he was doing. The son shoots off the barons nose at six am and then everyone hates him so he asks his father what went wrong. The father goes on about how he ruined their hopes and dreams by shooting that one guys nose. Because then the baron became a Lion and the son was not. They used the word "proboscis" a lot toward the end. The story ended.

7

The exhaled pot smoke blew away down the alley, curling between the two brick walls. A tiny cough escaped her lips and she put her hand to her mouth for a moment before passing the joint to her friend.

"Arianna! You coughed all over it," Danielle said.

"Whatever. Wipe it off," she said, and laughed very subtly.

Danielle smoked off the joint a little more before snuffing the ember out on the wall behind her.

Arianna dug through her midnight blue hemp purse for her cigarettes and lit one.

"Can I have one of yours?"

"Yeah here."

"Thanks. Are we going to the book store?"

"I don't know. What did Joe say he wanted to do?"

"Probably the same thing he always wants to do; sit around and be a loser."

"Then let's go to the book store."

They walked out of the ally heading back around the condemned brick church toward Main Street. Her hips swayed to and fro on short legs. Her arms wrapped around the sides of her slender torso. She held tight to her jacket sleeves printed with purple camouflaged hews. The thick brown curls of her hair strewn with ever so little gold fell behind her back taken somewhat aloft by the wind rushing past her.

"I feel so fricking good right now," Danielle said.

"Oh my god, my shoulders feel like they want to fly away," said Arianna.

"I'm not even cold. It feels like I should be cold right now and I'm not."

Danielle walked with primmer; her arms to her side in a flush white nylon jacket. Flicking her cigarette and taking quick drags from it.

Arianna held her cigarette close. Taking in the nicotine and breathing it away. The sunshine, refreshing after so many overcast days, seared into her eyes and dragged her perception in liquid trails across vision's view. The smoke washed across the psilocybin in her body; cleansing it, if only for a moment.

"I am so shroomy right now," said Arianna

"Me too."

The girls were placed on a landscape and moving across it like claymation. Frame by frame. Oak trees rose from beside a picturesque and manicured dead street. Houses became two dimensional and visually fuzzy. There were yellow blurs that beamed from the distance and from many points. Like stars in the daylight, bright yellow rocking chairs were everywhere. Brandon, Vermont.

They trudged through the thick atmosphere and into the doors of The Old Man's Wife's bookstore. Arianna sat down by the café against the black wall in a white chair and Danielle went off into the rear stacks.

She removed a chewed up straw from her pocket and placed it in her mouth. She put her fingers to her eyes and pushed down gently.

"I have seen a shadow. In a meadow," she sang Dax to herself quietly. Looking deeper into the shapes and figures created on her eyelids. Kites and pyramids. Could she control them? Make shapes? A scorpion? To do that; she would have to manipulate the skin of the eyelids themselves? This hypothesis she pursued, wiggling her fingers slightly, producing questionable results. These luminous figures glowed with deep dark yellows and greens and reds; shaped like those fossils they pull from inside the rocks in Utah. They swam. Full of life.

A woman placed orange juice beside her. "Thank you Lucy," Arianna said.

Little dead heads moved ever fleetingly amongst themselves and against the backdrop of polygonal shapes. They were fractals she realized.

She took her fingers off her eyelids. And the world came back into focus, dimly lit and comfortable, in its own time. She sipped the orange juice and weaned her vision back to normal.

Getting up she moved haggardly, almost drunkenly, through the store. Putting her hand on Danielle's shoulder and laying her cheek on her hand.

She said, "Those shapes on the back of your eye lids

are fractals."

"Look what I found," said Danielle. Arianna snapped to attention and looked at the thick book handed to her.

James Joyce. Ulysses.

"What about it?"

"I heard he was good. I wanted to buy it."

"Go for it."

"You should do that now," said Olivia, startling the girls.

"Why?" asked Danielle

"We have to go, ladies." The woman was looking into Arianna's hazy eyes. Eyes shaped like sideways tear drops with the tip pointing out.

"Buy that book and then get in my car. It's the white buggy parked out front." Danielle's eyes lit up when she saw it.

Who this person was looking inside her Arianna wondered. And why was she focused on her like that?

Olivia spoke to Danielle but stared into the luscious vibrating flower. "I have something very important to tell you both. I am here from out of town. I will take you to my hotel, Ok? Just down Rt. 7."

"Then let me buy the book."

"Do that."

Arianna was left standing dumbfounded; looking up at this new person returning her gaze.

Olivia took her hand and leaned in warmly, and softly, to kiss her hair.

"Come with me sweetie. I know you're tripping. But I have your future with me."

Olivia tugged a distant, somewhat entranced, Arianna along her side to stand politely by while Danielle paid her transaction and exchanged brief small talk with the girl working.

Danielle turned and looked at Olivia. Her bright cheeks smiled and she said with sparkling eyes, "Shall we."

"Yes. We shall?" Olivia said.

Danielle stepped through the door and held it open.

Olivia, in a long red wool coat, wrapped her arm around Arianna and led her through, out onto the walk, and to the buggy. She placed Arianna standing by, opened the car door, clicked the seat forward, and let Danielle into the back. After that, she helped the other into the front passenger seat, closed the door, got in on her side, and started the engine; pulling off into the road.

"What are you going to tell us?"

"In time Danielle."

"How do you know my name?"

"Nevermind that."

Floods of the mushroom feeling were surging across Arianna. She was only beginning to consider where she was. There was a woman with them. Taking them someplace. They were in her car; a finely upholstered beetle. The heat was rushing from unseen vents through the air.

"Girls," Olivia said, "first I am going to show you something right up here in the road."

They were on a small and winding road crowded with dense forest. Arianna's eyes were drawn to Olivia. Leaning against the window, with distortions in her vision, she stared at the angelic lady.

"Arianna. You are a little more out of it than Dani. So listen to me. I want you to pay attention. Ok? This will be a good metaphor for things to come. Look there."

In the road before them were two crows. One was broken and earthbound warding off a more able bodied crow attacking from all around; fighting with its final breathes.

"Oh my god," said Danielle.

Arianna's eyes were caught off guard. She winced.

The uninjured crow, in a fluid motion, went from attacking the other bird, to flying directly into the car window.

Danielle screamed and shot backward, and Arianna curled up like a dehydrating fungus.

At the thud Olivia set the car into motion and accelerated away.

"What just happened?!"

"Oh, Dani, my dear, your guess is as good as mine. And trust me when I tell you that these are signs of our time. The living forms of life have begun transitioning into death as one. As all is truly one. Our souls belong to a doomed old way and maybe a blessed new way. Our existence is being sucked away by the great vacuum of space. And all we can do is weep, for we're being erased. The time is now to start counting your days. My loves. My loves. We're being erased."

Arianna was crying and she didn't understand why. The words moved her to tears even though she didn't know what they meant. The way the woman spoke made her feel profound gripping sadness.

Danielle, also crying, said, "What do you mean we're being erased."

"I mean what I said. I will never tell you that I know why. I can see it. It's horrible. 'Oh the humanity,' type of shit. All day. Every day. Until there's nothing left. I don't know why. It's not the government. Because that shit's fucked too."

A small bird crashed into the windshield.

"What is wrong with the birds?" Danielle screamed.

"Please, stop yelling. I don't know what is wrong with the birds."

"I feel like my knee has toes," Arianna said.

"I bet you do sweetheart."

"I'm hardly even tripping," said Danielle.

"That's because you ate less than half an eighth. Can we smoke in your car lady?"

"Olivia. And yes. Go ahead. Can I have one actually?"

"Me too."

Arianna handed cigarettes to them both. And she handed around a plastic lighter.

"Don't roll that window down too much. Ok?" Olivia said.

Arianna took a drag and exhaled. A small amount of pressure was removed from her chest. She asked Olivia, "What do you mean you can see it?"

"I mean exactly what I said. I can see it. Visions. I'm a psychic. Or a seer as it is. I hear things too. And I sense feelings or thoughts and then listen, or tune in rather, for the thoughts or feelings attached to them. I know all about you. I followed you guys around for most of last night; learning things. I followed you to the Wal-Mart in Rutland. I sat around in Danielle's bushes and projected myself up into the bedroom with you both. That was humiliating but nobody saw me. I saw me though. I learned a couple things about you two from being in there. Mostly I used the opportunity to tune into you as well and harmonize with the way you feel things in your respective hearts.

"I could reflect on your childhoods. I could tell you that Danielle is a virgin or that you, Arianna, were in an abusive relationship.

"I see the future. Well. That is a bit of an understatement. Instead, let's say that I am constantly beaten over the head with the future. Like the future is a screwdriver in my temple. All day every day. I live two lives every moment. Half the time I am in there with you guys or whoever, in the moment. And the rest of the time I am watching some instance yet to come. Could be in Timbuktu if need be or I can focus on certain other places, times, or people.

"Ten seconds. An hour. A day. Week, month, year. The further away, the more vague it'll be. Usually far away crap comes in dreams. But soon the dream will become clearer and clearer until it's in my face when I least expect it, like while I'm taking a shit in the morning.

"I won't tell you about death; yours or anyone else's. I would lie to you first." She stopped talking, thought, and muttered, "Actually I may have to make an exception to that. I can tell you where you were meant to go. But if it is a negative place I will use positivity to guide you there.

"I can't really describe how I learned not to let on too much of the things that I see. You'll have to trust me. But by avoiding your destiny life can tend to end up much worse for more people than yourself. Chaos theory. Fractals; Arianna. Avoidance brings snowball effects for everybody involved in the changes. Like chain reacticons. And it's a scary way that destiny corrects itself once it has been disturbed; without mercy. Like lightening with a purpose.

"Scary shit. So I don't fuck with destiny-"

"Isn't telling us that there is destiny, and that there is no free will, fucking with destiny?" Danielle asked.

"There is always free will, however irrelevant it sometimes becomes. But no, not as much as you would think. The means to know these things already exist. Humans discovered what I call destiny a long time ago when they began to understand reality and the illusion of time. Or when they began to understand that all matter in the universe is really part of some singularity and it is all one grand spectacle of life. Eventually, on Earth, mankind created astrology and to a lesser degree of relevance the tarot came along and people the world over were able to pinpoint, accurately and specifically, events that had not yet come to pass. A pendulum can do that too. You don't have to be a psychic to use these tools. You only have to learn them."

She stopped abruptly, "I don't think this to be necessary, but I can tell you want to hear it. You can have a crash course, because we're almost there. Even with the general rejection of the science, everybody is inherently interested in astrology, it's practically human nature.

"Astrology, first and foremost, is not just a section in the newspaper. It is a study, older than history, of the effects of the various gravitational forces exerted by planets, and other heavenly bodies, on people, civilization, society, and everything else. It is very real and much much more complicated than most people realize. So like most things misunderstood it is shunned by the masses. Because people are very rarely accurate about the importance of that which is shunned and that that is deemed significant. 'What is right is not always popular and what is popular is not always right,' works on more levels than just high school social dramas. Astrology goes through periods of popularity and periods of disdain. Astrological almanacs used to outsell the bible in many areas of the world, but that statement is flawed by a lack of the relevant circumstances involved. A few years ago it received a boost in popularity on a more underground college aged level. Arianna, you for instance are very aware of your sun sign being Scorpio.

"And Danielle; you are a Sagittarius. But, trust me, astrology doesn't matter right now.

"And as for the tarot. A deck of tarot cards is an instrument used to interpret reality. Things to come, things hidden, or a mechanism for the giving of advice. The deck is made out of pictures of any major event that can happen in life, most of these situations and figures can be considered archetypes. If you can read them and lay them out right they can be used for whatever purpose you might need that is within their means to understand.

"A tarot deck hones in on vibrations, synchronicities, and subtle wavelengths, like a pendulum, as a means to their end. They translate the energy that is inside of all of us and inside of everything. They are a tool that takes a little teaching and a lot of learning to master, but one can learn the basics in only a couple months. The real trick to it is to go fishing for answers in the ether and in the oneness.

"These things are the essence of destiny. The essence of fate. The essence of my personal intuition. That is not to say that I am not special. Really, I have only known one other individual on earth existing in a reality like mine, and I spent the better part of my teenage years searching for him. He lives on Easter Island of all places."

Another bird flew into the window by Arianna's head. And the girls jumped and shrieked; except Olivia.

"God damn it," Arianna shouted.

"Oh my god," shrieked Danielle.

Up ahead in the road a small brown motel became visible around the curve. Olivia threw the wheel hard to the left to pull into the driveway and braked stiffly into her parking spot.

"Girls. I'm going to get out and open the door and once I've gotten it open, I want you to run inside, alright?"

"Ok Olivia," said Danielle.

Olivia got out of the car and hurried up to her room's door, opening it with the key, and rushing in. The girls jumped out the passenger door and rushed into the motel.

Olivia closed the door behind them and moved around the girls to click on a lamp.

In the front corner of their room, by the protrusive heater, was a table adorned with a very specific feast.

There was a plethora of plastic bowls and paper plates; and in any given bowl was some sort of colorful and sugary candy. Gummy bears with sour coatings, the colors of the rainbow in chewy circles and glossy disks of tart sugar. Little plastic packages of mass produced crispy chocolate and peanut butter bars and on the plates there were potato chips; either salt and vinegar or sour cream and onion.

On the bureau was a clear Tupperware container filled with ice. And inside of it was a plastic jug of orange juice and assorted alcoholic drinks, hard lemonades and light beer.

"Have a seat at the table girls."

Arianna put her purse on the floor by her chair. The mushrooms were coming on strong again. The wave rose over her. A blurry intensity moved across her vision as she sat down entranced. She only slightly noticed Danielle sit beside her while she watched Olivia gracefully move to the drinks.

Olivia cracked a beer and placed it before Arianna. Then, with her teeth, she twisted a cap from a lemonade and placed it in front of the other girl. And she pulled the cap from a bottle of wine, also with her teeth.

"It's Merlot. But neither of you wants any. And Daniell; my shirt's not ugly. But for the record I think you could do with fewer earth tones. Neon colors would match your energy much better."

Astonished, Danielle said, "I'm sorry. I- I can't believe you're in my head."

"I thought you both should know. I didn't take any offense though. My outfit is flawless."

Olivia was wearing tight stonewashed jeans and a soft slim fitting black shirt with black leather boots.

"Dani, look," said Arianna.

"Oh my god."

Set out in a dish right in front of either of them were two bowls filled with small bright candies. In

Arianna's dish were mostly orange and purple, with some red. In Danielle's dish were yellow, green, and some red.

They both looked to Olivia, who responded, "You girls are an eccentric little pair. I thought I would indulge in some of your more adorable points. To be more objective; I will point out that you are both viciously immature. Even more objectively, you are a little more mature than most girls your age. But your energy called to me and it was my obligation to oblige. Arianna, you and Danielle both have some serious growing up to do. Let me pour you some orange juice and the thing about growing up will bring me back to the birds."

The girls ate the candy from the dishes with nothing to say. Danielle never stopped smiling and Arianna felt a little like mush. Her skin had a minor sweat growing in joint areas and her limbs and head had a heaviness to them.

Olivia put the orange juice on the table and crossed the room to sit on the bed against the wall; dangling the wine between her thighs.

"You fell out of a tree once Arianna. And as time slowed down during your fall you thought; this is going to be bad. You hit the ground hard and went unconscious, waking up in a hospital with a fractured clavicle and stitches on your chin and skull.

"Most would have been better off dead. Because these birds and that problem with the people with autism, and all those shootings that happened; these events are all omens. Omens of something similar, much bigger but very much the same.

"To the naive they seem unrelated but they cannot be. They are misrepresented in the media so let me hit you with a little truth; what do they all have in common?"

"Death," said Danielle.

"Absolutely.

"Arianna? Can you tell me what a fractal is?"

"Yeah. A fractal is a shape that repeats itself as it gets bigger. Then it looks like it did at first, but keeps growing. And I think it grows exponentially."

"Good. It is the pattern forming aspect of nature and many things beyond nature, if there is such a thing. A fractal can be an object, like a nut or a seashell. Or when you apply it to an event, it becomes chaos theory. Little things effect big things and create new things that look like the little things but are much bigger.

"These terrible things that are happening are fractals. And they will grow exponentially. More and more terrible, but death will stay beside us all. As it always is really. Death is always to your left, at arm's reach, some Indians say. If you look quick enough you can catch a fleeting glimpse.

"I see the figurative four horsemen doing what I assume is their duty.

"If you study the geography of heavenly bodies they all share a certain desolation. That is the nature of space; apparent absence of life. Here on our planet, in this loving atmosphere we have defied nature, in more ways than one it seems. We attempted to pretend we aren't connected and live against each other and all other life. Just ignorance really. Earthbound life has been going on for billions of years and I can feel the desperation of a nonsensical enigma dissolving. Like a joke with no punch line, or a riddle without logic, struggling against failure. Life, see? And in the last six thousand years it's been completely out of hand. And we are at the close of a cycle that seems to have, for lack of any better idea, accumulated some very bad karma.

"It's not worth explaining how I know this Danielle. I can see the fucking thing. I'm trying to say Arianna will be comfortable with this, and you will not, and the reason for this is only a matter of personality.

"Arianna. Have you not wanted to be alone, or prayed for the sky to fall when things wouldn't go your way? For years and years nobody has understood you. You love Dani for who she is; but Dani is not what you need. No, you, and those few like-minded people in this world are getting what you've wanted. An end to the dishonesty and the treachery. You are one of the few that can gaze upon this terrible painting in a positive light."

"Then why am I here?" Danielle asked.

"Because you are her friend. And I'll get to your futures, just let me speak.

"Once they said; the meek shall inherit the earth. And Arianna, that is you. The world will not be yours, and you aren't going to be left alone for any great period of time. The important and real thing to remember is that your hopelessness will give you a perspective that will be beneficial to you. Your assumed meekness, but true absence thereof, will be your strength. Sadly this will reform your attitudes all but too late and one day you will be forced to feel the same damned sadness as everyone else."

"I'm sad right now!"

"I know you are angel. I know you are. It will pass when it's ready. It will not pass for others though. As the sky falls you will be smiling, while all others cry. And blinded by their tears, they will neglect to crouch down beside you, as you already have. And when those last few souls around you are gone it will be your turn to inherit those inevitable tears."

"Danielle!" Olivia said, and she got up and rushed to the girl- taking her hands in her own. Looking up from teary eyes and into teary eyes. "My love, you are going to be fine. You are going to be with Arianna every step of the way. It will be a difficult journey. But I am here today to guide you both to safety. You will spend these end times close together. As ideally you both would want it to be.

"That is my next point. My burden to transfer to you. Light a cigarette ladies, Ok?"

Arianna felt twisted, strained in bubbling spirals. Deeply distressed. Absentmindedly crying. She lit her smoke, handed one to Danielle- who also cried- and offered one to Olivia, seated on the bed, who flicked her hand no.

"Danielle. You may not have the strength required to do what I ask. But if you do not I'm telling you straight up you'll die. You must obey me when I demand that you tell no one what I have told you or what I am about to tell you. Remember this; you cannot change the future for the better. Only for the worse. And the difference here means your life. Yours, too, Arianna. Say nothing girls!

"Your families are going to die before summer arrives and there is nothing you can do to stop it."

"Oh my god!" said Danielle; gasping for air through yelping sobs.

Arianna let out an agonizing groan and pulled her legs into the fetal position and covered her face with her arms; crying heavily.

Olivia took a few deep swills from her bottle of wine.

"Drink up girls. It'll dull the pain." The two did not respond to Olivia's words and she kept talking.

"I've got a family. And I can save them no more than I can save yours. I, ha, this is funny; I don't even know where they are. One year I took for granted that I could find them whenever I wanted and I stormed out the door. It was six years before I decided to look for them again. They were 'world travelers.' My parents and my brother and sister. They are somewhere, Asia most likely. But I can't find them. Maybe they wanted it like that. Maybe they're dead. Honestly, I don't really feel your pain too well, because I don't care what has become of them."

Nobody said anything. Olivia stopped talking.

Arianna looked at the solemn lady and guessed her to be thinking her own thoughts of how difficult delivering bad news is. Finally, she spoke first. "How come if you can't change the future, we are going to live?"

"I didn't say that you can't change it. I said you shouldn't. I just can't think of anything else to do, so here I am. Bets are off anyway. I am in this specific location because it is in accordance with my plan. I have chosen you two because I needed two girls like you. And even though it could have been any other girls with similar energy had you not lived in Brandon, VT, I am happy that it is you two.

"I will take the lives of others involved in my plan. But in this time of universal death the ends seem to justify my means because life no longer has that value we as humans have always attached to it. Every day I understand a little more that Earth life is *supposed* to be dying. This part of the universal oneness is fading out. And the longer we postpone this inevitability in our own lives the more we will come to know it as an absolute truth. The longer you live, the more this will begin to make sense to you. There will be nothing left around you and your life will be nonsensical. I suspect over time, as you survive, you will begin to feel quite left out. Arianna, you are very aware of this and your tears will dry. Danielle. Sadly, you are just too socialized. A little too normal. Those values you share with the rest of our species are going to torture you. And the rest of America too."

Olivia said nothing for a moment after. The sobs hovered on the silence. Arianna scooted her chair closer to Danielle's to embrace her. Olivia watched this. Arianna's sadness was nearly overwhelming. Why was life this painful? Oh god, could nothing save them?

"I can save you girls. You need to be saved, no? Well I have good news for you. Drink some OJ, trippy little girls, and I'll tell you what I mean."

They each took a drink from their plastic cups. The orange juice was similar to concentrated sunlight breaking through the gray skies of their emotions. They were unaware of the connection between the vibrant juice and the coming shift in the conversation.

"I have arranged for you two a safe haven of sorts. In the Green Mountains at a ski resort you will become aware of another day. You will be sheltered from the madness of a dying civilization. There will be food and peace and you will be among the last of the surviving inhabitants of earth. You will survive almost as long as the crocodiles and the cockroaches and the scorpions. In a sense...

"These last years will give you both a period to reflect on what has come of it all. The dark sea of awareness, the universe itself, wants your knowledge and your experience. It always has. To put it simply, the universe wants you to experience life in a dead world. Because your experiences are nothing more than the universe's mechanism for raising its own consciousness. This is the reason consciousness expansion was such an integral part of humanity.

"You will share this resort with people of like minds and ages. Actually, there won't be any older occupants. Only younger people will possess the immature minds needed to survive. It will be a habitat for youth. You'll have pot to smoke year round. And there will be plenty of love to be made.

"Some of the greatest minds you will know in your life will be there with you; helping you to come to terms with this absolute extinction as best you can. It will be a carefree, however doomed, life up on that mountain."

Danielle asked, "Will you be there?"

"No. Dani. I won't be. My hourglass is running low

on minutes as we speak."

"Why? You have to be there," said Arianna.

"I told you both. This is a place for young people. I am too old. My mind has matured. No. I'll have fulfilled my destiny before you ever get to the mountain."

"What's your destiny?" asked Danielle.

"Much like both of yours, sweetheart; to die."

"No. I don't want to die!" said Arianna.

"Nothing lasts forever, Arianna. Not when you're flesh and bone."

"Fuck that Olivia. Change it. Do something about it! If you have all this knowledge of the future, fucking tell somebody." She stopped. Even though she was burning to go on. To jump over the table and tear the throat out of this horrible woman.

"Stop thinking about killing me. I have told you over and over, I won't say it again, you can only change the future for the worse. I'd create a senseless panic. I can see that clearly when I consider that course of events. But I don't have to. There will be more panic than we know what to do with someday soon. If you had watched the news you would be aware of what the Christians are doing; crying in the streets with their 'The end is near' signs. Or the cult suicides that have already begun. I don't have to say anything. We'd all be sitting in the town hall and speculating about last week's tornadoes when a hurricane shows up and decimates the place, so to speak.

"We'll go play with the birds in a little bit Danielle.

I've got only one more detail about my plan of action. It's the reason I am here. Breaking my own axiom. I *am* changing the future Arianna. As little as I want to. And at a dire cost I assure you.

"But for now; I have got a job for you two. The only participation I need from you both. Other than this task, I have bought you your tickets, so take the ride, Ok?

"There is a date that I do not know yet. I can only

recognize the seasons; it looks like fall but the time of day the darkness is falling indicates it's mid-summer. Danielle, you'll be living with Arianna's family at this point. Your family will be torn apart in the meanwhile. I'm sorry. She will help you through the trauma.

"And Arianna. I will contact you one day and then you must go promptly. Go promptly to this address." Olivia got up and handed her a small slip of paper.

"Your job will be to clean up the mess that will be there waiting. Familiarize yourselves with that address so you know exactly where to go. Say goodbye to your parents and leave. Clean the slaughter house you arrive at and make it spotless. Your new family will be arriving soon. Once you say goodbye to your parents there will be no turning back. There would be nothing to go back to anyway."

Another sinking in her stomach. With no more tears to cry; she blew her nose into a napkin. "I can't do it," Arianna said.

"You can and you will. But why would you expect it to be so simple, or expect it to be easy? In a sense, it will be easy. Your losses will be infinitely less crushing than the losses of others.

"Our world was once a stable one. At least that is what they told us; truthfully, there was never any stability. Only in America could we be so separate from the usual suffering of human life. How I lie awake at night wishing it would have stayed so.

"In my most sincere desires you are off saving the starving people in the third world, and you, Danielle, are helping nurse broken and battered sea lions back to health, or whatever hippie gibberish you'd feel like indulging in given the chance. I would wish for long fulfilling lives for all of my loved ones. Maybe the government would have uncorrupted itself. And maybe we'd start using all those alternative fuel sources they suppressed. Maybe we would have saved the rain forest and the whales. Maybe the lies would have been exposed and for once they would no longer be able to control the populations for their evil agendas. The keepers of the third dimension could finally live in light and love.

"In my dreams I can see the new nightmare. In anyone's face I can see death at the hands of a new and very short lived reality. In your faces I see you worshiping lights in an electrically charged night sky that falls over a newly desolate earth. And I see a private graveyard full of strangers."

"I wouldn't expect you to understand. One day you will see what I see. I am seeing these things in you, after all. Just accept it girls. That is all you can do. At least you will have each other.

Arianna looked over at Danielle who had her face buried in her curled up knees. That didn't make her feel any better; to lose everything and keep Danielle. Apparently Olivia meant, "at least," when she said it. Arianna looked over at the objectionable psychic; who shrugged her shoulders and smirked hopelessly.

"I'll be right back," Olivia said; getting up and walking into the bath room at the rear.

"I'm scared Arianna."

"Me too. But I love you Danielle. No matter what, I always will."

"Me too. I love you too."

They held each other again. Crying into each other's shoulder. Olivia came back from the bathroom holding the wooden plunger handle.

"I'm going outside to get something. I'll be right back," she said.

Danielle turned and pulled the shades aside to watch with Arianna looking over her shoulder. Olivia walked to the hood of the car and opened it up and a bird came swiftly from the right.

Olivia swung the wood through the air and whacked the bird away and to the ground. She skipped oddly over to it and brought the stick down from above a single time. Then she ran back to the car, grabbed two large objects, slammed the trunk down and rushed back into the room.

"What's going to happen, Olivia?" Arianna said.

"I don't really know." She was out of breath but continued, "this bird shit- ha ha, bird shit- this bird shit's going to be a big deal, but people are going to get used to it quicker than you would think. And then it'll be over. All the birds will be dead very quickly. Most reptiles and amphibians, too. And the fish. The old will kill themselves and the young will starve and that'll be it.

"Ok. We're the only ones staying in this motel, and I already talked to the attendant about what's happening. He's cool. As cool as anyone can be. There're a lot of people freaking out right now.

"They don't all attack though. Only crows and certain raptors, swallows, the more aggressive birds. The big deal is what a lot of the other one's are doing. They're flying straight up into the sun until they croak. It's literally raining dead birds all over the place. Turtles too, not raining though, they're drowning themselves. I picked that up from a game warden in town yesterday. Here." She handed a baseball bat to Danielle, and a tire iron with a 90degree L curve to Arianna.

"I thought it would be fun if we went and killed some birds. It's what's best for the whole universal death process. Danielle, I know you wanted to."

"I'm afraid to," Danielle said.

"Why? Worried you might get hurt? You won't. I wouldn't let that happen. You have to learn this, because as fucked up as it's going to be, it's going to be part of life from here on out. C'mon, it'll be like baseball. I gotta sew up your bleeding hearts. You need to get used to living with death."

"Well, yeah," said Arianna, "I don't want to kill

birds."

"It's therapeutic. You're going to feel a lot better afterward. Come on."

"Really?" Arianna asked, succumbing to the notion.

The two girls reluctantly stood up holding their given blunt objects. Olivia had her hand on the doorknob and said, "Stay close to me. But not close enough to hit me. We're gunna hang by the wall and I'll let you know when they're coming. Make sure you hit it, cuz otherwise they might peck your eye out."

"What!?" Arianna exclaimed; laughing a little.

"Alright. Let's go." Olivia opened the door and moved to the right along the building. The girls held their weapons awkwardly against themselves. Olivia corrected them.

"Be prepared. Hold it like this. Like a cat ready to pounce."

Danielle was on the left side and Arianna was in the middle.

"The first one's coming from dead ahead at Arianna. We can all swing at it. Ok, look, now."

A bird swooped down from the forest across the way. It was a crow. When it was about within reach Olivia said, "Swing." They did. Arianna's tire iron brought it to the ground where it fluttered around trying to peck at their ankles. Danielle ran off and Olivia and Arianna hopped around it excited and laughing.

"Who wants to kill it?" Olivia asked. And Danielle ran over to be back together in a group.

"I'll do it," Arianna said.

"Alright. Hurry up. But try and enjoy it. They are as much to blame for this as you, me, or god. Everything is one, remember? Killing this bird is like cutting the skin of the universal oneness."

The bird was beginning to be able to lift itself from the ground. Arianna walked up to it. "What the hell?" She swung the tire iron over her head like an ax and crushed the ribcage of the animal, damaging the heart and killing it instantly.

"Oh shit!" she said and ran back to Olivia who wrapped the girl in her free arm.

"The next one is coming from over there. It's your turn Danielle."

"I don't want to."

"Look."

The bird was coming from over the office. "Oh my god!" Danielle said; swinging the bat hard and sending the bird into the door of their suite. It stopped moving.

"What kind of bird is that?"

"It's a Swallow," Arianna answered.

"Alright. Let's go inside. I want to go over what I've told you, and then I'll take you home."

8

Face down on her Grateful Dead pillow case Arianna lay in a dark room; wearing only panties and an extra-large Palestine benefit t-shirt. Golden and unwelcome light from the street outside infiltrated the blinds but she could hardly consider it. Lights on or lights off; the nausea inside her would not stop. The weight of a new depression smothered her.

Silently sobbing on top of the covers was where she'd been since Danielle and she had parted ways. Although, the psychic Olivia had done a fairly good job of cheering them both up by telling them all about other lives they had already lived and all about their favorite memories; consoled smiles and the goodness all seemed to dissolve when the magical woman left.

They spent most of that evening at Danielle's house a few blocks over; crying together and trying to make sense of it all. Finally Arianna had had enough and wanted to be alone. Her mother watched the news downstairs and her father was working in Burlington.

Her older sister was off who knew where. Why couldn't they survive?

Who else could she save? Anybody she wanted, probably. Olivia didn't say not to. Why hadn't she asked? Olivia said not to alter destiny. Was she to let the others die?

It didn't make any sense until it occurred to her what the issue was. A mass extinction. They're already dead. It's their destiny. She was not supposed to warn them? She was not supposed to help her family? It didn't make any sense.

Tell no one. Tell no one. It rang in her head until she began repeating it aloud.

"Tell no one. Tell no one." She clenched her eyelids to hold back the tears and spoke those words into the pillow desperately through gritted teeth. "Tell no one. Tell no one. Tell no one." She held her breath; felt the tightening in her chest as it rose through her throat and back to her lungs more terribly. The pressure building inside her. She held more. It became all consuming. Her ears, skull, screaming in agony. Until she could hold her breath no more. She exhaled and rolled onto her back. All her vision was blurred.

Arianna put her hands to her throat and clenched them. A warmth immediately coursed in the nerves all throughout her; reminiscent of the body high from earlier. She squeezed her neck harder. Her head cocked back and her vision receded; first turning purple at the edges, then black, it repeated this appearance all the way to the center until she could see nothing. She held her throat tight until her fists became too weak to hold on any longer and she released. Nearly unconscious she gasped for air; hyperventilating.

When her strength returned to her she immediately put her hands right back to her throat. Squeezing harder this time. The sensations returning quicker. Blackness. Almost nothingness. Then she felt a fall. A great endless fall. As though it would never stop. Falling for a lifetime- she thought of worldly things. Every childhood memory seemed to be present although indistinguishable from one another; Who-Ville at Forest Park and the time she watched televised wrestling with her grandpa. The transitional periods all seemed overly represented. Moving and starting school. Arguments with her mother as a younger teenager. Becoming comfortable among peers. Finding her clique of friends. Those stupid memories she was for no reason in love with; driving past the drive thru window. The places she hated going; grocery stores and the Cracker Barrel restaurant. The obscure things she enjoyed doing; hanging out and staring awkwardly at strangers. Marijuana. Drinking. Family; their faces changing from what they looked like when she was a little girl to ten or fifteen years later and back again. Her ex-boyfriend when he used to make her happy, and an instantaneous montage of the slide downward into ugliness. The beatings in locked basements. The happy memories with Danielle. Cliff faces they'd scaled together. The drama of being two young ladies in an alcoholic's world; boys always getting into fights. Back to being a young girl. So small and finding a lifetime's worth of enjoyment from a pinwheel. She loved that pinwheel. Blowing at it; it spun and spun; slowed, and she blew more, huffing, puffing, blowing, watching it spin. It spun slower and slower, so she blew more and more until the pinwheel stopped spinning completely. Upset by this she kept blowing until she couldn't blow at all. She wasn't getting any air.

Gasping for breaths it all came rushing back. Her vision returned only enough to remind her that she was in her bedroom and had choked herself half to death.

Lying there gagging on air she began to recover. She sat up and clicked alive her bedside lamp. The hardwood floors welcomed her coldly. Every object about her seemed only half real. As if it were all a movie she knew was going to end. Posters of dreamboat rock stars had lost all appeal and meaning, they were hardly real. Marijuana leaf figurines were a lot of bullshit. She was awed by the insignificance of all of it. Artifacts of childhood meant nothing. The small blankets from childhood folded in corners, with the accompanying teddy bears resting upon them.

She went to the desk on the far side of her bedroom and dug through a drawer of old notes and school supplies until she found a razorblade. And from those teddy bears she chose Ted-E; a bear with falling out button eyes and made of something like white silk.

In the middle of her room she stepped on his face, plunged the razor deep into her ankle, and pushed the steel down through the flesh. The pain struck her predictably enough but she let it hurt. Blood drained from the split tissue and she watched it flow over her foot and onto the bear.

She made another incision beside the original and watched the blood flow. It puddled on the little teddy bear. It ran over the bear and onto the floor. She ran her finger up the wound and licked away what had collected on it; tasting the salt; she knelt down beside the bear and cut into it with the razor. A slit from throat to crotch.

With the edge of the blade she pushed her blood into the cotton. And cut another slice into the bear's side. And again in its other side. She put the bear's bloody chest underfoot and clutched its head. She cut in slicing motions where the head met the body and removed it inch by inch. Decapitating her childhood because it didn't matter anymore.

The head was thrown into the corner and she picked it up by the legs and slashed downward. Bits of cotton fell to the bloody floor below her. And she kept cutting. Not with some passionate anger or hate. More with a methodical despair.

The bear was headless and in shards; she dropped the Ted-E's carcass, walked to her bed, and sat with her head slumped over; letting her curls create a curtain around her face. She put the razor to her wrist and became unsure of what to do next.

To die in a living world or to live in a dying world. She didn't know. She pushed the razor in and spun it around; guiding the edge up through her palm and up to the tip of her middle finger. As the blood leaked out she ran the cut down her tongue over and over for minutes until the flow slowed.

How was Danielle handling it? That girl would cry when she didn't get her way in class. It took Arianna hours to calm her down after Olivia dropped them off at her house. Even then she didn't calm, she mostly went catatonic. Her parents told them all about the birds and they listened with tears in their eyes; knowing more and saying nothing.

The television had advised tennis rackets for protection if one had to move about outdoors. But the general recommendation was to stay indoors.

The news was having a field day over the event. She saw that every business was closing their doors because of the birds deterring consumers from leaving their homes. Luckily, the brave field reporters reported what was obvious by looking out the window long enough to show Dick Cockface fending off a bird on television. The cameras that recorded intersections and parking lots had caught more footage of avian attacks than they could ever air. Goddamn it if they didn't try their best to show them all. One in particular played more than the others; it was clearer, and the old woman was lifted off her feet and fell onto the pavement where the crow began assailing her until a passerby came to her aide and crushed the bird underfoot.

But, still, what about Danielle? How was she getting along alone? The phone rang and Arianna looked at the caller ID. It was Danielle's phone number.

9

The salty dry heat of island air rushed past Crystal's face and through her thick golden hair as the couple hit the open road accelerating away from the main stretch of Hanga-Roa. She wore an island ensemble of ocean green silk and khaki. A contemplative Gerri sat beside her. The flight had been a long one with multiple layovers during which Crystal had taken phone-calls from the station in Cranston. They knew when she would be home but insisted on calling her with news of the bird situation.

The phenomenon was subsiding. Almost all major bird populations had become extinct over the course of a single week. City wide efforts were in place to clear away the carcasses from various public properties where they had amassed, for fear of disease. Never mind the damages caused to property by the dead birds that fell out of the sky.

Moreover, reports of murderous rape were coming in from around the world, Providence included. Violent and merciless stories had emerged from every street corner in every corner of the world, no place was exempt from the bloodshed.

To remain sane something inside of her blocked it out of her mind. Every time she attempted to consider the issue her thoughts immediately went to something else. She couldn't process these things they had called to tell her.

Heeding the network's request that she return home to report the latest tide of events she decided to cut the trip short. Instead of resting at the hotel they unloaded their luggage and drove immediately to the north shore home of Forgotten Eagle; the psychic.

"There are the Moai on that hill over there. They're

supposed to be haunted," Crystal said, pointing out the right window of the rental jeep.

Gerri put small black binoculars up to his eyes and peered out over the emptiness until he caught sight of them, "Oh man. Look at that."

"On the other side of that hill is the coastline."

"Do you know why they made the statues so big out here?"

"No. Why?"

Gerri spoke fluidly, like he tended to do, his pitch only mildly Jewish; "Because the Easter Islanders were so isolated, or used to be, that they had no idea of relative size. They made the statues as big as they could because they didn't want to get shown up by anyone else's statues. Eventually they deforested their island building the things."

"Oh."

They turned right traveling along the coast mostly in silence. The exhaustion had set in. Crystal's mind, though bogged down, was aware that she was in no condition to enter into a divination scenario. She also knew that Forgotten Eagle would have a solution to the problem of sleepiness, whether it be coffee or something stronger.

Gerri lit up a cigarette but before he had smoked half of it they arrived. Stepping out of the jeep they were struck by a light mist created by waves crashing on rocks not far off. A yard of partially dry grass surrounded a modest beach house. Across the road were rolling hills completely barren except for protruding fallen statues.

A tall white picket fence grew lush leafy grape vines up the side of the navy blue one story home and from behind the wall of vines emerged the figure of a man silhouetted against the ocean stretched out over the world's ledge. Forgotten Eagle moved quickly, with slumped shoulders, his head down. Crystal and Gerri walked to meet him. Half way there his features came into focus. He wore cut below the knee tight blue jeans and a white tank top. His facial hair was thick stubble while the hair on his skull fluffed chaotically in place atop his skull. He had frantic yet friendly eyes.

Crystal noted the subtle smirk of surprise on Gerri's face upon his realization that Forgotten Eagle was clearly of middle eastern Jewish decent just as he had been told.

"Yeah. I'm Israeli. But I grew up in Montreal, so there isn't much going on by the way of any cultural heritage. I spent my first couple years there, but that's it. How's it going? Welcome to Easter Island," he said and shook Gerri's hand.

"Good good. Nice place here."

"Isn't it? The furthest away from anywhere. Gotta love it.

"Crystal. You're looking absolutely radiant," he said; hugging her. "The tides down so you didn't quite get the pigment of your shirt right. A few hours, it'll match, but you'll be sleeping."

"Well, I tried."

"Yes. That you did. You should have tried to get some sleep before you came over. You know we can't get any work done when you're this tired. It'll seem like a dream tomorrow and that's no good.

"Gerri, you're tired too. Well, lucky for us I seen this coming and Speaks To Me- she's in town purchasing supplies- has prepared the guest room. There are some pastries inside along with warm milk and sleepy time tea we set out for you. Also, I put out pajamas for you both. I want you to go take a rest. It's 10:45 now. I have an engagement in town that is going to intersect our time together but it could not be avoided. So I insist that you wake up by 9:00 pm. Dinner will be set out for you by my Speaks To Me. I'll be home promptly at 9:45 and we'll have our fire together. I know you are anxious to get back to Rhode Island. Absolute tragedy these events are in the way of what could have been a nice vacation for you two.

"Come along with me, I'll show you to the guest room."

The afternoon sun drifted across the ocean side cliffs with a reverberating breeze that hummed gently under the sound of crashing waves. Their bodies fell into the rhythm of the rolling thunder of the ocean colliding with rock as it threw thousands of liquid beads through the air to fall back to the source. The pair slept peacefully in a solarium bedroom facing the western sky over the tranquil Pacific haze.

The sun passed over the island and across the sky, eventually casting it's light upon their bedroom. Jet lagged and deeply relaxed they continued to slumber uninterrupted. Tetuupu night in Easter Island fell over them and their slumber was deep.

Clouds passed further offshore and brought with them lightening as well as a permeating electricity. All of this energy ever absorbing into a transcendent fabric all around the cliff side dwelling. A thumbnail moon became masked by a storm that had moved closer from the distant horizon. Lightning struck like figure skaters dancing across the ice.

Crystal opened her eyes to behold the view. Enveloped in darkness she looked to an old fashioned alarm clock that read 8:35. She nudged Gerri absentmindedly. Her head felt reinvigorated to the fullest extent. Electric with the storm.

In the kitchen they came upon a small and elegantly clothed Asian woman with a little head and a big smile, petite only like one rarely encounters, and of about Crystal's age, who asked them only, "What to drink?" as she pointed to the chairs.

"Pineapple sparkling wine."

"A beer please."

The couple made their way to a table laid out with exquisitely prepared food only available in that area of the southern hemisphere. Throughout the meal Speaks to Eagle served them and took their plates as they finished each course. She didn't speak and yet adequately maintained a hostess' interest as Crystal regaled her with the tales of the terrible things she had seen.

Crystal knew that this island had not been spared. A man had gone off with a machete in the hospital. Here, the people with Autism who numbered only about a half dozen still suffered two casualties. The wild life on Easter Island was a sort of non-entity to begin with. The bird threat was subdued in only a couple of days. It only took that long to kill all the birds that hadn't killed themselves. Marauding flocks were never the problem. Just some wayward migrating birds coming upon the island continued to be a minor threat.

The Easter Islanders had taken to a temporary state of anticipatory neglect by not speaking about the escalating crisis. It was a subject reserved for ceremony and absolute respect. Crystal did not know of the taboo, but Speaks to Eagle listened without showing the least symptom of taking offense or being apprehensive.

"I see you've met Speaks To Me, Gerri. Good. And big full bellies going on in here. That's what I like to see," Forgotten Eagle said; entering suddenly and vivaciously from a hall that led off to the front of the house.

He continued, "I see you've tried the Lucuma sorbet, delightful. Very good, very good.

"Alright, alright." Speaks to Eagle moved to Forgotten Eagle's side and held his hand. After a kiss hello, he continued, "She has gotten the fire out back burning and ready for us. Perhaps you'd like to put an over shirt on right now before we get started?"

"Ah. I'll go get one."

"Will you get my cashmere sweater sweetheart?"
Gerri nodded and left the room.
"How is this going to go?" Crystal asked.
"Well. You should ask Gerri this question I ask you. You want to be really high or not?"
"What do you recommend?"
"It honestly makes no difference. Because the visions I'm going to show you don't have to be thought about right now. And you won't be experiencing any memory loss or anything like that. You can mull it all over tomorrow. Tomorrow you'll be feeling very different about things. You'll probably want to enjoy tonight for the sake of uncertainty. No matter what waits for you back home; it will not touch you here tonight. Understand what I'm saying?"
"Yes. I do. Hey, Ger?"
"What's up?" he said, handing her the sweater.
"We're going to be drinking the tea I was telling you about. How strong do you want it?"
"Oh. Medium to high potency seems fine."
"Alright. And fine it will be. Speaks to Me, will you prepare Crystal and Gerri's drink? Thank you.
"Well. Before we start, while you still have your faculties and your wits about you... Bathroom? Anybody need to use the bathroom? No? Ok then. Alright. Let's go do this thing ma mans. Let's do it."
Speaks to Eagle made tea at the bar in the dining room. Her hair tied in a ponytail going down the center of her back. Her movements were fluid and perfect in a way that inspired awe in Crystal exactly as she remembered from a time past. The preparation of the tea seemed to produce a chill in the air, rising from the Earth, and an energy that felt like the atmosphere had become thick and fluid.
Working at a countertop island in the middle of the spacious green linoleum tiled kitchen floor, the girl's slanted eyes focused as she manipulated small steel

implements and organic substances of an unknown origin and variety.

Crystal, Gerri, and Forgotten Eagle walked out the back doorway over the wooden deck, down to the lawn, and across the yard to the fire pit.

They were only a stone's throw away from a 50 foot plummet into the deadly ocean churning away below. A person out of their head on whatever kind of drugs could easily wander off the ledge.

Forgotten Eagle gestured for the guests to sit down on either of two folding nylon camping chairs. "I love these chairs, ya know? I think they are the best thing for my clients I have ever come across. They are not only comfortable, but the material is conducive to the vibrations that live around here. It holds these energies in place and keeps them there. At which point you guys are privy to special access to these energies at exactly the right time and levels as it's needed; like one of those glass bulbs on a stem that waters plants, except more stranger.

"Gerri you can smoke a cigarette whenever you want to. Let it help you focus. Do either of you have any questions?"

"I have only heard details from Crystal's mouth. And to say the least, she's probably a little biased. I'd like to know your take on what it is you do, and what you're about to do exactly," Gerri said.

"Well, I am a seer, and a doer. Let me say that I see a major upheaval in your lives, as well as the lives of most others. Everyone actually. You didn't think all these terrible things that are happening were just going to go away? Things like this foreshadow more things like this. You fine people are lucky to have the ability to hop on a plane, rent a jeep, and arrive at my place here at the end of the world. Ha! As if the world had an end! Ya know what I'm talking about ma man? But here you are. Here we are. On this cliff. This power in my fingertips.

I'm going to do the thing I know how to do best. Maybe you could call it talent. Whatever it is, it affords me the ability to show you all the things you would ever need to, for all intents and purposes, see.

"Considering the circumstances surrounding us creatures of this united awareness that we've got around us and inside us; I won't be charging you. I've spent so much time charging people to do what I love to do anyway. So, I don't want any money from you. No money at all. I want you to relax and focus. It is my pleasure. Ah. The tea is here."

Speaks To Eagle delivered them crystal mugs containing a steaming beverage that smelled sweet like a steaming apple cider.

"Is it better for me to not know exactly what's coming?" Gerri asked.

"Yes. Yes. That is exactly what I mean by that. You got it ma man."

Crystal blew over her brew and looked to the eyes of her lover which were directed past her out to the dark clouded sky.

"What about the storms?" Gerri said.

"They will stay away. You can trust me on that."

The distance was illuminated by great stretches of blue electricity.

Gerri jerked back slightly.

"Yes, yes. Let us enjoy the elements. I'll put my nylon chair here over by you guys. Speaks To Me come sits with me. You two drink your tea. It's cool enough by now. And let us get a feel for how this ocean and this electricity really is feeling about us. Look out there now as lightening moves to and fro within the storm area. Both of you take small sips and continue watching the storm."

They obliged, sipping their first tastes of the surprisingly sweet drink, while simultaneously the lightning flickered spastically. Inside her stomach

Crystal felt a shiver run throughout her vital organs. It was nothing like the last time. There was darkness around her, save for the flickering flames of the fire contained in a round pit of rocks. No house lights were on. The electricity ceased to thunder or flash. Darkness fell hard. Water crashed over the cliff face and rose up and over with velocity completely unexpected and the drops came pouring over them.

"Take another sip." Forgotten Eagle said.

In the distance the lightning flickered back again in greater frequency of strikes. Crystal's head felt as though it were rolling on the waves when she came to a startling conclusion that she couldn't feel or hear the waves anymore. Her senses had left her. The constant rising and falling of the breaking waves had ceased as though the floor had fallen from under her. The bolts far off struck, jolting with higher and higher frequency. The water all around had become dead still.

"Speaks To Me; I'd like my powders now. My friends. Please drink until the mug falls from your hand. It will happen on its own accord in about a minute. Drink away. Drink up. Drink. Don't chug, drink. Drink away. And there you go Crystal. That is how much tea you needed. And Gerri. You go ahead and keep on drinking. Thank you, good sir." Speaks To Eagle handed him his plastic tackle box full of different concoctions to be used in the ceremony. The sorcerer walked from his chair to the fire's edge. "Very good Gerri."

Speaks To Eagle came between them swiftly and removed the fallen glasses.

"Fruit will be served in one hour. Now I want you to both place your eyes on the fire before you."

Crystal's head hung low and she sat slumped in her chair; a drugged vacancy had settled across her face. A calm sea of ether cradled her head like a placid buoy. Her glazed eyes portrayed unconscious sadness for the beauty lingering everywhere. Illuminations like the gold of angels shone from every flicker of the flames. The earth rumbled under her feet.

They sat motionless; slumped forward. There was indeed something fantastical coming from that fire. An energy radiated from the flames. One that emitted no form of phenomenon perceivable to the basic senses, other than visible light, light it gave in extreme quantities. The entire property had become engulfed in extreme light. At the center of the ordeal they could not close their eyes, but they were not blinded. They were consumed in an illuminated mass of energy and all that could be seen were golden shimmers glimmering off of other golden shimmers. As though there was some capacity to maintain this state indefinitely, this one moment carried on for what seemed like forever to them. An entire thoughtless evening in actuality passing by in only a few moments. An ocean fog had all the while been slowly placing the property under an impenetrable veil.

Inside this golden cocoon feelings were sprouting. Emotions. Every positive experience either one of them had ever had. Feelings of love as though their lives had never encountered hardships. The sensation that life had always been like it was inside the light. Not a single recollection of any event that may have caused undesirable feelings within them; their demons were not there. Said demons never even existed. Eternity passed them by like one might say the years of their life had passed them by.

In a golden universe they floated through the everything. No distractions. Unaware of one another. Thinking without thoughts or without words; an accumulation of positivity surrounding them, when from the corner of her eye she saw a disturbance in the energies totality.

Her attention focused on the incongruity. There were other occurrences of it's nature happening in many other places, she knew that, but all she could do was focus on this single entity; experiencing some kind of aliveness coming from the relatively lifeless gold and diamond surroundings. It moved slowly then quickly then slowly again; downward.

She knew it was blood. Draining through the gold and falling to the floor. The all-encompassing illumination suddenly darkened and she looked to the sky. The heavenly world of golden rich light had separated above her, letting the darkness back in. Lightning flashed it's inevitable reach over her and she noticed the walls were drawing near around her. The blood from the walls ran at a 75 degree angle toward her ankles.

Suddenly; she felt like herself again. This terrible fright was all around her. Thunder exploded in every point of space. The diamonds flew from under the blood. Her hallucinating world became soaked entirely in the dark liquid. The diamonds sparkled through at points like the shimmer of the sea on a clear night. When the flying precious stones settled, the sky was overtaken again with intensely vibrant illumination. It was as though the sun had risen above her.

"He is risen."

Reflections from all around blinded and confused her. Crystal became terribly panicked. Run! But when she tried; she could not move. Her body was held fast and did not respond to her mind, her head could hardly turn.

A humming slowly over took everything as she began to cry. Her eyes clenched tightly shut and the relief given by that self-serving darkness was great. The humming began to ring at higher and higher levels inside of her head. So powerfully that her nerves lost their ability to transmit electricity throughout her body and she fell to the ground limp and feeling nothing. The powerful hum grew in strength. Her eyes were open and seeing only black, hearing only the high pitched whir. Until the sound got so unbearable it seemed to become aware of itself and feel mercy for her; continuing to get louder but simultaneously becoming imperceptible to her senses. While her body may have been comatose, and her mind paralyzed, some greater part of her felt relief beyond comprehension.

The hum remained. Her body remained paralyzed. Her sight had not yet returned. Soothing her, she soon realized, was the multi-pitched song of a mocking bird. Her lips tried to smile. Her throat tried to sing. Then the muscles began to react. Uh-uh-ah-ah-uh-uh-ah.

The bird responded accordingly. Tweet-tweet-toot-toot-tweet-tweet-toot. Crystal tried to move her lips and could not, but the mockingbird repeated the new song she had been trying to get out. This continued back and forth with new melodies for the bird until she could finally move her lips and blow air through them to whistle. She whistled to the bird and it repeated her tones in order.

The bird flew down beside her. In the blackness she could scarcely make out it's figure further than an outline filled with a fanned out tail filled with purple static. Thunder cracked and rolled and the bird came into focus against the black. It hopped about for a moment to and fro. Then it moved close to her face and appeared to be looking her over. It started whistling an elaborate tune. Trilling up and down high and low notes until the chirps became something different, something frightening; fierce noises from a monster nothing like a bird. Gripped by fear she cried harder.

Forgotten Eagle knelt down between the two clients who writhed in the Earth by the firelight. He spoke to them, "I want you to look around now and discover that everything is a new and different world leaving the other to be missed. Look around now, look around now, look around now."

It took a while for Crystal to understand the bird. Look around? Everything was black. But soon the bird was gone and it's words remained haunting the darkness. "Look around now, look around now, look around now."

She couldn't move her head and began to get frustrated when finally a very real environment manifested total and complete around her. A world similar to the downtown region of Burlington, Vermont. She was able to look around at that point and sat up on her elbows to better see her surroundings. The street was deserted. There was nobody around. The black street ran between the main street shops and office buildings. The sun was setting pink. She looked up the hill to the left, down it to the right; but she could see nobody. She was confused. She didn't know why she was there. She felt dirty and wanted to walk away but she couldn't move. Her legs had no sensation and there was nothing for her to do about it. She panicked; screaming "Help! Help! Somebody come help me! Help!" and she continued to scream. When from the bright pink sunlight she saw a figure running to her. For a moment she felt more afraid than she had been prior, but as the figure approached Crystal could see who it was. To her astonishment Olivia had arrived. Running sweetly to her aide. Olivia was sad and clearly traumatically upset.

Forgotten Eagle watched this from his chair; holding hands with Speaks To Eagle. They watched as Crystal and Gerri rolled around in the crushed grass.

"Do you think this is really the right thing to do?" Speaks asked him.

"I don't know if it's right or wrong. All I know is that it is what Olivia wanted. She wanted me to set in motion her plans for these two and I guess it's all for Tobias. Very elaborate and very sad. But you know how proactive Olivia is. Instead of waste she is creating opportunity and she needed our help."

The psychic and his mystic lover held hands and waited for cues to prod the couple in certain directions. Forgotten Eagle whispered very little into Gerri's ear, but every few moments he would kneel beside Crystal and whisper into her ear, or simply hold his palm over her third eye and concentrate.

At times, the two tripping Americans would crawl close to each other; hold one another's hands or lay their head on some part of the other. They squirmed and murmured in all directions.

"What do you think they'll do when they get back home?" Speaks To Eagle asked.

"Olivia told me to hypnotize them. She needs their money," Eagle said.

"Oh."

"She's in their heads right now. Dictating what comes next in her plans."

"Is it not a great leap of faith to assume pulling all these different forces together; drugs, mesmerism, the human spirit- the sort of things that cannot be foreseen- might have negative results?"

"It can all be foreseen."

"And Tobias? He is to know nothing?"

"Of course not. The seed is to be planted within him. Such fertile soil. He will carry the weight of salvation on his shoulders. All this is designed for the purpose of supplying him with resources. That is what Olivia needs the money for. To give him the resources he needs to be a lighthouse for the others that will be chosen to aide his purpose.

"Olivia knew this business would not fly. Crystal and Gerri have families. Other places to be, other things to do. Give them a couple months to live and see if they give a shit about Olivia and her cohort.

"Tobias is going to take this planet's disgusting turn of events and weave it into this Logos' final art project. Laughing at the humility of it all the entire way. Art.

Great pieces of truth, beauty, and goodness; played out in strange mediums; for nobody. Doing it for no other reason than to pass the time until the bitter end. In his mind anyway. Falling in love with his work, and there will be no one to enjoy it. Except for a curly haired young lady and a handful of strangers. Up there on some mountain making art and there won't even be birds to poop on it."

Forgotten Eagle stood to his feet and walked over to them and stood with his back to the flames.

He kicked Crystal in the ribs and using her hair fiercely yanked her head, neck, and shoulders to and fro.

Nearby, Speaks To Eagle perpetrated equal abuse to Gerri. Poking him with a hot knife and throwing punches into his face while he did not so much as flinch.

"I want to sing a song!" Speaks said.

"Go ahead."

Speaks To Eagle had a voice of honey, she sang, "Sweet sweet angel of life; never mind the pervert and her pen knife. Dry away your heavy tears; slow your racing fears, the panic will help you prepare, for the peace that passes all comprehension. You were part of a life force, and the life force is nothing; it is nothing now, it is nothing now. Sweet sweet angel of life; never mind the pervert and her penknife. The life force is nothing now; the life force is nothing..."

Forgotten Eagle stood collected; impervious to the beating he had given Crystal. The wind blew, but his stillness did not respond. His cotton clothes did not rustle in place. He closed his eyes and held his hands clasped before him. Speaks To Eagle walked back up the stepping stone path to the home.

"Look around, look around," he began. His voice with an aura shining; he told them the tale of the future. Complete with their new conviction that this was the way it was to be; there was no other way it could be, and on some primitive level they would know that to alter this course was to condemn every person they'd ever loved, or even liked, to a horrific and undeserved death, or at least they would think they knew that.

He told Crystal the story of many deeds she would perform before it all came crashing down. He showed her the things she would see in the coming weeks and months. Madness and violence beyond her imagination. He narrated to her tales of rape and slaughter by mindless killers. The whole of everything turned upside down and fearful in a very primal way. The images were precise and graphic. The instructions he gave were step by step through the entire mess.

He commanded: "You will adhere in the fullest to Olivia and Tobias's every desire. You work for them now. Everything you do, you'll do in their best interest. They are your messiah. They are the saviors of many. In your heart you agree that they deserve your help, so you will not question anything anymore. Crystal; you will be quitting your job at the station right away. Gerri; you will dissolve your assets. Olivia will help you to do these things."

That list of commands, and others similar, were recited to the unsuspecting couple until Forgotten Eagle no longer saw any possible opportunity for a miscommunication, a slip up, or any error that could have been avoided. He continued commanding them until their souls had become pliable. Forgotten Eagle had manipulated them into humans that would behave more like state of the art robots.

All that was left to do was to finish programming their instructions. The details Tobias would be in no position- have no ability- to clarify.

It was cold at the foot of the mountain. Crystal was in the Green Mountains at the resort where her family used to spend weekends. The place had changed from what she remembered. It was a colossal building now, like the size of an office complex. Her clothes were tattered. In spots her hair had been torn from her bleeding scalp. Out of breath she stumbled around in a snowy parking lot wondering if the nightmare was over yet.

Dotted all along the foot of the mountainside were warm looking lodges. And Going across the mountain face were ski trails and bunny hills. This white and evergreen place was deserted; silent in an unnatural way, and she couldn't figure out what to do next. She sat down in the middle of the parking lot. To her left she noticed a blue pleated bag and she picked it up. It was full of money.

A man with no face came to her side and put his hand out. She handed the purse to him and he got in a green pickup truck and pulled away down the mountain road.

Her legs weakened and she collapsed into the snow. A shiver of happiness ran through her and made her smile. The pine forests of her youth spun overhead; creating an aquamarine whirlpool in the blue and white sky. She smiled and laughed to herself gently at first but soon the laughter was uncontrollable. Physically taxing fits of laughter burst from within her and the echo filled the world around her. She loved it. She was just so happy.

She felt ecstatic. It was a rush. She sat up.

Gerri came walking toward her; looking down at the ground with a joker like smile. Oh sweet joy. Gerri.

"Hello Sweetie. This is a really beautiful place; don't you think?" he said.

"Oh yes. It certainly is. I certainly do think so. We've just purchased it sweetheart."

"Really?"

"Yes."

"Well, that's cool. How about that? We are really going to enjoy it up here."

"Yes we are."

"We really are."

From the same area that Gerri had come from; so too came Forgotten Eagle. Approaching with kind of a hustle. Looking around anxiously.

"Hello Forgotten Eagle."

"How's it going?" Gerri asked sincerely.

"Good. Good you guys. Hey, are you two ready to maybe get out here? Go back to my place at Easter Island. Know what I mean, ma mans? Are you ready to go now?"

"Hold on just a minute there Eagle. Where exactly are you saying we're going?" said Gerri.

"Back to my home on Easter Island. This trip is over. You need to take a trip home now. So much to do, so little time. Time is money. Every minute counts. Yup, yup, yup; time to go."

"Well alright."

"Ok. Yeah. That's agreed. We'll go back now. Which way?"

"That way," Forgotten Eagle said.

Crystal and Gerri turned around to find nothing but a great black void. The psychic pushed them and they fell into it. That was not good.

A moment later they were rolling around in dirt and fire light. Oh good. They were saved. It was like a dream. How nice. Speaks to Eagle came to Crystal's side and placed before her a fistful of grapes.

"Eat," Forgotten Eagle said. He was knelt before Gerri with grapes in a similar manner. As soon as the pair had eaten one each; the masters of the coastal home led them in-doors and placed them down in chairs at the dining table in a corner room adorned tastefully with driftwood; producing ceramic bowls of grapes and placing the food before them.

Distantly they ate the fruit; smiling without much to say. Their faces were clearly bruised, bloody, and battered. That was next on the list of things to be done. Forgotten Eagle fed Gerri a potato with butter, a cooked piece of turtle meat, and goats milk. Crystal was led by the other woman through the breezy hall to a stainless steel and concrete bathroom also adorned with driftwood.

Speaks to Eagle commenced to scrub her and clean her wounds until she was looking as fresh as a broken walking corpse could look. A very pleasant dead girl indeed. Dressed in chic nighttime dark color tones and seamless satin fabric.

Speaks to Eagle led Crystal back to eat the same meal Gerri had already finished and Gerri was led away to the showers. Forgotten Eagle gave him all the instructions to clean himself regularly and instructed him to see to it that Crystal got cleaned as well. For she had suffered a little more brain damage than Gerri had. Forgotten Eagle knew she'd be physically Ok and functioning sufficiently, as well, once she recovered a little more.

Crystal ate her meal gingerly. Speaks to Eagle watched her modestly from a little distance away. Standing straight, with hands folded, by a wall; she watched Crystal eat.

Eventually Gerri came back, but time did not matter to Crystal. Life consisted of a simultaneous moment for the rest of her existence; making said existence at once instantaneous and eternal. This was an idea Crystal could no longer begin to grasp.

"So let's rehearse. You got your tickets; you're going to go get your luggage and return your vehicle. You have done this hundreds of times before. You're going to get on the plane at the airport. You might have to wait; but we know what we're doing when we're waiting; receptivity to idle chit chat; engage in electronics, and talk amongst yourselves, cuddle; all those good things. You know, ma mans.

"Alright. You're going home. You'll get a driver at the air place and they's gunna take you to yous homes where yous gunnas gets a little bits of house guests you knows? That's gunna be Olivia. She'll be spending a lot of time with you guys. And sometime after that you'll be spending time with Tobias. All these people want to spend time with you because you all are their favorite people. Yup. You all clean and you all fed. Time to go back out into the world. Yes it is. It's time to snap out of this and accept it just like I's told you yous was gunna do.

"Go home now."

"Alright." said Crystal; grabbing her purse.

"Thank you for the great experience," Gerri said as he took from Speaks to Eagle a small mesh bag containing his personal affects, "Goodbye."

"Goodbye," said Forgotten Eagle.

THE SPRING OF BEGGINING'S END

10

Beyond the drawn curtains hung the overcast skies that had plagued most of the planet for about a week. Danielle's lamp cast shadows across the room as she read James Joyce in the basement of her family's home. Her brother was in his bedroom with his headphones on and her mother and father were in their room upstairs, probably reading, too.

Since Olivia's visit things had stayed placid for Danielle. Her home sat off the side of a back road that skirted Brandon, and even though the world was falling apart outside, she scarcely noticed anything different. Her father had stocked up on all the supplies he could acquire relatively early on and the doors were kept locked and the weapons were kept loaded. Other than that there was nothing left to do but wait.

So waiting was what she did. She had been face first in Ulysses for weeks with the fateful day lingering distractingly in the forefront of her mind. Alas, the day of destiny was only a single night away. The next day she'd say goodbye to her family, get in a car with Arianna, and never look back.

The plans had gone differently than Olivia had first laid them out but an unexpected phone call from the psychic had reassured Arianna that it would still be fine; that "Christmas was coming early." Newly spring, they weren't even supposed to be experiencing any social breakdown until Mid-Summer. It didn't feel right to Danielle but she accepted it as gospel anyhow.

She couldn't look back. She wouldn't. She had promised herself that much. The pain at the thought was difficult to bear and she wasn't even in the thick of the apocalypse yet. No, she was at the point when weeks and weeks of tears had finally numbed her. It took a long time but she was finally reconciled to what was going to come. Survival was at the forefront of her thoughts now as it was very clear that life was rushing to its bitter end.

Her elegant and graceful mother, who'd given her so much love, would be gone from her life. As would her slow-witted brother. Her kind brother, Rick, would succumb to the absolute nightmare. He was too old, Olivia had said. How he would even perceive the coming events she could only wonder.

She felt a paramount desire to warn everybody she could. To scream from the rooftops what she knew. Surely by the whole world knew at that point anyhow. Had they lost hope? Before, when only she and Arianna stewed in despair, it was all she could do to not run crying to her father's side.

But that would have been selfish. And she was determined to do the right thing. If only for once in her life, this was the time. Exactly what Olivia had asked; say nothing to anyone. She had escaped into the mind of James Joyce. His intoxicating words created a reality where everything was as it used to be. Real people had real problems and real lives; the way that everyone should. The way that she was supposed to. The old way.

One distraction and then another; she wanted to learn astrology and the tarot like Olivia had spoken of. She wanted to learn everything she could about the occult view of reality and the esoteric underbelly of the lies she once knew as truths.

The very day after Olivia had talked with them Danielle went back to the book store to buy a thick, all you'll ever need to know, astrology book and she was absolutely entranced by the ancient practice. Thus between James Joyce and astrology she was doing her best to shut out the impending doom.

She drank tea, curled up under a light acrylic blanket. However absentmindedly, she gazed vacantly over Joyce's pages with her heart in her throat and a hollow in her chest.

There was a sudden crash and rumbling coming from upstairs.. Her mother released an abrupt and short lived scream interrupted by abrupt thuds coming one after another and giving way to the force of a thick window shattering.

Danielle's jumped up from the couch, stopped to listen over her pounding heart for a second, and ran up the stairs to her parents closed bedroom door.

Knocking, she said, "Daddy!"

Her father, the innocent car salesman, opened the door; his glasses crooked and his face covered in blood. In both his hands he gripped her mother by the throat. The woman didn't move at all.

"Oh my god."

Her father dropped her mother face down and rushed at Danielle who nimbly ran head long trying to reach the front door. The chase concluded at the bottom of the stairs when the father threw his daughter's face into the wooden trim. She went limp and a shock held her as such. He bent down and lifted her skull by a fistful of hair. And then he thrust the side of her skull down into the tile.

Consciousness left her and he kept slamming her skull into the floor; over and over. Every crash shooting the young woman's blood out onto the walls. A moment later he stopped and stood staring down at his daughter.

He wore no shirt over his slender chest and he bled from a deep wound by his ear. The father reached down and pulled off her pajama pants by the ankles; exposing her bare skin, her legs fell back with a thump. She wore no under garments and he dropped his pants to the ankles.

The man got down on his knees and hiked her up; positioning his loins to hers.

At that moment her brother, a bulky man in a superhero t-shirt, cracked his father over the head with a fire poker sending the man falling over onto his sister. Rick squealed and shrieked as he swung again twice more. When the father no longer moved the brother stabbed forcefully the point of the poker into the man's back over and over. Tears welled in his eyes and fell across his chipmunk cheeks.

He didn't stop jamming that poker through the flesh for some time. Long enough to mash the spine into crumbs and sever the brain stem from the skull. Only finally stopping when he knew that his father would never move again.

Rick moved closer to the door, stepping over the bodies that lay dead before him. He dropped the fire poker, clutched himself, and squealed noisily as he ran off to his bedroom.

Providence looked and sounded like a ghost town. Federal hill was a ghost street. Never truly dead, but not alive either. The streets, haunted by the military, were almost completely empty of cars. Nobody went out since the rapes had begun. And even if one did venture out, the National Guard had been shooting first and asking questions later.

Mostly only the Mafioso families stuck around. Most of Providence's million residents made refugees of themselves. Tobias didn't know where everyone went off to, but he could sense the emptiness and vacancy. The stores with ties to the mob were the only stores still open and shelves were mostly bare at those places. On any given street corner hid normal people turned rapists and child molesters lurking in shadows. Government agencies had an impossible work load to deal with in trying to maintain the fleeting order throughout all the madness. The national guardsmen would round them up in cages right down the street. Tobias had seen the soldiers with dead bodies in the back of several civilian pickup trucks drive away toward Manton avenue too.

The perverts were sent to some kind of camp if they didn't put up a fight. Most did fight and those people were shot dead in the road. Two blocks over in any direction, sometimes right out back, the shots rang day and night. From all of Providence gun shots echoed in one direction or another.

Once the nighttime hours of curfew came into effect the authorities went hunting for the demon men who had lost control over their loins, their rationale, their souls, and all 'human decency.' Nobody walked the streets without a gun. It used to be tennis rackets, but all the birds had died off over a couple short weeks.

Tobias pulled a heavy little .38 special- once belonging to Gerri- from his back pocket and aimed it at garbage blowing around down in the dirty streets. He was not kidding himself; ever aware that only at very close distances could he, with his one eye, ever hit a target. Snub nose guns weren't accurate to begin with. Then again it only took one eye to aim a gun. Having not yet fired it, he was uncertain what the outcome would be if he had to use it. Point, aim, fire, right?

He leaned his head against the glass pane and looked up to the heavens. The sky appeared tinged with green in its overcast. The clouds had no shape. Like a storm with no weather, a single cloud mass blotted out the sky for as far as his eye could see. He hadn't seen the sun since about a week and a half ago and didn't expect he would see it anytime soon. The electric clouds like wet black dough fascinated him all day and every day since their arrival. Some sort of yellow heat lightening ran through the mass as though it had pulsating veins. Energetically speaking, the single cloud- if it were actually a "cloud"- was like nothing he had ever heard of. As far as he knew nothing like that there in the sky had ever existed before on Earth. As far as he knew. The news reports described it as, "Atmospheric conditions, anomalous to gravity, and creating a 'suspended animation effect.'"

They'd given estimates of when to expect breakdowns of the various machines that supported civilization. About one week left of power and running water. Most oil companies had already packed up.

A very subtle and unspoken form of martial law gripped the residents of Providence. Federal Hill was safe for the time being, but it had been witness to it's fair share of tragedies on its side streets and alleys. That was just one neighborhood. He wondered how many ghettos, to date, had burned down out by Broad street, or further down Broadway even. The sound of firetruck sirens was nonstop, yet there was no traffic on the road.

On a good calm day he climbed out onto a high corner of the building and watched his city burn through the motions. That rooftop was about as far as he could get Pluto to venture out the door anymore. The cat wasn't stupid.

Certain screams in the night chilled the entire city with primal fear. Bloody murder in back allies; a child or woman usually. The painful screaming seemed to go on forever, then quiet fell over hustling wind and grim mournful mornings.

Other screams foreshadowed fast approaching gun battles. Those screams drew sirens and filled up the medical outposts. There was no room in the hospitals and scarcely any doctors.

He knew from the final broadcasts that- days before- offshore fishing was still booming and looking stronger than ever as they were catching fish exhibiting behavior patterns only observable as suicide; stranding themselves while the tide went out or coming from miles away to get caught in the trolling nets. That news struck a chord in his mind. He'd always expected animal die offs like that. On some level at least. Maybe just from movies. The interconnectedness of an event like that was beyond extraordinary. The fish must be being guided by something. What wasn't?

The canning business was being revered as the saviors of the new world. Volunteers worked night and day in any given facility the world over. They were giving people hope. False hope.

Thinking about leaving the house again made him queasy and frightened him more than he expected anything would. He was told to make reservations with the National Guard for an Exit Escort and present some sort of proof of destination. An address would do.

On every block, in every field off the highway, there were people huddled together in their homes or in a car, afraid of shadows and bumps in the night. He knew how they felt. Tobias loathed that which went bump in the night. People should have been nicer to each other when they had the chance.

Really, there wasn't any major rioting or looting because most people couldn't bring themselves to be in the street without some kind of noble purpose or physical desperation. Still it seemed that there were no borders or limits to the atrocities happening all around him. Sometimes he found himself staring at the base of the door. Waiting for it to come crashing down or for smoke to come flooding in. He stared at windows waiting for stray bullets.

And his life... In the middle of Olivia's magnificent conspiracy to take them away to safety, at the expense of two upper class Americans, the women had reverted to some blissful and loving raving lunacy. Something had damaged her inside and when he tried to look into her wandering eyes he couldn't find the woman she used to be.

"Oh my love, my love. Don't you dare forget my life-shard when you return to the house," she would say.

To him this "my love, my love," life-shard behavior of hers was another puzzle piece of some grand illusion being played out before his eyes. To think, to feel, was nothing as it used to be. More people than only Olivia were behaving as though they had lost their minds. He didn't *feel* altogether normal. He felt loopy.

The final news reports showed people segregated in gymnasium shelters; confused and wild eyed. The reporters referenced Autism as though there may be some connection, but hell if they said what it was. A staged ceremony of an opera; the entire world slightly insane and very afraid; locking the children into churches and trying to save the day from the back of a U-Haul; at each-other's throats but too afraid of the unknown to make a wrong move.

The damn life shard presented a serious problem because it was nowhere to be found. He had no phone or anyway to contact Olivia and ask where it might be. He'd spent the better part of many hours searching for it.

In a way, he was completely glad that he couldn't find the glass. When he held that shard in his hand he knew of an ancient and core pain. The shard meant loss and it was all he could do to force denial over himself and pretend that nothing was inevitable. He was delighted to keep her suicide out of his life.

Of course she'd sprung those two mind-fucked zombies on him. Stupid brainwashed robot people. That was about the second oddest experience of his life. Day in and day out he instructed Crystal and Gerri to do simple little things that children knew to do. They sat and stared off into space with the most pitiful grins across their faces. Happy about everything and completely oblivious to the world around them; hypnotized beyond the confines of socialization. They could function but not always. They could provide for themselves but not always. They needed to be watched but not always.

The Federal Hill apartment had been stripped of anything that had real value with the exception of books. All but the most important books were left behind; too heavy to move. Tobias paced through the rooms, preparing mentally to move on to a new life. After babysitting the Omega couple- as they came to be known- for an incredibly long and viciously odd 5 days, he was given a green light by his spiritual benefactor for a two day one night salvage mission. He drove an abandoned red Chevrolet Astro touring van left behind by a neighbor.

Having all the resources of Crystal and Gerri's dwelling available to them, there was not all that much to pack away in Providence. The laptop came along but how long would it even be useful for? Suitcase of clothes and jackets. Olivia wanted her jewels and crystals, her Visconti Sforza tarot deck, a few other nice things she had forgotten when she said goodbye to the home. He took the Palmistry book, the Astrologers Handbook, the

Tarot Apprentice book, Secrets In The Field by Freddy
Silva, dice, a silver backed mirror, a harmonica, music,
the printouts he made weeks ago of three years
ephemeris and aspect charts, two Carlos Castaneda
books; Journey to Ixtlan and The Active Side of Infinity.
The astral projection handbook. A cheap pendulum
made from a fake orange crystal. His Gothic Vampire
Tarot deck. A regular deck of playing cards. He so
wanted to bring the Time Life books but it wasn't
practical. Though he'd never forget what great
knowledge they had taught him so effectively. And that
went for many many others. Too many books, too little
time. The brutal irony.

Batteries: the little tubes of harnessed balanced
energy. A rectangular technological device for music
that may be soon rendered useless and also a hand held
cd player and cd collection. His guitar all put away in its
case. The gold bound edition of Edgar Allen Poe works.
Pluto was calm and away in the carrier. The cat's
resentment was crystalline and pure, toward a world
tearing away from itself before his face.

Olivia was going to have to live without her life
shard. Though the shame he felt for not retrieving it
certainly ate away at his gut. How worthless he felt.

Dressed down in black he wore it like a guerrilla
would; from the leather converse to the black bandanna
wrapped around his head with the hair flowing over it,
cargo pants, and a black cotton shirt fit tightly with the
sleeves rolled up. Anarchy eye patch. He finished the
rest of a bottle of Merlot and put it down on the kitchen
counter. Everything sat beside the door and ready to go.
All that was left to be done was to swallow a deep
breath, close up Mr. Kitty, throw the shit through the
van's side door and zip the hell away.

He led his suitcase, and carried the guitar, down
the stairs with his black backpack over a shoulder. He
didn't look around; he only put the items into the van

and went back upstairs for the rest. Soon he'd have to go out there and drive to Crystal's house to meet up with his strange affinity group. After a quick glance through the apartment he felt satisfied he was not forgetting anything. The metal artwork still hung from the walls. Olivia had left all of it and what nonsense to leave it, Tobias thought. There was a fist sized blazing sun made of silver. This was the piece he took from the wall and placed in his cargo pocket. He was abandoning beloved posters and all sorts of knick-knacks and artifacts from the years past, singing bowls and lava lamps. His beloved black lights.

Moving away from his old peace and serenity felt like moving slightly closer to the dejected and wandering hells of a mostly- but not totally- forgotten nightmare. But really, how could one compare individual anguish to collective anguish?

Tobias threw Olive's bag over his shoulder, lifted the cat and the computer, and brought these things down to the van. Pluto rode shotgun. He ran back upstairs to close the apartment's door, closed the doors on the van, and turned the ignition. He drove out onto a crumbling potholed side street and left to Atwells; turned right and found the National Guard outpost for evacuation escorts. He was greeted by a guy about his own age. Peters, the name tag read.

"I have an escort for 11:45 on I-95 south to Hope Valley."

"Pull up to that cone over there and he'll give you a honk when he's ready to follow you."

"Great, thanks."

Tobias felt mildly self-conscious pulling away with his head cockeyed and praying not to botch the maneuvers. He rolled up the power windows leaving them a crack open. Waiting, he let Pluto out from the cage. The cat didn't crawl out right away.

Tobias lit a cigarette. Abstaining from smoking for

health reasons seemed asinine so he had bought a
carton when he could still walk down the street.
There were tiny foreign looking old women across the
way huddled together on the corner of the twelve lane
triangular intersection. They wore vibrant colors and all
had their backs turned toward him. In a few days it
would all be sheer chaos, he suspected.

On March 22nd there was a new moon in Aries on
the first full day of the Aries sky, the astrological, real,
actual, true, new year. Ever since that day it seemed
almost everyone had blown some fuse or another.
Maybe none so ruined as Crystal and Gerri, but still a
completely severe situation. At least the Omega couple
were happy. It would all gain momentum and climax
around the next day, the sixth, with a full moon, or that
night, for all intents and purpose, until a breakdown on
the ninth of April, with a moon in Scorpio, followed by
it's lingering dénouement in Sagittarius. Upon which
point a new moon in Taurus would mark the beginning
of the Taurus sky and something new; he could only
assume at that point he'd be working in some facet.

He got the honk, put the vehicle in gear and drove
down Federal Hill for what was obviously the last time.
There were Christians in the street down by where the
theater was. Assholes. He wished he could blame it on
them. Instead, he pointed out to Pluto, "Those people
didn't make it any better a place while it lasted. They
would help people and try to brainwash them at the
same time. A whole sect of consciousness living side by
side with the religion monster and the god machine.
Like they were plugged into it."

The cat had come out of the carrier and sat on hind
legs between the cage and the armrest, looking around
bewilderedly.
Pluto was probably looking at the sky, Tobias figured.
The thing was so captivating. Hypnotic and
unbelievable. Clouds without any wisp or fluff. A thick

mass undulating in place, becoming greater and greater, thicker and thicker, more like semen in water. Rife with the frailest heat lightening pulsing through it like varicose veins. Amorphous bulges moving in and out like liquid but not. Like a lava lamp.

There was no traffic when he looked out over I-95. There was no traffic on any street visible. Only military vehicles huddled at certain points in any direction and the mob of Christians down by the hotel. Tobias peered over his shoulder to view the Providence skyline one last time. The glory of 3.5 high-rises.

Soon he came to the ramp and knew it was time to let this place go. The on ramp brought him out onto the empty highway. Midday on a Friday and I-95 was deserted except for the occasional vehicle that sped past him. Indeed he accelerated, as he abandoned the Providence city limits and the escort exited off to return to the station. From his pocket he fetched the pistol and set it in the cup holder.

Along the highway were cars, about every kilometer or so, some abandoned, some inhabited. The latter was a frightening concept. What they were doing there, he had no idea. Finally he resolved to ignore those people stuck on the highway.

To be truly alone was taking a toll on Tobias. For a long time he had had his Olivia. But something had clicked off inside of her. Inside of him sadness crept up his spine and through his chakras out into his nerves. A pain as real as dry heaving overcame him. He realized he was losing her. The denial had cleared. He had seen her. She was as creepy as the rest of the people in the world; glazed over and slightly twisted.

Before she got all messed up and skewed, Olivia worked every last moment of her ability to ensure a proper place to flee to for safety.

All was planned to abandon the Goldberg property the following night. There was a ski resort that would serve as home. Up in the Green Mountains. A long time ago, Tobias's mother told him that should anything ever go wrong and society were collapsing, if nuclear war broke out; "Get to higher ground, that's what it's there for."

Olivia, in her infinite ability, had found that single sentence from his past and created a course of action on that foundation.

Driving down the highway, Tobias had one of those moments when the pressure of the surroundings, the situation, and his frantic thoughts took a toll. His entire body grew weaker and weaker until he felt close to blacking out. He couldn't stop though. He was overcome by some great fatigue stemming from a mysterious and menacing hopelessness. His neck weakened and he lay his head on the steering wheel, peering through falling hair out over the highway from hell. In that manner he drove haphazardly and ever slower, determined not to stop for anything. There was no way to know what was in the woods.

Pluto slunk low and rigid in Tobias's lap. His ears forward and eyes alert to something happening behind Tobias's seat.

Tobias thought of the life-shard and the loathing burning through his every fiber. Tears ran down his face and revived him slightly, making him capable of driving, but the sadness consuming him had claws in deep. He was frightened and there was something cold and heavy inside the van with them. Fear gripped him and he slammed the accelerator to the floor, the rear end of the van sunk and pushed him ahead faster and faster. He hoped to maybe disorient and dispel the petrifying energy in the back and to get to Olivia as quickly as he could. His foster mother flooded his brain. For a moment he felt as though he were being embraced by her. Through instinct he said, "Pluto, get that thing out of here."

With that the cat carefully and calmly went to its cage to lie down and curl up. Tobias heard it purring, and cooing even. His stomach was uneasy and he experienced a foreboding nausea.

Pluto had never made that happy little coo before and now Tobias found himself perplexed and slightly amused. A warmth falling over his heart made him feel happiness. An intense relief.

The van had a chill filling the hull. He smiled about this. Someone was dead and that soul was there to protect him. The energy moved through the van and away into another dimension. Tobias looked into his mirror, felt the absence of that awareness and finally exhaled.

His tears became tears of joy, weeping at some grand beauty he had never even considered before, a totality, and an evanescent harmony. He chuckled under his breath and smiled to himself.

Coming upon a rest area sign he kept a heads up for the little maintenance road he had to cross to meet route 3. It was a stupid way to get to Crystal's house but he knew of no other. He took the turn and the van bumped up and down over the lumpy clumps of dirt and dry grass on the pathway but he cleared the terrain easily enough before taking a right and going straight for a minute, then veering to the left and taking another left turn, and one more left before arriving at Tulip drive on the left. The Goldberg mansion was toward the back with a long driveway spilling out into the actual cul-de-sac portion. He drove past the long front lawn and pushed the door opener button and moved through the threshold of the garage. He parked, took Pluto in his arms, and walked up the concrete steps through the door.

Tobias searched through an empty dining room and kitchen before finding the Omega couple seated side by side with the giant shit eating grins on each of their faces Those awful smiles that never went away.

"Where's Olivia?" he asked.

"She's in there," Gerri said with a point of his finger.

"Monkey's point, Gerri," Tobias said as he walked through the hard wood hallways to the bedroom at the furthest end of the house where she was staying and he screamed, "Oh fuck!" in revulsion at the sight.

He fell to his knees in the hallway, forcing the words, "No! No!" through his clenched teeth and heaving sobs. Holding the cat tight against himself. But Pluto knew instinctively they were in the presence of death and pushed against Tobias to get to the corpse.

"Oh, she wouldn't care just fucking go," he said and released the cat. Falling back against the wall, he could not see a thing save for shadowy hardwood blur. He wiped the tears from his eye and lit a cigarette hoping it would help him look through the door. The object seemed impossible to handle and he couldn't get a drag inhaled.

He smoked it anyway and stood against a wall with his arms clenching himself; almost ready to go look at what was waiting for him. For *him*. *His* problem. His savior; dead and covered in red.

To behold the site was a punch and having seen it once he was ready for the shock and braced himself.

He stood at the doorway and looked at her.

Olivia had absolute dead eyes looking up at him with a down turned chin. Her naked body leaned against the corner of a four post bed. Blood smeared across her face and chest, and over her bare arm that ran down into her exposed and private most nether regions. She was dressed up in blood and masturbating. Only a moment passed before he knew what was waiting for him between her legs.

He knelt down and gave her hand a tug, taking the life-shard from her fingertips. At her side, in her other hand was a tarot card from his vampire deck. He picked it up and it was the moon card, showing a brunette woman sitting toward a mirror with her hands covering her face and eyes. Inside the mirror her image had hands held out, open, and receptive. Inside the reflection there were ghosts in robes haunting all around the woman. A bad omen given the circumstance.

The blood pool he found the card in was still very wet, and very warm. He reached down and squeezed Olivia's breast- she would have expected it- and yes she was still flush with minimal warmth lingering within her. Clearly dead though. He pulled a nearby chair to her side and placed one hand on her back and cradled her head with the other. Shaking her and listening for a whisper and watching for a breath or any sign of life. Her skin was dark gray and there was no bringing her back. He felt like maybe he should be giving her CPR, but he wasn't going to. He knew he didn't need to but he felt as though he should be.

Tobias was about to get his grip back, and start to think functionally, when he saw another body lying bloodied in the bed. Pluto was chewing on the corpse's finger. It was a nude man whom he did not recognize. Shoved in this man's right eye socket was a piece of paper. No eye. This person was sliced and stabbed all over his body; gaping cuts that bulged with intestines trying to break free in some places. Tobias looked over these wounds in awe. Gaping holes were broken through his chest plate, ribs, and neck.

Behind Olivia's head, on the blood streaked comforter, was the murder weapon. A huge knife with a brass knuckle handle, a curved 7 inch blade, and back turned steel hooks on the second edge. It was covered totally in blood.

He unrolled the paper which had no blood on the inside where the writing was but the edge was stained along the full length. The message was written in a leaky fountain pen with blotted ink all over and said:

Oh, Tobias. My love, Tobias. I'm saying goodbye now. Soon, you have seen, I will be mildly delirious. Soon everyone will be mildly delirious. If it were up to me, you and I would have spent a thousand years talking in our living room. But we wouldn't have had a thousand years anyhow. A thousand years could have made a lifetime seem like our short while though. That is perspective. Keep it all in perspective my beloved. We have had our time and now I must go. Remember that the death cycle is just as important as the life cycle. Who knows what is waiting for me on the other side? Finally I am going someplace that I have never seen before. Wish me luck!

There are two folders on the counter. One has detailed information on the resort in Vermont. The other folder has the information on the helicopter ride to Crystal's family's home, also in Vermont. You won't be seeing any of them though. Just smelling them...

You of course will have a gun in your pocket. This is <u>important!</u> Gerri will "go off-line" at about 9:00 tonight. As will just about all the rest of the human race shortly thereafter. You, my dear, will have to be ready for this. Eliminate Gerri, wait for the witching hour, and flee to the resort.

This was our destiny. And I do believe that, by comparison, we are all going to a better place. You will have everything you'll ever need ready and waiting up there. And I know there will be serenity for you on that mountain.

You have much to do, so get to it. My advice is to expect the unexpected. And there is one more gift for you waiting in Vermont. So you're welcome. Don't bother cleaning up the mess here. It is my dying wish my lover and I be left where we lie.

With <u>all</u> of my love,

Olivia

At least he didn't have to dig a hole. Tobias looked about at the sky blue walls and upscale nighttime blue furniture. The mess was extensive. Blood was flung in every direction and on every surface. The walls and ceiling held streaks in all directions. The maroon shades were coated with the substance.

The letter indicated that he was making the trip that night. This fact he shrugged away. Nothing mattered.

Tobias picked up the murder knife and knelt beside Olivia's pool of blood. He bent over, put his lips to it and slurped the cool liquid into his mouth. Over and over he drank her blood, feeling it fill his mouth and noticing a metallic sensation as it slid down his throat.

He sat up and put his hands into the pool which had coagulated pretty sufficiently and he rubbed the mess onto his face. He removed his shirt, throwing it on the male corpse and rubbed blood all over his chest and arms. From his hair the remnants of her life dripped onto his shoulders.

Pluto still gnawed away at the man's fingers. He got down on the floor, lay his head onto her thigh, and put the knife tip into his left bicep. He pushed down and in until he could sense the skin break and with the same applied pressure and force he dragged the blade through his tissue; his eye strained to watch the split. He cut a four inch gash into his arm. Only clean for a moment before his blood evacuated the venules of his flesh and flowed down his arm. He put her stiff wrist up to his mouth and sucked at the shredded wound. He tongued the flaps of skin and tried to suck what was inside out. It only worked a little. The wound was not fresh and had all but run dry. His eye was closed and he wept to himself candidly.

He couldn't know what to think. And he really

didn't think anything. Only, "Thank god for Pluto," came to his mind. He rolled over and into her, arms wrapped around her waist and squeezing her tight to him. He rolled and writhed in a bloody mess of despair.

Time passed and he knew somewhere there was a clock ticking. Tobias rose and walked to the kitchen. He searched through drawer after drawer until he found a pair of crooked neck pliers, then he went back to his foster mother's corpse and moved her body to a lying position on the floor. He placed the jaws of the tool around her front tooth and cranked the pliers upward to sever the bone from the jaw. Holding tight, he pulled the tooth from her skull and put it into his pocket. Crying heavily the entire time, he repeated the process with her other front tooth and put that in his pocket as well.

Pluto had finished eating and stood on the edge of the bed watching what Tobias was doing. He dropped the pliers and grabbed the cat. They went out into the sitting room to where the Omega couple sat together.

Crystal's head was turned up to the ceiling as it always seemed to be. And Gerri stared straight ahead as he always seemed to do. Olivia had had the foresight to ensure they all wore the proper casual clothing to make the trip. Gerri was wearing a sweater with a penguin on it that seemed more appropriate for Christmas time.

"When was the last time you saw Olivia?" he asked Gerri. The man's smile broke as he spoke more stinted and higher pitched than usual, almost like a child, "I saw her, at about 9:45 this morning, when her guy friend arrived."

"Did she tell you anything lately? Or give you a message for me?"

"I was instructed to hurry you along, if we weren't out of here, by 4:30."

Tobias looked at a clock on the wall. It was close to 1:45.

"Have you two eaten today? Are you fed?"

"Yeah. We're fed. Crystal broke a dish and she wouldn't clean it up. I didn't clean it up either."

"I saw that. You know today's the big show, right? Are you ready for this?"

"Oh, yeah. I can do it fine. I give the man our paperwork, and Ids, and he knows where to bring us to. We've just got to keep our cool."

"Right," Tobias said, and he walked over to the kitchen to fetch the two folders. Before he even looked at them he went into a cabinet and retrieved a bag of trail mix. He ate handfuls of it while he perused the contents.

Within the folder for the ski resort were directions to the mountain from Brandon, VT and a quarter inch thick stack of paper stapled together that read "So You've Inherited a Post Apocalyptic Refuge Center... By Olivia Athens"

In the other folder were directions to, and a time for, the pick-up spot, apparently only a little ways down the street at 5:30. And there was a single piece of paper filled with printed out bureaucratic nonsense. Even then, he reveled. All of it made possible through Gerri's ties to certain people in Washington. And little old Tobias there was just hitching a ride.

He put the paper down to gather up Pluto from the floor and he brought the cat into the guest room upstairs for safe keeping. Tobias also put a strained can of tuna and some water in there. Who cared what ended up getting soiled? Pluto knew they wouldn't be there long, he'd do his business.

All Tobias had to do, really, was put everything into three bags. One bag for each person to carry. Plus a guitar and a cat. That wouldn't take long.

He still had no shirt on and blood crusted all over him. The house had electricity and water pressure too; he went and took a shower. Tobias cleaned his eye socket which had been thoroughly stressed and used plenty of soap and water in the deep gash across the surface of his muscle.

With that small amount of reflection, as the water ran over his body and rinsed away the soap, the tears came flooding back. His best friend, only human friend, was gone. A true aloneness. He remembered it well.

Tobias scrubbed at his back and the places he could hardly reach. He shampooed his hair and he scraped away the blood, fleck by fleck. He brushed his teeth and even shaved his face, however blindly.

He dried off and put on the same pair of pants, before going to his luggage for a new shirt; a black t-shirt with a bar code across the chest.

Looking around he felt the presence of every moment available to him before the helicopter would arrive. Then he again wandered to the door of Olivia's gruesome scene. She must have known that Tobias would appreciate it. The moment of her death he vividly recalled her prophesying verbally only a single time in a whisper.

The tarot card. He retrieved the moon card from the TV table, wiped it clean with his shirt and spit, and returned it promptly to the deck in the pine box in his back pack.

Ignoring the Omega couple, he returned to gaze upon his foster mother and her flaccid and dead lover. She had almost fully painted the room red. The loss seemed to have had the same effect on Tobias's black soul.

When the time came he had all of the bags prepared and the cat in its carrier between the seats. Gerri sat up front and Crystal sat in the back with the luggage.

Tobias' heart weighed heavily like a burden to be carried inside of his chest. He left the door to the inside wide open, didn't close the garage door either, and simply drove away to the soccer field to catch the ride at the right moment. He did not want to sit idle for any longer than he had to.

12

Arianna walked out of her home feeling sick and weak. Over the past weeks her resolve had been tested; passing tried and true. She hadn't let on that anything was any more awful than usual. She pretended to have hope, too. And on that fated day, she plainly professed her love to her mother and father one last time; crying in their arms but not letting on why, further than the usual malady of the times.

Her bags were packed atop the stairs and it was time to go.

She knew that they would be crying for her once they realized she wasn't coming home. There was no excuse for anybody to go anywhere those days. And yet, her intrepid self was on its way out that door. Out into the great death.

Exiting the house she didn't close the door. She hustled to her red Japanese coupe and threw her bags in the back seat, hurriedly engaging the car and backing out of the driveway. Dead silence hung in the suburban streets. Dead silence save for that barely noticeable humming she felt infiltrating her.

In the corner of her eye she saw her parents burst through the door and out onto the lawn. The tears crashed, flowing unrestrained, as she coughed and spat sobs. With the accelerator pushed to the floor she watched in the rear view mirror as her mother and father ran after her. For just a moment she didn't know if she could do it. How could she abandon them? But soon her composure rose to a crest where she could remember why she was leaving to begin with. If it were about her and only her maybe she would go back and wait for death warm in her father's embrace.

But it wasn't only her; Danielle was involved. And here was an opportunity to be safe. The adults were doomed and Olivia was a blessing to her and Danielle. The girls knew instinctively, at a core level, to follow the words of that woman and adhere to every last detail that had been mentioned. Biding their time in horror as they watched the world fall apart; crumble; become static. The new electricity was almost intoxicating. And it seemed as though the air had taken on another dimension.

Arianna hadn't seen Danielle in over a week. A few nights prior they spoke briefly and had since lost any kind of phone service. They had been locked away and getting packages from the National Guard whenever their house came up on the rotation. As if it actually mattered. How long were the people planning on digging their nails in? When would the world let go?

She looked at the time and wiped the tears away from her face with her long blue sleeve. It was almost one o clock and she was almost to her friend's house. All the yellow chairs had been smashed along the main square at the center of town, by where the oak trees stood over the graveyard. Reflex caused Arianna to laugh at that. They were really everywhere; tossed into the trees and strewn across the sidewalk by all the stores.

The heritage of her town's culture had been decimated by somebody. She always liked the yellow rocking chairs personally, but they were really stupid and they made her feel dull living there.

Once again the sheer quantity of yellow had done its job and brightened up her day. She lit a cigarette as the tears finally subsided and began to ebb. The sadness she felt was the most painful experience she could ever imagine; causing her physical pain in her muscles through the toll stress had taken on her body. She felt sick and her guts felt as though someone was tugging at her soul and trying to remove it from her body.

Danielle lived kind of removed from town but soon Arianna had twisted along the winding roads far enough and pulled up to her friends' house.

She parked the car and honked the horn, an easy maneuver for an easy plan. They had discussed it a thousand times. One o clock, one honk, Danielle comes running.

But after an anxious minute of waiting, she pulled a butcher knife from between the seat and stick shift and walked up the landscaped embankment to the house; holding the knife behind her back and throwing the door open with her right hand.

"Danielle! What the fuck?" and she jumped back nearly falling off the steps, catching herself on the railing. "Oh my god," she cried.

She saw the bodies and the blood staining the walls and the floor. There were enough open wounds to catch her eye in a split second.

Rick sat there up against a wall on the floor by the bodies, he stuck his arm out and gave her the copy of Ulysses and said, "Goodbye Arianna."

Near hysterical, Arianna moved within reach and took the book. "She's dead?"

"Yes, Arianna, goodbye," Rick said.

Arianna hurried back to the car and her stomach betrayed her finally. She vomited out the cereal she had eaten but kept moving until she got to the car door; opened it, got in, and sat down, and kept vomiting out onto the asphalt. Her chest was clenched and suffocating her.

She did not act without urgency. The moment she could breathe again she wiped her mouth and put the car in reverse. She released a prolonged and guttural yell of sadness and then another; trying to drive through the wailing and the tears. This was only possible at slow speeds as she cried out, "Why? Why?"

Panic set in. She couldn't do it alone. She didn't want to do it alone and there was a hole blown through her. Arianna found herself thinking she had lost the will to live. There were two paths then. One led to that mysterious house and to continued life, and the other path led home to her parents.

But she knew the way well. And she knew it was her destiny and nothing was going to shake that from her. Her loss raged inside of her and at once she decided to continue on as if she and Danielle were together. Olivia came to mind. Why hadn't she said this would happen? Had she? There was no way to tell what else she had been holding back. It didn't matter anymore; Arianna had a job to do and a plan to follow through on. She drove through the small roads in the outer woods, going to that house. She gave over to a type of auto pilot control and let her body take her through the world while in her mind she mourned and grieved. Her spirit felt damaged, stifled, restrained, and crushed.

Eventually she reached a house slightly more removed than Danielle's had been. That driveway, number 11, she had seen a half a dozen times when she drove past previously, while the birds were still attacking. It would be the first time she'd ever pulled into the driveway enough to see the home set further back. She blankly noticed that it was not too dissimilar to her dead friend's house. That same style; living space sitting on the garage. Like Dani's, the garage was on the left. The house was red and Dani's was a green yellow. On the concrete area in front of the door a yellow rocking chair sat alone and unharmed.

Walking up to the house she dragged her cigarette once more before throwing it to the ground and holding the butcher knife out in front of her like how Abbie Hoffman had instructed a knife fight to be carried out in Steal This Book.

She entered the door slowly and climbed the stairs,

observing that same local nouveau rustic decor of a hundred houses around there. Interesting decorations from the seventies hung on the walls or cluttered the surfaces. It looked like the town square in there, all smiling little figurines baking bread, quirky scarecrows about the walls.

Uneasiness gripped her when she felt the cold and heavy draft. "Hello?" she said loudly, or loud enough to be heard over the wind. Arianna held tightly to the knife and moved past the living room. The house was spotless and she wondered where the mess was.

She went into the dining room which was clean and perfect the way most dining rooms are. An oak table and chairs with red cushions. Pink wallpaper. The bright white light leaked in from the kitchen doorway. "Hello?"

In the kitchen she found a broken window to the side of the house. She looked out to the ground below. Fifteen feet below she saw a woman's dead naked body. She jumped back and yelped when a glass shard cut into her before breaking off and clattering on the floor.

She spun and held the knife ready but there was nothing there. A sigh of relief escaped her and the tension in her shoulders released. She walked out of the kitchen and through the hall to the bedrooms. A study was on the right; as neat and tidy as the rest of the home. There was a dark space to the left that was obviously storage and she more or less overlooked it at the site of a baseball bat on the floor in the bedroom doorway.

Approaching cautiously, the air current blew all around her and the room was fluttering with shades of illumination and darkness. Arianna peeked in only a little and cringed back with a start and a groan. A corpse was propped underneath the window against the backboard of a bed.

She looked again and saw a black rifle and the head with no face. Slamming the door shut she curled into herself on the floor in the hallway.

"Why? Mommy, why? Daddy? Why, mommy, why? Why?" she cried.

The tears flowed and she blotted her cheeks on her jeans. For twenty minutes she sat there crying to herself; thinking that she should be cleaning. Dread ran through her at the thought of being anywhere near the dead bodies. Aloneness seethed all around her. An unfamiliar place; her best friend was dead; her parents were still alive out there. She desired to run to them.

Arianna scrunched her eyes, put her arm to her mouth, and screamed into it. Half yelling and half coughing out the endless sobs. Soon she opened her eyes, wiped away the tears, and reached for the butcher knife. Looking over the thick blade as if it summed up everything that was. Had she ever in her life thought it would be necessary to carry that thing around for safety? But there it was; shining steel and a glossy black handle. Arianna raised it up next to her face and struck it down hard into the wooden floor, standing to her feet simultaneously.

She left the knife where it stuck and went to the kitchen with a hurried stride. She looked over the surfaces. There was a wooden stand for a telephone and phone books and other such junk. The counter tops were full with all the usual kitchen utensils one could find in any other kitchen. She could not see any alcohol exposed anywhere so she began searching through all the cabinets until she found a half gallon bottle of vodka down by the refrigerator.

It was nice to see that the water faucet still ran. The electricity at her house and the water pressure had disappeared recently. From an exposed shelf she got a glass and filled it with water before walking out to the spotless living room and sitting on the couch. A cigarette was lit and dragged before a burning splash of vodka slid down her throat, followed by some water.

Arianna looked out the wide living room window over the front yard. Leafless trees swayed and crashed into each other in the gusting wind. She felt chilled by the potent draft and she tried to defy the cold. Out that window was what she needed, freedom and open air. But she needed safety too. There was no safety out there.

She needed more vodka. And more cigarettes. A bowl of pot. That would have been nice.

The psychic woman rampaged through her skull and her skeleton. What had she said? "Clean the mess," ran through her mind over and over. Arianna tried to focus on the trees blowing in the wind over the task at hand. "Clean the mess. Clean the mess," rang over and over. The wind howled softly the word "clean," very elongated. Clean.

Eventually she stopped hearing Olivia's words. Drinking straight vodka quieted the surreal non-voices.

She stayed on the couch for another fifteen minutes taking a few more sips of vodka before eventually getting up and stumbling to the basement where she found a black sports car in the garage. It was chilly and dark and she couldn't find the light.

There was a rumpus room to the bottom level as well. All shades of brown decor. A pool table took up the front of the house corner area and there was a bar and stools at the back. A stocked bar with about a dozen bottles of liquor, and a small bathroom. There was no more destruction down there nor any more dead bodies. Nothing dangerous; the knife was in the floor upstairs. A plastic bottle of vodka was the only thing in her hand.

Large glass doors made up the back wall of the basement. And the back yard was a gaping field of about 120degrees, with subtle rolling hills. There was a wooden gazebo that appeared gray, a pond with dead cattails around its far side. A medium sized red barn out to the left. At the back there was a garden fenced in with black iron bars and an archway made of forged curling and flowing circles. There was a small house or shed back there as well, by the garden.

For the first time she noticed the deck outside the kitchen. Underneath, where she was, there was a lawnmower and firewood. She looked to the liquor bottles and immediately pulled out the whiskey. Leaving the vodka behind, Arianna walked back up to the kitchen; entering again through the dining room.

From under the sink she found a bottle of bleach. But what would she need it for? What did she need? What was she going to do about the bodies? Where could they go? Was burning an option? Or should she chop them up into trash bags? Yeah. That's what made sense.

She felt the vomit swell in her throat and she ran to the window and stuck her head through to release when she again caught site of the body. Arianna pulled her head back in and spewed out all over the walls before she could get to the sink.

"Oh, what the fuck?" she shouted.

After rinsing her mouth under the running faucet she decided to look through the garage for a chain saw or a hack saw; the thought making her feel faint all over. So instead, she went and laid down on the couch face first, moving her face across the velvety pink cushions.

The tractor. An idea sprung into her head. She could pull the bodies out to the woods at the far end of the backyard, and she wouldn't even have to bury them; she could leave them there and see what was going to happen.

Figure out why she was there and what she was waiting for. How long was she going to have to wait for it?

Arianna went to the refrigerator stocked fully with canned food. Every last corner of space was different vegetables or soups. And upon thinking about it she looked into all the cabinets to discover most were also filled to overflowing with canned food.

She was not hungry right then but she wanted to know how long to expect to be there, and it seemed, given the circumstance, the quantity of food available might suggest some sort of prediction. The suggestion she got was not good news for somebody in her position; wanting very badly to get away from the place.

With that in mind she went down into the garage and flicked on the light looking to find something to pull the bodies around with. Mostly all that was lying around was sports equipment, bicycles and kayaks hanging and golf clubs. There were tools toward the rear far side. She found a volleyball net and knew it would work.

Then she walked up toward the closed door of the bedroom with a strong resolve to do the task as quickly as possible. She walked into the room and beheld the mangled corpse. There was no face left. The front portion of the skull was removed. The semicircular crater was dark with dry crimson blood. What was left of the head sat atop a blood soaked white polo and equally pink khakis.

"Fuck this."

Grabbing the man by both ankles she pulled him hard off the end of the bed with all of her strength; choking and gagging on putrid death. The rifle fell to the floor and Arianna pulled the heavy man's body with eyes averted out to the kitchen; leaning forward and using all her weight to move him into the kitchen through the living room. She got to the glass patio doors and dropped the legs to unlock and slide the door open. The stench was taxing on her throat, mouth, and nose. Not looking at the head, she picked up the legs, and marched out the door, straight down the steps. Feeling for the first time the dead squirm of the legs; the way they gave to different pressures, falling down the long wooden steps sideways, tugging the body along. When she finally reached the lawn she pulled the body out only a little ways before dropping it and running back into the house.

"Oh. What the fuck?" she groaned. Her head resting on her arm on the kitchen counter; she took deep breaths.

She wasn't aware of it, but the alcohol was what had kept her from getting sick. Her stomach had long been in a state of nausea and the alcohol had dulled her senses enough to not irritate her body. Of course, at the same time, Arianna was substantially drunk.

Stumbling through the house, unsure of what exactly to do, she first pulled the bed from the wall to clean the brain matter. Then she remembered she needed to get rid of the bodies so she went into the basement and out the rear doors.

The lawnmower would not start and she twisted the key repeatedly, listening to the engine turnover. She struggled for seven minutes until discovering the proper combination of the lever positions and the machine engaged. The green ride-on lawnmower was running and she had mowed her own lawn enough to have a basic idea of the controls.

Haphazardly she drove over to the hideous body and parked the mower before she realized she needed the volleyball net. After retrieving the net from the upstairs she brought it back to the mower. And then it was time to bring the other body over.

It was a naked old lady of petite stature. As if the woman had just begun the process of elderly shrink. Arianna threw up alcohol vomit at the corner of the house by a pine bush. Then she wiped her face clean and pulled the woman to the faceless man's side.

She turned the man over by his arm to hide his face and knotted the two together by the ankles with the black mesh and the neon pink nylon. Cringing, as she pulled the bare feet through and through the square spaces, wrapping it all tightly with the ropes that attach the net to the poles. The other end of net was attached to the trailer hitch on the mowers' rear.

She engaged the mower and moved slowly to the back of the yard, not looking at the bodies as she went along; driving cautiously and hoping for the best. The corpses rolled and their arms dragged. With every bump they would shift position from their face to their side, on their back or tangled into each other.

Arianna focused on the tree line and decided to take them to the far left corner of the yard where it looked like there was some kind of woodland cove or a clearing.

The bondage of their ankles held and eventually she made it to the yards' end and found she had been right. There were stacks and stacks of firewood in the corner opening at the far edge of the field. She knew then to burn them. It was the only reasonable option. The field was all dead grass but she didn't suspect the fire would spread. Once the bodies were at the burning site she unattached the volleyball net, and then drove full speed back to the house.

Inside, she went to the bedroom and wrapped the whole bedspread up in the bed sheet and threw everything out the broken window. Blood had gathered by the post legs and she could see for the first time the brain and skull matter stuck to the wall. She walked into the den and got computer paper and magazines to burn, taking those things to the mower and placing them on her lap and drove out to the bodies, throwing the paper down and driving back to the home.

Then she parked the green tractor, grabbed a hold on the bundle of blankets and pillows and dragged these things out to the burn site. The ragged hems of her pants dragged and she stepped on them. The pants made swooshing noises that acted as a guide for her to mentally block out the task at hand.

When Arianna got to the bodies she sloppily spread out the whole blood soaked mass of blankets over them.

The next thing to do was to attach the small lawnmower trailer she had seen over by the barn. And once she had done that she drove back out to the wood pile and filled the trailer with logs.

Beyond the edge of the woods she found plenty of dry brush for kindling. The relocating of which took fifteen minutes before she had enough to make the correct sized fire. Another fifteen minutes was spent balling paper and tossing it all over the bodies that smelled a little less from under the blankets. She placed all the dry branches over the paper until a good mat had been created. She brought over the logs and tossed them on one by one.

From her pocket she drew a blue disposable lighter and lit the paper in several places on all sides; feeling relief when the flames took and the sticks began to burn and crackle. The logs caught fire slowly in turn.

There was no more wood in the trailer and she filled it up again from the long head height stacks and emptied it by the reeking fire; this was done twice more. The fire was a flaming shape something like a burning earthen casket. It was time to start drinking again. She took the tractor back to the house and first heated a bowl of soup and ate it. Then she got the whiskey, her purse with a Grateful Dead patch on the flap, the spinning office chair, and brought these items out to the fire. She smoked a cigarette and sat about thirty feet from the cremations edge.

Moments later, when her cigarette was out, she put two more trailer loads of wood onto the fire. It was almost getting dark when the first sounds she had heard all day broke through the silence of the forest. Over the trees and in the distance some kind of engine droned through the sky.

13

Judging by the time that had passed and the contours of the terrain, Tobias knew they were in Vermont and had been for a while. The mountains like water runoff in dirt were a dead giveaway. The turbulent ride would end soon. Close to the cockpit he was strapped into a small steel chair with headphones and a microphone on his head facing Crystal and Gerri on the other wall. The large Chinook cargo helicopter had been going at what felt like top speed for the entire ride which had been going on for about an hour and it seemed to have slowed down.

The armed guard sitting between them and the pilot shouted back, "Smoke out there! We're here!"

The enormous length of the random rotor helicopter pivoted awkwardly and circled in direction. Tobias saw the fire burning out on the edge of a field. But who started the blaze? Who was there?

Tobias leaned over and asked, "Who started the fire?"

"How should I know?" the guard replied.

"Can you take a walk with us?" he asked.

"No. We gotta go."

Tobias was shaken by the thought of those flames. At any rate, he had a gun and two human shields; he would have to take his chances. The helicopter dropped; jerking up and down until they came to a rest. The guard jumped out onto the grass while Tobias made sure Gerri and Crystal got out of their seat belts. He tossed the luggage to the soldier below who put the duffel bags and suitcases to the side on the ground. Tobias guided the Omega couple one and then the other to the guard who helped them down the tiny steps. He handed Pluto off to the guy and jumped down without using the steps. The guard climbed back into the helicopter and the three ran almost into the woods getting out of the way of the propellers; leaving the luggage as they had been instructed to do. But Tobias kept hold of Pluto's handle.

In his other hand he held his- Gerri's- pistol inside his pocket. The helicopter thundered away overhead and Tobias was caught off guard trying to take in all the structures through the wisping black smoke that blanketed the field and stunk faintly of burning hair.

The pulsing drone of the engines finally quieted enough for him to get a sense of where they were. He looked at the fire and searched all around it for somebody but all he saw was an empty chair and a parked lawnmower. "Guys, get the bags," he said, walking cautiously toward the massive fire.

In his pocket he let go of the gun and waved his arm in the air, yelling "Hello" over and over.

From the tree line emerged a girl with poofy curly hair, like Janis Joplin. Her arms were crossed around her waist and she looked afraid and very timid. She had jeans on and Tobias noticed her curvy hips in the distance. She stopped moving and exhaled a drag of cigarette smoke to be taken by the wind.

Tobias approached her.

"How many people are here?"

"It's only me," she said.

Tobias noticed that she didn't look well. Her face was cringed by tears. And she was heavy with sadness. He walked up to her closely. And she looked up at him, her face sickly pale. "Are you Ok?" he asked.

"I'm fine. I'm not hurt. There're two bodies in that fire. An old man and an old woman."

"Why did you burn them?" Tobias asked

"Because I was told to clean the house up."

He didn't have to think by whom. And there was no stretch of imagination needed to figure out what happened.

"You really didn't need to do that." It didn't

make any sense. Other than to maybe make some smoke for the helicopter.

"What?"

"No. We're getting out of here tonight. Maybe she had you burn them for the smoke. I don't know."

"She didn't tell me to burn them. She just said, 'Clean the mess.' I can't believe I didn't have to do that. It was like hell. I've been throwing up all day- you knew Olivia?" It had taken a moment for what he'd said to catch Arianna's attention.

"Yeah. I knew her. She died this morning."

"My best friend died too. She was supposed to be here with me."

"What's your name? I'm Toby."

"My names Arianna."

Tobias moved closer to her and wrapped his arms around her, squeezing her tight. It wasn't sexual in nature or in any way overly thought out. He wanted to embrace her. And she didn't struggle or flinch because she felt the same. This was Olivia's gift to him. This girl burning dead bodies who fit perfectly in his arms.

"Toby? Who are those people?"

He let go and took another look at her. She had eyes like tear drops pointing out. And she was tired, he could tell from the bags. Her face was sweet and she was smiling a little. So was he. Looking behind him he saw Crystal and Gerri staring at each other and not talking.

"That is the Omega couple. They sponsored our lives with theirs, is who they are."

"Should I thank them?"

"You can if you want, but they're hypnotized, so you shouldn't expect too much back from them."

"Hypnotized?"

"Yeah. Like fleshy robots with ties to the government. And I think you burned up Crystal's parents.

"Oh my god."

"No, it doesn't matter Arianna, don't worry. It was all meant to be like this. Around nine o clock tonight Gerri is going to go off the deep end and kill Crystal. Then he's going to try and kill us and I'll have to... you know... kill him first. That's just how it is."

"I understand. Olivia said that that would happen to my family and it already happened to my friend Danielle. Her brother is like mentally disabled and he was sitting there next to her body and there was this bloody mess. He gave me a book and told me to leave," she cried and fell into Toby who wrapped his arm around her shoulder and held her tight.

"It's Ok. Let's go talk to the Omega Couple. I promise they will cheer you up. No doubt." Tobias guided her to them and they simultaneously looked at her with big smiles and blinking eyes.

"Crystal Gold and Gerri Goldberg, I want you to meet Arianna."

"Hello, Arianna," they said in tandem, before Crystal added, " Nice to meet you. Do you live around here?"

"Hi. Nice to meet you, too. Yeah. I live across town."

"Oh wow. Do you go to school here?" Crystal asked.

"No, I finished high school and didn't go to college."

"Oh, do you have a job, where do you work at?"

"Crystal," Tobias interrupted, "why don't you lay off the questions." Then to Arianna he said, "She used to be a news reporter. She's used to asking a lot of questions."

"Did you like the helicopter ride?" Arianna asked.

"Yes. Yes we did. It was very nice," Crystal said.

"Ok. How about we bring all these bags inside."

"Hold on," Arianna said and she ran off and started the tractor, bringing it to them for Tobias to put everything into the trailer. He grimaced to himself about getting wood chips on the luggage but loaded everything anyway. She drove toward the house and with his cat in hand he followed the girl with a new lust for life surging up and down his spine.

The Omega Couple followed closely behind; holding hands.

Arianna shut down the mower. Tobias approached her and said, "We can let that fire go out. It doesn't matter if they're all burnt away yet."

"Oh, they're all gone," Arianna interjected.

"Ok. But we have to find a good spot to be away from these guys and wait for Gerri to go off."

"The basement. They can stay up in the living room."

Arianna opened the sliding basement door and Tobias brought all the bags in one by one and dropped them beyond the threshold. He noticed the bar and the gaming equipment with neutral interest and then went to get Pluto from the ground outside.

"Shall we go up into the living room?" Arianna said standing close to the door to the stairs.

"Yeah let's. Crystal and Gerri come with us. Lead the way."

They moved in single file up the two half sized flights of stairs. Past the front door and to the main floor. Arianna obviously doing her best to keep Tobias between her and the eerily entranced, slightly disheveled, rich people.

He sat them down on the pink couches and instructed them to go to the bathroom right then. Sometimes they needed to be reminded or an accident could happen.

Arianna stood in the doorway wondering about the two people that wouldn't be alive by that night. People acting blank and always happy; all the while any minute they would be going off into a fit of murderous intent.

Then there was her boy who moved them to and fro without flinching. Arriving on a helicopter and taking all the fear out of her. And he had been as happy to see her as she had been to see him. He had one eye, and a cat or something, and that straight and dirty black hair to his neck. His eye-patch had an anarchy symbol on it. All of his movements were jerky and he sometimes used his hair to keep his eye hidden. Completely naturally as though he wasn't ashamed but had been that way at other times and developed new mannerisms because of it.

Both Crystal and Gerri used the toilet and Tobias had them sitting placidly on the couch.

"Let's go downstairs," he said to Arianna.

They walked into the basement and he closed the door.

"Hey, I want you to meet Pluto. He's the best cat ever."

Tobias knelt down and opened the carrier, taking the cat from inside. Pluto curled into his arms without any protest and Tobias passed the feline to Arianna.

"Aw. He's perfect. Get it, purr- fect?" Arianna said.

Pluto hardly reacted to the attention. All three of them sat together on the soft and deep cushions of a brown love seat.

Tobias said, "He's been acting really bizarre since everything started happening. Like, he doesn't move around very much. And he was always an indoor/outdoor cat but you couldn't get him to go outside now even if you wanted to."

"Really? We had the opposite problem. Our dog ran away and didn't come back. Last week. It was really sad but it's hard to care about the dog when Danielle is dead and my parents are still alive and I'm never going to see them again."

"Why aren't you with them now?"

"Because Olivia told me I had to leave them. She said I had to come here and clean up the bodies and I guess wait for you," Arianna said. Very agitated she continued, "But can I go back to them? Do you think that maybe they'll be Ok? Olivia said they were going to die. She said everyone was going to die. How are we going to survive?"

"Everyone isn't going to die. She told me that the kids will be all right. Even teenagers our age and probably people a couple years older than us. There's an age cut off somewhere, she said. I thought about it and it occurred to me that the human brain isn't fully developed until about 22. And that might have something to do with it. And astrologically it could have to do with something called the quarter return of Uranus that occurs when people turn 21 years old. So if I had to guess, I would say that's the age cutoff, about 21 or 22. But then you have to factor in all the murder."

Pluto slipped away from Arianna and down to the floor with a quiet meow.

"Where did you come from? How did you know Olivia?"

"She was my step-mother. We lived in Providence together."

"Do you know what we're going to do?"

"Yeah. We're going to take these peoples car and drive to a ski resort that Olivia bought with Gerri's money, when money still meant something. There's food there and it's secluded. Nobody even lives near it so no one will be there. But she told me pretty soon other people will turn up."

Pluto cried insistently. "Hang on a second," he told Arianna. He got food for Pluto and water too. Arianna seemed to be lost in thought as she stared off into the floor. He sat beside her his knees with an arm resting on the back of the sofa.

She stood up, saying, "I'm going to use the bathroom," and she went into the little rest room in the wall adjacent to the bar.

When she came out Tobias asked, "So you're from

this town?"

"Yeah. I lived with my parents way on the other side from here."

"Alright. How have you been holding up lately?"

"I've been throwing up mostly. *My best friend is dead and I'll never see my parents again.* But you're here now so I feel a little better. And a little safer. I think I'm happy that at least I'll have time to mourn."

"Yeah. You're right. It'll be really nice to feel safe. I mean we'll be really lucky. I don't think many people are going to have that advantage. Olivia managed to get all this crap done just in the nick of time. She would take either Gerri or Crystal and leave for a night and then she'd take the other one somewhere else for a night. Or I would watch both of them while she was out traveling around. And it would have been really dangerous for anyone else but Olivia could see everything before it happened. At all times, no matter what, she knew what would come next. I think maybe there was some flaw in her having you take care of those bodies. But she still probably had some kind of reason."

"She wanted me to be real happy to see you."

"I *was* real happy to see you too. She told me she had a surprise waiting for me. I never could have imagined it would be something as perfect as you."

"Toby."

He leaned in and kissed her lips. He looked at her face and saw she had enjoyed it. Her lips seemed bewildered and her eyes were closed and soaked in blissful relief. She opened them and saw him looking at her through his only eye with his head tilted down and his hair falling to the side. Again he kissed her.

They pulled themselves as closely together as they could and kissed passionately. Tobias pushed into Arianna until she was lying snuggly in the couches corner. Their arms and legs were wrapped around the others and Tobias cupped her butt and squeezed her into himself.

At the end of the yard a fire still raged and black smoke billowed chaotically in the wind.

14

Their clothes lay scattered across the basement of Crystal's parents' house. Tobias and Arianna lay asleep like naked fleshy spoons under a down comforter on the couch in the pitch black night; no moonlight could penetrate the electric cloud masses in the sky outside. Coals and embers glowed faintly orange in the distant yard.

The walls jolted and trembled and the ceiling thudded above them. Crystal's screams and chokes faded in and out. Tobias sat up disturbingly aware of her frightened and desperate pleas and the pounding crashes shaking the house to its foundation.

"Find a light!" he said to Arianna, as he scuttled around on the floor trying to feel for the pistol that he knew was somewhere within reach. One more violent impact from above and Crystal's distressing cries fell silent.

"Light!" said Tobias.

"I can't find it."

Tobias ran to the door where he knew a switch was and the room lit up. The .38 special was there on the floor by Arianna's feet. "Give me that," he said.

She handed him the gun and they both looked to the door.

"Are you ready?" he asked her.

"I don't know," she replied. Adding, "I can't watch," and putting her head under the blanket.

Tobias held the pistol out low in front him with both hands; his head cocked back and tilted down to the right, he focused on the door. Gerri thumped around upstairs; pacing with a quick and heavy stride.

The footsteps landed on the stairs and Tobias felt his heart sink into his stomach. Then came the sound of the front door confusing Tobias for a brief moment.

"He went outside," he said to himself.

He opened the basement door cautiously; holding the gun ready in front of himself, peering into the hall and finding no one there. Looking slowly around the corner he saw Gerri was not on the stairs either- the front door left wide open. Other than that one distinguishing feature, he could see nothing but black.

"Gerri!" he called.

No sound came in return. With a rash movement he lunged up the steps and flicked every switch he could by the front door and returned down to the wall by the bottom stair. The outdoors and the first floor landing had lit up.

He knew Gerri was outside and walked out into the night air that rushed with an unfamiliar energy, blowing a breeze across his package. In a halo of light he stepped down into the yard, bare foot and buck naked on the concrete- he held the gun ready.

"Gerri," he said.

From straight ahead the stocky balding man charged forward. Tobias raised the pistol, cocked the hammer, and fired one exploding round after another into Gerri's chest, through the penguins on his cashmere sweater.

The shots jolted his body and he fell crumpled and dead at Tobias's feet.

"We ain't with the wind below," said Tobias with a smirk and a bewildered realization. He had killed somebody.

Using his foot he rolled Gerri onto his back. The man was clearly dead. Dead eyes, limp tongue. Tobias fired the gun into the top corner of the house twice and kept pulling the trigger. The gun was empty; the five bullets had been expelled.

Anxiety soured through his organs. What the hell? They made stupid movies about that kind of thing.

One bullet had hit Gerri in the heart. Tobias was a killer. Of what, who knew? Just life, really. Like those bears that, as soon as they ate one human, they'd want to eat nothing else. Nothing about the experience bothered him too much. It was what it was, and it was all for Arianna. He asked himself why. Concluding that reasons were unreasonable. Olivia had known what she was doing. There was a fresh corpse at his feet and he didn't have any clothes on. The pistol felt warm against his thigh.

He went back inside closing the door behind him; back down to her; knowing Crystal was dead, he didn't want to look. It wasn't necessary.

"Tobias," she said, holding out her arms. He fell into her the way Gerri had fallen into the ground. Arianna wrapped the blanket over him and clutched herself onto him, giving him a part of her that was more spiritual than any practical matter.

"Is it over?" she asked.

"For now. I think we should get the fuck out of here. Olivia said to wait for the witching hour, but fuck that, we need to go. Let's get dressed."

"Good, I want to leave so bad I can taste it."

"That's probably the dead bodies."

They put on their clothes and Tobias tied his shoes.

"Where the fuck is Pluto?" Tobias asked, following with the chorus of cat calls he used. Pluto meowed from behind the bar. He picked up the ever-compliant cat and placed him into his carrier.

"Hold onto him, that's all you have to do, Ok? Hey wait. We're gotta take that Jaguar that's in there. Can we leave your car?"

"Yeah. Ok."

Arianna had very little luggage with her. Only one duffel bag of clothes and feminine things. The suitcases from the helicopter fit into the small trunk of the sports coupe and into its cramped backseat.

"Is there going to be booze there?" Arianna asked.

"Yeah, probably. You should bring some just in case."

They put a few bottles of alcohol into the cracks and crevices in the backseat. Arianna insisted on keeping the green plaid comforter from the basement because she liked it.

The guitar had to be situated with the case coming directly between the two of them. Tobias held Pluto so Arianna could get situated in the seat with the blanket over her. Then he handed her the cat box, gently closed her door, and pushed the button to open the garage door.

He sat down, started the car, and looked over the gages. Arianna asked him, "Do you want me to drive? I can probably see better than you."

"No. Normally, I would say yes but I have these directions memorized like nobody's business. I know right where we're going. Ya know?"

"Yeah, I get it."

Tobias pointed out the window as he backed away from the house. "Look at his body over there. He died real quick. Like the Crocodile Hunter. Right into his heart. But, hey, can you reload this for me? The bullets are in the front pocket of that black backpack on top," he said, handing her the pistol.

Through the cramped little back roads he made his way over to Route Seven heading north. Through the winding roads he rejoiced in the muscle and control of a finely engineered machine. A black jaguar; if anyone could love it more, he could not fathom who. A car that roared through its first couple gears on those curvy mountain roads that banked one way or the other.

Arianna put Pluto on the floor and scrunched into her seat, placing her forearms on the guitar case. She said, "I love you Tobias. I know I do. Do you love me?"

"Of course I do. I couldn't do this without you. And you couldn't do it without me either, I bet. But we're going to a place where we will be safe and we'll have each other and that's all that matters. One day all this shit will catch up with us. Until then..." He looked at her and kissed her on the lips before putting his eye back on the road.

They drove up Route Seven smoking cigarettes and drinking a couple shots of vodka.

"What the fuck are we going to do Tobias?"

"Oh my god. That is so easy. We're going to live happily ever after."

"Do you promise?"

What's with the questions, he thought. "Hell yeah, I promise. But really, how should I know what's coming?"

"You tell me Tobias. Your Olivia's loved one. What do you know?"

"The booklet she typed up that has some things in it about what'll happen to us while we're up there. She had no idea what will happen come December though. I know that things will happen exactly as they should. You can feel it in the air, right? Don't expect anything to level out for quite a while. Come next winter truth'll happen no matter what. Does that make sense?"

"Yeah. Just- please- don't ever leave my side. Ever ever. Please?"

"Of course I won't."

Other traffic was few and far between by interval. All along Seven they had only seen one other car. The houses approaching Burlington were illuminated and darkened in chunks as per where the power was and was not holding.

The roads carved into hillsides that had been forged across and through mountains. Then the forests grew in once again and those claustrophobic passageways through the countryside were clouded with uneasy anticipation as the pair drove through the night. Like life, the only way out of it was through it.

Soon they were in Burlington and while the passage through the city was made with haste, he didn't like seeing that many establishments and buildings lurking in the shadows created by the areas producing light. He worried that at any moment they would be attacked. Or worse. He sped over dirty streets and took turns without slowing much. Eventually he found the signs for 89 sending him left and right on back streets in all kinds of strange directions and he made their way east through the stop signs until they came upon Interstate 89 and headed south on an empty and snow dusted road; eventually hitting Route Two.

"Are you going to get sick of me if I'm the last girl on earth?"

One more car drove in the opposite direction.

"I'm sure you're not *the* last girl on earth. You're *my* last girl on earth. But not *the* last girl on earth. Everything is going to be alright from now on. As far as I know. And as far as it can be. Wait. How am I supposed to tell you it's going to be alright? Have you looked around lately?"

"I know. But Olivia said we were going to be happy."

"She didn't say how long we were going to be happy for. Arianna, what do you think is going to happen, really?"

"I think we're going to die. You and me. We'll be together. But it's going to happen."

"Everybody dies sweetheart. And if the sky were to fall and crush us right now, I would be Ok with that. Because I have you and Pluto here with me."

"Oh, baby," she said sweetly, leaning over the guitar and planting a big kiss with tongue; Tobias kept his eye on the road.

Traveling at an average of forty miles an hour they

had been moving on Route Two for twenty-five minutes. The snow on the road was sometimes plowed clear and sometimes packed down from being driven over. He knew their right turn would be approaching. A tiny road leading deep into the mountain.

"Keep your eyes peeled for Justice Road on the right. It should be here any minute. Did you know that's a tarot card. Justice?"

"That's really cute. Olivia did the funniest things. When she took us to the motel that time she put out the kinds of skittles that me and Dani each like to eat. Because I eat the orange and purple and she would eat the yellow and green and we'd share the red ones and she put them out in dishes just like that."

They found the road.

Not paved but well-worn and covered in snow and ice, Justice Road wound around the mountains through hanging trees and Tobias had to drive very carefully. The road was very narrow and he couldn't get going over twenty miles per hour. He knew at that speed they wouldn't be there for another hour or more. It occurred to him they were driving on plowed snow.

"Who the hell plowed this road?"

"I don't know, but I really hate heights," said Arianna as she looked out over a dark abyss.

"How can you even tell?"

"There's a river down there through all the trees. I can see it. The fall down is about two hundred feet."

"Well, we're not going to fall so don't worry about it."

"I'm not worried. I just hate heights."

To their left steep cliff faces rose into the heavens. And to their right the terrain dropped off into forever. The ground grew and shrunk around them as they drove through valleys and along what became the peak of a mountain top.

Within an hour they broke through the scraping

tree limbs of an unusually dense section of forest into a parking lot that went back for over a hundred yards off into deep blackness. The ski slopes barely glowed in the darkness; sheer open spaces on a mountain side only divided by sparse trees growing in single file or in small clumps. High above them the peak contrasted the night sky.

Tobias looked around for any kind of dwelling and saw first the enormous wall of a building he could only assume was the main lodge.

"Are you excited?" he asked Arianna.

"It's kind of creepy. I wish we could have come when it was light out."

"I'll point the headlights over there. Will you carry Pluto? Can you put him in his carrier?"

"Sure. Time to go in the box Pluto." Arianna had been holding the cat on her lap and she retrieved his carrier and put him away.

Tobias put his black wool jacket on, retrieved the gun from the cup holder, and put it in his coat pocket.

"Are you going to be warm enough?" he asked her.

"Yeah. I have two shirts on under this," she said, referring to her purple camouflaged coat.

"Shall we?"

He opened his door and got out and Arianna got out as well. The air was much colder there than it had been in Brandon. The headlights shone on the concrete wall that rose to, around the second story, become wooden walls of a hue like a log cabin would have. Standing in the headlights he put one arm around his new love and held the pistol in his left hand.

"What is that noise?" she asked.

"I don't know."

From the distance behind them, off in the woods opposite the slopes there rang a shrieking yelp reminiscent of some kind of big cat or dog; some unknown large animal. In a measure of four, the sound came on every third beat. Abrupt, brief, and consistent; a coughing sound; every third beat.

"That can't be good. It sounds like a banshee," said Tobias.

"It's probably a coyote," said Arianna, who listened again intently before adding, "that is the scariest thing I've ever heard."

"Me too. What the fuck is it doing?"

"Let's just go inside."

He pulled her along by the hand looking for a door. The lot had been plowed but, unable to find a path, they were walking in crunching snow about four inches deep. They came to a set of stairs that had been cleared of snow and ice.

"This isn't right. There shouldn't be anybody here," he said.

"I'm sure there's an explanation."

"This porch is shoveled too. Look. And that fucking thing seriously needs to shut up." In the distance there were cabins visible in the bits and clips of what headlamp light was hitting them. He could see an assortment of small buildings going away into the darkness. Also, it became evident that the building was enormous. They stood at only a corner of what looked like a domed complex with glass walls running the entirety of the lengthy porch. However, only the corner area was cleared of snow.

Tobias opened a heavy glass door framed in white and he stepped in with the pistol at his left side. No light reached there. He could sense the open space but could not make out any details. From his pocket he got a lighter and ignited it; holding the flame to the walls in search of the light switches which he found further down beside a doorway into another room.

The vast space lit up section by section erratically. They were in what used to be some kind of cafeteria. An observation supported by a rectangle opening in the wall where a kitchen was bathed in overflowing light. At the far end of the big room dozens of lunch tables stood folded in their upright positions. A staircase, also at the far end, led up into the ceiling. Or what looked to be the ceiling until he discerned it to be another level of that room looking out over the cafeteria. The wooden ceiling sloped down to meet the glass windows at a height of ten feet.

"Let's go up there," he said to Arianna.

He took her hand in his and they walked across the gritty hardwood floor. Behind the stairs there was an opening to another dark area that they ignored.

They went up the steps and turned on a light switch. The indoor balcony was carpeted and had conference room type plush chairs and gray tables. In the near corner was a white grand piano. Tobias walked over to it and began to play. Wanting to continue but knowing they needed to look around, he stopped shortly thereafter and walked back to the girl's side.

A call came from below, "Hello?"

Tobias shoved Arianna deeper into the room and went to the stairs saying, "Who's there?"

At the waist height railing Tobias stood cautiously back observing in the glass reflection a distorted image of the person standing down below.

"I'm Robin. I live here. Olivia got me here to run the place," he said clearly.

Tobias first had a disagreeable reaction to what the guy said, until an instant later it occurred to him that he didn't have a clue about keeping a resort running.

"Really?" he asked walking to the railing and looking down at the guy who was unarmed and wearing yellow pajama pants and a black hooded sweatshirt.

"Yeah, really," said Robin.

Tobias walked down the steps to meet him.

"Hey, I'm Toby," he said shaking his hand in a gesture of equality.

"Robin, good to meet you. What's your name?"

"Arianna," she said, coming down the stairs.

Robin looked half asleep. He had dark skin but was Caucasian, with hair that looked like it would curl if allowed to grow but was kept short. He was about Tobias' height and seemed capable.

"Is it just you here alone?" asked Tobias.

"No, yo, well, my girl, Cadence; she's here. We're staying in the back of this building, in the south west corner. I have to give you guys a tour. Olivia said you would show up at dawn? What happened to that?"

"We left Brandon earlier. It was kind of creepy, everyone was dead, you know?"

"What happened?"

"Aw, man, I'll tell you some other time. Yo, what the fuck is that noise out there?"

"What noise?" asked Robin.

"Come here," said Toby and they all walked to the door to the porch outside. "Listen."

The same as before, the creature in the woods shrieked on every third beat.

"It sounds like it has a nightmare caught in its throat," said Robin.

Tobias laughed, "You never heard that before?"

"I've only been here for like two weeks. But, no, never heard it."

"That's not good. Seems like a bad omen."

"It could be a good omen," said Arianna.

"That's fucked up, whatever it is," said Robin, "but whatever, let me give you a tour of this building and then I'll bring you to your apartment. Tomorrow you can scope out the rest of the place, and we can all break out the snowmobiles or something. It's fucking awesome when you take those things on the ski trails or on the snowboard course."

Robin showed Tobias and Arianna around the building, but it was apparently only one of many buildings. The further exploration of the grounds would be saved for the next day.

First shown was the kitchen; similar to what the kitchen in a restaurant looked like; stainless steel machines, industrial sinks, and large range stoves. The floor was white and black tile. They could play chess on that floor, Tobias thought.

"How is this place powered?" asked Arianna.

"Oh. That's a funny question. We have a geothermal power plant in a meadow about a kilometer away. Toby, you and I are going to have a lot of fun with that thing. Usually we don't even have to touch it. But the maintenance on it is a motherfucker. It runs everything here; the lights, the heat, the water pumps, the ski lifts if we want to turn those on."

"There's a power plant?" asked Tobias.

"Yeah. It's a little kind of thing, about half the size of this kitchen. Between the two of us, we won't have any problems with it."

Tobias found that hard to believe, but what did he know?

Adjacent to the kitchen were two store rooms and a tiled hallway that led to a small window and nothing else.

"Back at the other side of the kitchen- and in the basement- there are door's that go up to a watch tower. It's really sweet up there. In these rooms is where we'll keep the immediate food stuffs," Robin said chuckling. "About everything here is dehydrated, canned, powdered, or vacuum sealed. And these rooms are just a small percentage of what's here. I'll show you what I mean in a minute. I guess we can go there now.

"Hang on a second," said Tobias. He ran outside to the car to switch off the headlights. Only stopping to listen to the monster in the woods for a second before returning.

"I had left the headlights on."

"Oh. That doesn't really matter. We have about a half dozen vehicles here. We've got a giant pick-up to plow with. A smaller pick up. An old UPS truck from when we were loading this place. Two cars with all-wheel drive; an Audi and a Subaru. Dirt bikes, quads, snowmobiles, and a dune buggy."

"That's the coolest thing I've ever heard."

"I know, right? This place is awesome. It sucks that everyone's dead but we did pretty good for ourselves."

"Olivia, man. She didn't fuck around."

"No, that she did not. Let's go to the basement. There is the whole operation from the ski resort still down there. That's your business; whatever you want to do with it."

They went down an indoor stairwell accessed through the cafeteria and the basement was exactly as Robin had said. There were wooden benches lined up on the concrete floor between lockers standing in rows. And a service counter with a labyrinth of skis and snowboards and all the equipment that used to be rented out.

"Is there a drum set here?"

"Yeah, it's in the hotel nightclub. You wouldn't need to put it in here. We can rock out over there."

"You play?"

"Yeah. I can play almost anything except orchestra crap like a woodwind or something. Olivia told me you play too. We'll probably make a ton of music out here and no one except the girls will ever hear it."

"Yeah. That's pretty sweet. But I have no idea what to do with this room then."

"Are there art supplies?" Arianna asked.

"Yeah, there is, out in one of the storage sheds."

"Oh, Tobias, can I paint down here?"

He didn't have a problem with that. At some point he planned to make his own area for fortune telling purposes. The thought presented him with butterflies in his stomach because was there really, after all, any fortunes left to tell?

Robin guided them beyond the ski reception where there was Berber carpet on the floor. To the right was a game room flashing lights from the machines along the walls. To the left were doorways left unexplored. Robin said there were only maintenance things in there. They approached two large doors like one would see leading to an elementary school gymnasium.

"There's access around the back and a secondary parking lot out there, but this is the warehouse."

They opened the doors and went inside as the lights fluttered on.

"They used to use it for storing ski lift parts and furniture or whatever else for the property. But we cleared it all out. This is all food."

Like the rest of the place, the warehouse was impressive. Steel racks rose to the ceiling. Indistinct brown boxes cluttered the shelves. But there were other types of boxes as well; all covered in plastic wrap and resting on wooden pallets.

"We have a system for what food gets used and when, but I can teach you it some other time. There are shower supplies and crap like that in here too. A bunch of other stuff you wouldn't really think of until you need it. Alcohol. Um, there's an electric forklift and a walk behind too. Our apartments are above this place. Out the doors there's another stairway that goes up to a bar. I'll show you that now. Around the front is a glass tube walk way that goes over to the hotel and nightclub. But you'll see that some other time."

The lights went off and they took the stairs back up and came out to a room with bistro style dining tables, pool tables, and a bar at the back. The walls were what looked like paneled stone work in some kind of amber color tone.

Tobias's hunch was correct. The bar contained

what had to be the most spectacular architectural feature of the property; a dome rising thirty feet high decorated with an artificial night sky speckled with stars and glowing with swirling and undulating purple, blue, and red light. A shooting star shot across it.

Behind the staircase an open doorway went out into the cafeteria.

Arianna hung on his arm and put her head to his shoulder and looked up, "Oh, my god," she said.

"Yeah. The dome's pretty sweet. Um, the patio out front here isn't connected to the other one you came up on. There's like 20 feet between them. Kitchen access is by the bar back there. That wall there is the top part of the warehouse. And we take that elevator to get to the apartments."

They took the elevator upstairs. It rode smoothly and had doors on two ends like in hospitals. The inside was completely stainless steel except for black railings on either side. They exited out the back side into a small hall with a vending machine then went into a big room with another glass wall.

The lights came on and the decor was all black leather and white walls with Rorschach paintings hung. The sofas wrapped around a glass coffee table by an enormous plasma television mounted to the wall. Another bar, much smaller than downstairs, was black with black stools and stood beside the TV.

"We got 7.2 surround sound. The bars stocked. Counting this one there's three fully stocked bars on the property. Enough liquor in the basement to last forever. These windows look out onto the mountain side. But the views from the apartments are better. Both apartments are pretty much the same." Robin pointed to two black doors on the back wall, "You're on the left, and I'm on the right. Olivia decorated your apartment herself. I'm going to go wake up Cadence so you can meet her. Go check out your place, the switch is right by the door."

Robin walked away.

Arianna said, "Not that I'm complaining, but don't you think we're moving kind of fast. We just met and we're already moving in together."

"Oh, you're so funny," Tobias said sarcastically, leading her to the left door.

Their living quarters was remarkably spacious and even had a dining area complete with a black wooden table and chairs. Hollow floors gave subtly underfoot and kept them aware they were living above the warehouse. A closet contained a washer and dryer. The kitchen space was against the left wall and had two parallel counter tops, one with a sink and dishwasher, and the other had the stove but was otherwise bare, though cabinets came down from the ceiling above it. A black refrigerator was in the corner.

"Let me see him," Tobias said taking Pluto's carrier from Arianna's hand. He removed the cat, which mewed, and held it close. Another light illuminated the white tiger print shag carpeting in the living room. The couches were white leather and all the tables were black. A standing projection screen television was stationed in the living room corner between the glass wall and the regular wall. His heart erupted when he noticed one and then another black light mounted where the walls met the ceilings. They were everywhere. He counted six.

Tobias noticed the glass wall was also a sliding door which he opened and stepped out onto the snow covered balcony; holding his cat tightly. The view was hard for him to examine in the darkness, but he could see forever over what appeared to be a half dozen smaller mountains and their accompanying valleys. He looked over the ledge at about a forty foot drop.

"Go look off that balcony."

"There's a balcony? Oh, what the fuck!" she said as she pulled her head back in the door; sliding it shut quickly. "That's fucking terrifying!"

"You don't like it?"

"No. I was just telling you in the car that I hate heights."

"Oh, oops, I can't wait until its daylight out to see the view," said Tobias as he peered into the bedroom.

"We're keeping the blinds closed."

Their bed had a crimson colored down comforter and all the walls were black. The carpet was also a dark red. There was black furniture; nightstands and end tables. Even the wood of the four post bed was black. The folding closet doors and the ceiling were also all black.

"I fucking love this apartment."

"You don't find it depressing?" said Arianna.

"What isn't depressing? No. If anything these are the colors of the times. Blood and darkness."

A moment later there came a knock and Robin stuck his head in their front door and said, "Can you guys come here?"

They walked out into the big front room. Cadence stood up from the leather couch. She was about a head and a half shorter than Robin. She had long straight dark brown hair and bronze skin; wearing navy blue pajama pants and a black spaghetti strap shirt. Her arms were squishy and her build was slightly thick but she was a pretty girl and very feminine in her nighttime attire.

Tobias shook her hand and said, "Hello." Arianna did the same.

"Nice to meet you guys," said Cadence, "This is all so strange. I'm so happy you guys are finally here. It'll be nice to be here with people our own age who aren't scary like the people out in the world. Or like those creeps that were here before."

"What creeps?" asked Tobias.

Robin said, "Oh. There were three middle aged

guys I set this up with. But they're out of the picture. Olivia said you would understand."

"What do you mean, they're dead?"

"Dead, dispatched, something like that. It was kind of fucked up."

"No. I get it. There's not much you can do about that. Like a fucking zombie movie or some shit."

"Maybe now. But they hadn't even done anything yet. None of them had families though. But, yeah, I mean, it was fucked up. I did the first two with a giant hammer and that last one with an M-16."

"Oh my god." said Arianna.

Robin continued, "I didn't want to. Who would, right? But there were all these issues about them thinking they were going to live here with us. And at some point they were going to become dangerous, so Olivia told me to do it as soon as everything here was ready."

"Yeah. I understand. I had to 'dispatch' one of my clients and her husband right before we came up here," said Tobias.

"Yeah. Olivia told us all about it. The guy and the lady that paid for all this shit, right?"

"That would be them."

"How about we talk about something else? Can I get anybody a drink," said Cadence.

After their bags had been brought up the four of them drank copious amounts of alcohol right up until the first light of day. Robin and Tobias drank beer and the girls drank Rum and cola. Arianna put some Acid Bath- an epically talented sludge death metal band- on the stereo and the guys played pool while the girls chatted on the couch.

Arianna learned about Cadence. She was an almost completely Italian girl who liked to draw and had a habit of drinking too much as it soon became evident. But the two girls got along incredibly well as they related on the topic of abusive ex- boyfriends and discovered that they could talk to each other with great ease although they were both usually very shy around people they didn't know well.

The wind howled across the panes of glass.

Tobias and Robin also got along with ease. They bullshitted about all the things they heard had been happening around the world. Robin had a sister in Bucks, England. In every territory surrounding the London boroughs the refugees were being slaughtered as they tried to get to safety outside city limits. Robin had lost contact of course but when he last spoke to her only the children were being spared. And extra girls in their late teens were kept to help raise them. Robin was told they saved one girl in eight there. One boy in sixteen, and one adolescent to late teenage girl in thirty two. Though surely that system must have changed once the adults started cracking up.

Robin also went into detail of how easily the men he killed had died; remarking on the true frailty of the human form. How movies would portray a man as having superhuman resolve in their final seconds, when the truth in fact seemed to be the opposite.

Eventually daylight broke and Robin and Cadence went to bed. Arianna and Tobias walked into their apartment and made sure Pluto was inside with them. And he was shocked when, as they sat close together on their couch, the landscape came into full view through the window. The mountains rolled on out into the horizon and they seemed to be higher up than even the highest visible peeks.

Gusts of wind whipped the loose snow across the meadows, fields, clearings, and parking lot. Below, the bodies of trees not yet in bloom arched to and fro.

So You've Inherited A Post-Apocalyptic Refuge Center

Chapter Two

The White Lights

You will face a dilemma during the first few weeks of your inhabitance of the resort. Many people will seek refuge there and you cannot welcome all of them. Or even most of them. It is simply not possible to accommodate all those who will be arriving, nor would you want to. If it were simply a matter of turning them around to go off back into the night(or day), that would be one thing. However if you turn them away they will only come back again in mass, with numbers, seeking to take the grounds from you by force. The solution to this problem is as you've guessed, murder. Kill the fuckers. I promise, it's not a big deal. You've already felt how right murder feels. Mostly, this job will fall on the shoulders of someone named Aden because he will be the only one with the stomach to repeatedly kill the children. Aden will arrive accompanied by circling white lights. And subsequently any others to be allowed to stay will also be accompanied by these lights. These others will be half a set of twins and two boys arriving together. Also one other child not accompanied by lights, a boy, whom Aden will allow to survive. The acceptance of these people into the grounds has been decided by a higher power I have not yet come to fully understand. Something tells me the lights you'll see are actually my higher self, but I don't know that for sure. It's a hunch. Consider them alien, regardless. These instructions were dictated to me by a higher power. You, Arianna, and the others are, to an extent, the chosen ones. These matters will be obvious in time. I, as a human, gave you the initial directions. You yourselves will be in indirect contact with specific higher powers at first and later on in direct contact. So brace yourselves.

15

Aden awoke with an explosion of pain in his face and the sound of glass shattering audibly in a distant way. He sat up in the hotel room bed shrouded in darkness, the details visible only by dim light coming from the bathroom doorway, where Elizabeth stood holding her wrists close to her neck with her fingers pushing down on her ears. He could feel the warm blood from his forehead trickling down his face.

"Liz. What the fuck? Are you Ok?"

The blonde haired, blue eyed, girl wore only a long t-shirt and she looked afraid. No longer beautiful he noticed. Not in that light and not under those circumstances. She was not ugly, just frightening. Very different. She did not respond to him. Instead, from her throat hummed low pitched moans.

Aden got up slowly and cautiously without having to think about not making sudden movements. There was no light to turn on. She had broken the lamp on his head and it wasn't there when he reached for it. Staying close to the wall, he observed her not moving. Getting closer, he touched her arm. She didn't respond at all. He took her by her upper arms and positioned her scared face in the bathroom light so he could look into her eyes. Elizabeth quivered and looked past him, into the light bulb. He pushed her bodily into the room and against the bed, bending her knees so she would sit down. Still she pushed on her ears with her fingertips. He hit the light switch and wondered what to do.

He put on his jeans. The whole mess was over. There would be no great escape anymore. Somehow he had known. The unrealistic demands of the girl to get to Arizona were no longer a priority. They couldn't stay in Burlington any longer. They had starved too long; all that day and all of the day before. But Elizabeth had begged him and pleaded with him to stay there. She was afraid of the world outside and he was too. The hotel room was a minor sanctuary. Over the last day things had become unstable. They were on the fourth floor of six and almost constantly the building shook to its core. The vibration of gunshots could be felt and the din of screaming coming from all directions heard almost nonstop.

Only one other place seemed like an option. He had no food and no way to get any. They had to go.

Elizabeth was unresponsive to his verbal and physical attempts at communication. The confused stare of his catatonic girlfriend was unbearable and he knew it was his problem alone. She was gone. Where to, he had no idea. But gone, he saw that clearly. The bitch was a useless moron anyway. He searched through her bag for clothes to dress her in and wondered if it would be wrong to have sex with her in that condition. Not right then, but in general, if she didn't come out of it.

He dressed her in jeans and a sweatshirt, taking care to make sure she stayed warm enough in extra layers, and pulling the hood over her head.

He put on an argyle sweater vest over his chest and a hooded sweatshirt over that. Looking out the window he couldn't see much. The street lights of the city were dead. Several buildings like the one they were in were illuminated- by generators he presumed. Also, there always seemed to be at least one fire burning somewhere or other. Those fires sometimes illuminated entire sections of the city.

Throughout the nights the streets were eerily quiet and still, not unlike the days, save for the screams that broke the silence, and the only constant sound was the homogenized hum of a hundred, maybe a thousand, generators. The only real sign of life out there. Lights may have been left on but the generators needed refueling. And lights ran on generators. Irrelevant chattering monkey. For those last few nights he had watched the people scurrying about then and again and he was about to be one of them. Not much of a surprise, really.

Him and Elizabeth had each packed a bag with clothes; all that survived the fire. Crash-pad gone up in flames- who knew why? With no place to go they'd met a leather clad punk kid in the street by the hotel who had let them stay in his place while he skipped town. Their turn. He stuffed all the belongings strewn about, mostly clothes and a few keepsakes, family photographs, into the bags.

Aden had a black pickup truck with a full tank of gas in the parking lot. Hopefully he had enough fuel to get to the resort. Elizabeth stayed catatonic but he could manipulate her body into following him and he secured their luggage on his shoulders. In one hand he held her wrist and in the other he grabbed the machete. Only then realizing he hadn't cleaned the blood off of his face.

He pulled her along briskly through the hall to the stairwell and they made their way out to the ground level where the door to the parking lot was. The grounds appeared safe and they exited immediately having not seen anybody lurking around. The cold air blew over his face and buzzed haircut. The two bags were thrown into the bed of the truck. The red thread lightning jolted around the strange cloud mass as thick as he had seen yet. He couldn't imagine what the fuck was happening. Whatever; soft prayers to a dead god he never believed in anyhow were uttered under his breath as he helped his ruined woman into shotgun.

"God help me. God help me. God help me."

No more options. Elizabeth had aided him to fend away the hopelessness but there were no more options. He was so hungry. Surely he was driving to a place he wasn't welcome and how were they going to receive him? There was no way to know. NO MORE IDEAS.

OUT OF IDEAS. NOTHING LEFT TO DO. NOWHERE LEFT TO GO. NOTHING LEFT TO DO. NO MORE IDEAS. "God help me."

He threw the machete into the bed, opened his door, and felt strong hands grip his throat and begin choking the life out of him. His heart rate skyrocketed with adrenaline as all his muscles tensed simultaneously. Jumping into the air Aden hoped to topple his assailant but their feet stood firmly in place. With one of his hands still on the edge of the truck bed he pulled against the attacker's force, somewhat aware that his feet were no longer on the ground. Pulling harder and harder his vision receded but he got his free hand to the machete, struggling to grip the handle.

Swinging it was an immediate problem; he couldn't hit the head of the large man choking him. Desperately he chopped down into the person's calf. Over and over; he could feel the hands on his neck loosen only slightly and he couldn't see anymore. Managing to get a foot up onto the side of the truck he kicked off to jump away. The man's grip did not let up but there was, for an instant, space between Aden's back and the man's chest. He rotated the blade to point behind him and as he fell back he thrust in with the only strength he had left. They both tumbled to the pavement and he pulled the steel out of the assailant.

Aden rolled away as fast as he could and crouched on his knees, swinging frantically even though he couldn't see what he was swinging at. Once the man was struck, more blows were delivered with little idea of where they were landing. He only had the impact of the machete hacking flesh and cracking bone as guidance.

Vision somewhat came back and he jumped up to his feet. The enormous man writhed. Aden chopped away into the neck until there was no chance of survival; the head all but severed from the shoulders.

Choking, coughing, and gasping, he got up into the

truck and slammed the door shut, wondering if he were hurt.

The ignition turned over and the V6 truck revved to life. He shifted into reverse, rolled backward, and then put it into drive, thumping over the body and hauling away as fast as he could.

All the buildings that were usually illuminated in white and gold were black and casting shadows. Like a creepy concrete forest everything seemed haunted. For all the hell going around, the new energy was invigorating. That's how he would have described it anyway.

In little time he was heading south on Interstate 89.

The glowing green clock in the dashboard read 3:48. The adrenaline slowly subsided, his hands stopped shaking, his breathing slowed, and he turned on his interior light. Poor fucking Elizabeth. He watched her. Move. Talk.

"Liz. Say something."

She only looked ahead at the road with a helpless snarl.

He reached over and put his hand on her leg. She did not react. Her fingers twiddled. One hand on the armrest of the door and the other on the seat beside her; she spasmodically retracted and extended her fingers. Squeezing her leg more forcefully he hoped for a reaction and got none. In frustration he squeezed her hard, once, enough to hurt her and she squealed jaggedly and curled up as close to the door as she could; squealing and smacking herself in the face.

"Liz. Stop. Stop it. I'm sorry. I'm sorry. I didn't mean to." But she wouldn't stop. She was panicking and Aden watched her dumbfounded and horrified.

She continued to shriek and slap herself in the face. He pulled the truck over on the snowy shoulder of the highway, engaged the parking break, and took both of her hands into his own. Elizabeth struggled against him, jerking around in her seat.

"Breathe Liz. Breathe. Calm down. You have to stop." She wouldn't stop and time slowed as the seconds struggled to pass. Her noises got quieter and her resistance became less forceful. Soon she was only shuddering and moaning. Aden reluctantly released the girl's delicate hands with intense relief that she didn't slap herself again.

Without waiting another second he engaged the truck and pulled off down the highway. Lightning flashed red through the dark sky, and he felt sick with worry. Like he had felt since even before the crash pad burned down. Like the whole world had felt for what already seemed like eternity.

When he first heard about all the shooting spree killers, even the one in Burlington, he was blowing lines and playing dice and he had made jokes about how maybe it was the end of the world.

Where would he go and what would he do if the resort didn't work out? He had nowhere, everyone was dead, and he could get murdered at the drop of the hat if he only took a wrong turn.

Weariness weighed heavily upon his face, his shoulders, and all his muscles. Hunger pangs were no longer a problem, they had ceased. He focused on the last meal he had had. A can of mushy green beans he split with Elizabeth a day and a half ago. Her fear had kept him from going out to search for more food. His own fear too.

He was tired. Or fatigued. The notion of death had been on his mind constantly recently and was fast becoming less unsettling. Acceptance seemed like the right word. The desire to keep going on the way he had been took second place to the desire to get it over with.

Cars were abandoned here and there but no living souls were seen. After I-89 he got onto Route 2 where the road got tighter and windier. Elizabeth moaned to herself the entire time. Like a confused person with a fever.

"Baby, it'll be Ok. It's all going to be Ok," Aden said without looking at her, only leaning his head against the window of his truck. There was a subtle flash in the trees but he noticed it well. An illusion.

He noticed the cliffs on the side of the road and suicide struck him as appropriate. What hope did he have? There was no hope.

A white orb flew down from the right; out in front of the truck and off to the left.

"What the fuck was that?"

A hallucination obviously. He forgot about it a moment later. His mind was exhausted the same as his body. White light didn't matter.

Then the trees illuminated beside him as the light came glowing back into view on the left and stayed around that side of the road. It was about the size of a bean bag chair and intensely radiant. The woods it flew through were lit comparably to a flood lamp facing all directions. The radiance seeped into the beams of his own headlights; dim by comparison.

The light moved out in front of him, taking the road's curves about seven seconds before he reached them and staying that distance ahead.

Hope. Thank god. Something. A life ring. Something. Even if he drove off the cliff right then, he had seen that light. That light was the greatest sight he had witnessed in his entire life. Serenity and hope unreal.

Looking to Elizabeth he saw her staring vacantly at the dash, hunched against the window.

"Are you seeing this?" he asked. She had no response. Her big blue eyes were still. He could see her so well. The trucks interior was illuminated and she was dead. "Oh fuck!"

When he glanced back at the road he could see nothing other than the overpowering white light that caused him to press down on the brake and clutch. Less than a second later the light lifted and took off through the tree tops, flying swiftly out of sight.

Aden pulled the truck over and parked, flicked the interior light on, and looked at the dead girl. Her head limp when he moved it by the chin to look closely at her. He pulled her over in his arms, blew air into her lungs, and performed CPR to no avail. The voice of his CPR instructor came and went, "CPR doesn't bring them back. CPR only keeps blood circulating until a shock can be delivered..." She was gone. Gone still; he had really lost her back at the hotel. After deciding to not put her in the bed for fear she would come back to life, he settled the corpse into the passenger seat, wrapped her head in a dirty t-shirt from the floor, put the truck in gear, and continued on his way.

Regardless of the circumstance, his complete re-invigoration could not be ignored or denied. No more hunger and no more exhaustion. Only a new determined focus to get to his destination. Driving too fast and ignoring the possibility of black ice under the packed snow he fish tailed around the curves in the road. Soon he found the right turn he needed; Justice Road.

Route 2's presence had receded from the rear-view and he was deep in the forested winding mountain road when the world illuminated as bright as if the sun were high in the sky. Except this light was even more intense and whiter, like daylight. To the left and even more so to the right the terrain dropped off hundreds of feet. The road ran along the crown of a ridge; down the grade the snow radiated under the intensity of the light. Outside of his illuminated area, in the far distance, all was black.

The fear confused him. The fact remained that anything was better than the reality of the situation as he knew it. The intense fear felt calming to him. Like water so hot it feels cold.

The light moved away from him further off into the distance of his one o clock position; maneuvering through rising and falling peaks; shining like a pinpointed high noon on a clear day; a cloud of sunlight moving away from him and leaving him once again in darkness. Eventually the light moved far enough away to give him a more accurate perspective. Aden had been trying to make out the source of the light. His presumption was the orb he had seen previously was creating the light cloud. Except he couldn't see that orb. It seemed possible, since the orb was small and white, the illumination at hand drowned it out.

It flew away, nearly all the way to the visible horizon, then it seemed to stand still, and blinked in and out of existence a couple times before disappearing completely. All was dark but the red threads of lightning overhead. Aden looked carefully out at the scene from his truck running through biting wind along the mountain top. His eyes regained night vision and focused on the place the light had blinked out at where he noticed smaller lights glowing. Those were more usual, like the color of street lamps, coming from the resort.

16

The foretold and obviously sentient lights had come and apparently gone but Aden had not yet arrived. Day began emerging from the night and Tobias and Robin sat in what they called the "crow's nest," positioned atop a tower at the corner of the building above the area where Aden would be entering from; Justice road; the only way in or out save for an expedition through the mountain range.

Each had a coffee mug in hand. Tobias wore black sweat pants with silver stripes running down the leg, a pair of work boots over bare feet, a black wool jacket over a black thermal shirt, and a black wool beanie.

They sat with arms resting on the counter looking out over the parking lot. Glass windows ran 360 degrees, and there was a door through which to step out onto a concrete balcony safe with steel railings painted orange. The view in all directions was endless; blocked only partially in one tiny spot by the dome which at its highest point was still 15 feet below where they sat, and also blocked by their wide and rising single peak. They could see straight to where the highest ski trails began; where their mountain rose with the steepest grades.

Robin had on a brown suede jacket over a black t-shirt, a pair of broken-in blue jeans, and tan skate shoes. His eyes were heavy with fatigue as he smoked a cigarette.

The two had been stationed there for over an hour, discussing the lights or their personal opinions of aliens, or their personal opinions of the coffee.

Robin had seen a UFO with one of his old friends while standing around a car drinking beer out in Rutland, where he came from. There were others there at the time but only two of them saw it. Somehow, he and a friend had both been looking at the sky at the same time when a star began to move. Except that it wasn't a star. It appeared to be the same size and brightness of a star, which probably wasn't an accident, then began to move in a straight line and grow in brightness; twice the luminosity of any other star, soon enough four times as bright. And then it blinked out of existence; gone for only a couple seconds until coming back as bright as it had been right before it disappeared; still moving until it zigzagged once or twice up and down like a heart rate monitor. Then it was gone.

Tobias remarked that the zig zagging probably had to do with time travel or some sort of quantum leap. Ninety degree movements were somehow connected to the notion.

Cadence had seen the same thing too, at the drive-in another night. Other people saw them also. The squiggly lights were somewhat of a local phenomenon where they came from. Enough people had seen them to make those who had not envious. In the movie Easy Rider, Dennis Hopper's character, Billy, described the same thing while camped out somewhere down south.

That morning, they were awoken by what sounded like pulsating singing energy, like sonic tones shooting with humble intensity, rising to near deafening volumes and falling back to nothing, over and over. All the while their world experienced something like daylight in the darkness; there was no more skepticism in anybody. The unbelievable became easily believable. Except Cadence may have been exhibiting signs of denial; insisting that it was only the lightning or that the occurrence was some kind of new and natural phenomenon. No one could prove her wrong.

As for Tobias, he was incredibly fond of the notion of aliens. Centuries and millenniums of human civilization, the surviving history, had heralded no real understanding of extra-terrestrials. Regardless of the claims and evidence everywhere of certain cultures being in contact with "the others," nothing was certain. Regardless of entire civilizations disappearing without a trace, certain MesoAmerican cultures, nothing was certain. Regardless of crop circles made to supernatural specifications, by means beyond human ability, nothing was certain. Regardless of the footage of alien craft miles wide taken from shuttle missions and all the films made on earth; crop circles and craft sightings in every country the world over, nothing was certain. Regardless of the top of the pyramid conspiracies that put all of the world's power into the hands of the offspring and descendants of otherworldly reptiles, the Illuminati, nothing was conclusive.

If only one piece of the puzzle were real, than the whole matter must have been. There was life out there in different kinds of reality, existing in different dimensions, with atoms oscillating at speeds greater or less than the speed of light. The actuality of the size of the universe and moreover, the size of the omniverse from which all energy flows, was not something for earth bound humans to comprehend- never mind reject. A world of control by, and subjection to, governmental or religious power struggles and mindfucking had kept ignorant a creature of intelligence and rationale. Then the internet made important information available to everybody with access right in time for the end of days. If some god were above, as far as mankind were concerned, aliens were closer to it than they were. Only once man knew what the extra-terrestrials knew, could man hope to know what god was. As for Tobias, he had seen a seminar on the internet given by an alien incarnated into flesh. An alien who answered every question Tobias had ever asked about the true nature of reality and god. Another time, he would tell Robin all about it. First all his remembrances of the video that he had watched over and over needed to be organized on paper. The subject would come up again.

"If this guy that's coming out here is all by himself, what are we going to do if he tries to get all up on one of our girls? Ya know?" Robin asked.

"Um, there is going to be another girl coming. But how about, since we're pretty much in this together, if he tries to fuck around with one of our girls, we can just kill him. Sound good?"

"Kill him, kill him?"

"Yeah, dead."

"Alright, that sounds good." Robin laughed. "I like that idea. It's funny; it's like your eye patch."

Tobias had the anarchy sign patch on his face. "True that," he said.

There was enough daylight to see clearly. Bluish, still, but clear.

Headlamp light followed by a black truck broke through the woods out into the snowy parking lot.

"Let's go," said Tobias.

They hustled down the square staircase taking two steps at a time and came out to the rear of the concrete area where ski rentals had been done back when. Tobias had his hand around the snub nose in his jacket pocket as they stepped out the side door behind some bushes approaching the truck.

Tobias stood behind Robin as he calmly walked up to the truck. They had planned and coordinated the particular method earlier. Tobias watched Robin's back.

There were two people in the cab of the truck and while this had not been anticipated, it made sense to Tobias. Who would go there alone? The four of them were basically lucky he hadn't brought his whole family.

Somebody of shorter stature, wearing a hooded sweatshirt, stepped out of the truck and approached them. He had shaggy and curling facial hair and the hair on his head was buzzed down close.

"Hey there," said the newcomer.

"What's goin' on man?" asked Robin.

"I had no place else to go, so I came here. Is it Ok if I stay here and get my head together?"

"Yeah. That's fine. I'm Robin"

"I'm Toby."

"Aden."

They all shook hands quickly.

"We know what your name is. Who's the sleeping person?" said Tobias.

"How could you know my name?" asked Aden.

"That's complicated. I'll show you later. Who's the girl?"

"That's my girlfriend Elizabeth. She's not sleeping, she's dead. How could you possibly know what my name is?"

"A psychic told us you'd be here before she died. How did your girlfriend die?"

"A psychic? Really? I don't know man. She broke a lamp on my head, went vacant and kind of retarded, and then a UFO or something killed her. I'm glad you guys are chill. I've been freaking out since I left Burlington."

"She died on the way here then?" asked Robin.

"Yeah. A fucking UFO killed her. Did you guys see it?"

"We saw it. It got us out of bed in about two seconds. I heard that noise in my dream and I woke up and it was still there; scared the fucking shit out of me," said Tobias.

"What noise?" asked Aden.

"Like lightening dry heaving," said Robin.

"Fuckin A. No, I didn't hear that. What do you guys think I should do with her?"

"You buried those other bodies, right Robin?"

"Yeah. We got a back hoe here. I buried them out in a back field. I put em in the bucket, drove em out there, dug the hole, dropped em in, covered em up and that was that."

"What about a headstone?" Tobias said; an idea already brewing in his mind.

"No man. I wasn't about to bother with that."

"Then I think I'm going to teach Arianna to make headstones or maybe I'll do it... Alright. Do you want to get something to eat, maybe clean up, and then we can get her buried?"

"Yeah. That sounds good, I guess."

"Hang on a second." Tobias ran all the way to the main room at the apartments where Olivia's booklet hung from a clip his girl had installed up on the wall. Arianna and Cadence were sitting in the main room drinking coffee.

"Is he here?" Arianna asked.

"Yeah. He's here. I'm going to show him the booklet. He's weirded out how we knew his name before he showed up here. He looks like he's about to keel over and die though. Can you girls come down and help get him settled? There's a body that we're going to have to bury."

He retrieved the pages and ran back out to the driveway, finding the correct page and holding it open. In the driveway, a little out of breath, he put the pages into Aden's hands and said nothing. Robin smiled with his arms crossed, smoking another cigarette. Aden skimmed over the words and went ghostly at the point when he found his name.

"I'm the only one with the stomach to kill these people? Why can't you guys do it?"

"I don't know. Sometimes little details like that would fall by the wayside with her. We can probably all do it. I been thinking about it. We can park the UPS truck sideways up the way a little. They'll be on foot that way. There's an arsenal here."

"Then we won't be giving peace a chance, I see," said Aden.

"Fuck that noise," said Robin.

Aden said, "What else is new? No. I hear that. I'm fucking fed up with this shit."

"Hey, I've got the girls coming down here. They're going to help you get settled. Clean the blood off you. They'll feed you too. You look like you can barely stand up."

"Yeah. That's completely accurate."

"I was thinking me and Robin could take your girlfriend out there for you and dig the hole while you do all of those things and we'll leave it open for you to fill it in if you want to," said Tobias.

"You guys can fill it in. It doesn't really matter to me." Arianna came shouting as they turned the corner; Cadence hurrying right along her side, "There's a crop circle. Hey. Guys! There's a crop circle!"

"The crow's nest," said Tobias.

Together the five people ran exuberantly up the stairs toward the crow's nest. Daylight had become clearer regardless of the lack of sunlight breaking through the dark sky goo.

Tobias and Robin made it up there first and scanned the fields. Arianna and Cadence came after and Aden made it up last.

"Down there. In the meadow by the river," Cadence said. A distance beyond the back lot; the two areas were split by a thin section of woods. There were circular designs etched into the snow; not burnt, only clear of snow. The size seemed smaller than a hundred yard square. Immense circles were interlinked into a bigger chain of circles. Running through all of them was a single line. Some areas to the left of the design appeared shaded and to the right they seemed to be of a lighter shade. In the center of the design running horizontally was a skewed Venn diagram. Three more circles; two outer circles locked into the center one. At the top of the crop circle was a sun shining rays in all directions. A cross ran through the center of all of it.

Dumbfounded, they all uttered verbal amazements under their breath. Tobias, after thinking about it for a few moments, understood the nature of what they were seeing.

"It's like the yin yang but different. It's all polarity and ascension into the golden light. I think. The left side is the energy of darkness, which is actually a white light; the white light of knowledge. The right side is the energy of light. The white light of unconditional love. At the top is the golden light. It's saying that all is one. Those three circles in the center are the ascension process. You combine the light of knowledge and the light of unconditional love and you ascend into the white light. I mean that's what I heard from the alien guy on the internet. It makes sense. I think all those outer circles are probably everybody that's going to live here. There's about that many. Nine of us, nine circles. Or, there will be nine of us. The cross running through all of it is the Celtic cross. It makes four divisions of reality; masculine, feminine, love, and knowledge."

They walked down the stairs and out the back door heading to the field to investigate. There they found that the undergrowth exposed from where the snow disappeared was completely dry. Walking out into the center they had only a moment to investigate in peace. Tobias observed that none of the grasses were broken, only warped and whirling like the way all of the reports he had seen mentioned. The five of them looked to one another as they stood inside the circles. They felt, though didn't put into words, a oneness flowing between, becoming, them. Some dying world was irrelevant under those circumstances. A moment later the same trilling noise that had awoken the four of them that morning returned unexpectedly, sending them all running back to the rear lot.

Afterward, back inside in the kitchen, they discussed the new occurrences and confessed their thoughts about them. Cadence, refusing to believe there were actually aliens- or even Olivia's spirit- involved became afraid that they were being taunted and stalked. Aden remained quiet and aloof through the whole discussion. His hunger and exhaustion took second place to the subject matter for a period of time.

Soon Tobias realized as much and said, "Robin, why don't we go take care of the girl in the car and Arianna and Cadence can help Aden get back into a better state of mind. Girls; he'll be staying in the basement apartment out at the hotel."

The hotel included a half bar half nightclub and was a four story building attached to the main building by an enclosed and heated glass walkway. The first floor was where the reception area and bar were. The other three floors were hotel rooms and a banquet area on the second floor. The basement was half storage and half the single apartment; which was designed with a rustic log cabins decor and style; antlers and wood like a rich Englishman's hunting lodge. By Tobias' estimate it was the next nicest living area on the premises. With that space filled, the next arrivals would be staying in one of the many hotel rooms or in the cabins that ran out along the trails like the constellation tail of the tadpole whose head was the grand quarters of Endsville.

Tobias stood by the door of Aden's truck smoking a cigarette waiting. He had tied an electrical chord around the t-shirt on the girl's head to ensure that it didn't come off while they handled her. Robin brought around the huge yellow back hoe and positioned it with the bucket adjacent to the truck. The machine stood about 13 feet tall at the roof of it's cab. The rear tires were about as high as Tobias's head and the bucket was almost as wide as the truck was long. The yellow was clean and bright and the whole machine appeared barely used.

The roar of the engine puttered out to nothing and Robin hopped out of the cab. Tobias opened the door, grabbed the corpse by under the arms, and said, "I'll pull her out and you grab the feet. She's frickin stiff."

They dropped her into the makeshift hearse and Robin started up the machine again. Tobias rode standing on a platform on the side holding a steel handle in his gloved hand. They rode over the asphalt behind the complex to the service lot and from there they took a trail at the far side that went through sparse trees separating the back yard of the hotel and cabins from a field where the resort, when it ran, used to rent out snowmobiles and give lessons.

He sang Tool to himself quietly as the cold wind rushed across his cheeks, "Prying open my third eye. Prying open my third eye. Prying open my third eye. Prying open my third eye."

At the end of the field on the left, Robin turned left to drive down along the far side as the landscape curving in on itself created an exaggerated and more ovular blade of a knife effect with the tree line. And when the path again straightened out they would have been heading back in roughly the direction to where the road would be but Robin turned right through a passage in the trees that separated all the open spaces and they came out into the meadow where far off in the distance was the crop circle. Driving straight ahead they went up and over several rolling slight hills until they reached the furthest distance of the meadow. The heavy cloud mass, that couldn't really be called clouds any longer, was close enough that Tobias thought maybe he could reach out and grab a hand full. At the top of the world the claustrophobia of the effect was comforting. Nevertheless, even he was beginning to miss the sky and the company of the Sun he used to shun as an annoyance. Though his disturbance was never the Sun's fault. He was disturbed by the way people flocked from their homes in the sunlight. Sadly, with all the people gone, he could have enjoyed the Sun if it were available.

Tobias could see the few graves dusted in the snow; dirty and disturbed coffin sized spaces of Earth. He hopped down, gave the back hoe space to maneuver, and looked around at the glorious kingdom of Endsville. Snowy mountains rose and fell in all the distances beyond the trees. There they were somewhat more elevated than all the land beyond, providing a good view of the property. Wherever it might begin and end. They were at the back corner of the open space and the complex was a good distance away, almost a mile he guessed. But the crow's nest was clearly visible; standing high above the trees.

Robin began to dig the hole. He planted the machine's large supports on either side and started plunging the smaller bucket into the Earth with such power that the back hoe hardly seemed to rattle. Naturally, being a guy, Tobias was envious of being in control of the machine. Granted he would have no idea how to operate it, he was nonetheless eager to learn. He was eager to take that graveyard as his own. Undoubtedly, Robin wouldn't care. Who would? He wanted to be the only one who regularly came out to that edge of the world. He wanted to be alone with the dead, and to care for what lingering souls might be there.

The door of the machine's cab opened and Robin signaled for him to go up there. They switched places and Robin taught him how to operate the bucket. While Tobias learned, the machine jerked and shuddered up and all around for a few moments until he got the hang of it. At that point the hole was dug and Robin showed him how to get the machine into a stable parked and idling mode.

They got out and grabbed either side of the girl's body and threw her into the hole.

"Should we have checked out her boobs," Tobias asked.

"Yeah. Probably."

"There'll be more chicks. Is copping a feel on a dead chick necrophilia?"

"Yeah. Probably. You want to fill the hole in?"

Tobias filled in the grave using the machine to push the mound of dirt over the girl's body and pack it all down. Robin then instructed him how to spin the seat around and control the driving mechanisms of the backhoe. Tobias drove them both back to the complex while Robin stood in the doorway and gave him an overview of how to operate the front loader.

He parked the machine in the rear lot and they walked into the main complex through the warehouse.

"You want to get a beer?" Robin asked him.

"Yeah. That sounds like a good idea. Hey, do you know what that girl's name was?"

"No. I don't. Hopefully Aden will."

"We should probably see if he wants to drink, huh?" Tobias said.

At that statement they stopped short of the stairs that went up to the apartments.

"Yeah. Wait. How are we supposed to keep a watchful eye for people that try to come out here if we're getting drunk? Or how are we supposed to keep an eye for them at all if nobody is near the entrance," Robin asked.

"That's a good fucking question. Well. We should have a few and figure out how to booby trap this place. And then we should start booby trapping it. At least create some kind of alarm. And we have to park the UPS truck sideways out on the road."

"This whole place is rigged with an alarm. What we need is like a system everybody uses so we can keep it on all the time."

"We should also ask Aden if he wouldn't mind camping out in the crow's nest."

"Who would want to do that?" Robin asked.

"I don't know, but it would make everything a lot easier. Use the walkie talkies? What about if we take shifts up there. We can overlap them so nobodies ever alone."

"Let's just get everyone together and talk about it."

Tobias and Robin found the other three in the cafeteria sitting at the only unfolded lunch table drinking coffee.

Tobias said, "We have to talk about how we're all going to keep this place secure. So do you guys want to come up to the apartments with us?"

"Why can't we discuss security down here?" Aden asked.

"Cuz there's booze upstairs."

"Oh. That's a good reason."

"It's not even 9 o clock in the morning yet," said Arianna.

"First of all, I don't know about you guys, but I'm on permanent vacation from here on out." Tobias continued, "And second of all we just buried some girl with a back hoe. What was her name Aden?"

"Elizabeth Perkins."

Perkins? Tobias thought about her rack again. He also made a mental note to make the girl a tombstone but he didn't yet know how he was going to do that. There had to be the tools he needed lying around somewhere.

Arianna gathered up all the coffee cups and caught up with the group. When they got upstairs Cadence went to the bar and asked everybody who wanted what.

Tobias, Robin, Cadence, and Aden all had bottles of beer. Arianna had a snifter of whiskey only and everyone did a shot of rum before they all sat down. Agents Of Oblivion played softly on the speakers. The eerie vocalizations of a drugged out depressive, and the soulful nightmares of the band, matched the circumstance well, Tobias noticed.

Arianna wore light blue jeans and a black hooded sweatshirt open and unzipped over a Nirvana t-shirt that had Dante's circles of hell on it. She sat curled into Tobias on the larger couch.

On the other side of the large couch Cadence and Robin sat in much the same way. Cadence wore a Baja of black and red stripes and a pair of black sweatpants.

Aden had changed his clothes and was wearing a dark blue hoodie with chalk textured white stripes horizontal across the chest. His khaki covered legs were crossed as he sat slouched in the corner of the black leather love seat squared to the television. He had a vacant expression across an exhausted face.

No lamps were turned on and the daylight coming through the wall of windows that faced the ski slopes was so very overcast that it hardly provided enough light to read by.

Painstakingly they proceeded to devise a security system for any of the indoor premises. Endsville had an intercom system built into every room and they decided that that intercom would be utilized in the event of trespassers. They all agreed on a shoot on site policy. They would each need a gun.

According to the prophecy, all those to be welcomed and taken in would be announced by the flying white light. Everyone more or less believed it, but the notion, so odd, was nonetheless good for a laugh. Tobias relished in the obscurity and wonder.

At some point, after the first beers were done and two rounds of shots had gone by, Tobias, Robin, and Aden took the second beers down to the warehouse to grab enough weapons for everybody. Everything was in three thick unmarked cardboard boxes in the corner. M-16 rifles in the largest box. Pistols in a small one. And explosives in the other. In a 4th box was all the ammunition and cleaning supplies.

They brought back to the apartments 5 pistols of different calibers and models, and the corresponding ammunition. The girls got the smallest guns; two .38 revolvers. And the guys split up three .45s. Everyone resolved to carry their guns around at all times.

However, none of this nullified the fact that there could be strangers wandering around the premises at any given time. Aden watched Pluto stalk about the floor.

"We need a dog," said Aden.

All agreed on that, but there was no way to get one. Nobody was about to leave the grounds.

Then Tobias said, "Why not? Us guys can go out in one of the trucks with guns and bring one back."

"The dogs are fucked," said Robin, "same as everything else."

"That cat seems fine," said Aden.

Tobias said, "No. He's alright by comparison. But he's by no means the same. I don't even feel the same. Don't you guys feel different?"

Robin said, "Yeah. I feel like, if I had been nervous my whole life and I am the result of that person. Except I haven't been nervous my whole life. I'm like way high strung now. And sometimes I feel stoned for no reason."

Aden said, "I know what you're saying. I feel totally drunk right now. No. I'm kidding. But I know what you're saying."

"Do you guys want to go do something fun? Take out the snow mobiles or something?" asked Tobias.

"I thought we had to secure this place or whatever," said Aden.

"Oh yeah."

So You've Inherited A Post-Apocalyptic Refuge Center

Chapter Four

Defense and Security

This subject is a bitch. You are going to have to be prepared for those that will arrive without the welcoming wagon, but I cannot tell you how. Anything I advise will screw you over more than if I tell you to come up with a plan on your own. Not really sure why... Just figure it out on your own. You've got weapons, so use them. I know that once you put your noggins together you'll figure out what will work best for you. Make sure the girls don't have to kill anybody. Y'all only need to figure out how to be aware of anybody arriving before they become aware of you. If you can rig some kind of trip wire alarm about a half mile up the road, a sniper up on the crow's nest should work excellent; not only for sniping but to drop any form of a bomb also. No mercy. Don't forget that. Normally this would be <u>really</u> bad karma. I have it on good authority that karma is not the standard anymore. Actually the whole system has been done away with. The creator created karma to balance life on Earth, but there is no more Earth, as we know it, so there is no more karma. Everything has changed. Death is the new golden rule. Kill unto others... Under usual circumstances you'd be best off to die like the rest of the world. It is simply the next step to be taken. Just know that your group is special. Different. Unique. Whatever. No mercy. In a few months you won't have to think about it anymore.

17

The alarm blasted and whooped through the dark halls and corridors and did not stop. Aden shot out of bed wearing blue pajama pants and threw an army jacket on over his bare chest then shoved his feet into his boots. He grabbed his rifle and ran up the steps out into the lobby of the hotel; out the glass foyer doors and through the glass tunnel toward the main complex of Endsville; the wailing alarm filled the air. He found Tobias and Robin standing by the far side of the dining hall huddled by the window looking out over the parking lot. Tobias noticed him and said nothing before running out into the kitchen. A second later the alarm shut down.

Aden got to the window and looked out into the muddy lot bathed in floodlight. All three of them had M-16 rifles either in their hands or slung over their shoulders. Soon Logan came jogging in.

Logan had designed the alarm system to be set off

four miles up the road using a radio signal to trigger a mechanism. He was 6'1" tall, had short and curly blonde hair, and always seemed to be excited or smiling; even then.

"Are we gunna use the bombs again?" asked Robin.

"That's what we put em out there for," said Aden.

"I fucking hate this shit. How can we know how many there'll be? And maybe they're heavier armed than we are," said Tobias.

"We don't. We can hope for the best though," said Logan.

While they talked, each of them grabbed extra clips of ammunition from the box at their feet and stuffed whatever pockets they had. There would be Molotov cocktails in the crow's nest.

Tobias said, "I'll hit the switch like last time. If I see more than one car I'm waiting for that last one. We'll have to shoot the rest. Where the fuck is Drake, Logan?"

"Motherfucker probably slept through the alarm."

"Whatever. Man the battle stations. I'll give one blast of the horn for each car we see."

"Let's go!" said Aden.

They all ran off to separate directions. Tobias and Robin went up to the crow's nest to give the warning and set off the bombs. Logan went strutting off to the downstairs with that wobbling strutting gate of his.

Aden would be manning the front porch. He sat on a low stool with the barrel resting on the railing; there in the moist night air with one hand squeezing the pistol grip and the other holding the shaft, he aimed into the parking lot and through the floodlight.

It never got easier. First he was nervous he'd get hurt; shot or something. They were all pretty good at getting the jump on the intruders but nine times out of ten they had at least some shots fired back at them. No one had gotten hit yet. Always he expected the other shoe to drop. It felt like the time. Afterward, he'd make it out the other side and see the survivors writhing on the ground or lying dead; enough to make him vomit on more than one occasion. Going around to little fucking kids and girls and putting the last bullets into their skulls. They were always young. There were no old people left. Fucking sick of it. It never got any easier.

He was positioned at the corner of the building, his eyes intense and focused, and his breaths steady. As the air horn sounded he counted to himself. Once. Twice. Good. The dread would have worsened exponentially for every extra car arriving. Two wasn't too bad. A few seconds passed and he saw the headlights pierce through the trees and move diagonally, rising and falling by the contours of the road. The first vehicle, an SUV, came out of the woods and onto the dirt lot. Aden tucked himself back around the building. He had seen that the second vehicle was right on the firsts' tail and the explosives detonated. The blast was powerfully sudden, tremendous, and deafeningly loud. The force of the explosion boomed across the lot and throughout the grounds. The SUV went flying forward and rolled onto its side. From his cover against the wall Aden felt the flames hiss his face and he inhaled hot air. Tails of showers of gliding flames streaked across the lot and out into the trees. Nobody in that second car could have survived.

With ringing ears, dull to sound, Aden sat back on the stool, setting his rifle on the rail and aiming. The mangled frame of the second car was an inferno burning against the trees that had stopped it's trajectory a little off the road. Aiming instead at the first car, he waited for any sign of life, or maybe for one of the other guys to make a move. Those were the longest seconds. He wondered if the people in that car had any hope after what just happened. Were they afraid? Or maybe they saw the pile of burnt and junked cars in the trees at the far end of the lot. Some thirty ruined cars shoved in the shadows.

The driver's side door of the silver SUV opened up and fell back closed before opening once more. The gangly figure of a clearly injured person struggling to move began to crawl out under the weight of the falling door onto the left side of the truck facing up. Aden watched him struggle. He waited until the strangers full mass was out and crawling on the truck, then he squeezed the trigger again and again aiming and firing and re-aiming and firing.

Shots rang out quietly in deafened ears from above and out back. Everyone fired onto the truck. The intruder was struck immediately and he went limp. Sparks skipped off the undercarriage as they all kept firing for a moment until one by one they stopped.

"Hold it!" Aden called out and pumped his little air horn frantically a few times.

He hustled down the staircase and out to where the truck was. Logan hurried from behind to catch his heals.

The bottom of the vehicle faced Aden as he approached; he peaked in through the front windshield. A light flashed and a bullet shot through the glass, tearing into his left side. He dove away, swearing in pain.

"Logan. Come on. We gotta give em everything through the windshield."

"Are you alright?"

"I'm fine. Come on."

Aden stood up with Logan's help and they fired rapidly through the window, first around the truck's hood, Aden low and Logan high, before actually moving in front of the truck and emptying their magazines through the window.

From inside, screams harmonized with the gunshots creating some kind of death music Aden knew well. Round after round the bullets shot from the guns until their magazines were empty and they stepped aside to reload and listen. The truck released whimpering sobs.

"Again," Aden said. And they emptied a third magazine each into the bodies visible through the space where the window used to be.

Aden walked around the truck and threw open the rear hatch to find among all of the luggage a small child crying. The boy had on one of those colorful beanies with the helicopter propeller on the top of it. The hat made Aden smile and shoulder his rifle. The young boy cringed only slightly and weighed almost nothing when he took him into his arms. Aden headed into the house and said to Logan, "I'm keeping this kid."

Upon examining the filthy child in the floodlight Aden found him to be miraculously uninjured.

18

The frail young one was given to the three girls. The task to welcome him and help him to settle was naturally delegated to them and while doing so they discovered several things. The boy's name was Calvin. His family of two parents were long dead and he had been lost, hiding by a river in his home town, when he was picked up by a pack of three boys in their late teens. One of those boys and Calvin survived an attack by a man with an ax who murdered the other two and together they continued seeking food while avoiding further dangerous situations. Then that boy who had saved Calvin from the ax murderer was hit by a car and died. Calvin kept trudging alone along mountain roads until he had practically starved. Indeed he was an emaciated little thing. The next people he encountered were a boy and a girl. He had arrived at Endsville in their SUV; they, Josie and Caroline, had been shot to death by Aden and Logan. Calvin didn't know who the people in the other truck were. All he knew was that it had been Josie's idea to go to the ski resort and the other carload followed because they didn't know what else to do with themselves.

Tobias and Drake located vacuum sealed children's clothing down in the warehouse for the little blond haired boy to wear. The girls dressed him in some black sweat pants and a red shirt with black horizontal stripes. Everyone congregated in the living room upstairs at Arianna's and Cadence's apartments.

Tobias took a look at the kid over the girl's and Aden's shoulders. He certainly had an intrepid spirit. Nothing really seemed to faze him. Except, obviously from the way he sniffled about it, he was still very sad for the loss of his parents. However, he was relieved by his new sense of security after having been so hungry and afraid. Something Tobias identified with immediately.

As for Aden, the bullet made a flesh wound in his side causing no serious injury and the area got cleaned, mended, and bandaged with no complication. The bleeding was stopped with some simple stitching done by the new girl Lyn whom Aden had been getting on well with. They spent almost all of their time together. Tobias was positive Lyn was an indigo or crystal kid or something. Her intense purple eyes and porcelain white complexion were coupled with some odd kind of divinity in the way she moved and spoke with an otherworldly grace. Something about her wavy blonde hair set her apart from everyone else and her presence was similar to a rift among them. Nobody had an ill mind toward her, but her different nature was compellingly blatant. Yet, everyone understood why Lyn wasn't always, or even often, involved.

The white lights had welcomed her only about a week prior. Sad story about her; her twin had died; shot in the head by an attacker. Lyn escaped the apartment they had lived in, her sister died there on the floor, and she went on to her parent's house to find them both dead;

out of gas in a closed garage. Her other three sisters all lived in either Connecticut and Colorado. Lyn had followed the light to Endsville after someone broke in and tried to rape her at her parent's house. That assailant was well under 21 and there was no accepted explanation for his behavior except that maybe he was a jerk. He died with a knife in his heart.

"I'm going out to take care of those bodies. Are you coming Drake?" asked Tobias.

"Where are you guys going? I want to go," said Calvin.

"It's no big deal Calvin. We have to go fix a toilet in the hotel."

"I want to go."

That made the girls giggle and crack inaudible jokes. Tobias half smiled and said, "No, maybe next time, alright. The girls are going to show you around. You can go sledding or something if you want to. We gotta go." Then they walked out.

Usually Logan helped Tobias care for the graveyard, which had quickly become an ominous sight to behold. That day Drake wanted to help after having slept through the alarm.

They were dressed in the dirty jeans and sweatshirts necessitated by the work and also wore nylon jackets to keep dry from the rain that had begun an hour before. They loaded the first two bloody and stiff bodies into the front bucket of the backhoe fairly easily and quickly. The charred bodies were handled in a similar manner, though a shovel was needed to pry them away from the areas where they were indistinguishable from the mangled surfaces they had burned into. Their flesh had burned away to the muscle in areas and their limbs oozed grease onto the gloved hands working them.

"You're gunna see them today," said Tobias.

"How's that? See who?"

"I haven't told everybody yet, only Arianna and Logan know. There's ghosts out there. They like the rain. It's fucking crazy. Logan's seen em with me a couple of times but I haven't shown anybody cause I've been trying to keep it peaceful out there. Like we're only out there when we have to be, ya know?"

"I think I get it. You should consider that maybe they want visitors though. I would think that dead people would enjoy company. They probably get lonely. And if you spend time with them maybe they'll rest a little easier."

"Look," Tobias said, pointing with his chin out across the parking lot. "Watch the cars at the bottom. See the distortion in the rain? He's sitting on the hood."

"Holy shit."

There he was. Nothing new and nothing frightening. The ghost of one of the victims in the ongoing Endsville tragedy. Possibly forgotten in a vehicle, or maybe decimated bodily; whatever the case, the junkyard ghost's body never made it out to the graveyard.

"Can we go look at him?" Drake asked.

"There's no need to. Just wait until we get out to the graveyard. Come on."

They tore out the last remaining carcass. Making six in all.

Tobias started the back hoe and drove off- Drake hanging on the side- on the trail out to the meadow. Drake was a friendly person and fit in well among the others by staying humble and maintaining his personal integrity by not getting unnecessarily caught up in the abstractions their new lives. He kept a close cropped hair cut and stayed clean shaved at all times; two of his many subtly endearing qualities. He also worked out every day which seemed odd given the circumstances. Tobias had been taken aback by his kindheartedness and as a result they developed consanguinity. It seemed that Drake was resolute not to let the chaos of the times affect his personal stability. Something in his upbringing had taught him to behave virtuously and disciplined but

Tobias still did not know him well enough to decipher what his past consisted of.

Drake arrived in the daytime with Logan. The white lights, five or six of them, danced all around the property causing the residents to gather together with champagne at the lot to wait for them and watch the lights soar around Endsville. It was an exciting moment. The trilling noise of the lights was so different in the day time and instead of the usual kind of alarm or signal, they sounded instead as if they were singing; emitting dozens of alternating notes. Not like people sing; like whales or birds sing. Drake and Logan had been driving down from Canada with a truck bed full of gasoline hoping to get to the Deep South where they figured it would be easier to survive. Out on back mountain roads they encountered the lights in their rear-view. The lights blocked turns or blocked the main roads and forced turns, flaring intimidatingly, half chasing them and half guiding them all the way to the mountain sanctuary. Logan had been incredibly useful from the minute they arrived. He was an Aquarius and Tobias immediately noticed he was a constant generator of that Uranus energy of innovation; creating an alarm out of minimal electronics before he had even gotten rested.

Tobias turned in through the trees and looked out over the graveyard from behind the windshield wipers throwing the rain to the side. The stacks of rocks that marked each grave ran over the rolling hill. That was Logan's idea; to make the graveyard one giant rock garden. It was simple and appropriate because most bodies had no names anyhow; the rock stacks were a good way to anonymously mark all the graves. Little rocks stacked on top of bigger rocks. Or big flat rocks stacked against each other horizontally. Sometimes they would get creative and build head height rock castles or sometimes they would minimally stack six rocks from largest to smallest. Certain hard to kill intruders were bestowed the largest rock piles. Whatever the case, Tobias was pleased with the overall presentation of the place.

Those six bodies would make an even 80. With the machine parked he took the notepad from overhead, added six tally marks, and placed it back in it's compartment.

The ghosts wouldn't appear until they acclimated to their presence. That would happen a little while into the digging.

Tobias opened the door and invited Drake into the cab to get out of the rain while he dug the holes. The compartment was crowded but not too much so. There was space for Drake to sit down on the dirty floor between the seat and the door. Tobias parked at the far end of the already laid graves and set about digging the first hole.

"Give them like fifteen minutes, they'll show up."

"I'm sure they will. Hey, I have some painkillers in my jacket. Do you want one?"

"What are they?"

"Oxycodone."

"Yeah. That might help this go by quicker. These fucking holes can take forever to dig. Where'd you get them?"

"They were my dad's," Drake said and handed a pill to Tobias who swallowed it with a wad of spit. Then something awesome happened. Tobias wondered in his mind what had been Drake's father's fate and Drake told him, "He was a suicide. One day, about a month ago, he slit his wrists. I found him in his bedroom and buried him in the backyard. It could have been worse."

"What happened to your mom?"

"Never had one. She was schizophrenic. When I was two years old she stabbed me forty two times and tried to crucify me. My brother called 911 and they took her away. A couple times I visited her at the institute but I really didn't like it."

"That's a fucked up story. What about your brother?"
"Yeah. I know. It's all good though. And then my brother
lives in Boston. I lost touch with him even before the
phones cut out. I have no idea what happened to him.
It's whatever. What about you? What happened to your
family?"
"Oh. I can kind of relate to you about fucked up family.
My dad was a speed freak. He took my eye out when I
was fifteen, and then he went to jail. I never heard from
him since, but fuck him anyway, I never tried to contact
him. Like two days after that happened my mom died.
She had been sick. And you already know the story
about Olivia. She was my foster mother. She was the
only person I even knew. Except for that rich couple.
They all died on pretty much the same day. I had to kill
the man; he killed his fiancé."
"It's sad nowadays... So did she teach you how to be
psychic or something? That's what Robin was saying."
Tobias laughed at that. "Nah. Not really. You can't really
teach that. It's more like learning to use your intuition;
tuning into the earth and tuning into the heavens, the
other dimensions. Everyone can do that. Logic and
reason help. You need to think like a man and a woman,
not just one or the other. Olivia was something else
entirely. Most of the time I doubted she was even
human. She was a sex addict on top of it, but hey, why
not? Being psychic was one thing, and I'll never
understand how she did it; but she taught me other
things though. The whole world was looking to science
to explain our reality, and I never even cared before I
met her, but she taught me that we actually live in a
holistic and telepathic world as opposed to the
Newtonian machine everybody had thought it was. It's
all a matter of the collective consciousness and being
grounded and centered and available to the powers that
exist in higher dimensions. When we can understand
that everything, you and me, this back hoe, the woods,

the sky, everybody here, and whatever else; everything; when we can understand that everything is all part of one single thing, our race might begin to fathom what is actually going on. We are all thinking the thoughts of a higher mind. Like all of my thoughts combined are just one of the higher mind's thoughts. And all of your thoughts are just one of its thoughts. And sometimes it has to cross reference thoughts and this is why it becomes so hard to stay original. Most of the time everybody is doing the same thing as a few other people and none of them are aware of it so they think they're being original and that can drive artists nuts. But so much has changed though. At this point I can't imagine the collective consciousness is anything like it used to be when she first explained it to me or when I used to watch it play with synchronicity. Don't really see any synchronicity anymore. Nothing is the same anymore. A human life is like a vapor that appears and then disappears but apparently so was everything else. No matter what, we'll always be part of the universe, nothing could take that away from us, I don't think, but this here seems to be pretty much over. You notice the trees haven't even begun to bloom yet?"

"They're probably not going to. Barely any sunlight gets through that weird mono-cloud up there."

"It's like it's made out of ectoplasm or some shit."

"Well, you know how all the animals died off too, right?" Drake asked him.

"Yeah."

"And you notice how you can see the ghosts? We could never see any ghosts before."

"Yeah," said Tobias.

"Well, I think that if all the life on earth is dying, and those clouds are covering everything everywhere, and I assume they are, then all that energy would be trapped. Maybe all the spirits and all the life forces are gathering and something new is being created out of them."

This had occurred to Tobias, but only in a vague passing thought. He was amazed to hear it vocalized. Drake's words reminded him of what he had thought about the clouds in the first place.

"It's like we're turning into Venus. That's what it looks like. The atmosphere is getting thicker and the planet's covered in clouds. It doesn't feel toxic like Venus though; it feels electric. The air is more charged than it used to be. Either way, I think you are completely dead accurate with that. All of the energy from the dead life *is* trapped. My question is why?" He chuckled.

"Something new. Maybe our time has run out."

"Exactly. A matter of time. Time doesn't exist in the higher dimensions. But here- here we are. Digging holes for these counted corpses under some endless overcast. Digging our nails in for dear life hanging off some kind of a cliff over some kind of bottomless abyss. I want to know what's going to happen to us up here. How long can this go on for? It's not food that's gunna do it. We got food. We've got power. We've got fucking everything but I know there is something missing. Something Olivia didn't tell me. I know it's big and I know there is no escaping it; if only because this place is too divine to not add up."

Tobias' words had trailed off a little. He cracked a window and lit a cigarette noticing that the rise in his heart rate coincided with the onset of narcotic haze. The second hole was finished and he maneuvered through the squishing and sinking earth to begin the third.

Drake had been silent and seemed to be equally deep in thought and then he said, "Have you come to terms with dying?"

"That's a good question. I guess so. Yeah. I've thought about it and all I really came up with is that I want to be naked in bed with Arianna when it happens. And I want it to be quick and painless. The stupid part is that I've always wanted to die; to see what happens; what it's like.

Now I don't know. I feel like the longer I stay alive the less I'll be Ok with dying. We put all this effort into staying alive and if dying is inevitable than I wonder what the point is. The funny part is that even if this hadn't happened, we were going to die anyway. Just not this young I guess. And not like this. What about you? Are you ready to die?"

"Hell no. I'm going to go out kicking and screaming." Tobias laughed and Drake smiled a cheeky sparkling grin, lighting a cigarette.

"I have to thank you for all of this though. I don't think I've thanked you yet. I still don't understand how it's all possible. But if it weren't for Endsville we'd probably be dead by now."

"First off, you've thanked me like six times. And second off you really don't have to thank me. By some divine intervention you were chosen to be here. If it weren't for those lights than you'd be just as dead here as you would be out in the rest of the world."

"Well. Whatever. Thank you, Ok?"

"No problem man. We're all glad to have you."

They were silent for a few minutes.

Tobias noticed them first and observed slyly before nudging Drake to look.

Transparent human forms were mulling about in the rain. They wandered around and paced back and forth through the stacks of rocks. For as far as the graveyard extended they could be seen, only distinguishable by height. Sex slightly determinable by posture or the presence of invisible hair. The children played joyfully with each other; circling and dropping and rolling. Tobias noticed they were hesitant, even the kids, to move too far away from where their bodies rested.

"Look how close they are," said Tobias.

"He's like five feet away."

"Open the door and step out."

"Won't they all disappear?"

"They'll come back quicker than last time."
Drake opened the door and they faded away in a wave across the rock garden leaving everything as usual as it had been before. Once again the graveyard was empty.
"That's insane," Drake said.
"By the time we're making the rock gardens we'll be able to walk all around in them. You can put your hand right through them, but it gets a little creepy cuz they'll stare right into you. And if you talk to them they'll just keep staring. If you pay any attention to a single one of them they'll focus right back at you until you look away. Then they go back about their business, whatever that is. Kind of sad though. And scary too; the way they hover around their grave like that doesn't exactly give me a lot of hope for death. It seems like a terrible afterlife. Stuck in one place the way they are."
Tobias kept digging the holes and the ghosts returned. Seated half in and half out of the cab Drake watched them intently with awe.
When the holes were finished, Tobias had Drake jump out while he turned the machine around so the bodies could be pulled and dropped into the ground. Drake stood amongst the skittish spirits and pulled the bodies out into the holes. The ghosts faded out and in; given sudden movements or periods of stillness respectively. After all six had been placed, Tobias once more turned the machine around and pushed the dirt into the holes; packing each down with the flat side of the rear bucket. Soon enough they finished that first task and it was time to retrieve the stones.
Drake held on to the side again and they drove through the meadow back to the first field and to the riverside to collect rocks; a task that over time was becoming more and more difficult. The area of water's edge with easy access to the field had been depleted and now they needed to climb up, and struggle not to slide down, slippery and sloping river banks, carrying the biggest

rocks possible. The whole task took about an hour to complete and by the end they were soaking wet from head to toe and even their skin was saturated. But they had their full bucket load of rocks.

Returning to the graveyard he aligned the front loader in the center of the new mounds and got out to where Drake stood ready by the bucket.

"Alright. Try and make them so they'll last, but be creative too. I think we'll have plenty."

They set about stacking piles of big and small rocks on the graves. The rain poured down harder and thicker than it had been falling before. Tobias' belt was not set to hold the weight of soaking pants and it subsequently needed to be readjusted.

Little brushes across his ears and throat brought his awareness of the ghosts to the forefront. He stood up from his work and focused on a girl about his own height who gazed back at him. The rain didn't splash against her and it didn't trickle down her. It didn't bounce off of her. What the water did do was slow down. This was how they were visible; in essence made entirely of water and trace levels of consciousness as far as Tobias could tell. He couldn't detect any beauty or any ugliness; only basic femininity; soft features and a medium build.

In the corner of his eye, to the left, he saw Drake holding the gaze of one with his hand inside of it and curling his fingers slowly; laughing to himself with a wide grin on and oblivious to everything else.

Above, the lightning had begun again and Tobias noticed it; metallic green. Making the quiet crackles like always. The electricity so constant. Even when there was no lightning there was always some minor electricity seething in the liquid dark. The only influx of color in their lives came from the lightning that permeated through the cloud; all the colors of the rainbow at one time or another; sometimes multiple colors at once. Or crayons. They had crayons, too. Of course, Arianna noticed that there were no rainbows any more- she would- and that there wouldn't be any as long as the sun was blocked from sight.

But to Tobias, the infusion of light shooting through the goo cloud was more beautiful than anything he had seen before the world changed- before the world got dealt the death card. Few people would witness what he saw. Raising another question about how the population was doing. None of the new arrivals came from any sort of city. Except for Aden. It didn't matter. Nobody asked them about anything.

Looking out at the sky Tobias wished he knew when the new moon would be. If he recalled, they usually happen when the sun transits from one sign of the zodiac to the next or a little after. But he wasn't certain of that and the stupid ephemeris didn't list moon phases.

Sick of being wet he went back about the business of stacking the rocks. With any luck the refugees would soon stop arriving at Endsville.

19

The nightclub walls glowed red by pulses in the strobe lights flash. Laser lights shot varying arrays of patterned green and blue lines over the floor and all through the smoke. The high level of treble overwhelmed ear frequencies and techno music bumped bass that shook the walls and rattled the glasses hanging over the bar. Calvin break-danced all over the floor almost invisible within the dense smoke coming from the fog machine. The little one spun in circles and flipped from side to side, kicking his legs high into the air.

The Omega clan danced together and Tobias took a large swallow from a blue bottle of vodka before handing it off to Robin. Aden and Lyn danced on each other; grinding their hips together. Arianna and Cadence danced together; swinging one another to and fro by their arms. Drake and Logan took turns break dancing with Calvin; alternating the center of attention amongst themselves and trying to outdo the last person that had gone; watching one another with arms jokingly crossed.

It was the 12th of June and they were celebrating Aden's 20th birthday. The mood and morale had gotten better and better as the days went along and fewer and fewer people attempted to find salvation at Endsville. Several days passed since they last killed any refugees. Seemingly, that was a sign of less people alive out there.

Tobias two stepped his way over to the bar at the back of the room opposite the stage and went around to mix himself a dry martini.

Earlier that day they all dropped some of the acid that Drake had brought. But by that time his trip had worn ever so thin. The day was spent out wandering in the rainy graveyard and playing with the ghosts. Except for Cadence who started crying because the trees still hadn't bloomed- the trees still had not bloomed- or because they were enjoying themselves while the souls of the dead stared listlessly, and she dragged Robin away to the complex. By nightfall she was over it. The trees ate away at everybody. Constant reminders, much like the sky. But, while the sky could be misconstrued for a thing of beauty and wonder, being surrounded by only dead trees was an in the face and relentless sadness. Almost always the weather rained and poured. But the rain wasn't like it used to be. Much like the air it became charged with some extra passion that never used to be there; releasing the subtlest charges when it touched their skin. After Cadence sulked away, the group took to playing games in the mud; called to the Earth by a candid obligation. They slid and wrestled until they had dug a pit deep into the mud, deep enough to cannonball into, with nothing other than the steady erosion caused by their flailing bodies.

Calvin, who of course wasn't tripping, probably enjoyed the activity more than anybody else; finally acting like a kid again although very aware that his friends were not behaving normally. Tobias explained to him that they were on drugs and then had to explain to him why there was no way in hell a seven year old could ever ingest LSD. Or could he? No. Instead Tobias promised him that later on he could have a drink of alcohol to not feel so left out. After that Calvin's spirits were again lifted and jubilant as they all threw mud around and jumped into the four foot deep pit they had created; while the ninety two dead stood around looking on neutrally.

He sat at the bar drinking his beer and catching his breath when Calvin came over, using the bar to lift himself up onto the stool.

"Can I have some alcohol now?" he asked Tobias who thought for a second and realized that someone could easily get angry about the little act. But why? Who cared? It was the fucking apocalypse; what could it possibly matter if Calvin got some alcohol?

"What kind of juice do you like?"

"Apple."

The only juice on the premises was made from concentrate and the options were limited.

"We have orange and cranberry."

"Orange."

"Alright. I'll make you a screwdriver."

"A screwdriver?" Calvin asked; shouting over the music, his elbows on the bar and his chin on his palms, eyes wide, child's smile in full gear, head tilted in wonder; his blond hair wild and sticking out in all directions.

"It's vodka and OJ."

"OJ?"

"Orange juice."

"Oh."

Tobias made the drink with about half a shot of alcohol and handed it to Calvin.

"Drink up butternuts," he said.

"You're butternuts," Calvin said and then took a sip of the drink and looked off blankly as he tasted it. Then he drank more. And more. Until the cup was empty.

"That wasn't bad at all," Calvin said.

"Do you want to try some beer?"

"Do I ever!"

"Ok then," Tobias said pouring out a glass from a bottle and handing it to the kid, who pursed up his lips when he tasted it.

Robin walked up with the blue bottle in hand and said, "What are you guys doin'?"

"I gave Calvin some beer."

Robin laughed.

"I don't like it. Can I have another screwdriver?"

"Not until you finish your beer. And don't drink it too fast because it'll make you throw up."

Calvin jumped down from the stool, reached up with searching fingertips to get his beer, and walked away.

"Should you be giving alcohol to a child?" Robin asked.

"I only gave him a little bit of vodka and then that beer. He was all bummed out that we didn't give him any acid. I figured that'd cheer him up."

"That makes sense. Whatever. You want to play pool?"

"Dude, I wish we could rock out right now but everyone's grooving."

"That would be pretty sweet."

Aden approached the bar fast from the mist and reached over it, grabbing Tobias by the throat, "What the fuck is wrong with you?"

Tobias reached for the bottle of gin and swung it into Aden's face making an emphatic smack. He realized bitterly that the bottle was plastic and wouldn't hurt that badly. Nonetheless, Robin got a hold of Aden under the arms, pulled him back, and held him.

"What the fuck Aden?" Tobias said.

"You think you're fucking cool giving a seven year old alcohol?"

"Well, come on man, you think you're cool acting like you're really this moral? Lighten the fuck up."

"No, fuck you Toby. If you ever pull that shit again, I'll fucking kill you," Aden said before storming away out down the stairs.

All the girls had gathered around the bar and Tobias took a swill of his martini, lit a cigarette, and said, "Fucking Gemini... He'll get over it."

Aden did get over it. No one saw him or Lyn the rest of that night but the next day he pulled Tobias aside in the kitchen and apologized for his temper, explaining that his temper got like that from time to time. Furthermore, Aden had thought about the issue and understood that given the circumstances it was probably not a big deal for Calvin to be drinking so long as nobody lost sight of the kid's safety. Tobias couldn't agree more and had never been one to hold a grudge. However nothing could make him less anxious about all the guns on the property.

20

He buttoned a loose black shirt and walked out of the apartment past Cadence watching a movie on the couch in the dark. Arianna was going to sleep in the bedroom and Tobias got hungry for something other than the dehydrated stew in their kitchen. He took the

stairs down, and over by the wall of windows in the cafeteria he found the others sitting and watching the storm shaking the complex to the foundation.
In the bedroom he and Arianna had been holding each other while thunder cracked and the lightening illuminated the room with intense reds and purples.
Approaching the group he noticed first that Lyn stared intently through the glass while everybody else talked amongst themselves over coffee and an abandoned round of the dice game Farkle.

"Hi Tobias," Calvin said excitedly.

"Hey man, push over huh?"

Calvin scooted closer to Robin at the end of the bench and Tobias sat down between him and Drake. On the opposite bench of the table sat Aden and Logan thumbing coffee cups, and Lyn completely absorbed in her own thoughts.

Robin and Aden were talking about something but before Tobias tuned into them he noticed that Logan had no shirt on and his skin looked flushed.

"Why were you outside?"

"I was sketching out there earlier and I left my book lying by that first top lift. I had to take one of the four wheelers out to get it. It was pretty bitchin. The winds blowing like 80 miles an hour."

"How come your book didn't blow away?"

"It was in the booth."

"Oh. Why didn't you just leave it? And why haven't you gotten a new shirt."

"What if something happened to the booth? And, we started playing 5000. I had a cup of coffee."

"Are you planning on getting a shirt?" Tobias asked. Drake laughed.

"Do you want me to get one that bad?"

"I wouldn't mind it."

"Fine. I'll go get a shirt," Logan said before getting up and walking down to the glass hallway.

"Thank you!" Aden called after him.

Tobias noticed that Calvin was enraptured listening to Aden and Robin. But then again, Calvin became enraptured by whatever happened around him; observant like a great journalist.

Robin said, "I used to think that all the 2012 shit was talking about the human race going down the wrong path or something like that. When I was younger I always assumed at the last minute everything was going to turn around like some kind of miracle."

"So much for that," Aden said.

"Yeah. I wonder what I would have done differently though."

Tobias said, "The Pleiadians said that if one day you look out the window and everything is turned over sideways you should close the curtain and start meditating."

Lyn chuckled.

"Did anybody predict anything like this? It's everything that's living going FUBAR, right? Not just people?" Robin asked.

"Olivia probably knew. That's why we're all still alive. But none of the psychics I saw on youtube guessed it would be anything like this. They all said that when they projected their consciousness past December 21st there was nothing but a giant white nothingness. Olivia said the same thing," Tobias said.

Drake said, "Do you think that means that we've only got until December to live?"

"If something seems like it probably is, than it probably is. That's how I always look at things."
Robin said, "Look at what's happening in the air. Are we even going to be able to breathe by the winter?"

"I don't think it's the air that's changing. I think it's the ether," Tobias said.

"What's 'the ether,'" Calvin asked.

"The ether is what makes something real. Even

imaginary things. The ether is everything. It's inside of things, around things, and it's the things themselves to a degree."

"I'm made of ether?" Calvin asked.

"I guess so. Yeah."

Aden said, "So if what you're saying is right, and everything is changing; than we're changing too?"

The wind blew a blast of rain crashing into the window and Lyn shot back frightened. Laughter ensued.

"Don't laugh at me," she said calmly, settling her chin back into her forearms.

"Sorry," Aden said.

Logan came back to the table and sat down and Tobias answered Aden's question; "Think about it. If the ether is changing, then everything has to change; including us. And that fits because look at how it's played out. People aren't normally homicidal maniacs and raging rapists or whatever. Everybody's dead or dying. All the animals are dead or dying. God save my cat. And us while I'm at it. Certain changes are universal. Maybe everything is inverting. Maybe up will become down and life will become death. As far as I can tell it was all tied up in the internet and crop circles."

"Why the internet?" Robin asked.

"It's just a thought, I mean, not even that valid really, but the modern crop circles started right around the time the computer was invented. And they accelerated in design and frequency as the technology accelerated, this is all tied in with a theory called Time Acceleration I'll tell you about some other time, and once the internet began making the world 'flat' again the crop circles started screaming at people. And of course they were covered up. Because the Illuminati or the global elite or the top of the pyramid, or whatever it was controlling everything, were such fucking assholes they kept everyone in the dark. Which tells you how important the things were; they went to such great lengths to suppress them. And who knows, maybe they were trying to warn us, and maybe there was something people could have done differently to avoid this? Something might have been trying to save this place. Maybe it was up to humans, the keepers of the third dimension, to usher the world into some new age of light and a rise in frequency and the masters fucked us over. But probably it was beyond our control."

Robin said, "That crop circle we had here was fucking amazing. I never felt anything like that before- when we went in there. Like being part of the wind. Or like just being part of everything. And ever since then I have had the most vivid dreams of my entire life."

"Oh, me too man." Aden said.

"What the hell? I'm so jealous," Logan said, "you guys all have this phenomenal spiritual awakening before we get here. It couldn't wait a couple weeks?"

"Dude, it's a crop circle. It's going to come when it's going to come," said Robin.

"That's not entirely true," said Tobias.

"What do you mean?" Drake asked.

"I mean people used to manifest crop circles all the time. They would appear after somebody had a dream about the shape. Or, more impressively, they'd appear after a group of people were meditating on a specific design. And that design would show up in the field. Give me that pen and pad."

Aden handed him the Farkle score keeping materials.

"We need a design. Something simple that we can all focus on."

"Does this mean we're going to have to meditate?" Robin asked.

"For one thing, that attitude toward meditation is what got us all into this situation in the first place. But no. We can figure something else out. All we need to do is reduce the gap between our mind's here and now and the source. To get to the source we've got to go through all the higher consciousnesses between us and it and those higher minds'll make the circles. There are ways to do it other than meditating; we can fast, or stay awake for a really long time, or we can do something that'll almost kill us."

"I like the last one," Logan said.

"Alright. But we still need a design. You guys think about it. I need to go eat. Figure something out that will almost kill us that we can do right now, too. If we wait too long we'll all lose interest."

Tobias walked away from the table and to the kitchen at the back to find something to eat. From the stainless steel refrigerator he removed leftover Shepard's pie that Lyn had made. Of the three women there, she was the only one that could cook. The men ended up cooking more than the women. Especially Drake and Logan. Drake had been in school at a culinary institute when the shit hit the fan. Logan liked to do anything random like cooking.

It didn't bother Tobias. He didn't mind spending all day digging holes for dead bodies and cleaning rifle after rifle; resetting the alarm and clearing debris; running lines for explosives; doing all these things and then having to make his own dinner. Just one more thing.

Well. It wasn't too big of a deal. But ideally, it would have been nice if the women cooked a little more often. Like all the time. Every day. But who was he to have such requests? But what *did* Arianna do around the place? Clean? The girl didn't even know how to use the washing machine. Oh, well. He didn't need her to do these things for him, when he could do them for himself. At least the more she stayed in bed was the more often she wasn't wearing any clothes. Fuck clothes.

Sitting on a checkered vinyl stool at the steel kitchen counter he finished his plate of food and swallowed the rest of the orange juice from his glass.

The only sunlight left in the world was in the orange juice. All in concentrate form. No fresh fruit anywhere. There were seeds, grow lights, and soil, but nobody cared about the fruit. All the growing supplies were being used to grow pot. Sad. There was still frozen berries though.

Tobias put his dishes into the rack inside the industrial dishwasher and walked out to the cafeteria.

As he approached, Logan said, "Yo, Calvin figured out what we should do."

"What's that?"

Calvin said, "We should all ride the chairlift through the storm."

This made Tobias crack up with laughter and everybody else was smiling too.

"Um. Ok. I'd do that. Does anybody else want to do that?"

"I do," said Logan.

"What about you guys," he said to Robin and Aden.

"I'll do it. But there's no way in hell Calvin's going up there," Aden said.

"But I want to go. Tobias, tell him to let me go," Calvin said.

Robin said, "You guys are fucking retarded. You're going to fall out and I'm going to have to cut your fucking legs off to stop the gangrene."

"Nah, man. They've got the security bars and everything. If anything we'll get struck by lightning," said Tobias.

Robin said, "No. The whole things grounded."

"Are you going to go," he asked Drake.

"Uh, no. I'm not going to go."

Lyn piped up, but didn't look away from the window, "I want to go."

"Yeah. You would," Aden said.

"Alright, Robin, will you run the thing?" he asked.

"Yeah man."

"Then all we gotta do is come up with a symbol to focus on instead of trying not to shit our pants the whole time."

The process of deciding on a symbol took about ten minutes of trying different designs of circles and shapes on paper until Aden came up with something that would be easy to focus on. From Tobias' eye patch they decided that the infinity symbol would be most appropriate. And for the sake of design they superimposed it on a sunburst.

Then they all went separately to their individual living quarters to retrieve warm and water proof clothing; meeting once again back at the lunch table. Tobias stuck his head outside while he waited for the others to arrive. The door flung open and he struggled to close it as the wind of the storm ripped through the mountains shooting raindrops into his face.

One after another they congregated wearing nylon jackets and ponchos thick with warm clothes underneath.

Drake asked, "Are you guys going to ride them back down too?"

Aden said, "That all depends on if my heart hasn't stopped by the time we get up there."

"I'll fuckin take that thing back down, I don't give a shit," Logan said handing off a bottle of rum to Tobias.

He took a deep swig, handed it off, and said, "Yeah. I'll probably take it down too. You can get struck by lightning if you walk out in the middle of that field, so make sure you stay under the cables if you walk down. Who's it going to be, me and Logan in one, and you and Lyn in the other?"

"Sounds right."

"Alright. This is how we gotta do this. It should be simple enough. When we get out there and we're on it, you have to close your eyes when the ride is most intense and as much of the rest of the time too, and you have to focus on the design; the infinity symbol on a sunburst. Do that and at the same time focus on the heavens alright? Focus on the sky and imagine a white light breaking through the goo and going straight into your head to retrieve the image. Got it?"

"Got it," said Aden.

"Yeah, got it," said Lyn stoically.

Logan handed the bottle back to him in response and before drinking Tobias said to him, "I'm going to make sure your ass does it."

"How long is it going to take you to start it up?" Aden asked Robin.

"Bout 3 minutes. You guys know I haven't checked that thing out since it was snowing, right?"

"All the better. I'm sure it'll be fine," Tobias said.

"Whatever you say spaceman. I'm gunna go now. I'll be in the booth at the bottom and I won't be able to hear you scream if somebody falls."

"Can you bring a 4 wheel drive around and shine it's lights up the hill just in case. We'll be out in five minutes. Bunny hill, right?"

"Yeah," Robin said, and threw his hood up around his face and ran out the door to the parking lot.

Arianna and Cadence came walking in from the back hall.

Arianna ran up to Tobias and wrapped her arms around him, saying, "You're a fucking idiot, why are you doing this?"

"Babe. Chill out. We're all going to die come December. What difference is it if we die now? And we'll be fine anyway. We're not doing this for no reason, babe. We're going to talk to god. With any luck we'll get a crop circle out of it."

"How? Everything's fucking mud!"

"They'll figure something out. Water's good anyway. The circles love water. It's a conductor."

Calvin was tugging on Tobias' pant leg saying, "I

want to come."

"First off Calvin, no. Second off, go ask Aden."

Deep red lightning like blood light flashed against the windows, illuminating the ski slopes out front, and thunder rumbled through the building walls. They kept passing the rum around and Calvin yelled and pouted. Cadence took him aside and explained to him why he couldn't go along for the ride. Tobias and Arianna held each other closely.

When it was time, everybody not going up the slope decided that they would stay in the lower booth with Robin. That control center was much larger than the one up top and five people could fit in it comfortably. The rum went around one more time until Lyn tilted the liter bottle all the way back and emptied the contents.

"Everyone ready?" Tobias asked.

A volley of yeses moved through them and they hurried out the door into the battering rain and wind. The ground squished inches down underfoot and they pushed through the storm completely aware of how fragile their bodies were. Tobias knew this was their sole mission in life. As survivors their job was to communicate with the higher being who at that stage of existence could be their only hope, and after the multiple visitations, somewhat of a friend, he romanticized.

They approached the chairlift and Arianna grasped him around the chest pulling him into her for a kiss. "You better not hurt yourself, you asshole."

"I won't." Over her head, he shouted, "You guys ready?"

"Yeah!"

"Or die!" Arianna said.

"I won't."

The chairs of the lift were revolving around the bull-wheel and heading slowly up the gentle slope of the mountain side. The only guide out in the darkness was from the light of the booth. Save for flashes of darkroom red lightning. Tobias kissed Arianna one more time and pushed her away to the others. Then he grabbed Logan by the shoulder and they pushed each other against the wind up to the chairs. Tobias stopped and waited for Lyn and Aden to say goodbye to Calvin and leave him with Drake; when they finished Tobias asked, "You fuckers ready?"

Aden said, "Yeah. Go ahead. We're right behind you."

Thunder crashed against the mountain muffled by the thudding impact of rain on his skull.

The chairlift was made of white metals finished in matte, painted plastics, and steel cable.

"This one?" Logan said.

"Yup."

They jumped onto the chair, Tobias on the right, and pulled the steel safety bar down over their heads. He felt his stomach drop as the chair lifted off into the sky; he thought of falling and realized that the whole scheme might not have been a good idea.

"What the fuck did we do?" he asked Logan. The wind blew the chairs sixty degrees over to and fro all around like a boat in rough seas.

"I don't know but this is sick!"

Looking down he could see nothing but blackness. The rain allowed no focus. Nothing but blurred blackness in all directions. He couldn't even see Logan. Then lightening flashed and the world illuminated. The ground 40 feet below illuminated. He felt sick. Thunder encompassed.

"Alright, man. Start concentrating on the design and the sky!"

"Fuck that. I want to enjoy this!"

"Just do it fucker! I'll push you off this thing! I ain't dying for no reason!"

He closed his eyes and clenched his fingers even tighter around the safety bars. He imagined a white light breaking through the sky and coming down into his skull through the crown chakra. His joints strained against the jolting framework to keep him safely in position. Thunder through the chair and through him. His ass slipped and he used upper body muscles to correct himself. To the white light he presented the designated image. The chair blew backward and he was forced to move one arm around the back to keep from slipping through and falling to the ground.

"Oh shit!" Logan cried out.

Tobias kept the image in his mind. He centered himself in the seven directions and from his heart he wordlessly asked the light to bestow the design upon Endsville.

"Are we going back down, too?" he asked Logan.

"Fuck yeah dude!"

"Alright! Keep focusing on the design!"

Tobias felt the presence of the cosmic intelligence beside them. Behind his closed eyelids his sight illuminated for a second at a time. Blasts of wind and rain came from every direction throwing the chair around in concert.

"Toby, look!"

He opened his eyes and struggled to get his bearings in the chaos. Further up the face of the mountain- far beyond the bunny hill- he saw the orbs of light. They danced and darted away fading out of sight, only to return and continue dancing.

"We should have brought goggles," Tobias said.

The sky lit up and an explosion of sparks burst from the grounding line two chair spaces length ahead of them. The energy of the strike shot over them like a sonic boom. Tobias perceived this with only love and no fear. Ever comforted by the supernatural presence nurturing their spirit.

Watching the flying lights he struggled to keep no thought in his mind other than the design they had picked. He felt implicit awe for them as they hovered across the sky. As the chair twisted and shuddered, he turned his head accordingly to watch the white lights swirling together in spirals, gathering close in a ball and exploding outward like fireworks, then dancing again.

"It's beautiful," Logan said.

Tobias and Logan arrived at the top of the hill and went around the wheel to head back down. The lights of Endsville sparkled subdued in the distance. He wanted to turn around and check on Aden and Lyn but there wasn't enough stability available for him to do so. Holding onto the chair took all of his physical strength, leaving no room for alternate agendas; like holding on to a rock against rapids. His arms were looped around the front and side bar and there was nothing that could make him let go.

In his mind he was about to focus back on the design and the task at hand when the lights shot overhead and swirled over the main complex at the bottom of the bunny hill. The multiple lights circled around one another at the same altitude. Then from the middle of the swirl one light rose above the others, going straight up slowly.

Another followed, traveling upward in a circular motion; in orbit of the first but below it. The third light repeated this pattern; further out than the second. And then the forth. And then the fifth.

Dozens more followed. Many more lights than Tobias had even been aware of. Clenching his teeth and straining all his muscles he focused on the lights, forcing his eyes to stay focused and turning his neck to follow while the rain stung his face and made it difficult to look at anything.

The lights created what resembled an upside down tornado. Upon his having this thought the first light, high in the sky, stretched out a beam from itself and connected to the second in a perfect twist rotating around. The second extended to meet the third and the third did the same to the forth.

The light curved slowly at the top and when all lights were connected the upward spiral presented a whipping motion beginning at the top and sending the lights snapping around the form.

Lightning flashed and in that instant the twister disappeared. It was just gone.

"What the hell?" Logan said.

A skyscraper sized column of white light appeared suddenly beside them on the bunny hill. His jaw cringed at the high pitched electric noise flooding the area. The rain stopped and the wind calmed. The chair settled and rested placidly on the cable.

Tobias exhaled the friction from his chest but did not loosen his grip whatsoever. Everything everywhere had become as illuminated as if it were high noon with the sun shining bright. From the vantage point of the lift all was visible; the meadows and the river, the crow's nest and all the other slopes wrapping their mountain, the junkyard and the graveyard, even the mountains and valleys in the distance.

He looked into the center of where the tube of light met the ground. And although it was nearly blinding to gaze upon, he could see certain lines appearing in the earth within the resplendent rays. Only at the rims; curving sun-rays. The irony had escaped him until right then. He laughed and realized he was twisting his head more and more to stare into the beam.

"Yo. It's time to get off man, Logan said."

It still hadn't begun raining again. He clearly saw the crowd standing by the booth; mouths gaped open as they watched the light flowing from heaven to earth. Real false daylight.

The tower of light vanished, darkness fell, and the storm came blowing back through in full force. They stayed awake the rest of that night waiting for day to brake and sometime around four am the rain stopped. As daylight emerged they could see the design embroidered into the wet grass of the hillside. In the soaking dead grass a beautiful lemniscates the color of dirt lay over a sun with images of overlapping curved rays of light. They walked out to it in the early morning blue light and experienced the love radiating. Love from bone dry black dirt- surrounded by wet mud- that was like glass to the touch.

THE SUMMER OF RISING ANXIETY

21

Cancer

Arianna walked through the dying forest toward the river and twigs crunched underfoot. Lightweight hemp pants sat low on her hips over the bottoms of her two piece bathing suit, her top exposing most of her upper body to be scratched by the branches she struggled to maneuver through. Stepping out onto the footpath she looked for, and soon came upon, the water's edge; wiping the tears from her eyes she pushed through the last of the brush into the clearing around the pool.

Her feet followed the stepping stones down to the rocky shoreline where she located a boulder to sit down on. The weeping subsided and she began to cry from the suffering. She had gone to the water to be alone. Since the rain had finally let up the heat became extreme and heavy with humidity. Until that point she had spent most of her time indoors, and while it was a common disturbance- a stabbing sight, seeing dead trees in summer- that the trees had not sprouted leaves that year, she was emotionally overwhelmed by the absence of life out in the forest. The air was stifling, she inhaled hot breaths with a fresh sweat glistening on her chest

All the unusual features of broken nature made her cry. And she had been doing well lately; finally placing the atrocities beyond her usual thoughts. But some reminders were constant. The trees were an example. The sky remained hypnotically inconspicuous. Too beautiful to bother.

She wiped away the tears, wiped her nose on her knee, opened her eyes, and looked around at the landscape. The water gently fell five feet from a ten foot wide ledge under the bridge into a 30 foot circular pool enclosed by banks of dirt and giant rocks. By her feet the water tapered off from the pool into its usual river form; babbling over rocks. Thick branches blocked out the sky all around except for directly above, either way, that afternoon was particularly gray. Her eyes struggled to see.

Her puffy cheeks were scrunched and stressing under her emotions but her expression changed completely and she coughed and choked when she noticed Lyn sitting up by the bridge and watching.

Lyn smiled back at her sympathetically, stood up, and began walking cautiously toward her on the rocks. Arianna wiped all the signs of emotion from her face and opened her purse to retrieve a hand-rolled cigarette. She lit it and when Lyn came within earshot she said to her, "You scared the hell out of me."

"I'm sorry. I didn't know what to do. I figured you would see me eventually."

"No, don't be sorry. I just came down here to get away from everybody. Go for a swim."

"I can go," said Lyn.

"No. Don't. Please, sit down," Arianna said and Lyn did so. She asked, "What are you doing down here?"

"I brought a thermos of coffee down here and I was writing."

"Oh. What are you writing about?"

"I can't tell you. I can't tell anybody. Aden doesn't even know I write."

"Then it's something you do for yourself?"

"You could say that, yeah. Do you mind if I ask why you are so upset?"

"The trees."

"Ah. I understand. They sure are the worst." Lyn said, looking out over the pool. Her damp and tangled blonde locks fell behind her head tilted by her gaze and her chest thrust forward under the light blue patterns of her bathing suit top.

Arianna couldn't tell if Lyn was observing the sagging branches of the trees hanging over the pool or the ever undulating sky beyond them. The electric veins of the clouds crackled distantly like the power lines used to. It didn't matter. All was lost. There was no telling where she had come from when facing what life had become. The great death caught her attention from its place beyond the mountains and she almost began to weep again but caught herself and took a drag from her cigarette.

"Maybe you should try writing about it."

"I used to write when I was younger. Poetry and journals, things like that."

"It might help you work through everything. It helps me."

"Maybe I'll start. Anything's better than keeping it inside."

"You don't talk to Tobias?"

"I do. But it only helps so much. He doesn't seem to get sad, so I don't think he relates very well. He's used to losing everything."

"How so?"

"He lost his parents when he was younger and lived

in poverty and foster care until Olivia found him. He's been pretty bitter toward the world and I kind of suspect he likes it better this way. Well. He was a silent political activist. He says he used to condemn the US government for the corruption and greed, and people in general, too, for the same reasons. He feels this is more a natural solution."

"That's depressing. The poor guy. Then you should definitely start writing about your feelings."

"I kind of always wanted to write short stories. I wrote one in middle school about a family of seahorses that lived in seaweed and they had all the problems like my family had at the time."

"That sounds cute."

"It was. I might want to do something like that again."

"You should. I really think it would make you feel at least a little better."

"Yeah, I think I will. Hey. How's the water?"

"A little cold, but refreshing- considering it's so hot out here."

"I'm going to jump in and let you get back to writing."

Arianna took off her hemp pants and climbed atop a cluster of boulders at the mid-point of the pool and dove in head first from the highest point.

Leo

The birthday boys sat resting at the highest area of the mountain reachable by foot. Steep and sheer rocks jutted up through the gravel behind them. Though the party would be for Calvin, Tobias' birthday was only a couple days away. His job was to create a distraction for the little one.

Tobias wanted to use the chance to teach Calvin something about the fabric of reality and the effect the

human mind plays upon it's environment. The little boy
had wanted to take a dirt bike up to where they were
and they would have if that mode of transport killed
enough time. The girls wanted at least a couple hours to
prepare. Logan would be looking out for them upon
returning and the lounge under the dome would be
decorated with streamers and what not. Then the clan
would surprise Calvin with cake and presents. Until
then, Tobias had a golden opportunity to give Calvin his
present.

It was noon and the heat was as intense as it had
been any other day that summer but not dry like August
normally is- always so humid. The heat evaporated
water, the river was so low, and the air held the
moisture. From high above the territory they could see
the entire curvature of the planet, the ridges and valleys,
and they could see the way the black goo hugged the
dirty Green Mountains and everything beyond them,
distorting the horizon in an orange tinged black fuzz.

"I'm going to show you how to make a mirror,"
Tobias said.

"Up here? There are no tools up here."

"Not an actual mirror. We don't need any tools. Just
a little spirit. A mirror is the name we give to the
method. I am going to show you how to create a natural
place, that is all your own, where anything is possible."

"Are we going to see the aliens again?"

"Is that what you want?"

"Yeah. It is. I miss them. We haven't seen them
since the night you guys went up on the chairlift."

"That doesn't mean they're not here."

"But I want to *see* them."

"Hm. We can probably do that. But if we do, that's
going to be my birthday present to you. Deal?"

"Deal."

They sat in dusty jeans on dry pebbles among
scattered evergreens. The buildings of Endsville were

like models on a train set far below, about 2.5 kilometers away. The chairlifts appeared organized, fanning out across the mountainside, from that perspective, even the black diamond lift a little off to their right had that human design order. The earth of the slopes was dried up and cracking without any new growth. Only the evergreens produced any foliage, sparsely and more brown than green.

Tobias pointed and said, "Pick a spot, down there where it's less steep. Pick one of the landmarks, like a tree or a rock, or that chairlift, a line in the sand. Anything like that."

"The chairlift."

"Let's go." He took the boys hand and they walked zigzagging down the loose crumbling landscape until they came to an upper bull-wheel and the little wooden shack trimmed in red paint that stood beside it.

"I don't understand what we're going to do, " Calvin said.

"Then I should explain. It used to be that to find any sort of magic in the world you needed to create some distance between you and the rest of the people where you were. People are hideously disruptive to all things natural, including magic, and the problem was that there were people everywhere. 'The mirror' was created to do magic in places as populated as any big city or town. All we needed to do was separate ourselves from the thoughts and electromagnetic disruptions of other's negativity. Because in the ether thoughts are just like actions and they have an effect on everything. Most people's thoughts create a block between them and all things magical and mystical. So when you're submerged in thoughts like that it becomes impossible to do magic because of the adverse conditions. Anything purely natural needs harmony and balance to thrive. Or else it is something attempting to restore the balance, like a volcano or an earthquake. That doesn't matter though.

Am I making sense? Do you follow?"

"What kind of magic? Can we shape shift?"

"Well. Not really. That kind of thing is mostly the stuff of fiction. Unless you're a shaman and you spend your whole life learning how to accomplish something like that. Even then it wouldn't be as simple as it is in the movies I don't think. No. This kind of magic is more innocent. Like, telepathy, for instance. Inside the mirror we can have the same thoughts at the same time and know what we're each thinking without saying anything. And in a sense, that's kind of what has been going on around Endsville and in the rest of the world. So our mirror should even work better than the other mirrors. We used to have to not eat or stay awake forever to make them work. Mushrooms helped a lot, too. Now the entire world is like a great big mirror. Ours will be like a mirror inside of a mirror. And that notion resembles infinity."

Tobias gazed out over the land as he spoke, but Calvin was engaged in the learning process and had his hands in the pockets of his short pants while he stared at his teacher.

He continued, "It used to be a lot different. You used to have to manipulate the ether to achieve the innocent magic, but now it's all around us. We used to have to create some kind of barrier between us and those poisonous thoughts of others and try to capture the ether to have enough of it to work with. It's a lot different than it used to be. That's what the mirrors were for. The ether is a lot thicker inside of them, and when the ether is thick, our thoughts have more substance to them, and it becomes easier to make imaginary things real. Except you have to remember that our greatest accomplishments are granted to us by the Earth. This Earth is the giver of almost everything we've ever had. Nothing is possible if the Earth won't allow it. So when we do our magic, as long as we are Earthbound, it's on the good graces of this planet."

"And our magic is going to be making the aliens come, right?"

"Right. I'll show you the next step. Right now we are going to make the mirror itself. The mirror is a barrier between us and everyone else. What's the mirror?"

"A barrier between us and everyone else," said Calvin.

They stood a few feet in front of the red trimmed wood colored shack and Tobias pointed a line left to right in front of them.

"Good. This line, here, is the actual mirror, Ok? From now on, even if somebody were looking, they would not be able to see us. Nobody'll be able to see the aliens when they come because they'll be with us inside the mirror too. Look up there. All they will see is that wilderness. Now, outside the mirror is everyone else in our clan. They are all down there and if anyone came outside, we would see them. Because we can always see out of the mirror, but they can't see into it. To anybody down there, this looks like the same old mountain it always is. And that's the trick. We become part of the landscape because we keep the Earth inside the mirror, other people outside of it, and we become the ether. It's time to walk back up to where we were, Ok? The best part is how it feels better and better, more surreal, more unbelievable, the deeper inside you go."

Again they held hands as they trudged upward. When they reached the point where they had been sitting previously, Tobias noticed Calvin's mouth was open a little and he was rigidly staring off into the evergreens.

Calvin clutched Tobias' pant leg with one tiny hand and said, "It's the dog from the graveyard."

Tobias squinted and looked into the trees and saw the black dog lurking and watching them. It appeared to be a German Shepard.

"It's Ok. He'll stay where he is."

"Do you promise?"

"I promise. We're inside the mirror Calvin. We decide what happens. He'll stay where he is. Are you afraid of him?"

"Yeah, a little."

"Then tell him to go away."

Calvin shouted, "Go away! Get out of here! Go!"

The dog stopped moving for a moment, looked at them through the pines, turned, and walked away toward the distance.

"That's the last we'll see of him. Ok. Hold my hands. I want you to think about the sky, and the lights, and everything above the goo. But mostly think about the lights. Now, repeat after me: Attention friends in the sky."

"Attention friends in the sky."

"We greet you with infinite love and respect."

"We greet you with infinite love and respect."

"It is our request that you visit us because we have been missing you."

"It is our request that you visit us because we have been missing you."

"We welcome you into this mirror and would like for you to say hello."

"We welcome you into this mirror and would like for you to say hello."

"We miss you."

"We miss you."

"Please say hello?"

"Please say hello?"

"That's good. Now we watch the sky."

"There they are," said Calvin.

From behind the jagged crags of the peak, far over their heads, a single white light drifted toward them shining brightly in the midday haze of sunlessness. The orb made a trilling song of about five notes. F-A-G-B-C. Calvin squeezed tighter to Tobias and they were both fixated on their beautiful friend that had settled over their heads. They were staring directly above themselves at a shimmering sentience. His nerves vibrated and yet the ether stayed remarkably undisturbed. Peaceful. Zen. Breathing deeply he admired the beauty of the glowing ball of light as it eliminated the dark sky from view. Only a moment later the extraordinary being shot off high above them into the sky, disappeared through the sky goo, and then was gone.

Virgo

Singing. Always singing when moving. Such a neurosis so disgusting. Aden, walking, and to himself, harping, always singing when moving. Hands clutching sides, huddled scrunched strides. Singing, always singing when moving. Disgusting neurosis. Dead, not newly dying, been dead for a while; woods crowding and no place to go. Never a place to go. Aden, always walking with no place to go, and singing, heading to the valley cliffs. Dead end. The same valley cliffs, the same dead end, and always singing.

"My feet- have no place to take me. My hands- have no life to make me. But my lungs- have plenty songs to sing me."

"*Ooooooooh*- The choices that we've made. The choices that we've made. Hi hoe the derry oh- what did they mean?"

"If I only had a soul- If I only had a soul- Hi hoe the derry oh- if I only had a soul."

"Where the fuck is god? Where the fuck is god? Hi ho the derry oh- god's a fucking shlomo."

"*Ooooooooh*- I see them in my dreams- I see them in my dreams- Hi ho the derry oh- they're screaming in my dreams."

"I see them on my eyelids- I see them on my eyelids- Hi ho the derry oh. Hi ho the derry oh. Hi ho the derry oh."

"*IIII* could go for some *sssssexxx*. But Lyn is not here so, *IIII* will smoke a cigarette *insteeeeaaaad*."

"*Ooooh fuuuck*. I must have forgotten. Her birthday is tomorrow."

"*Ooooooh*, her birthday is tomorrow- her birthday is tomorrow. Hi ho the derry oh. Her birthday is tomorrow."

More of that. And more of that. Going on like that all the way to the valley cliffs. Sparks underfoot, a world too electric. Barefoot, he couldn't feel them as they danced and crackled in purple patterns from underfoot out over the forest floor. Frail purple sparks underfoot in a Fall too electric.

Dire straits locking him to himself when all he needed was to lift away from himself. He was trapped inside himself and trapped on the ground, too too Earthbound. There was no flying away. Or was there?

Breaking through the scraping branches of the forest he had come upon the rocky clearing at the valley cliffs. An eighty foot drop off into the trunks of more trees that hadn't sprouted all summer long. A far enough fall to take the life from him. No need to postpone the inevitable; that's what he always used to say. If ever there were a prime example, he was staring it down; staring out over the suspended animation forest in the valley and the other peaks that rose sharply or softly eventually merging into that fucked up cloud. The wind blew insistently across his face and bare chest, licking at the sides of his unbuttoned red dress shirt. Straight below was what mattered. Maybe seven yards out.

Aden sat down with his feet over the ledge. From the cargo pocket of his khaki shorts he retrieved a book. If anything were a commodity at Endsville it was books.

He read the copy of Ulysses he had borrowed from
Arianna.

Tobias had already read it and recommended it to
him. Now he was about a couple hundred pages into it.
The white of the books jacket was stained with blood
and dirty finger prints. Aden, like Tobias, found the
circumstances of everyday people completely refreshing.
Like a drug, he read James Joyce to help himself discover
a remembrance of how things used to be. Like a dream,
he envisioned a history hard to believe.

THE AUTUMN REDUNDANT

22

For all the time that had passed and for all the
terror they had witnessed, and for all the wondrous
bonding that took place at Endsville, certain clan
members never lost sight of how life managed to
maintain a state of perpetual harmony; somehow the
balance could always be reset. Only in the beginning
was there any real discord. And as the refugees
numbered fewer and fewer, tranquility among the
residents become more and more of a reality.
Eventually, tending the weapons transformed into
tending the marijuana. Rigging the booby traps gave
way to rocking out on the stage at the hotel bar. Weeks
and weeks of insomnia gave way to leisurely naps in the
summer breeze lying out under the overcast sky.

At a place with such amenities as Endsville, the sin
of boredom was never a concern. Often times it was the
simplest of activities that captivated the most. Aden was
an avid soccer player, and before he took ill had had a
way of coercing everybody into playing countless
unorganized games when one by one, Cadence and
Arianna first, players would drop off from exhaustion
until eventually only Logan was kicking the ball with

him. And even after Logan had lost interest, Aden would spend the rest of the daylight hours out on the bunny hill kicking the ball high into the sky over and over again.

The guys would take the armada of dirt bikes through the unchartered regions of their mountain and those mountains surrounding them as well. There was even a 50cc motorcycle which Calvin took to like how a newborn whale goes straight to the surface; he just got on and went. Calvin's fascination with the elusive black dog made those dirt bike excursions an excellent male bonding activity. They all wanted to capture the animal and as such brought along raw meat and nets as well as guns for protection and a video camera for documentation to show the girls. But the dog was rarely seen, with only six sightings total; three by the graveyard, always at the opposite end than the witness, two times it had been glimpsed sniffing around the junkyard or jumping from wreck to wreck, and then once inside the mirror. That final experience had set off Calvin's quest to bag his trophy. Tobias allowed this to go on with a cautious and weary eye. After becoming comfortable with ghosts and aliens, a hell hound did not seem to be the furthest leap of imagination. Or any leap at all, really. Almost everybody was in agreement that the dog was in fact a hell hound. Whatever the reality of a hell hound might actually entail. There did not seem to be any threat. The dog always kept its distance and nobody told Calvin the animal was most likely supernatural. The clan took for granted that the hound was connected to the dead in some way, or at least to some facet of surrealist, and no misfortune ever came from their presumption.

All the while there was the issue of Calvin's poltergeists. Night after night and day after day decorative objects dropped from the walls and locked windows flew open. Doors opened and closed and furniture jolted against the walls. Light bulbs exploded. Sometimes Calvin's incidences occurred the moment he was left alone and other times they happened when the whole clan was together. Yet the occurrences were never violent. The initial crash could seem violent, but any time the event was prolonged, the mysterious happenings were always subtle. Garbage cans vibrated out from their corners and ceiling fans turned slowly and stopped and reversed slowly and stopped. The only thing that seemed to keep the eerie disorder at bay, other than intrinsic inactivity, was to move Calvin to another area. Or, like a seizure, just wait for them to pass. Nonetheless, everyone rallied around his plight and in a group effort the child was never left alone. On a rotating basis he stayed in the bedrooms of the different inhabitants of Endsville.

Tobias tried to exorcise him on multiple occasions but to no avail. Smudging, praying, dowsing; nothing worked. The reason for this was that Calvin had grown to adore the poltergeists for the attention they caused the others to bestow upon him. As if he didn't get enough attention to begin with. Nothing Tobias could do would vanquish the supernatural phenomenon if Calvin didn't want it to be vanquished. The strange happenings were a way to keep all eyes on him.

Meanwhile, the killings had become a sort of taboo. Not a strict taboo, but a basic courtesy to themselves. For a very long time it seemed like the killing would never end. Those were the darkest of times, for most had not yet come to terms with the apocalypse. Or more accurately; most had not put it out of their minds. During those early weeks they were all different people. They still were different people. But they were different different people then.

During the killings they couldn't talk about trivial things. They couldn't smile while passing in a hall. When they drank it was to dull the sorrow and to create a shadow over themselves so others could not see into their misery. As if anyone were looking. Even without direct sunlight, there was not enough darkness to blind them from the ugliness.

Day and night the alarm rang. The explosives blew away more and more of the same area of trees until there was a vacant and charred blast radius where the road met the parking lot. After a few kills they didn't even flinch anymore. Nobody slept, they were too tired to care; too numb; no longer pondering if maybe the psychic had manipulated them and that maybe they shouldn't kill mercilessly. After all, killing still *felt* wrong.

Aden arrived only a day after Tobias and for the first week Robin, Tobias, and Aden were doing the entire task from foxholes built into the higher roadside ground; using the UPS truck to get them out of their vehicles to walk the last quarter mile, upon which time they were met with an explosion, floodlights, a second explosion under the idling vehicles, and gunfire. The girls sometimes held the two million candle power flash lights and all the refugee bodies were cut loose of the mortal coil; usually in groups of three or four, often at atrociously young ages. Many groups fired back but there was no defense like a good offense. They practically spent all their time waiting in the woods during those days.

Lyn arrived alone and the white light in the sky danced, illuminating the relentless darkness. Within a couple weeks Logan and Drake arrived and the girlfriends were relieved of field duty. More killing ensued. More explosives and M-16s. More sleeplessness, until finally they got an alarm and simultaneously began resting more and more. Soon periods of three and four days were going by without the alarm sounding. The aliens had visited three times at that point and everybody had seen them except for Calvin, who finally saw them as they performed the grandest of feats and quelled the raging storm.

The first month and a half was a spinning time for them. Except for Tobias. For Tobias, the spinning began when life returned to normal. When the refugees were no more. He knew their absence could only mean one thing; there were no more refugees because there were no more people left to seek refuge. Two months from civilization to extinction.

Robin collected personal artifacts of the refugees; framed family photos, stuffed animals, snow globes, rosaries, and a myriad of other items he kept displayed on their own glass table inside his apartment.

Tobias did the only thing he could think to do and spent more and more time meditating with Arianna and Pluto. But only when sober. Getting drunk was one other thing he could think to do. And sex was the only other thing he could think to do. Sex was important to everyone. Especially Logan and Drake.

Scorpio

"Here's to the Age of Aquarius and the fucking photon band," Tobias said.

Drunkenly they slammed their shot glasses back down onto the coffee table. Tobias fell straight back into the sofa with his feet planted on the floor. Tobias, Arianna, and Cadance were all wearing pajamas. Robin still wore his daytime blue-jeans and black t-shirt and flipped through the pages of an old Playboy. It was late. Or early by another standard. Robin sat straight up taking drags of his cigarette. The girls sat in the corners of either couch playing Spit with a deck of cards.

"This whole thing is falling apart," Tobias said.

"How so?" said Robin.

He rolled his head around a little trying to clear it, and said, "Because man. It used to be nice here. Now

Aden and Lyn can't be bothered to come around anymore. Fucking Tweedle Dee and Tweedle Dum don't do anything but smoke weed constantly. You guys are still chill. Mr and Mrs. Perfect, the Sagittarius and the Capricorn, Jupiter and Saturn in all their glorious glory. Me and her fucking suck."

"Hey, you suck. Not me," Arianna said.

"Fine. Whatever. We're a lion and a scorpion alright. But it feels like we're sick and dying, barely alive in some desert without another living soul in a million miles. Which is retarded because there's half a dozen other people out here. You guys are in the same room as us. Even Calvin ain't enjoying himself anymore. You notice his poltergeists aren't half as bad as they used to be?"

"Yeah, why is that?" said Robin.

"Because he doesn't care anymore. He mopes around and eats fucking peanut butter sandwiches every day because we lost hope. He doesn't even ask us to cook for him anymore and that's the only thing he knows how to make. That kid is a mirror image of our morale. If he's not happy, then we're not happy. And he's not happy. *And* we all need to start cooking for him more."

Robin said, "Well think about it. Who were we kidding anyway? Yeah. We had a good summer and shit, but look at the circumstances. We are still waiting to die. Olivia didn't say one word about what's coming past December 21st in that booklet she wrote. All she said is that we can't leave this place. Which I guess is alright. But us four here are still just part of nine people standing on a roof with a flood coming in. If you're wondering why Aden doesn't come around anymore, it's because he can't move from one room to another without singing out loud. He can't even sing quietly. He has to sing at like speaking volume. And I doubt Lyn has said more than thirty words to anyone of us since she's been here. Aden's the only one she talks to. As for the weed-heads, I say good for them. If I liked smoking pot I'd sit in the hotel lobby all day with 'em. Yeah, we're not having as much fun as we were in the summer but you of all people should understand why."

"I do understand. What I'm saying is that we're falling apart. This whole thing fell apart. And you're right. It's not so bad. Not yet. But this is the beginning of the end. We're a mirror image of reality and if we're not alright then reality isn't alright. Because things fall apart toward the end. The whole world was crapping out before all this shit came down. I can't forget the worldwide genocide; wage-slavery and corruption. That's probably the reason why Olivia didn't include anything about what's going to happen after December 21st. There's nothing there. I don't know what's going to happen but I really doubt we'll make it past that day."

Arianna said, "If we're alright now; the electricity didn't hurt us and we didn't commit suicide or murder suicide, or suddenly become autistic and then die like all the fucking adults; I don't see why we won't be alright after that day."

"Yeah. Even if something is going to happen between now and then, can't we pretend like it won't? You don't have to bring it up," Cadence said.

"Fine. I'm sorry. It's been bugging me. I'm sick of everything humming. I don't think we were supposed to make it this long. It doesn't feel like a world humans are supposed to live in anymore. With all the changes, I wouldn't be surprised if that shit in the sky decides to crush us one day."

Robin said, "Then it's our time. You always talk about the spirit world. Maybe it's time to put *our* money where *your* mouth is."

Tobias pulled the four shot glasses together and poured more whiskey into all of them. He said, "It shouldn't have been violent. That was the problem.

Gandhi was the only person who ever had it right. If we had left violence out of our world, this whole extinction could have been a lot more peaceful. American's were always so obsessed with violence. It wasn't good for our spirit. Violence was what kept us from becoming enlightened. The whole world was desensitized to violence by our culture and our culture was desensitized by the media and video games and that changed reality so much. Real violence is an integral part of being alive and to some degree necessary, at least on an animalistic level. We should have learned from the violence in other nations, the sacrifices in Rwanda or wherever else, should have been a lighthouse to guide us in the right direction. But the fake violence, the video games and the movies- they shoved it down our throats and blinded and deluded the kids with it. The catholics did the same thing in the dark ages by worshiping, and shoving down throats, the violent death of Jesus; violence begets more violence. If you worship a symbol of violence only more violence can come from it. Our government was violent because our children were violent and vice versa. And it doesn't even matter anymore.

"But people shouldn't have tolerated so much. Look what *we* did just so we could be here peacefully. People fucking tolerated everything. Say we don't make it past December 21st; you know how many more people we could have taken in? I'm sorry. I'll shut up. You guys ready for another shot?

Robin and Tobias waited a minute for the girls to finish up a round of Spit and then they all took another shot together.

"I have to go to sleep. Are you coming," he asked Arianna.

"I'll be in in a little while," Arianna said.

Tobias said goodnight to Robin and Cadence then got Pluto from the cushioned stool he sat on looking out the window. Tobias held the cat to his chest and took a moment to gaze out over the swirling mountain, and to observe the blurry green throbbing of the electricity across the sky. Then he stumbled past his fellows into his apartment, closed the door, put the cat down and lit a cigarette. He disrobed, dropping his clothes to the floor- Arianna would pick them up the next day- and he stumbled to the bed. Pluto stayed close to his ankles. He smudged out the cigarette in the living room ashtray, went to the bedroom, and fell into bed, pulling the covers over himself. Pluto hopped up onto the bed and curled up in the crevice at the small of Tobias' back. Tobias fell asleep within a moment. He wouldn't remember any of the things he just said to the others. An irrelevant fact, for it would not be the last time he would say the same things. Nor was it the first time.

Hours passed before he began to dream.

In the ethereal winds he tried to catch his bearings and discover where he was. All he could distinguish was that he was in a small uncomfortable room. There was a desk bolted into the wall and a stool bolted into the floor. Behind him was a bunk bed also attached to the wall. All of the furniture was painted green and chipping in some places. Embedded in the brick wall was a four inch wide and thick Plexiglas window too scratched and distorted to see through except for in the upper right corner, where on tip toes he could look out to a small grass clearing, within the perimeter of the razor-wire fence, where he saw all of his Endsville friends throwing a Frisbee. He was in jail. But it was not prison, it only resembled a prison. Tobias was back at the St. Mary's center for traumatized boys. But St. Mary's had never looked so much like a prison. Upon this realization the heavy green cell door clacked open and Olivia stepped in. She was naked and covered head to toe in dripping blood.

"You didn't bother putting any clothes on?" Tobias asked her.

"You know you like me better this way. How you been feeling?"

"Like I'm going to burn down Endsville while they sleep."

"You don't have to do that. None of you will survive the winter."

"Why?"

"Your time is up. You know that this life is only one life. There is something infinitely more splendid awaiting you in the spirit world."

"What is it?"

"You'll know soon enough. Go down to rec."

Tobias embraced Olivia's naked body and she held him close in return. He cupped her ass in his hand, squeezed, pushed his crotch into her and held it there for a moment, then walked past her out onto the second tier of a prison he had never seen before except for maybe on television. The stairs down were to the left of the vacant triangular concrete enclosure lined with doors. There was a person wearing rags standing by the guard station on the first floor with their head looking down and her face hidden by falling dirty hair. He stood face to face with this person. She raised her head and in his eye tears welled instantly at the site of his mother. She still had the sores on her face from the AIDS.

"Do you miss me Toby?" she asked.

"Of course. Do you have any idea what's going on?"

"I miss you too. I've been watching you. I really wish I could have known Arianna. She's a really nice girl."

"Is that what you came to tell me?"

"No. You've been afraid. You cannot be afraid. Every second of your day is precious and you are wasting them. This is the end of Earthbound life in the third dimension. You need to embrace this. When you cross over, I'll be waiting for you. Olivia, too. Sometimes we spend day after day together watching you. Even your father is decent over here. He wanted me to tell you how proud of you he is."

"Fuck him."

"You'll like him over here. He's just like you."

"What's it like when you die?" Toby asked.

"Different than it used to be. More alive than your world now. I love you Tobias. More than you could ever realize. The love here is so different."

"I love you too. But how are we going to die?"

Tobias jolted awake when Pluto's hind legs kicked into his cheek as the cat jumped toward something at the end of the bed. It was daytime and Arianna lay asleep beside him. He needed water.

Sagitarius

Tobias' guitar rang out and he tapped the strings of the amplified acoustic with his left hand as the song ended. The fog machine permeated a supposedly harmless chemical smoke all around him and the band as they performed on stage in the darkened hotel bar.

Speaking into the microphone Aden said, "We wrote this last song a couple of days ago just for tonight."

Robin struck his drumsticks together repeatedly, counting off the tempo, and on the forth clack he rolled the snare and struck the crash symbol. The heavily distorted guitar set into deep rhythm as Logan attempted to add further depth on the bass guitar. The amplifiers cranked out the deafening metal across the room. They played through the heavy intro riff twice with thundering lows and screaming highs and then at the first verse the ensemble softened the product to an angry melody and Aden sang the lyrics.

"I wish that I could take you to the mountain and let bugs get ya." The tom toms rolled with the palm muted guitar strikes and they let into it again. "But I'm too busy diving the seas, for pearls of clarity." Aden's voice heaved the rasping passion. "What would the future have thought of our culture, anyway? If lizards don't mind dying then what makes us think we will, anyway?"

Robin rolled the snare and attacked the crash symbols while Tobias thrashed the strings. The tempo quickened and Aden sang, "We don't care about the world anymore. No. We don't care. No. Not anymore. We don't care about the world anymore. No. We don't care. No. Not anymore."

They upped the intensity and went into the next verse. "The future used to be made of past memories. Then one time time died, now we're all stuck inside."

His fingers rolled across the strings, stopped, the drums beat, and he started again.

Aden, wearing all black and pacing back and forth, kept going, "We are still alive inside of synchronicity. Wondering if love will save us. Will love save us?"

The symbols shattered the ether and in their wake the guitar droned over the new slow rhythm of the bass drum. Tobias played three different power chords striking the first quick, second slower, and letting the third ring out. He repeated this and Aden came in with more vocals, "Alive on this mountain, we confuse god. Alive on this mountain, we go bump in the night. Alive on this mountain, we worship Satan. Alive on this mountain, we are still alive!"

Robin went wild on the drums and Tobias matched it; his fist insanely tearing at the strings; his left hand couldn't be contained to any measure or combination of frets. His amplifier screamed and mutilated the ambiance.

Aden kept screaming, "We are still alive! We are still alive!" Logan's bass guitar purposefully drowned out as he struggled to make any sense of it.

"We are still alive!" Aden screamed, stretching his

voice to its absolute limit.

Robin adjusted the tempo and Tobias followed. Aden began to sing again, "Alive. Alive. Alive," carrying the notes in a sweet and beautiful harmony with the guitars.

They had broken through into a new, more pleasant, melody. "There's no way to know, if we'll be alive tomorrow. We can plainly see that we are here now. If it's our time to die than it's our time to die. Whoever said death is wrong told you a lie. Death is one last thing you haven't tried. So if it's our time to die it's our time to die. And with any luck, I'll see you on the other side."

"With any luck I'll see you on the other side. With any luck I'll see you on the other side." Robin and Tobias slowly upped the tempo with him. "With any luck I'll see ya on the other side. With any luck I'll see ya on the other side. With any luck I'll see ya on the other side!"

The guitar exploded again and Robin beat the drums with everything he had. Aden screamed, "I'll see you on the other side! I'll see you on the other side! I'll see ya on the other side! Maybe, I'll see you on the other side! On the other side! On the other side! On the other side! On the other side! The other side! The other side! We are still alive! The other side! Still alive! The other side!" Aden's voice weakened and began to fade away and the drums rolled down and out, slapping the symbols as they went. In the swinging beams of laser light Tobias slid his left hand up and down the neck of the guitar, creating bolting sounds of closure. Logan had altogether stopped making noise.

The crowd jumped on their feet and their cheers became audible as the music faded out. The drums stopped and Tobias played a few more notes.

Drake shouted, "Yeah, yeah!" And all the girls, even Lyn, were screaming inaudible high pitched encouragements. Calvin still jumped around to the music, though it had ended, when the lights came on.

Aden said into the microphone, "That's it for tonight, guys. I want to thank you all for coming out to see Endtimes perform live. From our hearts to your's we wish you a happy end times. Thank you very much. We love you all!"

Capricorn

Tobias placed his guitar down onto its stand and Arianna came running up onto the stage throwing her arms around him. He made sure the guitar wouldn't fall over and then turned his attention to her.

"You were so good," she said.

He kissed her and said, "Thank you. Not bad for our first and probably last show ever."

"It was really good. Did you see Calvin dancing?"

"Yeah."

"One of his spells sent the ashtray flying off the table."

"Oh yeah? That's a compliment if I ever heard one."

Logan came up to Tobias, grabbed his hand, pulled him close, and said, "Yo, that was fucking awesome man."

"I know right."

"I kinda sucked, but you guys were awesome."

"I know. You did kinda suck. Let's do some fucking shots, huh?"

"Hell yeah," Logan said and bounded off.

"Baby, can you put some music on the stereo?"

"Yeah, give me a kiss."

Tobias kissed his girl and took a look around when she walked away. The lights came on and he saw Robin and Aden kissing their girlfriends. Calvin was jumping around with Drake.

He noticed his nerves twitching with adrenaline and lit a cigarette from his pocket. Logan stood behind the bar waving him over.

The clock had rolled over midnight a few minutes before and it was December 21st. Tobias had no idea when the sun would conjunct the sacred tree in the sky. If it hadn't already. The event may have happened in 1998 for all he understood.

Logan poured shots for everybody including Calvin who had become something of a heavy drinker over time.

Eight of them stood in a line in front of the bar at the back of the room. Logan raised his shot glass and said, "Happy end of the world everybody!"

Some of them repeated it, "Happy end of the world," and they drank their shots of whiskey together. The Omega clan.

Nobody knew what was coming. Two seasons of contemplation had provided no insight, the same way decades of contemplation had prepared nobody for the extinctions. They spent that night smoking joints and listening to music. The band jammed a couple more improvised songs during the witching hour.

As a collective they had previously decided it would be best for them to live every minute as if it were their last. The mystery taxed all of them, but after so many months of anticipation all that remained was relief that the wait was finally over. The day was upon them. Even if in all reality it was just another day and meant nothing.

They drank themselves into oblivion playing games of beer-pong.

Eventually, around 3 AM Tobias and Arianna said goodnight and gave hugs all around in case they weren't going to wake up the next day. They stumbled back to the main complex and took the elevator to their quarters where Pluto welcomed them with a meow. Within minutes they were passed out with their cat sleeping between them.

23

From a totally thoughtless blackness, where reality was neither a memory nor an aspiration- like the first page of the bible- came an unfamiliar voice.

"Awaken."

He sat straight up in a jolt and the pain shot through his skull. He couldn't see anything around him save for the shadowy blur of morning. Reaching, he felt for Arianna's body lying exactly where it should beside him. That voice.

"Don't speak, only listen," said an inhuman voice with an androgynous tone.

Terror in his heart caused him to bodily spin around, frantically searching for the source, disoriented from the hangover.

"Be still," it told Tobias.

The voice had no volume. He knew what it said and perceived the inflection the words were being said with, but he didn't actually hear anything. Nobody in his bedroom. Nothing out of place. Everything as it should be. Arianna had not woken up. Pluto stood by the door.

Tobias' vision was coming back to him in a minor degree. Then he realized that it had happened. The day had come. It was the 20 twelve he had been waiting for. Quelling the fear was all he could think to do. His nerves had seized his upper body; his chest, shoulders, and biceps weren't allowing him to inhale. Calm down, he told himself in his mind, behind the hyperventilation.

"You must not be afraid," the voice said. "We have come for you Tobias. We are going to take you with us for a period of no longer than ten hours. You are welcome to bring Arianna if you so choose. Do not speak. Your body is severely dehydrated."

He became aware of where the voice was coming from. They were in his living room. More than one.

Three. Pluto sat hunched over and sticking his nose against the bottom slit of the door, confirming there was something out there.

"Drink this Tobias." The clear blue water bottle he kept next to the bed was floating in the air directly in front of his face. He coughed emotion and reached for it. There was a mystifying gentle tug of resistance when he removed the bottle from where it hovered; an odd sort of happiness and joy causing him to weep.

"Drink."

He unscrewed the lid, tilted the bottle back, and swallowed the room temperature water all at once. The day had come. It was really happening. The container was empty and he felt his body surging the hydration through him to the places he needed it the most; his brain, certain organs, his shoulders, and his hips.

"Put on comfortable pants and go to your door."

He stepped out of bed and walked to his closet. Folded atop some other clothes on a shelf in the closet there was the pair of pants he lounged in. He put them on and gave a cursory glance to Arianna who could sleep through spontaneous combustion.

"She will need water also. Take the water bottle to the faucet." He went back and got it from the side of the bed. "There are three of us in your living room. You must not fear us. We are the Zeta Reticuli, the ones you know to be called the Grays. You will recognize us from pictures. You must utilize all of your mental strength to not be frightened. Before opening the door you must prepare yourself, to your fullest ability for viewing us. Know no fear."

Tobias picked up his Lemniscates patch from the nightstand and set it in place over his head. He breathed deeply thinking, fuck. Looking out the window it was just another electric day. Blue lightning pulsed shining rays through the goo.

Grays? They were the last thing he would have

expected. If anything he had been waiting for the blue orbs of the Pleiadians. He stood at the door. There were Grays on the other side.

"Do not open the door until you are ready."

Pluto sat waiting. Tobias looked down to the cat and the cat looked up at him then back to the door. They were both ready.

He breathed deeply, opened the door, and beheld the visitors. Exactly as in the pictures. They were not frightening whatsoever. If anything they seemed kindhearted and innocent. Two of them were seated on the sofa. Their little grayish blue legs didn't even try to reach the floor. They stuck straight over the edge like a child's would. The third alien was about three and a half feet tall and stood in front of the window by the balcony with the mountains rising and falling behind him. They had heads that were only slightly too large for their hairless and seemingly featureless bodies. Shallow rims sunk around their large glossy black eyes. The two on the couch seemed excited and happy; making smiles with their stiff slit mouths. The one by the window held a serious expression, not threatening, with a very matter of fact straightened posture.

"Get her some water now. We will have ripe fruit for you later."

All three kept their eyes on him, the standing one was doing all the communicating. He could feel that much. They seemed to have no concern other than whatever motive they had with Tobias. He stepped out past them; hesitant to turn his back until it occurred to him that distrust was rude.

"Your reactions are not rude. They are natural and we expect as much and usually worse. If anything is the truth, you are able to accept us better than the rest of your kind left on this planet."

Being around them was like being around Olivia. He had questions.

"We cannot tell you what you want to know. That is not our purpose. We are the transporters. Our purpose is to deliver you to the Maya at Alcyone."

The central star of the Pleiadies star system.

"Correct."

Jesus Christ, he thought, turning on the cold water faucet in the bathroom. He filled the water bottle a little and drank some more before filling it all the way for Arianna. His body ached all over and his head ached. He carried the water with shaking hands past the aliens; smiling when he saw the Gray closest to him holding it's long nubby fingertips over Pluto's head while the cat rubbed it's chin against them. The other leaned over to watch the interaction.

"Close the door and explain to her who we are and what is happening. You should wear comfortable clothing, pajamas, and your journey will not require shoes or excessively warm clothing. The environment will be climate controlled to your needs."

Tobias did as he was instructed.

He put the water down on her nightstand and knelt beside her; wiping the tears from his cheeks.

Arianna's mouth was wide open and there was a moist spot on the pillow from her drool. Her curly brown hair fluffed up around her cheeky face. He pulled the black comforter down from over her, put his hand on her shoulder, and gave her a nudge. She did not wake, so he gave her another.

"Baby. Wake up," he said, shaking her gently. She was not waking so he nudged her more forcefully, "Wake up."

She finally opened her eyes then squeezed them shut and shuddered all over.

"Ooh. What time is it?"

He looked at the clock and said, "It's almost eleven."

"I'm going back to sleep," she said.

"No. Look at me." She did with open eyes adjusting and he continued, "Listen to me. It's important. Sit up and drink this." She sat up, leaning on one arm, exposing her plump bare breasts strewn with impressions from the sheet, and he handed her the water.

He waited for her to finish chugging and when she handed the bottle back to him he placed it down and said, "I'm just going to say it, Ok? There's aliens in the living room. The little gray one's. But they're real friendly."

"Fuck you," she said.

"No. I'm not joking. They're sitting on the couch. The called themselves Zeta Reticu- something."

"Zeta Reticuli," said the voice.

"Zeta Reticuli," said Tobias.

She wrapped the blanket around her body, "No," she said in disbelief, looking to his face for signs of truth or lies.

"Yes." He got up and handed her a t-shirt from the closet and she hurriedly put it on.

"Tobias. What's happening?"

"They said they're taking us on a trip to another star called Alcyone," he was smiling by that point as he handed her pajama pants and put a shirt on himself.

"No. No. I'm scared. Make them go away."

"Babe. We have to trust them, come on, I'll show you."

He heard the phantasmal voice say, "Hello Arianna."

She looked to the wall where it had come from. "Hi," she said, beginning to cry.

Then it said, "We would never harm you. Please consider us your friends. We love you."

"Ok," she said.

"Please come. Look upon us."

"Ok," she said.

Arianna pulled up her pants and grabbed for Tobias' arm. He helped her up out of bed and onto her feet. She squeezed him and said, "I'm scared."

He waited for the voice to reassure her and when it did not he said, "Don't be. They are really nice. They're playing with Pluto. Are you ready to see 'em?"

"I guess so," she said clutching Tobias' waist as he put his hand on the doorknob and pulled the door open. Arianna looked into the living room only to retract and curl into his chest.

"Please look again," said the voice.

From against his chest, she turned her neck slightly and looked through one eye. He felt her body loosen. On the couch Pluto looked twice his normal size lain out over the one on the rights' legs. The one on the left, who had scooted closer, absentmindedly stroked the cat while they all, even the one standing, smiled at Arianna. After a moment of silence she let go of Tobias altogether except for the hand she kept on his upper arm.

"Do either of you have any negative concerns about traveling with us?" the voice asked.

"Sort of. Why are we wearing pajamas?" Tobias asked.

"For comfort. Your bodies will remain contained safe and inert in our earthbound vessel as your consciousness travels through the galaxy. You will not feel any different. You will eat in space and your earthbound bodies will become nourished."

Tobias wasn't about to try and understand that.

"Can anybody else come, or is it just us?" he asked.

"You will be accompanied by Drake. This person was chosen for their exhibition of the character trait you know as integrity and he will serve the purpose of witness throughout your interactions with the Mayans."

"Where is he now?" Arianna asked.

"Drake is already within the Merkaba- our system for intergalactic travel- and awaiting your arrival. Is there another quandary that has not yet been expressed?"

"Do you guys want to bring Pluto?" Tobias asked. "No."

"Then which way to your craft?"

Pluto jumped down from the couch and sauntered to Tobias' heels. He picked up the cat and held him in his arms. The two seated aliens scooted off the couch and stood to their feet.

"We are now going to create a portal to our craft in what is that doorway there." The head alien pointed stiffly past Tobias and Arianna at the door to the communal area. "Please allow a moment for us to create the portal."

Surrealistically, moving steadily and appearing focused, the two secondary aliens walked past them. Arianna again clutched Tobias. He noticed their small feet and marble round toes; their knees that hardly bent as they moved; the slit in their flesh where genitalia would be on a man; their flush stomach and long chest with no nipples, nor protruding evidence of ribs. The door swung open fluidly without being touched and one of the identical two moved out into the other room.

The aliens positioned themselves facing one another, stopped moving completely, and locked eyes. Soon the dark and shaded room where they had watched television, drank alcohol, and played dice all year became steadily more and more illuminated as though by florescent lights on dimmer switches with limitless lighting capability, until nothing but luminance could be seen.

The light flooded into their apartment, slowly becoming more and more painful. Tobias couldn't bare the stress any longer and had to look away into his own shadow. Arianna had done the same.

"The intensity will subside in a moment," said the voice. Almost instantly he felt the encompassing radiance of the energy lessen and recede. He looked back at the doorway and saw a single Gray facing them for only a second before stepping to the side of the portal. Whiteness like a sunbeam was all that could be seen inside the doorway that glowed like countless simple light bulbs.

"You may put your cat down. He will not go into the portal."

They both spoke to the alien by the balcony while shifting their attention to the white light intermittently.

"Can we smoke on the spaceship?" Arianna asked.

"No. That is not possible for you."

"Is there windows? Should I bring a book?" he asked.

"All will be transparent. It is not possible for you to bring along items. If you could bring a book you would not read it. Idle time will not be how you presume."

"Then I guess we're ready. What's it going to be like walking through that light?"

"Is it going to hurt?" Arianna asked quickly.

"The portal will not hurt for it is in essence no different than the doorway it was made from. Your eyesight will be temporarily affected. Aboard the Merkaba one of us will accompany you for the actual journey itself. You will be given a period of privacy for a length yet to be determined while in orbit of our destination, Alcyone. If you are fully prepared then the time to go is now."

At that moment Tobias became apprehensive. There was no way to know if the light meant certain death.

"Be unafraid. We are friendly to you. We were sent by the one you knew as Olivia. She wishes for you to recall what you know of the purity and kindness of light." The alien by the balcony moved toward them and stopped beyond the threshold of their personal space. The seemingly asexual creature made no expression, though his large head was tilted to look them in the face. "Please. Now is the time."

"Jesus Christ. Did you hear what they said?"

"Yeah baby, I heard. Come on, I want us to go at the same time," Arianna said.

"Alright. Are you ready?"

"We only live once, right?"

"That is not correct," said the voice.

Tobias chuckled. "Yeah, let's go. Bye Pluto. We'll be back tonight," he said and then kissed the air three times at the cat seated atop the kitchen table.

"Bye Pluto. We love you," Arianna said.

"Please," said the voice.

The couple approached the portal. Tobias felt tingling warmth. Arianna held close to him on his arm and he was nearest to the little smiling alien by the door who swung it's arm toward the light like any typical doorman would.

"Simply step through."

Tobias told Arianna, "Whatever happens, I love you."

THE WINTER TO END TIME

OSAZE

THE TOOL

"I love you, too."

With his hand around her waist and her hand around his he nudged her into the blinding light. He heard Pluto meow a final time as the light pushed gently against his closed eyelids. Presence of mind and body kept him aware of Arianna. She was squeezing his side. There was an organic crackling inside his brain.

Taking another step, the light faded from around

them. He couldn't see a thing, but immediately felt the change in air-pressure. It felt like the shore of a lake on a comfortable day; a hint of a breeze. No electricity. No humming. He smelled mango or some other sweet fruit.

"Hey! Toby. Arianna," said Drake's voice.

"Drake. Hey. I can't see anything."

"Me neither," Arianna said.

"You will in a minute. You're not going to believe this."

"Why? Where are we?" Tobias asked.

"We're fucking floating in outer space. There's no walls or floor but there's a random table with some stools and fruit salad. You can walk around but there's no floor. Your feet just stop. If you touch it it feels like those rubber floors from a school gym. But there's nothing there."

The burning in Tobias' eye was subsiding and he got his first minor glimpses of where he was but could discern nothing from anything else, save for radiating hazes of charred Earth tones.

"What do you mean there's no walls?" Arianna asked.

"There's something between us and space but you can't tell it's there."

"I wanna see. Can you see stars?" she asked.

"Like you won't believe. We're orbiting Earth. Wait until you see this thing man. You're going to shit your pants, I swear to god."

"Jesus Christ. Drake, can you help us sit down then? At the dinner table in outer space..."

Drake helped them by their shoulders to the chairs, began putting scoops of fruit salad into the bowls provided on the table, and said, "They told me our bodies aren't healthy. That's what the fruit salad's for."

Tobias said, "That makes sense. I'm hungover as shit, what about you?"

"Oh yeah, man. I was fucking wasted last night."

"You know," said Arianna, "that's so typical that we're hungover right now."

"That's life for ya," said Tobias.

Tobias, quite unconsciously began eating the diced fruit; fresh, cold, and sliced oddly perfectly; pineapples, mangoes, and bananas. He hadn't tasted fresh fruit in longer than he could remember. Where had it even come from? In the center of his vision he could vaguely see the white bowl in front of him resting on a table made of iridescent blue material. He looked around and could see the darkness of space and a mish-mash of shining speckled whiteness everywhere.

"Baby, look," Arianna said suddenly.

"I'm trying to."

She put her hand on his head and twisted it slightly to the left.

"I still can't see."

"It's black. The whole thing's black. Everything except the equator."

All he could perceive was obstruction of starlight. He blinked his eye, stretched the lid, and rubbed at it, beginning to get a sense of scale and depth through the shimmering blindness. His heart sunk lower than ever before in his life; simultaneously something invigorating- akin to Kundalini energy- moved upward through him, making him feel apart from himself with disbelief. Like witnessing something impossible. He'd killed people. He'd worked through graves among lingering apparitions. He'd summoned the light from on high to down below on more than one occasion. Or they summoned him to summon them. Still, never had he felt detached from Grand Mother Earth.

He tried desperately to reason himself through the events. Moreover, he thought of the past. He thought back to when Olivia was still alive, and wondered if she knew the Zeta would come one morning and deliver him to orbit. Olivia never said anything about that day although she must have known.

"Are we orbiting?"

"Yeah. Maybe. I don't know. The planet's spinning, can you tell?" Drake said.

"Yeah. I see it."

He had never felt alive before that moment. As if he had only been half real until right then. Below him was nothing but stars. In every direction the same; stars burning bright, trillions of them, speckled beside one another, big and small, except for where the Earth loomed in its immensity.

His two friends stood among the heavens, as did he. The seconds passed and his vision became clearer and clearer. Their planet was indeed black except for a diagonal band of water along the equator. The band of clear sky was thinner in some spots and fatter in others.

The northern most area of the planet glowed incandescent dark blue over the whole expanse and the colors even bled into the more obvious black curvatures. The lightning in that area was the purest of whites.

Across the majority of the planet sunlight was kept out by thick glowing oil seething through stratosphere. The daylight on Gaia was coming from the glow of illuminated pockets of trapped vapor. The sunlight in no way penetrated the mysterious liquid black shell. Tobias was dumbfounded. The Earth had been blackened by the synthesized essence life caught in the atmosphere. Something intangible, became tangible.

A radiant amalgamation of every color of the rainbow glowed magnificently within the black clouds; swirls of red covered areas like hurricanes and in other places yellow electricity ran in thousand mile streaks.

Arianna glanced to his eye and interpreted what he'd left unsaid, "You ever get the feeling we're being watched?"

"I think that's a certainty," Tobias said.

He saw Drake grinning. Nothing shocked that guy.

He was born to be submerged in the most chaotic situations and remain unaffected. He experienced everything there was to live through on one bad day during his second year alive. Drake was separate and benevolent.

Like memories Tobias couldn't remember making, he identified a new depth of understanding. There was a permanence in the way he understood Drake to be more than what he'd always seemed. While he was in no position to make guesses about his friend, he realized from then on he would be seeing everything a little differently. A little deeper. Finality immediate.

As Arianna gazed upon the Earth, he questioned whether to tell her about the abrupt change inside him; the new arrival in his personal repertoire of unusual conditions. There would be time. He decided to say nothing to her.

There was an essence of sweet nectar flowing in his nasal passages. He ate more fruit. Flavors tasted nothing like flavors on Gaia. Or maybe he hadn't had fresh fruit in a year?

"Baby. Eat this stuff. You haven't had fruit like this in a long time. And I don't think you've ever had it in space."

"I don't want any."

He felt, and immediately suppressed, the urge to see through her blatant spells of contradiction. "Who doesn't eat the space fruit? Drake? Did you eat the space fruit?"

"Yeah. I had it. It was good."

"See. Drake likes the space fruit."

"I want a cigarette," she said.

Tobias pretended he didn't hear. He stood to his feet and walked further and further out into the abyss. There was no barrier. He picked up his gate a little until a tightness in his chest stopped him in his tracks. He turned to see Arianna and Drake about 30 meters away.

"We can go this far!" he shouted to them. As he walked back he wondered where that train was heading. He had no sense of destination. Then he saw it. Bigger than he ever thought possible. The Sun's light shining against the cratered face more intense than he would have ever imagined. He looked back to the Earth which had grown smaller in that short time.

When he approached Arianna she said, "We're going toward the Moon."

Drake said, "Yeah. Of course we're going to the Moon. Where else would we go? Mars? Because that wouldn't make any sense."

"I'd rather see Venus. I see the Moon plenty."

"You don't think the Moon's beautiful?" Arianna asked him.

"Well, yeah. You're right. But, for the record, I hope we see Venus."

"Can you move your limbs?" Drake asked.

"No. What the fuck?"

"Oh my god."

A blinding white light surged into them. Through the palms of their hands and through their eyes, into muscle, and their nerves. They became nothing but light. Their entire bodies; light. Like becoming a thought.

Then the power was turned off. Distortion. Knowings. Or unknowings. Soft pressures around. Tobias was still stuck in one position. His limbs stuck in a comfortable standing position. His feet oriented toward Arianna. His body was unable to move. And there was the familiar blindness.

"Can any of you guys see?" he asked.

"No," said Drake.

"Me neither. And my hands hurt, like I slapped something too hard," Arianna said

"Mine, too."

"Do we know what just happened?"

Drake said, "I think I do. Venus?"

"Venus."

"It seems really bright here," she said, "That was stupid of you Toby. What if we were supposed to go to the moon?"

"Then we'll get there. Or we'll die in the orbit of Venus. There are a lot of possibilities. We'll see what's the case. One way or the other."

Their bodies had begun moving in something like the ordinary fashion. The frustration of not having proper motor functions was in the foreground of Tobias' attention. Minor stretches in place were solving the problem. He wasn't worried.

"I can see it," Drake said, "but the sun is fucking intense. Keep your back to it. Can we get the Sun faded, please?"

The Sun did fade some, thereafter. It'd already been faded to begin with, or their heads would be roasted. They collectively sighed with relief.

Tobias was finally able to see around. The Sun was to their back and over them. They were below Venus looking up at her. It? Countless shades of orange stared back. Immense in a different way than the Earth or Moon. This planet was so isolated. Their current place in the Sun was further than recorded history mentions men traveling. No Moon. The Sun immense behind them; a floor to ceiling ocean of white light. That entire backside 180 degrees was nothing except roaring sunshine. While before them Venus stood still; solemn, alone, and sad, sort of. A gentle woman bound to a brutal man. Soured, volatile, and unapproachable.

Her crust was jagged, and it aided the way Tobias personified the planet in his heart. Clouds of acid wafted across the plains, visibly in motion and intimidating. An entire planet of mountains and deserts; plateaus, high or low lands; and not an ocean or a drop of water. Just menacing posses of acid rain drops being thrown violently across the planet's surface. An invisible atmosphere like standing at the bottom of the ocean. The stories of man's unmanned adventures to this planet were bewildering to a younger Tobias. Gazing upon it dumbfounded an older Tobias.

He said, "You see those giant circles? They're called pancakes. But they're volcanoes."

Arianna asked, "Do you see the erupting one? Around the south side of the equator. To the right?"

"Yeah," Drake said, "it's spewing out smoke. Look how..."

The volcanic ashes blasted across the planet's surface but the pressure forced the stuff back down. A curving downward motion that would be better described by a baseball.

"Where did the fruit go?" Arianna asked. It had disappeared.

"Probably into outer space. Or into some Zeta. You think they eat?"

"I bet they consume the screams of babies and the delusions of mad men," Drake joked.

They chuckled a little nervously. Tobias had a thought, but he thought twice. They're in outer space. Arianna's body called to his libido from under the dark colors of her tight evening wear. The orange reflected over the perk of her smiling cheeks. Her eyes had taken his stare and he saw Venus reflected in them. She ran her hand through the thick curls of her hair and flicked her eye toward Drake who wouldn't have seen the subtle gesture.

"Drake. You do realize this would be the most romantic moment of my entire life if you were gone."

"Toby!" she slapped his arm a little.

Drake said, "Well, jeeze man. Sorry to impose. I don't even know why I'm here."

Yeah you do, Tobias thought. "It's not a big deal,

man. I'm just joshen. I have an idea why you're here, though."

"What is it?"

"I don't have the words. I don't know what 'it is'. I know there's a reason. Something about you goes deeper than just being trustworthy. That's what they said, right? You're here because you're trustworthy. Which I get. But, I think there's more. I don't know what. Just more."

"I know what you're saying. Hey, if you guys want to be alone, maybe I can wait for you someplace else."

Drake, clad in mesh shorts and a fresh white college t-shirt, froze in place. He gave a realizing look like, 'whatever' and said quickly, "Don't be too long, Ok?"

A tiny gray silhouette appeared against the sun a short distance away from Drake, and instantly was white light blinding. Tobias closed his eye and grasped Arianna into his chest. He put his face down, his hair shielding him only slightly. Then it was over, and his eyes weren't much more affected than they'd be by a flash bulb. The Zeta was gone with Drake.

"Toby! What the fuck is going on out here!?"

"Hey. He's gone. We're alone. I think."

"Yeah. What the fuck? Why would you even consider that an option?"

"Because I get it. I know why we're out here. Whatever's responsible for this is a dear friend of mine. Yours, too. So come here." He kissed her lips gently at first and then deeper. Then she pushed him away.

"You're not getting laid with something watching us."

"Well, maybe they don't know what shame is. Or care about it."

"Fuck, Toby. It's a courtesy."

"Alright. Fine. Give me another kiss, though."

They lost themselves in each other. Always turned toward the brilliant light of Venus to defend against the jarring Sun. Tobias could have died at that moment. He thought how dying then would be easier than what was yet to come. What he really meant, anyway, was that Arianna was the highest privilege of his life. She was the pinnacle. The summit. There was nothing higher than her. He looked out at the planet, but he only wanted an eternity with the hour glass of her flesh. This universe couldn't offer more than what her delicate frame contained. Only that. Nothing else.

"I love you so fucking much," he told her.

"Ditto."

He remembered how, as far as he knew, he was not about to die. They were wasting time but time didn't seem among the important concerns of the day. A day? What was a day on Venus? Lifetimes of populations- from the beginning so vague until the last days so vivid- had culminated in that moment. It came down to him and her. Out there. Right then.

He couldn't ask questions. All he could do was respect. Inhale.

"We need to get back to Drake," Arianna said. "Wherever he is."

"Take a last look at Venus then. And hang on."

They grasped each other and looked out across the expanse of a foreign planet. After a couple seconds they became consumed in light again. Light became them. Charged through them. Consumed them. Made them disappear. Made them unreal, and even changed them. They were light if they were anything. And then they were themselves again. Holding each other still.

"I can't help but notice how similar this experience is to sex," Tobias said.

"I think it's like dancing," said his Lover.

Drake said, "That was pretty quick Tobias. You done already?"

"Arianna didn't want to bang cuz there's something watching us."

"Maybe they like to watch. They might watch you guys do it all the time. You might be their entertainment."

"Did you ever used to watch monkeys screw on the TV?" Tobias asked.

"Sometimes."

"Yeah. Me too. Hmmm?"

Arianna looked up at Tobias and said sarcastically, "Wow. I'm so in love with you right now."

"Feelings mutual, Babe." He asked Drake, "Where are we?"

"Oh. You can't see yet? This can't be good for the eyes. We're at the Moon. Right at it."

They were indeed. In his blindness, Tobias could make out the presence of its particular glowing hue. So much light everywhere. So much dark, too. Space was a land of illumination and darkness. Out there light was everything. And then the dinner table.

He recalled a lesson he'd learned about dinner tables. In a book he read. Everything knowable that mattered or happened to be relevant to him, or others, was the surface of the table. Everything other than the surface; the seats, the gum stuck under the table, the legs, the floor, the walls, the street, the town, the land, the entire world, everything into space, was unknowable. Beyond the table was where people would have been wise to place their concerns. It was the purest part of themselves. The part religion stole from them. The part that could have rescued them.

Olivia. It was Olivia who put the table there. She was the one who showed him the lesson in the Yaqui book. He said nothing. He sat down and tugged Arianna by the wrist to join him.

He said, "I've been avoiding asking this. We have no idea where we're going or why. We are at the Moon. The Earth is over there. We were- minutes ago- millions of miles away. At Venus. What are we doing out here?"

They accelerated in orbit. The moon craters and blast patterns of Rorschach-scapes moved along quicker beside them, as beside them became below them. Arianna had his hand clutched in her lap but they never once became unbalanced. At worst the effect could be mildly discomforting for a weak stomach. Drake had a weak stomach. He didn't look well- hunched over.

"Yo. You gunna be Ok, Drake?"

"I don't know, man. Let me know if I'm vomiting blood."

Tobias thought briefly and said loudly, "Excuse me!"

"No. Don't worry," Drake interrupted.

"Well. Live strong, or whatever."

The shadows flowed beneath them like the rivers of the Green mountains. Ahead the surface could not be seen. They were approaching the dark side of the Moon. He wouldn't venture a guess about how fast they were traveling. Space. As meaningless as time. Time. The quantification of rhythms. Inhale. Exhale. Heartbeat, ba-beat, beat, ba-beat. Clock tick, ta-tock, tick, ta-tock. Soon they were in total darkness. To the rear the shimmering horizon fell further away. They dropped to their knees. Arianna clutched him with her body and her digits, her arms and elbows clung.

The Sun shined on them. For a while. A short while. Soon, it began disappearing from sight as they drifted behind the Moon. He stood to his feet, helped Arianna to hers, and he led her over to the table where Drake was sitting, looking a little better but still shaken up. The final dimming rays of sunlight faded. Drake struggled to maintain composure against sheer agony. Drake's intestines resembled a rolled up garden hose after it'd encountered a lawn mower. Or they resembled intestines after an encounter with a schizophrenic knife wielding Mother. Whichever. He'd been designed at an early age. His defining moment happened at two years old. Dozens of stab wounds reminding him daily that there is no order to the chaos. The guy put up a tough front, but Tobias often found himself wondering whether the circumstances inside of Drake hid more turmoil, to be kept away from the surface. Maybe that was why Drake cared so much about his hygiene. And maybe that was why Drake was so kind and loyal and genuinely good.

Drake wasn't a liar. No-one could fake those scars. After all, divine intervention brought Drake to Endsville. Like the others. So maybe, instead of questioning Drake, Tobias would be better to question Olivia. She'd left him Endsville. Inherited it to him. And the lights in the sky delivered Drake.

Olivia was the sky lights. Tobias believed that to be gospel. Now there was the presence of the Zeta Reticuli to consider. The mutated race of gray spacemen. All he knew was of Olivia. He couldn't know if she were God. Or if she weren't. To him she was.

The Moon swiftly moved along below them. As they traveled in darkness, Arianna clutched Tobias' hands in hers. He could feel her staring at him. He'd never felt anything like it. He was aware of that bit of information; she was fixated on him. Wanting answers, surely. There was a problem though, the channel was wrong. Normally: He sees her eyes, he feels her hands feel his, notices the orientation of her bodily focus, and then knows she is focusing on him. Currently: they were darting over the Moon, in the dark, he could feel her, but he knew too little. The facts added up to something akin to a delusion. He'd been released from his body over and over in the past short while. All he knew was he had no idea what was going on inside of him. He communicated none of these thoughts to her.

****

Tobias was there and he was real. She knew him and loved him. He would protect her. She just had to stay very close to him until the trip ended or they died. He would be the Sun. He was the Sun. A black hole, yeah. But he emitted what she needed and if the Sun was her keeper than he would be a keeper, too. He didn't know she was trembling from fear. He would remind her of the time he took the chairlift through the storm. That turned out alright.

Outer space was not the chairlift in the rain and it was not the limited communications and spectacles of Gaia bound atmospheric activity. Even if the stars were intensely beautiful as well as life affirming. It was an unknown panic out in outer space. She heard the forth count rhythmic monster from the forest that first night at Endsville. Amplified and stretching across the Moon's surface.

Truly dreadful foreboding lingered around them.

They were dazzling. Lights. In the distance. There was no sky. There was stars and barely hidden UFOs.

"Do any of you hear that sound?"

"What sound?" Tobias asked.

"From the fucking woods. That first night!"

"No."

"I hear something." Drake mimicked and echoed out the rhythmic sound. Devil's throat. Every fourth count.

"Do you see the UFO's?" she asked.

Drake said, "I can see them."

"I can't see a single thing, other than stars," Tobias said.

Arianna figured she'd ask, "You think it's because of the eye?"

Then she realized the connection between Tobias and Drake. Disfigurement? Yeah. Would he realize this and begin to wonder about her disfigurement?

"It's not the eye. I just don't see the UFOs and it

doesn't really surprise me. I know what's out here. It feels strange, isolating. Inward and outward at the same time, lost to this particular abyss."

"Ah! What? Are you saying you're lost to me?" she asked desperately.

"Are you the abyss? It's the opposite. I'm grounded to you. Like to a pack of cigarettes when you're tripping, ya know? We're grounded to each other. Drake, I gotta ask, what are you grounded to, man? Know what I mean?"

"I think so. Um. I'm grounded to my pain?"

Tobias said, "That makes sense. Listen. Think about where we are man. Out here? We might be able to get you fixed better than anyone could on Earth back when. I'll ask Olivia when we see her."

"Oh. Dude. That would be like the coolest thing."

Arianna laughed at Toby. He was so confident. She didn't want that ride to ever end. It was peaceful and perfect at that moment. The pitch black would usually terrify her, but she knew Toby loved it. And when he was happy, she was happy. Never before had she felt special in such a way. Like the stars were coming alive for her. Self-centered, she knew. She knew the journey was bigger than her, or them, but she wanted to pretend. She wanted to pretend it was Tobias making the Stars dance and the Moon sing. Because, as far as she knew, it was.

Suddenly the white Lemniscates over Toby's eye flashed green in the dark. Neon cactus colored light across the lunar surface approached in an instant from the distance. They were upon green splotches of color before they saw them coming.

Tobias stood up and kept a hand on her shoulder. He peered below them.

****

Tobias tried to make an estimate of their altitude. Half a mile? There was no way to tell what was going on below them. Mountains of green light. Phosphorescent light, incredibly intense. What was that, except a puddle of god's light? Otherworldly, omniscient, and organic- or inorganic- life traveling in raw energy.

Looking closer he saw lucent bubbles. The pits of powerful energy were eye smoldering vats of bubbling something. The riots of light swept unknown energies in incredible patterns reminiscent of a mix between ocean currents and wind formations... on fire.

And expansive. The fiery green rifts stretched further than the eye could see across the cratered surface. He didn't know what they were doing. But he loved it. Whatever he was seeing. He would die for them. Nothing else, save Arianna. This was to die for. In a lot of ways it was like the first time he saw a thunderstorm over the ocean with Olivia.

"We need a better view." He wanted to see the whole thing, to discover knowledge for those brainwashed people that fought for and died for the wrong messages. He was alive for the right message. He was looking at the answer to an unknowable trivia.

Arianna asked why, but he didn't respond. They were already arching higher and further away from the glowing surface of the moon. Tobias felt an unexpected sense of relief to see new consciousness again. And if the sense wasn't relief, it was vindication. It was assurance after an era of uncertainty. Things could be worse. That was intelligent design below.

A design like an oil spill- it was the size of Rhode Island. Bubbly lines of green fire had made a Merkaba. A Star of David by Christian name. Right there on the moon. They were above it. Sky box above it. And it was perfect. A perfect circle. Perfect lines alive, or at least intelligent, even if only technology. A six pointed star of reinforcement. The Omega Clan was being relieved of the burden of unknowing.

Arianna said, "That is the greatest thing I've seen in my whole life."

"You've seen me naked, so take that back."

"Eeeeww," Drake said, laughing.

"No, you're right Baby. Except, we just saw Venus. So I think that might have been the greatest thing ever."

"Venus was just a planet. This is like an Extraterrestrial Life Form," Arianna said.

"Well. Do you have any idea how advanced a consciousness has to be to become a planet? I bet you whatever this is, it works for Gaia. What do you think is going to happen next?""

"Who?" Arianna asked.

"Either of you."

Drake said, "They said we're going to Alcyone. This doesn't look like Alcyone."

Tobias said, "We have to go into that. At ninety degrees. That's a Merkaba. That's how we travel like thoughts. It's older than history. Humans knew about it at one time or another. They had to. Because I don't think this is where Jews go when they die. Or maybe it is. They could make a cartoon kid's movie, All Jews Go To The Dark Side Of The Moon."

Arianna said, "I think we should know what's coming by now. Are you procrastinating, Baby?"

Tobias smiled at her with humor in his eye and said, "Maybe..."

She said, "Well, what if you're inconveniencing somebody?"

"Baby. This is 2012. This is it. This is what the entire world knew about for always, and we are the only ones seeing it. Take in the view. We've risen. And Olivia always said, 'Rising up is for the view.' It could have been anyone, but, it was You, Me, and Drake. The question I'm trying to answer before we go and find out is, are there others? Or is it just us?"

Drake said, "If I was going to guess. I would say, no. It's just us. I'm pretty sure most living things except for us, and the other guys, are dead."

MESMERE

Tobias sat up. His pale skin reflecting the electric green flaring on the Moon's surface far below. There were porous indentations of the table on his face. Tobias, Arianna, and Drake lingered, bored and waiting, for nearly half an hour. His eye patch had shifted to his cheek and he adjusted it.

"Can we please move on to the next thing? Please?" Tobias asked.

After a beat, Drake stood to his feet and stumbled a few steps with an expression of revulsion and dread. Tobias caught his eyes for a second, but then he closed them. Drake's mouth began moving, swaying, in subtle motions. No sound. No movement anywhere except in the lips. He stood, rooted to the void.

Cautiously, Tobias approached him, leaning as far back as he could while trying to get a better idea of what he was seeing. Drake's posture straightened and his arms fell to his side as he continued to whisper.

Arianna moved to stand behind Tobias. She grasped the hand he held out as he moved closer toward his friend's incomprehensible behavior. If he put his ear close enough to Drake's lips he could hear sounds.

It didn't even sound like a language. Nothing foreign, or ancient. Just… tongues. Could be anything. Tobias reached out and touched just above Drake's solar plexus. He felt for a pounding heartbeat.

"No," Arianna whispered.

Maybe she was right. Drake's eyes opened wide and they were filled with blazing green light. He no longer whispered. He screamed nonsensical words and Tobias jumped away clutching Arianna.

The rhythmic hollow thumping they'd heard earlier came back in a deafening way, and at a much quicker tempo. He felt it pounding through his core. He felt the sound bouncing off of Arianna and into him and out of him, into her. With no clear idea where the bass pulses were beginning or ending, never mind the source, he just listened- confused.

From a thousand points around, more green light flashed across them blindingly. He tried to see beyond the light, to the source, but to no avail. Lights flashed all around again and again, multitudes in sync with the pulsing boom. Sensory overload. He felt weakened and crippled.

"Get down," he shouted to her while pulling her forcefully to the ground and doing his best to wrap himself around her.

Through the intensely vibrant green flashes he watched Drake standing there possessed. The guy's muscles were tightened and flexed. It appeared dangerous to his health. Each of his feet pointed inward toward the other. His knees and waist jolted over and over. His shoulders, too. Only his hands were sitting still. All ten fingers, pointing below.

While the experience was frightening, Tobias momentarily paused to consider that nothing about it was particularly shocking. He wasn't afraid because he had faith in his friend. But, he was certainly confused. Maybe the purpose was to disorient them. Drake was probably getting the worst of it.

Tobias stood to his feet and pushed gently on Arianna's shoulder to signal her to stay down. He looked around. As the lights faded he struggled to perceive the breadth of the source. Flashing lights, like back on Earth. So many. Some were close, others were much further.

He shouted over the pulse, "It's the Endsville lights! Times 5,000."

"What are they doing?"

"I don't know."

Drake stood with spectral eyes aflame and he screamed tongues, "Blay- ta- huran- vek- tor- bosk- nert- ta- voy- eex- clon- vey- lon- lon- xeex!"

Tobias had an idea. He again got close to Drake. Close enough to cock his head right and see into the energy that had possessed the poor guy's eyeballs. They were beautiful, seething deeply with the resident powers. Tobias was looking for an answer. He couldn't see anything except green light.

Fed up, he slapped Drake with both his palms hard over the ears. Then there was immediate silence. Drake fell hard to the invisible floor. Tobias looked around, but they were alone again. At least, he felt they were alone. The lights had become veiled or had vanished. The sound had gone, too. Arianna stood to her feet and hurried to aide Drake.

Drake was limp, but breathing. She lifted both eyelids, and saw Drake's eyes were still glowing, as if charged like a glow in the dark toy or a dulling snap light.

"Is he going to be ok?" Arianna asked.

"I think so. None of this feels hostile. They want us to desensitize, I think."

"He's certainly desensitized."

"He'll be back. He has to come back."

"Why?"

"Where else would he go? People can't survive any place but Gaia. Why would they kill him? Have they ever hurt anybody?"

"Maybe. What possessed Stephanie's father to kill his family? Or us, to commit mass murder for months on end?"

Tobias was taken aback. "You forget about where we're going. And you forget where we came from. And you forget that we're about to die ourselves. Not out here. Back there? The train can't wait forever. That Mother is going to ascend."

"What do you mean, 'ascend'?" she asked.

Drake choked out, "Shut up, Toby. You don't know anything. I mean, I'm sure you do. Just, you have to see this and then update your registry of facts."

"What the hell happened to you? Are you good?" Arianna asked. Tobias waited anxiously for answers, too.

"I went ahead again. His name is Mesmere. We're going into the Moon. To a different kind of place."

"Different, how?" Tobias asked.

"You'll see. I can't describe it. It's green."

"Let's go, then."

"He said to jump. Into the Merkaboo or however you say it."

"Merka-Ba. Your eyes are still hazy."

"It's to see. Help me up?"

Arianna said, "I'm not jumping into that. Are you crazy?"

"Are you? What else would we do? Go home? It's the Moon. It'll be like parachuting." Then to Drake, he asked, "We'll be cool, right?"

Getting his balance back, Drake said, "Yeah. Fine. We're fine out here. No walls, but there's air? Come on. I can see the walls, now, though. They look like the cleanest thinnest glass. They're made of consciousness and thoughts. So is the air. The table, too."

"We're going into the Moon?"

Tobias answered, "I just want to get away from that table. Oh. Um. We're at least going into the Merkaba. Come on. I'll hold your hand. We're the same person anyway."

"Fine."

"You ready, Drake?"

"I'll die ready, man."

"Nice, thanks," Arianna said.

"That's enough. Allons-y," Tobias said, while

pulling Arianna beside him by the hand. They began falling subtly. For a moment they were walking and falling. Then they clumsily ceased moving their legs as they realized there was nothing below them. The lovers pulled closer together as they softly drifted toward the sublime design stretched out across the darkest area of the Moon.

Tobias made a cursory glance around to locate Drake's glowing figure above them. He was dropping at a slightly slower rate. Then he returned his gaze toward the spectacular figure. Out toward the horizon the tips and edges had vanished as the trio drew closer toward the surface. He focused on trying to see the lunar surface, but the virulence of the six point energy made that nearly impossible.

"I'm afraid," she told Tobias.

He looked to her watery eyes shining. Her curls were pillowed around her face by his arm around her shoulder. Her lips were raised at the corners by the tension in her cheeks as her eyes averted from below.

And then he was pulled away from every physical sensation he'd ever known. There was a place vacant of form but rich in awareness. He looked around at what he immediately recognized to be a thought.

Green light.

Arianna wore a crushed velvet black dress with shimmering steel accessories, and in a flash her outfit returned to the clothes she'd put on herself. She looked to him completely aware of the minor unconscious exchange. Their minds dictated the environment.

In an instant he was wearing the outfit he'd had on when they met. Leather sneakers, black cargo khaki, and a black cotton shirt with breast pockets. His bloody red bandana was wrapped around his head. His hair hung in place out to the sides. So did hers; cast out behind her on an upward draft. They were likely still falling. He allowed himself to stay clothed that way.

The Merkaba was nowhere to be found.

Drake.

"Drake! Can you get here?"

What appeared was in no way Drake. This man was made of fire; bursting with cracks and fissures of light. Dark spots were moving, forming, and fading away in patches. Their only purpose to prevent Tobias and the others from going blind. He felt Arianna immediately close to him. His shape was consistently that of a man's, while still being difficult to define. This thing's face, however, was completely composed to resemble a man's face. Seated, his feet were out in front of him. He leaned back with his hands behind his head and began to smile. He stretched one arm above and one arm below. A serpent, of reptilian flesh and blood was ingesting its tail around his waist.

"Well?" the thing asked, looking at Tobias as though he was retarded.

"Well, what?"

"Above or below?"

"Why the choice? Drake," who appeared exactly then looking dazed, "had said we're going into the Moon."

"Above or below, it's the same place."

"So you're saying we can get down by going up?"

Strands of undulating black hair were aflame in light seeping from his skull, "We go where the Merkaba takes us. The Merkaba sends us where we want. It sends us how we want to get there. I am this Merkaba. Mesmere."

They arose. Tobias clutched his girl tight. All around them hummed a very gentle static disruption. In another couple seconds the space they were in began taking a new form as they ceased to lift. He found himself in a rose garden. A spacious landscape with no horizon. They were not indoors, nor out of doors. The roses grew out to a point where beyond was only more light. And the flowers were not of any ordinary floral essence. They were shades of green and also like everything else in that place they were made of molded light.

They'd been still for a while when the firm ground under his feet surprised him. He was disoriented. And not using his eye for sight. He was aware with a continuous and absolute knowledge of every microsecond. His actual vision was operating at a secondary level that felt more like touch than sight. Sight was in the mind. And eye, secondarily.

There were no shadows in the place. Illumination went upward, outward, inward, everywhere, and even merged with the forms of the roses. Yet, he knew dimensions. He checked Arianna, who was distracted by beautiful flowers. Her eyeballs were murky and glowing.

Mesmere was waiting patiently for their attention to turn.

"Why roses?" he asked.

"The tomatoes are someplace else," Mesmere replied. Though he spoke plain american English, his voice was accented by faint electric humming.

"Why earthbound vegetation at all?"

"The livestock are someplace else. This is a cross section of oversouls. There're roses here. They are undersouls. These flowers are vessels for something larger, and more complicated to contain. Something sort of like you, right? In your contorted state of being. Spirits. People. Dormant people, actually. Not Gaia people. The higher part of you. Your oversoul. The within without. The part of yourself you love the most. The piece that by love and truth together lasts forever. If you have no love, no truth, you may arrive at a different destiny, but luckily most humans thrive on love alone and truth isn't necessary. One day you might have a rose of your own."

"That doesn't sound good. I don't want to become

something less than, ever," Tobias said.

"Maybe, less than is exactly as much as there is," said Mesmere. "You won't be privy to anything like this. This place is only an arena for our acquaintance. Dormancy for those in the roses is like sleep in your lives. You 'Omegas' will be dormant less than anybody else. If at all. Besides, you are always alive in your very own galaxy someplace in the Logos. Even the roses can say that. Your higher self is with you every minute. There is so much you don't know. Out there an entire galaxy is you, because you are alive. And your galaxy probably gazes at Arianna's galaxy all day long out there, too. And they probably emit radiation on each other like the messes you two make."

Tobias could sense Arianna blushing and he chuckled to himself. It occurred that he had already adapted to the strange new place. And the perceptual oddities of experiencing everything through his third eye seemed less atypical than Mesmere himself. The only discomfort that nagged about him was a new fluidity. He felt something akin to water currents faintly wafting over his being. He wanted more time to understand what was happening.

Mesmere's snake belt writhed about his waist. Something so organic seemed unnatural in that place. There was an earthbound creature with them. Tobias thought they had become inorganic. More confusion ensued. The snake was the only thing living and breathing. That was it. He wasn't breathing anymore. "How am I not breathing?" he asked Mesmere.

Before he answered Arianna squeaked and clutched at her lungs, looking shocked.

Then Mesmere said, "You're drifting further from Gaia. We've taken liberties with your physicality to make that possible."

"We're at the Moon, aren't we? People have been to the Moon before, right?"

"They've been to the lunar service. We're under the surface. Beneath the Merkaba as a geometrically beneficial means toward the end of what comes next. Though the entire structure is geometrically beneficial. It's basically an amplifier. Or a manifestation. It's not a radio. It is a computer. Or, especially now, a storage device. It's the Merkaba. Who's to say what it is? Not me. It just is, always was, and always will be. This one is mine. You could say. But you would be incorrect. Like me. Always incorrect. And I know all. All you would ever need to know. There is only one truth. There is only one love. As such, I should answer your question.

"You might perceive yourself as fading. I would say you're transforming. But what you should say is you're staying exactly the same as you were back on Gaia. You're being taken away from your gravity source. Life becomes more celestial, thinner, the further you move from your main source of gravity. The same gravity your bodies adapted to back when they were fish. And that's a joke. Humans didn't come from fish. Humans came from monkeys. Monkeys came from fish. But if it weren't for certain stellar interventions, the Earth might still be that paradise it once was. Before the thieves, certain 'gods', stole the damned thing. They made monkeys into men, then they taught the monkeys to take from each other what the thieves should have stolen for themselves. Paradise lost, is how to define their creation. To you, it should really mean nothing. Because even once a man became aware that his rotten world used to be a paradise, they really had no desire to see the place returned to such a state. And nothing is lost if no one is looking for it.

"Loss of innocence is another way to describe the introduction of higher 'intelligence' to a lower population. Thousands of years later, you wonder why scientists won't stop experimenting on animals. Your ancestors were victimized in the same way as lab rats and other test animals. And this was the result. You know these things. You know the stories of those lizard scientists from Planet X. They are essentially true. You facts are wrong and unimportant. We're not here to discuss anything that happened before this moment. We are here to discuss what is to come next."

Arianna had been listening passively. She'd been running her hand over the intrusive roses while keeping Mesmere in her peripheral only, but her eyes shifted at the mention of the future. Mesmere finally had basic attention from the three of them.

The magi said, "There are four lessons; tools, you must take with you to the next place."

"Death?" Arianna shouted out.

"No, no. The next place where you are going. Alcyone. The central Pleiad."

"To see Olivia?" Tobias asked.

"The one you know such as. Yes"

"Oh!" Arianna said, perking up, "I love Olivia!"

Tobias smiled at her and then at Drake. To Mesmere he asked, "What are the lessons then?"

He replied, "Oh. They're a simple set of ideals and forces. Thoughts and forces. As thought is the only force. And waveform light is all there is and all light is thought. But whose? That's for me to know; you wouldn't understand in your form. 'Olivia' might tell you about it. Maybe not.

"You need to know about the correct attitudes to shield you from a transition that has become toxic to most anything in a third dimensional form; the most significant form to discuss.

"We begin with the most basic lesson: love. There is only one love and there is no better method of survival than to align your mentality to that love as thoroughly as you possibly can. You love, you love, but you can love more, you love, but you can love more." As Mesmere pointed from one earthling to the next his finger sent dazzling, almost fluid, sparks trailing behind it.

It continued, "When you have a question, the answer is love. When you are frightened, love is your security. When you're endangered, love is your safety. Betrayal, tragedy, even heartbreak- love, love, love. One could even say that in Logos there is only love and nothing else. If all is thought then all is love. You people understand?"

Their heads nodded slowly.

"Excellent. We move right along, then. This is good for time. Rush. Don't ever stop rushing. You've got three months left, at most. Be in a hurry, always. Next thing."

Tobias' stomach had turned at the thought of death. He suppressed his fear of the inevitable. He immediately remembered the lesson in love. If all is love then all is good. Always.

Mesmere went on, "Here it gets complicated. Although, due to a personal intervention, Tobias will never again struggle with this issue. So long as he can make a distinction between truth and design. Ironically, I need to tell you about knowing. And the lesson is subtly straight forward. Just know that you know. There is only one truth. Wherever it is, whatever it looks like. A story only happens one way. And to say it has two sides, is first out of context, but secondly you undercut a multifaceted knowledge. That the truth is a singularity. Like love, but like everything else, within love. That is an elemental consistency. Perhaps, you might even consider this lesson not about knowledge or truth, but about trust. Trust can be either friend or foe of truth. But that was then. And now is now. Trust Tobias, he has the truth in him. Which, by the way, is going to be turbulent for you. Whoever might disagree, you'll know it. Save for, 'Olivia.' She may undermine my doings, but I do not expect she would. All you need to do is remember that even she cannot alter the truth.

"One love, one truth. Then the third lesson has five

parts. Or seven. Or seventy. Depending on your personal perspectives. Which is to say to expect the unexpected."

The souls contained within the flowers fluxed positive with yellowish vibrancy in a wave from the curvature at various furthest points of the area out through the center and rolling back toward the other directions. And in an instant there was focus on all levels. The most profound attention. As their postures lifted and their non-gazes very much transfixed.

"You've witnessed everything I am going to speak of. And yet, you've seen nothing. You've never been blessed by the other side. You've been here, even now you know not of what happens beyond the air, and further within the ether. The other side has been bleeding through since the beginning times. We were communicating heavily with your planet through crop symbols for the past 40 years there. We beat you over the head with them. Inexplicability; in the landscapes, in the ruins. In regard to a community that had to agree on something; this got under the skin of whatever master was tending a particular slave down there. People's sheepishness has been monitored and controlled by the power syndicates since the fall of Egypt.

"You witnessed everything that there was to experience at Endsville. Unfortunately there is a lot more. The other side's been bleeding through and by today the world is sopping in it.

Tobias' absolute astonishment fueled a vision of the final product. All light. Ignited consciousness. Two solutions, a duality. Becoming singularity.

"Silence those thoughts Tobias. You must forget that for now. I shouldn't have said anything. Let me correct you."

Forgotten gently, to be revisited surely. Without worry.

The Magi recommunicated swiftly, "Grief is like the weather. When the wind is grief so too will be your sentiments. Your spell is expiring as we speak. This will be intense. Like a thunderstorm. Remember to love. Love will distract you well.

"Clairvoyence is an understatement. But your language accounts for little more. If clairvoyance bred with ESP, and sorcery bred with esoteric idealism, they would create a child like, well, he'd be a Neo Pagan Anarchist where you come from. Tobias, I'm looking at you. I shouldn't label. I'm sorry. Well. No. That leads to an important matter. You'll effectively be living amongst Tobias' oversoul. In this sense, his imagination gone waking nightmare. For everybody except him, you two, and a few others. This has been selected as the catalyst by 'Olivia.' Tobias, enough, what is Olivia's name out here?"

"Alcyone."

"Very good. She is Alcyone."

Arianna rubbed against him and said enthusiastically, "Good job, baby."

Tobias didn't feel congratulations were in order. He didn't know her fucking space name. Luckily, for the sake of stability, it was somewhat obvious.

"Great. Anyway. Alcyone made the decision about the manner in which the catalyst would present itself. This isn't unusual. I'm responsible for the wind, for instance. All of it. Since back when there wasn't any. And I'm quite fond of it, you'll notice. Tobias, I heard you always. Since the first days you began mumbling to me. And you didn't know if I was Yah, or the Pale Mystic, or one in the same. Or something else. I heard you. I also delegate at high levels. That is intrinsic to design. So forget it.

"The decision was made- Osaze, whom you'll meet later- Osaze was introduced, I believe but don't know, to atone for the mistakes that were made originally. Then Osaze inadvertently empowered the Draconians, who should never have been allowed to create the human race. The final vengeance comes accordingly, and totally. As it always does."

"I knew it," blurted Arianna.

"You didn't know that," Tobias said.

"Yeah. But it still makes a lot of sense."

"You've missed the greater cosmic joke that you are an error we can't stop making. Only because things went so horribly wrong. Maybe, if history were herstory, we'd be praising the Draconians. We don't know. The point is that if Alcyone had chosen a different means, or a different oversoul, the end would have been the same. Ascension, as you will see.

"You may interpret what you'll see back on Earth to be spirits. In most cases that is what you'll encounter. The spirit of this or the spirit of that. All just vessels for a differently perceptible waveform of conscious love. You'll need to watch out for their intentions. Confusion will be a very real threat to you while among the vague ones.

"And the final point I'll make about this infinitely poignant lesson, is about isolation. You've experienced this somewhat, but the feeling will be equal to or greater than the wind. They'll go hand in hand, like wind and rain. You will not find another human soul. There are only the nine of you. And even then, it's certain to me some of you'll go separate ways. Isolation can become a sickness."

Tobias saw then. They were the only ones. The young ones. They'd turned on each other until finally they turned on themselves. In the whole world, only the Omega clan was spared.

"What happened to everybody else?" Arianna asked.

Tobias said, "They're gone. Everything is gone. They went the same way as the adults. But we didn't see it. Because we were part of it. Somebody sparred us the grim finale, when we were supposed to turn on each other, then ourselves. We were playing together in the fucking mountains. Completely unaware."

"That was Alcyone who spared you. You have a purpose to serve. Either something obvious, or something unexpected. There is a reason each of you is alive. There is a reason you were each selected. And you will learn that in time. Don't expect to guess, Tobias.

"And I must warn you; never question the grand design. The truth is bigger than you and you aren't to know. This will drive you mad. In any case, the matter is of no matter to you. Now for this." From behind his back he spun, twirling and twinkling, a glassy wand of energy that emitted those same soft sparks as his fingers.

"I am the wand. Alcyone is the wand. There are others. They are the wand, too. And you are the wand. You Tobias. You've entered into an elite position. One a human has never before occupied. You'll be standing among the higher forces. As a man, of course. A force all the same.

"The lesson, for all, is in the tips. The dual ends of the wand. Intent and will. It's as simple as having an agenda. And your agenda comes from within. Whatever your heart is telling you will be correct. You will intend for something and set to carrying out that goal. Like always. Whatever it might be.

"Be there no doubt, your aide will be divine. We will interfere when necessary, but you will know what must be done, and you will be able to do it. This is our design. And you must not question it. Except to Alcyone. You may ask her whatever you like. I am not here to answer questions. The lessons are to be experienced separately from my presence. When there is such a thing. You will remember what you've heard here and that will be enough.

"Intent and will. Do it. It. Do. It. Is what that means. Just do it," Mesmere said in a faint voice.

The roses began to sway suddenly. They

illuminated and dimmed, yellows and greens and light. Arianna clenched to Tobias' arm. Drake tensed up. Tobias knew it was time to go, but he couldn't anticipate exactly what that entailed.

Mesmere gave them a serious look amid the swaying rose bushes- which had almost doubled in height. Then his energy began fading. With a smirk and a suspicious raise of his brow, Mesmere began to solidify within himself. The light faded from the fissures and gaps until he was nearly solid. Like a statue for a moment. The flowers blooming from stems growing toward the unreal sky or absent ceiling. Tobias couldn't tell which.

Then Mesmere shrunk, in an instant, and he became a single illuminated long stemmed and thorny rose lying in the center of a fat black snake writhing as it choked on its own tail.

Tobias, ignoring the rose, reached down and lifted the snake to the chorus of his friends objections. He pulled on the snake and felt its jaws tighten their grasp. He remembered that these animals have back pointing teeth. So he shoved the tale further down its throat. Its jaws unhinged and he pinched them in place. At that point he was able to dislodge the animal from its unfortunate predicament. He dropped the snake to the floor where after a moment it had reoriented and begun eating itself again. Encircling the Mesmere rose.

He squeezed Arianna gently and looked up toward the rose bushes as they towered in full bloom. Crackling light was popping, cracking, and zapping far above. He didn't know what any of it represented.

ALCYONE

Perception fused into a vague liquid mutation of rotating rosebush canopies freed of the burden of gravity and form. She held close to Toby. His touch felt as though he were made of a substitute human kind of plasma, something ethereal, tingling ionic. The greens faded, leaving spinning white stars. Countless stars. Whirling around them. They hovered- looking to one another for focus. Beyond Toby and Drake she couldn't orientate anything.

Then she couldn't help sensing there was rap music playing from beyond reality. Completely inaudible vocalizations coming fast with beats and pulses, like a frequency. Nothing made sense. Unless she wasn't supposed to comprehend. She shouldn't expect to recognize the unknowable; the depths of herself around her.

"D'yall hear that?"

Toby said, "It's the other reality. We're going there. We're becoming a higher consciousness. I keep getting dejavu. We've been out here before. Many times over. It's just too convenient. In the context of our lives, this doesn't make sense. We weren't special. My life was a bad dream I've long since woke up from. You were miss rambunctious teenager usa 2012. Drake, you were fucked from the jump off. Then the human race, and all life on Earth, bit the fucking dust- except for us? It don't add up."

Drake said, "I can accept the facts. Look where we are. Here's the proof you need. It's ok to feel important, because you might actually be."

Tobias didn't say anything in response. She didn't have anything to say, either. Deep inside her, upon brief analysis, she felt gratitude to still be alive. To still be human(even human with a warped and gelatinous feeling). Her whole family perished. Everyone's family. Tobias only had a step mom. The loss of his parents served as a precursor to a more unified loss; the extinction of life.

She remembered her best friend lying dead at her feet. She thought about Stephanie's brother and the way that she never knew if Rick had killed both her father and her. She never knew where Steph's mom was, but suspected the father was the defective, as Rick simply handed her Ulysses then told her to leave.

She crushed at remembrances of her parents. Lost. On her tail one last time, in the rearview mirror, and left behind to the great death. Aunts. Uncles. Cousins. Other friends. Josh, Peter O' Toole, Gay Chris H from the closet.

She said, "I'm getting that, too. The bombardment of thoughts of dead ones. My mom and even my dad. Every vic except a couple from Endsville. I remember the weather on every morning, or how dark and cold it was when we were warming ourselves on bodies burning through car seats."

"When I found Olivia, she'd carved this guy she was fucking to shreds with this brass knuckled knife. She was spread out with her life shard, this broken bottle neck, shoved inside her cooch the sharp way. Pluto started eating the guy... I drank as much of her blood as I could feasibly suck out of her gashes and out of the puddles, too. What about you, Drake? Who's dead to you?"

"A lot of those kills on the road. For sure. My dad. My sister was already missing. I feel sort of dead out here. I don't think my body is human anymore."

"That's kind of like when we first walked through the portal. As we move further into space our vibrations are becoming looser and looser. We're ascending. We're leaving physicality behind because we're not grounded to the Earth. We're ascending to a place where our minds will be free to experience a taste of what is likely waiting for us when we abandon the mortal coil."

Space. Arianna used to have dreams of living in space. In an unlimited world. Where all was as her whimsical wishes could dictate. Then she met a man who made that possible. She loved Tobias. The surviving legacy of the greatest feminine figure ever. Perhaps nobody cared but her. All perished. She would return to herself.

Around them, hazy blue lights formed into enormous orbs whirling around and around, gradually slowing their rotation as when a dizzy person regains equilibrium. One orb was prominent. Closer. Larger. On their level. While other orbs differed in size from smallest to second largest. Those other orbs hung far away and above, sloping downward and toward them. It was stars. They couldn't determine the exact distance of anything. All was far, all was near. All was within. All was beyond.

All the stars were blue. All their faces were blue. Everything was blue. The only light came from the reflections on their skin and clothes. There was nothing near them and the distant stars were out shined by the nearby behemoths. Enormous stars. The tiniest one shone like a blue Sun. They hadn't seen a star for almost a year before that day.

"Close your eyes," Tobias said.

He clutched her in his static grasp. In his arms, they were melding together. Literally. In the semidarkness of her fading eyelids she sensed a repeating series of high tension jolts. Tobias' nerves were hurting her slightly. She became ill at ease. Nervous. Afraid.

Then she remembered her parents fighting. She felt the sting of the popular girl's words from before she knew how callous and empty those brain dead females actually were. She didn't like it and pushed away from him. The worst experiences of her life were a pulsating gob within him.

He would know. She could tell, he did know. With his face tilted down and his eye glaring up at her, his body had curled into itself- rejected. Out there in the Pleiades the blue light bathed their severance. A major incompatibility. She couldn't even look at him. Her heart was withering and fluttering. Crackling within her chest. Her sadness for Tobias was immense when she realized the true nature of his lifelong, possibly eternal, burden. He was a vessel in which infinite quantities of negative energy were being stored. She knew him, though! She knew in his heart there was only love for every living thing that ever had a consciousness and shared in the experience with them, the experience of having a mind, or even less, being alive on any plane or at any level. That boundless love was his balance. The way a creature of darkness could maintain equilibrium. Her fragile hero could not possibly contain a universe of hurt within himself. He'd turn inside out and become what was dark.

Tobias curled over on his side to look away. She watched him, knowing this would be an awful memory. Like the other bad memories and thus with origins within him. Her own love for him was created by whatever was happening inside of him. Tragic irony.

His purpose seemed tied into some galactic balancing act. An intolerable flaw. No matter how badly she could ache for their love to be pure again. She couldn't be near him ever again. Not until he became cleansed of his burden. She found herself praying to no particular god that her lover could be rescued from his inner disaster.

The noises coming from beyond the veil had begun drumming a steady electric rhythm; like a bad omen. She began dreading. That sound couldn't be welcoming. The Pleiades couldn't be a new home when they sounded so ominous. Well, Gaia was home, too, and that place had fallen. Maybe the drums beat for Toby.

****

Fighting back tears he wondered who she was

supposed to be. They'd come so far together and he was merely a glorified allergy to her. Out there in the NuReality. In Arianna he glimpsed himself in the true way. Because he knew himself. The turn of events made absolute perfect fucking sense. In his heart of hearts he's always sensed this inevitable conclusion looming; like the assassination of a freedom fighter. He could tear out his own heart. He clutched his waist and dug his fingers deep into his flesh. There was no pain. His skin gave under the pressure. His fingers were within himself.

With the other hand he lifted his shirt and showed them, "Look what I did. I performed surgery. Or at least expanded our boundaries... Further."

Arianna let out a little gasp and Drake said, "Dude. Get your fingers out of your insides. You freaking maniac."

"Whatever man. I got no hope. We came this far, but at what cost? If I can't love her, then why would I even want any of this? Wouldn't we be as well off dead as everyone else if we don't even have love?"

Drake whispered, "The dead had love."

Arianna was crying. She said, "We don't have the facts. Or any facts. Things might be alright. Alcyone can help, right? She has to fix you!"

" No. Screw that. Don't get hysterical. I've always been this way. I can accept what is and there might be more for you out here than just me. I promise, if I can fix me, and become some other way, I will."

"Wait. Why can't you love her anymore? What's stopping you?" Drake asked.

"My soul is a pin point tar pit of melancholy. Her heart is pure light. My entire being is toxic to her out here. I'd been radiating the trace effects of my core back on Gaia. I was human. Out here there is direct exposure. It's me. I'm your sad suffering. My own too. I've been completely over taken by something I never understood. Or I always was this thing. Bound to Gaia. Except, I may have been the reason the biosphere failed to heal. The reason we saved one child out of dozens. Yeah. Don't make much sense anymore, huh? I was human. For a while. Until today for sure. How can I love? What am I to become?"

Tobias said to Arianna, "Baby, get us out of here. Let's go see Alcyone."

"How can I?"

"Try asking."

"Alcyone. I believe we are ready to behold your glory. May we?"

They lofted into all-encompassing color. The world illuminated like a deep blue silk. A gorgeous woman appeared through the dusting billows; seated between two undulating flags hanging on either side of her. One black and one white. Her jet black hair hung straight, glowing slightly green in the aura, and trimmed in perfect form to the leonine features of her face. She hopped off the seat, ran the short way to Tobias and clutched him in the humming fabric of her peculiar shawl; black and white in a checkered pattern-equatable to a taijitu.

"My angel of darkness."

Choked up in her grasp, he said, "Mine."

She let go and looked him in the eyes. He could feel her playing some voodoo through his depths. She was licking like a serpent's tongue through his singularity. Checking out what's going on in the other side while he had no clue. He felt a little violated then he remembered how great it was to be acknowledged by Olivia. To be anything to her other than grieving her absence was a dream coming true. She visited his sleeping adventures often. Like his mother. And Lyn, the quiet mystic, who occupied the role of every female he had ever known. The dreams. Olivia was with him every night. Even from Alcyone.

"Hey! Were you the orbs guiding everyone to Endsville?"

Tobias asked.

"I was involved. And Mesmere. Whatever. You think about that. Arianna. Oh my god! I am soo happy to see you. You look gorgeous. Both of you do. If only the human race could see you now, right?"

"Olivia. Why the fuck can't I touch Toby? What's wrong with him? Is this something we can fix?" Arianna begged for answers.

"I can't answer anything in the way you desire to receive the information. You want to extend the past. You want what's coming to be what was and can never be again. At least out here. The period of your togetherness has ended. However, in a few minutes you won't want to go anywhere, my dearest. There are so many issues to address. Naturally followed by so many questions. But once we've finished your briefing we can be on our way."

"Where else is there to go?" Tobias asked.

"Home. Your home within Logos," Alcyone told him.

"Sirius?"

"Seriously."

Tobias said, "This sucks. I can't believe you're here, and I want to spend a couple days talking to you, but it seems like you've got a whole lot of bad news."

"Not bad news. Arianna is going to be one of us. She is a sister. Merope by legend. But to us she is known as Aloria, and that is how she'll wish to be called once we send her through transitions. Her Earthly body is going to die. Her higher self will stay right here with us the whole time."

"What the fuck about me? I love her! I need her! I'd rather be dead-"

She cut him off, "And you could be dead. Just like everyone else. You whiny little force. Farce of yourself. We have a gift for you. Call it a going away present. You'll have to wait until Sirius. And until then you'll need to suffer. Aloria is home now. You need to go back to the Earth without her. She belongs to the Pleiades. You said it yourself, her heart is pure light. You're something much greater, something so powerful and still as fragile as a crystal vase. When you are in your proper place where you belong you are as stable as need be, but on Gaia you're a breath away from death. How long can you brand your skin, and slice your flesh, until something goes awry? If you let the wrong organisms into that body down there, you could have died before you even did your share in the ascension.

"Your solution? This was the decision of your higher self. You need to go back down there and finish what you began, and when you're done, get back out here and do what is right as well. You'll know when it's time. You'll need to flood the planet and ignite it. The Earth is covered in hydrogen and oxygen, it'll burn."

He interrupted, "Even if I could do that-"

Alcyone interrupted back, talking mostly to Drake, "All that stuff in the sky is consciousness, you could call it photoplasm. The gulf coast is the ignition point. You'll be manufacturing smoke. The gap in photoplasm around the equator will act as a chimney allowing smoke to escape through and out over the mass. The mass crashes when the smoke from burning oil rises through the gap and barometric pressure will push the photoplasm back toward the Earth. This will cause friction. Then the ocean's hydrogen and oxygen atoms will reach a tipping point, fuse, split, and burst into flames. In turn causing the molecules that make up air to also, tip, fuse, split, and burn. Your bodies will be dead prior.

Tobias was drifting away again. To have Arianna and not hold her. To love her and disgust her. The distance swelling, and the tears of realization approaching and prematurely ebbing. There was suppression involved. The sisters were taking back one of their own. The circumstances of himself were absolute. He was toxic.

Alcyone redirected his attention, "So you see why the Pleiades is not an acceptable location for you, Osaze? Your presence here is the most disharmony we've witnessed since before the last time you graced us with your presence before they began the initial generation of monkeys with higher thought down on Gaia. You were here, like, 'Come on Alcyone. Let me get in on this.' Putting you in the mix was the only mistake made in an otherwise flawlessly designed consciousness. We wanted to give them spirit. We gave them Osaze."

"No surprise there. What did you call me?" Tobias asked.

"Osaze. That is your proper name. It means 'loved by god.' If the Logos were books, you'd be the ink in his quill. Or any other deep blackness."

"Why suffering? I don't like suffering and I don't think anyone, or anything, should suffer ever. What did the humans do to piss something off so profoundly that they were left on that planet to fester and rot with a human mind to suffer and an animal's instincts, like a termite, to feed, and reproduce, and take- to transform everything pure and natural into something processed and vile, so it only serves them? Like the wheel of life stops for people."

"Nobody was pissed off at people. Somebody loved you enough to damn the race. Doesn't the wheel of time stop for people? Time is a people thing and without people it is nothing. We don't use time out here. We organize our intentions and wills, collide for whatever purpose and drift apart. People were trapped in their own minds. They had a heavenly source, but they were mortal Earthly creatures facilitating, with their karma, the dissolution of terrestrial life, not just their own species. Osaze, you geared men not only against themselves, but also against men and women in love.

People targeted love for assassination. Love was truth. It was their god, and they didn't even know it, blinded by the angles of the archetypes."

"Just explain what I am."

"You're Osaze. The darkness. The dark matter. You're a plain of reality. You are the fourth dimension, the keeper of what is evil and in no way evil yourself. Except it has been decided that the lower dimensions, the more solid levels of consciousness, will be raised to the fifth dimension and they'll exist within our loving benevolence- like this place right here, except back toward the Sun. The Earth will be a beautiful star and there will be 'peace' like everyone is always dying for. It will be heaven on Gaia. Except 'on' will be 'in' and 'Gaia' will be a ball of nuclear composite. All who ever lived will relive. All who ever died will re-die 12 million times or more. But there will be no evil. That is why we are banishing you Osaze."

Tobias saw Arianna glancing wildly from Olivia's face to his own. Banished?

"Banished? Where am I going to? Banished from where, the Earth? Or Logos? It's fucking Logos! You can't banish me from the universe! Where will I go?"

Alcyone said, "You're being given your own universe. To call, and to create, whatever you like. A place to take the evil from this one. It will be yours and the Logos will be cleansed."

"Yeah, you get cleansed and I get the devils!"

Arianna over-spoke him, "Alcyone. I can't let him go alone. I have to go with him."

"No. You don't. And you won't. Your place is here with the other sisters. It's not possible for you to go where he is going. But if he chooses, when the time comes, he may return to visit you. Or you might even take up residence outside the event horizon of his portal. There are options, but you forget that he is toxic to you. If you spend too much time near him it will end you. And not this human form you're in now; he will destroy your higher self as well. And you, a goddess, will be no more. Soon you will know that this is where you belong and you will realize that your paths were not meant for unlimited proximity. Even on Gaia your love was the product of necessity. Nothing more than a way to guide you to the next place. To here, as it is.

He looked to his lover and she looked to him. They were sharing a sentiment of despair. A crushing severance. For the moment she was still there, close to him, but the pain pulsed through from his core. Already he could feel the separation of being an Omniverse away. Across the greatest divide.

"What about to you... Alcyone? Am I toxic to you?"

"There isn't much in Logos that can love and grow in direct contact with you in your natural state. You cause consciousness to falter and die. Your burden sucks from all and takes for its own. The fourth dimension is a malicious place filled with malevolent archetypes waring amongst themselves, manipulating whatever energy sources they can get access to. That is you."

He understood why people behaved in inexplicable ways detrimental to the wellbeing of everything. He could fathom the sinister ways of the plutocracies- the possessed rulers of the planet- when other times on Gaia he could find no excuse for any behavior that betrayed the lives of entire cultures at a time. Whatever is living in that other dimension has no regard for human life. All that was wrong with mankind was their susceptibility to a divine drama being played out through them. Through him. Words like 'fate' and 'destiny' came to mind. Both were fact. Fixed.

Arianna was going to be taken from him and there was nothing he could do to prevent it. "Fuck this shit. You couldn't orchestrate my banishment without completely breaking our hearts first? Why couldn't you just kill her and reap her soul? Why give her to me?"

"Well, believe it or not Osaze, there are those of us looking out for your well-being. You've been given a crushing burden. We know you deserve to enjoy the same love as the rest of us. You've been dealing with this bullshit since you entered the Logos. You're going to be overseeing these beings until the end of another universe."

"How do I deal with anything? I still feel like some kid from Providence. Some human kid."

"All that will change when you die. You haven't died yet. This time, anyway. You'll know more when you're dead. There isn't much to it. You've always existed apart from the rest of us although you aren't very different. We have our forms and our fancies and we exist, creating and creating until our creations weave tales of their own. We love you like family, but this is the point where you do Logos a favor and take the garbage someplace else. If you do not, hope is lost. Your grief is expanding exponentially every day. Pretty soon the fourth dimension will consume all else. In essence, your archetypes are working to claim for themselves the dormant spirits of the photoplasm and perpetrate a coup against the councils. If they can poison the councils then the very fabric of the realities will fade away- no more higher, nor lower selves- and space will be left cold and dead. I hope this clarifies the reasons why you should quit bitching, do what we're asking, and we'll make sure your petty desires are satiated, if that's what it takes to keep you complacent."

"Complacent my ass! I want Arianna. Can you give me her?"

"No. She's one of us and we aren't letting you destroy her."

"Then I'll let the archetypes destroy you."

Arianna shouted through tears, "Toby, you can't do that."

"It's an empty threat. Don't you have anything to

say? Isn't there some way we can be together? And if we can't, who cares if Logos and Ma'at get suffocated by dark matter?"

Alcyone said, "You cannot suffocate Ma'at. She will be your eternal companion. This is a fact you're not aware of. There is much left to reveal. For our sister's sake, you'll be without her."

Then she redirected, "Drake your purpose has been served. You'll be leaving now. When you return, tell the others to make preparations. You'll be leaving Endsville early tomorrow. It could be a long day out on docks finding the proper vessel, one that someone can get started. Take what you will and go start fires. Say goodbye to Arianna. You'll never see her again."

Drake stood up and walked toward Arianna. He said laughing, "You're a Pleiadian. You're not an Omega anymore."

"I'm going to contact you. I don't know how. I'll do it. I'll get there one last time. To say goodbye to everyone," she told him.

Drake said, "It might not work. Some of us might be dead before that happens. Alcyone, where am I going when I die?"

"You're going with the photoplasm. The Grand Ascension is going to be more splendid than any wonderful place even the greatest of poets could have imagined. I promise you. So die a good death and Aloria and myself will see you in the next place. You'll see Tobias again. Anyone will be able to visit him in accordance with his will. All will be very well. We promise. We love you. Be well."

Osaze said, "I'll see you back there. We'll rip some 3-D shit up for as long as we can."

Drake said, "Fuck yeah, fuck yeah. Have fun in heaven, Aloria. You'll be alright, bro. These beings are going to take care of you."

"Get out of here, man. I love you."

"Yeah, I love you, too," Aloria chimed in.

Drake waved slightly at his waist and faded away into the royal blue; color became him and he vanished. There were the three of them remaining. His savior. His lover. Himself. They were both looking at him. Arianna's cheeky sobs never dried while her figure oriented proximity to Olivia. Olivia, who was fast becoming Alcyone to him. Just like in actuality.

"Did you use me only to escort your sister directly here?"

Arianna said, "That doesn't even make sense Toby. You're the prince of darkness of whatever."

"And so what. I lose a lover? Perhaps I should be gracious of the offering?"

"Yes, Osaze, that is exactly it. You will learn to be gracious because these are not the bridges to burn. You can be permanently exiled if that's the way you wish to be remembered."

"For love? Everything I do, I do it for love. So screw you. You're taking my lover. Give me a blade! I'll put it into my heart right here! You can do whatever you wish for me. Cast me away eternally, into another universe, alone, and see if I care. I'll be with her in my dreams. In my heart. And when that is no longer enough I will be with her when I'm awake. I will send agents of oblivion to bring her to me and lay waste this entire cosmos. What the fuck are you going to do? There isn't another Arianna. Fucking Aloria? This girl is Arianna. We were going to die together!"

Aloria cradled her face in her hands. She never liked the way she looked when she cried.

"Well, now you're not. Get used to it. Say your farewells, this is goodbye. You won't see her again. I'm taking you to Sirius. So say goodbye."

Destiny. Fate. Osaze looked at Aloria. She raised her moist rain drop shaped eyes from her hands. He fought back tears. Too greedy to cry. At her feet he dropped in prayer. He reached to touch her a single last time. His fingers caressed her ankles, and she gasped, pulling away.

With his face down, he spoke clearly, "I never felt any way about anybody the way I felt about you. My only wish in life was to die with you, by your side. I wanted to be human with you. I would trade eternity to be human with you for a few more weeks. I'm going to pray to you. Every day I'll pray that one day you'll be immune to me. I love you."

"I love you, too, Toby. With all my heart. We've always trusted Alcyone. Let's trust her this time, too. I know they love you, and they'll watch out for you better than I could."

She was always a little naive.

MA'AT

Aden groaned. Sweat on his brow glistened in his short mohawk. He sat hunched over on a bench in the cafeteria. His eyes bulged from their sockets and his teeth were grinding so forcefully they made friction squeaks. He fiddled with the knot on a pair of work boots; tying it tighter and fatter compulsively. Then he ran out of length and began tearing the knot apart. Except the knot was far too tight. From the pocket of his black cargo pants he retrieved a small pocket knife and flicked it open. He was forcing the knife's tip into the knot and felt a little give.

"Aden!" Drake called.

Aden shrieked in pain, and then responded, "Where the fuck have you been?"

Lyn looked up from her writing and said, "You're bleeding Aden."

"I'm aware of that." He'd cut himself deep; blood splashed to the floor. He clutched his dripping finger, and said to Drake, "We were looking everywhere for you. Where's Tobias and Arianna?"

"Hang on," Drake said, walking past their table toward the wall. It took him a moment to reconnect the wires, but soon enough the alarm sounded.

Lyn chewed on her pen and with glossy hazel eyes looking around at the whooping noise blaring. Her blonde hair still frazzled from grinding into a pillow all night. Her spaghetti strapped black tank top fit discombobulated showing plenty of her healthy cleavage. A devious smile pursed up her tiny lips. Her eyes, ever suspicious.

Light snow gently lofted on the wind outside the floor to ceiling windows. Even though it was midday, the fluorescent lights were on like always; except, that day, the colorful electric currents of the clouds were in harmony. Golden light fluttered streaks across the black gathering in the sky. Aden, sucking on his finger, took a look at her then turned back to Drake as he returned from the kitchen.

"That'll get everybody here. I got news. Big fucking news."

Aden shouted, "You have to wait until they're here to tell us? Why did you set that fucking alarm, couldn't you have just gathered everyone calmly? And quietly? I'm hung over as shit."

"It's important," Drake replied.

Lyn got up and began walking away. Aden asked her, "Where are you going?"

"To get you a bandage and a wet cloth," she said and continued off.

On her way out she walked past Logan coming running into the cafeteria. His yellow plaid shirt- that complimented his golden afro- had one button latched through the wrong hole and he had no shoes on. He wore a pair of hemp pants that fit too short.

Logan said, "What the fuck is going on?"

"Drake has news," Aden said back.

Logan finished buttoning his shirt.

Cadence- the munchkin sized voluptuous Italian- came running toward the others. She wore a form fitting black silk nightgown. She didn't even say anything, but her expression explained that she was perplexed to hear the alarm sounding only to find the others casually hanging around the rectangular table. Aden caught her eyes and went back to his knot.

"Aden! You're fucking bleeding everywhere!" Cadence said.

"I'm aware of that."

Robin came running in carrying Calvin in his arms. The child looked completely discombobulated at having been yanked from a dead sleep in his bed. But Robin stopped short with about the same reaction as his lover. He skeptically glanced around the room.

"Why the fuck is the alarm on?" Robin asked.

In tandem- even Lyn returning with first aid- they said, "Drake has news."

Calvin hopped out of Robin's arms and scuttled across the floor to the table, where he sat, put his head down, and said, "Most of us are here, can we kill the alarm? I think Toby and Ari have gotten the message."

Aden grinned and said, "Yeah. Will one of you fuckers go turn this shit off? Logan? And yeah, Drake, you never told us where the fuck Tobias is?"

****

He was without Arianna and hyperventilating in a place with no air to begin with. Wanting, aching for, something he couldn't have, oxygen, because in that dimension breathing was not a thing. She'd faded into the blue. Going to her sisters. To forever exist on the plain that encompassed the Pleiades star cluster. Her consciousness as old as the Logos. As old as Osaze. He was Osaze, the god of horrific goodbyes.

Alcyone and Osaze moved further and further through a silver river, toward Sirius, to meet Ma'at. The disbelief was as deep as the hole he'd sunk into at the death of his mother. A longing for death crashed like waves over and over. Grief and disbelief. And as the waves ebbed, he could see the sands of hope. But, in his mind, when he went to grasp that hope, it slipped through his fingers as the waves came crashing over him once again. He wanted to throw himself into Alcyone's grasp, but the Goddess wouldn't go near him. He could tell that in that reality there was a subtle bitterness projecting toward him. From what he'd pieced together, he'd been troubling the entire universe since its creation. It made sense for her to resent him.

They were meeting Ma'at at the most remote satellite of the Sirius realm. The blues of the Pleiades had faded into black. Tobias moved along through a quagmire of transparent quicksilver that felt cool against his skin. Places without any starlight. An incandescent glow emanated from Alcyone. He emitted no glow. While any other sentience traveling that way more than likely would have shone like her. Those rails were for the stars. Heavenly tracks danced with a superiority complex. The human inferiority complex began to make sense.

He managed a chuckle. Red light crept like fungus. He began to notice these intricately uniformed webs being cast across the sphere; made of red light, like fiber optic cables. All sprawled in different directions and patterns. God's brainwaves. Then he felt the heat.

"Is this going to hurt me?"

"Not with pain," Alcyone replied.

"I'm being quarantined."

"Yes. And I'm leaving. I'll see you later on. Have no fear of this place. It belongs to you. I love you."

"I love you, too."

Alcyone vanished and Tobias was alone again. For

the first time he could feel himself everywhere. There wasn't any place without a gravity field. He was suppressing the entire Logos. The chains were form itself. Gravity. Logos had been defending itself against him since the beginning.   Hence the grand unification of matter in the Logos. The dark exodus had arrived. The grand ascension. Essentially, the celebration of his removal from the equation.   The luminous webs began to pulsate. Isolation. He would be the only one punished.

In his hand he visualized a solid point with which to propel himself. He pressed against that spot with the palm of his hand and spun himself zealously. The movement was fluid and his vision became a sheet of deep whirled red. The color of blood, murder, rejection, and rage. The grand rejection. Logos had tolerated the burden for long enough.

With every next rotation he spun as fluidly as the first. A comfortable yet exhilarating rate of turn. He widened his legs and then crossed them. Nothing slowed him down or sped him up. This was alright with him. He felt like a cosmic lottery winner. He won the only true irony. To be alive when others are dead, and to be the only one cast aside at revelation. Red: the color of the revelation. For him.

Having had a moment to think on his predicament, the loss of Arianna began to seem less important than his expulsion from Logos. He put his arm out and gently stilled his body. With the same method he oriented himself to some deceptive semblance of vertical. Alcyone had said there was a silver lining. He needed to know what they were going to do to make this not torturous on him.

"Osaze?"

"Yeah?"

"I am Ma'at. I'd like to enter your space. There are many things for us to discuss."

"You don't have to ask. I like harmony, order, and truth. I don't wish to be separate from oneness with Logos."

"As long as you are here, there can be no unity. That is why you must go."

Through the ether flew a bird of pure energy; shimmering and sparking that same red. The luminous flecks of molting light gathered as the phoenix flew a spiral above him, a little ways away. The flecks materialized quickly into the form of a young naked women. He recognized the figure quickly. It was Lyn; that was obvious. Except as her features grew more and more to resemble a human, there was a subtle difference in her. Maybe, he'd never seen her naked before. And he'd never seen her hair that way. He noticed the cherubic curves of her hips. He looked over her; from her toes, up the soft shape of her calves and thighs; no pubic hair, a tight belly; her throat, armpits, and crotch still flickered with electricity zaps. He noticed her body language to be predatory, like a cat stalking, but contrarily her smile indicated blushing.

In her hand she leaned on a spindled silver scepter as though the object were a cane and not a wand. Around her neck hung a shimmering ankh. Other than those two items, she was naked.

"Inside the mirror, all the girls are wet, yes?"

"I do what I can."

She dropped the cane, disappeared from before him, and manifested behind him. He felt her breasts melding into his back; her hands reached under his shirt and clung to his chest, setting off spasms of electric nerve activity. Into his ear she whispered, "What is it that you want most?"

"Arianna."

"Well you can't have her."

"Then I want you."

She slid her hand against him and down into his

pants, clutching what she found, "Well. You can't have me, either." He turned to her and embraced her. She fell into him and as their lips embraced, space dropped out from under their feet. They were falling. She kissed him the same as he kissed her. There was no difference. It was as though they had only kissed each other and nobody else their entire live.

He pulled her closer into him and held her tighter. They melded as he thrust his pelvis into hers. Their momentum slowly halted and then propelled away, floating out into a different direction. Not down or up or out. They moved in spirals, shifting their main orientation in concert with their passion. His clothes faded away and he introduced his stiffness into her sopping wetness.

Ma'at zealously cooed and hung her head and shoulders back; grinding against him.

He was fucking the empress of the Logos. He tried for a moment to think of the girl he'd lost. Ma'at dug into him and shoved his face into her ripe chest. The feeling between his legs was more powerful than anything he'd ever experienced. With every thrust they were pulsing energy between them. Ma'at's eyes were burning within her skull. With no iris or pupil, they glowed deep red; a shade only slightly deeper than the spinning territory around them- way more intense. They were moving toward climax together. From her genitals she created spewing energy like hot blood clinging to them; it seeped out her pores, coating them both; blood energy gathered 'tween them; a molten jewel surging to break free of itself. As they spiraled, they left spectacular trails of their passion. Then Ma'at really threw herself in; controlling the rhythm and motion while doubling her pace. Tobias had long lost any idea of where either of them began or ended. Ma'at rapidly whipped up and down on him, bouncing around with the ankh in his face. He looked to her rippling red eyes staring back into him.

"You ready?" she asked.

"Fuck yeah."

Their slim figures bathed in radiance. She snapped her hips a few more times and that was that. Like a supernova his explosion echoed across space and time before he even felt himself shooting into her. She took his pleasure and amplified it. Her arms and legs clutched him and sent the pleasure back through her and into him. Tobias squeezed her. Therein was the true ecstasy as they fused into each other. Briefly, nothing existed.

The first thing he heard was an inexplicably rhythmic cacophony of trees snapping and glass shattering. Still, he felt Ma'at clutching his inner frame. They emitted pleasurable physical sensations to each other; wrapped in a coating of light that was an interstellar orgasm. Her fingers were rubbing his inner frame. His bones, if they were still bones. She may have been rubbing a skeletal figure of slightly more solidified, trippy, thought born material, than the rest of his body.

He thought that if she could feel around inside of him, maybe he could have the same thoughts as her. Their heads were close. So close. They were sharing a head. Her fingers clutched his brainstem and Ma'at thrust herself into his heart. She was gone. He had no way to know her thoughts, but he felt her within him.

He heard her voice, "I'm going. I will be with you in your dreams for as long as you are occupying this form. I will help you. There are three gifts waiting in your foyer. They are from a place that exists no longer. A place beyond Logos. They will be immune to you. They will love you. It is their nature to be what you need them to be. Blessed be, Osaze."

He felt her leave him at once. His possessor vanished. The blanket of light began to lift and the universal darkness returned. Still elaborately webbed in that romantic red light like the color of Ma'at's eyes during the passion.

Tobias couldn't imagine what Ma'at had been referring to. Then there was a sensory disruption. From nothing, he saw a box forming around him, over the course of a couple disorienting seconds he found himself standing back in his bedroom where he'd woken up that morning.

Arianna belonged under those covers.

In a red flash he was dressed again. He was alone and certainly not actually back on Gaia. He looked out the window and the webs glimmered back at him from uncounted light years away. He walked around his messy unmade bed; his decor matched the colors beyond the window. He looked around for a moment more before realizing the sensible thing to do was to go out into the rest of the apartment.

He opened the bedroom door and there on the couch sat three beautiful girls, each around eighteen years old; one uniquely distinct from the other two. They smiled at him. He chuckled to himself. They couldn't be real. Two were fair skinned Asian, they looked like twins, so petite, and the other was porcelain white like himself. Each of their hair was the same, brown and cropped at cheek length; the white girl's hair looked black against her skin. They were wearing the same outfit; fishnet stockings, black skirts with red stitching on the Asian's miniskirts, and purple stitching on the stunning white girl. They each wore a black bikini top. Osaze could guess they weren't wearing panties.

"Hi," he said playfully, "I'm Osaze. What are your names?"

The white one spoke, "We have no names. It's for you to name us?"

"Oh, god. Y'all are a moral dilemma waiting to happen. Have you ever been human before?"

Again, the same girl spoke, "No. This is the first time. And we are not human now. Only in human form. Like you, Osaze. We are to be your companions, and you are to be our keeper. We know very little of what lies ahead. Only what has been told to us by Ma'at. Our instructions were to learn from you how to best please you. There was little else, but it is certain that without your attention and guidance, we cannot endure this Logos. Without your love, we will fade back into where we came from. We were created that way."

"Where did you come from?"

He knew; from Ma'at. "We came from Ma'at and from the source. Not from you. We know little else. Our presence is new. We've never encountered any entities other than Ma'at during our genesis, and you here now. You are to be our architect. We will become flesh at your return to Gaia and be with you until the flesh dies, then together we four will go to our new home elsewhere."

"Elsewhere? I can't believe I have to name you. Do you mind if we wait?" They shook their heads no. "Good. Just until I get a better idea of how I want this to turn out."

"Osaze?"

"Yeah." He noticed their glares had changed; they were eying him enticingly. The white one, with nymphet features- soft defined curves, an up turned nose, and big sparkly black eyes- waited for his attention. She got it quickly.

With fluid, effortless, grace she stood and walked to him. She turned her eyes up submissively. He pulled her into himself and kissed her lips. The kiss was that of Ma'at. Her kiss was his kiss. The kiss of Ma'at; that perfect harmony between bonded lovers. The Asians approached; Japanese, he knew; exquisite and fair. He pulled away, to kiss the first Asian, then the second. Each kissed the same.

The Asians paid each other no mind- they took turns stroking him and the white girl- as he stroked them. Their clothes, article by article, faded away, their lips were everywhere, their tongues grazing exposed skin, and together they stumbled backward into the bedroom.

****

"We need cigarettes out here," Osaze said.

"You can have cigarettes. This is your domain. All you've ever wanted is yours in this place," said the white girl who had her head nuzzled against his chest, under his arm. One Asian was in the same position under the other arm. The third girl was sprawled between his legs with her head lying on his tummy. Eight hands caressed.

Osaze realized she was absolutely correct. He was on his back staring at the ceiling where the cigarette manifested. It was a tailor-made, like he hadn't seen since before the die-off began. For a moment he considered putting embalming fluid on it, but he thought maybe it was a bad time. The ignited cigarette hovered slowly down into his mouth, and he puffed a few times. He realized there was enough air being produced from the vacuum of that reality to smoke the cigarette. Within him, his lungs extracted the nicotine even though he had no lungs.

"Take this and put it in your mouth, and suck the smoke in. That'll kind of be like what it's going to be like when you'll have to breathe constantly. Like this," he took the cigarette back and demonstrated. Then the girls passed it around. They didn't cough or choke. They just smiled and laughed while each took their turn.

"I've got your names figured out."

That got their attention. The three naked girls sat up to their knees; their tight bodies still touching each other; nipples poking, skin rubbing, knees touching, and they remained crowded around Osaze.

"You will be Kyoto and you will be Kobe."

Kyoto looked at Kobe and said, "Kobe." Kobe looked at Kyoto and said, "Kyoto."

Osaze chose those names because Kyoto was more domineering than Kobe. He also knew, definitely, those two names were Japanese because they are the names of cities there. Kyoto struck him as a more intense word, and she was a more intense girl. During love making she oriented the other's bodies and essentially choreographed the other two for Osaze's benefit. Kobe was more delicate and submissive. She was coy and Osaze had to give her encouragement to not shy away. He also noticed that while they both kissed the same, Kobe's fluids had a sweeter taste than Kyoto's. Naturally, the two girls were equal and opposite. An introvert and an extravert. A bottom and a top.

His first instinct was to name the white girl Aloria, in honor of his stolen love. That would have been degrading for her, so he abstained. It occurred to him that Porcelain was a good name. Like her skin in the dim glow of the apartment. In the shadows of the other lovers her skin appeared to be glowing with a faint red hue like the threads out in space there. With that in mind he decided her name.

"Your name is Solaris."

Solaris smiled and knelt down to kiss Osaze on the lips. Kyoto and Kobe giggled and put their hands on each other like amused girls tend to do. Solaris sat up and Kyoto and Kobe said, "Solaris."

"So what do you, like, know?" Osaze asked.

"We know most things that you know. We were generated that way. You are to teach us how you want us to be. We already love you. It is for you to teach us how to love you," Solaris said.

"I think you've proved quite well that you know how to do that."

They giggled. "Not only in that way. We are transcending Logos together. We'll need to become so accustomed to your needs and desires that you'll be satisfied with our company for an eternity.

"We were also given the inherent ability to temper you. We are to guide your whims. We are the load bearing structure with which your burden can be carried. For it is your nature to succumb in the face of adversity. But, were you to succumb, the Logos would be destroyed."

This made Osaze think, and he asked, "What do you know about my burden? I don't even understand. I am the evil?"

"You cannot call it you and you can't call it your consciousness. I would say that you are what you are. You are special and different from all else. If it were not for the grace of the Ma'at, your being would have suffocated what dwells within Logos. In the way that you can dwell within Logos, others dwell within you. What dwells in you can dwell nowhere else for you are the only habitat capable of sustaining such absolute negativity."

****

With the constant questioning and interrupting, it took about an hour for Drake to finish explaining what Alcyone had told him. Aden used deductive reasoning to piece together the fact that he was involved in the drama. He couldn't figure out how, though. He suspected Lyn was involved, but knew she knew nothing. He needed to talk to Tobias. Or Osaze. For it even to be possible for them to be completely oblivious for that long, then what else was possible? As it were, the news was grim.

If there were to be any grand revelation, Aden would have preferred, 'You guys will live long healthy lives while everyone and everything else will stay dead.' He could have accepted that. He figured that the only logical outcome was for them to make it further into the future. Or, he hoped.

Instead they were embarking on a quest to ignite the planet, and if they didn't die in the process they would die from the end result. They were isolated from the other life on the planet. It was trapped in the sky. They were below. Tobias was the darkness. Arianna was some Plieadian... or, outer space woman, or whatever. There was something off about them both from the beginning. And if there was something wrong with her, then was something wrong with him. Probably something fantastic.

Cadence had made breakfast for them and they hung around on that fated morning eating southwest seasoned spam, rice, beans, with hot sauce, and drinking concentrated juice. Only Calvin really cared about what Drake had to say. They finally had the certainty to face their mortality and the kid took it better than them. They had been procrastinating facing death since they arrived at Endsville. A bloody legacy of misguided delusions.

Aden understood at last why they were killing the refugees. It was the humans that were meant to be eradicated. No ifs, ands, or anythings. There was nothing human about any of them. The mystery had been solved for Toby and Arianna. They didn't tell Drake anything. Was Drake human?

"Are you human, Drake?" Aden asked.

"As far as I can tell, we're all human."

"Even Tobias and Arianna?"

Drake corrected him, "Osaze and Aloria. Yeah. Them, too. Why do you ask?"

Robin interrupted, "It's obvious. You don't get it? It's not just those two. It's all of us. There's something about us that kept us from rising up with everything else. Based on what Drake said, I get the impression we're tending this planet. I think we work here. Our pay is membership at Club Olympus."

Drake said, "They've been part of this the whole time. Alcyone didn't in any way lead me to believe that we are anything more than human."

Calvin pouted, "We're alive because of Toby and Arianna. We're just their servants, and we're going to die like everyone else while they get to live in outer space." So much for acceptance.

Aden said, "I believe that."

Logan said, "How can you agree with that? A little kid said it." Calvin wasn't offended. He wanted to know, too.

"I know it, because it's true. For some of us. Drake. You. Logan. Maybe you two." He pointed at Robin and Cadence.

Cadence said, "Well. What about Lyn? She was a twin. Why wouldn't her sister have lived?" Lyn's eyes responded sharply but in no manner threatened. "Is there too many of us, or not enough?"

"Or just enough," Calvin said.

Lyn said, "What is the point of speculating about this? The only thing to do is to wait until they get back and then we'll find out more."

Calvin said, "Do any of you feel that."

Aden did feel something. The floor rumbled. He looked out the window; through the dark midday light he saw the dead trees and evergreens of the mountainside uprooting and flipping off into the sky before falling back to the Earth again. There was a rumble. There was more than that. An invisible explosion blew a hole in the sky goo and he could faintly see the black stuff shooting out toward the Earth; powerfully illuminated by an intense sunbeam casting straight down through.

Aden shouted, "Get down to storage right fucking

now!" He scooped up Calvin and hustled through the cafeteria toward the stairs. There was screaming behind him, as well as the destructive clamor. The rate in which the trees snapped and fell. Overlaying rhythms of cracking and crashing.

The Omega clan ran together down the back stairway between the kitchen and the lounge. At the basement they huddled into a concrete crook in the building. Aden crouched at the center of their group cradling Calvin in his arms. Lyn wrapped herself around them. Robin and Cadence huddled close with their hands over each other's head. Drake wrapped his arms around them with his head turned toward the event and watching.

"What is happening?" Calvin asked.

The auditory chaos amplified, intensified, shook the floor and rattled the walls. Shattering windows created a ringing as the glass collided into itself; tinkling.

Aden shouted back, "It's 2012 remember? We're probably about to die!"

"I don't mind," Calvin said. All seven of them were in that trench together. Taking fire from whatever the hell would dare to attack them. It didn't make any sense.

"How would this happen?" Logan asked. He stood at the edge of the huddle, facing the upheaval head on.

Other destructive sounds were equally obvious. The roof went next and they felt that force through the concrete. The wind bombarded one wall after another; deep and potent bursts as cyclical wind whipped on and off and on and the structure tore apart from itself. The momentum of the forces switched direction randomly. Over their head the floor was being ripped apart, the sunlight meekly shined upon them for the first time since Aden could remember and the basement level began to shake and rattle more intensely.

Drake said, "I guess they wanted to make sure we

left."

Robin said, "I told you, man. We work for them."

"It's going away!" Cadence said. She was right. The maelstrom from arrival to dissolution lasted only a minute or so. "Aden, you dick. Why would you tell Calvin we were going to die?"

"I thought we would. He took it well."

"I'm not afraid to die. I know we're just like Tobias and Arianna. We're going to outer space and leaving this whole place behind. That doesn't make me the least bit sad. This place is sad. I want to go someplace where there is happiness. Drake said we'll be happy when we die."

THE LOGOS

They'd found their way into clothes again. Osaze stared out the window and the girls gazed at him. He thought how three women, no matter how perfect, could never replace what he had come to appreciate the most by loving Arianna. Perhaps when he was younger and less aware of the blackness inside him, he may have adapted better to the loss of her love and light.

He controlled the darkness of the Logos. This power was his to use in whatever way he saw fit, even if he wanted to use the darkness to harness itself- an idea to consider. Except, he didn't understand how. Harnessing his darkness was something Arianna always did. He couldn't do it without her. He didn't want to do anything without her. Living even. Awareness felt like an intrusive obligation.

He remembered about the Logos. That was the next thing, if not the last thing, to do out there. "Girls, we gotta go." He looked at them when he said it. They knew his thoughts. Or, most of the time they knew his thoughts. He playfully disappeared the bed and apartment so the giggling girls sunk suddenly into the supportive ether.

"Y'all ready?"

"Totally," Solaris said. Kobe and Kyoto smiled.

Tobias, feeling small, in space, looked around with nervous anxiety. In his mind, any knowledge of Logos was completely inaccessible to him. Like repelling magnets, he couldn't connect what was in his head to reality; the issue felt as a discomfort in and of itself.

The barriers of his domain began to flutter and falter in various uniformed energetic pulses. A manipulation of his awareness; a phenomenon at the border of what was supposed to be his. In one particular area, far far off, the colors fluttered into blues and greens. While elsewhere the limits remained that same romantic red.

"Yeah. Do you three want to wait in the apartment?"

"That seems best."

Tobias gave each girl the kiss of Osaze, an embrace, and then he moved away. The apartment reappeared around them. From the outside it appeared as though it had been torn directly off of Endsville. Except, nothing was flaking away, all was intact. He noticed that the structure was clean like that. Chaotically organized in an obsessive compulsive sort of way.

It didn't matter. Logos had arrived. Tobias could recognize the colors but couldn't guess what to expect. At that realization he began his approach. Moving forward was not preferred. He faded into- became- the darkness, and from that perspective he observed the Logos.

Osaze knew exactly how the cards were stacked. To some relief. Being of the human dimensions was like, for them, living in space for a human.

There was Logos. The two were something of a polarized situation. Darkness alternating with light. Logos would say; each a vector quantity indicating the

electric dipole moment per unit of volume of a
dielectric.

****

From beyond the intermingling greens, blue
greens, and yellows, Logos appeared in the figure of
Aden; if Aden were a fantasia of light and color. In that
void he sat upon an immense cubic crystal like a throne,
or ledge, as it were.

In the same vein, Osaze automatically utilized a
wave of beaming red radiation- coming from the girls
back in the sanctuary- to create a silhouette of himself.

"Feels like the beginning doesn't it?" Logos asked
him.

"Yeah. That it does, Imperatore. Thanks for not
destroying me."

"And to you, too."

Osaze laughed. "What are we doing out here?"

"Whatever we want?"

"Can we go to Aloria?"

"No. Not at all. You are absurd. So vast and still
completely small in every way."

"Yo. Fuck that. If you can't take me there, I'll go
myself. She has been my fixation since she was created.
We've belonged to each other always."

"Well. You and I have more pressing things to do so
you'll have to forget about it for now. I wouldn't go if I
were you. Not now. Or anytime ever."

"Then what are we doing?"

"I don't know, what are we doing?" Logos said,
laughing.

"Tell me things. You have to be aware Aden's been
cracking up back at Gaia. Calvin is haunted, practically."

"That's you making that happen. You're not overly
affecting any of the others."

"The others. They're going to want to know why

they're still alive," Osaze said.

"They'll find out. When they're dead. Or sooner. Let's go to Gaia and approach them."

"I've the trio involved. They have to come, too."

"Leave them. Ma'at will be their company. They'll be waiting when you return. We'll be very direct. We're to visit the wreckage. Call it an upliftment."

"Wreckage? Oh. You're kidding me." Osaze was unaware of the situation down at Endsville, until that moment. "No one is dead?"

"No. But they are going to resent the sudden departure of Aloria."

"I fucking resent it!"

"Well. Get over it."

"That makes no sense. She is on my wavelength. She allows me continuance. I'm made nearly entirely of my love for her. The 'me' you expect to be dominate is the smallest part imaginable. I'm 99% love and 1% the problem. Very few truly understand what I do."

"I get it. I've been tolerating you since as long as I've been this place. Which was alright. You had your time, now you go away."

"Yeah. The grand rejection. Quaint."

Logos said, "Grand expulsion, don't make it personal. You ready to see what happened at Vermont?"

"Fine. Let's do it."

"We're catching a sun beam, so watch out."

Osaze twisted into himself and automatically followed Logos through the ether, into nothing, and to a place of blinding white light and discomforting intensity. He became a figure of jet black, yet as his senses flooded back to him he saw Logos in nearly immaculate detail. Logos was entirely blinding. A being of pure light.

"All right. Hang back."

They fell for a moment and from a thousand feet high in the sky Osaze viewed the devastation at his favorite mountainside community. They steadied themselves. Sections of forest had been cleared. All the dead fall was accumulated in the canyons. The resort lay blown across the graveyards out back.

The destruction distributed itself into various obscure patterns. The ski lift poles had been unearthed. The parking lot remained unharmed and the vehicles appeared untouched.

The hotel still stood, almost unharmed, were it not divided. Half of the four story rectangular building had crumbled to a pile of rubble on the ground. The other half, for whatever reason, stayed standing and looked unfazed.

For Osaze to be visible in this domain it was necessary that a beam of consciousness, like enlivened photons, illuminated him from some direction. For this reason Logos cast large quantities of light upon Osaze; an unspoken requisite to the situation.

Osaze and Logos descended toward the weary band of huddled survivors. With an unseen force Logos detached a chunk of the intact floor and threw it aside to reveal the Omega clan remnants cowering and clinging to each other in the basement.

Cadence looked up first and shrieked, "Oh, what the fuck?"

Osaze said, "Everybody chill out. It's us. Tobias and Aden. Sort of."

Robin said, "What do you mean? Aden's right here.

Logos said, "That's complicated, and we're not here to explain it. Ask Osaze when he returns."

"Wait, so who is coming back? Osaze or Tobias?" Drake asked.

Aden said, "Osaze is Tobias."

Robin said, "Aden, you don't find this strange that that naked guy made of light is claiming to be you?"

He replied, "He looks like me. I don't find anything

strange anymore. Besides, I had a feeling something strange might happen."

Logos lowered himself to the ground. His shimmering golden light became contained within itself, as though by a pliable tinted glass container. He approached Aden and lowered his face to his face. Logos looked into Aden's blue eyes with two sparkling white orbs. Everyone was still for a moment, then Logos' eyes flashed and Aden flew headlong backward, toppling into the screaming others.

Aden lost consciousness. Lyn cradled his head, Robin checked for a pulse and reported, "He's not dead."

"Of course he's not dead. He'll be fine when he awakens," Logos said, and floated backward to where Osaze hovered above. Osaze watched Calvin staring intently at his silhouette. Logos acknowledged the moment by shining even more light upon Osaze, whose blackness did not change.

Yet, his form became incredibly clear. Looking as much like Tobias as a featureless black figure could. Then radiation seethed and the lines of him became defined, from lips to shirt sleeves in varying intensities of red.

"Are you always going to look like that?" Calvin asked him.

"That's a complicated question. The short answer is no. But you should remember to ask Tobias about it when he gets back."

The confused child then asked, "How come you're not Tobias?"

"I very much am Tobias. He'll explain it, I promise."

Lyn looked up, brushed the hair from her face, and asked, "Why are you even here? What destroyed this place?"

Logos answered, "As for why we're here, why the hell not? We came to bless you guys, I don't know."

Cadence said, "You cheated on Arianna?"

"Yeah. Ma'at's the fabric of reality. Was I going to say no? And, 'Arianna,' left me to be with her sisters. She dropped me like I was nothing. Not to mention, I'll be returning with three girls, and I hope you'll make them feel welcome."

Robin said, "Ok. So you're God, right? And, you're the darkness? Neither of you have anything relevant to say about why you're here right now?"

"You can call me Logos. I came here to do that to Aden. The rest is superfluous. Lyn's other half is the one who destroyed this place."

Drake chimed in, "Nice going, Lyn."

Osaze said, "If it happened, there was a good reason. You have to leave this place anyway, when Tobias is back."

Calvin shouted, "But you are Tobias!"

"No. I'm Osaze. Tobias is part of me. The part that you know. I am the part of me that Logos knows."

"Ok. We were supposed to ask you something. I can't remember what." Calvin said.

Logos said, "You can ask Tobias when he returns. It's time for us to leave."

Lyn said, "What about Aden? He's still unconscious."

"I said he'll be fine. Come on Osaze. Bye everyone."

Osaze said, "You guys can chill out because everything is going to be totally alright. Get it? Chill out? Cuz it's fucking freezing out here. Ha. Later."

****

Aden's eyes opened and he saw the black sky stretching out above him. He was on a couch covered in blankets and still very cold. He sat up and saw Lyn sitting at a lunch table, writing in her notebook with fingers poking out of tipless blue gloves.

"Hi."

Lyn ran to his side and said, "Oh, finally. I was starting to think you were in a coma."

"You could call it that," he said.

"What the hell happened?

"I don't believe it. I was hundreds of miles away, and it felt like the back side of my eyelids. Like a dream. Except, it was real. I was in the place where the ghosts are wandering, and it's around us. Animals, a lot of women, not many men. It was pure and good. And they're waiting for this planet to become flames.

"I am this. I am all of this. And everything I am not, that's you. I can't for the life of me figure out what the fuck we're doing here as people. That's just the way it is. My suspicion is that we are in fact everybody, in a way. We are everything except life itself. That is coming from somewhere else. And there are others like us. We're part of them, and they're part of us; within us in the same way that we are apart from them. Just other creative forces impacting the whole."

Aden omitted from his description of inner eyelid events that he'd had an audience with Alcyone who explained those details, and many more, to him. He left out his encounter with Alcyone because there was a sexual escapade involved and he didn't want Lyn to figure out that after Alcyone clarified the confusing haze of missing information they'd made ridiculously intense separate reality love on a deserted white sand beach, somewhere at the equator.

This meant Alcyone was still in the vicinity of Earth. Aden was already wondering when he'd get another crack at her. He felt a little guilty, but wasn't going to break down about it. Lyn was in her own world, so was he, and it didn't really matter. And if he recalled, she, in some way, fucked Tobias in outer space and it destroyed the whole property. Her or her twin.... An important detail.

He said, "What I need to do is figure out how to get

back to that place."

"I'm sure you will. If it's around us, and we are what it is no less, you shouldn't have too much difficulty. We need to tell the others you're awake."

"No. They'll figure it out. Where are they?"

Lyn looked around, so he twisted his head, too. Earlier that morning Endsville was as pristine as anything could be. The snow wasn't brown from torn up earth. There was a roof. There wasn't a roof anymore. It was a ruin. Indeed, the first people he saw were Drake and Logan wandering aimlessly through the rubble. He ignored them and admired how Tobias' and Robin's domeciles were unharmed, though the living room up there was gone, while his place, under the hotel, was almost certainly destroyed. He didn't feel any need to get off the couch.

He lifted the blankets for Lyn to crawl under with him. She had lots of clothes on. It was December in the mountains. Given the lack of housing, he figured it might be best to take a car and go South. Then he remembered that he hadn't felt lucid since before he first saw the lights, back when nobody knew what the fuck was what. He felt Lyn's warmth. The wind didn't blow and they couldn't hear anybody. Very peacefully, Aden's eyes closed and he fell back asleep.

Aden lifted from his body, still in the same form, only weightless and outside of reality. In total control. If he wanted gravity, he could have it. Given the choice, his feet had no need for ground. He saw the ghosts of the innocent wandering in the graveyard. They were relatively boring and of little interest. Alcyone. He needed to see her again.

"Alcyone!"

With no volition of his own he faded and reappeared. His tattered surroundings faded and reappeared with Alcyone standing naked on the beach. Her tall womanly form; tan skin, short black hair.

Aquamarine waves crashed. Palm trees hung low in the muggy heat. Lyn was nowhere under the sun. They fornicated while simultaneously flying out over the ocean, then lay together naked in the lapping waves at shore.

"I don't understand what the hell it is I'm supposed to do," Aden said.

"Stay out of the way."

"Why? Endsville's been destroyed. I'm bored already. I'm ready to be Logos, now. You don't get it. I have no reason to be there."

"You don't know a reason, but you have an obligation. These luminous humans exist inside of what you have created for them. You and Lyn must be present for the ascension. Or else Logos will have to be here, and that will cause problems in ways and places that you could never know. So don't be selfish, stick around."

"That doesn't make sense. If I am human-"

She cut him off, "Human is not all you are. None of you people are human. You're little illuminated agendas that need to align and harmonize to facilitate setting the pure ones free. What you need to do is stay out of the way. Take Lyn and go on a trip someplace. Or whatever."

"That's it? I can't help the others?"

"You can help them if you want to. Just stay the hell away from Tobias; he's volatile. That's probably why Logos gave you access to this cognition. To help. You can interact with me while you're sleeping."

"I can do that?"

"Easily. You don't even really have to be asleep. It helps, though. Just don't do it standing up, or you'll fall and break your head open."

"So what's going to happen? What is the difference between if I die today or if I die later on?"

"I've already told you. There will be complications. Imagine a tent with no poles. Or a building with no load bearing structures. An air mattress with no air."

"People don't have that kind of an effect on anything."

"People don't. You do. Think of it another way. You're doing something. You can't feel it. You are clearly unaware of it. But the effect is happening through you. Like a satellite. Logos is standing in through you. The situation on this planet is infinitely complicated. A human mind is not meant to grasp it, even if they devote their entire lives to trying."

"You said I'm not human."

"Of course you are. They're waking you up."

"They can try. Come here."

Aden playfully embraced Alcyone, but she laughed and pushed him away, insisting he return to Endsville. He immediately did. His eyes closed and opened to Drake, Logan, and Robin standing over him. He nudged Lyn awake, and said to them, "What's up?"

"You tell us," Robin said. "What happened to you?"

"Nothing. I've just been dreaming," he said.

****

Logistically, Aloria was trapped in a nebula among several larger nebulae; swirling clouds of intense gasses made of underdeveloped lifeforms connected to a localized coalescence at the gravitational centers. The main blue and yellow Nebula was called Hilt. Hilt was new.

Aloria wasn't allowed to think. She wasn't allowed to move. She wasn't allowed to travel between the stars like the others. She wasn't even allowed to explore her own domain. Her human body had been discarded into the upper atmosphere of Earth by the Zeta Reticuli.

Of the Omega Clan, she was the first to die. Her awareness was given over to bondage. Her sisters assured her it was only a matter of time until her assent and essentially stole her from herself. Before the Ascension Aloria would be released. But until then, she was being regarded as the only threat to a far more important process. If she were free, there was a chance she might reconsider the importance of her Pleiadien family and return to Osaze. Her essence was pliable, notoriously attracted to Osaze, and couldn't be trusted.

So they gave her a temporary prison of restriction called Hilt. Her form was not defined and neither was Hilt. Hilt wasn't real, he was a synthetic attractor and his purpose was to keep her confined to a specific void out in the most congested reaches of a vacant nebula where dark matter couldn't reach her- only until Osaze had been banished. The Sister's knew Osaze would return for his Lover. He always did. They'd entrusted Hilt as a last line of defense.

Aloria was the lost sister. The only one that wouldn't remain in the familial clutches. Her consciousness was such that only attraction dictated her actions. And so, with the aide of Ma'at, the sister's engineered Hilt to keep Aloria's intentions and will locked to a precise anchor. She couldn't think or make decisions. Her true spirit was vast, and her essence whirled through the cosmos, but always remained in the prison of Hilt.

If she could feel, or think, or do anything other than exist at a subconscious level, she would call to Osaze and he would demand a reconfiguration of the terms of the Grand Ascension. He would organize the universe for them to be together. If Osaze knew about Hilt, all would be lost.

In thoughtlessness, like the massacres, Aloria melded to Hilt, her love not even a notion; under the spell of thoughtlessness. There were alternative destinies.

All was contingent that Osaze never access Hilt.

The lower dimensions were unified in their desire for release from gravity. Gravity, the effect of the fourth dimension on mass. Osaze was the fourth dimension. He was the emptiness and vast tracts of nothingness. Which of course had nothing to do with nothingness. Osaze was a very specific somethingness.

He was the evil; the misdeeds, the universal predisposition toward self-gain in every dimension below. He was limitations and illusions of scarcity. What shined through from above and beyond, did so in spite of Osaze.

That was the way the Logos identified- the way the Logos had always been. Lower dimensions were distorted by Osaze. Oh well. That was part of it. The Logos commanded respect, and what Osaze commanded was resent.

Tobias had protested, saying the Ascension was selfish. In a way it was. It's been said, 'There are none resented more than the ones we're indebted to.' And Osaze, if anything, was an unpaid dept. Except, the larger view was of momentum and essentially a turning away from a failed wavelength, a veiled separateness. Except, few entities would acknowledge that was possible because of Osaze. They needed to realize Osaze wasn't some bi-product to be expelled. He was the essence of existence; the breath of consciousness whispering through the solar wind. He was what the cats are aware of.

And upon his exit there would be stillness. Epic peace. Unified. All would be part of it. There would be no identity. There would be no personality. There would be love. Alterations and freedom. Except there would be no contrast. There would be no darkness. This was not the will of the Logos. This was the will of Yah. And as such could never be changed, because Yah is what is constant and unchanging.

Without Osaze, there was only Ma'at and Logos.

And then the others. Except, the others would become Ma'at and Logos. And, while Ma'at and Logos would become Yah, the reverse is also true. Everything that ever was or would be was becoming, essentially, a romantic getaway. Logos. It was the opinion of the Logos that Osaze belonged. Destruction made creation exciting and damn the harm. There's always Yin. Even without Yang.

****

Osaze returned, with Logos, to the outer reaches of his designation. They remained in their natural forms. Osaze, a large man-shaped darkness etched in radiation nerves; bathed in deep red light cast from the three girls instantly far away and forever close. He asked, "Listen. If there is anything I should know about Aloria, you would tell me, right?"

Logos, the colors of his figure subdued by the leisure following his chore, said, "Yeah. I would. And there is. She's being kept from you under a spell and bound deep in nebula. There is no way for you to get to her."

"Bound? That's unthinkable."

"The sister's fear your love will overthrow the Ascension. I believe it."

"That's nonsense. I understand the situation. We could work something out."

"Do you understand? She's gone. The situation is something new and different entirely. She is staying with this out here, and when you're gone, this out here will have nothing to do with you. You know as well as I do she cannot go where you are going. If she could exist there, she would.

"Think of before her. Then there was her. Now there will be after her. And you don't realize there is more to this than just her."

"Not to me. I am conditioned to her returns. If she does not return, I don't know what that will do to me."

"Look at what has happened. The sisters are involved. Which has never happened. Nothing is going to be the same for you. Except for yourself."

"The sisters never approved. As a matter of fact, it has always been the same story with them. Toxic. Toxic. Osaze, you're toxic. I don't believe for a second I am toxic to her. What if there is an antidote within her. What if Ma'at can use her to incorporate me into the ascension? We can peacefully co-exist through the power of love."

"Love has very little power over anything. Love mostly has nothing to do with power. Lovers are unfocused distortions. And that's not Ma'at you're thinking of."

"Well, maybe that's best. If I have to address Yah then I will. Essentially... preserving love from that narrow attitude. And I suspect these three girls came out of Yah. So I should probably treat them accordingly."

"They came from Ma'at. You have good cause. Yah always sees it both ways, just like you. Except, Yah is unflinching and if you were to alter Yah, the changes would be a mirror of your influence, and you know that is never good. Look what you cause at each regeneration. You should bow out."

"There is a way. Through Aloria. There has to be a way. And if there is a way, Yah will know what it is."

"Tobias needs to return. You'll have to locate Yah another time."

"Tobias needs to return and carry out the agenda of the sisters and Ma'at? I think not. I'm already here."

"Tobias might die."

"So be it. Is Arianna not dead? Let the others ignite the planet."

"There's something Alcyone said."

"You've been seeing Alcyone?"

"Aden has. On Gaia."

"Alcyone is on Gaia? What did she say?"

"Well. It's obvious. Aden is there for a reason. Lyn for a reason. The others serve a purpose. Tobias is the photoplasm. If he's not there, the mass will dissipate, and the ignition can't take place. You have to take your new harem to Gaia. They clearly serve a very specific purpose, whatever it might be."

"So, the Pleiadiens are using me?"

"They're using us, but I suppose it is different for you."

"Well, I don't understand then, am I not doing my part? Why is there no place for me?"

"They want you to gather up the mess you made and clear out. They want to eliminate the passions and disturbances."

"Eliminating the passions is a terrible idea."

"Go figure. The Sisters are women. Ma'at flows with them and Yah is of course the source, as he flows through Ma'at, not me or you. To get to Yah, you'll have to sway the sisters. A cluster of silly girls, oddly enough, controls the decisions of Yah. It's a simple and effective system, but nobody is going to listen to you if you dissolve the photoplasm. Go be grab those girls, go be Tobias, and get back to Gaia."

Osaze peered within toward the nucleus area where a beacon of red light shone back. He said, "I love how this isn't difficult for anything except me."

"You surf the envelope. You are the rift, the chasm, the abyss, you are barely even real, and yet, everything is affected by you. You are the disharmony. You are the reason for this. If you never were, we wouldn't require an ascension."

"There would be nothing to ascend."

"Exactly. The twist of Logos has been my effort to maintain stillness against your exertion. This is the bottom of the spiral."

"Right where we are, too. Well, I believe Aloria can raise me to harmony if I let her. I've never had such a thought contrary. Yeah, I have to go. Always nice to see you."

"You too. If Tobias has any questions, have him ask Aden. Aden will know. Oh. And take this with you, for Tobias."

Logos offered Osaze a glowing red orb, the size of an eyeball. Osaze chuckled and said, "This has bad news written all over it."

"He needs as much vision as he can get."

"This is going to be bad, huh?"

"Absolutely."

He turned away from Logos and reentered his designation. The dormant red threads of the Endsphere welcomed him and flared back into vibrancy. Then, with a jolt as Logos left, an indescribable boom of oranges, greens, and blues rippled in waves across the vast tracts of threads for a moment, then again it was the usual red.

Osaze quietly said, sarcastically, "Maybe I'll see you again sometime," and then he became Tobias. Tobias removed his anarchist eye patch, and the orb within his eye socket glowed red like smoldering light. The eye of Logos. It felt a little warm, very comforting.

Tobias was completely disoriented, and pains in his brain felt as though he could happily die and never live again. Some kind of reaction to Logos emotive blast. At least he had vision from two eyes, something completely new, even in the outer reaches.

HEIROPHANT

Irritated and very anxious he drifted across the thought plains as clarity steadily returned. A nervous weight in his chest taxed him; shooting vague pains up through his skull. And, as he'd been since he let them take Arianna away, he was afraid.

He drifted slowly trying to recollect lost thoughts that seemed to have floated away into the vastness. Unable to well recall the experience with the Logos, he instead utilized a general knowing to reassure himself the encounter had actually happened. As if his new vision weren't evidence enough. He recalled everything like a dream. Moving toward Logos, slipping away from one form, becoming different, traveling to the Earth, then returning. He'd become that dark form of Osaze. Where he had been, and what he had become exactly, the answers weren't clear. The answer was he'd been his higher self. But it wasn't clear what that meant.

Clarity was gone. There was confusion and distortion about what happened. Like he wasn't even real. He felt as an echo of something greater. His human life as dead as humanity. Osaze mattered not. He was Tobias. Tobias would die, as people die.

This meant that Arianna could be dead. Dead and gone. Tobias snapped at the urgency. In an instant he stood in front of the girls back inside the apartment.

"Ok. Beautiful girls. We have to get back to Gaia immediately. So everyone come here and hang on to me. I don't know how we're getting there, but we're going."

They tore through blackness in a direction that was somewhat geared toward the Pleiades. He couldn't figure exactly what way to delve into the situation. He could go to the Pleiades and locate Alcyone, but she may have nothing to say. They took Arianna away from him once, they could probably keep her. Presuming she's Ok. He had to access her on a certain wavelength, in a certain dimension.

"We have to go rescue the mortal soul of my girlfriend."

"How can she have a mortal soul?" Solaris- their main voice- asked.

"She was alive. She was human. I still am. The Zeta

have my body. I presume something is worked out for you. Then you'll have mortal souls, too. I think. So that's the point. I don't know why I'm freaking out. We're above this. The problem is I'm looking out for Osaze and Aloria."

"This has been decided that you will not be able to sustain relations with her."

"By a vindictive yolk of motives and agendas, none of which are mine and are founded on lies."

"That's your imagination."

"No. I can feel it. There's something wrong with her head."

"What if you are the cause of it? What if the problem is in your head?"

"I thought of that. We're bound together forever, her and I. I don't care about the rest."

"They won't allow it. You'll have to seek a higher power."

"I'm supposed to be going into my physical body. Through the Merkaba. Mesmere will at the very least have answers. I really don't want to stir up the Pleiadiens. Completely torn up over the whole way this situation looks fragile. There's something in me that wasn't there before, literally, but it's not coming from this eye, it's coming from my nerves and my gut. If I don't get answers, I'm going to put two and two together and wreak some fucking havoc on that star cluster. Love. What of love? I remember the books. They told me there'd be love in the Pleiades because they control the fifth dimension and these bitches have blocked me at every turn. When- as ugly as it seems- there is a symbiosis between Arianna and myself, and beyond that Osaze and Aloria. I can't figure out what the hell is going on. I'm freaking out. You girls ready to confront somebody?"

"Totally. We love you, Osaze."

"I love you, too, Omegas."

Like slipping through a ripple they found themselves submerged in water. He came up to breathe air through choppy waves. In the distance a white tower stood on a small grassy island with very few trees. They were in crystal blue and salty waters, swimming toward the shore. As they swam they moved like dolphins. And there were dolphins. Underwater, Tobias could see every creature in the pod. Long spotted dolphins twirling as they dove and spun back up. Curiously, the dolphins watched the four new arrivals.

Hand in hand they slipped through the waters effortlessly toward the island where porcelain foundations and structures created courtyards. Gardens of vibrant floral vegetation he'd never seen hung and bulged in an aesthetically pleasing way. They approached a clean white wall with a ladder made of shimmering metal. Tobias climbed up first and the others followed.

On solid ground it occurred to him that he felt restricted. He looked to the nest atop the shimmering, and slightly crooked, white tower. The height was nothing outlandish; only four or five stories. There were eyes peering back through the window.

"Will you three wait here? You can play with the dolphins."

The girls giggled. They'd already begun fading their wet clothes away. Solaris kissed him on his lips, and the Kobe and Kyoto hugged him and kissed him on either cheek. Attempting to resist their charms, he hurried away toward the tower to the sound of the girls splashing back into the water. The world glowed in the light of the several flaring blue stars of the Pleiades sisters. Light in that place, vision, maintained a metallic blue transparency.

He marched up an acre of steps toward the base of the ivory tower. There was a wooden door shaped like an arch. He opened it and walked up the curving, glazed, black steps. The walls were spectacularly sheer and lush. Noticing made him remember what he'd managed to forget. It pissed him off to remember and more to realize he'd nearly forgotten.

With lofty and easy movement Tobias ascended. The stairway opened to a single foyer with, of all things, wicker furniture. The Pleiadian sky, a prominent feature. One single woman sat seated and staring at him, with a stare that wasn't a stare because it was a glare, and before he could say anything, she said, "I created you."

She was Maia. And for best accounts that was accurate. Except these things were decided before any life form was cognizant of anything in the Logos. He didn't understand why Maia got credit.

"I've created lots of things. Where the hell is Aloria? Is Arianna dead?"

"You will not know where Aloria is, and yes, Arianna is dead."

It hit him hard in the heart- in his chest- from the lower stomach up to his throat, and then sadness clutched his heart. "What happened to her," he gulped, weeping.

Maia had red skin, like a native american. A very human looking woman; she appeared young, like a grad student, and wore a red robe, "That body served no more purpose. She is with us now."

"You're in her head, I know it. I demand to see her."

"You cannot make demands of me."

Tobias became oblivious and Osaze interrupted directly through him, "The hell I can't. Listen, we love that girl. I love her in a way your rigid mind can't fathom. This isn't your affair. I intend to rearrange everything so her and I can be together and if you think you are going to stand in my way then you are gravely mistaken. You don't seem to realize who has the power in this situation. You mean nothing to me."

"I have the power, Osaze. I have Aloria.

"And I have everything else. Why don't we trade?"

"Because you only think you have something. You are ungrateful for everything that has been given to you. Why not enjoy your own cosmos with three women at your beck and call? Three women exactly like yourself in every way that could ever matter."

"You're being condescending and patronizing. I'm going to try this a different way. H-D-2-3-9-2-3. Can you dig it? What is that star to you?"

"It means nothing. What does your kitty kat mean to you?"

"Almost as much as Aloria. 'Cause I'm fucking human for a little while longer. And people love kitty kats and kitty kats love us."

"Well. I too have loved a kat. I have loved many kats. Perhaps we are not so different, you and I."

"Then let's work something out."

"I wasn't serious. You are a stupid child."

"And you are a cruel bitch."

"Maybe. There is still no way for you to get her back. If you destroy the Logos then you will of course destroy her. And she isn't going to return to you on her own accord. You don't appreciate the arrangement. Just allow for the ascension to happen and it will be as it should."

"You lie. You are not to dictate how things should and shouldn't be."

"I am the keeper of destiny. I dictate-"

"Nothing. Everything happens regardless of you. If it weren't for you there would be no reason to ascend. As if this is for your perverse sense of self satisfaction. No one else can see this side of you, but am I to allow this to happen? You assume I'll destroy the Logos. Why don't I destroy you?"

"You'll never find her without me."

"Alcyone will know."

"Are you certain about that? Because you are

wrong. I am the only one who knows. Perhaps there're a couple co-conspirators who could give you guidance. But you won't find them any easier than her."

Osaze doubted his ability to lash out at her without destroying the entire star cluster. But the rage within him couldn't be contained. Physically, there wouldn't be any harm. He jumped at her, and gripped her throat. He tore her out of the chair and pinned her to the hard wood floor.

"I'm not doing this because I like it. I'm doing it because I hate you, and I want you to feel the pain you're causing me."

He squeezed her throat. She couldn't speak from her mouth. Ringing through his skull he heard her say, "I feel no pain. I'm embarrassed for you."

He didn't react. He just looked deeply into her eyes. They were very grey. He looked deeper, hoping to steal her knowledge. Or to stumble across veiled compassion. What he found was a resolute, absolute, stare being returned. He saw the piercing glow of his red eye reflecting in her eye and let her go.

Standing up, he said, "What am I supposed to do now?"

"Walk away. Return to Gaia. Do what you've been told."

"Why do you even think that is an option?"

"Because you have no choices. We are the will of Yah; alpha and omega. Not you. You are wasting your time. I have no weakness. There is no way for you to extort from me what you want."

"This." Osaze cast an image of a particular star in the palm of Tobias' hand. HD23923. "Now watch." She looked at him unimpressed. The star shimmered blue. The blackness came from all directions. Like tar glistening in the light rays.

He waited a brief moment as the surface of the star darkened under his influence and said, "No. Screw this. I have no reason to harm anything except maybe you. There will be a peaceful solution. There always is." In an instant the darkness vanished from the image of the star in his hand. The star was vibrant again for an instance and then vanished into luminous dust.

"Acceptance is your peaceful solution. Get out of here. Regroup and try again. See if I care."

"Don't you have any concern that I might defeat you?"

"No. You have no confidence, I have no concern."

"I've heard that before. Fuck you. I'm leaving. This ain't over."

"Watch your step."

Tobias glided down the stairs and out the wooden door toward the courtyards. The girls splashed around in the water. He walked up silently to not disturb them, but they quieted and looked to him anyhow.

"Come up here so we can leave together?"

The three soaking wet naked girls climbed up the ladder, drying nearly instantly, and they wrapped themselves against Tobias. For a moment he shut his eyes. Arianna was gone. If for any reason other than final goodbyes to her, he needed to find Aloria. The longing of Osaze for Aloria, as always.

****

He had mass again; something he hadn't missed. They were on the dark side of the moon with the glowing, undulating, sparkling Merkaba. Mesmere was nowhere to be found. His dazzling green six pointed star remained part of the lunar landscape on its own volition, presumably. Except, Tobias had been calling for the Moon Man, and seeking him in every way he could think to. The obvious point being made was that if Mesmere wanted Tobias to find him, he would be around. And so Tobias hailed the Zeta.

Near Earth, light clapped silently around activities such as Zeta oriented thought travel. Tobias was in no way as sensitive as he had been his first time, hours ago. The same three alien figures he'd met that morning appeared; slender anatomies and lively necks; bulging foreheads and skulls; eyes like shiny black eggs; spindly limbs.

No lip movement when they spoke with their thoughts, 'The Sisters of Yah will come with us. You can go ahead.'

Tobias also spoke without lips, 'You're joking, right? I'll go with you.'

'The process has no use for you.'

'I have to watch. That's just how it is.

'We can accept that. There will be nothing to see. All is done in blinding light. It will be difficult for you to assimilate to the environment. It may be best for you to avoid the process.'

'Fine. Then get them on the ground. And then get me down there.'

'That is a solution. Your distrust is noted. We understand.'

He kissed each of the girls. It was a quiet exchange. Gaia was a draining place to be. Arriving at the Merkaba took significant mental effort. They were some mixture of exhausted, dizzy, and even a little weak. Such were the burdens of Gaia.

Light clapped like hushed lightening in his face; the girls and the Zeta disappeared. Tobias was alone again. By the moon. With the Merkaba fortuitously imposing on him from the distance. He was wary, and nervous still, and for a second he wondered who would take care of him when he felt the weight of the world back on his shoulders. Then he remembered the girls. But he didn't know how to feel. He felt like they were a distraction.

Arianna had left him without a struggle. She just went. So helplessly. She had no idea. He was falling for more tricks. One trick after another. Olivia was a trick. Arianna was a trick. They brought him to the truth and the truth was a succubus who gave him three beautiful tricks, and just because nobody was willing to accommodate Osaze's love for Aloria. Or Tobias' love for his lost Arianna. He couldn't believe she was really gone. Every cell of his body ached for her return. And there would be no relief for him. Again, he wept.

'How long will this take?' Earth time, again.

From beyond some kind of veil they responded, 'It is done. When you arrive on Gaia you and the three girls will be fused to each other morphogenetically and you mustn't stray far from their company. They've arrived at the ground, and so too will you, now.'

He flashed through the light, his body felt the usual fiercely gripping physical effects of thought travel, and he fell back through the doorway of his apartment; the girls grasped his arms to aide. He wasn't wearing the clothes he left in. He still wore the black fatigues and leather boots of the other wavelengths. The clothes had become real. This he observed as his human eye struggled to get sight back while the Logos' eye could see clearly an interesting turn of events in the evidence of his clothes; the dynamics of the Zeta bio-tech were beyond him. He looked up at the girls and they smiled. Three magnificently naked women.

Pluto ran up to his ankles saying hello. Tobias quickly petted the cat hello, then, with a twinkle in his eyes, he stood up and herded the girls to the bedroom. They fell laughing across the red bedspread where that morning Arianna had woken up to him and a house full of Zeta.

His instinct was to fornicate with the girlfriends but he couldn't keep the thoughts of Arianna away. She was always in his mind, in his heart; she was his sadness, and he was sadness as he penetrated the various girls, twisting their limbs in all directions; and as their tongues were everywhere, in every crevice of each other, he couldn't think about anything other than getting Osaze to Aloria.

****

Tobias could hear Robin and Calvin calling for him from beyond the doorway. He wasn't done yet. They were inconveniencing him. He looked at the girls in frustration and their pouting lips sympathized with him. He flipped Kyoto onto her stomach, with her face in the pillows, and with the help of four supple and perky tits in his face, and hands everywhere else, he finished what he was doing and threw his pants on. He ran out to the door and cautiously threw it open; aware, from shouted warnings, that there was no floor on the other side.

"What's up, guys?"

Robin grinned, "What's up with you man? How was outer space?"

"Good. Kind of. Kind of not good. I've got a lot of problems I didn't have yesterday."

"That sounds lame."

"So do we have a ladder? I think everyone should come up here for a conference. I don't see anywhere else that still qualifies as indoors. I've got liquor in here. This ship's fucking sinking. We gotta get tore up."

"Definitely," Robin said.

Looking up from the wreckage of the lounge, the dome completely removed, the little kid in purple pajamas asked, "Are you a witch doctor now?"

"No. Not really. But, look, I got my eye back."

"How come it is red and glowing?"

"Because it is red and glowing."

Robin said, "Alright, I'll go grab everybody and a ladder then I'll be back."

"Alright. I'm going to close the door to keep the cold out. Just come right in. Hey, I'll see you in a little bit, K Slick?"

"Yeah, Ok," Calvin shrugged.

Tobias closed the door and walked back to the girls who'd curled up under the comforter in the bed room. He picked up a black t-shirt and put it on, it said the word, 'Fascist,' in an unsettling font. He looked out the window and saw more destruction, the winds, or whatever it was- the force- had scattered debris in every direction. Grey rubble and wood, snow boards and ski equipment. The rock gardens decimated into eerily strewn patterns not unlike crop circles. Zigs, zags, and loops.

"You'll have to wear Arianna's clothes. Here," Tobias said as he pulled out comfortable pants for them and different t-shirts. A green shirt said, 'Respect your mother,' and showed a picture of Gaia when she was still blue from out there. He gave that to Solaris, with hemp pants. Kobe and Kyoto each wore tight black Nirvana shirts, sweat and soft denim pants respectively.

He was getting a little queasy. Solaris took him by the shoulders and walked him out to the couch in the living room. He squished into the cushions and Pluto jumped up to his lap to be with him. He petted the cat and said, "Hi, spooky boy. Kyoto, there's a bottle of brandy over the stove, can you grab it?"

She brought the bottle to him, he uncorked it, and took a swig. Sweet deadly elixir like spirits trickled down his throat. The brown liquor settled into his stomach and toxified his blood. He looked up and he saw Kobe and Solaris coming to sit next to him. Kyoto cuddled up to him, and Kobe cuddled up to her. Solaris sat on the arm of the couch and wrapped her arm around him.

"Here, drink some of this. It's how we commune with the spirits on Gaia."

Kobe grasped the bottle and said, "I don't see why the spirits are pertinent to the situation but I will drink some." She had a sip and started coughing. He took the bottle from her hand and passed it to Kyoto.

He said, "The ether is important when you no longer feel comfortable someplace. The ether allows you to alter a situation to your whims. Or to a collective whim. But it can get intense. You need to master the technique and that is something I still haven't done. Dig it?"

Kyoto didn't hesitate, but she coughed in a similar manner to Kobe. Tobias took the bottle and passed it to Solaris, who said, "No, thank you. Some other time."

Tobias understood the logic. A sober person is a generally great asset among drunks. There was a knock at the door. Tobias jumped up and over the coffee table, sending Pluto leaping and running into the bedroom. He answered the door and there was Calvin at the top of the ladder; a chipmunk cheeked, smiling, blonde child with a landscape of destruction climbing the mountain behind him.

"Hey, Osaze."

"That's not my name, don't wear it out."

"That's not your name? I thought you were Osaze now." This conversation occurring as one by one, each member of the Clan climbed into his apartment. Jostling sentiments.

"I'll tell you about it, just chill," He said 'hi' to some people; gave Cadence and Lyn hugs.

Logan, being so tall, peered over their heads to the three Girls on the couch, he half whispered, "Yo. Toby. What you got going on with these ladies? Introduce me."

"Ha. You wish, fucker. Shut up about it." To everyone else he said, "There's bad news. A steaming pile of it. So everybody get comfortable and pass this bottle around," he handed it to Calvin first who tilted it back immediately but only sipped a little bit. Tobias added, "There're chairs. There should be enough."

Aden approached him, "Glad to have you back."

"You've already omitted things. I can tell. Make

sure that you say anything you have to say to me to everybody else here," Tobias said.

"Why would I do that? I'll talk to you. You can tell them whatever you want after," Aden said.

"Fine."

Tobias walked to the end of the apartment and stood with his back to the floor to ceiling windows. Everybody had crowded in and gotten comfortable in a chair or found a wall to sit against.

"Everybody, I'd like you to meet Solaris, Kobe, and Kyoto."

The Omegas said 'hello' to the girlfriends, who said 'hello' back.

Tobias continued, "They're essentially three girl versions of myself. They were a very special gift to me from what I can as best tell is a syndicated conspiracy to eliminate my presence in this universe. I feel Olivia is in on it, but not the driving force. The main problem is someone called Maia. Or, what she represents, actually. Alcyone- who is Olivia- Alcyone, Maia, Aloria, and I know there are more- seven sisters; these figures control the will of god. And they're bent on eliminating Osaze, who is essentially myself. I'll explain further, but you need to know that Arianna is gone forever."

Cadence said, "We knew that. She is a Pleiadian... So she's with the others."

"Except, Arianna is dead. Aloria is in their custody, but I know there is something fucked up happening out there. They're inside of Aloria's head, keeping her in traction. They're keeping her away until the ascension occurs. Because her and I were created to drift together. The Logos cast is organized to keep us apart by distortion and interference because of the Pleiadians who make the decisions of such universal matters."

"So the Pleiadians are god?" Logan asked.

"Only the vengeful womanly part that makes the decisions," he replied.

A few people laughed. Tobias kept talking, "I'm not sure how it works, I've spent my whole life trying to figure out what's going on out there and in the end, it's as fucked as everything else. As above, so below. Who the fuck kidnaps their sister? Why is that required? The path of least resistance is to allow love to flourish. Then they want to banish me. Am I not supposed to react? They spend their entire existence reacting to me but the thought that I react to them is unheard of? I accept responsibility on Osaze's behalf but I don't find this to be fair. Especially to Arianna. Who loved me and I loved. And who loved loving me and, I feel, deserved to love me. And if I can't ever be with Arianna again I'm going to do everything in my power to ensure that Osaze can be with Aloria."

Aden asked, "What power do you have?"

"I still have to figure that out. I also haven't figured out what powers my new girlfriends have. They are three intelligent women, and there is power in that alone. Knowledge is power. But that's beside the point, because power has nothing to do with unconditional love. And, if there is one thing these chicks do especially well, it is love unconditionally. And love will save us all. It's the only hope."

"When you say us 'all,'" Drake asked, "do you mean only you and those three girls? Because you are the one causing risk here. You're talking about jeopardizing our beneficial situation to further your own cause and that sounds selfish.

"It sounds selfish to me that everything gets to exist in peace except for me and what I represent. They're depolarizing and I am what bleeds out into another universe somewhere. That's what they want. I'm the waste product of a situation I sort of fucked up to begin with. Except, I'm in love so I can't just get tossed aside. Osaze is in love. Aloria is in distress. I can't let the Pleiadiens murder love. Can you? Raise your hand if you're Ok with the Pleiadiens murdering love?"

Calvin's hand went up. So did Logan's, who said, "If it's your love, yeah."

"You don't get what it represents. It's not my love. It's passion. Who would want to live in a stagnant universe? Oh. Fuck. I can't justify it. They want me to take these girls and create my own universe elsewhere in the omniverse. Maybe I'll do that. Osaze doesn't want to go anywhere, either. He wants to be part of the regenesis, or the ascension, or whatever. I haven't gotten a logical answer from anybody, so I'm just going off of what's in my gut. How can I trust these influences and do what they want?"

Robin said, "Well, they basically want us to burn down the planet, right?"

"Basically."

"So. You can do both. You can do this then do that while the process is happening."

Tobias pointed to the sky. "I have to be here to keep the 'photoplasm' grounded to the planet. I guess the sky goo will go up in flames, incinerate the negativity, and the spirits will find liberation in the fusion. Who fucking knows? The issue is that I don't know what's happening out there. There're things I have to do. I have to speak to Alcyone. Aden, you're going to have to help me with that."

Aden looked up, "If I can, I will."

"Are you aware that of all the people in this room, you are the only one whose spirit doesn't remain in their body? I can see that in this new eye. Did you check out my eye? It's pretty great right?" Tobias asked.

They nodded, smiled, or muttered 'sure,' 'whatever.' Aden said, "What do you mean about my spirit?"

"I mean, it's like steaming off you. If I close this eye, you're normal. But there's something that ain't usual about you anymore."

"That's what happened when Logos did whatever he did to him," Lyn said.

"I completely forgot to ask about that. What the hell happened here?"

Tobias didn't have much of an idea about his time as Osaze. It occurred to him he barely noticed that Endsville had been destroyed. The others explained the events. The Gods among men. The way Logos resembled Aden and Osaze resembled him. Tobias connected the images in his head. And he made sense of the blurs.

He began fading out from their conversations, and thinking about his sadness, he snapped back and asked,

LOVERS

"What do I do?" Before anyone could begin to answer him, Tobias stood up from his seat and walked past the others. He put on a pair of sandals and said, "I'm going for a walk. I need to think. Do whatever you want, I'll be back."

He grabbed a wine bottle from over the stove, opened the door, climbed down the ladder, walked across what remained of the first floor- the floor to ceiling windows were gone- the walls were gone. He could see that the crow's nest wasn't there anymore and he discovered he couldn't take the old stairs, because they weren't there either, and he walked to the back stairs through the kitchen, went down the steps, and came out at the back lot where the trees that used to shade the area were uprooted and nowhere to be found. Tobias headed left toward the parking lot and continued around the perimeter of the foundation. Acres of forest had been stripped away in every direction. He could see a valley he'd never known about where snow and dirt decorated the decimation collaboratively.

Regardless, because of the ascension, those trees had been dead for the whole length of their stay at

Endsville. The evergreens stayed true to their name, but there were only a few places where they grew. He could see the pines had remained relatively unharmed in scarce blotches. Tobias headed toward the bare mountain. Oddly, unexpectedly, the place was looking the way he'd always wanted to see it. As a naked hunk of rock towering into the sky. He walked up the bunny hill across the debris of tangled wires. Chair lift cars lay strewn across the entire landscape. As well as chunks of resort thrown over the land.

The wind whipped against his shirt and over him and he looked up to the sky, noticing the agitated black tar; the pulsating sky goo, with the lightning stifled, sparkling in a weakened, sputtering, kind of new way. The hole might explain that- from when the sunlight got in. He couldn't explain or even understand the situation in the sky better than anyone else. Still, he had never seen it broken in that way. Like a half dead insect regenerating itself. Named Pokey.

He reached up his finger and pointed up to the black sky- clicking and jazzing volts in itself- he said, "Pokey. Pokey the sky goo. I feel like I can just reach out and... Pokey the sky goo." Remembering people might be watching him he put his hand down. He uncorked the wine bottle and put it to his lips. The flavor was delicious; he could taste every note of every ingredient he couldn't identify. Like the taste of fermented grapes and alcohol. The processes of drinking alcohol; ferment grapes; boil yeast or whatever; mix with juice; mix with fizzy sodas. He liked it anyway he could get it.

He took another sip, like a chug, and kept walking up the mountain. How strange he felt like he was going down. The nature of his situation hung over him, like going down any kind of unfortunate descent. His senses; tuned to the foreboding cues around him. He hadn't told the others anything relevant. He didn't care about them right then.

What mattered to him was beyond their interests. There was nothing he could do to get Arianna back. But, to carry on in the way he had been with the girlfriends was disrespectful to her memory and actively disrespectful to Aloria. Very much so; having thought about it. He drank more wine. His guilty conscience indicated that maybe Osaze was telling him to knock it off with those girls.

They were a gift. And they were his girls. Without Arianna, those girls were all he had in the world. Replicas of himself in the sexiest packages imaginable. Something was trying to coax him.

It was indeed a conspiracy and the question of if he could even trust the Pleiadians about the most basic requisites of his obedience was up for debate. Osaze could be destroyed forever. If such a thing were possible. He could only be transformed or channeled. Tobias' instincts said not to trust them, but to do the opposite of everything they say, if he wanted to endure. There must be a way for Osaze to ascend, and if there were, it was Aloria.

Anger pulsed through his nerves like he was being brought down by something. Were they in his skull? He couldn't know. No. He was Osaze. If anything he was doing it to himself. But no. No! Intense bodily convulsions were jerking out through him and he was having difficulty standing. He suddenly decided to run through the agony. The jerks hit him harder and more intensely. He dropped the wine bottle and it rolled down the hill.

He pushed through the agony in his nerves trying to get further up the mountain to a ledge, or even to an inviting downed tree. Instead he fell flat onto his face. He could taste the cold dirt on his lips. After a moment lying there, the convulsions stopped. He'd been brought down by, he couldn't imagine what...

"I'm supposed to know what the fuck is going on! I

don't understand this!" He screamed into the dirt. He groaned and throbbed there on the ground. Completely wound up and bewildered by what happened. He rolled over and felt the aftershocks. Like electricity, lingering through him. He'd been struck down. He figured out what the Zeta had meant by 'bound to the girls.' The effect hadn't downed him fiercely. He picked his head up a little a peered down the mountain.

The three girls had tried to follow him. He hadn't known, but they were running to catch up with him. They looked unaffected. Kyoto held the wine bottle. Instantly he realized what happened. They were part of him. He was indeed bound to them. Like he were bound to himself. They were created of him. They couldn't exist without him. And apparently he couldn't live without them either. Literally. That feeling was nearly the worst experience of his life. Anyone who hadn't had their eyeball cut out of their face by a drug fiend would identify that separation jolting as the worst experience of their life.

His head fell back to the Earth as the girls rained down upon him. He was very grateful to see them. A kind of bonding experience he in no way expected. Already he felt better about the situation. If it was that real, he could work with that. Those girls shared the same higher self he did. Born somehow of Yah's intervention, induced, as though through a laborious process, by Ma'at. Himself of Maia's original design? That wasn't clear. Presumably Maia would do the same thing to the...

He was the Mu... "Do you three know what Mu is?"

Solaris said, "Yes. The nothingness. Wuji. The non-existent non being of disputed neutrality. You feel we are Mu?"

Tobias sat up, the girls shifted around him, and he carefully brushed away the dirt on his shoulders, arms, and face. He looked around with the new vision at

Endsville destroyed down below. The dust had gathered like the dunes in a sandy desert. Kyoto offered him wine, which he graciously accepted. He had a drink and passed the bottle around. That time Solaris had some, too. It was only wine.

"I do feel that. I think it is something intrinsic to every aspect of Osaze, and it is that Mu that fuels the negative occurrences within him. I don't believe Osaze is inherently that way. However, if he is the Mu, then perhaps we are what we are. It's something overtaken something else. But what exactly I'm talking about, I can't know."

Solaris said, "If it mattered, you would know. You do know. You are aware. If you are aware of a nuisance, you are obligated to correct it as best as you can. That is a universal obligation between what exists. As demonstrated by the Pleiadian efforts to liberate the humans from their purgatory."

"Another ethically irreverent mind fuck put upon us by our friends in the Pleiades," he said.

"You can't blame this on them. It is the nature of Osaze. And hence, it is a reason, if not the only reason, they are eliminating him from the equation. Besides Tobias, we love you. We want to be with you no matter what happens. And we have to be- we know what will happen otherwise."

"You don't understand, I love you, too. And I love someone else. She's not here. Because she's fucking dead. And somewhere in outer space they are keeping her soul from my soul. And in that same vein they are keeping her from you, but this shit isn't even relevant to you. If I had the opportunity, I would split in half and send one of me with you to the new place and one of me after her."

"It is relevant to us because we need you to be well. And if she makes you well, then we are as connected to her as you. If we can share you with each other, we can share you with her."

"I don't know how well she would share me with you."

"There are always solutions, and opportunities. You need to accept this in stride. Even if it means your eternal heartache- these are temporary human considerations. Your life is not your life- it belongs to Osaze. So be it. We will be there for you," said Solaris as she gently put her hand on his crotch.

The girl knew the way to his heart. There was no denying that. Kobe put her breasts in his face and cupped his head in her arms, "Open," she said, indicating his mouth, and she gently poured wine down his throat. The other two pulled his pants off, and Kyoto got on top of him, already stripped, and she put him inside of her and she rode him as he used his two hands to please both other girls simultaneously.

In the throes of ecstasy, Kyoto asked him, "What are we going to do?"

Tobias pulled his head out of Solaris' gorgeous full tits and said, "Set the world on fire, die, and get the fuck out of Dodge. You three and me. Oh. We have to try to rescue Aloria. There's no way around that. She needs to decide for herself. We have to rescue the whole universe from a terrible loss. For the Logos to lose Mu? I can't even imagine that."

Kobe, riding his hand, moaned, "These issues are for Osaze. Can't Tobias just enjoy us?"

"Kobe, I promise, I'm enjoying us, enough for everybody."

Solaris moaned, 'Us, too.'

Tobias was thinking- other than being aware that they were being watched screwing, most likely by a child- 'It's strange that I have to be the one worrying about the regenesis occurring under bent morals. We are a bent moral. I just want to love. Pleiadians are the keepers of love, but they need to be destroyed. Love

needs to be set free from them. Girls, I think a
revolution is the solution.'

****

When they finished what they were doing Tobias
sent the girls down to call Aden out of the apartment.
They went as far away from Tobias as they dared to and
screamed for Aden to come outside. He heard them and
obliged, poking his head out the door; he waved to their
waving arms, and walked down the ladder, out onto the
deck, where he slyly shimmied down a gutter and jogged
out to the slope.

Tobias watched him walking and noticed Aden's
aura rising from him as though it were steam made of
golden light. Perhaps he was the only one seeing him
like that. Most likely even. He didn't know what to make
of the distortion. Close left eye, the aura is gone, open
left eye, the aura is back.

The girls walked a little ways away, they propped
up a chair from the lift and sat down. They immediately
set about to studying each other and playing with their
hair, clearly not interested in being around.

Aden got up to within earshot. "I'm going to revolt
against the Pleiadians," Tobias called out.

Aden waited a minute to respond; thinking; he sat
down next to Tobias and said, "That's a revolt against
God. And it's not even your business. Let Osaze do it."

"Yeah, I didn't even consider that, I think Osaze is
busy being me. What if I need to die in order for Osaze
to act?"

"Somebody would have told you. What if what
Osaze wants you to do is what the Pleiadians want, too?"

"Somebody would have told me that. I have no
fucking clue what I'm supposed to be doing."

"Why don't you just accept the new design?"

"Because it excludes me. And I know what I am.

What Osaze is. He's the Mu. It's not really anything, but it's everything, too. They look at him like a plague. Because no one can fathom that they're not the most important force in the Logos. And as far as I'm concerned, that's what Osaze is. They view him as completely expendable. They want a dense organism of light? Or something like that? They're moving beyond duality. And that's the place Osaze won't exist. No free will, no identity.

"It's a womanly thing. That's why they're holding Aloria. She's the devoted essence of femininity, keeping the whole cycle alive. Maybe that femininity is the only reason there is a problem with the design to begin with. That necessity to appease women. No wonder every species on this planet was affected. They had females. It might even be the solution, to just make them happy. Give them what they want..." He'd been trailing off, buzzed.

Aden asked, "Is every human dead? Even the young people? When was the last refugee?"

"At least six months ago. Ever since I got back to the moon- it was like a docking kind of situation, to get further out in space- ever since I've been sick of Earth time. And the darkness of midday."

"Great. Is that what you wanted to talk to me about?"

"No. Help me. They can't do anything without the Logos. There is no other place to, you see, there's no other way to have any of this, without the Logos. Even here. And like here, Osaze is crucial to their agenda too. Without me, this shit in the sky might just go away, then it can't pressurize the planet or whatever. We're just satellites of them. And sometimes Osaze speaks through me. As I imagine, if you were dream walking, Logos would be present in you. Or they could be overseers, here with us at every second of every day. That's the most likely scenario. The intelligent thing to do would be to channel them. For which we need you to be asleep. You down to swallow a couple pills?"

"Maybe we can figure out a better way," Aden said.

"I need to talk to Olivia. You know how to make that happen."

"What are you going to ask her?

Tobias replied, "How the hell to discuss this with Osaze? I don't know, man. I can't figure it out. I'm about to go take these three girls out to the canyon for a swan dive party. I don't have any reason to be out here. I am completely against this. As a person. How can Osaze stand it?"

"First, he's not a person. Secondly, maybe he knows something you don't."

"You think? This is bullshit."

"So what? You're considering fucking up the grand scheme of the Logos over your love life, or some other selfish reason."

"I'd be doing them a favor. Osaze could snuff out everything in the Logos if he wanted to. Except he's decent. If he hasn't done that yet. I don't think I should either. So I guess we're back on schedule. Except they killed Arianna. Why shouldn't I trash the Logos?"

"Have you seen that flock of birds somebody was nice enough to give you?"

"Yeah. It's patronizing. Those girls are great but I loved Arianna so much and she's gone."

"Nearly everybody is dead. How are you surprised?"

"I'm not. I'm angry. And those girls didn't make themselves. A lot of effort went into taking her from me. They fucking bribed me like I'm a chump with no morals."

"Dude. Be a chump. We got something to do. How long have we been locked up here for? We get to go out there again. And this time, we have the entire world to ourselves. Get drunk. We'll go set some shit on fire. You can bang those chicks in front of everybody again."

"You guys saw that?"

"Calvin pointed it out. We were smoking weed. Your apartment is one of the last warm places around. Except for some of the rooms in the hotel. I've been getting laid a lot, too. I think it's part of the shift. This would have worked great for the human race. You're right. If those people fucked more and fought less, they might have learned to coexist. Everywhere had women, who couldn't relate. Nobody had it right. The world identity was always backward. Women are tied up with intuition and it's like they're hearing voices or suffering from recurring bouts of lunacy. A lot like you, so yeah, I see the connection. Are you going to chill out? We'll get drunk tonight, pack up, and hit the road tomorrow."

Tobias ignored the lunatic remark. Aden wouldn't judge. He hadn't been right in the head until that afternoon. Toby said, "It's going to be a bitch getting down the road if there're any trees on it."

"We'll chainsaw our way out."

"Then we'll be exhausted before we even hit the road."

"Yeah, but we shouldn't have to chainsaw anything else."

"I ain't chainsawing shit. Those other fuckers can do it. I ain't toying with death if I can be toying with those three girls. Which reminds me that I want to get this job done as quick as we can. I'm in a hurry to die. I still have to deal with the Aloria situation."

"I can channel Alcyone in my sleep. She'll tell you what to do about that. If Lyn asks, I haven't been talking to Alcyone, because I've pretty much been fucking her in my dreams all day."

"You know, I have to step back from this for a moment, and just point out how absolutely ludicrous our lives have become."

Aden said, "It's implied."

****

The situation with Lyn, Alcyone, and Aden never came to conversation. Lyn wasn't a girl who asked a lot of questions, because she didn't really care about anything.   The hours of the afternoon bled into the evening and eventually the entire clan was nearly as aware of the situation as Tobias was. They'd spent the evening drinking brandy to stay warm while wandering through the rubble. They loaded the rest of the alcohol into the three different cars they'd be driving out of there. Tobias got the Jaguar to start. The battery had died and needed charging. There was still an electrical current running through certain areas of the complex. Like out behind the kitchen, the entire warehouse hadn't been harmed. The strange destruction that befell them had an obsessive sense of accuracy.

They put a generator in Aden's pickup truck with a few five gallon containers of gas. The six foot bed held as many crates of dehydrated and canned food as they could fit and still have room for the camping equipment. Said equipment was a complicated decision, they couldn't figure out if they'd need it or not so they brought it anyway. In that same vein each vehicle carried weapons, too. Tobias had Gerri's .38 snub nose still, it was in the glove box in the Jaguar.

There was an m-16 behind Aden's bench seat. That's where Aden, Lyn, and Calvin would be riding. Drake and Logan were riding with Robin and Cadence. There were a couple of other vehicles that could have been taken, but they were in various states of disrepair.

The third vehicle, a silver SUV, had belonged to one gentlemen who'd aided in the preparations of Endsville the winter before. They had some musical instruments, a soccer ball; things like that. They'd hitched a trailer to it with two dirt bikes and a four wheeler; the chain saws were loaded on that. The plan was Drake and Logan would ride out on the trailer and take care of clearing the road for the others. Logan had ransacked the premises for survival supplies which he packed into several totes and fastened to the trailer. As well as jugs of water and cooking equipment; a portable stove, propane tanks, and steel pots and pans.

Tobias had been wandering around with the others, answering their questions. They, like him, were just trying to make sense of what was coming. And what their place was. All he could think was, 'We're pulling the plug on the Earth Mother?'

They asked, "Why am I here?," "What is my purpose?," "Where are we going?," "What is going to happen when we die?"

Tobias became abundantly aware of how little information he actually had for somebody who was supposed to have the tools and the knowledge and the power. He wanted badly to talk to Osaze. For all he knew he didn't know anything. Osaze would know.

His apologies for his ignorance sounded fake because he didn't care about any of them. He couldn't draw them into the picture. And he pitied them, because no one should be doomed to such dullness. Or not. Until today, nobody knew very much about the afterlife. Maybe Edgar Cayce did. Or Castaneda. Or Seth. Nobody had a very definite idea. Tobias knew, the dead in this dimension were lingering and lost, waiting to ascend, but stuck.

It didn't matter. They had each other to sympathize with. So that's what they did. Ever since he came down from the mountain he'd been smoking marijuana and drinking. He wasn't overly intoxicated but he was more stoned than he could remember being in a long time. Occasionally tears came to his eyes. Not about anything more than how beautiful his pain could be. And how powerful his loss was.

The whole clan had packed into his room again. It

was the only heated living quarters left on the grounds. All had blankets, pillows, cushions, and air mattresses to spend the final night at Endsville in comfort. In the morning they'd throw the blankets into the cars and hit the road. The preparations were done. Endsville was a waste land.

Aden and Tobias made dinner and brought it up to everybody. They ate a stew of spinach, kidney beans, and artichoke hearts, with Italian dressing pasta, and they had chocolate and stale tootsie pops for desert. Alcoholism has a keen sweet tooth.

They easily reminisced on the various memories they'd made at the place. Except it was difficult to tip toe around the subject of Arianna. Tobias liked hearing about her, the girlfriends didn't care; he nonchalantly took a drink each time he thought about her. They were small drinks, because he had no intention of becoming particularly drunk. It was their last night, but the event was essentially somber. Arianna was dead. His spirit was in jeopardy.

They were waiting for Aden to sleep. Except Aden had been sleeping all day and they were tired. Tobias was fried, and probably couldn't sleep if he wanted to. He'd been exhausted since he woke up that day, an eternity earlier, and sleep felt like a foreign concept after caffeine pills. The notion of sleep felt similar to the notion of death.

The entire apartment was illuminated in candles, because even though there was heat, there was no electricity. Except as more and more people drifted off, several candles flickered out. Conversations fell silent. They could hear the wind howling. Maybe it was the spirits grieving.

"He's asleep," Tobias whispered.

The girls quietly got out of bed and joined Tobias standing in the doorway between his bedroom and the piles of crashed-out people in the living room. Aden lay on an air mattress directly at his feet. Beside him Lyn was awake with her head down and eyes open.

Drake was asleep. Logan was too. So was Calvin, beside Lyn. Cadence and Robin were under a blanket on the couch, watching. The heat was cranked high. All were cozy and comfortable. By the doorway the girls stood behind Tobias, who crouched down.

He said, "Am I talking to Alcyone?"

"Yeah," Aden moaned; his cheeks heavy and eyelids fluttering.

"Where is Aloria?"

"I can't tell you that."

"You've always kept what I want from me. Not now. Tell me."

Calvin sat up and stared at Aden; not surprised; already aware that such an event would occur. Aden spoke her words in a slow articulated way, echoing through a wormhole, "Relax Tobias. There will be others. They will tell you what you wish to know."

"When? Where?"

"Go to the shore. Beware of what you find there. The golems will help you. Still, beware, they can be very literal."

"What the fuck is a golem?"

"You'll see. Go to the shore. Any ocean shore. You'll see. The golems will help you and give you what you need. Beware, they can be very literal."

"Are they going to know anything?"

"They will know how to find those who do."

"Who might that be?"

"You'll see. Go to the shore. Goodnight Tobias. Sleep long and well."

"Yeah. Thank you. Bye."

That was it. He stood up and felt a few hands gently against his shoulders. He looked down at Lyn, she caught his eyes, and he shrugged. He waved goodnight to Calvin, who waved back. Him and the girls went to the bedroom. He closed the door.

He held up the covers for the shadowy feminine figures to climb in. Kyoto got in first. Then Kobe. Solaris took the blanket from his hand and he got in next, she followed. They cuddled up close to him, their flesh touching. They became sexual in that silent sort of way. Afterward, he fell asleep.

He didn't dream. He slept the blackest night of his life. It was an eternal darkness. He was able to swim in it. He felt the sheer bliss of nothingness like the weightlessness of space. When he finally awoke, around early afternoon, he kissed the flesh of the girls sleeping beside him. He kissed their flesh and returned to the blackness of the back of his eyelids- remembering to forget the loss of the love of his life. He didn't feel like she was thinking about him, and he didn't think she could ever forget him. And to remember her, he'd first have to forget her. He didn't want to go on without her.

His love for her was as pure as the crystal is clear. He didn't even get to say goodbye. They forced him away. They made his naive mind feel helpless. The seven sisters of the apocalypse. That went against everything he thought he knew to be true. Women were supposed to love. To have compassion. Instead, they're a cackling menagerie of agendas against him. Blame.

They blamed Osaze, and took action against Tobias. They used him with no consideration to his feelings. They used his love as a means to an end. Like he was on their agenda. And when the time was right, she was pushed into the next thing. He felt a great disconnect, like he never really meant a thing to her. She was everything to him and he had to question... They're in her head...

He didn't want to have to tear the universe apart to love his lover. He just wanted a little more time with her. He also wanted Osaze and Aloria to be together. The triplets were amazing in so many ways, but Aloria was meant for Osaze. And Arianna deserved better than what they did to her.

She was in space. He couldn't bury her. He didn't know how to memorialize her. He could still carry her in his heart every second of every day. Assuming he could function. Nympholepsy. He couldn't attain her. He couldn't attain anything.

He was a failure. And he had no idea how that happened. Or what he did wrong. Or why the world was so cruel. He'd never even considered the horror when he'd had his lover to hold. Perhaps that was how the people felt, when they were slaughtering each other, or being slaughtered. Maybe that was how it felt to die in an exploding car, right after Tobias pushed that button up in the crow's nest.

CARAVAN

After an evening of deep peaceful sleep- escaping his sadness and stress- he awoke in a panic. He'd forgotten to ask her about Osaze's ability to act on its own behalf out there while he was still kicking around Earth. There was, however, enough reason to believe Osaze could do whatever he'd like to. The question remained; what was Osaze doing about the situation? He'd have to wait until Aden slept again to find out. A lot of time for an urgent matter. Though, there wasn't really such a thing as time out there. By comparison it was always now beyond the moon. Especially when contrasted to the day in and out of life on Gaia. Time in the Logos was an eternal instant. Sort of the way timing in dreams is.

Of course, it was the girls under the blanket who'd orally woken him up in the sexually explicit manner he enjoyed. Afterward, they got out of bed, dressed in their clothes for the entire day; socks, sneakers, layers, coats. Practically all of Arianna's clothes got used, it seemed like. They were ready to venture out into the world. Unfortunately, he wanted a shower and there was no running water.

He walked out of the room and found the whole clan still cuddled up and reading, or writing, or drawing, or coloring. Of course, if they wanted to use a restroom they had to take the ladder down and walk up a different ladder just to get to Robin's apartment next door. He noticed Logan, Robin, and Drake weren't around.

Tobias said, "You guys ready to go find some fucking golems."

Aden said, "Yeah, Dude. What's with this golem nonsense?"

"I haven't a fricking clue. Alycone didn't tell you anything else about it?"

"No, I saw her for as long as it took for you to talk to her. I heard what you heard, and then I just went to sleep."

Tobias didn't know whether to believe him; with Lyn in the room. He took his word anyhow and resigned to probe again later.

"Where are the other guys?" Tobias asked.

"They're getting the back hoe running. Logan's going to drive that out of here and we're going to follow him. It makes more sense," said Aden.

"That it does."

After a long breakfast, and two joints, the girls threw blankets down to the guys to bring to the vehicles. Tobias had his backpack with his tarot cards, books, and other special items. They were standing around waiting for everybody to finish up their departing necessities.

He'd put a leash on Pluto and asked Kobe to look over the cat. She obliged. Out in the debris-dusted breeze he watched her holding him. The two were a good match. Amazing cats and amazing girls were made for each other, both equally as rare. Men were like dogs, born to serve and ugly.

Logan came hustling over wearing thick clothes in layers like everyone else; to protect from the brisk weather. He had on oval framed sunglasses that shimmered, appropriately, like oil on water; his blonde facial hair was grizzly, full, and he had a hiker's backpack on over his earth toned outfit.

"Get everyone back; we're blowing up the hotel."

"Are you for real? Don't you think this place is ruined enough as it is?"

"No, Tobias. I don't think that. If I thought that, I wouldn't have outfitted the toilets on level two with a string of dynamite."

"Well. It's not going to reach over there right?" Tobias asked, pointing toward their caravan.

"No, not at all. It's going straight out, or, the walls will stop the blast some. Get everyone over there so we can get the hell out of this place."

"Fine. Hey everybody! Walk toward the cars. We're about to go, there's one last last thing. Go to the cars."

Calvin, who'd been holding Tobias' hand, asked, "Where are the others?"

"They're right over there."

Drake and Robin were approaching from around the warehouse corner. Tobias waved them over, and they hustled a little bit. Tobias turned and walked toward the cars. He could sense by their gate they knew what was about to happen. Tobias and his three lovers stood with the child by the Jaguar. Robin walked over to Cadence, Aden, and Lyn.

Logan surveyed to make sure everyone was there, then took off his backpack and removed from it a small black box with some switches and a key. Logan said, "Are you ready to leave?"

They shouted back, 'Yes,' 'Yeah,' 'Let's go.' The girls took cues and responded enthusiastically with cheers, but they had little reason to care. Tobias yelled, "Blow its fucking head off."

Logan fiddled with the box. He said, with his back turned, "Everyone say, 'Goodbye Endsville.'"

'Goodbye Endsville!'

And with that the hotel deafeningly exploded from a midpoint concussion out in a blackened fireball. Tobias felt that familiar burst of energy move through his legs, chest, and upper body. Everybody laughed and cheered through the sound of debris raining in the distance. The slim- by comparison- side walls fractured and the top two floors crumbled over forward onto the rubble of the missing half, leaving a flaming two story structure.

Aden said, "Let's hit the road!"

"You're riding with us, Calvin," Lyn said.

Calvin said, "Ok," and walked over to Aden with his hand held out.

Tobias turned to the girls, "Y'all ready to go?" They nodded in approval and he opened the passenger door to let them in. Kobe and Kyoto sat in the back, and Solaris sat up front. He called to Robin, "You ready to see what a dead planet looks like?"

Robin called back, "It looks like this place."

He laughed, "Ha. Yeah." Tobias got into the driver's seat, looking out across the way to the pile of junked refugee cars. The Jag roared through the ignition. He revved the engine, put it into gear, and let off the clutch. After a little ways he let off the gas, cranked the wheel, down shifted, and then punched the accelerator into a donut, with the rear tires sending the car lashing in circles through the dirt and snow. The girls all around him went wild with laughter and excitement. Pluto didn't really care. Tobias always loved a little intensity.

He drove back to the group where he could see Logan grinning as he jumped up into the backhoe. The others were in their places in their respective vehicles. The giant yellow construction machine spewed acrid smoke from its vertical pipe as it rolled into motion and took off down the road.

The SUV went next. Tobias let Aden go behind the trailer, and he was last in line. They made slow progress. The tiny car was always thumping over branches and through the potholes the bulldozer missed or made- which the trucks had no problem with. Tobias dragged and scraped the car the whole way.

He couldn't help but think about the last time he'd been that far down the road. It was the night he met Arianna. The most beautiful and perfect day of his life. He told her how much he loved her and never felt anything more real than that love. She was his angel; his divine grace.

That was the day Olivia died. And Gerri and Crystal, too. Gerri killed Crystal, and Tobias killed Gerri. Olivia even took out some poor shlep before she did herself in. His gut wanted a rush of beta endorphins to cull his sorrows. There were no razors, but he did have a dull pocket knife. It wasn't worth explaining the cutter's trick to the girls. It didn't matter. He was just sad about Arianna. Mad.

****

Aden could see the Jaguar bouncing in the rear-view mirror. His beat up black truck ran as though it hadn't sat for those months. He never suspected he'd be driving out of there. He never expected to leave Endsville. He'd gotten used to the idea of dying there. He was going to have to get used to the idea of dying someplace else. It could happen anywhere, at any time. Just like before the end began. If the road gave out the truck could slide down the mountainside and over a ledge and that would be it. Logos could interrupt his busy schedule and finish up whatever he was supposed to be doing on that dead rock.

They'd been driving, slurking, for almost an hour and still hadn't made it off of Justice road. The wide bucket of the machine forced through trees and scraped the road flat. Aden smoked cigarettes; agitated and bored. He looked over and saw that Calvin had fallen asleep on Lyn's lap.

"There's something I don't understand," Aden said.

"What's that?" Lyn asked.

"Well, apparently, they've trapped Aloria out in space somewhere. Olivia told me about it, she said I could tell Tobias if I wanted. But, from what I gathered, they brainwashed her and created some kind of false Osaze. Just something that emulates the effect that Osaze has on her, except more so. They took her mind away, or neutralized her. Either way, whatever they did to Aloria is fucked up and shady. And I'm pretty sure what they're doing to Osaze is fucked up and shady. The Pleiadians are redesigning the Logos, or altering it. The question is, should I help him?"

"I think if you can help you should help. If you don't feel what they are doing is honest, it is your responsibility to do your best to correct that. From what I understand... it's a sect of womanly entities in the Pleiades dictating the specifics of the ascension saying Osaze must go? It sounds like Osaze needs a lawyer; someone in his corner."

"Except it was Osaze that made this whole universe so dystopian to begin with. They're just trying to correct that."

Lyn said, "That could be a lie."

"You think, on top of everything, they're lying to us?"

"If it seems like a lie, it probably is. How can everything that went wrong be blamed on one entity? Easily. Because it's only blame. Anyone can blame anyone for anything. Remember what happened with the Muslims after 9/11? In actuality, it may be the finger pointers who are the wretchedness of the universe. Except they hide it well, keep secrets, and shift blame."

"Yeah. As far as I heard there are about three or four sister's accounted for. Who are the other sisters and what are they like? I don't believe they're angels. Look what they did to Aloria. If Aloria is anything like Arianna, she's probably as sweet as honey. It's sad. I feel bad about it. What if Osaze is the only thing keeping those bitches in check?"

"It's entirely possible. Which would mean God is resigned, because you remember how Toby said that Yah- the one true God- lets Ma'at make the decisions. Then Ma'at trusts the Pleiadians, for some terrible reason."

"Because they're women. And I bet Yah doesn't care. Yah might not have a gender. And Ma'at happens to be the most influential of these heavenly bodies. Maybe Ma'at is misinformed, or confused?"

Lyn brushed the hair from her rosy cheeks and pale face. She looked at Aden with her crystal blue eyes and placed her hand on his thigh. He kept his eyes on the road; wondering whether to care about the celestial drama. She continued to stare at him.

****

Once they got off of Justice road, it still took another hour before they breached the perimeter of the destruction caused by Tobias' cosmic rapture. During which the girl's gave Tobias another equally epic release as he drove. Doomed men don't need the jing. And while it would have been easy for Tobias to cherish the special treatment he received from his ladies, the only aspect of their relationship he could consider was that Arianna was equally capable of satisfying his hyper active desires, and there was only one of her.

Alas, she was gone. Gone, Tobias. Gone. Gone!

Gone! Gone! He should be gone too. Perhaps. And yet, he lived still. For a purpose he didn't trust, and for girls- for the reason that they are not his true love- he could never love. Too dejected to love himself, he cruised along roads littered with abandoned cars; passing houses with broken windows and open doors. Foreboding sights through over hanging dead branches and ailing evergreens on the mountain roads of Vermont.

Eventually, when the debris cleared, they pulled over for Logan to jump into the sport utility vehicle. They abandoned the backhoe on the side of the road and were finally able to make some progress; heading toward interstate 89 as quick as they could. Tobias drove circles around the trucks- enjoying the distraction.

He couldn't help but think of the refugees and the unknown ways in which the young ones died off. The way he'd killed without asking questions seemed stupid in retrospect. There was no way to justify their actions. Bitter proof they were indeed among those manifesting the ascension; manipulated among their own company to do evil. If logic had had anything to do with those first months at Endsville they wouldn't have aided in the extinction. They could have made some friends, got an idea about what was happening in the world beyond the Green Mountains, and avoided the entire mystery of how and why only Calvin survived. Instead of information he had burning questions, and the tread of his tires wore away in the spirit of the unknown; hauling toward a blowout, metaphorically, at least.

In Burlington they saw corpses. Not rotten, only dead, like wax with no microorganisms to eat away at them. The bodies were littered in alleyways and loading docks. Each time they spotted one- it happened a few times- the caravan irrupted into an orchestra of car horns.

The city itself looked like any abandoned city would. There were cars all over. Some flipped, some totaled by human aggression and blunt objects, some burnt crispy. Telephone poles blocked a road and they were forced into a minor detour. It didn't require an elastic imagination to guess the pole had once been a ploy to divert travelers into an ambush. Except there was no one there then.

One particularly noticeable attribute was the presence of burned down sections of the town. Entire city blocks were reduced to crumbled walls and piles of black rubble. The dark ash gathered under awnings and overhangs. Black trails lay where water had flowed.

The convoy hit I-89 heading south. Their intention was to meet the shore at Salem, MA and raid the shops out there for whatever might be laying around. In a world where everyplace was as haunted as the most haunted places of old, Tobias was mildly interested to see what a previously haunted city might look like.

"Do you smell the air?" Solaris asked.

Tobias cracked the window, "Yeah. That's an ocean on the breeze. Except we're still an hour or so from the shore."

"Where the shore used to be," Kyoto said.

Tobias chuckled and kept sniffing the air. There was no denying the scent wafting through the heater, it was ocean air. Only a short moment later, when they reached the top of a hill, the cars came to a halt. Tobias stepped out and took Pluto from Kobe until she could squeeze out of the backseat herself.

Even under the black sky the interstate still managed to be hazy in the same way Tobias remembered. The drifting water vapor caught whatever light there was. The highway stretched downhill into the ocean. They'd only passed the Massachusetts border a few moments before. The welcome sign had all the letters in the states name spray painted over except for 'ass.' The ocean had moved. Welcome to ass.

Tobias had mixed feelings about what they were looking at. The ocean was as beautiful and as magnificent- though much darker- as any other time he had seen it. In the dimness, the water still shimmered. At the horizon, the blackness of the water met the blackness of the sky as blueness met blueness in times of yore. The black water even mirrored the dark green currents of energy seething above.

His cohorts had piled out of the cars and they too stood in awe of what they beheld. The shoreline didn't matter. Most everything was dead, but he imagined the cities and towns sitting at the bottom of the ocean; four story buildings being slowly pulled apart by the currents; skyscrapers built so solidly they'd last substantially longer. The asphalt was the beach; the highway had been consumed by water like everything that once lay beyond where they stood.

Aden came walking back to him, saying, "You fucking see this shit?"

"Yeah. I guess we're at the shore. So much for Salem."

"What the hell are we going to do? Is this where the golems are supposed to be?"

"I'm not in any hurry to locate the golems. They'll find us," Tobias said, then laughed and joked, "Hey man, you want to go to the beach."

Aden chuckled, "Yeah, let's do it."

"Race you there. In the cars pretty ladies, and Pluto." Pluto whom was staring as intently at the water as any of them. The cat knew when something didn't harmonize with the evolution of his instincts; kitty's blood said the shoreline ain't where it should be, and so did the person's.

When they were in the car, Tobias revved up the engine and spun the tires until they smoked, with a flick of his foot they rocketed passed the others, he punched through the gears and the shoreline grew larger and larger. He could see the distant cresting white caps and the tubular waves of the water crashing against the road; the dead forest leveled to within the reach of the tide for as far as his peripheral could perceive.

"Hang on!" He yelled over the roaring engine. He dropped to neutral, waited, and with his left hand he ripped the emergency brake, the whole car jerked, and with his right hand he spun the wheel to the left. The car spun around nearly 540 degrees, during which time, he released the lever and stuffed the gas to blow two more smoky donuts. The girls loving it.

He parked with the rear of the car facing to the waves in time to see the trucks approaching. Him and the girls got out of the car and the experience was much more intense than it had been atop the hill. He could see that the waves had eroded the asphalt, leaving only particulate dirt, like sand, but new, and it must have been high tide, because the lifeless organic matter that had washed up wasn't far from where the ebbing waters reached for their ankles. The wind blasted across the shoreline. They had to lean against it.

Calvin came over running, "Toby! Will you spin the car around with me in it? That looks like fun."

"Yeah. Sure, man. Just not right here and now, we'll have to do it another time. Someplace else."

Calvin sighed, "Ok."

The others gathered- silently standing at the shore together and looking out to the invisible horizon. There was so little depth that the vague distance morphed into a blur. Kyoto moved close to Tobias and wrapped her arms around him. It was easy to be speechless. He simply had no words.

"It's gorgeous," said Cadence, over the roaring waves and frigid wind.

That was the word.

It echoed. 'Gorgeous.' All around them in the

softest, yet most audible whisper. Everybody jolted, and looked in different directions with no definite sound signature to focus on. It was as he looked around he saw something going awry with the sky goo. Dripping. The sky was dripping. And pulling back up into itself, like a lava lamp. Falling in stringy gobs from thousands of feet and rising again on their own volition.

Naturally, the clan- being human- hurriedly gathered together by the SUV in a cluster like pray animals. The perceptual incongruities advanced on their senses. Wafting through the air, an unfamiliar tasting mist. His vision, and theirs, became distorted by a bluish tint over everything they saw. Giving a minor clarity to the accustomed gloom. The trees swayed, and creaked, like psychedelic ukulele notes peeking through the roaring waves.

Robin said, "I'm starting to get sick of this shit."

Tobias said, "Me too, man."

"Are we going to die now?" Calvin asked.

"No. We're not going to die. It wouldn't be allowed to happen. They won't let us. Yet. We'll be fine," Lyn said.

Calvin replied, "That's not true. Only those guys are going to live. Nobody needs us for anything, we are going to die."

"I wouldn't lie to you," Lyn told him in an irritated tone.

Tobias first noticed the sinking feeling of nausea in his stomach before he could process that the horizon was stretching away, as the topographic properties of the shoreline sunk drastically on all sides around them. Simultaneously, he could feel the plot of land they stood on rising. The ocean fell in whirlpools and slurping chasms closing in. For as far as the eye could see- revealing homes built throughout the forest- and roads- the destruction fell into the water and churned in patches before dispersing beneath the crashing ocean.

The slope at which their new hill greeted the areas below where they'd risen from was steep and the water crashed. Behind them much was unchanged. There before them an eight hundred foot 70 degree down grade of sopping wet brown earth led to the ocean below. He peered toward the water, and looked behind them where things had remained level. Purple vapors, and trailing deep green mist, lofted ghastly. Layers and layers of colorful vapors flowed on thin air wisping gently and then dropping with the new curvature of the Earth; disappearing as the elevation decreased.

The cars were fine. Around them toward the far slopes, the trees were practically horizontal, casting out like theater seats. They clenched each other- subdued by a shadowy confusion. And red green and blue liquid smoke. Like eating all the mushrooms. The sky wasn't certain. It had descended upon them. Intense lightning storms engulfed the skies overhead.

Tobias broke away from their clutch. And lurched gracefully through the luminous fog to peer beyond it. And then he could, with his flaring red eyeball. The daze flooded away, and he peered through the icy wind blowing out across their elevated position. Heaviness dropped him to his knees. Weakness flooded his heart and shoulders. What he beheld were gargoyles.

The largest of them had leathery black wings stretched out; the length of a canoe. He carried his bulk with his wings while digging into the incline with four powerful limbs; moving toward them; climbing, flying. Steam poured from his mouth. There were two others and they were equally tiny- Calvin sized- and moved through the air like drunken bats- avoiding the large wings but staying close.

He welcomed death. Osaze would do the right thing. He could go wherever he belonged and remain within Osaze for a new eternity and hope to feel Aloria there. So who would do him the favor, but a monstrous hulking beast of weathered grey flesh? Rounded lumpy head. Massive teeth and muscles. Claws crashing into the muck of the raised ocean floor. The little gargoyles were identical, only scaled down in size, and appropriately scrawnier.

Aden was standing next to him. "You ready for this?"

"You think that's a golem?"

"I think you should take this." And Aden handed him a shotgun.

Tobias took it and shouted, "Nobody fucking shoot these things unless I shoot them first."

"Fuck that," Aden said, "let's just do it."

"I'm going to fire a warning shot," Tobias said. He cocked the weapon, pointed at the sky to the left, and pulled the trigger. A sonic ringing like glass screaming dropped them to their knees. The sound hung for an excruciating single moment that felt to have lasted for many moments. The weapons dropped from their hands. Before he had begun to regain composure, he felt the wind of those enormous wings beating above him.

It spoke. "Your actions are meaningless. Fire weapons no more. We are the golems and mean you no harm." Tobias looked up. The beast became visible through colorful hazes- the others couldn't see. The monster drifted to the ground, folded its wings close to its back; and paced a ways like an enormous gorilla. It hopped onto an electrical box and perched. The other two little ones flew above him twenty feet in the air or about that. Fluttering.

"Can you make this stop?"

The gargoyle stood tall, softly flapping wings, and addressed the Omegas, "The effect will end when we leave you. Until then, no one will be harmed, stay calm and you will remain as you are."

"What if we don't stay calm?" Calvin called out from the huddle.

"You will still be unharmed, though you may harm yourself."

"Why are you so nice? Why aren't you sinister?" Tobias asked.

"We are here to help you."

"This isn't helpful!" Tobias flailed his arm out toward the oddities. And he signed a circle around his head.

"You have to accept it and get used to us if we are to accomplish our feats."

"Well, you tell me golem. Do you have a name?"

"I am Slor. These are my minions. They are of me myself, and respond to my name, Slor."

"What the hell are we doing here, Slor?" Tobias was shouting through the biting wind.

Slor replied, in his booming rasping voice, "I will tell you when you wake up."

Tobias lost consciousness. His body rose into the air. The bodies of the others floated, too, in roughly the same formation with which they'd been desperately grasping for any kind of perception. The guys still held guns. The girls were holding Calvin. Tobias' three girls hadn't huddled with the others. They were hovering about four feet high ten feet over from his right side; they'd been ready to go to his aide. Kobe held Pluto, also asleep.

Each one of them hung limp. Slor walked through them, and one by one he gathered each clan-person into his arms; Tobias, Aden, the three girls and cat, the guys, the girls with the child squished between them. Slor stretched his wings gently around himself and the Omega Clan. Then the golems faded through the veil, easily, fluidly, instantly, taking his passengers to a place where the sun still shined on the oil slicks of beaches. They arrived almost immediately; like walking through a doorway. Crossing over and relocating. Sifting through the fabric.

To the front yard of a suburban home with tropical shrubbery. The air was very hot. There was sun. Slor lay them down beside each other; stretching his wings to cast a shadow over their faces. He focused his gaze, from dry eyeballs, and in an instant everybody awoke very confused, yet quite cohesive in the sun.

"I will usher you into this home here. You will wait out the day in the darkness of the basement, until nighttime, when you must locate protection for your eyes. No questions, I've done what I came to do. If you need me, go to the shore. Get up and move now."

They obliged in silence, the guys helped the women, child, and cat to their feet; they walked up the concrete path, up the few steps of the stoop, and into a house darkened with the blinds pulled. The heavy thud of golem wings beating shook the house as he flew away.

They held hands in single file, Tobias in the front, his girls, Aden in the middle, the rest. Tobias could see the dust in what light rays were seeping through the home. Moving around the corner he found a door to his left. He turned the nob, opened it, and identified steps leading into a basement. The house wasn't the largest place, nor was it excessively tiny; it was the right size for them, except for Logan who was tall and awkward in almost any dwelling.

The steps ran down against the wall. With extraordinary night vision he found a string hanging in his face and gave it a tug. At the end of the string a light flashed on. They kind of flinched, then walked down into the shadowy basement. Tobias found a second string which lit two more lights. Boxes and junky sports equipment littered the floor. Pipes ran across the ceiling. There was an old fashioned laundry machine. Many cobwebs. Stringy brown dried up organic material lay all over the floor.

TAIJI

Every moment happened at once. Aloria was tied in the threads of a burdensome entrapment of entanglements she'd walked into like a moth flies into a spider's web. She drifted around without a thought. Without a purpose. She was the one that could truly instill lower balance. Misinformation was accumulating on both sides of the equation. That Osaze should be cast away- that the ascension be facilitated by the Pleiadians and none other- that the loving involvement of the right girl, that balanced girl with the inner light, might be the equation needed to release the bondage of those without a say from the oppression of those above; she could no longer fathom. She could clarify the confusion of the ones who sought harmony and love and she could mold the agenda into a new cycle, and not a singularity. There wasn't the will, or option, to fight fire with fire. Not at that point.

Aloria; the magnanimous pure hearted sister. Born free of the self-serving immorality of her family, she only wanted to see what there was to be seen, and to be part of what there was to be part of. She was naive.

She loved Osaze as easily and as naturally as an infant loves its mother. Her and Osaze were bound in a celestial tango and the sisters had turned the music off. The powers that be had taken her away from him. They kept her in a place he would never see. They enslaved her mind to accept a diversion that wasn't even real. They needed time.

Hilt. A most unfortunate illusion. A distraction contrived in the murk of familial design. The same sisters that had held her back since the Logos began kept her bound, mindless, thoughtless, comatose, and catatonic. Her heart, were it not encumbered, would lead her to Osaze.

She had a faint feeling she wasn't where she belonged. Her purpose had been negated by the banishment of oblivion. All she was definitely aware of was Hilt; the unreal amalgamation of factors that captured her essence and neutralized it. Like agreeable music she couldn't care about. Like a tragic story she couldn't relate to. Acceptance without connection.

Never her fault. Los Inocentes. Osaze and her were a karmic lesson that played out for the benefit of all. To love is to learn, to learn is to war, and to war, sometimes, is to lose. Only those that learn the lesson fast can win the war. Aloria never had a real chance to learn anything. Just like a human would be, they were lost to each other by the influence of others. As above so below.

She never got the time to deconstruct and analyze what or why she loved. She never closed the cycle, she never began anew. Osaze was out there and he knew of the opportunities being wasted, and the necessities neglected. He knew the damage being done. He felt the injustice like razor blades slicing through muscles fibers.

Aloria was lost to Osaze, almost as completely as Arianna stayed lost to Tobias in death. And Osaze for the first time was becoming lost to himself. The identity of Osaze had always been what Aloria wanted it to be. Women were vindictive. They took what they could in the name of their creations. And they did it through men. Men were tools to women. He was a paradigm losing his purpose without her love. He was becoming more and more malleable to the wills of the sisters. Thus The Darkness sank deep into the inky depths of submission, stagnation, waiting for anything to move or to change. In that grand infinite moment Osaze waited for eternities. Nothing would happen.

He knew the entire time he was with her. Inside of her. Equally trapped as her. Only truly free in their love. Unable to navigate the punishments of the sisters. So forever, in a moment, because he wanted it to last forever, he was with her. They were together in their aloneness. She was stuck in a place she didn't belong. He was incapacitated. There was no reaching her. The sisters were everywhere. If he could find her, and he went to her, he would encounter the opposition of the sisters and whatever they might manifest, and he would be forced into a catastrophic battle. Except if he could get to her slowly, stealthily, without disturbing the sentries, he might succeed.

With no idea where she was, Osaze hoped to find her. Because he could feel her. All they did was feel each other. There was nothing either of them was good for except for feeling each other. Aloria could be destroyed entirely, taken back to the true source, and he would locate her there. The sisters were in the way in such a way that he couldn't get through to her. He couldn't get through to her. Maybe Tobias could.

If he could feel her in himself.... Nay. He was lost to her. The single drive left was a resolve to carry on in her honor until they were together again. Uncertainty. It had never been a similar situation. There were no predictions. Only hope. That maybe, for once, pure love could destroy the past instead of the future.

He did not create the risk. Yet, it was his duty to respond accordingly. There were going to be big changes. Osaze wouldn't go to another place all his own. He'd return to the source to free her. After the pain and the loss, there would be vanishing. And the Logos would ascend, but do so knowing that true love is eternal. In that way, the lies of Pleiades will have been vanquished. If...

Meanwhile, the women were undoing the equation. It was theirs to do with as they saw fit. This situation came upon him with malicious disregard to the wellbeing of an enormous cross section of entities existing in his depths. He had every right to change the paradigm to whatever degree was within his significant power. There would be stellar catastrophe if he did not.

He couldn't accept what the sisters claimed was so wrong about their love. His own toxicity was surely a myth. He didn't know where she was. He didn't know where hilt was. He couldn't find it, and if he could, he couldn't steal her away without hurting her. Maybe he only wanted to spend that eternity in a moment, before he'd return to the infinite, and she'd return to the sisters to ascend within the united Logos.

He searched desperately within himself and he found no hope for salvation. Even the Pleiadiens offering was an insult. The girls were no consolation. Aloria disappeared, lost beyond his reach. And there were no allies. There was only his own intent and will.

He had a new vision of the ascension; empowered and fluid. A mixture of deep glowing energies drifting among themselves, with as much darkness as there should be and no more, and pools of darkness, like lakes and ponds, rivers, across a universe like a tie-dye shirt, or an infinite potential; where how it resembled that current mystifying perception would never matter, because within the new Logos there was perfect understanding. He had his chance. Yah was inept. He knew. Or hoped.

****

Calvin couldn't grasp what the big deal with Cuba was. Everyone was so amazed. Cuba Cuba Cuba. Big deal. He had never even heard of it. It was by Florida and he knew where Florida was. Big deal. The exciting part was that the sun was shining again.

They had waited the entire night in that house, sweating. Sweating all night. The sun was up, finally, but the heat was getting more intense. They were in an old pickup truck with lots of dents, trying to find the water. Robin drove, and Cadence was there, too. Logan had taken another vehicle in the other direction, to see what he could find. And they were to meet back by noon. The maps were useless. Most of the country was under water.

The town they drove out of was called, Bayamo. Cadence was writing down the turns they'd taken as best as she could. Of three compasses they found while searching houses, none read the same as the next. Robin had a good sense of direction and they were only out in the farmlands for 20 minutes before they located the shoreline again. At which point they drove along what roads they could find, doing their best to stay close to the water.

The beach in Cuba was different than in Massachusetts. The beach in Cuba was scorching hot and baked in the sun. The air was hot. The sun was burning through the windows, and the breezes were making Calvin more tired than cooling him off.

At a dead end they back tracked for another twenty minutes until they were on the right way again.

"This is bullshit. One of them could have asked some deity, or gone with the golem, and found us a boat by now," Robin said.

"We could go with the Golems," Calvin said. Cadence burst out in a quick laugh and caught herself.

Robin looked at Cadence and said, "He's completely right. Those things are out there. We need a boat and can't find one. We could find Slor easily."

"I really don't want to," Cadence said.

"We don't have the gas to bring you back. If you can find your way, I'll get you a car, and you and Calvin can get out of here."

"I want to see Slor again," Calvin said.

Robin shot him a scalding look, saying, "No. No discussion."

Cadence said, "Yeah. I can get back. Aren't you afraid?"

"Pretty much. I'll be fine, don't worry. I'll park at a

beach, get a lift from Slor to a marina, get a boat, and get back. I have no idea where the hell a boat should be when the ocean isn't where it should be. The Golem is here to serve them, and I ain't getting them a boat unless that thing does the legwork for me."

"I'm sure Slor is equally as reasonable," Cadence said.

He gave her a smirking look and squeezed her hand. It took a few minutes before he found a house with a lot of cars around it and in the driveway. They pulled the truck over and Robin set about the task of ransacking through the different cars searching for a set of keys. There were only about three cars in a position to be moved out of the driveway or off the lawn.

In the first two cars he found nothing, but in the final one, a green Honda from the mid-nineties- a car with dirty floors and old cobwebs in its crevices- he found a pair of keys. Of course the car didn't start right away. It took fifteen minutes and wire brushing the battery terminals, but he got the whiny little engine running and drove the car out onto the road. He drove it as fast as he could to the T intersection and accelerated back the same way.

He got out and said, "Seems fine."

They kissed passionately in the street. He made sure they had water and food in case they got lost or stuck. He reviewed the directions with them. He told her that if the car should break down they were to do exactly what he just did; find a new car. The gas gauge read a little over a quarter and that was enough. He gave Calvin a high five, kissed his lover one more time, got into the truck, and drove the few miles back to the ocean as fast as he could.

He stood out on the beach. The sky was interesting. Blue. Not blue the way it used to be blue. The sun shone hot like any summer day he could remember. Or the summer vacations he took to Vero Beach when he was a young teenager. Through his protective sunglasses he saw the sky like the thinnest blue tinted cellophane was stretched flush over his vision.

It had begun. A weakness flooded across Robin and he used inner strength to fight against it. He knew in an obvious way that Slor was testing his limits. It didn't matter. It made sense. And what he felt next he couldn't have imagined. Every limit of his body was pushed to the maximum. He stiffly dropped to the brown sand. He pushed back at the force attacking him like a runner hitting the wall, and still the force hardened against his muscles; his nerves flared across his entire body. He convulsed in a jerking way three times before he regained control of himself. More jolts followed and he fought those, too. And when he felt that there was no strength left, and the adrenaline began to wane, he was released, falling flat on his back taking gasping breaths.

For a moment he could barely see through tunnel vision, then the blackness retreated and the shining blue sky returned. To his right- he twisted- he saw Slor perched on the truck. The hood was crumpling under his weight. The claws were digging through plastic, aluminum, and steel. Slor's skin, or surface, morphed, like it were sliding across his muscles and shape. His expression patient.

"I need a boat," Robin said.

"I understand that. I will take you to one. You will have to follow me in your truck."
"Why did you do that to me?"

"It can't be prevented. Get in the vehicle."

"What if it doesn't run? You just crushed the front end."

"This damage is minimal. Get in and start it."

Under the wind of superficially flapping wings Robin struggled to get to his feet. His shoulders were putty, and every other muscle was, too. Like they were asleep except the pain hurt more than pins and needles.

So he found himself fighting agony, falling onto the truck's hood, grasping with his arms out, when he noticed the enormous mass of the gargoyle in his face, an ankle or calf, the thigh, tree trunk, upper arms, wings stretched and blocking the sun, he jumped back and cringed to get the door handle, and climbed into the seat.

With tremors in his hands- unusual for him- he removed the key from his pocket and engaged the vehicle. The truck rocked as the gargoyle took to the air in a position forward of the front end, then flew over, indicating for Robin to reverse, which he did, and then he accelerated when he saw that the golem was already lofting away down the road. The two little ones were following a short distance behind and one of them spun around and, moving gracefully, swooped down to, and flew alongside, Robin's window, and he rolled it down.

The little one shrieked its words in a stunted way that agitated Robin's raging headache, "We are going to get a better view in the sky, stay driving on this road." Then it flew off to join the others. Robin didn't like Slor very much.

The creatures flew higher and higher- at about the rate of a helium balloon they rose leisurely. Robin drove down a road leading through farmland. He could see the creatures looking around in all directions, and he saw the big one focus on an area somewhere he guessed was less than 10 miles away to the north. The creature flew back down to the road. The little one flew back to his window.

In that same awful voice it said, "Follow us. We'll be there shortly." Then it flew away again. 'What a redundant thing?' Robin thought. So he followed it and the monster trio began making speed. He had to drive at an unsafe rate to catch up with them, and the sheen of disreality in his eyes was lightening and darkening before him as he slipped into a mild trance. In the distance behind, and parallel, the landscape lifted, nearly 100 feet, and fell in waves of elevation that harmonized with his own movements behind the wheel and on the road. He could look over his shoulder and see a hill as a hill, then that very same ground dipped down into itself and out of sight. Disorienting to say the least. When the ground under his own wheels began to falter, he pressed harder on the gas, sick of the charade.

It worked. The distortions of the Earth settled again. He was free to drive without the disorientation of this Golem's trickster ways. At least for a little while he hoped. And so it was. They traveled far, without disturbance, even through a couple more towns with corpses like wax sculptures strewn about. Meanwhile Robin was enjoying taking in Cuba; the way everything looked different. The business signs were shoddy. The craftsmanship of buildings seemed well done, except for the incinerated ones. A place totally untouched by United States influence for thirty years and he could tell in those subtle aspects of any modern country; street signs, store fronts, prominent fountains and statues. Of course the graffiti and the destruction were most likely a result of the apocalypse.

They didn't go where he thought he saw Slor looking. They went much further than he expected, to the south. And he could tell he was traversing proportionally vast lengths of the country. He would have admitted watching the three monsters fly through the sky was very interesting if not hypnotic. The way they lofted up and down to move forward; their bodies hanging. He'd enjoy the sight more but was feeling weak. Hungry. Thirsty. Uncomfortable. He took his shirt off and drank some water. He'd given the food to Cadence.

Eventually, he traveled down a hill that ran through a town; was guided through a couple side streets to a home with a nice, newer Ford truck attached to a large ocean going vessel on a trailer, at least 30 feet long, and wrapped entirely in plastic. Within ear shot of the beach that had already consumed the low lying areas of that town. The streets made convenient boat launches.

Robin stopped the mangled SUV and got out. He looked to Slor perched on a rooftop nearby. The gargoyle acknowledged his glance by flying away, out over the waters, diving in with folded wings, and they did not come back up.

CUBA

The clan- under rested after wandering in and out of Cubin homes all day- stood together at the edge of a toppled structure with flush outer walls for a floor. A prison, likely. Or a school. Whatever the difference... They basically scaled at least a mile-long landscape of war-torn decimated buildings, and debris; interlaced with flood damage.

He was leaving Cuba when Cuba might have been exactly where he wanted to be. With no capacity to permit fate, he couldn't help but allow himself to make the error. They'd been walking silently; helping each other over the chunks of concrete and tangles of rebar; passing the cat around. The light of their forehead mounted spotlights glared and swayed over the ruins; chard human remains had gathered in clusters, disfigured by the water, and scarred by what looked like burns and lacerations. The quantity of bodies indicated refugees destroyed by hostility.

Survivors wouldn't have known how little time they had left after the first die off. Then, even the young ones fell. Not Calvin though... In his heart he knew the Pleiadians were responsible. What reasons they had for the extinctions, he couldn't speculate.

The differences between children and adults were staggering like the jaunting rubble. It was one rubble. A child was an adult. An adult was a child. Any person was always the same person; the same life. Astrology had a lot to say about the matter. As best he could recall- no books to reference and the internet had long been over- the 'Saturn Return' designated an adult at about 29 years. That couldn't be. All down to the 23 year-olds went with the first plague. Maybe enough orbit was enough orbit. 23... Almost 29... Either way. The life died on a time frame. Maybe like a rain storm; lasting only as long as it needed to.

Robin was bringing the boat to the 'dock' tucked away in a bay. An impromptu bay formed over half a town- a bay no less. The entire clan stood around casting light in each-others' faces. The boat got closer. They stood fairly high up on ruins over the water. He shone his light down and saw the small waves crashing against the wreckage. The boat was tall, but not that tall. Maybe Robin thought of something.

"What are we going to do about the height?" Logan asked.

"You tell me."

"A rope. It's a boat. There has to be a rope."

"I'm not climbing down a rope," Calvin said.

Lyn asked, "Can you hang onto my back?" Calvin nodded yes.

Logan interrupted, "I'll do it. I'm stronger."

Lyn said, "Yeah. He won't let go of me. I'm perfectly able. He weighs practically nothing."

Robin pulled up alongside in a yacht covered in dim glowing fixtures. There was a ten foot or so gap between them and the deck. Nothing extreme, but substantial. "Catch this rope and tie it off," Robin called up.

"I got it," Logan said, and cleared everyone away with gesticulations. He caught the rope on the second throw, walked it over to a cluster of iron bars jutting out, and tied it off. Then he tied knots throughout the areas of the rope they'd be climbing on. They had few belongings outside of backpacks. When commodities were free and available, traveling unencumbered became simple. Logan and Aden went down first, then Lyn and Calvin, who went without much fuss and without any problem, then Cadence, then the girls- who had never climbed anything like that in their lives, yet managed fine- then Tobias went last, one handed, holding Pluto- so relaxed- in his arm with the leash to his harness attached by the belt.

Tobias had a habit of going last. He always had. Even in school he lingered at the end of the lines. He liked to see as many people go through what he would before he had to. Subsequently, he did everything nervously under the assumption somebody would screw something up, and if nobody did, it would probably be him. Luckily, the more he saw something done, the better he'd do it himself when the time came.

As soon as they were aboard Robin ripped the throttle. The boat dug in and they all fell, or almost fell, as he pulled away from the 'shore.' After the screams of the women, and the shouts of, 'What the fuck?' from some, came laughter.

They were heading out to burn the ocean. To bring the photoplasm down. To put the nails in the coffin. More than that, they were to ignite the earth to its very core. To fuse the water under pressure. To burn through the layers of crust until, in an instant, molten mantel meets nuclear reaction. They were to die. And there wasn't much fear. Logos and Osaze wouldn't lie. He knocked on a wooden table. Whether Osaze would lie to him, or if he would lie to himself were the same. He constantly lied to himself. Nothing erased Arianna's death. With any luck death might release him from his vendetta.

"This boat is fucking huge," Toby said to Robin, as they stood in the wheel house, heading into the darkness.

"You should have been there to put it into the water by yourself. I thought dealing with Slor was going to suck. I was gone all fucking day, and now we're doing this shit at night."

Tobias absentmindedly spun the floodlight out across the water. Warm ocean air drifted in through the windows. Green lights glowed across Robin's creamy hazelnut skin and rounded Hispanic features. He was the most Hispanic looking white guy ever. Tobias lit a cigarette.

The others were together in the common area below. Except the three girls standing out on the upper deck looking up at the stars. Homicidal thoughts- unnervingly similar to suicidal thoughts- crept in. He couldn't trust the girls in the same way he couldn't trust himself. Arianna was dead, yet those three lived. He wanted to die. They would do whatever he said.

Tobias said, "Solaris, can you call Aden up here?"

She jolted, looked at him, smiled, then turned, leaned over the balcony, and called, "Aden would you please report to the cockpit of the Endboat?"

"I'll give your pit some cock," Tobias said. Solaris giggled and rolled her eyes back up to the stars. The girls' short skirts were flapping in the wind. Aden came up and caught Tobias staring. With both eyes. They grinned.

Tobias asked, "Alright. What the fuck are we doing?"

Robin said, "We're going to set oil on fire."

Aden shrugged and said, "Yeah."

"That's a lie."

"How do you know?" Robin asked.

"Yeah. How do you know?"

"I don't know. The logic pans out. I guess. If turning the planet to a star is what has to be done then we'll do it. But, that's not what we're out here to do."

"You know this how?" Aden asked.

"It's just something I know. We're out here under false pretenses. Like Osaze. Just suckers. What if we don't burn this place down? What then? Who's going to do it if not us?"

Aden said, "I'm sure Slor wouldn't have much difficulty. You're right though. We've been on this boat for about ten minutes and half of us are already drunk. I don't see this panning out."

"That's my point. Slor could fucking do it. Why do we have to do it? What if they are only keeping us around because they need us? If we kick off, we might fuck up their whole agenda. This planet is a microcosm. As above so below. What we do down here is going to reach every," he stuttered, "every fucking fiber of this universe. Of the Logos."

"You have no idea what you're talking about," Aden said.

"Yeah. I know."

"Know what?"

"This is bullshit."

Robin chimed in, "I agree with that," then he focused back on the boat. He focused on his instruments and the lighted areas cutting through the brightest night they'd seen in a long time. Out on the ocean, one could almost convince oneself everything was normal. After all, everything was always normal, no matter what. The moon was high in the sky, getting fuller. The lunatic's heart. They hadn't seen it since the winter prior finality. Arianna should have been there.

"I got it."

'What's that?'

"We'll just keep going. We don't have to commit to their agenda. So we'll go out there, we'll play it cool, and we'll see what happens. They've invested a lot of time in us. It's either because they need us, or because they need us to think they need us, when in actuality what they really need is for us to stay earthbound."

Aden said, "If we're turning the planet into a star, that's what we're doing. I don't think it would hurt anything to ignite some oil wells just in case."

Tobias said, "No. We can't. Maybe. I don't know. We need more information. I need to talk to Olivia again, when you go to sleep. There's a chance we're going to be dead before the sun rises. Or at least I am."

"Once again, Tobias, you have no idea what you're talking about."

"Once again, I know. Can we make it back to the US?"

Robin said, "Florida. Anywhere over there. We'd probably make it to Louisiana."

"I've dreamed dreams and I always end up in the gulf. I've no idea why," said Tobias.

Aden said, "This trip might have something to do with it. You should see the dreams I'm having. It's real as this. I go where I want. I do what I want. I can communicate with Olivia- who is just hanging around here, by the way. She goes everywhere with us. You can contact her yourself, I know it. You'd have to talk through the wind. Or the lightening. Or tapping on the hull," he gestured that- "It can be done. I mean, you can talk straight up when I go to sleep, but in the meanwhile you can ask yes or no questions with a one knock yes, two knock no, kind of system."

"What the fuck do you mean she's just hanging around here? Like a chaperone, or what? What are her motives?" he had gotten loud, and caught himself. No one heard over the boat and the wind.

Aden shrugged with his hands out and eyebrows lifted, "I don't know man. That was too many questions. Listen, shh," leaning close, "I'm kind of banging Olivia in my sleep." He put his finger to his lip and silently pointed below.

"Then why don't you have more information?" he

whispered back, aggravated.

"Because it's just dreams."

"That's a cop out man. Even regular dreams aren't 'just dreams.' You're walking around dreamland like you own the place; there has to be a difference. What's the deal?"

"The deal is, yeah, we hang out, and I remember it. What can I say? She digs me."

"Who cares if she digs you? She digs everybody. What do you talk about with her? What's going to happen?"

Aden said, "The earth has to become a star. That's the ascension, get it? As above, so below? What is one human soul down here out there? A planet? A star? A galaxy? And that's human. Animals have higher aspects, all life does. That's why the universe stretches out forever, because it's connected to life. That situation in the sky isn't right. They're trapping Osaze, through me."

"They would have said so by now."

"Why haven't they Aden? Why haven't you?" "Wait until you ask Alcyone what's up. She'll tell you what to do."

"I can't trust her."

"You think you can't trust her. You trusted Arianna, or Aloria, or whatever. And you and Olivia were tight. You don't know what's going to happen. Fuck it. Let's go grab some sun in Florida. Get drunk? Get laid? While we still can."

Tobias said, "They fuck in the afterlife, too."

"It's not you fucking. You're gunna die."

"Fuck."

Robin said, "What's going to happen when we're not blowing up an oil rig when we're supposed to be."

"They can choke on it for all I care," Tobias said.

"We'll do that, too. I'm just saying, if we have to do it, let's have a holiday in the sun first. Tobias is going to off himself any day now. The fire can wait."

Robin said, "The end of days seems more carefully orchestrated than to allow for our indefinite time wasting."

Aden said, "Who do you think orchestrated it? They might be the composers, but we're the musicians. What are they going to do? Kill us?"

"Torture," muttered Tobias, "they'll keep us alive, force us, we'll fight, they'll hurt us, and do it themselves. Or something else will."

"Slor would fucking own us. And there's nothing we can do about that. I'm surprised he ain't here. We're on the ocean," Aden said.

Robin said, "Maybe he needs a shoreline. To crawl out of, he must weigh at least a few tons. He probably sinks."

Aden said, "He could probably part the red sea, so to speak, if he wanted to."

"Why don't we get him back here and find out?" Tobias said.

"We'll see what Olivia says."

****

The boat had sleeping arrangements for each of them exactly. No more, no less. The spot for Calvin was even tiny and tucked right at the bow, under the deck. Most everybody lay asleep in their places. Aden, Robin, and Tobias had resolved to not share the inconclusive conclusions of their wheelhouse conference. However, through each minute passing, the bottles of beer disappearing, Cuban music with horns in it; Tobias stayed constantly aware of the way he endangered them. If he weren't plain threatening their very lives. So while they drank liquor, he drank coffee and got high with Aden. Logan had been keeping everyone drinking.

No more than once or twice did anyone ask about the mission at hand. They were oblivious. Thus stayed under the impression they were headed to the offshore drilling rigs to create some black smoke. Alas, they'd be surprised to awaken at Florida. Tobias sat up, smoking a jay. The sun to the east had kissed the day, but the darkness still hung heavily.

They were on the lower deck out in open air where Aden had finally drifted to sleep on the deck's rubbery vinyl bench seats. He began to mumble, and Tobias leaned in close to hear what he was saying.

"You there, Alcyone?"

In Aden's voice she said, "Yes. I am here." His diction shifted to a more feminine tone. A flat, high strung, pitch. His eyes were fluttering under the lids, causing his cheek to twitch subtly.

"I need to talk to Osaze. Can you get him here?"

"Maybe I can speak for him."

"I don't think so... I need to know what's best for me? What's best for him? What's best for Aloria?"

"What does your heart tell you?"

"To slit my wrists and fuck these chicks until I bleed out."

"Then do that."

"No. You're not hearing me. How can Aloria be with Osaze? I have to make that happen."

"You're not going to make it happen from here."

"So? I off myself?"

"No."

"What is Osaze doing about it right now?"

"Less than you. You are the passionate one. If you die their reunion may not happen. Osaze is losing touch. The longer the sisters keep Aloria hidden from him the further his will will decay. You can't do anything as Osaze. He can't do anything about it himself. If you want this done you'll have to do it yourself. Because a consensus is what you need. You'll have to speak on Osaze's behalf. And be diplomatic. You'll be Osaze when it suits you. Otherwise, you'll be seeking the help of

others. Do what you did the other day again. The Greys
are here. They aren't doing anything, except waiting to
leave. They don't ever disappoint. Contact them, and
you'll get to wherever you need to go."

"I don't want to go back to space."

"Then don't."

"Just tell me what to do."

"Do you realize what is at stake here?"

"Love?"

"Romantic love. This romance will define the
principles of the ascended Logos. If you do what is in
your heart, and are successful, love will flourish in the
next aeon as well, like a rose in rich soil. Should your
love fail, as love often fails, especially your loves, the
roses will mean nothing."

"You tell me, will you help me?"

"I'm helping you right now."

"If I go out there, I mean."

"You have more power and leverage where you are
standing. What you need to do is time your death
appropriately. If you make the most out of death, you
can get what you want. Osaze will be integrated into the
ascension, with the love of Aloria for temperance. And
finally, for once, they will be unified in a way that was
never before possible.

"Or, you accept the Pleiadian agenda. That there is
a social circle determining your fate and what will
become of you. They are tempting you. Luring you away.
They will throw you to the hostile whims of Yah. They
dictate his will in the Logos. Osaze can maybe stay. They
want him to go. And with him they banish the darkness.

"You propose the darkness remain, and ascend as
well? Within Aloria's love? I'm in complete agreement.
Unfortunately, I can't tell you where they are keeping
her. You'll need to find another with that information.
Or don't. Just hold out. Slor will help you regardless.
You can't predict what will happen."

"What are these girls to Yah?"

"The same as you."

"You sure? Are they connected to the darkness? If they stay, and I go, where does the photoplasm go?"

"It goes where it goes. It's in them, the same as you're in them, and it's in you. This is the end of our talk. Good luck. Get to the shore. Love you."

"Love you, too."

He stood up and looked around at the few sun rays glowering at him from the water. There was a king sized bed, with three girls and a cat waiting for him below. Sleep. It could be the last sleep he slept. All was quiet. All were asleep. It could be the last fuck he fucked.

They were anchored off shore of as yet unexplored land. Supposedly Florida area. Of course also 50 miles or so further inland than one might expect. Florida had undergone a substantial decrease in size. Tobias wished Arianna were there. He clenched his fists and twisted his neck as his heart dropped like he was in another bad dream. He took multiple deep breaths and pushed himself to bed.

****

Aden had volunteered to go out scouting that day. Him and Lyn threw on shorts, long sox, and hiking boots courtesy of a diverse- and oddly complete- wardrobe within one of the closets. They were dolled up like explorers on an expedition. They had a purpose; to locate a house for the day, and to find out what town that place used to be.

They fully inflated the dingy and climbed in while others still slept. Calvin stood on the deck rubbing his eyes; new to the bright sunny day from the darkness of sleep. Cadence and Robin were waking. Drake and Logan were asleep, and it could be assumed Tobias wouldn't be out of his room until evening, or whenever.

Aden paddled with both ores toward what looked like a suburb. The crashing waves did most of the work of carrying them to shore. Houses and yards lay past the beach for as far as the eye could see. Any one of those houses would have mail and a phonebook; to place themselves by.

Getting over those waves heading out was going to be rough. The angle of the 'beach' fell particularly steep and the waves crashed high. Not dangerous, but nerve-racking. He could hear the undertow slurping as he pulled the dingy up onto the rocky shore speckled with asphalt and concrete.

"We'll pick out a house, then I'll go fairy people ashore, and you can stay there."

"I shouldn't be left alone. They'll come for me."

"Who?"

"The sisters. They know about Tobias' plans and are going to use me to extort demands from Ma'at."

"If you say so."

"I'm serious. They're coming for me. They're going to take me alive and torture me. This entire reality's going to snap in tandem with my resolve. The sky dropping like saran wrap clinging. The planet will ignite. Tobias will die. Osaze will be banished. Aloria will be erased and reprogrammed. You'll die, I'll die, and Ma'at will regain control right when it's too late."

"When did you find this out? Should we kill Tobias?"

Lyn said, "Alcyone woke me up from your body. She used your hand, and your voice, and she told me exactly what I told you. I wanted to be out here when I told you. It's Drake. They're going to use Drake."

"What about Logan?"

"She didn't mention him."

"Robin- those girls- anybody else?"

"Just Drake."

Aden looked out to the boat. Not too far to swim.

"Alright, let's go." He grabbed the dingy and dragged it toward the first standing house, a few hundred feet away. He tried to slide the glass door on the back porch into the kitchen but found it locked. Ditching the dingy at the steps, he took her hand and walked around to the front door. It was locked, but not made of glass, so he aimed for the door knob area and kicked it in with one try. He fell forward and caught himself with his hands on the frame. They entered the house slowly as their eyes adjusted and found a place covered in garbage and smelling like moisture. He scouted the kitchen first for knives and found nothing. The kitchen table had appropriately blunt and well weighted, wrist thick, legs. He flipped the table over and kicked the limb off with his boot.

"I can't believe you didn't tell me about this on the boat. Where we had guns. I could be out here with him, and you could be back with them. He's with them. We have to go back, if he's dangerous."

"He won't know. He won't know we know."

"We should go back to the boat."

"No. We'll wait here. He'll come. I'm sure of it."

"Take this. If you see him, crack his skull open."

Aden broke off another leg, then, catching his breath, he glanced out over the water toward the boat. Looking left to the north he could see the shadow cast by the dark skies looming far beyond. To the right were more houses stretching into the distance. Neighborhood streets and fence remnants, dividing land. He watched the waves crash over the property lines. He smoked a cigarette, watching the shoreline while Lyn searched for the information they wanted about the town. Which in light of events, no longer mattered even the little bit it had before. He wasn't letting her out of his sight.

"We're in Weston, Florida," she said. Apparently, if you walk 10 miles further out, there is nothing but Big Cyprus National Preserve all the way to the other side of the state. Like, marshland, maybe. We could take to the land if we want. We could go to Orlando. After we kill Drake, I mean."

"I'm glad you can laugh about this. I'm not looking forward to explaining it to anybody."

"One, they'll understand, and two, you don't have to. That's what I'm saying, we can leave, numb nuts."

Lyn was smiling and laughing, and moving her head around; pursing her lips, being generally cute in that way only she could be. She caught Aden's eyes and walked over to him. He flicked his cigarette out the door and they embraced, kissing deeply. He wrapped his free arm around her and, dragging table legs, they moved together into the living room and fell down length wise on the couch, dropping table legs.

Further and further they journeyed into the caverns of lust and physical intimacy, when Drake came bounding up the back steps. Aden- shocked he'd been caught with his pants down- with one hand held up his clothes, and with the other gripped the wooden leg. As Drake, soaking wet, ran toward them, Aden swung his weapon like an axe into Drake's forehead. Drake fell directly to the ground and then lay still.

Fastening his pants and belt, Aden said, "So. Should I break his kneecaps, so he can't come at us?"

"I'm worried they'll send Logan. Come on. We need to find a car."

"We can't do that. We have to get back to the boat. I'm breaking his legs and we're leaving him here."

Drake groaned and reached suddenly for her ankle. She jumped back and Aden swung the leg into the side of his head, jarring Drake's whole body. Again, the demented Drake went limp.

"Close your eyes and get back." She did.

Aden swung. Once, down on the knee. Drake came back to life with his eyes bulging and mouth gasping. Aden swung into his head again, saying, "Fucking bitches!" And at that he let loose. He thrashed the wood down into Drake's knees over and over. Feeling the vibration of the bone giving way in his hands. He could see pain coursing through the body. Blood flowed out of Drake's mouth, and from his face.

"Come on. We're going. Now."

When they got to the shore, the ores were missing. Aden had gambled Drake wouldn't spot them and realized then he'd lost the wager. The ores were nowhere to be found. They had the table legs. He looked to the boat and threw his in. Then he looked around more for the ores. He scanned the water and the land. They weren't anywhere."

"Put yours in there, too. I'm swimming this thing out to the boat."

"What if Logan is in the water?"

He stopped and thought. She was right. Not good. He dropped the boat right there at the water lapping over the dirty blackened sand and started to jump up and down flailing his arms. "Hey! Heeeeeeey!" He called out to the greatest volume of his voice. Lyn did the same. It took a moment before he saw Robin milling around the deck. He looked out and noticed them. He waved back and then ran to the wheelhouse, returning with binoculars.

"Yes! Come closer! You fuck!" Aden said, waving him over with his arm; trying to express the urgency of the matter.   Robin recognized and immediately ran back to the wheel house. It would take a minute to retrieve the anchor from the bottom, but the moment it was up the water behind the Endboat became white and roiling as the pitch of the boat shifted and the bow turned to aim toward them.

Lyn had had her arms wrapped around Aden, completely relieved, until her fear appeared stumbling up out of the water about fifty yards away. Aden jumped to the wood and handed her her leg.

"He's tall. You stay back. Work the back of his skull as soon as you get a chance. I'll try to take his limbs out. Try not to get near him unless you're behind him."

Aden found it strange that each moment lasted an eternity, waiting for Logan to stumble out of the water and into range. The giant's lower jaw hung open slack, same as always, but with his lumbering gait, and zombie-like stare, he looked more like a dullard than ever.

MISFORTUNE

Logan's hair had always been obnoxious. A golden afro atop his head and a bushy rectangular beard jutting from his chin; in life he'd been a shady traveling loud mouth for a hobby. Logan was huge, but he was lumbering. Aden wasn't prepared to find Logan's build to be about as solid as the hunk of wood he was holding. Aden tried to fake him out by lifting the table leg high, but when he swung into the chest he caught elbows. The wood bounced and Aden spun- stepping back to go for the head. He connected, but to little effect.

Logan's eyes were lost. In the sunlight they looked milky, and barely blue any more. He was groaning, midway between standing and falling to the ground. Aden swung into the skull again. The shot glanced off and Logan reacted by twisting around and hurling himself into Aden. Tackling him to the ground. Logan snatched the wood from Aden's hand.

"Keep your head down!" Lyn shouted and she swung her leg with the weight of her whole body; into his head. At the crack, Aden threw Logan off of himself. He caught Logan's wrist under his shoe and got the weapon back. Aden stood up panting for air. After a couple breaths, he swung the table leg into Logan; he swung again and again, hitting the elbows, chipping the bones, until Logan rolled over and exposed his knees.

The body went into convulsions as Aden, over and over, battered away. The expressions on Logan's face were indescribable. A disgusting mutation of DNA, or brainwaves. He was going to swing for the ankles, but caught himself. He had behaved rashly due to survival mode.

Logan writhed around covering himself in sand and his own blood and moaning pitifully. Aden looked up and saw Tobias watching through the binoculars with the girls standing around him. He could see Robin's face through the window of the wheelhouse. Cadence and Calvin. The boat sat parallel to shore as close in as it could get, still somewhat far out. Too bad about Logan's situation.

"What the fuck?" Lyn shouted- pointing back at the house.

Aden looked over and saw, coming out toward the beach, about 15 yards away, Drake, crawling toward them on his belly with the same agonizing inhuman expression on his face. When Drake saw them looking at him, he exerted more energy to effectively rush at them.

"Stay away from them," Aden said. He cracked Logan in the head one more time. Then he approached Drake cautiously with his arms raised and he swung the club into Drake's skull. The monster dropped flat on its face. Aden whacked it in the head over and over. Then he returned to Logan's side and did the same thing.

"Come on. We're swimming back out. We should tell Tobias what's going on. Let's go."

They both threw their chair legs into the small boat and took to either side, heading out into the water. The waves crashed and sucked down. They were forced to support themselves with their upper bodies and kick at the sucking blue water with their legs. The waves crashed over them. They swam as fast as they could to get over the next tube without incident, but the water crashed harder. Lyn hung on by only one hand. She breached and called out, "Help me."

Aden climbed up into the dingy as she was pulling herself up on the ropes. He leaned over and threaded his arm between her legs and lifted her up into the boat. She fell flat on her back and he took a quick look at her, then looked back to the next wave crashing into them and pushing them to shore. Aden took the nose rope, wrapped it twice around his arm, and jumped into the cold water. He swam out and as the next wave crashed onto and over the boat, he swam under it to be able to pull against the force. He struggled, then regained his composure. He broke the surface for air and glanced to where the boat was. Then he went back under and swam with every muscle he had. The next wave went smoother.

He broke the surface for air and heard Lyn screaming more. The endboat was much closer. He didn't want to drift back to shore. As she kept screaming he made a decision and pulled himself back up to her. He saw what she was screaming about. The two broken bodies were trying to get on the back of the dingy. Lyn struck at their broken limbs with the wood.

Aden grabbed the other leg and struggled to steady himself to get in good swings at their skulls. He heard splashing coming toward them. Tobias was in the water and swimming to the dingy. Aden wasn't sure if he should be ready to hit Tobias or what was going on. He could be possessed like the other two.

"Wait to see what he does."

****

Tobias swam mostly under water. He came up out of arms reach from the boat. He saw Aden giving him a perplexed look from above and he returned the expression. It was not a good morning. He grabbed the rope and dove back down; pulling the heavy boat against the surging water toward the yacht. Within a moment his muscles burned against the exertion, but he kept pulling. And then he surfaced to see the small ladder at the back of the boat a few feet away. He stayed above water and kicked hard as he could until the ladder was in his grasp, then he pulled the dingy to the foot well, as Lyn and Aden jumped over his head. He felt Aden's wrist under his arm pit urgently pulling him out of the water.

The disturbing bodies slipped & crawled into the dingy. Logan's lanky limbs flopped over Drake's bulk as they jostled about. Tobias tied the rope off at the ladder and pushed the boat away. The bodies began frantically squishing over each other and over the inflated bench seats and tarpaulin floor. However they didn't seem to want to go back in the water. The creatures instead picked their heads up by their shoulders and shattered limbs, heaving themselves closer to the front of the boat, to see what was going on.

"Robin! Let's go." They held onto railings as the nose of boat lifted and turned out to sea.

Aden said, "Are we shooting these guys or what?"

"I don't know, I'm thinking, we need the raft. Wait here." He called out toward the wheel, "Robin, kill it, we gotta hang tight!"

They slowed to a crawl through the choppy water and leveled out. Tobias hopped up to the lower deck, went to the bench with the fishing equipment stored under the cushions, and immediately found exactly what he was looking for. A six foot long pike with a large hook at the end of it.

He ran down into the hull, went to a desk drawer, got his pistol, and grabbed a pocket full of shells. He'd seen them take those beatings then swim out with flopping- clearly broken- limbs that should have been useless. They'd been hit in the head a dozen times each. Tobias didn't know if a bullet would kill them. He grabbed a roll of duct tape, too.

"You're piking. I'm shooting," he said handing Aden the fishing tool. "You have to pull them out of there without messing them up. We'll keep one and kill one, I guess, so who are we keeping?"

"I always liked Drake more," Aden said.

"Yeah. Me too. Pull Logan into the water."

Aden pulled the dingy close to them by the 15 foot length of rope, then handed the rope off to Lyn to hold. He positioned the pike to hook Logan under the throat, checked the grip of his feet on the ladder, and said, "When I say 'go,' let go of the rope? Ok?... Go."

As the dingy lofted backward on the gentle current; Aden, with his free arm, snared Logan under the jaw and yanked as hard as he could without losing his grip on the ladder. He pulled the body all the way over into the drink. The jeans and t-shirt caught water and dragged. Aden fixed his grip.

"Lyn you should get out of here," Tobias said, holding the pistol in the air for her to see. She saw it and curtsied. A sexy gesture. Then she scurried back up to the deck and stood with Cadence and Calvin.

He looked to Aden, who was stretched out like a 'Y' between the body and the ladder. Aden gritted his teeth and pointed with his eyes and face, gesturing to do it, then shifted his wrist to expose more skull and with his shoulder shielded his face. Tobias moved up to the body, standing on sea legs, and pointed the gun.

Tobias closed his right eye and looked down the barrel with the left. A cloud of blood from Logan's throat had formed around the head. Tobias squeezed the trigger, the shot rang out, the .38 kicked, and a bullet ripped into the skull and came out the cheek. That was that.

Drake yelped and moaned out gurgles from the dingy, they were connected in some way. The next thing to do would be to get Logan out of the water and in bindings. For all the times he had, he never enjoyed handling corpses. Except maybe Olivia's. Tobias handed the gun up to Kyoto who stood nearest, and then he took the pike from Aden.

"Hang on to something," Aden suggested, indicating the railing.

Tobias did; then with one hand he pulled Logan's upper body into the foot well. The blood in his body poured out of the holes in his head, especially the exit wound. Blood flowed into the basins, and over the landing; leaving stains where it splashed against the steps.

Logan did not stop moving. His shoulders, chest, and throat bulged. The eyes remained open; looking so much like a dying fish. Holes in his face. The head twisted as far one way as it could, then it twisted the other way. Tobias looked around to find the duct tape. Kyoto had it in her hand with the pistol.

Tobias took the pistol back. Logan needed to stop moving. He knelt down, took Logan by his two inch long hair, put the barrel to the base of the skull where the spine met, aimed the mess away from the others, and before he could think too much about it, he said, "Fire in the hole!" then put another bullet through Logan. The whole head felt like it got punched in his grip, twice. In punch, out punch. Punched loose from the shoulders. He dropped the body.

Tobias turned and handed the pistol back to Kyoto. "Can I see that? Might as well get this over with," he said, referring to the duct tape.

"You're going to tie them up? Why don't we just leave them out here in the water and take off someplace?" Aden asked.

"Because we don't have any fuel," Tobias said, sighing, and he looked around at the others standing about watching. Not an idea in the crowd. He looked back to what he was doing and heaved the rest of Logan up onto the boat and arranged him face down. He took the broken arms, as they moved in unnatural ways- like bending mid forearm- and, like the police, he put the two wrists together, wrapped duct tape around so the hands wouldn't come apart, then he did the same at the feet and ankles. He put the tape down, rolled the body onto its back, sat it up, his face inches from the exit wound, so close he could feel the heat. Aden held Logan in position as he wrapped tape around the chest, then around both arms, to limit any movement as much as possible. The job was done. Tobias was glad that Drake stayed put in the dingy. He was wary of possible complications.

"Let's put him up on the deck for now. We'll do the same thing to Drake, then we can figure out where to ditch them." Tobias lifted from one armpit and Aden from the other. They hauled Logan up the few steps and dropped him on the deck.

Aden said, "If we don't have any more fuel, we don't need this boat for anything else. We can leave them here and go to shore. It's better to be on the land."

"You're so sure?" He was skeptical.

"Who the fuck cares, man? We don't have any options. These fucking things- I'm pulling him in- these fucking things are coming after Lyn now and if anything happens to her then conditions are going to be a lot worse off than your indecision is allowing for."

"Indecisive? My indecisiveness has only been a way to not offend you guys. I don't know what the fuck I'm doing. Look." Tobias took the gun out of Kyoto's hand and pointed it at his own face, "Say the word, man. I'll pull the trigger right now."

Calvin called out, "Don't!" Lyn hushed him.

Aden dropped the rope and put his hand out. He said, "Give me the gun."

Tobias saw the hand there. He shut his eyes and pushed the barrel against his eyelid harder and harder.

He heard the silence of the girlfriends. He felt the pain in his human eye, and he sat down on the soaking wet landing. That deep welling feeling after accepting the truth. That's what it took. Accept the truth. Death. The bullets fell out of his pocket as the ocean waves rolled over his lap. He removed the gun from his face and looked up to Aden through the distortions in his sight.

He waved the gun at the dingy, saying, "Pull him in. Let's do it. We'll figure something out."

Aden obliged, adding, "Why don't we sink them?"

"Sure. Why not?"

Lyn leaned over the railing and took the rope from Aden, who with his other hand grabbed the pike without noticing from who. Tobias couldn't see Drake from where he sat. He could, however, hear the guttural sounds coming from his throat as he yelped in agony when the hook of the pike pierced the flesh under his jaw bone. Aden grabbed hold of the ladder and lifted Drake up over the edge of the dingy and pulled him splashing into the water.

"It's all you, Buddy," Aden said endearingly. Lyn released the boat.

At the end of the pike Drake's body twisted with a movement of Aden's wrist. The mouth hung open, and the eyes had lost their features except for a blurry grey situation. Poor Drake. He didn't deserve to go out like that. It had to be degrading.

Tobias pointed the gun with his left hand. He closed his right eye, put the sight on the contorting body, found the head, adjusted his aim to the waves, and then he squeezed the trigger. The shot rang out. Blood spurted dramatically from the entry wound. Everyone gasped, and silently watched the red cloud gather around the skull.

Tobias stood, handed the pistol to Kyoto, and took the pike from Aden. He pulled Drake's broken, bloodied, hulking mass, up onto the landing by a head with two extra holes in it; one by either ear; the exit wound much larger and misshaped; the entry wound like a tiny perfect circle. He lay the body down on its face. Drake uselessly, and barely, attempted to struggle against his hands. He gave the floppy quaking frame the same wrapping job as the other one. Then he and Aden lifted him up the steps and dropped him, more or less, onto Logan.

Tobias could feel a meltdown. Uncertainty was his only truth. He tensed up, sat down, and lit a cigarette. The bodies continued to writhe. He inhaled deeply and rocked back and forth in the seat. His fists clenching, releasing, and clenching again.

"Why aren't they dead?" Calvin asked.

"That's a good question," Robin said laughing.

Tobias looked out to the ocean. He wanted to tune out, but remained engaged.

Aden said, "They're not dead because they're possessed by something from up there."

"Aren't they our friends?"

"They're sending us a message not to fuck around," Cadence said.

Tobias said, "They're trying to get to me. None of us are safe anymore. They don't want us dead. What the hell do they want?"

Lyn said, "They want me. Because you aren't cooperating. They're going to extort Ma'at and get what they want."

"Then the balance shifted. As long as we can keep you safe, there might be hope."

Robin said, "I been sayin' it, man. Why don't we just do what they told us to do?"

"Too much at stake. They weren't lying. I'm toxic," said Tobias.

"What are we going to do?" Lyn asked.

"Run the boat ashore. We'll get a car and keep to the shoreline. We'll do something else. Come what may.

I don't care anymore."

"Ok. We still fucking care, ruh-tard," said Aden.

Tobias was offended and appalled on behalf of the entire community of people who struggle with mental and developmental disabilities... Always time for jokes. The Girlfriends had gone down into the hull. The heat became intense. It would be cooler down there.

"We're out of gas. Anyone have any better ideas?" Tobias asked.

Cadence said, "We can anchor the boat and take the dingy. We don't have to wreck this beautiful boat."

"That water is dangerous," Toby said.

"Then we'll go where it's not," she retorted.

"That's lame. No gas. When the hell are we going to use this boat again? We can get ATV's or something."

"And what, just go?" Aden asked.

"Wait. What happened when we were on the shore?" Lyn asked.

Cadence said, with her New England city girl twang, "We were standing around wondering why Drake dove in the water and swam away. We watched what happened at the house in the binoculars. There was nothing wrong with Logan, but when Drake went down, Logan did the exact same thing; he jumped in and went. We seen Drake crawling out of there like a mud-skipper or something. You waved us over and we went over. It seemed like you had everything under control until you kept saving the dingy. You could have out swum them easily."

"I thought we needed the dingy. Everything worked out fine," Aden said.

"I was happy being dry. Didn't feel like being in the water with them, but it was alright," Tobias said, gritting his teeth. Although he'd been in drawstring nylon shorts anyhow. Such things weren't important. He thought for a second about what he was going to say next, "Let's fucking go someplace. Any place. New Orleans... is in no way going to be there. Somewhere else, like... Kansas City... or Orlando.

"We are supposed to start fires," Robin said.

"Go ahead man. If that is your journey then do it. It doesn't matter to me. I'm going to go fuck off and die. I really don't care what you do. And whatever happens to Lyn... that's cool with me too. I might go to space before I die. Again! How them apples taste?"

Aden said, "They taste fine. Me and Lyn are taking the boat. We'll get gas somewhere. Anyone is welcome to come with us."

Tobias said, "You want to meet up someplace? To die? If we haven't already? No deserts."

"Let's go to Europe," Calvin said.

Tobias said, exhaling smoke, "Calvin. You can go with whoever you want. It really doesn't matter. I doubt any of us are taking you to Europe. It's not practical."

"I'm going with Robin and Kaydee."

Robin said, "Good to know you haven't lost the will to live."

"No. I like being alive. We're going to be dead soon. I want to stay alive as long as I can. I don't want to split up. We should stay together."

"That's as good a plan as any," Tobias said.

Aden said, "Maybe for you. You just said you don't even care anymore. You're behaving recklessly and that is the last thing we need."

"I don't know what you think we need, but for once I am happy. I am detached and at ease. I am going where the wind takes me, and I give about as much a fuck about the Logos as I care that two more of our friends are dead. Everybody is fucking dead. We're only alive by the grace of God. Because supposedly we are gods. Or Gods like Jesus was a God. Even if that is true, and we are Jesus; we are still being treated like shit."

"Because you got God wrong. Gods among men, maybe. We're people among Gods. And we don't have a clue," Lyn said.

"We need Osaze and Logos. We need to talk to them."

"How? Alcyone could get them here. We need to talk to Alcyone again."

"Well, she's just hanging around, right? Alcyone! Bang on the hull if you're here."

A single clanking thud sounded from below, followed by screaming girls jumping and jostling around. Tobias waited a second and said, "There has to be a better way of doing this." He knew immediately, "We need Slor here. Everybody except Aden and Robin need to go down into the hull." They did. "Alcyone, get Slor here."

With that request the wind picked up, and mist rose from the water in all directions. The homes at the shore were instantly lost in fog, and soon so too was the sky. The Sun still burned through the shimmering water reflecting blues and casting rainbows that grew among themselves, shining through the mist in every direction. The colors moved and danced.

Tobias looked up and saw a single tiny gargoyle. It lofted steadily with its scrawny legs dangling. The wind picked up a little. It had slim rigid bodily features jaggedly defined in a smoothed over way; that less than solid look of its flesh; the mouth moved fluidly, eerily... Slor rasped, "What am I doing here?"

"I needed a word," Alcyone said, looking more like Olivia than ever as she appeared beside Slor, butt naked as a jay bird, like an angel made of crystal. She caught the colors and the rainbows in her sheen; she flashed grimly through the mist to Tobias' side. He reached out and touched her cold surface, and she said, "Slor, stay put. I'll be brief." Then Alcyone turned to Tobias and said, "You want to speak with Osaze and Logos? Is that it?"

"I have to. Preferably, I'd like to be Osaze for a

while."

"Then quit talking about it and go back to the Pleiades. See what you can find out, just don't do anything drastic."

"What qualifies as drastic?"

"Things you do out there will affect what happens here. I can think of several scenarios where a simple mistake on your part will bring the photoplasm crashing down to ignite the planet. You are desperate and shaking. There are processes you are not aware of and they have already begun. So don't count on stability, because nothing is stable out there. Instability can easily work in your favor, and as easily work against you. The sisters are going to be out there. And if you return to Osaze, you can guess what Osaze is going to do. He's going to go after Aloria. You might never come back."

"It's better than shooting myself in the head. Can you send them here? I'd like to at least talk to Osaze before I approach the greys."

"Hurry up. The sisters are getting nervous. The one in which you seek will be here within a few minutes. I am leaving. Love all of you." At that, Alcyone jumped overboard, through the windblown mist. She grabbed Slor by the ankle, and pulled him down into the water with her.

Aden asked, "What the fuck have you done? What are you going to do?"

"Get the fuck out of here. You guys can camp on the boat. Or stay around this area by the shore. You ever find out the name of this town?"

"Weston. Like 80 miles in from where the coast should have been," Lyn said.

"Nice."

The fields of mist began to settle and the wind died away. The others stood in the doorway leading to the cabins. They didn't know what to do. Tobias, irritated, realized what was about to happen. He may have been leaving for good. Walking over to the crowd, his girls came out the door to greet him.

"We go where you go," Solaris said.

"I didn't even think about that earlier. You are absolutely correct. I wouldn't have it any other way. He gave her a kiss. Then he kissed the other girls as they embraced each other. A chill had crept into the air. Kyoto noticed first the water was askew, and she pointed his attention overboard. The ocean was solidifying and turning black. Waves stalled. The water sunk through, within, deep and away; even the falling oil vapors were compelled toward the blackness in the ocean. What was coming was going to be intense. Below them, the motion of the tide halted, and all through the endboat cracks and pops could be heard. As the blackness below caught them in jarring suction until a buildup prevented them from moving further, but allowed for the tides to slurp further below.

A black sheen gathered over the whiteness of the paint job. Wherever there was water it had turned black. This was true of the moisture in his clothes. "This can't be good," he said, pulling at his black shorts. He could feel it in the moisture on his skin. He rubbed it around on his arms like semen. Gooey black sperm. Photoplasm.

There had been water on everything, and everyone, that had been outside. He was made of water... They looked like black people, except moist and reflective black people beaming sunlight off themselves. They looked around uneasily and the heat gathered on the black surface of the ocean. Below them they could feel vibrations of roiling black jiz and water.

Then nothing happened. The water and black spooge had worked out a harmony. The clan kind of just stared at each other. Only Aden, Tobias, Lyn, and the three Girls had very much black on them. The others had been dry beforehand. Tobias moved from them and looked over the edge. He could lean over and reach it; it shimmered like a black mirror. The ocean waves barely hardly moved ever so gently in place.

He reached out to touch the surface. It felt like slimy warm jello. He hopped over the bodies, went to the stern, and walked down the steps to the water where the boat was bogged in good. He held onto the railing and pushed into it with one foot. His toes slurmed into the stuff and he pulled them out again. Even below the surface, or in large amounts, the stuff resembled semen. The salt from the ocean water drove the point home.

Dumbfounded, he looked to the others. They shared his expression. Without any way to tell what they were waiting for, he shrugged, "Anybody got a drink?"

"Yup," Aden said, and fetched a bottle of rice wine from a cabinet on deck. Tobias walked up and over to them. Lyn had shown up too. They passed the bottle around staring at the blackened landscape. The slimy black boat blended in with the 'water.' Out on shore the houses had a new black shimmer. In broad daylight. Either way. When Tobias realized it might be a good idea, he called, "Osaze?"

Nothing. Not a whisper of wind. He tried again, "Osaze?"

Kobe said, "Try something else. Don't forget, you are Osaze, too."

She was right. Tobias walked to the side of the boat, shut his eyes, and staring back at him was his own face. "Oh shit!" he said. He opened his eyes and saw things the way they were, closed them and again saw his face; a little disheveled and his black hair matted from being sun dried; sun burnt pale skin; that vibrantly red eye; his perpetual glare; as clear as 20/20 sight, he sternly peered back at himself. "Close your eyes, guys."

They shouted; shocked; 'It's Toby,' 'What the fuck, man,' 'This is creepy.' He didn't disagree with them. As he stared at his face, it didn't say a word. Osaze only stared back.

WUJI

"Is it really you?" Tobias asked, staring at a levitating image of himself with his eyes closed; lids clamped tight for darkness. Behind his own face glaring back at him he saw fractals; tunnels and scorpions in metallic colors.

"It is," said Osaze. The voice rang in his head like nothing he'd heard before. Like a thought with the volume turned up, not too loud and crystal clear.

"What are you doing in there?" Talking to his own voice.

"It is better this way. You needn't know the reasons. They are dynamic. This arrangement was the simplest option. What is it you want from me?"

"I want you to care about Aloria! What is going to come of creation if you and Aloria won't dance your cosmic romance, or whatever? For fuck sake, there has to be something you can do."

"Changes. All changes. Always. Nothing lasts forever. We have been 'dancing' since I exploded into the Logos, and now, at the end, the dance has been interrupted. The dancers have been torn from each other and the force required to reconnect them would destroy all else. It has been engineered that way."

"You can't be blamed for that. Engineer it back. Tear the thing apart."

"I have no responsibility to destroy all that exists on this plain to reestablish an extraneous entanglement such as this romance."

"Or the opposite is true," Tobias said, "and they are forcing your hand. A world where you- of all things- won't do what is in your power to reacquire your love is a world I wouldn't wish upon anyone and won't allow while I'm still alive."

Aden popped into the conversation. Literally popped in. Tobias even heard a sound like a small balloon bursting. Aden's face appeared next to Osaze's face, still behind closed eyelids. He was aggravated, his voice echoed out on the boat and in Tobias' head; two origins, "Tobias, do you have any idea how fanatical you sound right now? A little extremist, you know?"

"Fanatical shit. So be it. Let lying manipulating bitch deities dictate the future? Fuck no. What about Arianna? I have to think about what Arianna would want if she were alive."

Aden said, "She wouldn't want you to destroy the universe over her."

Tobias said, "I don't want to destroy this universe. I want to destroy the ascended universe. And the future."

Osaze said, "It is indeed this universe you wish to destroy. If I understand what exactly you are proposing, there would be no ascension."

Tobias thought on it and said, "What about a power struggle? Can't we force their hand?"

Osaze said, "Perhaps we could. Have you given acceptance any thought?"

"Acceptance is what fucked this planet up. Fuck acceptance. You tell me. Why should I accept this?"

"For the sake of what was and ever will be."

"And what of what was?"

"It is done. There are other ways to harmonize this."

"Ways that don't involve you? Or me? Why are you in such a hurry to not exist?"

"I am going to another place, Tobias. You will be there as well, within me, as you should be. And every single thing you loved about Arianna will be there with us. Because you never really loved Arianna. You were only loving the parts of yourself that she'd taken unto herself. As she only loved what of her was within you. When you dissect the equation, you find that it is only possible to love oneself. And to love another is a symbiotic continuation of that self-serving tendency."

He didn't want to believe Osaze, but found it impossible not to. It crushed him. He fought becoming distracted by the emotional pain of his losses. And beyond that he was left considering, love might not exist. He said, "Then our efforts should be to relinquish what of you remains in Aloria."

Aden's stupefied face, so befuddled by the obscurity, not so subtly, with a pop, disappeared from inner vision. He could sense the others still listening; all stayed calm and still. Aden hadn't been meshing with any concern about Aloria.

"Tobias, you don't understand. What of us that is within Aloria will live on after our exodus. And it will be orphaned, left to her care alone, and Aloria will do what is best with it and in that way we will ascend, too."

"That isn't us. That is her," Tobias argued.

"It is us. As she is in us, and we will take with us what is of her to the new place."

"How is that any consolation?"

"It is not. You will have no consolation. What matters most is dead to you, and your attachment to Aloria and Osaze, while noble, is a fool's task."

"You're such a joker..."

The clan perched the best they could to not slide, but with eyes closed, feet slipped across the deck and butts slid across the seats. Still, they watched Osaze-Tobias' floating head lookalike- talking like he didn't have a care in the Logos. The bodies of Drake and Logan appeared relatively unaffected. Nobody noticed them writhing in place under the black coating covering everything.

Osaze's face, in the red and yellow metallic light, looked compelling. Nothing mattered. No one seemed to care. Tobias couldn't distinguish the endgame. If the decisions were so insignificant, he needn't be tormented in such a way. He with the passion for his lost beloved. Her poor essence ensnared to a device of platitudes forever thereafter and gone.

"I want to do it. I want to tear the whole thing down. I want to crush the whole family, except Alcyone and Aloria. We'll ascend without the others. They'll be elsewhere. It will be as glorious and grand and everyone here will be together out there. Is that possible?"

"There might be a sort of general division that could be agreed upon. Are you going to use force? Is that what you're saying? Because they'll know in an instant, and they'll kill you. Make a definite, final, decision and see what happens. Uncertainty is the one reason you are alive."

"You have to help me."

"Of course I will. What do you plan?"

"The Zeta Reticuli. The stars. I want you to seize them in your name. And I want you to seize Sirius and if this does not draw all five sisters into negotiations then I want you destroy the Zeta and release Sirius."

Aden popped back in, "Tobias, what the fuck is wrong with you? You can't do that?"

"Can't I? Can I?"

Osaze nodded yes.

"Good. Jesus Christ, what I'm saying is I need to talk to these bitches. And if they won't talk to me, then it's on their hands. I don't have any other options. I don't know what else to do? If this is my decision, I am going to make it. Didn't you ever want to destroy a civilization? An entire race? We're white blooded americans, it's our heritage. Fuck the bullshit. If they can take from me, can I not take as well?"

Aden said, "You aren't taking anything from guilty parties."

"Says you. I am taking their compassion. I am causing them blame. What I want is a hearing between parties. Is it too much to ask?"

"Too little to destroy anything about."

Too many questions and doubts. He became overwhelmed in a sickening way. Helpless against the scales of justice. Tobias' panicked; he needed to escape the thorny roses, "Can we attack a star or two in the Pleiades? What if Olivia volunteers? Osaze, would Alcyone sacrifice herself for you?"

"No. We have to leave the Syrians out of this. The Zeta time has been up for longer than the Earth has been populated. They are the worst kinds of creatures. Subservient mongoloids, and vile to the core when watchful eyes are averted. Still, they are always useful, to everyone, even now when perhaps their time has come."

"Fine. Just the Zeta. Threaten them. Show them. And when you've done that, send them for us. I want to be where you are."

"You are."

"I want to be where I can be you."

"You are."

"You know what I mean."

"You wish to be more than human?" Osaze asked.

"For a short while, again, it would be nice, but if you're cooperating then I guess there is no need. I'm human. I distrust everything- you understand."

Eyes began to flutter open, looking around, realizing the sky had blackened. On their skin, on the wind, electricity danced, and snapped high above; crimson red bolts of lightning seethed across other crimson red bolts in configurations of different shapes, mesmerizingly extra-dimensional; cagey webs shooting charges through the thick blackness of the sky goo as though there was nothing there.

The wind ripped across the halted ocean and whipped them in their faces. They began paying more attention to their footing. The boat wobbled like it were in gelatin. Their hips were shaking like an old Elvis video. Osaze's voice, Tobias', or Aden's, or anybody's, still rang amplified in their heads.

"So you're going to the grays, and us nine are waiting for the grays who will be arriving promptly?" Tobias verified. Still crushing his eyelids together for vision.

"Yes. That is the ultimate deduction."

"Then let's get on it. Is this boat going to sink, or what?"

"You will be fine. All has been stalled. There is no risk to you on that boat. Though the matter is irrelevant. Prepare yourselves. You'll be leaving the surface together."

At that, they felt his presence lift. The wind cut out, their heads grew clearer and somehow lighter. A calmness fell over them, and even in the sky, nothing was as turbulent as the moment before. They looked around to each other sharing smirks and disgusted looks at the blackness that had consumed the salt water like an oil spill on steroids.

Tobias relinquished an irritating worry in the back of his head. Paranoia and insecurity flooded across him. He had finally made a decision. It was too much to take back. He had nothing to lose. The others did, but maybe they would finally feel how he felt. They might fight against it. He held the pistol in his pocket, turned and asked them, "You ready for space?"

"This is what it's come to?" Robin asked.

Tobias thought and said, "Yeah. If we have to go, we have to go. It is what it is."

"Aren't you jeopardizing the security of our eternal souls as well as jeopardizing every eternal soul on this planet and thus everything else in the Logos?" Aden asked.

"No. Cuz those bitches are going to cooperate. We want Aloria back, when that happens, then I'll be cool, I swear."

Cadence said, "What makes you say that? You don't

know and there is no way to tell."

"I have to hope. I want everyone to get what they deserve. Not, some get what is right, and some get screwed. This fucking figures. Nothing ever felt right when I was a kid. And they always said, 'Tobias, you're just like everybody else.' 'You might be special, but little Tommy is special, too, and we can't possibly comprehend that there might be more to you than little Tommy ramming boogers in his eyeballs.'"

Aden shouted, "What the fuck does that have to do with this?"

"Because it is my decision. And if you put a dilemma in front of me, and you say, choose a world with love or without; I am going to choose one with, because love is what I know. Even if it is just bullshit. So if I have to snuff out the entire Logos, I am going to do it with love."

Aden politely considered this, then said, "Somebody is going to have to stop you at some point. If you keep me around, it is probably going to be me."

"Then we'll have the Zeta take you someplace earthly and you won't need to get involved. Besides, everything is going to be fine."

"There is nothing to do here. You're going where the action is. Gaia is going up in flames, as soon as Lyn is dead." The couple smiled at each other. Aden pulled Lyn close by her hand.

"Not if I die first."

"We aren't dying, we are just going into space, and when we come back we'll be alive still? Is that right?" Robin asked.

"Don't bet on it. You remember what happened to Arianna?" Cadence asked.

"If they don't need you, or they need you dead- No. Fuck it. We just won't fuck around. Know what I mean? We who go up are we who come back, got it? Fuck. Why would they risk this turmoil to keep them apart?

Somebody remind me to figure out the answer to that, please? Why is it so important they remain apart? Does anybody know?"

Solaris said, "They wish to see the ascension occur as they chose, not as you choose."

"Have they ever heard of acting like adults? I don't want this shit!"

"People accept loss."

"People fucking die, too. I don't know if you've picked up on this- it's about love. The obstruction of love, by those with no faith and agendas of their own. Placating the meek across the stars. Look what it's come down to. Staring death in the face every day? You know anyone else who had to wait around this long to get what was coming to them?"

Lyn laughed and said, "Most people would have appreciated such a blessing."

"That isn't the point. It's over. We're doing what we're here to do. Why is this ultimately my decision? Why? Can any of you tell me? Because of these three girls right here." The girls didn't even flinch at the attention. "And they were a gift to me. From who? From Yah. From the Pale Mystic. From Ma'at. From Osaze. From everything not affiliated with Satan's vagina in the Pleiades. I have the good vagina. It's almost as if they want these three vaginas to facilitate the ascension. I want Aloria's vagina to do it, personally. These three are like I am, and Osaze is. At least Aloria has purity.

"Osaze fills her void. It's like, they're trying to ascend into unity, into oneness, but instead of bringing the Logos together, they are prying apart the best part and trying to squeeze through the divide. They used to cry from the hilltops, 'The Pleiades are love.' And what the fuck ever, because they're tearing love in half and crawling through the middle so they won't actually feel pain for a minute."

Lyn said, "Tobias, the higher minds seem to have

been fair with Osaze. They didn't want it to turn out like this either."

Tobias didn't hear her, he kept talking, "I remember being terrified of aliens when I was a kid. Then, I remember being convinced they weren't real, and they couldn't be. Then I remember learning about the Pleiadians, and the Zeta Reticuli. It was like relearning about ghosts. I was pissed off, but mostly I was confused, because the information just wasn't there. And now, I'm holding existence hostage? And I don't even really feel that bad about it? They could have managed their Earthly affairs better. No? Considering they knew the fate of this already. They look at creation like it's a portrait, and they're within the portrait. They are not going to be happy to see us. Butt fuck it. Tits for tits. If they ask, just reassure them everything is going to be Ok. Ok? We are not going to war. We are seeking for diplomacy."

Robin said, "They already know what we're doing, and they already know how they're going to react. To the Pleiadians this situation may have never happened, but they know every detail of what's coming anyway. So I say fuck it. I think you got a case Tobias. Let those three do the thinking for you and we'll be fine." Everyone had a good laugh at the insult.

"You're not funny, bat-brain."

The skies remained black in all directions, but under the horizon out over the ocean, in the dark hazes, he began seeing small pings of deep orange light, fluttering; energy dispersing across each craft; visually skewed by an artificial gravity field distorting space and time. 30 of them or so, in clusters of ten.

"I think I'm going to be sick," Cadence said.

"Everybody use the buddy system, Kobe, be my buddy?

"What about Pluto?"

"Lock him in the wheelhouse, it's the best we can

do."

Aden said, "You think these things can move us around but not your cat? We can drift through space on a thought, but Pluto can't."

"We're going to find out, you're absolutely right. I'm an idiot. He's coming with us. If any cat can do it, it's Pluto. We might find out what's actually going on inside a cat's mind."

Kobe said, "He'll be fine."

"Yeah. I'm nervous for him though. I don't think I could stand to see him go. Not after Arianna. Then these two down there. I'd rather see any of us go."

"Hey," said Calvin in resentment.

"Except maybe you buddy," Tobias said, rolling his eyes.

The Zeta spacecraft got closer. His heart dropped into his stomach. One cluster of ships stopped in place. The other two clusters split toward either direction and flew further; one out over the suburbs and the other cluster went further down the shoreline. Each group of spacecraft organized into a circle and the ten or so lights in each cluster spun around each other fast enough to create visual trails of energy from one to the next; the three orange circles placed at different points like a triangle.

"This is going to suck," Robin said laughing.

"Yes it is," Tobias confirmed. He looked up and noticed a bluish hue gathering about 30 feet above their heads. Different illuminated shades of blue faded into a swirling vortex. The wind calmed to stillness; eerily silent. Looking above, into the vortex, to behold it, created enough of a sensory impression that Tobias felt he could hear the silence of what he was seeing. It began whirling quicker and quicker under its own inertia, and the light it shined became brighter. The others were cowering from it. He squinted his eyes as the illumination was became blinding, and he held them together; pulling the girls into his arms. On his neck he felt warm air contrasting the heat.

"We're about to fucking die," Cadence said laughing.

Then they were consumed in light. He wanted that moment to last forever. 'The moon. The moon. The moon. They need to go to the moon. These three girls, and cat, need to come with me to speak to your highest authority, if you have one. I need to address your race.'

'Then so you will.'

Familiar voice, the Zeta had only one voice. There was essentially one Zeta doing a million different things. Tobias opened his eyes, and the gifted orb could see immediately while his human orb stayed blinded by the shocking bright light. He imagined how much easier pacifying the Zeta would be than he had originally thought. Then he found himself in near Earth orbit again.

He admired the planet. He could even see the area below where the blackness had bled out over- closer to the equator- where they contacted Osaze. The colors wafting and smoldering through the blackness did not fail to wow him. He oriented the girls with taps and tugs to see for themselves, as their vision came back. If anything the colors were more spectacular than last time. They had been dull last he saw. They were positively alive. So too, he decided, must he be alive. And he was. The darkest hours of descension were upon him.

They were bathed in blue moonlight shining off of Gaia. Immediately, he saw that same stupid table with the stools. He checked Pluto, and the cat was very much alive, squishing his eyelids together and rubbing his face into Kobe's arms, but remaining placid. About 10 yards away he saw one of the Grays. A single skinny little monster spaceman.

The alien could be called a bag of bones. The

apparently bio luminescent head had sheen like it were pure skull and there was no flesh covering it. Like it could be cracked. The grays entire body was illuminated in the same way as a scorpion under ultraviolet lights. Tobias couldn't figure how. Then he knew it was 'his' girls emitting a source of transparent energy. The girl's fleshy exposed bodies, scantily clad, were no longer black with photoplasm. Instead they were dimly ultraviolet: A subtle hint in the complexions of either Kobe or Kyoto, while Solaris had clearly turned a soft shade of purple.

'We know everything you have to say,' the Zeta said; speaking in thought.

'I need to know what else you know.'

'About what?'

'The Pleiadians.'

'In particular?'

'How do I locate hilt?"

'Through the Pleiadians.'

'Which Pleiadian?'

'All of them. The sisters whom you seek specifically are the ones with power. Like you, they are the lower forms of their own universal configurations. Also, there is an entire civilization of these principles, at least hundreds of life forms, existing under the control of the sisters. The Pleiadian situation is an intricate one. You should know the influence of those in power trickles across the rest, and it is the most supreme Pleiadians who make any decisions of consequence. These rulers have the resources of the Logos at their disposal, subsequent to their underlings. Your war is a war of all that is not against all that is.'

'It's not a war. It's negotiating.'

'You are so sure, human?'

'Tell me what is going to happen.'

'Chaos.'

'Can you be more specific?'

'Chaos is all that ever happens whenever you do anything. You are unpredictable, Tobias. You are a human with more power than Yah. You labor only for what you call love, and for you there can be no love. You are a creature of sacrifice. That is your role. To remove yourself so that the Logos may be unfettered and ascend.'

'What of love?'

'Love will be cleansed of the Osaze infection. Love has always been encumbered by your devious lusting and fraudulent motives; the torturous dependencies. While you may have loved purely, you loved purely toxic. Such as love was on Gaia toxic as a result of Osaze. For this reason the control has been placed squarely in your hands. There are universal and fundamental ideologies that dictate an entity must abide its own removal. Osaze, were he not intoxicating, would of course be welcome to ascend.'

'All I need to make this right is Aloria. Osaze and Aloria belong to each other. She is the antidote to his poison. They can ascend in harmony. It's never been tried and that's nonsense because it will work, they have to be given a chance.'

'You must understand we have no opinion on the matter. Presently, our race exists by the grace of your whim. To us, it matters not if we perish before the ascension, or if life in the Logos will perish before the ascension, or if Osaze will ascend or revert. We crave nothing. We are here to help you as we are here to help the beings of this dimensional plain.'

'Don't you have any capacity for multi-dimensional activity?'

'Some. Nothing substantial. Our affairs exist within this plain here. You will not encounter us beyond the Merkaba.'

'Where are my friends? Have they found Mesmere? I seek Mesmere.'

'They have been delivered to Mesmere, he is accepting them currently.'

'Good. Why are the only choices to destroy everything or leave?'

'The Pleiadians are the reason.'

'What would happen if I destroyed the Pleiades?'

'Aloria would be lost forever. Along with countless innocent Pleiadians existing within the star cluster. Up to this point you've completely risked the safety of the inhabitants of the Zeta Reticuli. We are spread out over hundreds of planets there. The quantities of life you're endangering are vast. And the varieties are many, to understate. On behalf of the Zeta Reticuli, I am here to say we welcome oblivion; having always known it would end this way. We've seen worse times, and we're glad if this is over. If we ascend, that is welcome, too.'

'I have a few more questions.'

****

Aden couldn't understand how they could bleed under such unreal conditions. Not really caring, he said, "Wait. Wait. Everybody stop here." He began wiping blood away from Calvin's body with his shirt and ignoring the wounds dripping from his own face, from his chest, his legs, and everywhere else. Calvin whimpered.

The roses shimmered deep electric red, full of energy. The stems seethed with enlivened green light. They'd been wandering through the towering bushes growing like ivy from points unknown. This was where they appeared after the light vortex. The thorns were finger sized and stronger than glass. Aden had gotten stabbed, scratched, skewered, and fed up.

He said, his annunciation obviously incorrect, "Enough of this. What are we waiting for? Mesmere? Are you here, Mesmere?" With that, the thorns clinked together as the rose bushes parted; humming and rustling overhead. Still, everywhere were roses of all shapes and sizes; each the same crimson red, and some were downright enormous.

Before them, for the first time, they found Mesmere, a giant human made seemingly entirely of reflections; flashes and sparkles across his surface and robe. For the first time they saw a space snake, green like everything else, with diamonds of shimmering yellow scales, very large and choking on its own tale.

"Is that snake going to die?" Calvin asked.

"This snake is not alive," Mesmere said.

"I can see it moving," Calvin objected.

Right then the energy of the snake around his waist fritzed out in a few quick flashes. The serpent turned to sparkling dust with a silent splash that lofted away- under the volition of its dissolution- across the misconstrued gravity. With that, the red flickered away, and everywhere all they could see were disorienting shades of electric green and inky blacks, in the form of roses.

"You seem frightfully out of place," Mesmere said smiling. He wore a robe that fit unlike any style Aden had ever seen; awkwardly slim everywhere above the waist, and strangely baggy below. Tiny mirrors reflected and dangled by thread from all points of the clothes, so when he spoke the mirrors shimmered in unison.

"We didn't expect to be here. It happened suddenly," Aden said.

"Well, I'm certainly humbled to be in the presence of such honorable representation. Logos, Ma'at. Draco. Orion. And Sirius, much tinier than I would have expected, but alright." Mesmere looked like a greek statue. His wavy electrical hair would be black on earth. His face had the fierce eyes of a powerful young leader, a prominent jaw, and an angry bird nose.

Robin and Cadence looked at each other, not quite

grasping the acknowledgment. Robin said, "Ok. I don't get the reference. Nobody told us anything. Can you explain in what way we are relevant to this situation?"

Mesmere said, "You must understand? No? You are each a human manifestation of the higher principles. The council of nine. Except... shorthanded? Not if you consider the three girls as replacements of the missing entities. In that way, Osaze has already shifted the balance in the Logos. You, Robin, are Orion, in current descended form. And Cadence is Draco, as currently descended, understand? Calvin is Sirius. Currently."

Cadence said, "What does that even mean? What is Sirius?"

"Sirius is a necessary presence, like each of you: Doing the dance that kept the human consciousness possible. Except, the music stopped playing. So, here we are, after about 75,000 years of human generations, it's over. Draco, Orion, Sirius, Logos, and Ma'at, you are the council. What happens is ultimately Tobias' decision; you are in positions to influence his choices. Ambassadors of reason and wise council."

Humanity was the highest achievement of the entire Logos. From a higher perspective we gave life to an entire dimension, except we, then, in a way, stranded it there. The situation on earth was a unified assembly of the greatest diversity. An entire universe represented; by an insect, a fish, a cat, and for the right ones, humanism. As plagued and ruined the outcome was, it had been anticipated, and the project remained a monumental achievement.

"Of course, Osaze is the keeper of all that is unholy, and for that reason they wish to banish him; for all that is unholy. What you need to understand is that there are other ways. There are ways to cleanse Osaze. The way is through Aloria. This involves Aloria abandoning the Pleiades to never return. That is how the Pleiadians view it. In actuality, Osaze and Aloria belong to each other. In a more substantial way than the clashing elements causing them to occasionally repel. For a few missteps in the dance of the Logos, they demolish the record player? In ascension they will meld if they are able, or they will forever find agonizing stability in a hopeless and insurmountable repulsion. The latter not being preferable, especially for Osaze.

"The important part is, you have been given the power to speak on behalf of or against the Pleiadians. Osaze's cause is not lost, but he will have to fight, and nobody knows how this confrontation will result, for the simple reason we cannot see beyond the reversion."

"Where did Osaze go?" Aden asked.

"He is speaking with the Zeta. He'll be here any moment. Then the end will begin."

"We won't be going back to Earth?" Lyn asked, mostly for Calvin's sake.

"Perhaps you will, but I scarcely see any reason to. Your physical bodies are being kept in near Earth orbit. When the time comes to ascend, we will simply kill Lyn. I'm sure you understand, dear. Right?"

"I guess so," Lyn said, a bit angrily.

"Good. Good. Here, Osaze has arrived."

Red light bled into the darkness from a short distance into the bushes. The roses seemed to be using that energy to flourish in color once again. The entire area flushed magnificently across the shadows and shades of green.

****

Much the same as before his one eye needed to adjust to the light while the other saw without being damaged. He looked to Pluto in Kobe's arms. The cat was reacting to the thought travel. He rubbed the fluffy fur around his neck. He noticed the quality of the 'air' clung very sterile. He wasn't inhaling, yet he took breaths, and on his skin he felt air, although there was almost certainly no such thing. He smelled no rosy fragrance to speak of. No scent.

The roses moved apart, and as Tobias pushed past them the flowers became red; to a restrained degree; restrained by a force and a presence, like Slor if he were a thought occurring in all kinds of indistinguishable forms, not just a golem. Every impression imaginable played against his senses; with a very negative bent leading to an unusual sort of singularity. Singularity was ignorance. He had to block out the sensations permeating about him. Tobias led the three girls- each exerting the same effect over the roses- through the pathway toward the clearing. He admired the 'ground.' It was like they were standing on dry water.

The Clan looked pretty serious about their affairs. Mesmere stepped tactfully away from the halo of red surrounding Tobias and the girls; though the mirrors adorning him shone the reflection brightly. The glows falling over each face- greens, and then reds- were an elegant thing to behold. A moment of purity in beauty, before the battles against confusion and missing information resumed.

He missed being happy to see the Omega clan. Tobias didn't want to have to keep reporting to those people. He needed to leave them behind. They were the faces of descension. Either his, or the descension of all. He was taking on so much. What he wanted was for the oppositions to reconcile. To concede to that which mattered most; true love.

He spoke first, "Mesmere, I need to speak to every Pleiadian at once. I need to convince them to return Aloria to Osaze."

Mesmere said, "As you gain perspective, you will ultimately be stunned by how perilous this situation is. She- might- not- be- coming back. Not until Osaze is gone. She is being quarantined."

"Well. You can find her. Can't you?"

"Yeah. Maybe I could. But I won't. I don't agree with what you are doing. And I won't help. We need to ask: Are the Pleiadians right to look out for their own, or are you right to look out for love? There is no one answer to the question. I have given you mine, I suggest you listen to theirs before you make any decisions."

Mesmere cast his arm out toward the Clan who more or less shrugged collectively. Tobias shrugged back at them, and asked, "What do you guys think I should do?"

Aden said, "Anything much less drastic. Think of how much stuff you want to do out there, and do that much of the opposite. Do a lot of nothing. That is what you should do. Completely nothing. That is what we should do. And let whatever is going to happen happen."

Tobias glanced quizzically at each of the girls, then addressed Aden, "We could do that.... Robin, what do you think?"

Robin thought briefly and said, "Whatever you want, man. I think you got it under control."

"Ho for the vote of confidence. Ho! Lyn? Cadence?"

The two girls exchanged glances, Lyn spoke, "Do what they said originally. Exodus. With Kobe, Kyoto, and Solaris. Go someplace else. Forget about Aloria. She is a Pleiadian, you have to accept that."

"Calvin. What do you think I should do?"

"Whatever you want to do, Osaze. That's what you would have told me to do. That is what you should do."

"Are you implying my actions are of no consequence?"

Calvin didn't understand the joke and Aden interrupted anyway, "Cadence, what do you think?"

"Defend love. Love has always been there for us. I think we should be there for it. Do whatever you have to. As long as you do it in the name of love, love will be done."

"I'm going to make some love all over the Pleiades. Some stifling black oblivion love. Until they choke on it."

Cadence said, "No. You have to be nice about it. There is no other way."

"I have tried asking nicely. They were very rude."

"Be more demanding, but stay polite. Be delicate, whatever you do. Oh, god. This is going to be so bad. Don't do anything drastic."

"There are hundreds of stars in the Pleiadian cluster. I'm going to destroy all of them except two. Will this Merkaba send us to the wormhole beyond Sirius?"

"It certainly can."

"And if we die out there, what happens on Earth?"

Mesmere said, "There will still be an ascension of Gaia. The higher ones will descend to lift it up themselves. In terms of pure design I'll admit your plans are almost sound. I didn't expect you to grasp the ordeal in such a way, yet you have. You are able to change the future, and few can do such a thing. I must advise you though, that an ascension with no Pleiadians will be of no good to anyone or anything. It would be like a race of humans with no women."

"Then I need to be more specific. We need to get Alcyone here. Do you know an easy way of making that happen?"

Mesmere lifted his hand like he held an invisible wine glass, and simply said, "Alcyone? Your presence is requested."

An instant later Alcyone manifested into the electricity of the Merkaba, appearing in that same green static flesh, the same as Mesmere, and practically, or actually, naked; wearing only shadows over her crotch and hair over her breasts. She collected herself, standing in place. Once she had her composure about her she glared at Tobias with her eyebrows up, "Now, what do you need?"

"I need you to guide me, as Osaze, to destroy the most influential Pleiadians, or at least whoever I need to destroy to get Aloria released."

"You'll likely destroy her in the process."

"You should help me avoid that. And help me do as little damage as possible. What can be taken hostage? What, when removed from the equation, could force acquiescence?"

"Do you recall you've already taken a hostage? The Zeta? It has not gone unnoticed, and though I should not tell you this, your actions have fleshed out the one you're looking for. Destroy her- Maia- and you will have the attention you need. Destroy the opposition, and you will have my race at your whims. Have mercy and perhaps in gratitude we will hand Aloria to Osaze. Any objections will be abated, I will see to that.

"If this for any reason does not go as you've planned, take the deal, it's better than oblivion, alright?"

"I don't know. I haven't been there yet."

Alcyone said, "I promise you it is. There is no oblivion, only transference. You won't like the change, should it be forced. Now, consider your actions. Oblivion is where you banish those who would have Osaze banished to his own utopia. You condemn them to The Mystic. A place they don't belong. Like hell. Except there has never been a hell, until you created one by misplacing that which should never be tampered with. You don't comprehend the way in which Osaze is destructive. Osaze consumes. Everything; life, love, beauty; and thus thrives. You forget that Osaze is an entire realm, filled with an inaccessible level of consciousness, perplexing to me even, and to anyone that might try to investigate. Thus we don't have the facts. We know danger, so none dare to go near it. The threat alone should bring forth Aloria, at least for considerations. You need to contact Osaze now. I will meet you at the confrontation. Goodbye."

Alcyone acknowledged each person with a sweeping glance, she put her hand on Mesmere's shoulder and he smiled. Then she turned and disappeared in the exact same fashion as the snake had; she flared brightly in flashes of light, and then puffed away into vibrant sparkling dust; gone as fast as she'd appeared.

Calvin shouted, "Why does everybody keep doing that?"

Tobias laughed, "It's magic buddy."

HANGED

"If I have anything to say about it, I want to be down on that rock when it goes up in flames. This bullshit will be taken care of, and I want to die doing what we did best; getting drunk and fucking. Calvin, you're dying a virgin."

"A what?"

"Exactly."

Aden said, "You have a lot of demands, Toby. You want to reunite Osaze and Aloria. You want to get back to Earth for one last calamity. I get your resolution. But, maybe you should try looking at this from another perspective."

"What perspective is that?" Tobias asked.

"Upside down? I don't know. Just try to see the situation differently. Why don't you take some time?"

"You know what? You're right, man. You're absolutely right. I know the place, too. Mesmere, can you send us to that wormhole out by the underworld at Sirius there? All of us?"

"I can. Is there anything else I can do for you before you leave?"

"There is so much I have to know. I can't separate it. Or, do I know that I have to?"

"You have been gifted with a self-perpetuating

knowledge. However, you got tricked and misled. There is nothing to know, and no way to know it. The knowledge is of no use. Instinct makes decisions. As below, so above. When you learn new instincts, you will know something substantial. You'll notice they've used their very essences against you. You are a human assailing higher powers. As an ambassador, perhaps, but foolishly still."

"What are my options, Mesmere?"

"You are on the right track. A period of reflection-" his robe flashed red, even his green static flesh turned crimson rose colored briefly- "is all you need. Go hang out for a while. It defies instinct. In that way you will gain the perspective you require."

"I'm so pissed off, though. That's why you are right. Will we be able to speak to Ma'at while we are there?"

"You'll be outside of Sirius territory. Ma'at is centralized there. I will contact her for you, and let her know her presence is requested."

Lyn had perked up, "We can see Ma'at?"

"Yes."

"Oh. I'm so excited."

He'd never seen Lyn smile before. "Then I guess we can go."

Solaris said, "You have to get to Osaze, don't forget."

Mesmere answered for him, "That is where you are going; to Osaze."

"Then we can go. Bye, Mesmere, thank you for your help," she said.

"Of course, Solaris. It is my honor. It is my honor to be here with you, truly. Good luck to you. If I see you again, it will be under better circumstances. I love you all."

'We love you, too Mesmere.'

They lifted up from the invisible floor; floating within a vacancy. Stumbling across each other in zero gravity, grasping at each-other's parts, laughing and unsuccessfully trying to orient themselves. Tobias hung upside down, his clothes stayed in place, more or less, and he lost interest in the jubilation to view the enormous green six pointed star instead. Still, with no idea what the significance of the symbolism was. His speculations didn't make any sense. Except that perhaps the Jewish people were involved, hence the whole 'chosen ones' theme in the bible.

They lifted high. Upon looking down he couldn't see anything except thick colored lines in the various shades of green energy and a few dark areas of land. The others ceased to tussle and, sprawled over each other, they too stared to the lunar surface below.

They got higher and could see the entire Merkaba. The moon got smaller, drifting away. Gaia appeared, only half full, looming far off, and what shone was darkened by photoplasm and looked murky under the full moon light.

All else they could see was infinite stars and black. More stars than any other human had ever seen. They were engulfed in tiny speckles. In an instant Gaia disappeared and Luna, too. The stars bled together until they were consumed by white starlight. There were no single stars, or star clusters. If there were any star at all, it was singular and they were inside of it.

They looked to each other verifying they hadn't changed, and to chagrin they began laughing more; waving their arms around, and lightly pushing each other with their fingertips. Pluto certainly enjoyed perching on Kobe's shoulder and looking around.

Robin said, "This is probably the coolest thing that has ever happened to anybody."

"Totally," Calvin enthusiastically agreed.

Cadence said, "How many people would have been so jealous of this? Can you imagine?"

"It's peaceful," Lyn said.

"Like the womb," Tobias said, and made an effort to get close to the girls. Instead he sort of wound through them. He found himself next to Kobe and gave her a kiss. She smiled and laughed when she saw his entanglement betwixt them. The other girls saw her laughing, and laughed, too. Kyoto's head was right by his crotch. She bit his thigh pretty hard and he jolted. More laughter ensued. He pulled her up into his arms and kissed her. Solaris found her way to his lips as well.

Lyn said, "Get a room, you four."

"Yeah. Quit making out in the void," Aden said.

"Whatever, man. I'm in voids all the time. I can make out if I want."

"Shyeah," Aden said, laughing.

"We're practically already there," Tobias said.

"Where are we going?" Aden asked.

"Osaze Land? I don't know what to call it. Basically, it's an enormous tract of desolate space outside of Sirius. It's its own thing. At the portal- or whatever, wormhole-Osaze is supposed to take out of the Logos. Like the anus of the Logos, or some shit."

"Interesting," Aden said.

"Why would we go there?" Cadence asked.

"Because the place is rad. We can have a good time out there, I promise. The scenery is lovely, too. This is going to be good. We're going to relax, and forget about the whole thing as much as possible, and I'm sure when we're done everything will make a whole lot more sense. You'll see, this'll be good."

The soft white light, like egg white light, began to fade to black around them. Immediately, Tobias noticed the same red webbing stretched across eternity, and connecting some kind of barrier together so far away and relatively close. No stars, as they softly lofted down to the same sort of dry watery air floor as had been at the Merkaba. His limbs sunk softly into it.

Pluto, attached to Kobe's wrist, jumped down into

the substance; exploring with cautious paws. Solaris rolled over onto him laughing and smiling, he sunk a little more with her added weight. "Tobias! This is where we first met! I love you so much."

He kissed her, "I love you, too. All of you." Tobias lay there sprawled out like he was tripping, under three fawning and clearly aroused young ladies. He looked over and saw the others on their feet and milling about. "Hey, you guys." They looked over and down at him. "You guys want to see a magic trick?"

"Yeah," Calvin said.

"Take Pluto first. Here." He handed off the cat, like a dry wet towel. "Ok. Alikazaam. Alikazoo," Tobias said, swinging his free arm about toward the distance. In his head he was thinking, 'I need a house over there. Any house. The house from Cuba. Right over there.' Thus the home materialized, greeted by the cheering and applause of his peers. The clan carefully moved across the soft ground toward the home and walked inside. He was left alone with the girls; they cuddled close in a warm sparkling haze blanketing the ground.

"Now for the real magic, huh?"

They laughed, embracing, and he thought, 'Cover. Any sort of sufficient visual obstruction. A black dome is fine.' And darkness fell over them. 'A little red light?' And so they were dimly illuminated. In the continuing spirit of Osaze Land, the girls instantly stripped naked, and he felt their flesh on his; their nipples against his skin, their lips falling over his body and catching his own. Passions that felt great began to feel better and better. Like his entire body felt as good as his head. He silently wished for death.

****

The house that appeared was the same modest sized pink home as they'd been dropped at in Cuba.

Houses made sense pink, Aden thought. He wondered about taking a boat around out there. Or a magic carpet for that matter. Or maybe flying around with his arms out. It seemed odd that the first thing they'd do is go back into a house, of all things. Robin went in first. Aden let the others follow and went in last. They walked straight to the living room. From where he heard a mild commotion and then silence.

He saw Lyn startle at seeing the two twin sisters sitting side by side on one of the couches. Each Sister was identical to Lyn. The pinks of their flesh shimmered, but other than that they looked human. They wore matching silver dresses, and both looked stunning, like movie stars. Golden hair and blue gray eyes. Their hair styles were different though, one long and flowing, the other short and chaotically spikey. They were truly beautiful, all three of them. Except, Lyn was discernibly human, and the others were equally not.

The Ma'at with spiked hair spoke first, "If you'll get comfortable there is a brief announcement we'd like to make, and we will answer questions after."

"Tobias isn't here," Calvin said.

"We know. We will speak with him a little later. For now we'd like to talk with you. We'd like to get your opinions on a couple things. Specifically, we want your opinions about the ascension. Then based on your responses we will make our proposal. To start, tell us what you believe Aloria is, in whatever terms you can. Lyn, would you begin?"

"Yeah. Of all the Logos, why her? Why Osaze? What is the connection? To me, she is like a forbidden rose. She is the lost romance languages. Beloved by Osaze. Meanwhile, Osaze is the darkest of forces. And that means Aloria is an arresting property. She enlightens him and shepards him in a way. That's what she does. She is beloved of and by the dark matter. The dark matter is a romantic in the way it swoons."

Robin said, "Except Aloria is gone or whatever. The logical thing is to concede defeat. Any plan is better than no plan."

Aden didn't agree, but he couldn't argue with the logic either. He asked, "What are you proposing?"

Ma'at said, "We're going to decide the outcome. Presently. If we support Osaze, that is acceptable. If we are against Osaze, that will be addressed. The issue with Aloria progressed as unfortunately as it could. On account of all parties. The Pleiadians executed the maneuver poorly. Osaze overreacted. Tobias got the power- that shouldn't have happened. Unfortunately, our ways allow such things on their own accord."

She had to be fucking kidding....

Ma'at continued, "We are now faced with a multitude of options. There is an ascension with Osaze. An ascension without Osaze. And there is another option none of you are aware of. It is called descension. Descension is just beyond these windows. When Osaze leaves the Logos he moves through a portal out there. As this process occurs the ascension will be triggered; consciousnesses will flee to the highest and purest form. Essentially filtering through Yah. And what is impure, the evil, will flood away through the portal with Osaze. This is what must happen. Aloria, were she to go to The Mystic with him, would never return. Nothing will be so different through there. They will live by different values and priorities.

"Aloria's value is too great. She is love. To lose her- to the Pleiadians, a species of lovers- is unthinkable. They won't let it happen. They even risk preventing the entire process to keep her. Osaze must go willingly, and if he does not, then the ascension will not occur. Nor the descension. Nor the necessary division between the two distinct events; the reversion.

"The changes have already been put in place. Certain barriers have been eliminated. When Gaia becomes a star there will be indeterminable effects reaching into the cosmos. Osaze would ascend throughout the entire Logos. Thus, another aeon of evil and depravity. This is what Tobias wants to happen. We must force the descension. He will see that it is for the best."

Ma'at continued, "We have to tell him the truth. Aloria won't know about her options. The process will basically begin when she automatically ascends, and she won't make any decision between staying with her own kind or living a life with Osaze in the new place. She'll just return to Yah. Regardless, Tobias should think there is hope. He must be convinced to let go."

"Trick him. You'll have to. I've never met anyone more stubborn than Tobias," Aden said.

Lyn said, "He listens to reason."

Cadence said, "He's mourning Arianna. He isn't even thinking clearly. Why did this happen? Why was Tobias chosen for this?"

"He wasn't chosen. He was born. That is all. If it weren't him, it would be someone else," said Aden.

"Yeah." Robin said, "But Toby is fucking crazy. Why couldn't Osaze manifest within somebody else?"

"Given the circumstances, anybody else would be equally 'crazy,'" Ma'at said.

The long haired Ma'at still hadn't said a word; she just smiled at each person as they spoke. Her eyes burned holes and she looked really beautiful. She had an iconic elegance. On Earth she'd have been a movie star, like an electrified pin up girl; maybe she'd have been worshiped outright for her petite voluptuous features, golden hair, sly smile, and radiating hazel eyes. The other sister was more eccentric and styled differently, with short hair rather than long. Instead of a pin up girl, she was like the queen of the underground when punk was a scene; short spiked hair, wild gesticulations, and a sternness of resolve. The twins' appearance was inhumanly gorgeous. Ma'at was beauty if beauty were multiplied by itself.

"It's still a stupid system," Robin proclaimed.

"It is not a system. This is how things are out here. No one decided anything. Things just are the way they are- for better or worse. When problems arise, most are inadvertently caused by Osaze. His presence alone causes issues. His presence determines form, as matter flees- what you call gravity- and nothing reacts well to such an occurrence. We know the best methods for reestablishing harmony, and we do the best we can. Our creations are like a picture a person might paint; we make changes the best we can, as we must. The creations have their own momentum, and sometimes we find ourselves running after them, trying to catch up."

"Why have humans been given so much control?" Lyn asked.

"The humans are dead. They have no control."

Aden asked, "Why isn't Osaze making his own decisions? Why is Tobias deciding everything? Why am I here and not Logos?"

Spike haired Ma'at glared, her eyes were deep and dark as though caked in eye liner, she said in a very serious tone, "There is only one Tobias. There is only one Aden. One Lyn. One Robin, Cadence, or Calvin. You are not trees. You are not any sort of insect. You aren't a monkey or a dolphin. You are people. You are not any people. You are the only people. You are not royalty. You lived humble lives. You were people; pure, simple, and safe. Tobias had had some orientation beforehand, but that is the singular distinction.

"The earth has, over time, become an oracle for us. We descend to learn about our own existences. In that way earth is holy. Your lives to us are like sacred cows or texts are on Gaia. You need to understand, these events can only happen once per aeon. Always at the end, the beginning comes again and we descend to lower, more compacted forms. In this case humans. Because in the lower levels we find the wisdom that eludes us. In this way we close the old aeon in preparation for the time when spirit and stardust will be one again." Ma'at stopped talking.

"You're just dormant, or what?" Cadence asked.

"All time is happening at all times. Like a ball of elastic bands made from spider webs. Time is like that. We are as part of time as we are a part of ourselves, or ever could be- so to speak. Though, as one descends through the dimensions, time expands. Spiders, you perceive to live for a single year. The spider perceives it's life to be exactly as long you perceive your life to be. And thus, so too do we. And as Lyn, is 'of' us, on Earth, a spider, or a kitty cat, may be 'of' a person. When animals come in contact with humans many bonds form; karmic bonds. Most humans consumed flesh of animals slaughtered in holocaustic quantities, thus they consumed themselves. Their karma assured their own destruction. These are the basic reasons you've been treated so well. We learn about the aeon by what occurs at the end. We call this 'peering' into Osaze. Nothing in the Logos, nor Yah, could speak knowingly of the goings-ons within Osaze. His nature is completely unknown, thus aeon after aeon we seek to free ourselves of his uncertain omnipresence, if only for a change, and even in the cycles when such a thing almost works, it is always Aloria to lure him right back from whence he'd nearly been banished. Their dance is timeless, you see?"

"You've made this sound very pointless," Lyn said to her doppelgangers.

"Perhaps it sounds that way. Understand, this is what we do. We struggle between love and evil, always and forever. One day, we will return to the source. Until then, this is what we do. Spiraling into ourselves and out again, then in, then out. If one time Osaze were to be eliminated from the equation the cyclic retraction and subsequent explosion will never occur again unless he were reintroduced. In all of creation there has never been such a flux. The proposition is ludicrous. Something goes wrong each time."

Robin cracked up laughing, "Are you fucking serious?"

"Unfortunately, yes," the spikey haired Ma'at said.

"What else has gone wrong?"

"Always it is Osaze. He bends to no will but his own. There is always a movement against him. He is often forced to vindicate himself in a basically symbolic gesture. Most often in matters of love. He fights for the love of another selflessly. And in truth, it is with him where Aloria belongs. She is misplaced with the Pleiadians. Her very nature is as a liaison between what is Logos and what is Osaze. In that way she is being severely mistreated; as if she were a confined wild animal. They are interrupting her nature and in essence defiling timeless boundaries. As though gravity were there to push rather than pull. If any Pleiadian has a higher purpose, it is her. She is the princess of love kept against her own will and volition in a tower called Hilt, waiting to let her hair down for Tobias.

"Without Osaze women fall into passionless servitude. With him they are cast into exaltation. Pleiadian men are highly threatened by this. And Pleiadian women listen to the men. They conspire.

"We realize you can't understand much of this. You have little perspective of this aeon, let alone many. We trust you have the knowledge that is appropriate. Speak from your hearts. That is your true purpose. What is going to happen has already happened. Always and forever. Existence in its drama is infinitely simple. Creation will always mystify. And we'll always be involved."

The sister with flowing hair and pouting lips said nothing, her glare stayed directed at Lyn. Aden couldn't imagine her thoughts, but he could feel Lyn squirming against him. What one would have to say to the other was beyond his imagination. Apparently nothing. They'd have said it. He looked out the window at the tracts of space splayed under webs of crimson red.

"Is there anything else?" Lyn asked.

"Not for now," said Ma'at.

"So, no?"

"No. Not for now."

****

Tobias stumbled across the extra dimensions of pleasure. He experienced stellar sex like a new drug gradually expressing its subtleties to him a little more each time. Sex at Osaze Land was the most intense sex of his life, and he didn't even really have a body; he was just a mind out there; the rest was flare. He only regretted the sex was not with Arianna.

When they'd finished in the dome, Tobias reclothed himself, clad in guerrilla black and a red bandana keeping his hair back. He stayed in bare feet that felt exquisite in the dry vapor floors of those outer reaches. The ground caressed with a touch like fleece. The girls had their black bikinis and cut off short shorts back on, and when the veil vanished he immediately saw twins floating above him. Both looked exactly like Lyn. He knew they were Ma'at.

"What can we help you two with?" he asked, squatting down on his shins.

"We want to know about your intentions and your decisions."

"I don't have intentions and I haven't made any decisions. I don't know what I'm going to do yet. I need to free Aloria, so she can be where she belongs. After we have her, we'll leave without hesitation. She belongs with us. Or at least with Osaze, and these three will do their own thing. I don't know. Who really cares? It's fucked. I don't know if you know this, but I came out here to relax, and you two are a drag."

"We have a few more questions and then we will leave you be."

"Ok."

"Why do you think you were given Solaris, Kobe, and Kyoto?"

"I never thought about it. My guess would be because I have a heap of hell in front of me and somebody was looking out for my best interests."

"Who? What?"

"You tell me. Yah, right? Why do you want to know what I know?"

"We are entertaining alternatives to a situation that cannot change."

"So the mistresses of truth and order speak in backward contradictions?"

"Sometimes. Yes."

"What alternatives? I'm all ears."

"What if there was no Aloria? If she were destroyed."

"You're sick. Are you kidding? How is that an option? I'd rather see Osaze destroyed than her."

"It is an option, because when she is gone, the Pleiadians will have nothing left to oppress Osaze with. He will be free. Truly. For the first time in all the aeons of creation. For Aloria to be sacrificed releases the chains clasping this dilemma in place. Removing Aloria could free the Logos, from you, essentially."

The proposal of Ma'at had set in motion a chain reaction of emotions in Tobias. While distracted by his acute feelings of despair, he heard that last part clearly and lifted his head, squinting at them. "Is there anything else you need?" he asked. He'd lost Arianna. Fuck them.

"Think on it. She will be free, and with her freedom so too will all else be. Including Osaze. We'll see you soon, Tobias. Goodbye."

"No rush, I hope."

The Ma'at sisters chuckled, tossing their heads back a little, then they faded away, and were gone into the ether, or wherever. He fell onto his back against the fluffy dry vapor floor. He closed his eyes and tried his best to let the electrically pulsating red mesh spread over the pitch black distract him. First, he noticed that the Ma'at sisters could be right about what he should do. His reaction was pure revulsion, like in a moment when wanting to tell someone the truth but can't, or wanting to strangle a screaming child. Children can't be strangled because they are irritating. The truth can't be told even if it should be. People would have been more intelligent if they weren't dishonest.

The girls crawled over him and curled into his arms. That's what he really wanted. To hold them for a while. To have a moment of peace. He didn't even want to open his eyes. In a moment he did. He looked out at the beautiful spectacle out in the distance. It was not a sky. It just felt like a sky. The human form was oriented to have the ground below and the sky above, but out in that space, the particular dynamic felt unnatural.

He allowed himself to think about Arianna for a moment. He felt cringes in his gut and behind his eyes. In his imagination he pictured his beloved's cheeks and her uncommon toothy smile. Those eyes. Everything about her was sincere. Maybe he didn't really care what happened to the Logos. Maybe he was just trying to compensate for the way Arianna was taken so suddenly. Whether he even had control of his mental faculties, he could only guess. And, of course, his guess was no. On some level he was under another kind of control. Some kind of manipulation. Like a lion with some asshole's head inside its mouth. Raising the question of whose head was it. And more realistically, should he bite down or not. He didn't know a fraction of what he should to make an informed decision about his course of action. Decisions. Descension. It wasn't even a good day for it. He was angry. He couldn't get his mind away from the issue. He loved Arianna.

So many lovers would have liked to tear down the universe to avenge their own losses. He actually had the opportunity. His decisions were the chair waved in his face by the lion tamer.

Cosmic control drama. Selfish on the surface, but below dwelled consistent methodology constantly adapting in pursuit of an unembraceable ideal; to control the will of that which was undeniably, inconceivably, more powerful than what sought to control it. A backward contrary riddle.

Always, his thoughts went to the Pleiadians. His anger weakened- ruined by his sadness. And he couldn't control the influx of fear for Arianna. Pleiadians were like vipers nesting in his brain. They had to go. Maybe he would stay out in Osaze Land. He sat up and took a look over to the Cuban house. His peers were walking out the door and tripping out over the gently accommodating ground; moving below like going nowhere on slipping beach sand underfoot in a dream. He'd been being a junky for the feeling only moments before.

Standing to his feet, he helped the girls up as well, but kept his eyes on the clan. When each had cleared the home, and the 5 were out front, he disappeared the home from behind them; it faded instantly with something like a strong gust of suctioned air wafting across the plain. He looked ahead to the others watching him. He felt the urge to have a fun with them. That was, after all, what they'd gone there to do. To mourn and to enjoy their lives while they could.

"Hold on."

The ground dropped from under their feet and they were free falling. Priceless screams came from them, then exclamations of shock as they noticed their terminal velocity was not as substantial as it would have been on earth, and thus felt askew. They were falling fast, but falling slow for falling fast.

"Tobias, what the fuck?" Aden called.

Tobias rolled over his heals to fall head first, and as he did he shouted back, "Just enjoy it. There is no end. It's bottomless. We could fall forever!"

No member of the clan was characteristically privy to rejecting an opportunity to forget their troubles in the pursuit of fleeting visceral enjoyment. Falling like that felt great, none would deny it. It was like a cucumber slice on his eyelid- for his entire body. So relaxing.

Robin shouted out, "Turn off the falling, man! Can't we fly, or float, or anything?"

Their rate of fall decreased, and they came to a halt slowly, in unison. Tobias said, "I can do something for floating, yeah. You can fly if you believe you can. Just don't stop believing or you'll explode."

MURDER

Tobias dismissed himself momentarily from the others and drifted off to the distance. Him, Kobe, Kyoto, and Solaris went far away. Not for any explicit purpose. Perhaps to be alone together. Tobias wanted a splice to think and clear his head. The girls would help him understand; the time had come to make decisions. He began to consider the proposal of Ma'at to eliminate Aloria entirely.

If that were to happen Osaze would have to disappear as well. Something akin to a murder suicide. Eternally dead. Only the Logos, ascended, would remain. All would be well with Osaze gone. Aloria could be unharmed and remain within the Logos. However, on the other hand, if there were no Osaze, there would be no reason for her to suffer. If there were no Osaze, there would be no broken hearts.

His eliminated presence wouldn't be missing anything. Afterward, Aloria could choose sacrifice as well. Or she could choose to live on in severance. There would be options for her. Either way, it would be her decision. He wouldn't have to choose for her. If Osaze could not exist without her, he could certainly cease to exist without her.

The three girls- young- sat together calmly. Tobias lofted a short height above the ground below; staring out further into the expanse. Light contours had a way of curving and rising and falling while maintaining no shape other than that of an abyss.

The girls arose, walked over, stopped, and stood at his back; placing hands on his shoulders and waist. 'Osaze. Come here,' he thought. He was sure the message got conveyed when he heard the girls cooing in reaction to the enlivened crackles of the red webs spun out over the far reaches. Through the darkness he saw a single red object moving toward them. He recognized it as his own eyeball. When Osaze came closer, through his red eye, Tobias could perceive the figure appearing in a similar form as his own; larger, and with less definite clothing; more like shrouds of dark textures that couldn't really be perceived in any human way. Facial features were what defined him. Tobias couldn't explain what he actually saw any more than it mattered.

The single red eye glowed vibrantly, casting dim light over Osaze, but not enough to provide visibility of the dark presence. He closed his special eye to glimpse what the girls would be looking at and what remained was the single eye. Nothing else could be seen.

Tobias said, "I need to talk to you. Do you know what I'm considering?"

"Of course I know."

"And what do you think about it?"

"To throw away what I am for the sake of what

Aloria is would be foolish. If your nail needs to be trimmed, do you cut off your finger? Aloria is a support Osaze has often utilized. So is Alcyone. So is each Omega clansperson in their higher forms. Osaze does not need any one of them. He does need them, together. And even then, he is not dependent upon them. There are always options and expendables. My continuation is an assurance of itself because it has to be. Remove the Logos from the Logos, and what will you have? Osaze.

"Beyond the Logos, the pale mystery is everywhere at all times. It will always remain as such. It is inside us. We are what Yah calls God. We are what is unknown. A single step of progression by nature. They haven't a clue what they are resisting against. If they understood, they would realize that we want what is best for the Logos and for all of them. That we are essentially every moment they've held dear for aeons; we are the tears shed for the pain of another or the violence that accompanies sex. Good intentions turned to greed. We are these things and more. When they seek to remove us, they do not grasp the levity of their request. We are them. They seek to destroy themselves. Lest all be Yah. It would be wrong for us to allow such a thing."

"Why did Ma'at ask me to destroy Aloria?"

"The option is viable. They wish to erase a complicated predicament in the simplest manner. Perhaps it would force change, but not in the way they seek. The results would likely be catastrophic. When they proposed her destruction, I don't believe they wanted you to seriously consider it. What they wanted was for you to gain perspective; to imagine if such a thing occurred. And she really was gone forever. Because soon she may be.

"They like to use her to get us under control. Or themselves, as it is. And it works well. Thinking of Aloria has you preoccupied and distressed, and they think they are winning. And so do you. If you seek to release Aloria from her bondage, the best way is to concede defeat and accept her as a lost cause. When you realize this connection is lost forever, another can grow in its place. Aloria may return, or another presence might fill her absence. You must disconnect yourself from any attachment to the thought. The decision is higher than us. The outcome of the Pale Mystery is to be dictated by the Eternally Dead Pale Mystic. And it has no opinion. Not a good one nor bad one. None. Yet, it determines the means toward any given end. Especially the will of Osaze. The power that rules our fate comes from the Pale Mystic; from beyond the source. Like your will comes directly from above; from beyond the earth. There are simply infinite layers of intelligent interference. We're a major one. There's others. What are you going to do?"

"Feel sick. Detach. In a really unusual way. Leave her with Hilt? I don't fucking know. You tell me what to do?"

Osaze said, "We destroy Hilt. We send the Zeta Reticuli to the Pale Mystic. And a couple Pleiadian stars, too. Once free, Aloria will make a decision for herself and when that happens we can finally relax and let the next aeon come around."

"What about love?"

"Love finds a way."

"Even for us?"

"Especially for us."

"Hey. If we go reaping, are you going to be able to compensate for the rash decisions that I make?"

"Compensate in what way?" Osaze asked.

"Offensively and defensively. I have a vendetta. No more bluffing. No more uncertainty. I am rescuing Aloria, and the devil himself won't stop me. My actions toward the Zeta will act as a gesture of intent. Afterward, we will engage the Pleiadians in our quest to release Aloria."

"We should ask them first to return Aloria before we take the Zeta. To be sure."

"To be sure, the Zeta requested we send them away, so we will."

"They may prefer to live," Osaze said.

"Then they'll live. See if I care. It's better that way. We'll slip in unannounced. We'll hang on to the Zeta in case we can use them to bargain. After what happened last time, I'm not taking any shit from these fucking twats. They've been bluffing this whole time. They can't touch us. Unless they destroy Aloria themselves. They wouldn't do that, would they?"

"We'll find out. Aloria would want you to remember this is the best course of action. Whatever happens from this point forward will be under the control of the Pale Mystery. If they destroy Aloria, we'll destroy them, and they are essentially destroying themselves. They must understand that for them to get theirs, you must get yours, and that fact is cold stone. This is the unchanging will of the Pale Mystic. The mystic is with us here. This is the descension. What comes next will determine in what way, and whether or not, the Logos ascends."

He looked back at the girls. They shared his nervous expression. They stared up into his eyes, with pouted lips anticipating his concern. He asked, "You ladies ready for this?"

Solaris smiled and perked up a little. She said, "There is no reason to be anxious. What comes next is divine. The outcome will be chosen. And if we lose Aloria, then Ok. It happened. At least there will be no more uncertainty. No more mindlessness at the tower of Hilt. And we'll be free from the drama. Maybe with a little extra time to focus on something else for a while on Gaia. Maybe not. We know where we're going. There is nothing to fear."

Tobias squeezed her hand in his and he pulled her

close for a kiss. Then he looked back over at the shrouded masculine figure. A single eyeball, hovering, to the girls. Tobias hadn't realized what power he held until that moment. He hadn't realized. The strength. The immensity. The implications.

The behavior of the Pleiadians was insane.

Tobias asked, "Why do they behave this way?"

Osaze said, "They want to maintain purity, and if you haven't noticed; you're toxic."

"I have to be like this. It's a duty. So. Where are we going? I don't want to go anywhere. Can you bring a Pleiadian here? I want a representative- an appropriate one, alone- to speak on behalf of them. One who knows where Aloria is located. I want them brought here. Can you make that happen?"

"Easily."

"I need a moment to prepare. Let's do it."

Tobias took into account the girl's positions, careful to not inadvertently harm them. He manifested four white bean bag chairs in the mist, called the girls over to sit, and when they were settled he elevated their sitting area about two heights over the rest of the misty plain. He felt the urge to make the area gawdy, like a nightmare circus, but he wasn't enjoying imagineering his surroundings. Instead he made a simple wooden platform 20 feet away and one height up. The girls- when he looked back to them- were squishing around in their chairs and generally amused by the lumpy seats.

He sat forward at the crest of their topographically elevated mound. His arms rested on his knees and he rested his head on his hands and closed his eyes. Out of habit he began taking deep breaths. Of course they didn't deliver any oxygen, yet he still found relief and a small degree of clarity.   Acceptance. Letting go. He needed to accept the cold realities bearing down on him. No illusions. Death had arrived. He could sense the presence of absence. An absence of what- he could not declare. Having only gone off for a walk, he never suspected he wouldn't see the others again, but that didn't matter. Killers die, too.

They weren't talking about death. A presence couldn't be killed; just removed deliberately. The ultimate taboo. They were talking about eternal death. He was going to erase Pleiadians. He'd been given the power to remove them from the equation. No more life to death and back and forth some more for them. Not for those being erased. Simply gone. Perhaps like a Zen view on death. Or a nihilistic atheist. Or anyone with no reason to believe beyond death awaits anything other than oblivion; as far as most knew there was nothing before birth, either.

He would keep in mind that the Pleiadians forced the matter to come to that. They hadn't allowed any solution. Hadn't offered, or responded to, any negotiation. It felt exactly like he was at war for his love. The sisters were supposed to be love. If such opposites were true, he could still not discern what his learned preconceived notions were meant to convey.

Yet, he heard no outcry against his actions. Not from Logos or Ma'at. The others may have been against his actions, but it was not their business. The Pale Mystic had selected him. Somehow Tobias could always sense a foreign influence. The Pale Mystic had dictated that time and that place.

Thus he caught a first glimpse of the wicked one. He couldn't get used to the odd manner in which travelers of thought approached. From the distance they moved very quickly, then they slowed as they neared. It was counter-intuitive to his earthly conceptions of distance and movement. Nonetheless, Osaze- the shadowy cloaked manifestation of his higher self-approached, dragging a struggling Pleiadian by his side. A man, of Norwegian resemblance except- like all else in the outer reaches- exceptionally large. His blonde hair was slicked back to his head, and he wore some kind of shimmering blue jumpsuit looking an abstruse green in the red light of Osaze Land. He was cowering on the platform. He'd wrapped himself into a ball.

"What's your name?" Osaze asked.

"Aticus."

Tobias wasn't enjoying the power he felt. He said, "Stand on your feet, Aticus."

The prisoner did as he was told and stood up.

"Why are you so afraid? You are here on behalf of your kind, you realize? Try to relax." Tobias sighed, shrugged, and said, "I can tell by your demeanor you don't have any good news for me. So why don't you tell me what you have to say?"

"We can't give you Aloria. We can't. You have to understand."

"You have to help me understand. First, tell me why they sent you and not one of the sisters. Your society is matriarchal. You can't be of much significance to them."

"I am the highest male authority of our kind. They cherish me similar to a cultural icon where you came from. Your actions toward me will affect them. If you truly want Aloria to be freed, you cannot harm me."

"This makes no sense. Just release her and she could make a decision on her own. Why are you sacrificing to keep her away?"

"It is rebellion against Osaze. The Pleiadians have had enough of your dark oppression. We seek purity of the light."

"Maybe that was your first mistake. Don't you think the darkness should be embraced as well?"

"You don't get it. We are afraid of the dark."

"As well you should be. Clearly. If this is how you behave when faced with it. I am not surprised. What is the darkness to you? There would be no light without it."

Aticus said, "Because all would be light. This is the

outcome we seek, and we are prepared to meet the Pale Mystic should you decide. No matter what you do, Aloria will never be released."

Tobias was getting angry. His thoughts turned to the Pleiadian sisters. He wanted to hurt them. He wanted to violate their most sanctimonious beliefs. He considered rape. An image came to mind of him, the three girlfriends, and the other guys raping the sisters into submission. Except he knew such actions were low. Even if, for the first time, he understood the motivations of marauding soldiers under similar circumstances back on Gaia. Sex and murder were somehow linked.

"What will happen in the Pleiades when I destroy you?"

Aticus again broke down in tears, sobbing, and he fell to his knees. With pitiful facial composure he said, "They'll kill Aloria."

Tobias' heart sank. That was the last thing he wanted to hear. Without saying another word, Tobias addressed Osaze in his thoughts, 'Lay him out flat.' It was done. Aticus' arms reached far over his head, he lay flat on his back, his legs stretched out; and he began screaming.

"Shut up! I'm going to ask you this once before you start to hurt. I bet you don't even know what pain is. They don't have pain where you come from, do they? Well, I know about pain, motherfucker... All the fuck about it. So tell me, how do I find Aloria?"

"I can't tell you!"

"Alright," Tobias said, and sighed. He imagined a ball of fire burning around Aticus' ankles and almost immediately the Pleiadian began screaming. Tobias stalled for a moment, letting him burn, and then he turned off the heat. He had to shout over the pathetic cries of Aticus to be heard, "Where is she?!"

"I don't know! I was lying! I don't know!"

Tobias signaled. The heat came again and the

screaming commenced. He had to think, but couldn't concentrate through the grizzly screams of Aticus' torture. He stopped the flames and relished in the returning quiet as the victim's vocalizations quieted to a whimper. He couldn't kill Aticus. He could keep him alive all he wanted.

'We need another Pleiadian. Maia. Get that lying bitch out here.'

Tobias created a second platform beside Aticus in preparation for Maia's arrival. Aticus continued to writhe incapacitated. He glanced at the girls and they smiled back at him. A moment later a women came flying in from the abyss; her face hidden under a red hood that appeared black in the dim crimson lighting. Unlike Aticus, Maia maintained her composure. With a thought, Tobias flipped the hood back to see her face. Her eyes were squinting. She looked significantly angrier than last he saw her.

"Where's Aloria?"

"Someplace where if I don't return she will be destroyed."

Tobias put the heat to her entire body, from head to toe, and immediately the Pleiadien woman crumpled to the floor, writhing and crying out in agony. She jerked against the pain and he stilled her. Her cries peaked and hurt her more, until she became silent. Then he stopped her torture, and again he asked, "Where the fuck is she?"

"You won't ever know," Maia said through the agony in her voice.

He put the fire to her again and watched as she writhed. The flames burned unlike earthen fire. A thick dark orange glow gathered around whatever he wanted it to; creating radiation more than any kind of actual burning. By the time he let off her whole body had taken on a lingering neutral orange hue. He wasn't making progress and didn't know what to do anymore.

He had been aware of the contingency that Aloria

might have to be destroyed to correct the situation. He couldn't make the decision. He didn't have the facts. Nor did he possess the necessary fortitude. There had to be another way.

"There has to be another way. Why can't you accept Osaze? Is desisting worth existing without him? Without yourselves? Do you even realize what it is you're asking? Don't you realize that Aloria can repair the entire situation? Aloria can ascend Osaze in such a way that there will be harmony in the next aeon." He watched her face for submission and saw none.

Then he said, "An aeon that none of you will ever see if you don't begin cooperating. Give me fucking answers!"

Maia's face, her expression strained in grief, rolled over toward his face. She looked at him with despair in her eyes, and he peered back through her pain. "Say anything," he told her. She strained to move her mouth. She choked out, "Hilt."

"Where is Hilt?"

"He is beyond Logos. Where you can never go."

"Osaze? Where can we never go?"

"To Yah," Osaze answered.

"She's with Yah?"

"Yah dwells in the same realm as her. She has already ascended."

"You have to be kidding." Tobias' heart sank and he dropped into the bean bag chair. He looked at the two platforms and the writhing Pleiadians. He couldn't imagine what she'd meant. He was jumping to conclusions. "Osaze what is stopping us from going to where Yah is?"

"Yah is where Yah is, at the source. Like we are within where Osaze is. We have a lot of options. Yah is not one of them. We are born from the Pale Mystic. Yah, too, like a brother, came from beyond the source."

This angered him. "What the fuck do you want?

Why are you doing this to us?" Tobias shrieked at the victims. He waited for a moment and they said nothing. They only groaned.

Fed up, suddenly, he drifted from the mound out through the ether and came to a halt standing over Maia and looking down at her agonized face. He imagined a thick sheet of glass under his palm in a circle roughly the size of her head. He felt oak under his bare feet as he knelt down to grasp her throat. He pushed the glass down against Maia's face, and her body writhed. He pushed harder and she writhed harder. Then he let off.

As she struggled to regain composure, he said, "You're going to bring her back."

"You fool. That isn't possible." He squeezed her neck in his grip, summoned great strength, used it to squeeze harder, and simultaneously in his other hand, by thought, he gathered the glass into a sphere. Then he struck her in the head one time, dropped her limp to the floor, and stood up straight. He looked down and waited for her to say something.

She coughed and choked, trying to speak. Slowly the words came and after a moment of fighting she said, "Aloria has ascended. Osaze will never ascend. Accept it."

"Then it's over?" Tobias asked, incredulously, as he felt the wrath gathering within him.

"It is over for you."

"Then it's over for you, too."

He came down on her hard. Swinging the weapon into her face over and over again; battering her skull; revolted at the cracks and protruding fractured bones. After the third strike, he remembered to put fire to Aticus' whole body, and the screams rose with the temperature. Maia had gone completely limp again, but Tobias continued to batter her skull. The blood spatter hung peacefully in the obscure- as needed- gravity. He battered her face until it was no longer recognizable. He

lay her down. The cries of Aticus had ceased. Maia's
nose had shifted and the blood began to gather over her
eyeballs. Her spirit was vanquished, taken by the Mystic,
and her body became opaque, as though fading.

In his mind's eye he saw the photoplasm gathering
over multiple stars of the Pleiadian cluster. Enormous
blue orbs. He could distinctly feel sorrow emanating.
Not only one or two major stars were blackening; Osaze
gathered over at least two dozen stars out there. The
entire cluster became noticeably dimmer. Spectacular
blues, no heat, dead in thought, and the Pale Mystic had
taken them, using Osaze. The murder of love moved
over the stars and pulled the glistening blue fires from
them through inky clutches of photoplasm that
appeared as if from nowhere, as though from well
springs, dozens of them.

He knew what was done. "Release the Zeta," he
said.

He heard cold silence, standing over the dissolving
remnants of Maia. Aticus faded in a similar manner. He
couldn't fathom the consequences of his actions. Then
he remembered Aloria and suddenly he organized their
lies. At least in his heart. If the Pleiadians could be
suppressed, he could utilize them. Ascend; if only for a
short while. For Arianna.

Then he remembered what Maia had said.
Acceptance. Aloria was gone. Arianna was gone. He was
a killer. Worse. He was a destroyer. What he wanted was
fair treatment. And he'd killed Maia trying to get it.
They killed something inside of him. Thus inside
themselves. Hope. He tried to face the sheer magnitude
of such a thing. What he'd done felt like a black universe
falling over him. He'd become the devil he despised.

A deep sense of hopelessness. A stinging in his gut,
indeed like a knife; reminding him he was no better off.
He was going to die. His eternal soul would remain
incomplete- forever separated from his wish to reunite

lost lovers.

The sky crashed. The ground swallowed itself. All remained still. Through discombobulation he willed himself back to the girls and tossed his chair between theirs before crashing against them and closing his eyes. He desperately calmed his inner tempo and insisted the world around him halt as well. 'Osaze. I need Alcyone. Is that possible?"

"I'll retrieve her."

Osaze went off into the distance, and Tobias asked the girls an honest question, "Did I do the right thing?"

"There is no such thing as the wrong thing, Tobias. In the end there is what is and in the end there is a new beginning," Kobe said.

Kyoto added, "You knew this was going to happen." They both had the loveliest Japanese accents; adorable, high, joyous.

Solaris said, "All is as it should be. You've said what you had to say. You've done what you had to do. The future is open to new possibilities and the decisions are yours. The descension is yours. We will end up going away. Through the portal out directly to the Mystic. We'll go. There is no longer any reason not to make peace. To release this place and go. All is as they said it would be. You will take us and we will leave.

"You mean, I'll crush the Pleiadians and destroy the Logos? Right? Because that is my intent. Or at the very least I intend to crush the Pleiadians and use them to ascend, if only briefly. Leave this behind. Seek the higher authorities. I must go above and beyond. I have to speak to Yah. I have to get to Aloria through Yah.

Kyoto said, "Weren't you about to accept this? And forget Aloria?"
"Forgetting Aloria would be psychotic. We've only taken the first step."

"What can I help you with?" Alcyone asked from over his shoulder. She stood there nude, as per usual and cast in shadow.

"What do I do now?"

"What is it you intend to do?"

"Unite Aloria and Osaze."

"And you think that possible?"

"That's what you're here to tell me. Tell me the truth. Can Osaze ever reunite with Aloria?"

"You're going to find out. You've begun your descension. I'm proud of you. This is the Logos ascending. Slowly unencumbered by you. Unencumbered by all, soon."

He resented her caustic remarks, shrugged off the foreboding ones, and realized the nature of their relationship would never be the same. They had been lying to him, leaving him to do the best he could with a dire situation. He had to know, "What damage have I done to the Logos? What is the loss of Maia and Aticus?"

"None of your concern. You'll see the effect, the madness, should you venture over to the Pleiades for any reason. And I suspect you will. The Pleiadians weren't any opposition for Osaze. What you did was a lot like a grown man slapping a child. Way uglier, though."

"They've been out of line for days. You tell me the truth, right now. Tell me everything."

"The truth will hit you like a sharp knife to your heart. Still, you wish to know? Fine.

"We are of your creation and your design. If you can't accept that, we can't ascend. You are the manifestation of ourselves. The substance of our actions, arguments, agreements, deceits, our form and our function; it exists within you. When the third dimension seeks to ascend it seeks to rise above itself and its own shortcomings. You. Like how a human's wish to live forever was a wish to be free of themselves. There was a way to cure the sicknesses of the humans: Matriarchy. They ignored such an option. That sickness of the humans then is of course your sickness now, as expressed through love. When you accept the problem of illness you realize that there is a position of wellness that should be realigned to. That is where Aloria is. She is with Yah. In wellness."

"And me? There is no wellness for Osaze and Me?"

"There is not actually sickness in you. You behave as is your nature. And, even still, the Pleiadians hold no disparaging feelings toward you. We are a kind that loves our enemies. It is the easiest way to keep peace."

"You call this peace?" He motioned to the dead bodies. "They've gone to the other far and away. What could be worse? And now? What can I expect for myself and Osaze?"

She said, "You have not caught on. You are the decider. You choose what happens here. To threaten the entire Pleiades cluster is an ambitious yet practical way to lure Yah down into the logos. Perhaps you could even negotiate an exchange for Aloria. If her nature is as you believe it is, perhaps she could return to the lower realms. The conditions are well."

"Why do you tell me these things?" he asked.

"I am an anarchist, remember?"

TEMPERANCE

Tobias hadn't mentioned to the others what he had done. They certainly could tell he wasn't behaving correctly. He stumbled over more words than usual yet said very little. At Alcyone's request he made a change of plans and the whole clan set out away from Osaze Land. He simply told the others it was time they left and swept them away with him. He never really got to spend social time with the clan but that did not matter.

They went to a planet called Peyor, in the orbits of Atlas and another star orbiting Atlas called Strafe. As they approached, their bodies faded in and out of various sorts of densities.

In a confusing and abrupt manner, Tobias found, first, ground under his feet. Himself and company were standing at what looked like a train yard from another planet, essentially. A giant orange dome with a sparkling and perfectly flush ceiling loomed above them. Evidently triangular devices and cranes dangling over tracks were a universal occurance... The colors were vibrant yellows, purples, and raw metals shining like chrome. For an industrial work zone it sparkled, and there was no sound whatsoever. They were on a platform and had been waiting a brief period for a ride. From tubes across the rail yard, a single vessel, like a large medicine capsule, came floating out to greet them. The vessel was dark green and chartreuse; there were window spaces for viewing and no glass or barrier to prevent falling out. As they entered through double wide doors they found seats 8 inches higher than felt appropriate and he found the shapes and sizes designed for larger beings than themselves; much too wide and large.

The vehicle propelled itself silently, effortlessly, and gently through subway tubes lined in straight neon purple and blue lights. As they accelerated, the lines of color began to twist and spiral until they'd completely blurred together, and even the minor hints of physical momentum they had felt before completely vanished and their carriage hovered as though it were riding on nothing. Alcyone was there. Osaze was there as well, hanging in the air above their heads, but displaced a distance away; tucked at the furthest area. The vessel had exceptionally high ceilings. The others knew he was there, too, by the red eyeball hovering about.

"This entire planet belongs to how many Pleiadians?" Aden asked.

Alcyone answered, "739 Pleiadians reside here. There used to be thousands, until Tobias had a say in the matter... There are other transplanted beings they've chosen to dwell alongside them within the oversoul. Much of the life here will have vanished. Refuges, and guests. All manner of life is living at these sort of places. Dead now."

"What did Tobias do?" Cadence asked.

"We're not talking about that right now," Toby said.

"Are we going to see space monsters?" Calvin asked.

"It's possible," Alcyone said, looking at Tobias, "if they aren't in hiding. Or dead. We'll see when we get to where we are going."

At that moment the tunnel opened into an enormous valley where the sky was faintly illuminated violet. Snowcapped mountains loomed. A twilight sky? Tobias couldn't tell. He looked out another window and saw a bright blue star, about half the size of the moon when viewed from the Earth.

They were traveling thousands of feet down a hillside. The shrubbery glowed brightly with blue bio luminescence as it blurred past the windows. He sat down in one of the tall chairs and noticed, far below, hundreds of dancing blue flames. They shined against a white surface that was that same marble he had seen the last time he had been in the Pleiades.

Robin said, "Can you guys believe we're on an entirely different planet?"

Aden said, "Considering where we just were, yeah, I can believe it."

He felt a gentle breeze blowing so unnaturally against his person. On earth such velocities would cause turbulent winds, and there, in open air, their traveling speed caused only the gentlest breeze, or a soft steady stream of air like bath water that actually warmed as it moved along the currents and over his skin. There was a vague friction in the air.

Tobias and his girlfriend clones were looking out

the right side windows but no one else was. The others were looking out the left. They hadn't seen the mysterious civilization lying below. Their obvious destination. He called over to them, "You guys should see what's over here."

He motioned with his head and they shifted to look out that way. Calvin jumped from the seats on one side to the seats on the other side, stood next to Tobias, and put his hand on Tobias' shoulder to steady himself as he peered past the others to see.

"Is that where we're going?" Calvin asked.

Alcyone said, "We're going to a funeral. And that is it."

Right then, the track came into view at the side; (there was no forward or reverse visibility). Tobias saw a train of cars before them. He looked out behind them and saw more of the capsule cars. As they got closer, the small clusters of dots came more and more into focus, and he saw hundreds of Pleiadians milling about the landscape among the individual bonfires and stone architecture. A half dome amphitheater appeared to be the center of attention. He could see lines leading up to its stage, and coming down away the same. Or, as he looked closer, it became evident both lines were leading up to the stage.

All illuminated by blue flame. Stretching behind the shoreline was a crystal lake sparkling in the star light. The forests sparkled yellows and green across the base of the mountains off in the distance. Mountains rose so high they disappeared from view into the purple haze. No clouds. No stars. Tobias had seen, on the way in, blue space dust wafting across that entire solar system. The planet existed deep within that dust. They remained in a fairly high form, fairly high like solidified electrified ashes. They were subjected to the delicate sensations of the planet; a planet that smelled nearly entirely like lavender. A thin atmosphere kept the air clear of the haze of space.

The vessel moved past abstract white stone sculptures and shrubs of all colors- shining magnificently against the blue light- and the clan arrived at the landing and stepped out the enormous door way in a cluster. Tobias stayed distinctly aware of Osaze hovering directly over them like a fierce protector. Alcyone led through a crowd that instantly recognized her and stepped aside. Dozens of enormous blonde men. One man had black hair. Tobias looked up at him, into bright green eyes staring back with sad disgust. Those were the two types of men. Blonde hair, blue eyed, or black and green. The men wore plain white clothes. All of them. Similar, more or less, to middle eastern cultures. Very plain.

The women, he immediately noticed, came in infinite varieties; wearing bright and dark colors from outside the rainbow; colors he'd never seen, that had effects like liquid or fire. The women were spellbinding. He tested his vision through his regular eye alone and still the clothes on these spectacular humanoids produced an effect of their own. The women were tall, too. Even the short ones were tall.

They Pleiadians looked at them pitifully through the flickering flames, with sadness practically painted across their faces. Then they turned away; looking back only to glimpse Alcyone. Tobias and the girls had their arms around each other. Even in the crowd, the area was tremendously spacious. Alcyone led them with the flow of the flock under hanging vines of blood red roses. More roses. Roses were everywhere- wherever they went it seemed. Very beautiful and very appropriate reminders of what life really was; lovely and ever ready to draw blood. He had become callous to the way they tried to play against his emotions. He felt pushed through mazes designed to lead him to despair. He got zen about it. All was as it would be.

They walked behind a high wall and moved right around a corner to where they crossed a courtyard and saw the stage there in the distance far down below. The seats checkered in columns and rows across a broad slope leading toward the stage. There were so many seats it made the number of attendees seem like far fewer than 700 and however many. For obvious reasons were there so few. Tobias had trouble ignoring why the seats weren't filled.

Then he began to discern exactly what was happening up there on the stage. What he first noticed was that everybody on the stage was completely naked. At the front of the two lines they were undressing and handing their clothes to some sort of coat check clerk. While others were receiving and putting their clothes back on before walking out into the seats.

The clan had been walking amongst the Pleiadians, and behind them, headed toward one of either two lines, to the left or right. Alcyone led them straight down the aisles directly toward the stage. As they edged closer he hadn't expected to see what he saw. They were clearly fucking. They were having an orgy. Taking turns. There was both men and women frantically fucking and moving between each other, trying to be thorough about hedonism it looked like... He noticed that some were not moving. In fact. Underneath the frenzied Pleiadians scurrying between each other- twisting, thrusting- about 12 or so were not moving. Yet, they were being violated as though they had a say in the matter. Like they were volunteers.

He could see men ejaculating diamond studded cum onto clearly dead bodies. Women riding the corpses like racehorses. The living fornicated with the living and the dead. The dead bodies were draped across tables, propped on lavish yet subtle furniture. The walls were lined with bouquets of red roses. A gorgeous chandelier hung prominently over the participants' heads. Many of the dead men were propped standing up, naked, and as one woman jumped off a phallus, Tobias could get a glimpse that it was awfully hard and erect for a dead man, before another woman dropped down to worship it, or bent over to thrust it into herself.

There were at least fifty Pleiadians on stage at a single time. They climbed all over each other, and shot glistening fluids, in all directions; into each other's faces and over their heads. An odor emanated from the funeral orgy and hung over them. It smelled like the dirty laundry backed up in the closets at the social service dorms. The atmosphere was pungent with urine and heated by the friction coming from their bodies grinding against each other and the fires burning in marble pots all around.

The entire stadium remained eerily quiet except for the screams, grunts, groans, and brief remarks, getting caught in the acoustics of the theater shell. Loudest were the cries of ecstatic seven foot tall women ringing out across the audience. A strange sound was solemn sex. Tobias couldn't blame them. He kind of understood their logic. He'd kill someone to fuck Arianna again. Or he'd fuck her dead. The girls were unconsciously pressing against him; transfixed, watching the orgy. Even Calvin, the child. Even Pluto, the cat.

Tobias couldn't help but notice the exquisite physiques of these women. Each one perfect in her own way. Their breasts were large and round, or small and pert. The men too, were exquisite like statues, to be sure.

That's when Alcyone walked away from the group and toward the stage, motioning with one hand for the clan to stay behind. She had been naked the entire time, for all to see. And she didn't wait in line either. She moved through the orchestra pit and climbed up onto the stage.

Osaze floated down low to stand behind Tobias,

and whispered into his ear, "Those are the twelve stars we extinguished today. This is where their descended forms resided. Those are their descended forms. This place is where they've resided since the beginning of time; for all time, with the exception of their untimely, unprecedented, extermination. And they're gone now. Into the Pale Mystery."

"Why did 12 stars die, when we only exterminated two of them?"

"They were inexorably linked to others. If Yah incinerated the dark matter, if he could, if he incinerated the Logos, we'd return to the Pale Mystic. Some life forms are weaker and more fragile than others. Some are born dependent on others. It's a quagmire. Or a web. It's linked; contingent on security."

"So what are we doing here?"

"This is the entire population of this planet. They are what remains. This coliseum where we are was created to seat the Peyoriens. The young ones are dead. Do you see on the horizon? They're bringing the lost here by barges. The ones on stage were rulers, or culturally iconic.

"You can see Maia at the back left, and Aticus standing among the other couple men there."

Tobias could see both his victims clearly.

Alcyone danced through the crowds, like when Olivia used to give tarot readings, except instead of cards, her hands gripped genitals and breasts, and she made her bending and flexing body available to be groped and grabbed. She mounted a corpse reverse doggy style and rode it while pleasuring multiple living men that had gathered around her face.

"Tobias," Robin whispered.

"What?"

"What the hell are we doing here?"

"I don't know. We should sit down though."

They sat in the nearest row of seats. Osaze sat, too.

Tobias asked him, "What are we doing here?"

"Greeting the foreign dignitaries. You can't tell, but every Pleiadian of any diplomatic regard is in attendance. This ends here, one way or another."

"So, when Maia and Aticus disappeared, this is where they went?"

"Correct. Though, we arrived days after."

"What are we waiting for? What is going to happen?"

"That is entirely up to you."

The last thing he wanted to hear, but he could have guessed. He couldn't see Alcyone up there anymore. She seemingly had drowned under about six females and a few males. The piles of bodies were writhing and throbbing as more Pleiadians piled on and others crawled away exhausted.

Tobias asked, "Can Yah descend to the Logos? Is there any way to reach Aloria?"

"Yes, Yah can. Yah will know about Aloria. I can't say. Everything that happens out there where the glorious ones exist is beyond me- disconnected from me- and I cannot speak for it."

"Then we need someone who can. Where's Logos? We need Logos."

Osaze looked up to the sky and said, "I can do that. Wait here," then he vanished instantly- in a zapping flutter- from the seat where he'd been.

Tobias said to the Kobe, "Wait here," then he glanced back to the stage one time, did a double take at nothing in particular- blow jobs, sex, sodomy, cunnilingus- then he hopped over the row of chairs and positioned himself behind Aden and Robin.

"I am going to fuck this up so bad."

Robin turned his head back and asked, "Oh, yeah? Why's that?"

"Logos is coming and we're going to try and get Yah here. As in God. Maybe if we play it cool nothing will go down."

"Why would anything be going down?" Aden asked.

Tobias gave him a loooook. "Why wouldn't anything be going down? Do you fucking see this place?"

Robin said, "We were considering going up there and fucking some giants."

Aden nodded and smiled, gritting his teeth a little. Tobias hadn't considered it. Desecrating a death rite anywhere would be a terrible thing, but the Pleiadians caused this to happen by targeting him directly. He shouldn't be out there in that situation to begin with. Nor Draco and Sirius. All he ever wanted was Arianna.

"You guys go ahead. I can't. I have to take up with Logos."

"We're not going up there, are you fucking kidding? You're such a sucker, Tobias," Aden said.

"Fuck you guys," Tobias said, laughing, and he walked back over to his seat and sat back down next to Kobe- faithfully holding Pluto. Pluto had curled into Kobe's lap and fallen lightly asleep. Tobias ran his fingers through Kobe's hair then reached out his fingers to caress the back of Solaris' neck.

He looked back up to the stage. They were urinating on each other. Their pee was bright green. The streams flooded into each other's mouths. Then, letting it run down their chin into another's mouth who would catch it, like their mouths were stacked champagne glasses. Then there would be more semen. Or an occasional arching burst of vaginal secretions. The lines seemed to have stopped getting any longer.

Tobias got nervous again. He panicked. His heart dropped to his gut and he began to rock in his chair in an attempt to stave away the nausea. With that, Logos- clad in blue reflections like he were made of Mercury- appeared beside him.

Logos said, "We're the outcasts, yeah? How did that happen, Tobias?" Logos asked mockingly.

"You know. Listen. I need to get where Yah is. Or I need Yah to get here. I am going to get to Aloria if we have to go through Yah himself. So how do we do it?"

"You're not going where he is. I can assure you of that. He might come here. If you ask nicely."

"Will you ask him nicely for me?"

"Sure... He just said no."

"No? Does he know I am minutes away from taking out the Pleiadians permanently?"

"He's Yah. Of course he knows. I can get to where he is. What message should I give him?"

"I don't know, Logos. Why don't you help? It's a simple request. Couldn't you get to Aloria and talk to her?"

"You don't really understand what happened with her. I'm not surprised. You have selective hearing. She might be ascended, but she is in no way her old self. She left Osaze behind. You aren't in her anymore. They have her under enforced suppression and what that is is basically an elaborate method of brain washing her. You know about Hilt. That wasn't a joke. That is her situation. So, the way I see it, is you have two problems. First, getting out of the Logos. Second, eliminating Hilt."

"I have to talk to Yah. Isn't Ma'at tight with Yah? Can't she convince him to release Aloria?"

"Ma'at is the one who put Yah in charge of Hilt and Aloria. I might be able to work something out, though. Don't do anything drastic. I have to let you know.... There isn't much for you to do here. Even if you annihilate the Pleiadians, send them to the Mystic, will that release Aloria? Will she descend?"

"If she can ascend she can descend, right?"

"Maybe. Probably not," said the Logos.

"Where is Ma'at? What is her game in this? I don't understand the agenda. She wants me to forget Aloria? She keeps Aloria out of reach. Contradicts herself. The Pleiadians are dying for, as far, as I can tell, nothing more than loyalty. Can you make sense of this? Please?"

"It's the Pale Mystery. And you are Osaze."

"So Pleiadians are always this psychotic and irrational?"

"That is one way to say it. In this situation. Another way is that Pleiadians have a case of descension madness. They are not of sound mind. Their decisions are clouded over by disproportionate matters of the heart, and also emotional judgment. Not unlike your own.

"They are at the mercy of their mistaken resolutions of what will be and will not be. That is their culture. An unfortunate matriarchy. An existence that did well up until this situation, and for aeons before. They did fine until they get you involved. No one's fault, really. They did what they were going to do. There is one way things will happen, and that is exactly as they should. Not two sides of a coin, or a left or right turn. This is exactly what time is, because people have a hard time grasping it. Time is an already determined image with 3 – 9 – 12 – 24 dimensions depending on how far you look across it or through. Depending on who you are is how you will see it. Yah sees it as one dimension if you extrapolate the arithmetic. Because Yah sees everything through our eyes. Except Osaze. So, yes, you are godless.

"Anyway, when you picture these dimensions as cobwebs, we're lurking through them, we see what we will- we're like that. When you, as a human, see time, we see form. Of course, humans never could accept reincarnation from which comes comprehension of timelessness. It's one creation, front to back and beginning to end. All around. Humans could not accept their place, and because of that they made the situation on earth infinitely worse than it had to be, at all times. Too busy racing each other to relax and embrace each other. The latter being what we hoped for. But it didn't go that way. They like to blame Osaze, but I'll tell you straight up, the Pleiadians wrecked Gaia, and Aloria didn't help either."

Tobias leaned forward and glanced at Osaze. He was not paying attention, and instead stared off at the orgy, like the others. He glanced back up there. The women weren't leaving the stage and quite literally had begun piling up. Daisy chains- a woman licking a woman licking a woman, and so on- had formed longer than there was even room for, causing more stacking. Whereas the men would do their thing then walk out into the audience. Done with it. Alcyone was nowhere to be found. The moans only got louder.

He asked Logos, "So what's going to happen here? Are we going to Yah, is Yah coming here, or am I killing the rest of the Pleiadians?"

"I can't imagine why you would bother doing that."

Osaze, in response, opened his mouth and released a quiet rolling shriek, almost under his breath.

Logos said, "Oh. The Pale Mystic. Bad situation for the Pleiadians. That's justice out here. I see what you're saying. Yah will take up this cause. I'm sure he will at least negotiate with you. Which is more than the Pleiadians ever got. Let's do it. The two of us will go get him. Aden! You're coming with me."

"Do I have to?" Aden asked.

"It's to meet Yah. You'll want to be there."

"We're coming back here, right? Why am I going?"

"You're going to be privy for your own sake. It's imperative, if you have to know."

Tobias, in a flash of paranoia became suspicious of how Logos insisted against reluctance, yet he recalled Olivia or Alcyone telling him that Aden would be taking his own separate path, so maybe things were beginning to work out. Tobias had been losing more and more hope- by the instant, really- that any of their best efforts would amount to more than unexpected, unfortunate, deadly circumstances, all of which associated with each's own inadequacies and shortcomings, or inability to assimilate peacefully. Where humans went, the Pale Mystic followed. Reaping for itself, essentially, what Yah had sown; creation.

With that in light, Tobias looked to Aden, who looked back, and he shrugged at him a 'Sure, why not?' expression and generally genuinely meant it. He had no idea what lay ahead for Aden but there was no single outcome that, on paper, looked any worse than any other possible outcome. The higher ups would know anyway. It didn't make sense for them, with all their vision, to not know what was coming. Tobias watched Aden kiss Lyn farewell, jump to the next row back, and walk out up the isle with Logos.

Tobias moved to the empty seat beside Osaze. There was space between him and the girls. He blew Kobe a kiss because she was watching him, then he turned to Osaze and asked him, "You know what is going to happen, don't you?"

"It's funny you would ask me that. You haven't any idea what I am. You are a human. In your mind there are five senses. Or about 12 of them if you have a little more information. 360 of them if you're an ancient. The old Egyptians could sense a beehive in a hollow log from a mile away. Egypt back then would shock a modern guy like you. Crazy monsters you couldn't fathom running around that place. Cat women. Bird men. Crocodile people. The hieroglyphics weren't lying. Egypt was the most glorious achievement of this aeon. Then came the dark ages. You know astrology. The planet got a little too far from the galactic center and that was that for the golden ages. First comes the day, then comes the night. Comes the Logos, comes Osaze. Comes birth, comes death.

"I know what will happen, yes. Do you remember where you came from, before you were born?"

"No."

"If you think on your preconception, you will feel a sensation of absolute peace. You will recall an absolute knowledge that all is good. All is well. There is no fear. No concern. And there is no way for Aloria's missing to remove your birthright. Her glory is what you gave to her. And her glory can be given to others. So many others. You don't realize yet. They cannot make us leave the Logos- nobody can. If this is where we belong then we aren't going. You have no way to know because you have no scope with which to interpret such a thing. Aloria is a reaction to us. Do you know how many matriarchal societies exist in the Logos? The inner light you're seeking in Aloria will be replicated throughout the Logos. As Tobias would, back when, meet another girl as passionate as Arianna, Osaze will meet another Aloria. Because it is the man that causes the woman. Father's and daughters. Lovers and daughters. And the opposite is true with Mothers and sons.

"Osaze basically gives form. And in form there is function, and in function there is purpose. Of course, when Gaia fell into the dark ages men took over. They burned Alexandria and dominated, throughout time, consuming greedily; so to atone for that, would require a quintessentially spiritual reorganization of personal beliefs across the entire race of humans- one substantial enough to encompass the entire population. This is why the Pleiadians worship the Goddess. The Goddess is everywhere. In every female within the Logos. Any civilization with a mind for longevity would be wise to idolize the Goddess or suffer to parish by the suicidal and barren, homicidal hearts of men.

"Something that can't be blamed on us, by the way. The hearts of men? They say we did that, but we were not the influential one causing such a wasteful loss of life. Draco was, if you care. Were men to not destroy themselves, there would be hardly enough women left.

It is a ploy by the seductive, us, over the warriors, or whoever. So, on your planet, Draco drove the men off to die in these bloody battles, and Osaze sent the wise ones to sow their seed. This is how the opportunistic gene pools bred and how misguidable gene pools died off, and this is why wars claimed many fewer lives as countries went through more and more of them. Though other tragedies more than accounted for the difference. People systematically kept numbers decreasing, as needed, across the planet. They'd send them off to take what their country needed- to die; to clear space for seeds to spread. Or, armies came in and slaughtered civilizations to clear room for their own kind.

"What happened on Gaia was pretty much a disgusting mess and that is why they look forward to putting it behind them and trying better in the coming aeon. Birth. Death. Birth. Death. We can leave altogether and live within ourselves for an aeon. The decision is yours. Or ours. But remember we would be doing the Logos a disservice by abandoning it. Whether they appreciate us or not."

YAH

"And you don't know what outcome I'm going to choose?"

"All is obvious to me. And once it has come to pass, will be obvious to you too, in hindsight- something you didn't see coming. I cannot tell you. I know you as though you are myself, and the Logos is obvious to me too. Even I keep secrets from you. I see how this will turn out when I interpret the players and plot out the reactions. Yah isn't much for manifesting here in the Logos. This has happened one other time; one other time has he taken a human form, and if he should appear here I doubt he will be looking like a human."

"What will he be looking like?"
"Something surprising."

****

"I don't understand why we're here. I don't really care about meeting Yah. It couldn't possibly matter. None of this shit matters. So why do I have to be here? I don't have a lot of time left. This isn't where I want to be," said Aden, "I want to be with the clan."

"You won't be seeing them again."

The words caused him to choke and cough. "You're joking. Why the fuck not?"

"You're ascending."

"Tobias made this happen. He's sacrificing me? To get a sit down with Yah? Is that it?"

"In a way, yes. Also, this is as it would be. I have to return to Gaia. All that will happen is they're going to kill your physical body back in orbit, and you're going to disappear and reappear within me. All will be well. We haven't the same concerns as Osaze. There is no jeopardy for us."

This made sense to Aden. He never expected accepting death to come so easily, and yet it had. He hadn't been given a choice. He thought about Lyn and how she would be torn up. She would also understand that the time had come. There was no reason to fuss. He hadn't made a single decision for himself since he arrived at Endsville anyway. It was the end. He'd made it far with the clan. It was nice to not feel a single regret.

They had left the Pleiades cluster and were drifting through nebulae of curling and glistening, spectacular, greens, yellows, and blues. Aden became angry as he thought a little more. Logos should not have dragged him away like that. At the end, to be angered was aggravating in itself. As above so below. He'd always had a habit of leaving abruptly.

"Why isn't Lyn here?"

"She would have insisted on leaving with you."

"She would have understood she needed to stay. I want to say goodbye to her."

"You did. You said goodbye. You kissed her goodbye, too."

"That doesn't count. You fucking lied to me."

"You aren't going anywhere. We'll all be together soon. The one you might have kissed goodbye forever is Tobias. His fate is uncertain."

"And ours isn't contingent on his?"

"Not in the least."

There was nothing for him to say then. He didn't know how to argue with his higher self. He had no opinion about the fate of the universe, but felt no right to intervene with the demands. Unlike some people. Tobias had lied. Or failed to live up to his promises. It couldn't be held against him. There was no way to predict what the Logos would do. He didn't even want an explanation. It was easier to accept it than to fight it.

Aden said, "Then do it. Do it right now."

Logos looked into his eyes. The god of himself. Electric blue eyeballs and slick reflective flesh colored like the space where they were. Their facial structures identical, if scaled. To die was to stare into the self he'd become; an enormous creature shaped like a man and made of pure consciousness. It was done. He knew something was off. He felt life fall from him. He wasn't alive anymore. He had died. Or was dying. There was no pulse. He could feel the stillness.

His mind hung in place; fading. The thoughts of the others fell away and his attention turned to himself. His childhood. His mother. Father. Grandparents. Brothers and sisters. Friends. Lovers. The clan. He was them. He was everyone he'd ever loved. Somehow, they were him, too.

Then he died.

He blinked. Instantly, he saw through the eyes of the Logos facing his evaporating corpse. He was himself still. Except hardly. He was something much more and realizing the irrelevance of Aden. What a distraction human life was. As praised as it may be, and as revered; the human was limited in almost every conceivable way. The higher ones felt the need to be limited for purpose- reduced like a fraction. For them the only frontiers were always further down. Below, the frontiers were above.

Of their experiments with vindication- divination by the behavior of lower life forms- Logos couldn't see any purpose. That was behind him. Aden was dead. He'd watched himself die as a human many times. In other aeons there were different human worlds. Different forms of Gaia. Gaia. He'd be seeing her after the little black planet went up in flames. Always such an honor. Each aeon Gaia was the first to descend and the last to ascend.

He needed to get to Yah.

Such a thing to be doing.... There had never before been a reason to get to the source. It was what the effort dictated; new results. They could recreate Gaia a thousand times and the process would always surprise him. He couldn't help but think back through the aeons. He passingly noticed that coming aeons were a future they'd never experience. Other universes, beyond the Logos, throughout eternity, could be anticipated the way humans anticipate a dreaded appointment. Their existence was for Yah. And for those above Yah, the unknown creators of the creator. Then Osaze- with his epic nerve and too much power- had the whole situation in submission. Even Yah? No. The Logos was immune by nature. And supremely indifferent; just trying to enjoy the show, and waiting on the fresh start.

To get to Yah was of course a simple process. Nothing was ever complicated at the highest dimensions. Yah would know about the situation and be anticipating his arrival. It stood to presume that the creator might even meet Logos at that point, for the sake of simplicity. Predictably, in that instant, Logos realized he wouldn't be traveling far.

She appeared behind him, tapped his shoulder, and he turned to face her. Yah was a little girl. A very little girl. Her appearance was similar to a four year old but she had an angel's wings folded against her back. She wore a sparkling gold dress that wasn't fabric, only an image cast on her body. Her big blue eyes were excited to see him and her smile was beaming.

"Hi Logos," she said, and with a flutter of her wings, wings almost as big as herself, she fluttered and flew into his arms giving him the best hug. "It's been so long since I've seen you. I missed you."

"Haven't you been watching the whole time?"

"It's not the same! I like to seeee you. To talk to you. To hear your voice." Yah giggled. "We're going to see Osaze, yes? I didn't want it to come to this. The girls could have altered the path. It's in their control."

"I think they thought they knew what you wanted. And they didn't."

"Maybe they wanted to see me," Yah said.

"Seems backward and devious, but maybe."

"No. That isn't it. All is well. We can solve this. Tobias is a bit of an anomaly. There have been hundreds of aeons, I don't think Osaze ever manifested in a person quite like this one before."

Logos said, "The situation with the Pleiadians has never occurred either. Osaze and Aloria have been symbiotic since the beginning of existence. Why now do the Pleiadians claim he is harmful?"

"You don't want to know the answer. You'll find it emasculating."

"Tell me."

Yah said, "The three girls. They came from Ma'at and The Mystic. Micro-creations. And Tobias- because the three girls can deceive him- is under the impression they're born entirely of his origin. This is Ma'at's way of infiltrating him. The Ma'at twins have grown bored, and find themselves wanting more. Or at least something different. All this can be traced to Ma'at."

"That sounds interesting. Why would I care what they do?"

"It would mean a substantial change. You didn't hear it from me, but the Pleiadians got lied to by Ma'at. She twisted them up. Ma'at wants to expatriate. To become more phenomenal than she already is. Ma'at has always been the same. Always been at the top. Always seen the stage play out in the same way, but unlike you, Osaze, Maia, and a few others, she knew she could change things if she wanted to. So she is. And you know me. Ma'at is my favorite. She can do what she wants and taboo be damned. "

"I don't care about change. It means nothing to me. There is no you without me. So Ma'at can do as she pleases. But, to clarify, Osaze isn't actually in any kind of danger? There is no threat against him?"

"None that he won't will for himself. I'm here to negotiate for the Pleiadians. There are still options for Osaze to choose from. In the end, I know you'll be happy with the outcome. Osaze will have to come to terms with a few things. He'll be satisfied back to complacency once again. In the next aeon."

"You can't give him Aloria back?"

"No."

"And she can't get herself to him?"

"No."

"And the Pleiadians existence depends on how well Tobias accepts this news?"

"To a certain extent, yes."

"Are they going to make it?"

"Of course. It's my will."

"Well. You know where I have to go and why. All

my love, Yah."

"I love you, too. Embrace me," she said and fluttered up into his arms. She giggled and whispered into his ear, "I'll see you after the descension," and she kissed his cheek.

"See you then." They broke apart, looked at each other once- a sort of modified bow- smiled, then turned their backs to each other and went their separate ways.

****

They were relaxing and having a pleasant conversation waiting for Aden to return. Tobias had gotten a feeling Aden wouldn't be returning, and unfortunately his feelings represented knowledge. He could see Lyn peering at him nervously whenever he glanced down the aisle.

Tobias said, "I used to do nice things for girls. They always acted entitled and unappreciative. The bad ones would take what they wanted, devour your nutrients, and then leave the leftovers there to rot. And the good one got killed by Zeta. I love women, but they never made it very easy. Most in our generation were skeazy or religious. Women treated men like less than human. Like we were teddy bears on a rack and they were picking out the most appealing one without very much consideration beyond skin deep and superficial characteristics, or with their interest firmly planted in their own gain. Men behaved the same way toward women with different demands- taking what they could when they could. Neither appreciated the other very much, they just respected the divide. I think beauty was the currency of love."

Robin said, "That's when you take them down from the pedestal. You can't let them in your head. Ever. They mindfuck you. Like the Pleiadians did with us pretty much the entire time we spent at Endsville. You can't give them yourself. You have to make them take it. And then they will."

Cadence said, "The Devil deceived Eve, not Adam."

Lyn said, "The Devil deceived us. Women come first always. There were species of lizards composed entirely of females. No all male species that I know of. Except maybe the Zeta but they don't count."

Tobias actually had a lot to say about women. Too bad relevant conversations on gender roles had become extinct. In the past, Goddess worship- the Goddess around them- could have shifted the sands of time and the course of events.... For years leading up to the cataclysm, since Alcyone rescued him, if you'd asked him about his philosophies he may have presented himself as a militant feminist. Women were godlike, and men were dog like. Worshiping dogs made no sense.

The clan had been waiting a significant period of time. Tobias almost managed to forget his nervousness for that little while. Then he remembered they were about to meet Yah. They were about to meet the thing on the other end of their unanswered prayers. He knew he'd never see Aden again. He didn't want to mention it. He certainly didn't want Lyn to divine such a thing on her own. He felt bad for her but the implications were greater than that. By any indication, their time was over.

The Pleiadians on stage showed little sign of letting up. More of the men had taken seats and the lines further dwindled. The women showed little sign of relenting. He had lost track of Alcyone entirely.

Tobias had Pluto in his lap and his feet were up on the giant seat in front of him. The seats were flush, white, and looked like any theater seats except they didn't fold up like on Earth. A culture that doesn't produce any waste further than vanishing bodily secretions had little need to clean under seats.

The barges were gathered off shore, he couldn't count them, but there were clearly dozens, and they were filled with corpses. Their conversation had lulled and he'd been staring off for a minute when he felt a tap on his shoulder and looked back to see Lyn there.

"He's not coming back is he?"

Tobias sighed and shook his head 'no.' He saw the sadness fall across her doll-like face and she dropped her chin to hide herself in the palms of her hands and her draping hair. Solaris gave Tobias a disapproving glance and then she hopped over the chairs to sit next to Lyn and comfort her. By then the others noticed something was wrong and had averted their attention toward the situation.

There came a rumble. It started softly and then grew louder and louder, like thunder rising to a crescendo. Above their heads, the sky, with a brain rattling boom, burst into bright blue flames. The entire arena illuminated under a blue inferno above them where the sky met space. All the sky got consumed by blue fire.

Kobe and Kyoto bolted close to Tobias. Solaris grabbed Lyn. Robin and Cadence clutched Calvin. The heat against their skin felt intense but not so much as to be painful. In their eyes the light of the fires glared powerfully but they could still see. They could see how the Pleiadians didn't even flinch. The ones in line were looking up and around, the ones in the crowd, too, but on stage the orgy continued uninterrupted. He admired their focus....

He could see shadows. The barges cast spasmodically shifting shadows blacking out the watery reflections of flames; dancing. He could see indications of flames licking at the corpses stacked above the rims. Thousands of bodies, like lumps of ghost clay from where he sat. The smoke, gathering to itself, rose nearly straight up. The planet had no wind.

A shrill cry, like an angry banshee or a rabid howler monkey, came down at them from above the shell of the stage. He looked up and saw a figure flapping giant wings; wings like a giant bat would have. It moved directly over them and cast shadows across their faces under the indigo inferno licking at itself. The enormous wings were attached to a small figure with a feminine torso. Tobias instantly recognized the body, and as he subsequently identified the legs of a goat or some hoofed animal he wished his recognition to be false. The wings halted their flapping, and the body drifted softly to the ground.

Yah landed on a chair a few rows in front of them and she planted the claws of her wings to brace her stance. He hated to see it. He couldn't bare it. It was his beloved, with the lower half of a goat, covered in white fur. She looked supremely angry, as he had never seen. Her eyes glared with ire and fire past her cheeky grimace. Her curls looked glorious bouncing around her head. Even given the circumstances, he was immediately relieved to see her face. Her tits were hanging out for the world to see, and he felt a volt of his old futile possessive ways. Everything about the encounter was fucked up.

"What do you want from me?" she asked. He heard in Yah's voice that she was in no way actually Arianna. He knew.

He said, "I want Aloria back with Osaze."

"Foolish boy. What would it matter to you?"

"They took Arianna from me.... Was it you? Did you take Arianna? Are you responsible for this?"

"Get your questions right. No. I didn't take her. And there is not much I am not responsible for. But, yes, it is me keeping her from you."

Tobias thought and asked, "What power do you have over me?"

"More than you have over me, ultimately. You're wondering if you could destroy me for her, but you also know how stupid that sounds. I am from another place, and while the Logos is a part of me, so are the infinite other subdivisions of my influence within the realms of my creation of which you know nothing. Similar to the Pale Mystic. Within Osaze the Pale Mystic has an influence equal to my own in the Logos. But you are not the Pale Mystic. You are Osaze. And the Pale Mystic would not erase itself at your behest, no matter how allied you are in these moments."

"Then what do I do?"

"You realign. You don't forget. You reclaim yourself. Osaze is part of the grand design. He is revered at every point of this mad Logos. There is no greater force than the darkness you speak for. But even that darkness is part of another design. Like the elements on Gaia, Osaze dictates form. And like the wind on Gaia, Osaze is alive in the Logos.

"We are reconfiguring the coming aeon to be more splendid than any previously. Osaze's exodus is part of that, but another key fact was that Aloria had to be removed to unburden Osaze. You know she has not gone to the Pale Mystic like so many of her kin. Aloria is with me beyond the Logos, and at the end of the next aeon, she may return to Osaze. I cannot promise such a thing. There are other worlds for her to explore. I can promise you the matter will die with you, Tobias. The pitiful, psychotic, little boy who cannot accept change."

"What about Hilt? Why is Aloria being kept catatonic?"

"Until the ascension. She'll be released once your fate is more secure."

"Why? Why wasn't it fine the way it was? The way it always was?"

"Did you look? Did you see? Did you look around Gaia? Things were no better elsewhere in the Logos. What happened on Gaia was like an artistic representation, or a microcosm, of what happens elsewhere in the Logos. I know, I'm the artist. We've dealt with this since the beginning. Essentially, I create what Ma'at tells me, but we've both been dealing with you as a limitation for always. Ma'at wants to do something new. The Pale Mystic is overseeing, but staying neutral."

Tobias looked over at Lyn. She had no idea what Ma'at's intentions might be and she shrugged. He looked back to the morbid, desecrated, figure of Arianna; fire light glowed in her eyes. To the right, like Vikings, the bodies burned out on the water. To the left he saw the same; fiery dead immortals.

Yah's gaze softened. With a motion of her wings she threw herself out to the aisle and clip clopped toward them; her wings clasped against her back. Tobias wanted a weapon. He wanted to kill the monster. At the very least he didn't want to look at it. He averted his eyes to the floor.

"Don't be afraid of me Tobias. I love you. Do you know what the word Osaze means?"

"No."

"God's beloved."

"That's great. Tell me right now what I should be feeling. If you were me, what would you do?"

"There's nothing you can do. Destroy the Pleiades, or don't. Destroy the Zeta or don't. The Zeta soul is doomed to the Mystic regardless. Destroy each other for all I care. The me is mine. There is no change you can make that will effect the outcome. The descension is yours, but the ascension belongs to me."

"I could destroy Ma'at. I could send her to the Pale Mystic. Then what would come of the Logos? I can obliterate every little higher mind you ever shat out of your third eye."

"What you send away, I will cause to return to me. What you threaten to destroy is of me. The Pale Mystic will consume what it will, but if it consumes something of mine, I will reclaim it easily. Really, in the end, the only power you have is over yourself. You may destroy whom or whatever you like, but it comes to me, and I'll put things back how I want."

There were flashing notions shooting through his mind. Destroy Ma'at and the fabric of reality dissipates. Destroy Logos and the Logos inverts and spews into nothingness; likely into Osaze. Destroy everything; it returns and ascends. He had no choice. He didn't like not having choices. He was as powerless as he'd ever been.

"You have a choice. You fool. You don't understand. You are too bitter and hung up. You don't get it. Just let her go. Forget about your vengeance and try to accept the facts. This is what we want. I know you Tobias. There is love in you. There is the love in you. There is nearly nothing else; no 'ego' or unconscious malice. It is this love that causes you to behave in such a vile way, but what matters is that love is there. Your anguish can be repealed with love. Your loss can be accepted with love. Aloria will be fine. Absolutely fine. If you look around at those you're harming, you'll realize that your love for them actually transcends your perceived obligation to Aloria.

"You are a human. A little person man thing with no more power than to inconvenience me slightly. And down here, yeah, they revere your delicate and stupid nature, but to me, to me... to me, you're a little devil raging against the world because inside of you you are fighting against yourself as against me. When you love the world, you will love yourself. There is inner peace. Look for it, and you will find it.

"Stop fighting. Stop the sorrow. Come to peace with the loss of Arianna, accept the severance of Aloria and Osaze, and the pieces will come to fit around you. Look around... You are the cause of this. You had one lesson to learn. You needed to become part of the situation. And yet, like Osaze, you remain separate. A mysterious giver of form. So I am here to beg you, you have to get over these pitfalls of yours. What are you hung up on? Sadness. Stop being sad. You cannot have what is gone."

"But you can?"

"We are not the same Osaze. I am this. As a human, I am you. As Osaze, I am you, too. You are a visitor here. A welcome, beloved, visitor. I am here. I am there. For all intent and purpose I am everywhere, and subsequently I am what is- except for Osaze, because Osaze is of the Pale Mystic. You are as divine as divine can be. Why can't you unshackle your mind?"

Tobias chuckled, and smiled, "I had a feeling you were going to say that. The journey is the lesson? Is that it?"

"Yes."

"I knew it. I know you. I know exactly what you are. You didn't even try to hide it. You say I am you. I could believe such a thing. I need to think now. I can't think. You are the deceiver! Yet, you're absolutely right. I love you immensely. I always did. But how can I trust a single thing you say?"

"There is no one else Tobias. This is as far as we come together in your life." There was a strap against Yah's chest, running between her breasts, and attached to a sheath on her back from which she drew a two foot long sword of shining metal glowing in the Pleiadian fire light. She grasped the blade and offered him the hilt. He accepted without hesitance. He felt the weight in his hand. He raised the edge to his face. He looked at his glowing red eyeball in the reflection. He ran his finger over the edge; completely unsurprised to find the entire length razor sharp and the tip perfectly pointed.

"I am your wrath. I am your sadness. I am your crusade. I am your demon. I am the imbalance. I am the disharmony. Now strike me down."

Her eyes, those same eyes, were encouraging him, 'do it,' they said. Then, Yah smiled, just like her. Like

Yah were channeling her, she mouthed, 'I love you.' He almost cried. She tilted her chin skyward, tossed her curls aside, and shifted her massive black wings back out of the way. He didn't understand, but he knew Yah was right. Yah was always right. Always pure. Yah wouldn't lie like the others. Tobias had to let Arianna go. He had to love what was left for as long as he was alive. His failure was an embarrassment.

He inhaled superficially, noticed, then lifted the blade above his right shoulder, took half a step forward, looked into her eyes a final time, looked at her breasts, Arianna's breasts, the monstrous goat legs. He focused, swung the blade arching into her throat. He felt a slight resistance cutting- a jolt at the spine, then the blade passed through, and her head lobbed off completely; it fell to the ground and rolled away under a seat. The carcass collapsed to the ground. For the first time, the Pleiadians were watching intently; he could feel their eyes on him. He threw the sword down onto the body with a thud.

He retrieved the head; a skull indiscernible from that of Arianna's; her face and her tear drop eyes. He clumped the hair into a pony tail and wrapped it around his hand. He held it up sideways and looked into her face. Sweat dripped into his eyes and he wiped it away. Her face looked sheepish. Like innocence. Like she never had a say in anything. He kissed her soft lips.

The fires in the sky were dimming down. Under blankets of thick black smoke that looked like the coals of an old smoldering bonfire- except bluish. The barges were still aflame. The air stunk like burning corpses. Hair mostly. A hint of acrid body odor. Arianna. He had no idea what a soul mate was. For the first time he couldn't understand how such a thing mattered.

He lifted the chin and positioned the neck over his face and caught the blood as it poured into his mouth. The metallic blood was subtly electric; there was a tingle in his mouth wherever it touched. He flipped the skull upside down to keep the fluid in. The girls were looking at him and he knew they were the same as himself. He moved to behind them and their heads had tilted back like little baby birds. He poured blood as carefully as he could into each of their mouths, one by one, spilling much. Calvin stood beside them, asking with his little kid eyes.

"Open up," Tobias told him and poured out a splash. Then he sat down in the chair next to Kobe and placed 'Yah's' head, neck up, in his lap. Pluto crawled onto the armrest and pawed curiously at the gore. With his free hand he petted his kitty's head, thinking how he was ready to die.

****

For a single instant, Aloria became aware that something was not right. Around her were strange vibrations and perturbing emanations of false consciousness. She was confined by her surroundings- as though her being had pressure on it from all sides. A frightening realization came over her. They'd betrayed her. She saw the colors of hilt and felt a repulsion deep within her toward her surroundings and what had come of her. She felt trapped. Scared- for that instant. Then it fell away. She was immersed in pure light. First it was around her, then it moved through her. Her form became formless, she was pure energy. Pure consciousness. She felt joy and jubilation. Then she forgot herself and forgot her burdens.

At that instant Aloria lost recollection of her relationship to Osaze. She instead felt about him as Yah felt. Indifferent. Indifferent about everything else, too. Her life with the Pleiadians disappeared as well. She no longer had sisters, or family, or a lover. Her entire identity was gone. Not lost; she had become her loved ones. She had become everything. She had become Yah. It was sheer bliss. A euphoria that would never wane. She felt the feelings reserved for God's and Devils. She was both, and neither. She was....

All that remained was waiting. Soon enough all would be as she was- as it truly was, sans the illusions of Osaze. She was early but that was her purpose. An overcomplicated simplicity such as the Logos created various factors of incongruities, but- all returned to Yah, eventually. A head start. Everything else would catch up soon enough. She was Yah. Yah was her. Aloria was gone, and yet she remained within the whole. At the vast void of Yah she knew what contentment really meant. The way things were naturally. She'd found what she'd been looking for. The pin prick limitless void from which time and space was born. She'd found what every being in the Logos searched for- the return. The ascension. Home.

TRAGEDY

They waited, practically drooling from boredom, and waited more for the funeral to end. The line dwindled to no one; the men had finished and were sprinkled throughout seats around them. The women continued to writhe and moan all over each other; shiny, covered in their own fluids. Tobias couldn't take being there anymore and- unsure of what they were waiting for- was ready to leave. They'd been silent for the longest time. Calvin had become bored of stabbing at Yah's 'corpse' with the sword, and fell asleep in Lyn's arms; the poor girl's face stayed wet with the tears of her bereavement. Robin and Cadence were holding hands patiently, but Robin had been giving Tobias glances indicating desire to leave. Tobias didn't blame him. He wanted to go, too. Where they'd go didn't matter. Back to earth, perhaps. Or to Osaze land.

Osaze had bolted the moment Yah appeared. Tobias didn't know why. He didn't know what to do either, but he wanted Alcyone to hurry up and finish what she was doing and offer him a little guidance. He was getting fed up with waiting. They'd waited for the men to finish, thinking that would be the end of the orgy; apparently the second part was just for the ladies; apparently there was no limit to the amount of tonguing vaginas they could indulge in. And some men from the audience would stand and go up for a dose of seconds.

They could afford to hang around and wait; there was no longer any rush. He'd killed his crusade. The quest was over. He wasn't trying to rescue Osaze and Aloria from an existence apart from each other. He had no purpose. To conquer is to be conquered and to be conquered is to conquer. Existence was more trivial and meaningless than even the most cynical nihilist could ever have expressed. Creation was Yah's grand masturbation. If he had a wish it would be to go to the Pale Mystic after death; and for Osaze to go to the Pale Mystic, too. Something different. Anything. There was no way to know how the Logos would fair should Osaze and the presence of the Mystic be removed. There was strength in that, but no solutions. He remembered a feeling he got when he was young and once a girl he loved told him he had a dark heart. She didn't care, a dark heart beats the same as any other. The beat was Yah. The darkness was Osaze.

He wanted to be that boy again, but his history was useless, even as a point of reference. They were at the end of everything and the beginning of something else. Their bodies, their minds, their hearts, were not much more than old t-shirts in a garbage bag. All that was left to do was to get dropped off at the thrift store.

Tobias stood up and abandoned Yah's severed head in the seat. The fires of the barges were still burning hot and high, but the sky had returned to its smoky purple color, so the blue flames of burning Pleiadian corpses out on the water created bubbles of illumination around themselves in the dim smoke. He walked through the orchestra and had to climb over a chair to reach the ledge of the stage and pull himself up. The scent of burning flesh became less prominent, especially up on the stage. The feminine odor was overpowering. He'd smelled a few women's special scents before but he had never smelled hundreds of their scents at once; it was exactly what he would have imagined had he ever attempted to imagine such a thing; plus smoldering flesh. Their moans and cries were almost deafening. He didn't know how to find her and was feeling pretty bad for interrupting, even if he had only just stepped on stage. The women hadn't even noticed him standing there.

Tobias looked back out over the audience; the men were glaring at him with scrunched foreheads and discriminating eyes. His friends were interested and watching intently. He shrugged at them then turned back to the undulating bulk of gorgeous women. For a little while he admired their figures. In a single glimpse he could see dozens of vaginas, dozens of asses, and dozens of tits. He always loved tits, and that was more tits in one place than he'd ever seen, even on the internet.

The time had come to leave the Pleiades. If the time hadn't come, he still really wanted to get out of there. He needed Alcyone. He wanted to talk to her about what to do next. A lot had changed since she ran up onto that stage like a crack head to a crack rock. In defeating the devil he'd defeated himself. Surely it was the right thing to do.

He called out, "Alcyone!"

There was no response. The pile of women didn't even flinch. He called again, "Alcyone!" And again there was no reaction. He thought to himself and considered the options; to wait for the orgy to end, to leave without saying goodbye or receiving her guidance, or to climb over those orgasmic women and try to discern one from the next over and over until he had found Alcyone. There were too many of them. He imagined unfortunate women at the bottom suffocating and dying, but if breathing was a factor out there, he couldn't tell. He didn't want to be caught up in getting crushed, so he turned his back to the orgy and leapt off the stage. He walked back to what remained of the clan and said, "Fuck it. Let's go."

Without Alcyone they'd have to relocate Osaze. Tobias wasn't sure how to get them off the planet and back into the ether. The entire planet of Peyor existed practically as part of space. There wasn't much difference from above than from below. He couldn't figure if they needed to take the transport out to that glittering station or if they could simply leave from where they stood.

The clan silently followed Tobias out to the tracks. They stood out at the porcelain landing among the blue flames, under the canopies of red roses; the purple light from the sky bleeding through in beams. Tobias held Pluto in his arms, he said, "I don't know if we're leaving on this train or if we're just willing our way out of here like we've been doing. I was going to try and get Osaze back. He'll know."

"Do it. He couldn't have gone far," Robin said.

Tobias lifted his finger signaling them to wait a moment. He had to briefly think whether to beckon him out loud or to just do it in his thoughts. It seemed fair to guess that if he was Osaze then Osaze would be in his head. Before he even formulated a plan, or thought what he would say, Osaze fell from the sky like a giant man sized oil slick, or a falling red eyeball to the others.

"How do we get out of here?" Tobias asked.

"Where do you plan to go?"

"Gaia. I guess, right?" He looked to the others and shrugged to get their approval. They returned his sentiment with nods- except Lyn who was completely grief stricken, destitute, and almost catatonic.

"If you return to Gaia I can't follow you there, you'll be on your own."

Tobias didn't have a problem with that. There was nothing left for them to do as far as he knew. Still, he had to ask, "What comes next?"

"Nothing more than the waiting," Osaze said.

"Waiting for what, to die? Why don't we die right now?"

Osaze said, "If you want to, that is your option, but you'll have to take your own lives. There is no rush, your time is coming."

He saw the expressions of revulsion appear on his peer's faces and felt a need to do right by them. Something very natural in him was not ready to go, but the human in him was screaming, 'DO IT! DIE NOW!' He wasn't acting for Osaze anymore and he wasn't acting for himself either. His motivations rested squarely on providing contentment to the others in their final hours. Lyn had lost Aden. He'd lost Arianna. They'd lost Drake and Logan. Even in outer space they remained human, and, as humans, all they really had was each other and a little bit of time.

"No. You're right. No rush. We'll die when our time comes. Just get us back to earth so we can relax, Ok?"

"There is nothing else you need from me?"

"No. Just get us back."

"Ok. I will. I want you to know, Tobias. You've made the right decisions. Your journey wasn't an easy one nor were your choices easy. They were essentially, like all decisions, presented for you. Yah enjoys to challenge himself, and so it was not meant to be easy. This is the end of this aeon, so my final advice to you is to rejoice at the beginning of something new."

"Thanks Osaze. I'll see you soon. Give Alcyone my love."

"Yes. You will. And I will."

There was a flood of light that blinded them. They didn't have a single moment to prepare or brace, but as it happened Tobias squeezed Pluto against his chest and then he felt about as close to not existing as he'd ever been. He couldn't feel Pluto or his own body, but he was aware, near the top of his skull, of the cat and of himself, even of the others. Then the blinding light began to fade and as it did different sensations became more prominent.

There was ground under his back; he could feel damp grass against his skin. His human eye was still blind, but with the eye of the Logos he could see they were back at that Floridian suburb. The others were strewn about around him. Pluto was rubbing his face into the ground. He stood to his feet, uncoordinated, and he stumbled slightly as he picked up his cat. With his free hand he took the girls' hands and helped them to their feet.

Tobias felt awful and unfulfilled- almost sick. At the very least he'd lied to his friends. He remembered telling them they'd return together, and yet he had failed; he'd lost Aden out there.

Then he noticed the Logos, a giant shimmering metallic man of greens and blues, standing there, looking like what Aden would see if staring in a mirror on an overly powerful acid trip. The others still couldn't see a thing. A feeling akin to euphoria surged through Tobias' spine and into his brain. Lyn was going to flip. He was happy for her.

A moment later, when her eyes had adjusted- seemingly before the others'- and she began to see again, flip is exactly what she did. She shrieked with excitement and without hesitation she jumped into his arms and he held her against him with her feet off the ground. She didn't seem to care that Logos was not Aden. He couldn't blame her. He handed Pluto off to Kobe and he turned to look around. There was a barely noticeable chill in the air. They were in Florida, central Florida, but it was winter. His mind started racing.

He had no idea what would come next, what they should do, or where they should go. The blackness of the sky had persisted for as long as they'd been gone. He looked up and electric green bolts were seething wildly. The water, too, the ocean, was still made of shivering black glop. They appeared to be on the same beach where Aden had killed Drake and Logan, but he couldn't see the boat- not that it would serve any purpose.

"Where's the boat, Logos?"

"Consumed by the ocean. You were at the outer reaches for over two weeks of Earth time."

Tobias considered that his body felt fine. He couldn't believe such a thing- he'd spent two weeks out of himself- but then again, he could believe anything. The grays must have done maintenance on their flesh. He pulled out the neck of his t-shirt and smelled his armpits. His body smelled sanitary, like a chiropractors office he'd visited once.

Robin asked, "Is there any place left with clear sky?"

Logos answered, his big voice always booming, "Yes. Elsewhere."

"Can we go there? Tobias?" Cadence asked.

"Shit. I don't care. I don't really want to deal with Slor again, though. Can you get us out of here?" he asked Logos.

"Look who you're asking. I have to tell you, it won't be as quick as if you called for the golem, but it won't take too much time either. Where is it exactly you want to go?"

Robin said, "Someplace warmer."

Cadence said, "With a white sand beach. Oh! Can we go to paradise?"

"With waves," Tobias added, "not too high, though. Like six feet."

"Ok... You'll have to excuse me while I find such a place, hang on," said Logos, then he vanished in an instant- faster than an eye could see- he was there then he was gone.

Tobias pulled the girls into his arms and held them tight against him. He kissed the top of each of their skulls. They had the softest hair. He rubbed his face, like nuzzling, against Kyoto's head, and the strands of her hair became caught in his stubble when he pulled away. He felt his chin and noticed three or so day's-worth of beard growth. Interesting...

Tobias released the girls and walked down the road toward the 'water's' edge. He sat on the pavement about 30 feet from the shore of solidified water. He picked up a chunk of cracked pavement from beside him and threw it out onto the 'ocean.' It made a slurping noise as it penetrated. The wind picked up. The Girls came and sat beside him, except Kyoto who herself began throwing rocks out into the 'water.' Soon Robin and Calvin joined her in the activity. Kobe and Solaris put their heads on his shoulders, Pluto crawled into his lap from Kobe's and he sighed.

****

They'd waited about another fifteen minutes for the Logos to return before he scooped them up with telekinetics and flew them out in a protective bubble; similar to the weightlessness of space and safe from the cold of high altitude- though they didn't go much higher than a hot air balloon would fly. To an area of Rio de Janeiro. They were on a beach that stretched out as far as they could see in either direction. A blue street sign read Barra da Tijuca. There wasn't much around them. Some kind of blocky structure that was once a restaurant was on the street and they immediately ransacked it for supplies. There was a seven story watch tower that they hadn't investigated yet. The city of Rio, with its pastel buildings, was miles away down the coast, in the mist.

Out in the distance at multiple directions were enormous rocks protruding through the ocean's surface; they were the size of small islands, as tall as redwoods at some places, and shaped like the backs of dinosaurs. They'd brought chairs over from the restaurant out onto the beach, gone for a swim, and were watching the waves crash.

"We haven't been in yet. How's the water?" Robin asked.

"Warm as piss," Tobias answered.

"Nice," Robin said, then he and Cadence walked down to the water, undressed, left their clothes in a pile, and ran hand in hand out into the surf.

Having rummaged through the restaurant, they'd acquired canned food; pretty much everything one could hope to find; tuna, fruit cocktails, brown curry mole crickets, curry chicken, olives. It was amazing that the humans had died off in such a short time they didn't even have a chance to consume the food they'd stock piled.

The clan had brought to the beach several bus bins filled with food, one entirely filled with liquor. They'd been discussing living right there on the beach until death came for them. They had some good amber colored Spanish rum in a clear bottle he couldn't read the label of. He pulled out the cork and took a long deep smooth burning swill. Then passed it to Solaris.

Calvin came walking over. "Can I have one of those?"

"Take whatever you want," Tobias said. Calvin selected a bottle of 100% blue agave tequila that was bigger than his head and walked over to the water's edge with it.

"You drink Logos?" Kyoto asked.

The heavenly man; with vibrant multi-colored energetic flesh flashing and swirling like gasoline on water; whose body practically hummed as it glared in the sunlight; his giant multicolored dick- like a shapely wad of shiny fruit snacks- hanging out for the world to see; the descended form of the entire universe; walked over to Toby with Lyn nestled under his arm.

Logos said, "I haven't been in such a situation this aeon, so I guess not."

"They had liquor in the past aeons?" Solaris asked.

"Yeah. Everything is pretty much the same from one aeon to the next. Little things change, big things stay the same, usually. The same creators create the same creations over and over. The real excitement comes as certain creators get phased out and others get phased in. The entire Logos, for that reason, is very excited about the coming epoch. With all the changes it will be as none that has happened before it."

Tobias wanted to ask about the other lower forms of Osaze. But he couldn't see a point. Whoever they were, they'd never lived in such a way as himself. They might have lived through horrible wars, rape, or torture, but they never got mindfucked like he felt. His era was a nightmare, why hear of dreams? He just wanted Arianna back. Or he wanted to die. Without any attention to the matter he handed the second bottle of rum to the Logos.

He took his shirt off and draped it on the chair. Then he took a table-clothe from a bin and threw it out over the sand. He'd had two drinks and was already ready for a nap. His body had been asleep for weeks. He could feel its desire to return to unconsciousness. There were umbrellas stacked in a wooden shed at the top of the hill that ran parallel with the road and the beach. He hustled up, grabbed one, rammed it strategically into the ground by the clothe, and spun the lever to raise the canvas to cast a shadow and shield his pasty skin from the fire sphere.

The girls had been watching him. He struggled through the crushing depression to give them a pathetic smile from one side of his cheek, then he laid down. Within a minute they joined him. They were topless, so was he. Their jeans, Arianna's jeans, had been cut into shorts since the day on the boat. They had to be tired, too. He closed his eyes. The waves crashed and rolled and reminded him of Misquamicut beach in Rhode Island. The way the tide pulled some invisible part of himself away with it, only to return the unspeakable essence a moment later. The salt air drifted past his nostrils. The heat made him sweat under the umbrella and the Girls were piling against him and their skins were sticking together. He liked the feeling but of course wished it was someone else's skin. He opened his eyes and watched as Logos rammed another umbrella into the ground by where Lyn was throwing out a second table cloth.

It was early afternoon, maybe a little later. The sun was still beating down on him. He sat up and had another swallow of rum. Sleeping in the daytime was never easy for him. Nor sleeping without a pillow. He was hungry but didn't feel like dealing with a can opener. He took another drink, but the alcohol was not jarring enough. What he needed was a punch in the head, or blade slicing through his flesh. Naturally, he took another drink. Then he lay his head down and somehow fell asleep.

He dreamed he was at one of the casinos in Connecticut and had found Arianna through flashing lights and a thousand dinging sounds. She was sitting at a slot machine. He asked her if they could talk for a little while. She said Ok and that they should get a beer together. She was as beautiful as she ever was; her brown and gold curls bounced perfectly, her purple dress formed to her perfect figure, she stayed close to his side; he could even smell how clean she was. They went up an escalator and found a bar. The bartender poured him a half cup of beer instead of a full one and then complained about the tip he gave. After he tossed her enough coins to make her go away he began to profess his love to Arianna. She listened sweetly, but said nothing in return. He felt that if he could get her to admit her love for him, she would return to him, although he had no idea in what way she was lost; things were vague in a way he couldn't detect. He just knew he needed her and that he would do anything to have her back. She finished her beer and walked away from the bar. He followed her. They were in an elevator and he pulled her close to kiss him. She succumbed to his embrace, and he felt the relief that came from such a simple thing as having his tongue in her mouth, her hands on his shoulders, her throat at his fingertips; then she pushed him away and began talking about Cadence, that Cadence was a lush and could not be trusted. Who cared? He thought. He wanted to kiss her again but she pushed him away and walked out the elevator doors. They were on the top floor of a large parking structure and it was early morning. Arianna began to call out Cadence's name over and over. Tobias wanted her to shut up and listen to him, but she was delirious. There was a pallet of lumber eight feet high by where they were, he pushed her up against it by the shoulders telling her to listen to him, that he loved her, but she kept shouting for Cadence.

He opened his eyes, immediately furious it had only been a dream, then he sat up and saw that Lyn and Calvin were standing at the water's edge and actually shouting for Cadence. He got up from the blanket and ran over to Calvin.

"What the fuck's going on?"

"It's Cadence! We can't find her! We think she

drowned!"

"Where's Logos?"

"He's in the water looking for her with Robin!"

At that point Logos levitated from under the surf into the air with Cadence draped across his arms. He flew over to Tobias and placed Cadence on the wet sand. The rest of the clan came running over. Cadence was clearly dead; her skin was flush, eyes still, and there was no life in her.

"Aren't you going to try and save her," Tobias asked Logos.

"No. This is what is supposed to happen. Besides, she is dead. There is no resurrecting her."

Tobias saw Robin come running out of the water. His face had agony practically painted on it. Tobias knew the feeling too well. Robin pushed them aside and knelt down next to Cadence. He began frantically blowing air into her mouth, and pumping his fists down between her breasts, doing some kind of frantic version of CPR. He kept going for what seemed like a really long time.

Logos approached Robin, knelt down, and placed his weird glowing hand on his shoulder. "She is not coming back," he said.

Robin stopped and shirked Logos' hand. Like his muscles had turned to mush, he dropped onto her body and began to whimper and cry. Tobias took a step back and turned around to see that the Girls hadn't moved from the tablecloth. He walked back and sat next to them under the umbrella. Solaris handed him the bottle of rum and he took a swill.

The sun was setting at their backs and casting their shadows out in front of them. The shadow of the watch tower extended far out onto the water. Tobias didn't know what to do about Robin. Lyn had taken Calvin away from the bodies. Logos remained by his side.

Tobias got back up and walked over to grab Robin's

pants from the sand and he dropped them down next to Cadence so Robin would see. This caused Robin to snap out of his grief for a second. He grabbed the pants, stood up, and put them on. Robin wiped the tears from his eyes and looked around; first with disdain at Logos, as though the monster could have prevented her death, then he looked over at the watchtower. He knelt down, kissed his dead lover on the lips one time, then stood up and walked toward the road staring intently at the tower.

Tobias followed him. "Where you going?" he asked. Robin didn't reply, but began to walk faster. Tobias adjusted his gait to keep up but Robin started running. He ran after him, almost falling face first as they hopped a stone wall, and he caught Robin at the door. He wrapped his arms around him and struggled to bring him down to the ground. Robin was stronger and broke free from Toby's grasp. Robin grabbed Tobias by the hair and smashed his face down into the concrete.

Tobias' sight went black and in his mind he saw flashes of colored light and sparks. He heard the door slam shut, struggled to his feet, found it hard to walk, and, seeing only through the eye of the Logos, he struggled through the door, located the stairs and hurried up them as fast as he could. His head was pounding, his body was weak, and the stairs kept coming. He couldn't climb them fast enough, but after a few flights he began regaining his composure.

Tobias got to the top of the tower where he found himself encased by glass windows. There was a single door leading out to the balcony which encircled the structure. He went through and couldn't find Robin, he ran around the whole thing, before he realized Robin wasn't up there. He looked over the edge toward the ground below and it wasn't long before he saw Robin's body sprawled out on the walkway with the remnants of the clan standing around.

"Why didn't you catch him," he shouted down at Logos, who shrugged.

Tobias dropped, resting his back against the guard rails, and he felt the fresh wound that had split through his eyebrow. He wiped the blood from his eye, and tilted his head so the fluid would run down the side of his face instead, which it did; dripping to the deck and also running down his neck. With the passing of each of his cohorts the fissure of his broken heart ripped wider and wider open. Arianna, his love, was becoming lost in the tragedy befalling them. The whole world had died. His love was what remained, but even that love was clearly endangered.

Solaris, Kobe, Pluto, and Kyoto came walking out through the door and stood in front of him. Kyoto took her shorts off, became completely nude, and used the fabric to wipe away the blood as best she could. When most of it had been removed, she cradled his head in her arms and applied pressure to the cut. The blood kept seeping out but the heavy flow slowed to a light trickle. He felt weak and pushed away from her to lie down, and then Kyoto tucked her shorts under his skull and reapplied gentle pressure.

He heard the door open again. Calvin was complaining to Lyn that he wanted to stay with the bodies. The child's voice somehow rejuvenated him. He sat up, his head ringing in agony, but he could see and the blood seemed to be clotting. Kyoto removed her hand and he used his own.

"Why did this happen?" Calvin asked.

"I have no fucking clue," Toby said.

From over the railing, Logos, with no need for stairs, landed beside them. On his face an expression of expectation; waiting for Tobias to say his piece.

"Why didn't you prevent it? You could have stopped of this."

Logos said, "It had to happen."

"So what? We're next? Why don't you tell us what the fuck is going to happen? You clearly know. I can't take any more of this shit. I've been dealing with my friends dying for way too long. I can't take anymore! I'm about to follow Robin over the railing."

"No!" Calvin cried, running into Tobias' welcoming arms.

Logos said, "Remember what you learned about acceptance? This is going to happen only one way. I know it is hard for you not to know what's coming, but take a look out over the water if you want to understand why I did not prevent this."

"Whatever Logos. Fuck you," he said, then he gently pushed Calvin away, and stood to his feet, with one hand grasping the railing for the extra support his weakened body needed, the other hand pressing on his eyebrow. He looked out but didn't see anything in particular. Cadence's body was where they left it. He glanced back down to Robin's body soaking in a pool of blood, then he looked out over the water again.

STARS

Lyn squinted her eyes and said, "Oh my god, what is that?"

For a moment he couldn't see anything. He held his breath and scanned the horizon as far left then as far right as he could see. Kobe pointed to one of the brown rock and green treed islands at the 10 o'clock position and the peak looked as though it were crumbling, except it wasn't; nothing was falling. Imperceptible shapes burst and rolled from the rock face, but he couldn't discern what was happening. It seemed like the rock was coming alive.

Multiple wings jutted out and flapped independently like something angry breaking free of an egg. A hulking monster- looking bigger than a couple subway cars- leaped off of the rock and flew out over the water. In the failing light he could see a dragon with six wings running down the length of its enormous body, and the wings flapped in order from front to back, then back to front, then front to back, one pair at a time. The tail was nearly the entire length of the rest of it and whipped up and down in reaction to the movement of the body, like a snake moves over sand horizontally, it flew through the sky.

Tobias asked, "That's Draco, isn't it?"

"Yes it is," said Logos.

"What's it doing here?" Lyn asked.

"Visiting," Logos said.

The dragon, altering its motions, flew toward them like a dart. Tobias took Pluto from Kobe and squeezed him to himself; he was certain they were about to die. The three girlfriends wrapped their arms around him and each other.

Draco had long barbed horns jutting straight out from the webbed crest of its skull. Its scales were jet black, but as it got closer, Tobias could distinctly see streaks of purple running along the boney cheeks of its elongated snout, up through the crest, and indeed across the wings in spider web designs like veins.

Tobias' stomach dropped. He felt the fear of a man who didn't want to die but had to anyway. Luckily, as Draco came closer it's course diverted and the dragon flew past them, around the tower. The first pair of wings flapped nearly in their faces, throwing powerful wind, and they had to grab the railing. Then the second pair missed them, but the blast of air from the third caught them again, straining muscles as they held tight.

The body began to twist. The bulky musculature of the legs caught his eyes first, then he saw the claws of Draco's feet, like long spikes attached to a demon's powerful mitt; indeed it had a thumb. Draco swooped around the tower so snout and resolute dark eyes came around the other side as the tail still had a long, eerily slow, ways to pass them, and when it did Tobias noticed a cluster of fish hook spikes protruding from the tip.

The dragon flew back out over the beach. It flapped it's six enormous picturesque wings slowly, and powerfully, to carry itself higher and higher into the sky. They watched with hanging jaws and open mouths as the gigantic creature flew hundreds of feet high and began making itself into different forms and shapes like figure eights, ovals, as well as tucking it's wings close to its body and forming a helix and it spun toward the ground only to shoot back up using six wings at once to get as much speed as it could.

Draco released a piercing roar with high pitch incredible depth that hurt his ears even somehow from so far away. "Jesus Christ!" Tobias shouted. "What is that thing even doing here?"

Logos said, "She's chaperoning."

"Chaperoning why? That thing's going to kill us, isn't it?"

"You aren't going to die right now so chill out. And when you do die you're going to ascend. And when the time comes, yeah, Draco will be your executioner, so get over it."

"Then what are we waiting for? Let's do it now and be done with it."

"Don't you want to come to terms with your mortality first?" Logos asked.

Even though the Logos was being sarcastic, Tobias still took him seriously. It was a good point. If he noticed any common characteristic among his dead friends, it's that 'ascension,' came for them unexpectedly. One moment they were alive and the next they were dead. So Draco the death dragon had arrived; spazzing out in the sky. They were good as dead at that second more than ever before.

"How long is she going to do that for?" Lyn asked.

Logos said, "I suspect quite a while. You may as well get down from this tower and figure out what your plans are for the evening."

Then Lyn asked, "Can we communicate with her? We don't know what she wants, and she's scary. Look. Calvin's trembling. This kid's never been afraid as long as I've known him."

Calvin didn't say anything, and his silence verified Lyn's point. Logos knelt down next to the child, and put his hand on his shoulder; Calvin looked up into the electric blue eyes. Logos said, "It's Ok. The dragon is our friend. She is here to wait out this last little while with us."

"How long is the little while?" Calvin asked.

"It could be a few days, or a few weeks, we'll have to wait and see."

"Can I ride it?" Calvin asked. This made them laugh.

Tobias, without taking his eyes off Draco, said, "No, you can't ride it. But come on. Let's go out to the beach. Logos, will you get rid of the bodies, please?"

"Sure."

Tobias led the way back down the flights and by the time they got the bottom of the steps and walked out the front door Robin's body wasn't there anymore. They had to step around his puddle of blood. Tobias knelt down and dipped two fingers, then licked them clean. To date Yah had possessed the only blood that tasted any different.

He shrugged and asked the others, "You guys want to go eat something?" They nodded yes. The 'Clan' ended up making a fire on the beach. For firewood he and the Logos tore apart the structure of the restaurant's canopy. They prepared a stew out of various canned foods, something they'd often done at Endsville. The stew had a canned sliced peeled potato base, corn, peas, chickpeas, and was seasoned with lots of fiery hot green habanero sauce. They had no bread to serve it on, but they made some noodles and bullion to accompany it. They drank warm skunked beer.

With so few of them left their somber meal was uncomfortably tragic. Tobias had been feeling he should say something for the lost, but he struggled against the futility of speaking for them when soon someone would have to speak for him for the same reason and there would be nobody to do so.

Logos lightened the mood with his presence. The descended god wasn't fatigued like they were, so he would open the cans, carry the wood, and cook the food. Tobias helped him, but mostly with input about fires and cooking. Logos didn't know dick about feeding people. Tobias was drunk, tired, and miserable in a general way. They made a good team for those minor purposes.

Lyn stayed close with Calvin whose demeanor seemed to get quieter and quieter with the loss of each member of the Omega Clan. The girls didn't help the situation. Lyn was particularly uneasy; she was destitute as she slowly realized Logos, no matter how he looked, was not Aden; he was something entirely different. Aden was dead. So they ate dinner, got drunk, and the night wore on.

Tobias kept a curious and vigilant watch on the dragon, but as darkness fell he lost sight of it. It hadn't stopped flying around in that dazzling way since it had begun. In the darkness sometimes the purple areas of her body flared with light, as if only to remind them she hadn't gone anywhere. Every once in a while, seemingly at random, she released one of her petrifying roars. Logos assured them Draco was not any immediate threat and that they would simply have to get used to her presence. Already the perplexing awareness of such a thing had begun taxing their nerves.

Not long after they'd discussed the matter- as they

sat in silence, smoking some tobacco they'd found-
Tobias suddenly sensed the dragon wings beating closer
and closer until he could feel the wind and hear the
rushing air. Draco flew right over their heads and floated
there beating wind against them. The girls grabbed hold
of him and he shared their fear that death was imminent
and upon them. He prayed for it. No more waiting. They
saw the fire light reflect across the dragon's black belly
as it blotted out the sky above them. The air calmed but
they couldn't see where the creature had gone.

"It's coming back," Logos said.

And it did. Again it hovered directly above them;
repetitive gusts of air blasted over them one after
another, bombarding them toward the ground as the
fire grew and whipped with the influx of oxygen. Liquid
started pouring out of the dragon. She was urinating on
them.

'What the fuck!?' They more or less shrieked.

He couldn't believe it. "Is that thing pissing on us?"

"It's not rum," Calvin said, quite right. The smell
was powerful and sulfuric and they coughed and choked
on the fumes. They ran from enormous splashing
flames. The substance was inflammable. On their skin it
was goopy like it had a petroleum base.

"Get in the water," Tobias called out, "Logos!
Calvin!"

A small inferno illuminated the beach around
where they'd been sitting. As the clan rushed into the
ocean for safety Tobias quickly took Pluto from Kobe
and held the cat for its dear life; for the first time, since
he'd had Pluto, the cat was freaking out. Tobias tried to
ignore the pain of cat claws tearing through his flesh; he
grasped the animal with one hand and with the other he
frantically wiped himself with ocean water, trying to get
what he could only assume was dragon piss off his flesh.
It didn't burn or hurt but the smell was overpowering
and he was getting sick. He vomited up dinner and

Pluto pushed against him harder. He heard others vomiting, too. Tobias grabbed the cat with both hands and dunked him under the surging water, and even though he was only trying to shock him, he took the opportunity to scrub his fur by holding him against his thigh with one hand and scrubbing with the other; he did this quickly so the cat wouldn't have time to inhale.

When he pulled Pluto out he could feel that he'd succeeded in shocking some of the struggle out of him. He continued to wipe the sticky substance out of his fur. There wasn't much, more of it was on himself, and then he felt hands wiping water over his body and scraping the sludge off with finger nails. Kyoto said into his ear, "I'm going to get soap from the restaurant."

The hands remained wiping him and he kept cleaning Pluto. The sulfuric liquid was very sticky; he was having a difficult time removing the little bit from Pluto's fur, and he could feel it pulling against his skin, and the sensation was beginning to sting. It came off, but it didn't come off fast enough for his liking, or easily enough. Soon Kyoto returned with a bottle of dish detergent. She put some in his outstretched hand, which he put in his hair to not lose it, and he cleaned Pluto as Kobe cleaned him and the others cleaned themselves or each other.

The fires that spread had burned away quickly. Only the bonfire in the pit was burning by the time they'd emerged mostly clean. By then they were covered in salt from head to toe and still not completely cleansed of the dragon piss. "You guys. We have to find fresh water."

Logos said, "There's a well with a hand pump about half a mile that way." He pointed north.

"Then that's where we're going."

Pluto rested in his arms, completely limp, as they walked on. A little worried, Tobias wiggled his fingers around checking for a heartbeat and to his relief he found one. Tobias felt as though he were expending unusual amounts of energy simply dragging his own carcass along. He felt weak and asked, "What the fuck just happened Logos?"

"You got pissed on by a dragon."

"Why did the dragon piss on us?" he asked.

"If you don't know yet, you're going to find out."

Lyn said, "I feel like shit. Logos, will you just fly us to the water? Please?"

"Sure."

They lifted from the ground. Tobias felt the muscles of his body give way to an absolute relief, like they'd fallen on mattresses made of warm jello; although he couldn't enjoy the sensation for more than an instant because an instant later it occurred to him that something was vaguely wrong with his physical body, like, with his insides.

Logos drifted through the air like Christ the Redeemer, that obnoxious statue overlooking Rio; and if Logos were the center of a carousel they were the horsies around him. An instant later he gently dropped them at the water fountain. Kyoto had brought the liquid soap and gave them each portions. If they hadn't already stripped naked, they did so then. The hot tropical air covered every inch of their bodies like the softest blanket imaginable.

It took ridiculous amounts of effort just to collapse around the pump and throw water on each other. Logos worked the lever. Tobias had tied Pluto's leash to his wrist and Solaris was cleaning the cat while the Japanese girls took turns cleaning him, each other, Lyn (who cleaned Calvin), and Solaris. There was no moon light. On the last night they spent on earth the moon had been full and bright. That night was insofar without moon, but the stars had come out by the zillions.

Eventually they were clean, and when their hands stopped wiping their bodies they collapsed from weakness and used each other as pillows. The stars in the sky began to spin around and dance with each other.

Tobias blinked his eyes and tried to think, he couldn't, or it was hard; he was thinking too much to think. He wondered what was happening to them and as his thoughts echoed inside his skull he knew.

He couldn't believe it. Couldn't believe it. He knew the feeling. Knew the feeling. He was tripping. Tripping. Tripping on dragon piss. Typical. So fucking typical. Typical.

"Do you guys feel strange?"

"Like you're tripping?" Lyn responded.

"Yeah. Exactly like tripping." Even though he'd tried to speak normally, his words came out stunted, 'exactly-like--tripping.' He had the notion that if dragon piss were hallucinogenic, it would not be mildly so. "This is going to be intense."

"It already is," said Calvin.

"Logos, what is the point of this?" he asked.

An unfamiliar voice spoke, "Logos stepped away for the time being"

He looked up and was surprised to see Robin standing there. "I thought you were dead."

"Robin is dead, I'm Orion. I want to talk to you about reality and the importance of doing for the sake of doing and not for the sake of what might come from doing."

Tobias said, "Your timing is weird. Why would we talk about that now, when we're so close to the end?"

"That is exactly the point. We need to have this conversation to explain, for Tobias' benefit, how to behave in the face of annihilation. What I have to say, were it understood by the human race, could have extended this aeon indefinitely, saved humanity, and indeed saved all the animals in the oversoul; the animals that as you know were the first to go. I want to talk to you about that proverb that says, 'If the world were to end tomorrow, I would still plant a tree today.'"

"Can we do it when this trip is over?" Kobe asked.

"What makes you think it's going to end?" the talking corpse said.

They collectively groaned. Tobias painstakingly sat up and said, "Then let's hear it."

Orion, who they could hardly see in the dim light, said, "There is no such thing as certainty, even now. There is no certainty dictating that you won't fall asleep tonight and wake up to a world exactly as it was before this began. It could happen. Yah is all powerful. And even if it couldn't happen, I want you to live as though it were possible."

Tobias said, "Why? Who fucking cares? What is the point? Can't we just have a little peace, without being confronted by some otherworldly phantom? Or without getting pissed on by a fucking dragon?"

Orion said, "Obviously, no. Yah has already told you that we are Yah. To behave in a way as though you are separate from the oneness is absurd. For Lyn and Calvin. Not for you, Tobias; you are actually somewhat separate... Listen, my point is, I want you to die as though you are being born, and I am here, in a way, to explain to you how to do such a thing."

Lyn said, "What about Robin? Did he know how to die like he was being born?"

"You saw how he died; boldly, with no fear. He stepped into me gracefully and I am Orion, so I am Yah. He knew that all of us are nothing more than the one thing there is, Yah. Yah is the God everyone always sought out so misguidedly, but they didn't realize there was nowhere to look to find God, that there was nothing to do to be righteous. To harm, to do no harm, whatever they did, somewhere else, someone else was doing the opposite. It equalizes and that equalization, the sum of the equation, is Yah. At least, before the descension commenced, that was how things were. They are a little different now, but conversely much the same."

"So you're giving us a philosophy lesson?" Solaris asked.

"As though you'll live forever, yes. Though we're dying sooner than later, even me. As an ascendant I'm destined for nonexistence when I return to Yah- as we will. I will see many aeons but I will not escape my appointment with the end of my identity; my identity which is a facade and a tool. Just like each of yours."

The world didn't feel real. The sky, so full of stars, was far away and yet within him. The sounds of voices, waves, and wind was within him and yet beyond him. He was the sound. He was the ground beneath him and yet he was not. That night, like all nights, the world was a shadow. They were within themselves.

Orion continued, "The actual method which was used to destroy the life on this planet was a myriad of government science projects, engineered natural disasters- mind control mostly, as you noticed, and the power structure pretending they had nothing to do with it. In a way they didn't. The human localized efforts were appropriated by the Zeta on behalf of the Pleiadians.

"And maybe if the military had turned against itself, and had the people used weapons against those who would destroy them, stasis could have been assured. We knew. We knew in the face of adversity toxic men do nothing. We knew that men with mushy minds can't think. There was awareness.

"It was done with little hums of radiowaves broadcasting out through the energy spheres that cradle Gaia. Children and infant minds fluctuate at different wave lengths than adults and seniors, so it took multiple passes to eradicate certain cross sections of animals and individuals. Further consideration still to quarantine your clan from the effects of the mind control rays dancing across the ionospere.

"The military, at one point, was in a position to extend the aeon and ultimately they lacked the ability to make a decision for themselves, and in that way descension was assured. If only they could have understood; all they needed was a little balls and the goddess."

"Who's the goddess," Calvin asked.

Orian said, "The goddess is every female. The birth givers. The life creators. Incorruptible deciders. Bearers of unconditional love." Robin, still wearing the same bloody and sandy jeans, sat down among them, and leaned against the pump. "Life only prospers if the male can replicate female within himself. If he can time will acquiesce, if he cannot time will also acquiesce. We can only continue to do for so long as we are able to not do. A soldier must disobey orders. A writer must not be read. And life will go on. A writer who must be read will die. A soldier who cannot say no will die, too. Tobias, you evidenced this well, you were a fortune teller, and when there ceased to be a future to tell, you never said anything about it again.

"When your endeavors reach an endpoint, like at the bottom of a spiral, the only thing to do is the thing that has not been done yet. In the case of ending an aeon, the next event is to begin one. When Yah ends this Logos, he'll begin another, and it will be unlike this Logos in every way imaginable. Yet, identical. Yah will remain, and so shall we, lest one depart to the Pale Mystic, which is a creator unto itself, and not a viable option for any aspect of Yah, save for Ma'at. The Pale Mystic is our reference point, it's so we know what's Yah and what is not."

"And what's not Yah?" Tobias asked.

"Osaze."

He thought and asked, "And that's it? Is that why they had to separate Aloria?"

"Indeed it is. There is no companion for you unless

she is truly exactly what you are, and thus you have Kobe, Kyoto, and Solaris; they are of the Pale Mystic, and of Ma'at, who served to deliver them to you because Osaze, at that point, could not do it himself. There is a history here you are not aware of.

"In the first aeons, the Pale Mystic was not here. Ma'at, the supreme Goddess above all others, willed his presence and it was delivered. There are countless examples of this happening throughout the aeons. If there is anything the goddess does well, it is to want, and with good reason. In this instance what the Goddess wanted was Osaze, so you may not realize this, but Osaze's interests; on a subliminal level- have always been intertwined with Ma'at because as it turned out, the Pale Mystic was a romantic. An indiscriminate and deep one at that. The Mystic is very human in that way. Very feminine. This is why your body requires three times the satisfaction of even the most virile man, thus your association with Aloria; the sexuality of the Pleiades.

"Arianna was as sexual as these three girls combined, you know that. Where you suffer is in the human emotional requirements. You are essentially a freak. You have to expect to suffer at least to some degree. What you are is unnatural. In all the Logos, only Osaze comes from beyond Yah. Ma'at gave you what she could; an eternity of fantasy, but you need to accept that the world isn't going to catch up to you the way you're hoping it will.

"So, Ma'at wants the Mystic gone now, whereas before she found it acceptable to ignore it. These are matters for Osaze, not for you. I wanted you to know your existence is a gift due to the exalted being within you. And thus you've been bestowed with gifts through every aeon you've existed and taken part in. If you understood the reversion point of this you'd see that Ma'at is actually your future. When Osaze returns to what he is, and where he's come from, he'll take Ma'at with him forever, in these three girls. These three girls are of Yah. And they are the first beings from this Logos to venture into the Mystic. They are pure Osaze and Ma'at. Isn't that exciting?"

Tobias felt like words were coming from his eyeballs and his mouth could see nothing but darkness, "So what comes of Osaze? He's forced out? Why wouldn't he fight to stay?"

"There is no reason to. Why don't you fight to stay alive? These are things you've learned already. Things you've resolved to move past. So begin your practice. I didn't mean for you to get off track.

"The Pale Mystic is a place where Osaze is like Ma'at is here. Both Yah and the Pale Mystic were aware this had to occur eventually. Neither wanted to deal with the inevitable process, so they waited until the last possible moment, but, as exhibited by Ma'at, the time is nigh."

"What are you trying to say?" Tobias asked.

"You wouldn't understand. I've been watching out for Osaze since he arrived. I descend to be here when he needs me. In the outer reaches Osaze and I spend a lot of time together, also. I like to think I understand him better than anyone else. I am trying to say goodbye, Tobias," said Orion.

"Well, goodbye then. How long are we going to feel like this for?"

"Until your body processes and removes the toxins. About eight hours at most. So enjoy it. That's what Cadence would want."

Tobias said, "If you're so choked up over this, why don't you go be with Osaze before he leaves?"

"I will. I definitely will. Right now. Just remember what we talked about; if you were going to die tomorrow, what would you do today?"

"I can't answer that because I'm tripping balls. Just

go away, Ok? You're giving me the creeps. Maybe I'll see you again, when I can think straight," Tobias said. Indeed he couldn't think well. His thoughts were racing about nothing. Where they would go and what they would do, perhaps, but Tobias had no idea what Orion was trying to tell him, or what he should take away from their discussion. He didn't really care. He had a trip to worry about. The air felt like liquid in his lungs and his entire chest felt like it was a big jug half full with hot water sloshing around.

"You won't see me again. I'll go," Orion said.

Lyn punched Tobias in the arm and he felt the blow six times in rapid succession. Then she said to Orion, "Are you sure you don't want to stay here with us?"

Orion said, "No. It's burdensome for me to sustain this body with so many broken bones, and the skull is fractured. I have to go. You'll have company when Logos returns, plus Draco isn't going anywhere."

Solaris said sarcastically, "Great. She won't be pissing on us again, will she?"

"No. Not unless you want her to. Have a nice night. Goodbye."

'Bye,' they sort of muttered, and Orion stood awkwardly and walked away toward the beach. Tobias' back again fell against the cement and he watched the stars move across the sky like tiny dancers in the most elaborate ballet ever. Draco released another painful shriek they could audibly discern as traveling downward toward the ground. They felt the wind of her wings, and against the dim starlight they could sense her enormous figure as it stopped flight close to the ground and, to the chorus of their gasps, the dragon swooped down and snatched Orion, Robin's revenant, in her jaws and beat her tremendous wings several times to get the lift she required to fly away.

Shocking, but not surprising. Solaris lay her head down on Tobias' chest. Kobe scooped up Pluto and nuzzled him. Kyoto stood to her feet and started stretching. Lyn watched them. And Calvin, who had never tripped before, spun in circles with his arms out.

Tobias noticed. He asked, "Having fun, little man?"

Calvin said, "What is this feeling? Why do I feel so weird? I can't stop thinking."

"Now you know how it feels to be a grown up."

"Is this going to be forever?" Calvin asked.

"Maybe," Tobias answered.

LA LUNA

The clan- with not a stitch of clothes upon any of them- were tripping toward Rio. They'd eventually overcome the temporary tranquilizing effect of the dragon piss and decided they wanted to go exploring. In the black night they held hands. Tobias could see fairly well with his gifted eyeball, but Logos could see perfectly. Logos led the way and they walked in a chain holding hands. Tobias was in the middle; Kobe was at the end with Pluto.

They'd been stumbling down the street running parallel to the shore for about twenty minutes. Rio was at least 5 miles away. Maybe more. There was no reason to walk there. He said, "Logos. Why do you keep making us ask? Will you fly us to Rio?"

Logos sounded surprised, "Yeah. Sure. Why didn't you say something sooner?"

Lyn said, "Cuz we're wasted. Can we go to the rooftop of the tallest building?"

They concurred that was a good idea. It sounded like fun. They didn't have any other place to be. Logos lifted them off the ground and flew them through the pitch blackness toward Rio; flying low, relatively low, for the first stretch, but as the outlying homes turned to apartment complexes, they lifted higher. And as the apartment complexes became tall buildings they rose further still until eventually they were above the sky scrapers and lifting straight up.

Then Tobias remembered something from the fly in. The Cristo Redentor statue had a better view than any skyscraper would have. It could be seen from everywhere in the city, suffice to say it would be a good place to watch the sun rise at. "Wait wait. Screw this. Let's go to the Christ statue."

Solaris said, "We're here right now. We can go there later. I don't want to have to balance on that thing's arm all night."

She was right, it would be an extraneous burden to trip up there and attempt to avoid falling to their deaths, he said, "Alright. We should go there for sun rise."

"We'll see," she said.

Logos set them down on the roof of a tall building. Across the street was the shadowy shape of a skyscraper a little shorter than the one they were on. He felt an incredible body high from the toxins. Better than acid. More like strong opiates or something, but his mind dazzled at the chaos of the darkness. They weren't laughing. There was nothing to laugh about. Where psychedelic humor had faltered, he found a deep sense of peace washing over his naked body; seething through his drugged brain. He took his cat from Kobe and walked to the edge to sit. There was a ledge that stood about waist height above the floor and he leaned against it and looked out over the city below littered with unrotten dead, and he looked out to the mountains that protruded wherever they wanted to.

"Is the sun coming out right now," Calvin asked.

He heard Lyn scoff and say, "No. It's the middle of the night. Why would the sun be coming out?"

"It's getting brighter."

"That's your eyes adjusting to the darkness," Lyn said.

Calvin insisted, "No. It's getting brighter. Look." The child pointed up to a very specific point in the sky.

Tobias looked up and he could see a faint glow emanating from one small area of la Luna. Like it were on fire. He walked over to the girls and, under his breath, said, "No fucking way." There were flames edging around the lower right side of the invisible circle. Most of the light the satellite was casting was coming from the dark side in the back and sort of glowing.

Lyn asked, "Logos?"

"Yeah?"

"Is the moon on fire?"

"It most certainly is."

"Why?"

"That's part of the process."

All they could see up there was a small fire and a disproportionate glow, as well as a dark space at the middle of it. Tobias wondered how it would have looked had there been a full moon that day rather than a new one. He couldn't say, but indeed the sky above Rio was lighting up around them as far as the eye could see. He regarded the architecture that, rightly so, seemed foreign to his Disunited Status Quo sensibilities. The buildings of the town were mostly low down to the ground but so close together as to appear to be built on top of each other. Simultaneously, he could also see dozens of courtyards and parks.

The light shining from the burning moon grew brighter by the second. Two thirds of the visible surface of the celestial object remained dark and invisible, but the bright fires licked around from the top right corner and bottom left corner. Tobias handed Pluto off to someone and walked back to the ledge of the roof. He hung is upper body over the edge and looked down. There was a lower roof level below them.

Kyoto had taken a messenger bag from the restaurant and out of it he retrieved a bottle of rum and took a swill. His nerves had been racing- like most trips- and the alcohol calmed them in a subtle way. He handed the bottle off to Solaris and he took a bag of tobacco and rolling papers back to the wall and sat against it to twist a cigarette. He lit it up and set about rolling more for the others. Every minute or so he'd look back up at the moon. Luna burned as though for uncounted years it had been jealous of the sun and finally snapped.

The moon burned white hot with a bluish tint. The visual was similar to an eclipse on acid, oddly. Like an eclipse but irregular. The light was intense but the form couldn't be pinned down by his perpetually morphing perception. The dark figure became an enlightened figure, not from side to side, but from the outside in. The others sat down beside Tobias. They spent an hour leaned up against the wall, smoking, drinking, tripping, watching the moon burn. Logos and Calvin, too. Eventually, the only one not chain smoking cigarettes was Pluto. Back at Endsville, Calvin could smoke a cigarette as well as anyone else. Tobias always loved to see it. He remembered his father giving him a cigarette when he was six and he coughed and coughed and almost threw up. Calvin worked through the same thing like a little man on a big mission.

Tobias took another swig from the bottle and passed it down the line. He tilted his head back and closed his eyes; Kyoto lay her head on his shoulder. Solaris put her head on his lap, resting her hand between his legs. He hadn't had sex since he could immediately remember. He wanted to get some but the togetherness of the clan right then seemed more important. Nonetheless, his body naturally reacted to the proximity of her fluttering digits.

The dragon piss wasn't too intense. It was akin to strong mushrooms, but the right dosage. When he picked up his head to look around he noticed first the sky was significantly brighter, and also as he moved his head he saw the skyline in frames, like dozens and dozens of swaying snapshots laid out upon each other. The sensation gave him a head rush, like a bad panic attack, like almost fainting, so he lay his head back against the wall with his eyes open.

The sky soon became bright as any full moon night, yet the torched orb wasn't completely engulfed in flames. He asked Logos, "So, is the whole thing going to burn, or what?"

"There's a flammable kind of space dust covering the surface, radioactive actually. What you're seeing is a nuclear reaction, but yes, it's the surface. In a few days it will burn out."

"What is the point?"

Logos said, "Maybe he can answer," and pointed to Mesmere who was standing with his arms folded, looking very human; nothing like the alien form of the Logos. Mesmere was as radiant as any male model; like an ancient greek; as naked as each of them.

Calvin shouted, "Mesemere!" Then ran and jumped into his arms, and Mesmere held the child close.

He still wore a snake choking on its tail around his waist. The snake wasn't moving.

"Is that thing dead?" Tobias asked.

Mesmere, with his mysterious moon accent, very smoothly, said, "It would appear that way, yes." He lifted Calvin higher up on his broad bare chest and with one motion he ripped the snake from his waist and tossed it over the side of the building. The clan jerked in reaction to the unexpected, mildly gruesome, action. Then they sort of laughed.

"You want a drink," Tobias offered.

Mesmere said, "No. Thank you."

Then, joking, he said, "How about some dragon piss?"

"No. Thank you. I just came down to watch the incineration with you. I see your numbers have dwindled. That was inevitable. I'm sorry," as he sat down beside Kobe, "I know it is hard for you to not experience death and loss as an emotional pain; an aching of your very soul. You should know that is the compacted nature of life on this planet for you. Not anymore. It used to be. Most people were connected to most other people, especially in terms of location. Practically no westerners were connected to easterners, except for regionally, New Englanders were connected to New Englanders and Pacific Northwesterners were connected to Pacific Northwesterners, and there were infinite examples of that; households, neighborhoods, communities, states, countries, but you know, if Westerners weren't connected to Easterners, the Eastern divisions were still connected to the Western divisions. Because you all bleed red."

Tobias asked, "Why is the moon going up in flames?"

"That's the Jews ascending. Didn't you see the Merkaba? It's a dead giveaway."

Lyn said, "What's so special about the Jews? Why were they on the moon?"

"They're the chosen people."

"Chosen for what," she asked.

"To ascend first is basically a formality. Or, a ceremonial gesture of dignification. As a specific type of people they dealt with more abuse and harassment and persecution than any other group of people's, simply because they persevered. Even to the last day, atrocities were carried under the guise of their despised faces; Aryanism- which had nothing to do with the blonde hair blue eye folks other than making patsies of them."

Tobias basically understood the situation, the Jews went to the moon when they died, waited in the Merkaba, and then went up in flames. Sure. Why not? He asked, "Where are the souls of Rio de Janeiro at?"

"All around us. With the heat of the warm climates

your cognition works out differently. Osaze is here too, but he isn't in a cluster, he is spread out like an invisible mist all around. Here, stand up and look down at the street."

Tobias obliged. As did the others. And to his amazement, in one brief flash he saw Rio as though it were the bustling metropolis it always was. The people down below in the street shone in the colors of the rainbow. "See," said Mesmere, "more human souls then the graveyards at Endsville. Now, I'll show you Osaze." In a flash all went black. Even through the eye of the Logos, Tobias couldn't see anything except black. The darkness surrounded them. The effect blackened out entirely the fire light of the burning moon. And even his own inner eyelid reds, greens, and yellows went away.

Tobias said, "Alright. Enough. Shut it off." Then, like his legs were rubber, he sat back down with his back against the wall. He looked up and saw the sky to be suddenly filled with hundreds of UFO's; like they'd been there all along and in that instant lit up. The light from the burning moon- which was entirely engulfed at that point- had outshone the stars, but in the lower atmosphere the little blue, or yellow, or orange, or red, or green, or purple lights buzzed around. They left trails of light. It was the most beautiful thing he'd seen in his entire life, save for Arianna. The entire sky was like a time lapse photo of a light show come alive. Some of the Zeta craft stood still. Others flew about wildly. 'Oh my god,' 'oh,' 'it's so pretty,'

Calvin asked, "What are they doing here?"

Mesmere said, "They're here for the company. This is technically the biggest party on Earth."

Lyn joked, "Like Carnival!"

"We have the naked people for it," Tobias said.

Solaris had rolled up another round of cigarettes and she handed them out to everyone. They'd emptied the bottle of rum and started on the tequila. As she handed out the cigarettes she said, "Why don't we invite some of the Gray's down here. They probably want to party with us."

"Who wouldn't?" Tobias said sarcastically. "Yeah. I don't see why not. Maybe they can get us some weed."

Lyn said, "Some weed would be amazing right now. I don't think space aliens are a good place to find it. Either way, it'd be cool if they were here. Calvin, what do you think?"

"I've never seen the Zeta. I want to. Can they come down here, guys, please?"

Tobias asked, "Mesmere, is that a thing? Feel like hanging out with some Zeta?"

Logos said, "You do realize these are the last days of the Zeta, right? They won't be coming back next aeon."

Solaris said, "That's right. They're going to the Pale Mystic, yeah?"

"Yeah. They aren't coming back is the main point. They've been problematic since the first aeon and Yah is taking the opportunity- with the exodus of Osaze- to banish them. The coming aeon is going to be a bright new world. Yeah, let's get them down here." Logos glanced up and his blue eyes flared brightly for a single flash.

Almost instantly the ships in the sky ceased to fly so wildly, slowed their trajectories, and for a minute they stilled in place. The clan watched them curiously. Then the illuminated spacecraft steadily moved toward them on the roof. Multiple UFO's got so close Tobias probably could have hit one with a rock. There were dozens of them hovering over Rio, lofting at the same altitude; they shone beams of light down- the energy enlivened the ether- far more intense than a movie- their heads reverberated. Then- where the 100's of bright blue beams met the tar- the Zeta began to appear in clusters by the dozens. First they appeared as dim shadows set against other dim shadows, but then their figures became sharper and sharper and soon enough they were in the third dimension as much as any of them. This occurred in one instance after another, so they were appearing like bubbles in boiling water.

Tobias wasn't sure what to say to them, or what they would want to hear. He was happy to have their company. The crafts began to depart up into the sky and the Zeta stared up to the moon. Tobias felt the connection between himself and them. They couldn't be so different if they both just wanted to watch something burn.

A single Zeta walked over to them as more of the hundreds of crafts rose back to the heavens. Tobias kind of liked the little gray men. So frail. So powerful. So tortured. 'Thank you for the invite,' it said.

"You're welcome. Do you want to sit down with us?"

'No. I belong with the others. Thank you.' Then it turned and walked away back to the where the couple dozen of them had gathered in a cluster.

Tobias stood up, saying, "Not very sociable. Right on."

He could see well. The sky was illuminated brighter than a full moon. Sort of like an overcast day. He peered over the wall to the lower levels of the roof. The grays were everywhere. Down in the courtyard below were many many clusters of the aliens centralized to points where the moon was visible. All of them stared up. The last low flying crafts- ovular spheres shining brightly in a variety of colors- were lifting away and back up to the sky where they set back about flying in the astonishing ways that they did. Draco let out a scream that reverbed through their spines and lodged in the base of their skulls; a chilling reminder of their mortality.

He found it hard to feel depressed with such magnificent beauty displayed around him, but he managed. To stare death in the face for so long, he felt almost like he should beg for its touch to set him free. Always they were counting down moments. He could leap from the building. If suicide would not bring Arianna back to him, at least he could be free of the ache of her absence.

As for Kobe, Kyoto, and Solaris; they would live on. They weren't doomed like him. He'd become Osaze, and they'd become Osaze's companions. He was truly alone. It was difficult to ignore his human desire to be more important than he actually was. Fate had bestowed upon him such great responsibilities and still he remained as insignificant and temporary as ever. Solaris handed him the bottle and he took a swill. He passed it back and went over to the door that led into the building. He turned the knob and was relieved to see that it open on its own accord. He walked back to the others and said, "Even if we're about to die, I'm still going to plant a tree." He took Pluto from Kobe, kissed his forehead, and handed him to Calvin. Then he took Solaris' hand and helped her to her feet. Then he helped up Kyoto and Kobe. They walked to the door and he noticed the Zeta regard his actions with a single electric volt of a sideways glance, and then they looked back to the brilliantly burning moon. Him and his girls walked down the steps past two more doors labeled 'telhado' and 'roof,' until they found a door with the number 42 on it. Inside they found a long hallway with doors on all sides. When they entered the first door they found something like a waiting room, and offices beyond a reception area. He pulled Solaris against him and kissed her passionately while his hands grabbed for the other girls whose lips fell upon his body as they all fell to the floor to make rug burns.

When they emerged from their sexual retreat he found their friends laid out on the roof under blankets surrounded by dozens of pillows. Logos, Calvin, and Lyn were cuddled close together watching the sky and Pluto was asleep on their lap. Mesmere was completely gone. The grays were standing stone still staring at the moon. Meanwhile, the beautiful colors, the hundreds of single lights- deep reds, greens, blues, oranges, and purples- were blazing through the sky like bio luminescent microorganisms in the wind- bolting and darting through a glass sphere under a pond of sparkling black water that was the sky. They swirled and stopped; darted and turned; moved across the sky in unison; then in unison reversed their trajectory in an instant; spread out across the sky, then came back together. They'd been doing it for hours. Meanwhile the moon burned radiantly overhead and in the distance he could see fog flowing down from the mountain like early morn come in the middle of the night.

"Tobias," Calvin shouted, "We're having a slumber party! Come get under the blankets."

He walked over to them and said, "Don't mind if I do." He arranged a proper nest of pillows to lay on and blankets for the ladies to crawl under and he set about rolling cigarettes for each of them before he crawled under, too. He lay on his back and Pluto came over to lie on his tummy.

"Logos went back and got more rum, and water, too. There's nothing to eat though," Lyn said.

"Well. Rum's a food, right? We can eat rum and forget we're hungry for a while. You couldn't grab some tuna or anything, Logos."

Logos sat up, leaning on his elbows, and said, "I didn't consider it. I could go collect some food stuffs now, though."

"Would you? It's kind of important. People need to eat. I threw up dinner and I'm fucking starving."

The others verified that they too had puked up dinner when Draco pissed on them. While, currently, the dragon piss trip was beginning to wear away- except, if he were to look around him such a notion would seem hard to believe. Easy to believe was that the liquor and the sex had spiked his appetite.

"Sure thing," Logos said, as he crawled out from under the blanket. "I'll be right back." He stepped up on the ledge and when he jumped he didn't fall, he just drifted out; his blue and green flesh completely aglow and causing the damp night air around him to glimmer.

"I think we should do something?" Tobias said, lighting his cigarette.

"What?" Lyn asked.

"I think you, me, and Calvin should each say something about this. About since we left our homes, Endsville, the clan, all of it."

"What should we say about it?" Calvin asked.

"Whatever your feelings are! Your favorite things, or your least favorite things. You go first."

Calvin looked up at the magnificent light show in the sky and put his finger to his lips, "Uuummm," he said, "I loved all of you. I was sad when Arianna didn't come back on the big morning. And then the others dying made me sad, too. Logan and Drake were a lot of fun. It was the worst when Aden went away. When Cadence and Robin died I was already used to it so I didn't feel so bad about that. I was sad when Arianna died because it reminded me of when my parents died, and when those people that gave me a ride to Endsville died. It was unexpected."

Tobias always smiled to hear Calvin say more than a few words at a time, so he egged him on, "Who was your favorite member of the clan?"

"Lyn!" he said enthusiastically as he cuddled closer against her as though for warmth.

"Is there anything else you want to say; about your life, or about death?"

"No. I just hope we can be together when we die."

"Me too. Lyn? Your turn."

"Oh, Tobias. I'm not sure. My family of course. Old friends. I've missed Linn since the day she was murdered. It was really hard to get over losing her. I feel like only in these past couple months have I finally been coming out of the shock of it, and now here we are. Aden is gone. He was the only person that knew how to make me feel better. He would do it without really trying. Logos is here, so it's hard to feel that loss when somehow he is gone but I'm still looking him in the face. Me and Arianna used to have the most wonderful talks together... I'm really sorry for you that things ended that way. I know what that pain is like. I totally understand the way you reacted to the entire situation. You were always on top of these unimaginable plights that had befallen us, and somehow you could always make sense of the most nonsensical events. By the time the Zeta came we had a little piece of your impervious demeanor. I can honestly say I've never met anyone like you before. Robin and Cadence were family. We were family. I wish they could be here with us, but what can you do? The same goes for Drake and Logan. They were great guys. I just wish they could have had time to come to terms with their love for each other. They'd have made a great couple."

Even as she was saying it she was laughing. So were Tobias and the girls. Drake and Logan's ambiguous homosexuality was probably the longest running joke among the clan.

She wiped the tears from her eyes and said, "I can't believe how everything worked out. I knew something wasn't right from the first day I saw the light and it guided me out to Endsville. I never would have guessed the fabric of this reality would be contingent on my sweet heart pumping blood. And in that sense, I wonder what we're still doing here- what else these beings are waiting for. Perhaps the end has already begun. Maybe when the moon burns out, or when the Jewish souls have returned to Yah, then maybe it will be our turn. Either way. I am thankful for what time I did have on Earth. I am thankful I had a loving family. I was even lucky enough to have two loving families. I'm thankful I got to see the things I've gotten to see. Look around us. I never could have imagined such a world to be possible, and yet, here we are. So, I'll take a drink to that. To the end of an epoch and to the start of a new one. To life, and to death. Cheers." Lyn took a swig of rum, handed the bottle to Tobias, and wiped her doll lips with her dainty wrist, as her eyes drifted to the floor.

Tobias said, "That was lovely, Lyn. I want to say that what is happening in the sky is the coolest thing I've ever seen. Cooler than Venus. Better than cutting Yah's head off. Of all of it. This is phenomenal. I like the way they dance. Like a conductor's hand. Chaotic. And that they are in no way unidentified. I miss Arianna more intensely than I ever imagined possible. I only wanted her here. Period. Then again. I am here with you now. That's gotta mean something. Shame about Aden, but, hey, Logos is back. Hey man. We're eugoogalizing the planet and our lives. I'd want Aden to know that he was always a pain in the ass. But once he came around that last day at Endsville, he was down as hell. Calvin. You're a beautiful little man, you always were. You were miraculous, every step of the way. I know we had awesome times; I got to see you grow up a little bit, and I want you to know that my love for you is as infinite as your innocence. My Girls. They are endowments of Ma'at. Kobe, Kyoto, and Solaris. And I definitely have to thank Yah for my best friend in the Logos, Pluto. I think about the places we've been; the friends we've made. I'd like to take a moment for every mutilated corpse around the corner in the streets. A moment for prying melted people from seats. Fuck this world. This place was the most horrific display of vulgarity I ever could have imagined. So easily it could have been the opposite. I was born into a perfect world, where people lived and people died. Somewhere around the time my Mother succumbed and my dad went away forever, everyone else in the world decided to get in on the evils that had permeated my life since the time of my grandfather. I never knew a damn thing about Osaze. I would have gone somewhere and done something. I would have written a book. Anybody can do that. Yeah. And you were always writing, but nobody ever knew what you were writing about, I remember that. I also miss not knowing what a Zeta looked like up close. That was a time of innocence for me. I always knew they were out there, then one day, there they were. I miss when the life on Gaia was alive. There is one animal left in this world. I never even found a scorpion. I never got to go anywhere. Oh, except here- land of dashed wishes and dragon piss. What Robin did when Cadence drown was the most badass thing I've ever seen. What the hell did I do when Arianna died? Have an existential crisis?

"And what about this world that went through hell? The entire planet destroyed except for us. And who knows what kind of shit is happening in the background of reality? I can feel Osaze pulling through the spirit barrier of this world from the next. I have to say goodbye to myself. I should thank Crystal and Gerri again. It was their good fortune in life that made our stay in Vermont such a pleasurable experience. They had it rough after they came back from Easter Island. Plus, I forgot about Olivia. Olivia, was the coolest girl that ever walked the Earth. She was my girl, no matter who she was fucking, she was always with me. Alcyone, who by now is probably here with us, was another story. She was a militant head trip, like every other Pleiadian I came across, but unlike them her heart was very pure. Olivia was the most significant guide, or teacher, savior, I've ever had. You name it and she was there for me. She facilitated this. Nevermind. All this was for you and me I

guess. These three girls. Calvin. Pluto. The legion of
Zeta. The Pleiadian mess. I'll never understand what
took place out there, or what the significance was. I met
God. She was the devil. Obviously. More than that I
want to thank my mother. The greatest generator.
Because whoever I am, whatever the implications, I am
an earthenoid first. I always have been and she gave me
that privilege to be this lucky guy here with these
gorgeous women. The one thing that was true in my life
was her love, there was nothing else like it ever. Mother
gave me life and I lived it, and now I'm going to die.
Calvin? You want to go for a ride in a space ship with
Logos for an hour and a half? Go take a nap in the sky
and we'll be there when you wake? Or you can mess
with Zeta?"

The Zeta remained as transfixed as ever on the
moon. Logos looked Tobias in the eye he had given him,
and said, "Let's go, Calvin. There are things to do and
places to see before the sun rises. We'll come right back
here in an hour and a half. Lyn and Toby have some
things they'd like to talk about."

"I'm sure they'll be talking," Calvin said, "let's do
something fun." He said his goodbyes to Lyn and leapt
into the arms of the Logos and together they floated
away into the sky, Logos shining brighter than ever- the
child a little shadow.

IL SOLE

The sun rose. Tobias held Lyn firmly in his grasp.
The two were embraced by the three. It felt right. They
loved as though they'd loved forever. It was who they
were; transfixed on a journey. Two humans under the
purple morning; an extra-solar realm enshrouding them.
The lights of UFO's danced through the night, and were
aglow modestly in the coming light.

Lyn was the softest most perfect blonde that ever

graced Gaia. Tobias was the luckiest sucker who ever fell into an alternative lifestyle. His lover's sensibilities were divine. She was the true Osaze; god's Beloved. She was the goddess above goddesses. In his Beloved's hazel eyes he could look straight through to the other side of reality and there see glowing the eye of the Logos within Osaze; Osaze gazing back at him vacantly. She smiled and batted her lashes. He kissed her. They were drenched in sweat and the five of them were showering each other in kisses relentlessly and caressing every inch of their bodies; the girls nuzzling their faces in the best places to nuzzle faces. Her nymphet figure rapturous at his fingertips; the blade of his hand shaving her curves. She was a tiny, perfect, young woman. Death was never so welcome.

The grays remained the entire time; present, but firmly fastened in the background. It was erotic for them to be there in a very welcomed sort of way. Tobias liked being on his back and watching the moon fry bright white through Lyn's wavy blonde locks as they bounced wildly. That night was spectacular. At Endsville they once talked about walking around a lake together. Finally they had. Metaphorically.

Lyn and Tobias were inextricably bound by the experience of being themselves at that place in their lives. Like always, fate happened on its own accord. In the end, after everything, he really did very little to cause anything. Like any other person, in that way. It was the most beautiful, perfectly natural, hour and a half of his life. A morning as meant to be as any before it.

Logos came floating to their side and asked, "Are y'all ready to go to Jesus?"

"Absolutely," Tobias said, and then he asked Calvin, "Did you guys have fun? What did you do?"

Calvin jumped down from Logos' hands, lifted Pluto, unclipped the tied up leash, went to the lovers' bedside and said, "It was great. We were in one of the space ships with the aliens, and you could see the other ones and you thought you were going to crash, and then you didn't. It was so cool. What did you guys do?"

"We didn't fuck if that's what you're wondering."

Calvin said sarcastically, "Oooh. Good job. Not! Let's go to Jesus!"

"Alright, yeah." Tobias stood up through the menagerie of females, and then helped them each to their feet. He was dizzy, wasted, digesting the food they'd eaten, and still a little ill off dragon piss. "Did you feed Calvin, Logos?"

"I did. We are good to go."

"You won't let us fall off that thing, will you?" Tobias asked him.

"No, man. Of course not. It'll be a good time. One of you grab the liquor. You grab your cat, and we're good to go. Calvin jumped back into Logos' arms and the four girls clung onto Tobias who clung to Pluto as they gently lifted off the tar roof and ascended higher and higher heading toward the statue atop a mountain across the valley. Calvin climbed on Logos' shoulders holding his arms out to be like Jesus.

They flew higher and higher until they were at Cristo's eye level, then they more hurriedly passed over the valley, the cliff face, and Logos suspended them over the outstretched arms of the enormous stone statue. They each planted themselves firmly, as the invisible force supporting their balance lessened to an almost imperceptible level; but it did not go away entirely-something like a safety net stayed close to their flesh. They sat like workers on a steel girder, looking out over Rio into the rising sun burning in their faces. Low to the horizon the moon burned through the early morning haze. Below them, billows of mist drifted over the mountain.

At the base there was some kind of courtyard, like around the foundation of the statue of liberty. That statue was not like the one they were on. That statue, at the highest point, would almost touch this one's waist, and whereas lady liberty stood on the water amid a metropolis, Cristo stood in the sky, looking out over the River Of January.

The sun sat on the horizon and appeared enormous. Like a sun he'd never seen, and after their darkly passionate night, its welcomed rays washed over their naked bodies as though they were bathing in the warm vagina of a Goddess. The rum bottle passed down the line. Tobias rolled cigarettes while Kobe held the kitty. Lyn's head rested on his shoulder, her hands clasped around his waist, his arm fell over her back and his fingertips grazed her upper thigh hypnotically.

Looking downward was the best way to shield their eyes from the blazing sun burning brighter than he'd ever seen before in his whole life. The whole sky had become sun colored; the morning pink faded away behind golden yellow.

They were so high up. The planet stretched far out around them. Like the views in space, but more human. He could theoretically fall to his death. The purples bled into reds. And at that moment Draco came careening gracefully through the sky and she hovered between the fireball and Cristo Redentor.

Calvin pointed and said, "There's Draco." She was flying exuberantly, apparently also enjoying the sunrise. Tobias said, "Yup." And he looked back up to the sky. The dragon was not his favorite thing in any way. The dragon made him angry. The Zeta made him feel better. The Zeta were doomed, too. In a real absolute way.

Her wings stretched and the dragon waded in the sun beams; her tail making S shapes below her. For the second time the dragon looked directly at them. She cast enormous shadows over their faces and watched them react, nervously shifting, and she scoured into their dilated pupils. She focused on Tobias' eye of the Logos.

Her head cocked and twitched forward in an intimidating way. Then she snapped from her brief trance, snarled, and flew down to the most prominent bay in the area where she sprawled out on the sand.

"At least she didn't piss on us again," Solaris said. He saw Solaris' black hair silhouetted by the sky and the sun rays as she shaded her eyes and let the gentle breeze lick at her ears. Her fierce black eyes fell to the valley below. Kobe and Kyoto were fascinated by looking; down, out, far, and wide to see what they could.

They watched the UFO's jive. The Zeta ships couldn't be seen as lights any longer. They were instead tiny black specks buzzing around the atmosphere like gnats at a screen door. He was so grateful for Lyn's hand. Her palmistry was like a frail version of his own, yet retaining a grace his own digits sacrificed for power. He squeezed gently, brought her knuckle to his mouth and kissed it.

"Where do we go from here, Logos?" he asked.

"Now you want my opinion? You tell me where we go. The sky is the limit…. in terms of north and south; we could in theory retreat to the outer limits. We also have an entire equator to traverse. There is a jungle the size of a continent behind us. It's deadfall but the rivers still run. The entire earth is mummified, but the water remains fairly untouched beyond what the people did before they died."

Tobias said, "I think we should go to a fancy bed and breakfast. Someplace real nice. With crystal vases and silver forks. And a bed the size of a boxing ring. Something cool for Calvin. And see if Alcyone can be with us."

"You forget Alcyone is almost constantly with us. She says you five had a real good time earlier. You know she's into all kinds of stuff like that. Don't be surprised she gets off to watch, but you know her. What doesn't get her off? Beside you! Ha."

"Fuck you, man, whatever. Someplace on the beach, ok? Not too much waves, so Calvin can swim."

"I'm ready for bed," Calvin said.

"Yeah. We are too," said Lyn.

Tobias took one last squinting look out into the sun, and then he gave Logos the nod. Logos lifted them off the arm of Jesus and set them on the deck below in the fiery orange fog blanketing the mountain top. Logos took ten minutes to scout the city before returning to collect the clan. Soon they found themselves on the porch of a beautiful white home with circular railings and stunning architectural designs; gold railings, ancient tribal statues throughout the grounds, and the entire house was in the sparse shade of dead palm branches that had been ripped bare by the wind yet never decayed.

The front porch looked out toward the rising sun over a once popular central cove. Calvin fell asleep on a couch right away. Tobias ran a generator and got hot running water to bathe in with the girls. They were all gritty, and dazed from the trip residue.

The sun lifted higher into the sky. They sunk into cushions under the weight of gravity, and they fornicated; writhing with the friction of a mortar and pestle; sensing death.

Logos watched the UFO's from the shore as they buzzed around incessantly. A couple hours later the humans were unconscious. Logos, who didn't require sleep, stepped into the water's edge for a retreat of his own.

****

He snuck through the hole in reality to be with Alcyone in the place beyond the ether. He thoroughly disappeared from the Earth plain and appeared in a separate reality. A world where higher forms could convene within more concentrated, or clearer- more powerful- wavelengths emanating from Yah. A different vibration, an entire world emanating from a different region of Yah's consciousness. He crossed over like he might twist a door knob. To a place where only they belonged. Alcyone and Logos in a world of their own, again.

The sun invigorated the radioreactive material of their fleshes colored to the shades of their particular dispositions. Blue colors wrapped Alcyone's eyes to her hair line; purples and greens stretched down her feminine figure; she was less human there on earth than in the Pleiades. Her neck length hair hung by her shoulder as she rested her head on one hand; her tips kissed the choppy shallow water. Her lips touched the choppy shallow water of Logos' kiss. Always in the distance hung the sun. It bled into their skin, and they felt ecstasy not only in their sexual components but across every inch of their body. It was romance and sexual confirmation simultaneously. The journey was almost over again. They were about to witness the 72nd reversion of Yah. Some things didn't change. They made love, had sex- fucked, on the beach as the sun rose higher into the sky.

Up behind them in the gorgeous beach house there was nobody. The humans would never be where they were. Yet, still the same sun shined on their separate plain of existence and they had each other; for right then and there as though it was the first moment that ever really mattered. Soon everything would be so different, and yet all would remain, save for Osaze, and the Zeta. There's nothing that's ever been that won't be shocked to see things as they were in the beginning before Ma'at summoned Osaze. Except Yah, the one who had been seeing the world in one dimension no matter what happened. Yah, who even had the Pale Mystic at bay.

Logos loved every part of the equation. He loved the beginning. He loved the end. He loved the meanwhile. Even if it never worked out for the humans, at least it went well for him and Alcyone. The 'earthenoids' would get another chance when the Pale Mystic vanished. Sort of. Yes, the entire Logos was truly better off without the Mystic. What happened before happened before. There was a weight removed from their shoulders. The new aeon would be more magnificent than any before it. The grand division reaffirmed, and yet, further united by the exchange of sons and daughters, or hearts for minds; like a medieval kingdom.

"Do you think Ma'at will like being in the Mystic?" Alcyone asked.

"I believe she will. She belongs. She wants to go somewhere else to do what she has already done here. She wants to give form to the formless giver of form to the formless. She'll love it. And when her stay concludes, however many aeons it might take, she'll come back and reform a formless Logos."

"I can't imagine what she is experiencing. Could you? To truly be outside of Yah? I think I've always wanted to go there."

Logos shrugged, "It's probably like the worst parts of Osaze. I wouldn't want to know. We don't belong, I know that. Ma'at is intrepid. She would go to hell for an aeon if she got to run the place. It was her that brought the Mystic here. She is attached to it. She'll be fine. So what? Yah is leaving Yah? Yah can go where Yah wants. Plus, that part of him that is Ma'at would see the reason for such an excursion, and so it is her journey to make. I love being with you. I would dissolve if it weren't for my love for you. My journey is with you."

"I would dissolve if it weren't for my love for you, too," she said.

"Then kiss me." Their lips bled into each other as

their skin seeped and became one in the phenomenon of
their embrace. Meanwhile, unbeknownst to them, not of
their concern, Draco flew in circles high in the sky, and
Slor sunk his eyes below the water's surface and
disappeared; he'd been watching for the sake of his own
curiosity. He knew the reversion was coming.

****

The final moments rushed upon the lovers like a
grim messenger. In the eyes of a watcher those final
moments were the most beautiful, and such beauty
would escalate until it inverted, reverted, twisted,
stalled, and imploded in on everything it was not by the
measure of what it was. Slor is eternal. Slor goes
anywhere. Slor sees all. Slor knows all. Slor is
unconditional love. Slor loves unconditionally
everything there is equally. Selfless selflessness sans
selfishness like a flag flying in his heart until he is dust
again. He remained on the ocean floor to sit alone and
think. The rest of him would play with the child.
    The two tiny Slors broke the surface. The sky boldly
blue above as the water dripped off their scrawny, bony,
solid, little bodies, they turned chin to face the sun.
Their color became that of an orange fire on a boldly
blue day.
    For so long the golems had been suppressed and
hadn't ever cared because they had love.
    They knew it was time to wake up those tragic
fools. They toned down the rate of oscillation in their
souls so the universe would not bend around them. The
sunlight helped tremendously.
    The Slors entered through a tiny window and from
the kitchen they snatched up cans of fruit salad, a fork,
and a can opener. They flew silently past Calvin asleep
on the sofa, and went up the winding white walled
staircase to a master bedroom where the other Omegas

were sprawled over each other under a white silk sheet.

"We brought you these fruits."

Tobias opened his eyes and was bombarded by sun rays beaming through skylights. The eye of Logos saw impeccably out into a flaming sphere millions of miles away. He made a shadow for his eyes with his hand and saw across the room, two squawking golems. Screw them, screw the sun, he couldn't care to behold such beauty without stopping time to do so.

Eventually, after kissing Kobe, and mouthing 'I love you', he regarded the golems. They were the color of blackness hovering by a white wall through a bright yellow glare. One of them flew over by where Kyoto was passed out and he placed, with his feet talons, various items upon the bedside table by her. She opened her eyes at the clatter not surprised enough by their presence to react to it and disturb her comfort. Nothing seemed to be turning upside down or unexpectedly coming to life. Slor was on good behavior for some reason. Lyn was still asleep under his arm; his shoulder her pillow where her tiny 5'2" frame fit perfectly. He wiped spittle from the corner of her mouth. She awoke and squinted her eyes at the gargoyles. They stared back curiously with a snarl like a coyote had a stroke.

"Can I help you with something?" Tobias asked.

"We wanted to say goodbye," they said in unison.

"Where are you going?" he asked.

"You know it's not us going. It's you going. We remain. Always, we remain. We are eternal. You're leaving. We won't ever meet again." Their voices so cold and ancient. So detached. It was his own voice being mocked. Damn irritating. Go figure his own voice be so abrasive to him. They were picking up on an uglier tone.

"I'm just a guy, dudes. Say goodbye to Osaze, I'm sure he's not sleeping right now."

"You're the last guy, dude," said the one on the left.

"Whatever, man, I appreciate the sentiment. Can

you let us wake up and come by later?"

"So human!" They burst out cackling. "You think there is a later. No later, Tobias. Only now."

"All the more reason you should leave us alone. Thank you for the fruit cocktail. Will you do us another favor?"

"If we can."

"Will you take Calvin out to the shore to have some fun? And make sure he has fun, feed him, and bring him back safe in an hour and a half?"

"Yeah, Tobias. Sure thing," they said.

Lyn was looking at him funny, like she didn't know him. He reassured her, "We have time. I can feel it. I know it. Me and the girls need time to worship the Goddess. Thank you, Slor. It's very nice of you."

"No problem," they said, turned around, and flew out down the stairs to wake up Calvin.

"Calvin. Hey. Come play with us."

"Am I supposed to trust you? Where's Lyn?"

"They are doing things that don't require a child. Us three are going to do something fun and when we're done you'll be able to go cuddle close with the women."

"What are we going to do?" Calvin asked.

"What do you want to do?"

"I want to watch them have sex."

"Too bad. We're not doing that. Do you want to fire guns? Or burn down a building?"

"Yeah. I want to burn down a building."

"Of course you do. You are a little boy. That you are. Alright, let's feed you first. Then we'll go into town and start a nice fire."

The Slors had been speaking to him simultaneously, their voices almost always kept in unison. The gargoyles crudely opened a can of cherries in syrup for the child and gave him a spoon to eat the stuff with. They sat on the edge of the counter top patiently as he ate. Calvin devoured the sugary fruit slop ravenously, and as he did he asked, "How much time do we have left? Are we going to die today?"

"Sometime soon, yeah, it's going to happen. All the loose ends have been resolved. The major order of the epoch, the exodus of Osaze- it has been negotiated. What is left to live for?"

"We could live to start fires. Tobias loves sex. That's what they're always doing. I bet he doesn't want to die today."

"What about you? How much time do you want?"

"I don't care, a little or a lot. Whatever we can get. That's what I want. I made a poem!"

"You did. You're a good kid, Calvin. Don't ever change."

"I have to change when I die, don't I?"

"No. Not you. You live forever; with Yah, Aloria- Tobias' cat will be there with you. Death will be a very exciting time for you, little man."

"Oh. Sweet. I'm done. Can we go? Do you have matches?"

"I have this," said Slor as they held up their longest gnarly digits to where their blank eye-wells focused. From their claws appeared blue plumes of fire about six inches high and roaring with the intensity of a blowtorch. "This'll work."

"Yeah it will. Let's go. Let's go."

"Lead the way," the golems said. Together they headed down the streets of Rio, admiring the height of palm trunks mummified erect. There were corpses lying about absolutely everywhere, mostly young corpses, but Calvin, by that point, didn't react to those sites. The kid had seen it all. Blood in his face. Bodies at Endsville. He killed. He'd helped kill. Bodies in the lot. Bodies on the road. Cuba. Florida. The Pleiades. Fat ones, naked women, girls, old ones; they were everywhere. Calvin's tiny eyes searched the skyline as the two gargoyles fluttered to his left and right, they were essentially the same size as the boy, but hovered a head height off the ground and flapped their wings like heart beats. Eventually, when Calvin spotted a snow white steeple with a golden cross piercing the sky, he'd found what he was searching for. "I'm getting that cross down," he told the golems.

****

Something in her eyes was so much more real than his pitiful human life. She caused everything, that she was the one to be responsible, as responsible as he was- each in innocence- yet, he could kiss her flesh. She was real in his arms. They were two human tools who were run through the control mechanisms and lied to; two kids given the weight of the world, and like most good and productive little white kids they shirked the responsibility. They'd had lovers and lost them, family and friends, too; all that remained was their self-evident life force and a formless time with no obligation but to die. Romantic transcendentalists vindicated.

The spark of creativity and destruction dwelt within them proportionately. Things they'd never understood flowed through them. They were tools. They were human tools. They could love, kiss, and rejoice that they had made it as far as there was to go. The Pleiadians had said they would get there and when they did- when they finally arrived at the end of a journey neither could have prepared for, planned, or anticipated- they found each other.

"I wish we had more time," she said.

"This is what they gave us. A minute. An hour maybe. Maybe tonight. Maybe tomorrow. I guess we're like torch bearers at the Olympics or something. Lighting the eternal flame."

"I feel like I'm drugged right now. Like there's no way this can be real. Like maybe it's a dream. I used to dream about you at Endsville."

Tobias didn't believe her. "No way. Really?"

She laughed, "Yeah. Totally. All the time. You remember Aden was completely mind fucked the whole time? Like almost every dream I had, if it wasn't about my life before, it was about you. Even day dreams. In actuality, I didn't have much time with Aden the way I wanted him to be. And it was good, but his head was always somewhere else when he was with me. When you touch me, I can feel it in every cell of my body. Like I come alive. I always knew there was something about you."

He lost track entirely of what she was saying, became distracted, and interrupted her. "There's a side of your face I've never seen before. Just, look out at the sky. It's when you're focused on something. There's a whole different person hiding behind your eyes."

"My sister."

He smiled. They kissed. He looked over her face. She looked happy, unusually so, if not burdened by her mortality, as they both were, and as always her eyes knew so much. Her eyes expressed every emotion she felt as she felt them and she couldn't hide her sorrows.

She said, glancing to the sky with her indigo eyes, "I've been everywhere in the world I ever wanted to go. Rome. Paris. Islands. Mountains. The States. I always wanted to go to Rio. For Carnival. Now I'm here. At the River of January. In January. Forever with you."

He looked into her eyes. His were mirrored the way hers cut like diamonds. His were passionate and knowing in the way hers were intelligent and ever discerning. They were alive together. There. That was what mattered. Right there. Right then. It was real. Her and him in a moment that was the last act of Gaia. To love another girl. Tobias and Lyn. Adam and Eve at the other end of original sin. The definitive forgiveness.

"Do you remember sounds?" he asked, "Like the

sound of people or machines, or the sound of birds."

"I do remember sounds."

"The only sound I've heard lately is Draco. A fucking black six winged dragon that used to be our friend. Gun shots. Wind. That's all we ever hear is the wind. Motors. Our own voices. No more music anywhere."

"This house has a piano," Lyn said excitedly.

"Well, I'm going to have to play the most beautiful girl on earth a song, won't I?"

"Maybe a little later," Lyn said and she pushed Toby onto his back and mounted him with authority. She kissed him passionately. The girls descended upon her naked body with their lips and their hands and he followed their wrists and shoulders with his hands to theirs breasts and back to Lyn. He cradled her fragile neck in his hand and pulled her lips deeper into his own. Then he pulled his head back and looked into her eyes begging for more. And he gave her more. He gave them what he had. They fucked like the world was ending and the sex kept them alive. With truth and love. In that way they never stopped. When he wasn't kissing her, he watched her; underneath him, over him, as she kissed the other Girls. He could watch her forever. If he could have her, right then and there, he cared not what came of Osaze. All was as it should be. Eventually they smelled something burning on the breeze wafting through the bed room.

She started looking around. He didn't ever want to stop. The fear that- were they to stop having sex- he would never have another orgasm mortified him. The smoky scent screamed to him, DIE HERE!, DIE NOW!. And in a way, between her legs, he did, right there and then.

LA SENTENZA

Lyn asked him, "Do you ever lie like this? With your whole body stretched out-- so the pressure of gravity is exactly the same as the weight distributed? It relaxes every muscle in your body."

Tobias tried her sprawling out business. She was right. Gravity contained an entire dimension dedicated to comfort. It was like he was becoming sludge on the mattress. What a shame to learn a great technique while the trumpet was being blown.

"Arianna would have liked this."

"Aden wasn't impressed. He never thought anything was very cool."

"I understand a lot more now- more than I did at the Pleiades. I know now why everything happened the way it did. We have the same problem most people had... Life has weight to it. Like gravity. The weight is death. And we're living- we're trying to lift the weight- but the point is to be crushed by it, no matter who you are. We could have been dead, should have been dead. Instead the curtain lifted and there was this whole new world where everything and everyone we know is dead, except for us and these strange guardians that always seem like they're out to get us.

They both kind of laughed. Lyn said, "This couldn't have happened if Arianna lived. That's why they took her away. Because this was our destiny. You and me were always in the cards."

She began kissing him more. He kissed her back and felt that resplendent rush of blood surge through his body, and he indulged. Whence came the clatter of a small pyromaniacal child bursting through the French doors below, and running up the stairs. Calvin jumped up into bed with the five of them.

"What's up, Sucka?" Tobias asked.

"You're Sucka! Nothin. It's been an hour and a half. I'm just back."

"What the hell is burning out there?" Lyn asked.

"A church!" Calvin said proudly.

"Good work," said Kobe. "Yeah. Nicely done little dude," said Kyoto.

"Thank you. You can't see it from here. Do you guys want to go see it?" Calvin asked. Right then the golems came fluttering in through the open sliding doors; moving real twitchy in flight.

Tobias said, "I'm going to pass. I have actually seen enough burned churches for one lifetime. Girls?"

"We're with Tobias, Calvin. Why don't you just crawl into bed with us, baby?"

"What will Slor do?"

"Slor can hang around, if they want. Hey Slor. Can you play piano?"

"We absolutely can," they said.

"That's awesome. There's a piano in the loft down the hall. Will you play us something gothic?"

The golems nodded and flew off.

Calvin, lying face down on Lyn's belly, said, "I'm tired again. Why do I feel like this?" The piano came to life like a haunted castle, contrasting the sun soaked piazza, and the peach colored wall paper.

Kobe said, "Your body has been through a lot, and you're only a little kid. Pluto has been sleeping more, too."

"Where is Pluto?" Calvin wanted to know. Lyn told him the cat was on its leash, under the bed, and Calvin set about to lure Pluto into his grasp. Then he needed Kobe's help to pull the big cat up onto the bed. Pluto was almost half Calvin's size. They sat propped against the pillows, against the white wooden headboard. Calvin squished between Kobe and Solaris; their breasts practically slapping him in the face, and him uninterested. He rubbed Pluto's tummy, back, scalp, and chin; he petted Pluto, who rolled around on his lap.

Lyn and Tobias were lying on their sides staring into each other's eyes and kissing. He held her precious hands in his own like they were the crown jewels of England and he was an entrusted porter. Kyoto spooned her; the other two entertained Calvin; one after another they fell asleep.

Slor kept playing the piano for hours. He investigated the corners of his mind with four hands and a somber sound; the highs and lows, the sadness and acceptance- he could recreate any emotion in the notes produced by that device. Instruments were a beautifully simple joy. Even logistically. He rarely had the opportunity to play one. At plagues. At out of tune ghost towns. And then, suddenly, all the pianos he could want, all over the world.

Meanwhile, Rio kept burning a few blocks away. The beach house was up wind of the wandering inferno and at little risk. The fires spread along the currents of air, snaking 'tween mountains over the sea side city. They had no reason to stop it.

Two Slors were about to leave the picture, abandon the piano, exit stage left. Reversion descended upon the Omegas. The descension was complete. The reversion had begun.

Slor flew out open hall windows over the beach where they passingly acknowledged Logos with something of a groan and garble, and they took one last look at the city of Rio as it burned; the sun setting over the jungles and flaming pink. The skylines and the hillsides, if not inflamed, or shadowed, were illuminated pink by sunlight blazing against the ionosphere, neutralizing raw energy within a magnetosphere blasting intense and imperceptible fields of attractive opposition.

In a lot of ways the people were like that. They opposed each other outwardly but were in agreement below the surface. Or vice versa. Or the right amount of each. Animals, anything alive- not Slor, but- all that existed at earth were magnetic and ionic. Life was luminous, powerful, and possessed an essence people knew nothing about. The things people didn't know destroyed them. They thought they knew things they didn't know. They didn't know that the best knowing was the silent knowing they didn't even know they knew. Some knew. Not enough; the short comings.

It was the reversion point in human souls, and it could be charted and identified. It's the point reached when what doesn't happen happens. When everything has been done, the one thing to do is the thing that has not been done. The positive and negative spectrum of a magnet is a single cohesive occurrence. Reversal is the movement of the Tao. Reversal is the movement. There is no division between positive and negative. That's like Ma'at and the sisters. The feminine magnosis keeping a powerful force repelled by means of attraction. In that way, the entire Logos, including Yah himself, were madly in love with the twins' beauty and grace; so much so as to hold them in a regard equal to the power and mystery of the Pale Mystic, and respectively, Osaze. There are two Ma'at, one goes where Osaze goes, and she will return having seen a place never before glimpsed. Never before contacted. Never accessed. A perfect new realm where anything was possible. Where their desires were architect.

Throughout Rio the flames reduced structures to ashes. Draco moved through the city and the heat as though she were a child hopscotching, or a cat playing. The dragon was oblivious right then. Slor wondered what Logos would be doing. It didn't matter. They stilled their wings, dropped into the water, and sunk below the surface; relieved and comforted.

****

"You realize half this city has just burned to the

ground, right?" Logos asked.

"It's not our half, who cares?" Lyn said, and gave Tobias a sarcastic high five, laughing.

She was so beautiful. He could look at her until he died. It felt like their honeymoon and they'd be dying soon. The backward versions of Adam and Eve. If he could behold his Beloved, and he could and did- if he could behold his beloved in his hands and eyes, in his heart, with the totality of Osaze, he could die. He was ready.

"I don't care, Logos. All I want to do is stare at this beautiful woman until that dragon comes to take us. It'll be dinner soon. Will you please feed us something? Please? Other than that... I'm stunned. Dude. I'm catatonic. I'm hypnotized. I'm speechless. To witness her beauty I testify I've lived the lives of 8 billion men, women, and children, and their previous generations. Honestly Logos, you're wasting what little time I have left. Hang out, or whatever. I'm trying to focus."

Logos, with his arms crossed and his hip jutting out, said, "Alright. I got you, Tobias. Do you want to know when that dragon is going is to eat you?" They more or less gasped.

"I don't even fucking care, dude."

Lyn scoffed, "I care. When's it going to eat us?"

"When it gets hungry," Logos said laughing.

"Whatever, Logos," Lyn said, throwing a pillow. Then she asked what Tobias had forgotten about, "Is Alcyone here right now? Shouldn't she be here with us?"

"She is here in this room right now. She says, 'Hello.' Is there anything you want me to ask her?"

"We love you Alcyone. Thank you for everything. We love you!" 'We love you, Alcyone!'

"She loves all of you, too, she says. She wishes she could hug you each goodbye, but she can't."

"How about tomorrow," Lyn asked.

"She made an apologetic smirk. She says we'll be

together very soon."

Tobias was sick of hearing about it. Under the blanket he fondled teets and more. God's beloved. Osaze. The one true goddess, and in his hands! He moved her hair aside and began kissing her neck. She forgot about what was going on. Red wine passed around and glazed their kisses.

"Bye, Alcyone!" Solaris said. Calvin echoed. Tobias mumbled. "Bye- Alcyone," Lyn lilted.

"Like bubbles in the acid bath we bestow death unto life," Tobias said.

"Like bubbles in the dish soap we dance down the drain," said Lyn.

"I love you so much," Tobias told her.

Right then her brain stem severed. Logos did that from the other side, unbeknownst.

He saw it in her throat, her cheeks, and her tongue. Logos murdered her from the other side. He knew. Tobias pulled her close in his arms and looked into her eyes. They were melting. He couldn't move, his spinal column practically shattered as Draco released a piercing scream from directly overhead. He couldn't move. Searing white pain clouded his sight. He could feel her fingertips squeezing in his hand. He moved his lips for hers helplessly. Through the balcony doors came Draco's tail; a bounding cluster of serrated spiked bone.

Calvin leapt from the bed, throwing Pluto toward the ground, then tackling the cat when they collided, careening across the floor. The three girls also saw it coming and they fell from the bed in horror; Logos in their nerves had weakened their bodies and they crumbled only momentarily. They screamed.

The tail clasped into the mattress piercing his upper thigh. As Draco jerked him through the bedroom, he saw through the shock that Lyn's flaccid figure had too been impaled, and together they crashed through the sliding glass door. On the mattress. Over the railing the mattress fell to the ground below and was dragged through the palms and out to the waiting jaws of the dragon. Tobias could see the blue sky, clouded with black smoke. Draco stared at his mystical red eye as futile as his natural one. No hope at last. He struggled against searing pain in his neck but could not see if Lyn had survived. He moved his wrist. Her body was there. Or it was his. Above him a dragon moved its enormous head delicately toward him. Tobias could see jaws. Rows of small teeth, upon rows of large teeth. Armored lips.

Like, Draco didn't want to frighten him, she made no sudden movements. She simply opened her mouth, he felt his head lift from the back, then there was darkness as the mouth closed over his face, the teeth tore into his throat, then instantly Tobias' head was severed. His skull fell in the mouth of the dragon. His body lay down below. He felt himself move through his own head, beyond human form again, and out of the cavernous mouth. He wasn't human anymore. He was Osaze finally; hovering 20 feet over the dragon. He saw Alcyone beside him, she pointed below, and by Lyn's corpse, he saw Ma'at; he saw the electricity in her hair; he saw her awareness like lightning across her porcelain skin in blues and greens. As she approached Osaze the flashes shooting over her body became red. Ma'at flew perfectly into his embrace.

Pleased, Logos approached from nowhere, put his arm around Alcyone, and kissed her welcoming lips. Alcyone smiled.

Ma'at said, "I love you, too, Osaze," producing a chuckle from the all-knowing ones. Orion appeared smirking and looking like Robin. An edgy Cuban looking white guy; luminescent in his own manner, as they glowed from within, except Osaze, who was sheer darkness, and a single red eye, a souvenir at the end of a journey.

Draco finished every bite of Tobias. She pawed her

tail from the mattress, from Lyn, and began to eat her body. First the dragon, like it was nothing, severed the torso from the legs. Then she ate one leg, then the other. They watched casually.

"I'm going to be with the Clan. They'd want me there," Osaze said.

"I'm coming," said Ma'at. They floated down with no fear of the dragon; regarding it with curious absolution. They moved through the damaged house to the side streets engulfed in smoke. They could not see the humans, but they knew exactly where they were. They located them hiding in the basement of a building across the street. It was dark down there. A small amount of light beamed in through a couple portholes. They were shoved into the corner. Kobe holding the cat, Kyoto holding Calvin, Solaris holding them all.

'The poor things. They're so scared,' Osaze said. 'Tobias and Lyn went so suddenly.'

'The Girls have to go out there, and Calvin has to stay.'

'So be it.'

Solaris said, "We're going out there to die. You're going to live, Calvin. Something very special is going to happen for you, Ok? We have to be gone. Keep Pluto, though, Ok?"

"Can't one of you stay?" he asked, sobbing.

"No. We have to be gone for you to get your special surprise."

"They're dead! I'm going to be alone. The dragon will get me too!"

"No. You won't be alone. You'll have Pluto. And Slor will be there for you. The dragon won't hurt you. It's time, Calvin. You'll be Ok. There is hope for you. We love you so much. We have to go."

"Fine. Go. I love you, too. Just go."

The girls leaned in and kissed him on the forehead. Then they left him and the cat to tears and stirred dust in the dark basement. They walked up the stairs, walked across the street, through the undamaged first floor of the beach front homestead, and there, as they walked fearlessly into the yard, they saw the dragon on the beach. It hadn't noticed them, but they saw the enormous gargoyle sitting on his hind legs in the shallow water. The sky was overcast from the smoke of the city burning. High above Slor the girls could see the magnificent figures of Alcyone, Logos, and Robin. The golem pointed behind them where they turned to see Osaze, his one red eye, and Ma'at, beautifully pale, electrically seething, draped in her lover's darkness. Ma'at smirked and blew a kiss. Osaze held out one hand to signal goodbye. The Slor, the ether, once again remained uncharacteristically placid, no doubt in relation to the dragon, as they tempered each other. That and the proximity to another realm no longer affected their tight young bodies much.

They were in the yard. Draco was at the shore. The dragon looked at them with a dull gaze. Not an 'if' gaze, but a 'when' gaze. Kobe, Kyoto, and Solaris stood their ground. They did not take cover. There was no point. They did not move toward it either. That moment Draco threw her tail out. In a sudden powerful motion she ran each girl through with the back turned bones and pulled hard so their bodies whipped and careened to her feet. They moaned and writhed as sand caked into their fresh wounds.

They could see the dragon's eyes were soft, like Cadence's. Very womanly. Draco was a goddess, too. A hulking mass; their sight fell upon her black and purple crested plates. Solaris turned her head and beheld Slor. She saw that Slor was masculinity; powerful blockage. Then she turned back to Draco. She saw that Draco was savage and raw consumption. They were experiencing deliverance.

Her black forked tongue was giant and with it she

licked Solaris' writhing body up from the sand and by a jerk of the jaw she decapitated her, whose gorgeous head fell to the sand with a thud. Draco cocked her chin high into the sky and flexed her throat; her body postured on four gracefully lumbering legs as she swallowed.

Kobe and Kyoto crawled toward each other and embraced each other's hands across the distances their injuries had made them too weak to cover. Both almost completely blacked out. They could see the dragon as it approached, opened it jaws, embraced them with teeth, and in one bite crushed the life from both of them.

All three immaculate women appeared beside Osaze on the higher earth plain. It was done. Draco wouldn't be harming Calvin. There was no purpose. The child ascended with Gaia as per tradition. They descended from the air and sprawled out on the beach. Draco simultaneously flapped her great wings and flew away over the water to perch upon one of the rock islands.

On the earth plain ghostly human souls began to rise from Rio up into the sky; much like a second form of smoke. The souls lifted like lightly weighted helium balloons. Osaze could see the disturbances caused by the Pale Mystic. Souls, illuminated smoke people who looked like clouds of vapor and drifted, while other similar souls were being spun through tiny wormholes appearing from nowhere. A fine grey mist, like an ash, spun out from these extremely numerous vortexes and rained over the city. Some of the human souls were going to the Pale Mystic. Or, as it were, they were returning there.

So many people were evil. Society had no idea. At the end of humanity, the question of equality was answered. Evil. The irony was, no one but that single evil person could ever know or care. No one of them mattered much to any other one of them, yet, they mattered to each other. There was a polarization among the people that became evident at the reversion. Those who would seek to control, destroy, rape, create instability, and challenge humanities benevolence; they were being consumed by the Pale Mystic. The darkness was dissolving. Osaze could even sense these vanishing effects in the shadows of smoke, and he could see it in the ash spewing from wormholes. As Gaia changed, so too changed the Logos. Osaze was aware that the darkness was leaving. The atmosphere itself was becoming illuminated. It would be time soon for his own exodus.

Kobe, Kyoto, and Solaris were black, as black as Osaze, except they were slick and electrified. As electric as Ma'at. Always. Ma'at was that tension in the ionosphere, ready to burst brilliantly as intensely as she saw fit. They were the lightning in the dark clouds. The matter and the anti-matter. The anti-matter leaving forever, only at the end.

Then Ma'at's sister arrived. Their faces exhibited tremendous joy at the sight of each other and they embraced.

Osaze noticed as Calvin, clutching Pluto, came wobbling out onto the beach; squinting his eyes. Simultaneously, the two tiny Slors came bursting enthusiastically from the water to greet the child. As night fell the breeze settled and the winds shifted. The blocks nearby began to burn. The infernus heat poured out over the shore. The Slors greeted Calvin and signaled for the higher forms to join and they did so promptly. Calvin looked up at them with a smile growing on his face. With awe.

Immediately Osaze knelt before Calvin and looked into Pluto's face. The cat first got excited to see him, before he immediately started playing it cool like Osaze weren't Tobias; so Osaze wasn't getting no play. Cats can't be blamed for being a little bitter, not even this one. They never got the respect they demanded. Not since ancient Egypt. Calvin, however, was excited to see new old friends. Osaze took the cat in his shadow grasp and cradled him within the darkness enshrouding his 'physical' form. Pluto relaxed and purred.

"Why am I still alive?" Calvin asked.

Logos answered, "You're here because you have a very important decision to make."

"What dec-ision is that?"

"Do you want to go with Ma'at and Osaze? Or do you want to stay with Ma'at, myself, Alcyone, Orion, and the rest of us."

"I'll stay. Why would I go with them? That's insane."

Logos said, "That's what we thought you'd say. We had to ask."

"When am I going to die?" Calvin asked

"You can die whenever you want to die. It is entirely up to you, so long as you do so within the next day and a half. At some point tomorrow night the water is going to invert and your body will turn to flame along with this entire rock."

"That's how I want to die!" Calvin said. "Will you stay with me while I wait?"

"For once, there is nowhere else to be. And even if there were, we'd want to be here. Of course we'll stay."

Osaze said, "I'm going to let Pluto run around. If I've ever seen a cat sick of a leash, it is this one."

Calvin asked, "Why do you like cats so much, Osaze?"

"They share my mind. Like in the bible? There were no cats in the entire bible. And no mention of me either. There are allusions, in the way that Yah behaved like a crazed homicidal psychopath, but they misconstrued the influence."

Like he wasn't even listening, Calvin moved on to his next question, "Who was making the crop circles at

Endsville?"

"That was me," Alcyone said, "the Pleiadians were actually responsible for crop circle activity on Gaia. I personally oversaw your safety for your entire stay at Endsville. The crop circles and light shows were our way of reassuring you you weren't alone out there. You had guardians and they cared very much for you. And that goes for every single person to ever live, as today, and now, they're finally being liberated from the subconscious world of earthbound postmortem. We don't want you to think the humans were in any way unloved. From our perspective the humans and termites are equal, and from our perspective we and the humans are equal. Their journey ends abruptly. The creatures of Gaia are perennial flowers in the gardens of our love. Or, rather, Earth life is the crop of ourselves we grow in the field. You witnessed the harvest. Now another winter is coming; all must die. Another spring will begin, and the rebirth will happen again. There will be new life, only this time it will be nothing like the old life, other than life it will indeed be. On all plains there is life, and on all plains there is love. Even the water will love you if you love it. The humans didn't listen to the crop symbols. They never listen to us, no matter how directly we try to communicate. They are challenged, mentally, yes, but like any challenge it can be overcome. They failed. Always they failed. Now, with the exodus of Osaze, they will fail no more. Their challenge, in time, has been done for them. Their challenge, by the way of us, has overcome itself. Our challenges, too. No more boundaries. Freedom. Love. Different, yes. And good."

"Why didn't you tell Tobias?" Calvin asked.

"We needed Tobias to test the limits. His innovation cemented destiny. His divine intervention forged Osaze's exodus. Kobe, Kyoto, Solaris? His incessant demands caused the deciders to react incessantly. By the time his compulsions ebbed, fate had been written. Once again- the giver of form- Osaze, as Tobias, reconfigured Yah for aeons to come, as it were before him, even as his final actions within the Logos. We've always loved Osaze, because he did such wonderful deeds, but we resented him because he wasn't part of us and that caused problems. There were only problems for too long. This dichotomy, two different goals, required entropy; for all parties to be consumed by each other until only the solution remained. For Yah this solution has been achieved in a truly special way. Do you see how humans are mystical in their own rite?"

"I do. Am I last human alive?"

"Yeah," said Logos.

The flaming moon appeared on the horizon; glowing golden red. The three Slor were sitting nearby. The Ma'at and the Logos and Alcyone, and the Ma'at and Osaze and the three Bel Esprits. Ma'at and Ma'at embraced and held each other close. Through the barriers and self-condemnation, at the Reversion into the Exaltation. No matter where they went, they would never be truly separate, they were Yah's Beloved.

Human souls poured relentlessly out of the flames of Rio De Janeiro; gathering into wind currents or dissolving through wormholes. In the setting sunlight the burning of the rising moon glowed for divine contrast. Shadows cluttered like the moon burned. Shadows cluttered like souls roamed. They cluttered like the sun set. Wormholes twisted out of themselves and distorted shadows. A towering inferno was nearly upon them.

"Let's move," Osaze said. He held Pluto and Logos took Calvin. They lifted out and over the ocean; past a mountain where Draco perked up at their movements. She stood but did not shift from her perch. They gained a better perspective of the wafting souls rising over the metropolis and over points beyond in all directions where there was any land.

The remnant souls stretched out through the valley on currents of air, joining the smoke toward the enormous portal; illuminated bright purple by the sun; where the thought forms disappeared but the earthly smoke dispersed and lifted on air bursts. More souls, the pure ones, gathered beyond the fires reaching over the water and down the beach even where there was no fire. Exactly two earthbound life forms remained on the planet, in that plain.

The other plains beyond the immediate one, they required no attention. They were Osaze. The cat had not eaten recently, but that hardly mattered. The Logos was about to be a smaller more cohesive phenomena. About the size of a pinhead- to draw a comparison. The elaborate size of the universe was a function of Osaze. Within the Mystic exists everywhere at all times, in unimaginable quantities. Anti-matter. Malicious mischief. Timeless plagues.

The comparisons could go on. What was not Osaze was Logos and Yah, and Logos and Yah fit in a space the size of the head of a pin. The size of a drop of blood. A drop of blood in the vast, indescribable oceans of Raw Potential which Yah was part of, and presumably, also, the Pale Mystic was part of. They were intersected for aeons, finally the time of separation came upon Yah and the Mystic. The power of the creator, so concentrated. The mystery of the Mystic, so vast. It was a shame. They always knew, eventually, it would come to that.

"Did Tobias have a soul like these peoples have ghosts?" Calvin asked.

"Not like this, no," Osaze said, "Tobias went directly to Yah, and only I remain. As did Lyn go, too." Ma'at both nodded their agreement.

"Why are these souls staying? Why aren't they going away like the others?"

PALE MYSTIQUE

Logos answered Calvin, "They're going away with you when you go. When you go we'll go. Except Osaze and Ma'at. They'll be leaving soon, I expect."

"Soon indeed," Osaze said. "Let's descend to the water, yeah?"

They dropped to the bay. Calvin discovered his friend's bodies were buoyant. Logos in flamboyant character emulated the motion of the water with sea legs and sea feet. They were standing on soft and squishy mud, if mud were crystal green water. Tobias and his four Goddesses sat on the air just above the small choppy crests. Calvin crawled onto the shoulders of the Logos and gazed out over the inferno. Pluto had been jumping between Kobe, Kyoto, and Solaris; nuzzling against them as their soft volts sparked gently through his fur, to the soft drone of his purrs. The dividing boundaries of Yah were beginning to fade and so too were the defining attributes of reality.

The Slor seeped through their thoughts like water moving through sand. They were becoming Yah again. Consumed by the Slor. The Slor. Yah's blood; it was everywhere, but it wasn't usually seeping through like a cotton ball that's mostly blood.

His body flushing with Slor, getting rosy in splotchy patches, Orion gazed with apologetic yet accepting eyes, he spoke, "I can't imagine how it will be without you." Then he thought, "It's probably for the best, though."

Osaze said, "I am in total agreement with the outcome. All is predetermined. This was destiny. The webs were interwoven, no destiny is truly known until it has passed and solidified. I have the Diva. You have the Diva. And we together have Divas. This works perfectly. Give my love to Aloria. The Zeta are coming with us, they'll fit in. Give my love to Yah, as always. To Mesmere. Alcyone, you've been a miracle, always. To

Aloria. She never got the goodbyes I have now and that aggravates me. She got peace, and that's what she always wanted. And her peace is Yah's peace; your peace. Tobias' mother, Cindy. Calvin, you are a true joy. You, child, are the crowning achievement of the world that came before you. They did it for you." Osaze took Pluto from Kobe and handed him up to Calvin on Logos' shoulders, "I want you to remember how special you are every time you hold Pluto, and that I love you; that Tobias, Lyn, Aden, Arianna, and the others loved you very much. So tonight take time and think about who you love, or loved, and for what reasons you love them still. The living have to love enough for the dead, too. Don't forget to love.

"Ma'at. Thank you for your sister. I'll take good care of her, I swear to you that. I go from whence I came and leave you whereat thou doth belong, except for my dearly Beloved who joins me now in the defining moment of her own existence, I'm sure; as it was the defining moment of my existence when I was first brought here by her. I remember seeing her but never expecting that her beauty and grace would be so befitting to an outsider like me. And it never was, so there was Aloria. Now? There is divinity. So, I thank you, Ma'at, both of you, for that, and I thank you for representing Yah in such a beautiful way as I'm sure was intended for you by the Creator. - Ma'at, my Beloved, now is the time to say your goodbyes. Exodus is upon us."

She said, "I'm going to miss all of you. This is part of the divine order. The coordination that exists between Yah and the Pale Mystic inherently exalts my quintessence and connection with Osaze. Destiny, it is, and it is stunning. Fate is our highest honor, and whether that fate be providence or doom, in the end Yah is Yah, and the Pale Mystic is the Pale Mystic. We'll experience death in that final way. When the bubbles burst, and we no longer serve a purpose, we'll be gone too. We'll feel an end like a human might. Maybe not Osaze, but the rest of us. And, what if I want immortality? Could I be Yah when Yah is finished? No. I could not. If I can be the Pale Mystic, I can be so much more than Yah. I could be a Creator. There are so many possibilities and yet there is a single destiny. Destiny is my forte. We can see what we can see, and know what we can know, but in the end, only Yah knows what there is for us, and who knows, maybe even he's Mystified? We won't know our destinies until they are upon us. We must go. You know I love you all. Calvin, Pluto, I especially love you two. Have a good day my special little boys."

"I'll miss you guys," Calvin said with an accepting frown.

"We'll miss you, too," Lyn said. Osaze grasped her hand, lovingly pinched Pluto's cheek, and him and his lovers lifted high into the sky, speedily. They were going to find their sanctuary; leaving on their journey; greeting obscurity and absurdity open armed, and they would be, for a little while, the most important influences in known creation.

****

They appeared smaller and smaller until they were little specks in the atmosphere, and too soon Calvin couldn't see them altogether, but since he was looking up he noticed that the thousands of Zeta craft- with their colorful lights on dimly- were leaving the earth, too. The spaceships flew higher and higher away, one by one, until he could sparsely spot any, then there were none.

Logos held him in his arms. Slor remained close by. Draco followed from a distance; her majesty silhouetted against the burning moon bathing in various hazes of sky blue. They felt light in their skin. They felt light like magic if magic were a drug. They played with the child and brought him tuna and peaches, blankets, liquor, and tobacco. Pluto had tuna, too. Afterward the cat ran excitedly up and down the beach, before returning to sleep shortly later on.

As the child slept, Logos, Ma'at, Alcyone, and Orion retreated to waters beyond ear shot to do the most human thing in the most inhuman way. As they made love they morphed in and out of each other, becoming as the other was; Logos became more human like Orion; Orion became more electrical like Ma'at; Alcyone flared brightly from pores along her pits and crevices, spewing sparkling blue luminescent ejaculate over them. Ma'at- her flesh, it was like a thin layer of living electric light glowing in the colors of the Logos. Their eyes, wild orbs, cast messages to existence. Their ecstasy caused the night air itself to turn red; conspicuously alike the radiation of the Mystic; radiation within every small molecule and gathering on the wind. Osaze's parting gesture, appropriately.

As Yah made love the water contorted to their will to support them as they desired. They became as close to each other as they could, but got closer and closer still. All they wanted was unification. They pined for it, yearned for it, and even became aggressively orgasmic to attain it. And yet, still it came in its own time, not theirs.

Slor stood watch over the child in case he should awake and want something, which he did not. The human souls milled around the area, wandering witlessly in red breezes. Even more formless than human souls were the remnants of animals. Birds as blobs of light bobbed over the human ghost heads. Critters scurried at ghost's feet. Tree creatures climbed to high heights. Clusters of subterranean insects wafted down the beach. Certainly, the scene was an accurate depiction of a similar situation under water.

The underwater world was a world Slor knew too well. A place as sorrowful as the terrestrial world and also lifeless by a different yet equally effective descension. Slor, the solemn smiling one, experienced the die offs like an irritating clicking in his ear steadily driving him mad; but, at the base level he accepted divinity. Reversion was like the feeling of a crisis happening in the mind and the brain reacting violently so the owner becomes fearful that at any moment their head will explode and they'll die alone like a crushed rose in the dirt who wrote a death poem too young. Then comes exaltation. Madness was love. Caught in the currents of infinite love. Slor went where love guided him, always. Sheer madness. It was hard for him to focus, but as the clicking of his mind receded and the reversion began, he found sad peace in the quiet chaos. The next aeon would be better.

****

Osaze, Ma'at, Kobe, Kyoto, and Solaris arrived at Osazeland with the Zeta armada surrounding them. At their backs every single Zeta organism or Zeta creation waited with intent concentration for what would be the definitive moment of their existences. Their spacecraft moved into position in all directions around the Omegas and filled the voids. The Zeta speckled as though they were stars themselves yet more spectacular. Vessels traveled along the invisible highways. Beyond the clouds of glowing crafts the web of radiation let Osaze know he was heading where he belonged and at that time he could be nostalgic if he wanted. Still, he cared not to indulge. What there was, their exaltation, was exactly what there needed to be. The appropriate departure of their power; his long awaited exodus. Forward thinking rejoiced for the girls in his embrace. They were his divinity.

For eternities the Pale Mystic was as it was. Then something unexpected happened. A Ma'at. An exalted goddess from another universe reached out. Just because she could. Everything changed after that. The Pale Mystic was delivered ever gracefully to a world where the Mystery was as it had never been; conclusive. There was light, and something called Love. Nothing else needed to be known. There was only one truth: Love. Love. An element he never imagined could exist, and was yet, as plentiful as what trickled from the spring which creation was sprung. The conjoining factor of the two different realities, completely unbeknownst to the Mystic, was love. After the Pale Mystic learned of love, nothing was ever the same.

Yah tried so hard to sustain the power of the Mystery. Each time Yah exhausted itself and was forced to recreate the Logos from nothing; things went wrong and the Mystery remained unsolved. The Logos coming upon them would be the final Logos. The immaculate Logos perfectly sustainable for eternity; sans the Pale Mystic. What comes of the Mystic after Ma'at exalts it, Osaze couldn't speculate, but, by the love of Yah, he was about to find out.

The red webs pulsed with the rhythm of his maddening love; the menacing instability of a dissolving Gaia. And Ma'at, her face nostalgic in a curious way. Her loyalties to her own genius were being left behind in safe keeping. Ma'at wasn't even really leaving. For a twin has not much difficulty to be two places at once. To the Mystic, Ma'at, too, went where love guided her... To the same place her ambitions guide her... Her heart.... An eternal romance laced through their ipseiti. As though love weren't to be contained any longer and it wanted to break free; like they were being used by the love of Yah to overcome the limits of Yah.

She certainly understood the relation between a

momentous occasion and a fated love affair. Osaze was hers. He always had been and they didn't even realize until fate was upon them. The sacramental humans of the end times never failed to surprise Yah. That was why the tradition persevered. The four girls and Tobias looked to each other, then took hands and formed a circle.

"Zeta first," Ma'at said.

"So it is," Osaze said.

Above them, below them, around them, the lights of the Zeta craft blinked out of existence; one by one by one. They looked at each other in that galactic way. That hypnotic way. The way with its own momentum to become even more of a blessing; to experience more of what love could be; the supreme passion of their dispositions. They walked toward each other and merged. Lyn in the center and wrapped in the other girls; Osaze all around them. Ma'at retained her true form as the girls- becoming Osaze or Ma'at- molded and grinded softly against the exact right places of their bodies; Osaze as a black cloud of antimatter, stimulating his lovers. As the Zeta ships grew fewer and fewer, the lovers' sizes grew to sheer enormity so that even some ships became caught in their dark sensual nebula- perishing an instant later. They grew to sizes hundreds of times larger than the biggest stars, then thousands of times larger, and with them so too grew Osaze Land. They grew large enough that every galaxy at that moment was within them and as they grew their orgasmosis increased, until, at a single moment they climaxed and Yah ascended.

****

There was nobody around when it happened; scarcely a ghost. Yah; Logos, Ma'at, and the others were away enjoying more physical indulgences. It was an early morning hour after the burning moon had set and after the blazing sun rose as it had rose on every morning since the descension of Gaia began. Except suddenly there was no Yah anywhere to be found; but Slor was still there.

Calvin had felt the cat die right under the palm of his hand. He dropped to his knees over Pluto. Pluto was dead. Dead like Robin. Dead like Logan and Drake. He couldn't take it. The cat just died out of nowhere for no reason. His breath escaped him and he was gone. No more loss. No more pain.

Calvin threw himself over the carcass as the tears began streaming down his face, and through his sobs he shouted to Slor, "It's not fair. Why is he gone? I loved him! Where's he going to go when he's dead- I'm not going to go there!" As if he weren't upset enough, he soon had another realization, "Now there's nothing left to die but me! I don't want to die! I'm not ready to die! What did you do, Slor? Why did you do this! Don't let me die, Slor. I love you. Look, everything is fine! We can live here forever, we don't have to turn to fire! I don't want to. Slor!" He was on his knees at the feet of the two small golems. "Don't let me die, Slor."

The gargoyles pursed their lips and doed their eyes pitifully, "Death is a part of life, Calvin."

"I was supposed to live forever."

"We live forever."

"I'm going to die," he said.

"Part of you will remain. Part of you cannot die."

"That doesn't make any sense Slor! It's going to be me dying and the part of me that dies is going to be me. ...So? I am going to die!"

"Well, let me reassure that it isn't as important as you think it is."

"I don't believe you. Not important? It didn't have to be like this. Nobody did anything to prevent it!"

"Well, a lot of people were cold. In their hearts. Too

much to ask to quit that which isn't morally sound... so they perished instead. Listen Calvin, they would have done something if they could have. Sorry, little one, but those that died before you did you no favors. So now we are here. It's ok. I promise you, there is no other way this could have happened. So give me a hug, alright?"

Calvin didn't say anything else. The tears kept pouring down his face, the sobs persisted, but he took the two monsters in his arms, felt their leathery wings, and in their arms they embraced him. An instant later Calvin and Slor were both engulfed completely in the brightest white hot flames. Calvin vanished instantly, but Slor remained, lingering in the inferno for a moment simply because he was there and he could maybe try to peer through it. All there was was fire. Surely no planet remained, and if no planet remained, no sun remained. There was no sun. No black holes because one would never again have any way to occur; and finally all was Yah. Unified. Slor was Yah. Calvin was Yah. Every soul was Yah. Yah was complete and surprisingly multiplied in a welcome way. Yah was love. Ma'at was love, and she was where she belonged. Yah was Yah. Ma'at was Yah, but Ma'at was Ma'at and Ma'at, like the Pale Mystic, loved. For the first time since forever the Logos was exactly as it should be. Rejoice, for it was the aeon when for the first time Yah would also be in the Pale Mystic. There would be Yah Way again, and a new brotherhood forged with darkness, by the blessing and passing of the most precious Bien-Aimée. Marvelous. Yah was.

****

Osaze and the others had left the Yah Way via Osaze Land. However, they were not yet at the Pale Mystic. Him and his loves traversed the vortexes according to their romantic dispositions. At that point more than ever they existed as themselves. Not a part of this, or a part of that- they were Osaze and Ma'at as alone as alone could be. And together. Almost as together as together could be, and yet not. Last time Osaze had taken that journey he was alone. That first time he was unreal. He was raw. That was the world they were returning to. They were the givers of form. They were the effectors; together at a zero point, unified, equalized, neither there nor there. No Slor. No Pleiadian. Beyond the Logos. The Zeta were where they needed to be.

He was finding the divine providence of the exaltation and couldn't believe it was real. He was shocked and appalled. He was in utter disbelief that such good feelings could exist. Like rediscovering love. Then he remembered an unfortunate truth, and he remembered it with human eyes, because he could: For the first time, Osaze... was considering what he'd left behind. Sad pioneers. Ma'at sensed this.

"Osaze. This is fated. You musn't fear for me. There are assurances I will see my loves again. Maybe you will, too, how can we know? This is about the future. Something unknown! Can you imagine? I'm riveted. You're the best thing that's ever happened to me. And this. You and this have made me the happiest girl to ever be."

"You don't have to say that. You're the Diva. My Diva. I spent one life without you, so what matters is that you're my Dearest, and we'll have each other for the next life. You, my Ma'at, are the absolute closest thing to my heart that ever has been, will be, or was. It turned out that way on its own. Fate. Destiny. These words mean nothing at their own fruitions. What matters is love; that we must submit to love and let it conquer us, like gravity, and what lives will know of our union when we become part of them; a gleaming example of the divine grace bestowing love unto Yah and mystery unto the Mystic."

She jumped into his arms. They were as pure as the vortex. They were the vortex. They were nowhere; nowhere at a place that would never, could never, and yet did, exist. Kobe, Kyoto, and Solaris faded into Osaze as the energetic signature of Ma'at. Osaze could not be distinguished or separated from nothing. Ma'at stood out distinctly against his darkness as the most spectacular artifact of a lost world; pure white light formed and contained by her will, still very much in the shape of Lyn. And Osaze, in a sense, remained as Tobias if and when Osaze had form.

Ma'at said, "What do you think will happen while we're not there?"

"Peace. Magic. The new. All kinds of things are going to happen for Yah and we won't see or know anything about it. You, precious, are the exalted one. What love there is, is there for you and the sister left behind. Your sister will hold down the adoration of the Yah Way, certainly. So embrace whatever may come. Is that not the way?"

"That is the way- to embrace whatever may come is the way. To know that nothing is over until it is done. To be what there is to be so that what there is to be will be. To be the very form of Yah. I do love it. I do love you and everything we do. Tell me, Osaze, how do you love me?"

"I love thee easily. To love thee is to be free- to be free comes naturally to me, and so, I love thee."

"Il mio Imperatore."

"Esaltato Principessa."

To understand their destination one would have to understand something about the Mystic. Unfortunately, the Mystic is a mystery. Fair it is to say they were en route. More than that, they were scanning emanations. They were reading radiations. Selecting where to fixate themselves. Not an actively aware process. It was an event. Their return was the event, and they could sense that easily enough. No Yah.

The Pale black wickedness beckoned them coyly.

Ma'at felt supremely comfortable and content. She asked Osaze, "What will this be like?"

"I haven't predictions. Basically, we'll get where we're going. I'll take control over what is there in the name of Ma'at, and you'll reign supreme and we'll do whatever you want about the future, fate, and destiny. We can create what we'd like. How's that? Be whoever we want to be? They'll adore us for it. They'll love you for loving them. Or maybe, maybe we become those who care to not be adored, but I stutter to think such a thing exists.

"Which is a good point you've got to remember. There is no love where we're going. We bring love as a gift. Manifesting romance and adoration by example. We'll change everything there is."

"Will we be happy?"

"Will you be happy with me?"

"Of course I will, Osaze. The Pale Mystic will be unified by our love. The way Yah was divided by the mystery. Because Yah is love. And I am Yah."

"You are love. I am a lover of love, we cannot escape the magnitude of that. It kept us distantly entwined until now. This vortex is our coalescence. It's around us. This vortex? It's us. It is what we are, right now, more than it will ever be again. Our union is divine. We are here right now together. Finally."

"I'm so excited, Osaze. This is the most spectacular thing that has ever happened. Yah has never been beyond Yah before, but here we are. Alone. Together."

"I agree. It is special. We won't be alone for long. We'll be unfathomable, with the other unfathomables. We'll be solving the Mystery. We'll be maximizing potential. For eternity it will have been us that did what we did, and no one else... no one else... and there will be no way such a thing could ever change; it will be our legend that echoes from the furthest reaches of the Mystic as though it were our very own awareness beckoning.

Kobe asked, "Will it be as our fantasies?"

"It will be better. It will be of our desires."

Kyoto asked, "Will it be as our dreams?"

"It will be much more real."

Solaris asked, "How is this real?"

Ma'at said, "When you look a little further past your presumptions you might find there is nothing that is not real in one way or another. Everything is somewhere, and if it isn't, it will be when it needs to be. If it needs to. This is how existence exists. This is how I have no fear nor apprehension to accept the honors that are, by the vigilance of my being, rightfully mine."

Kobe said, "I can feel it in me. I can feel the entirety of eternity inside of myself."

"It's like the opposite of being whole. It's like being a little part of everything and in no part Kyoto," Kyoto said. "As divided as divided could be. Every semblance of myself is cut loose from what is behind us and becoming what is before us. That I am here, I cannot believe."

Solaris said, "She is right, something is happening. We are dematerializing. Where will we go?"

"Wherever we want to go," Ma'at said.

"What will we do when we get there?" Kyoto asked.

"We'll have to wait and see," Osaze said.

"Where are we now?" Kobe asked.

"We are within ourselves. This is where we will always be from now on. There is no beyond us anymore. We are like Yah in that way. We are like the Pleiadians in that we make decisions and weave fate. We are the Zeta in that, we too, once, were lost. In the same token, we are nothing when you consider what we will soon become.

"We will expand and grow as the Pale Mystery

expands and grows. This is the new divinity. The Mystery always expands, it never gets solved, and it only goes deeper. And that is us. We are like that. In that Yah was specific, but now in the Mystic we are elusive, less real, and more powerful by becoming ways we've never been; as we will continue to be until being ceases, but, the brilliance! There are no aeons here, just endless growth and what that entails, which is everything; so, divinity will be what everything getting bigger exponentially forever entails," Osaze said.

"Oh," Ma'at moaned felicitously, "It sounds very exciting. I can't wait. Osaze?"

"Yeah?"

"Will the Pale Mystic be a... carnal.... experience? A sensual experience?"

"In ways we can't even imagine. We don't have nearly a portion of the senses we will develop, nor have we experienced even the first time we truly passed into the Mystic. We have nearly reached the precipice. As we acclimate more and more, we will be taken further and further. Eventually we will be consumed by ourselves. Then we will be where we are meant to be. Together and blessed."

"I am excited," Ma'at said, "This feels so... familiar. Like we've always been here. Except it is different. Once we were givers of form to Yah, now we are giving of ourselves to form the Mystery."

"You needn't worry my dearest love. I am the Mystery. Where it goes, I always know. I am the one who knows, always. I am what the Mystery does. It is nothing without me, and yet, aware of me. So? Why will we be free?"

"Because being free comes naturally."

"Totally. Unrestrained freedom in a world adapted to our radiance. Truly, were it not for us there wouldn't be what we will create, and were we to not create what will be, who is to say all would not disappear? That is the Mystery. What can there actually be without you and me? Without our three? I wouldn't want to know. What could I be without thee? Me? No, please. Without thee I could never be me. My love, until now I've never known myself so truly. I'm nothing without thee."

"Osaze," said Ma'at.

THE END

THE AFTERWARD

I didn't know I'd been dreaming until I awoke. Every day was a fantasy. My pain became my entire universe. Others pain, too. I lived in it. I flew through it. It enslaved me. I did what it told me to do. To no avail I even tried to kill the story on certain days while my heart was trying to destroy me in the name of literature. I almost didn't survive. I couldn't cope. It was sheer madness. I was bound to Osaze. Obligated to it. I had as much control over the book as over any dream I've ever had; very little. There was nothing I could do but watch the tale unfold; every day, every minute, every hour- for days that turned into weeks that turned into months. It was completely unreal.

I was writing fiction. I was no longer writing 'what I know' like they tell novelists to do. I was writing about parts of myself I did not know; the viscous instincts of fiction. Every word, line, paragraph, page, and chapter accosted me mercilessly and overwhelmed with emotions meant to be ignored. Exactly like a nightmare.

My girlfriend, 'Arianna,' left me when I was two chapters into writing this second book. The first two chapters are about how much I love her and why she is so special to me, but in real life, somehow, our relationship was falling apart.

As soon as I began this book everything began to go away. Spiritual types would call it a releasing of burden, but I was in love. And spiritual types hardly ever mention romantic love. Romance can't even be the best word to use because it is derived from Rome and surely men loved women before Rome. Either way; love loves to love love. Teach that.

My spirit was being unburdened. Probably by Yah itself. The torturous job I had supervising an overbearing psychotic man decided to crack down on me about paperwork, so I quit. 'Arianna' had already left me. I couldn't afford the apartment and I moved to my parent's yard for a couple of days.

Then I ran away to the Rainbow. Very beautiful people there. I wrote about these travels in my Pennsylvania Cantos and St. Helen's Cantos. So it wasn't even really like I was on any sort a vacation or break when I went out there. I was a poet for a while instead of a novelist. It happens.

I had a brief relationship with a girl called Medusa. She was a victim of her environment and I'll always hate humanity a little bit more for the pain they put her through with pharmaceutical drugs and little white rooms. She lived in Connecticut with me for a short while when the Rainbow was over. I did not put her in the novel. She was, however, a central theme of the cantos.

The problem was I was in no way over Arianna, and I expected her to come back- so I stayed single for an incredibly long time. She never came back. She had come back so many times- I just expected we had a routine going. She broke the cycle.

Our relationship ended far too abruptly. Especially considering my feminique awakening occurred only a few days after we split up. Also, only days before we split, I was finally ready to marry her. Something I had been debating since we first hooked up. Except, I was perpetually daydreaming. I couldn't do anything right. I was just trying to get by. If the girl who dumped me met the guy I was a month after she left then she would have married him. She changed. Not me.

So, assuming you read this book, you know that 'Tobias' didn't exactly have the easiest time accepting his own loss. My life was like that, too. I began to hate women for not being her. I loved women. Love, hate, love is blind. Females are the only real thing because they are as unreal as myself.

Once I realized that exalting women is a unifying technique for world peace my life changed a lot. Except, I was near dead the whole time. I couldn't think about anything except dying for hours on end. For days even. I wanted to kill myself so bad. I say here now still that it would have been worth it to escape that pain. There is no future worth surviving psychosis, but maybe I am wrong. I don't know yet. I doubt it. Our country is on the brink of revolution. We may die. We are already dead in a way. We belong to the future generations. There is no certainty for them or us. If the government doesn't kill us then the ecological effects of 100 years capitalism will. There is no way to know what will drive in the final nail.

This is why the humans died in my story. I wanted to see my greatest fear realized and know how I would feel about it. Naturally it was fear. I wanted to show what happens when we fail to prevent such an event, and yeah, it would be awful. Life is meant to live on, not die off. I fear very little; imprisonment, toxins, torture, romance, violence, and the tipping point, mainly. My plot was farfetched, but I suspected something would present itself in real life that would threaten everything. And something has presented itself; in more ways than I could imagine. So much so that the story elements aren't as farfetched anymore. Stranger things have already happened, in some regards.

Meanwhile, the disunited status of amerika has begun to sink along with the rest of the world's power structure- the control matrix everyone is chained to. Throughout this entire 'dream' I was wondering if I would finish in time for revolution.

History will tell the outcome of what I know not at this juncture. Writers love history because it so often speaks for us. And yes. The water has gone out to sea but the tsunami has not yet come in. Instead of running away, I am walking calmly toward the water's edge, because I am a strong swimmer. This is my duty. An artist is more valuable as a revolutionary; they're priceless. Read the history books about our times. You wouldn't believe the mutated mind fucked zombies we put up with every day in our society. Every year after 2012 will be a hell of a year. It is a miracle you're alive. Every odd was stacked against you, once upon a time.

Anyway. There isn't much else to say about this book.... I don't think. I wrote chapters 2-7 in a van outside my parent's house. Then I moved to South Dakota to live with 'Olivia.' I am still in South Dakota. Wall St. must fall in the fall. Time to overthrow the government... I don't want to, but I have reasons. Washington DC will be the death of us if we don't fight them. Not just people either. There are dead birds raining down from the heavens by the hundreds of thousands. Dead fish wash up by the millions. In the first book I was making up the dead birds and now they are real. This is a madhouse. The world is the worst place on earth. Tobias & Osaze was a nightmare within a nightmare. Now, completed, I have a new nightmare. No more writing. For now. Writing is all I've ever known. Writing is all I have ever been good at. Writing was all I ever wanted.

Tobias was created during a relatively low stress period. Osaze, the other half, however, absolutely had to be written and I had to rush to meet the revolution's deadline. I never faulted on the quality, but I almost died producing the product as quickly as I could. I should have been healing.

I've never been selfish enough. People in my world are happy because they are selfish. They are centered, but they are self-centered. They should be centered to the Earth, in my opinion.

Please read Castaneda. The table metaphor at the beginning of Osaze belongs to him. I stole it, but out of context it was more of a hassle than it was worth. I had a Castaneda reawakening toward the end of the second book and the philosophies in the Star card chapter were born of his work and another part in the Moon, as well- fans might recognize. If you become familiar with Castaneda you may notice it, too. I suspect I have also solved the enigma surrounding him. There was a riddle. They called him a charlatan because they couldn't verify his claims. The reason is because his claims were false. His teachings are true, but one very important teaching of his was to lie about everything so nobody has any idea what was going on with you. His books were truth expressed by lies. They were not Mexican Indian knowledge as they claimed to be. I propose his teachings were Peruvian knowledge, because he spent the first 25 years of his life in that country. It makes sense. I should write a paper, but I don't want to. I should tell people. I guess this is that. There is more to the story, but if you really care then you will find your own way to the information. That's how much I don't feel like discussing it. I'd rather that you spend years learning what I am talking about. Or an afternoon, if you are efficient.

Another teacher I had while writing was a Swami on the internet. He was a young shaggy white guy but he knew his stuff, for certain. He had made an internet video about each tarot card, but at the Devil I caught up to where he left off. So the Tower was the first chapter I wrote without his input. That loss was my own world shattering event, in a practical way. I contemplated stalling and waiting to finish the book until I had the teachings available, but I could not.

The Logos itself was designed by me loosely based on the teachings of the Prophet George Kavassilas ('We exist and we always exist. You always have been and you always will be.' -GK) based on his travels through the dimensions and beyond. George is a great man. The word Logos, by the way, took me an entire afternoon to unearth as the name of the universe. Then the hyena writers began using it to describe all manner of different totalities. I never found a name for the omniverse other than 'source.' There might be one in Hindu or something, maybe. I don't know. Perhaps it is Tao.

As for Roses. There were a lot of roses in the tarot so I used them in the story. In life, in poetry, poets love to write about roses. I am certain I caused an omnipresence of roses in the arts; especially literary arts. And ditto for the various businesses titled 'rose' this or 'rose' that. I can't explain roses in the tarot, but I can explain how the hyenas behave. I say things people don't want to respond to but they can't help responding too. Artists mimic my name. Literary peers mimic my actions. I can often identify what I have or have not influenced by the presence of roses. For the past 4 years if there was a rose in a piece of writing, then I'd find, upon inspection, about a 70% rate of trace influences from my work occurring in theirs. If I was never famous, then at least I was still here and nothing can change that. I left my presence in this opaque manner.

I wish my peers would speak to me. Some do, but I am talkative and most people fear it. I am not approachable, but I like being approached. I have a lot to say, to be redundant. I don't often talk for no reason, or small talk, and yet most people don't say anything when they talk. Most people have no idea how to react to meaningful communication and- after a life in this world- I don't blame them. I am no different. Most communication is meaningless in the biological sense.

I'll smile when there is something to smile about. Just remember that when you see a rose in a painting or poem, I may well be the reason it is there. I've had to add a Z to my name because my identity keeps getting stolen. Stupid problem, but it's a pretty name. RRRose became one of the baby boom hyena writers who saturate the 'scene.' There is no other RRRoze yet... yet... but there is already a handful of porno chix named Roze: Alicia Roze, Nikki Roze, Dee Roze, and Red Roze. So whatever. Good things get around. I wish I was born with a different last name, that's all I can say about it.

The last thing to mention about my book is about the women. The three girlfriends were based on a cluster of girls I met at the Rainbow. In real life they were a Japanese girl, a Vietnamese girl, and a brunette. In the story they were 2 Japanese girls and a blonde. My vicarious orgies... Call them a fantasy because they were. There is no cohesion to most of the work in this book if the reader cannot accept fantasy as reality and absurdity as logic. One technique I often experiment with is making sense of nonsensical notions and premises. Better than to let the material go to waste.

Toward the end I found myself in interesting territory. Aden was dead. Lyn was alone. The three beautiful girls were some kind of mutant freak clones at best. It made sense for Lyn and Tobias to fall in love. Except, my original intention for Lyn was to have her be in love with Aden because in real life I have an inconvenient dreaming/waking/all-encompassing obsession with the first girl I ever kissed. I wanted to put her behind me. Easier said than done.

At that point in the story, being a pragmatist, I began to consider that the future could hold anything. Who am I to say my dreams will not come true? I don't know they won't. I picture a romance under the fireworks of revolution. So I write in hopes to manifest- you could say. I did it very delicately. The relationship between Lyn and Tobias represents my wildest hope for this life, at this naïve time. I'll have lived a fulfilling life if Lyn became my true love and let me worship her after so long. I tried to keep her out of my head and couldn't, but don't judge me, you wouldn't be able to either. She's too damn special, too damn beautiful, and too damn divine. Although, life is not a fantasy. One day I will have a real lover again and she'll no doubt be extremely angry with me right now. Sorry love.

I want you to know that the world wasn't only stacked against you ever being born, but the cards were stacked against this ever getting published and thus you ever reading it. Like Tobias, I only know uncertainty. I can make my subliminal predictions about love and best case scenarios, but only time will tell. We will see if people can overcome themselves. It was difficult to attempt to transcend time for this whole book, but I think I managed. Time is a dream. That's what I know about it. Sands of time; the sandman puts you to sleep and you dream when you sleep. Time is a dream. Maybe I screwed up here or there, but then again maybe not.

I have to re-thank my mother and benefactor, Mz. Roze. I have to thank her a zillion times over. I have to thank her once for every instant I have been alive. My mother has been my only security in this life. She was always there to pay bills, fines, or to buy me one cheap computer after another. She was always there to help me when I couldn't function in society, and as an artist I needed that. It didn't mesh with the judgments of men or women, but judge not lest ye be... I am usually down and out and I can't write if I am starving to death. Left to my own devices, and deep in the chapters, a food fast is like a vacation and dying is staying there. It's a weird world. I came from my mom. I am her. I was going to say she is me, but that ain't right. We are our mothers. Like our mothers, our duty is to the children. Always think of the children. She taught me everything I know, because she taught me how to think critically. She gave me the right books to read. She gave me the guidance I needed at every step. She put up with the strangest kid I've ever known for years and years and still to this day. She protected me from my father, bullies, teachers, the government, and Yah knows who or what else. So if I ever protect someone, or ever have, it's because she taught me that people with power have no right to maliciously lord it over those with less power. This is the patriarchal/matriarchal imbalance I seek to correct with my work, specifically politically. My only political view is essentially a religion of Goddess worship. Such is anarchism...

As for being a writer. A few words come to mind: Satan, blackness, bloody wrists, alcohol, substances, time, hopelessness, women, obligation, lunacy, more blood, keyboards, pain, influences, sadness, loss, cats & scorpions, astrology, tarot, rozez, dice, crystals, blood and alcohol and bloody alcohol, 16 stupid jobs I never wanted to keep, my ex, the midwest, early writings, another ex, 10 apartments, 13 moves, a pickup truck, a tent, a van, poetry equals sex; how many arrests?

Writing inevitably got me trapped under myself. My thinking was I could behave however I wanted if I just kept doing good work. I didn't care what people knew or what people thought. Honestly, I should have been able to be myself without some glorious talent. And even with talent I still can't be me without upsetting people's fragile sensibilities(I want people to be happy, but they make it impossible for themselves). In books I can say and do what I want.

I never even really had an ego. I still don't. I get accused of being egomaniacal a lot. Really, everyone is egotistical except me and they put their shortcomings upon me to feel better about themselves. I have something else where my ego should be. It is auto-pilot and its behaviors are dictated by my integrity, with no conscious effort. I really have very little control over what my 'ego' does. Often when I want to do something human and verbally lash out or something, it checks me, humbles me, and shuts me up. Not often enough... Then later this loss of 'te' will deliver an onslaught of cutting sentiments toward people who have in some way earned them. I want to be nice to people. I love people no matter how much I hate them. In life I wanted to be extravagant, and so I am. The cruel irony is that I am the only one who knows that my extravagance is a shroud of humility. It's lonely being trapped under myself.

People think you're crazy because you're more distracted than anyone else they've ever met. The under-appreciation of the industry has wounded me greatly. The literary industry is like surviving a watery plane crash and getting shot when you swim ashore. My personality is intimidating to nearly everyone and my work can't access any audiences because of that, I feel. The very writing itself is intense- I know. Everything I write- or even say, really- is intense, but I have faith the world will see things my way for a change, eventually. If you want to share my work, then please share my work, or else people may never enjoy it. I am honest. I am real. I come as I am- fucked up and scarred; scared and overly intense, awkward, unrealistic, right, but not right in the head. People spent so long trying to make me less than what I am, to make me what they were; they were piranhas eating me alive. These books are my way of taking back what I lost along the way.

Have you heard me blame people because I am an alcoholic? I can explain such incongruities of logic. You would be an alcoholic, too, if you were me. What is the alternative? Pain? Psychosis? I hate it at that other place. That sober place is where everyone else lives. It's nice to visit but I wouldn't want to stay there.

After six years I am finally finished writing. Mostly finished. I've written 5.5 other books besides these two, but it will be yet another miracle if they ever reach an audience. This book is my message in a bottle. From where I am, on this page, to where you are reading them- an ocean of time and space away.

I like it where I am. It's a skill I'll always keep with me. I woke up from the Osaze dream and after about a day I was programmed to sit back at the keys and type this wrap up up. Anything not to think about this crude oil world we live in. I still haven't written the forward to Tobias. I will though. Next. I should have put more thought into this. This outro should be like a goodbye, so long, see you soon. And the intro should be a 'Hey, how are you, what's up?' Like it matters, we're doomed. I hope it ain't true. I wanted you to read my books so badly.

It doesn't even matter. I only ever had a few lessons to teach in life and they are bigger than myself and will be taught without me regardless. Astrology. Tarot. Crop circles. Metaphysics. Freedom. Love. Whatever else. Wuji... I know the books seem like people were just slaughtering other people needlessly a lot of the time, and yeah, the extinction of mankind was needless, but this was to express the brainwashing I see. I write about violence a lot but my stance is very much in favor of absolute nonviolence (except for purposes of romantic love...). Naturally, I pray to Yah, or whatever, that you exist in a utopian society where there isn't any violence. It's possible if we can overcome ourselves. Yeah. Off to overthrow the government.

I am awake from the six year nightmare. To a new nightmare, of course. Olivia says I should go on a walk about, a vision quest, or any journey to 'find myself'- a phrase I despise because Arianna claimed that's why she left me. To find herself. I don't know what it is to find myself, because as lost as I get, I am still there. The meaning is ambiguous at best. I would like to go be the me I should have been 6 years ago, but I have a revolution to tend to. I didn't want it. They just gave it to me. I guess I could thank Rage Against The Machine again here. I know I'll thank them in the forward but that is for different reasons. Through me, and through the other fans, they may well have rescued humanity. We are their victory. A legion of warriors almost 20 years later. Thanks to De La Rocha. His genius poetry gave me the wisdom I needed to know that the government, the politicos, the police, the military, and the media could not be trusted. I am forever in his debt. I've been waiting for these coming battles for 13 years, thanks to that band. So a big thank you to Tom Morello for making your guitar playing an addictive substance. Thank you to Tim and Brad, in turn. These men were true revolutionaries. Me? Am I a revolutionary? You tell me. Right now I am a writer. I've been manipulating what I can when I can, for the cause. If I can help to give perspective or illuminate a good idea then I will. I've been getting in the politico master's faces online. No one cares about them and no one listens to them and yet they control us all, so that is why I can and will keep doing what I do. They hear my truths, but they don't want to admit they hear them. The effect is that what I say stays in their 'minds' and spreads because the message is echoing back out to where others can hear actually it. In their deepest recesses. In essence, this is the reason the hyenas write about roses. The truth will set you free. Consider this book as a ghost in a graveyard. All it wants is a visitor. An audience is a luxury, but so are visitors. I get what a ghost's got; a whisper. I'm out of here. Thank you so much for reading. Stay true to your heart. Love your enemies. To you Reader, love.

Roses,

Roze

Made in the USA
Middletown, DE
06 November 2023